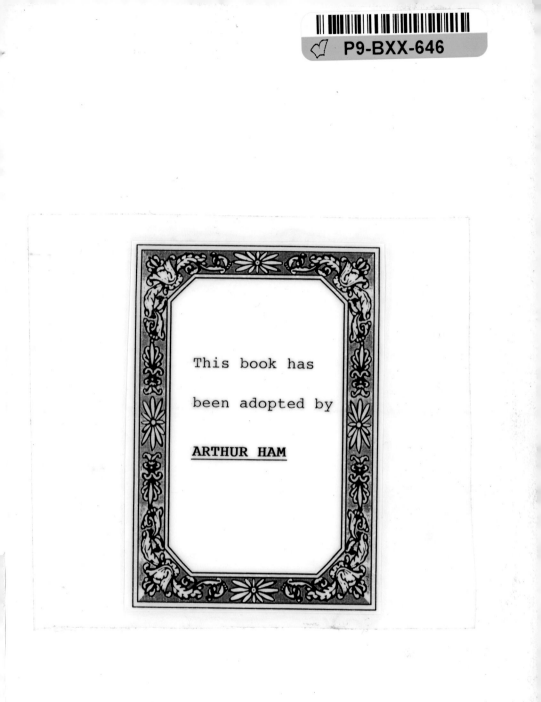

This book has

been adopted by

ARTHUR HAM

AT ALL COSTS

AT ALL COSTS

DAVID WEBER

AT ALL COSTS

This is a work of fiction. All the characters and events portrayed in this book are fictional, and any resemblance to real people or incidents is purely coincidental.

A Baen Books Original

Baen Publishing Enterprises
P.O. Box 1403
Riverdale, NY 10471
www.baen.com

ISBN-13: 978-1-4165-0911-0
ISBN-10: 1-4165-0911-9

Cover art by David Mattingly
Interior map by Hunter Peddicord

First printing, November 2005

Library of Congress Cataloging-in-Publication Data

Weber, David, 1952-
 At all costs / David Weber.
    p. cm. -- (Honor Harrington ; 11)
 "A Baen Books Original."
 ISBN 1-4165-0911-9 (hc)
  1. Harrington, Honor (Fictitious character)--Fiction. 2. Women soldiers--Fiction. 3. Space warfare--Fiction. I. Title II. Series: Weber, David, 1952- . Honor Harrington ; 11.

PS3573.E217A94 2005
813'.54--dc22

                                                            2005022402

Distributed by Simon & Schuster
1230 Avenue of the Americas
New York, NY 10020

Production & design by Windhaven Press, Auburn, NH (www.windhaven.com)
Printed in the United States of America

10 9 8 7 6 5 4 3 2 1

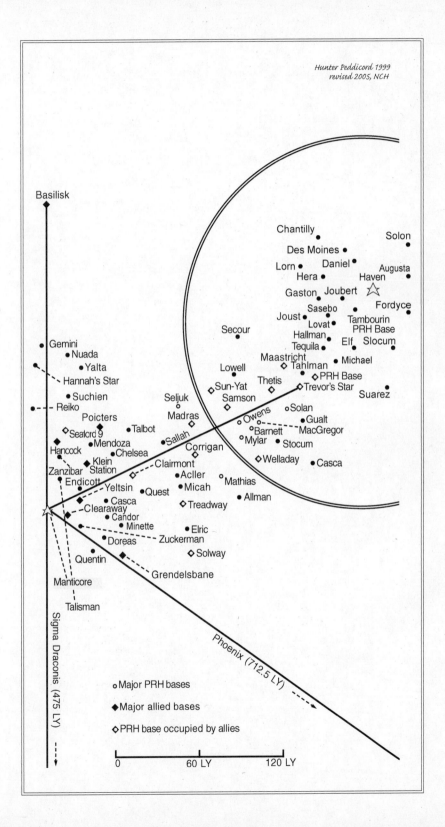

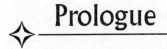# Prologue

The big *Aviary*-class CLACs and their escorting battlecruisers crossed the Alpha wall into normal-space just outside the hyper limit. There were only three of the superdreadnought-sized vessels, but their LAC bays spat out almost six hundred light attack craft, and if the Republic of Haven's *Cimeterre*-class LACs were shorter-legged, more lightly armed, and nowhere near so capable as the Star Kingdom of Manticore's *Shrikes* and *Ferrets*, they were more than adequate for their current assignment.

They accelerated in-system, building vectors towards the industrial infrastructure of the Alizon System, and discovered an unanticipated bit of good fortune. A pair of lumbering freighters, both squawking Manticoran IDs and bumbling along on the same general flight plan, found themselves squarely in the path of the incoming storm and already within extreme missile range. They accelerated desperately, but the LACs had an overtake velocity of over a thousand KPS at the moment they were first detected, and the freighters' maximum acceleration rate was little more than two hundred gravities. The *Cimeterres* were capable of very nearly *seven* hundred, and they were armed ... which the merchantmen weren't.

"Manticoran freighters, this is Captain Javits of the Republican Navy," a harsh, Haven-accented voice said over the civilian guard frequency. "You are instructed to kill your impellers and abandon ship immediately. Under the terms of applicable interstellar law, I formally inform you that we do not have the capacity to board and search your vessels or to take them as prizes. Therefore, I will open fire upon them and destroy them in twenty standard minutes from . . . now. Get your people off immediately. Javits, clear."

One of the two freighters killed her impellers immediately. The other skipper was more stubborn. He continued to accelerate, as if he thought he might somehow still save his ship, but he wasn't an idiot, either. It took him all of five minutes to realize—or, at least, to *accept*—that he had no chance, and his impellers, too, went abruptly cold.

Shuttles spilled from the two merchant ships, scuttling away from them at their maximum acceleration as if they expected the Havenite LACs to open fire upon them. But the Republic hewed scrupulously to the requirements of interstellar law. Its warships meticulously waited out the time limit Javits had stipulated, then, precisely on the tick, launched a single pair of missiles at each drifting freighter.

The old-fashioned nuclear warheads did the job just fine.

The *Cimeterres* sped onward, ignoring the dissipating balls of plasma which had once been somewhere in the vicinity of eight million tons of merchant shipping. Their destruction, after all, was a mere sideshow. Ahead of the Havenite units, a half-dozen destroyers and a division of RMN *Star Knight*-class CAs accelerated to meet them. The range was still too long for the *Cimeterres* to actually see the defenders, but the remote reconnaissance platforms spreading out ahead of the LACs were another matter, and Captain Bertrand Javits grimaced as he took note of the drones' relayed report of the defenders' acceleration rates.

"They're not killing themselves to come out and meet us, are they, Skip?" Lieutenant Constanza Sheffield, his executive officer observed.

"No, they aren't," Javits said, and gestured at the cramped, utilitarian LAC's bare-bones plot. "Which probably means Intelligence is right about what they've got covering the inner system," he told her.

"In that case, this is gonna hurt," she said.

"Yes, it is. If not quite as much as they *hope* it will," Javits agreed. Then he punched a new combination into his com panel. "All Wolverines, this is Wolverine One. From their acceleration rate, it looks like they've got to be towing pods. And from the fact that there's so few of them, I have to assume Intelligence is right about their defensive stance. So instead of walking obligingly into the inner system, we're shifting to Sierra Three. We'll change course at Point Victor-Able on my command in another forty-five minutes. Review your Sierra Three targeting queues and stand by for a defensive missile engagement. Wolverine One, clear."

The range continued to fall, and the recon platforms began to report widespread active sensor emissions. Some were probably search systems, but the primary search platforms for any star system were passive, not active. So the odds were high that most of those active emitters were tied into fire control systems of one sort or another.

Javits watched his own platforms' telemetry as it streamed across his plot's sidebars. The far more capable computer support aboard the CLACs and battlecruisers which had launched the platforms could undoubtedly do more with the data they were acquiring, and he knew how the tech teams back at Bolthole would salivate when they got a look at it. All that was rather secondary to his own calculations, however, since those calculations were mostly concerned with how to keep as many as possible of his people alive through the next few hours.

"Looks like we've got four main nets of platforms on this side of the primary, Skipper," his XO said finally. "Two of them spread to cover the ecliptic, and one high and one low. Gives them pretty fair coverage of the entire sphere of the limit, but they're obviously concentrating on the ecliptic."

"The question, of course, Constanza," he replied dryly, "is how many pods each of those 'clusters' of yours represent."

"Well, that and how many pods they want us to *think* they have, Sir," Lieutenant Joseph Cook, Javits' tactical officer pointed out.

"That, too," Javits conceded. "Under the circumstances, though, I'm prepared to be fairly pessimistic on that particular point, Joe. And they've clearly gone ahead and deployed the sensor platforms to *control* the pods. Those're probably at least as expensive as the pods themselves would be, so I'd say there's a good chance they wouldn't have deployed them if they hadn't also deployed the pods for them to control."

"Yes, Sir."

Lieutenant Cook's expression and manner couldn't have been more respectful, but Javits knew what he was thinking. Given the totality of the surprise Operation Thunderbolt had achieved, and the equally total incompetence of the previous Manticoran government, it was entirely possible—even likely—that Alizon's defenses had not been significantly upgraded in the immediate run up to the resumption of hostilities. In which case the defenders might, indeed, be attempting to bluff Javits into believing they had more to work with than they really did. On the other hand, there'd been time since Thunderbolt for the Manties to ship a couple of freighter loads of their multi-drive missile pods out here. And however incompetent Prime Minister High Ridge might have been, the new Alexander Government knew its ass from a hole in the ground. If those additional missiles hadn't been shipped out and deployed, the recon platforms would have been reporting a far heavier system picket than they were actually seeing.

"We're coming up on course change, Skipper," Sheffield told him several minutes later, and he nodded.

"Range to the nearest active sensor platforms?" he asked.

"Closest approach, twelve seconds after we alter course, will be about sixty-four million kilometers," she replied.

"A million inside their maximum effective range from rest," Javits observed, and grimaced. "I wish there was another way to find out if Intelligence knows what it's talking about."

"You and me both, Skip," Sheffield agreed, but she also shrugged. "At least we're the ones calling the tune for the dance this time."

Javits nodded and watched the icon representing his massive flight of LACs sweeping closer and closer to the blinking green crosshair which represented Point Victor-Able. By this time, the *Cimeterres* had traveled almost thirty-three million kilometers and were up to a velocity of over twenty thousand kilometers per second. The Manty picket ships were still accelerating to meet them, but it was obvious that they had no intention of entering standard missile range of that many LACs. Well, Javits wouldn't have either, if he'd been towing pods stuffed full of multi-drive missiles with a standoff range of over three light-minutes. However good Manticoran combat systems might have been, six hundred-plus LACs would have swarmed over that handful of ships like hungry pseudo-piranha if they could get into range of their own weapons. If there'd been heavy defending units in-system, things might have been different, but in that case, Javits would never have come close enough for them to get a shot at him in the first place.

"Victor-Able, Sir," his astrogator reported suddenly.

"Very well. Order the course change, Constanza."

"Aye, Sir," Sheffield said in far more formal tones, and he heard the order go out.

The green beads representing friendly units on his display shifted course abruptly, arcing back out and away from the inner system on a course which would take them right through one of the more heavily developed and mined portions of the Alizon System's asteroid belt. For several seconds, nothing else changed on the display. And then, like a cascading eruption of scarlet curses, dozens—scores—of previously deployed MDM pods began to fire all along the outer edge of the inner system.

The range was incredibly long, even for Manticoran fire control, and one thing Thunderbolt had taught the Republican Navy was that as good as Manty technology was, it wasn't perfect. Hits at such extreme range, even against all-up, hyper-capable starships would have been hard come by. Against such small, elusive targets as LACs, they would be even harder to achieve.

But of course, Javits thought, *hyper-capable units could take a lot more damage than we can. Anybody they* do *hit, is going to get reamed.*

The missiles streaked outward at well over forty thousand gravities. Even at that stupendous rate of acceleration, it would take them the next best thing to nine minutes to reach his ships, and his missile defense crews began to track the incoming threat. It was hard—Manty ECM had always been hellishly good, and it had gotten even better since the last war—but Admiral Foraker's teams at Bolthole had compensated for that as much as they could. The *Cimeterres'* point defense and EW weren't in the same league as Manty LACs' systems, but they were much better than any previous Havenite LAC had ever possessed, and the extreme range worked in their favor.

At least three-quarters of the total Manticoran launch simply lost lock and wandered off course. The recon platforms reported the sudden spiteful flashes as the lost missiles detonated early, before they could become a threat to navigation here in the system. But the rest of the pursuing missiles continued to charge after his units.

"Approximately nine hundred still inbound," Lieutenant Cook announced in a voice which struck Javits as entirely too calm. "Allocating outer zone counter-missiles."

He paused for perhaps a pair of heart beats, then said one more word.

"Engaging."

The command *Cimeterre* quivered as the first counter-missiles blasted away from her. They were woefully outclassed by the missiles racing to kill her, but there were almost two-thirds as many LACs as there were attack missiles, and each LAC was firing dozens of counter-missiles.

Not all of them simultaneously. Admiral Foraker's staff, and especially Captain Clapp, her resident LAC tactical genius, had worked long and hard to develop improved missile defense doctrine for the *Cimeterres*, especially because of their small size and the technological imbalance between their capabilities and those of their opponents. They'd come up with a variant on the "layered defense" Admiral Foraker had devised for the wall of battle, a doctrine which relied less on sophistication than on sheer numbers and recognized that counter-missiles were far less expensive than LACs full of trained Navy personnel.

Now Javits watched the first waves of counter-missiles sweeping towards the incoming Manticoran fire. EW platforms seeded throughout the MDMs came on-line, using huge bursts of jamming in efforts to blind the counter-missiles' seekers. Other platforms produced entire shoals of false images, saturating the LACs' tracking systems with threats. But that had been accepted when the missile defense doctrine was evolved, and in some ways, the very inferiority of Havenite technology worked for Javits at this moment. His counter-missiles' onboard seekers were almost too simpleminded to be properly confused. They could "see" only the very strongest of targeting sources at the best of times, and they had been launched in such huge numbers that they could afford to waste much of their effort killing harmless decoys.

A second, almost equally heavy wave of counter-missiles followed the first one. Again, a Manticoran fleet wouldn't have fired the salvos that closely together. They would have waited, lest the second wave's impeller wedges interrupt their telemetry control links to the first wave's CMs. But Javits' crews knew that at this range, the relatively less capable onboard fire control systems of their LACs had nowhere near the reach and sensitivity of their Manticoran counterparts, anyway. Which didn't even consider the effectiveness of the Manty missiles' penetration aids and EW. Since they could barely see the damned things in the first place, they were giving up far less in terms of enhanced accuracy than a Manticoran formation would have sacrificed, and the larger number of counter-missiles they were putting into space more than compensated for any target discrimination they lost.

The *Cimeterres'* own EW did what it could, as well. The first-wave counter-missiles took out over three hundred of the Manticoran missiles. The second wave killed another two hundred. Perhaps another hundred fell prey to the LACs' electronic warfare systems, lost lock, and went wandering harmlessly astray. Another fifty or sixty lost lock initially, but managed to reacquire their targets or to find new ones, yet their need to quest for fresh victims delayed them, kicked them slightly behind the rest of the stream to make them easier point defense targets.

The third and final wave of counter-missiles killed over a hundred more of the incoming missiles, but over two hundred, in what were now effectively two slightly staggered salvos, burst through the inner counter-missile zone and charged down upon Javits' LACs.

The agile little craft opened fire with every point defense laser cluster that would bear. Dozens of lasers stabbed at each incoming laser head, and as the attack missiles rolled in on their final approaches, the targeted *Cimeterres* rotated sharply, presenting only the bellies and roofs of their impenetrable impeller wedges to them. The targeted LACs' consorts continued to slam bolts of coherent light into the teeth of the Manticoran missiles. Over half of those missiles disappeared, torn apart by the defensive fire, but many of the others swerved at the last moment, either because they'd been executing deceptive attack runs to mask their true targets or else because they'd lost their initial targets and had to acquire new ones. Most of those got through; only a handful of the others did.

Vacuum blazed as the powerful Manticoran laser heads detonated in vicious, fusion-fueled chain-lightning, and immensely powerful X-ray lasers stabbed out of the explosions. Many of those lasers wasted their fury on the interposed wedges of their targets, but others ripped through the LACs' sidewalls as if they had not existed. These were capital missiles of the Royal Manticoran Navy, designed to blast through the almost inconceivably tough sidewalls and armor of ships of the wall. What one of them did to a tiny, completely unarmored light attack craft was cataclysmic.

More explosions speckled space as *Cimeterres'* fusion bottles failed. Almost three dozen of Javits' LACs were destroyed outright. Another four survived long enough for their remaining crewpeople to abandon ship.

"Wolverine Red Three, Wolverine One," he said harshly into his microphone. "You've got lifeguard. Pick up everyone you can. One, clear."

"Aye, Wolverine One. Red Three copies. Decelerating now."

Javits watched the designated squadron decelerate slightly—just enough to match vectors with the skinsuited crewmen who could no longer accelerate—and his eyes were hard. Under other circumstances, delaying to pick those people up would have represented an unacceptable risk. But at this range, and with the range already opening to the very edge of even Manticoran missiles' reach, it was a chance well worth taking.

And not just because of the "asset" those people represent, he thought. *We left too many people too many places under the People's Republic. Not again—not on my watch. Not if there's any option at all.*

He watched the plot's sidebars silently update themselves, listing his losses. They hurt. Thirty-eight ships represented over six percent of his total strength, and he'd known most of the four hundred people who'd been aboard them personally. But in the unforgiving calculus of war, that loss rate was not merely acceptable, it was low. Especially for LAC operations.

And we're outside their reach, now. We've confirmed what they're deploying for system defense, but they're not going to waste more missiles on us. Not at this range . . . and not when they can't be certain what else *may be waiting to pounce if they fire off all their birds.*

"Sir," Lieutenant Cook said. "We're beginning to pick up active emissions ahead of us." Javits looked across at him, and the lieutenant looked up from his own display to meet his CO's eyes. "The computers assess them as primarily point defense radar and lidar, Sir. There don't seem to be very many of them."

"Good," Javits grunted. "All Wolverines, Wolverine One. Stand by to launch on Sierra targets on my command."

He switched channels again, back to the civilian guard frequency.

"Alizon System Central, this is Captain Javits. I will be bringing your Tregarth Alpha facilities into my extreme missile range in twenty-seven minutes from . . . now. My vector will make it impossible for me to match velocity with the facilities or send across boarding parties, and I hereby inform you that I will open fire on them, and on any extraction vessels within my missile envelope, in twenty-nine minutes."

He looked down at his plot once more with a hard, fierce grin. Then keyed his mike once more.

"I advise you to begin evacuation procedures now," he said. "Javits, clear."

"So what's the best estimate of the results, Admiral?" President Eloise Pritchart asked.

The beautiful, platinum-haired President had come across to the Octagon, the Republic of Haven's military nerve center, for this meeting, and aside from one bodyguard, she was the single civilian in the enormous conference room. All eyes were on the huge holo display above the conference table, where the reproduced imagery from Bertrand Javits' tactical plot hovered in midair.

"Our best estimate from the recon platforms' data is that Captain Javits' raid destroyed about eight percent—probably a little less—of Alizon's total resource extraction capability, Madam President," Rear Admiral Victor Lewis, Director of Operational Research replied. Thanks to venerable traditions of uncertain origin, Naval Intelligence reported to Op Research, which, in turn, reported to Vice Admiral Linda Trenis' Bureau of Planning.

"And was that an acceptable return in light of our own losses?" the President asked.

"Yes," another voice said, and the President looked at the stocky, brown-haired admiral at the head of the table who'd spoken. Admiral Thomas Theisman, Secretary of War and Chief of Naval Operations, looked back at her steadily. "We lost about a third of the people we'd have lost aboard a single old-style cruiser, Madam President," he continued, speaking very formally in the presence of their subordinates. "In return, we confirmed NavInt's estimate of the system-defense doctrine the Manties appear to be adopting and acquired additional information on their fire control systems and current pod deployment patterns; destroyed eight million tons of hyper-capable merchant shipping, better than five times the combined tonnage of all the LACs Javits lost; and put a small but significant dent into the productivity of Alizon. More to the point, we hit one of the Manticoran Alliance's member's home system for what everyone will recognize as negligible losses, and this isn't the first time Alizon's been hit. That has to have an effect on the entire Alliance's morale, and it's almost certain to increase the pressure on the White Haven Admiralty to detach additional picket forces to cover the Star Kingdom's allies against similar attacks."

"I see." The President's topaz-colored eyes didn't look especially happy, but they didn't flinch away from Theisman's logic, either. She looked at him for a moment longer, then returned her attention to Rear Admiral Lewis.

"Please pardon the interruption, Admiral," she said. "Continue, if you would."

"Of course, Madam President." The rear admiral cleared his throat and punched a new command sequence into his terminal. The holo display shifted, and Javits' plot disappeared, replaced by a series of bar graphs.

"If you'll look at the first red column, Madam President," he began, "you'll see our losses to date in ships of the wall. The green column beside it represents SD(P)s currently undergoing trials or completing construction. The amber column . . ."

"Well, that was all extremely interesting, Tom," Eloise Pritchart said some hours later. "Unfortunately, I think we're into information overkill. In some ways, I think I know less about what's going on now than I did before I came over here!"

She made a face, and Theisman chuckled. He sat behind his desk, tipped back comfortably in his chair, and the Republic's President sat on the comfortable couch facing the desk. Her personal security detail was camped outside the door, giving her at least the illusion of privacy, her shoes lay on the carpet in front of her, and she had both bare feet tucked up under her while she nursed a steaming cup of coffee in slender hands. Theisman's own cup sat on his desk's blotter.

"You spent long enough as Javier's people's commissioner to have a better grasp of military realities than that, Eloise," he told her now.

"In a general sense, certainly." She shrugged. "On the other hand, I was never actually trained for the realities of the Navy, and there've been so many changes in such a short time that what I did know feels hopelessly out of date. I suppose what matters is that *you're* current. And confident."

Her tone was ever so slightly questioning on the last two words, and it was his turn to shrug.

" 'Confident' is a slippery word. You know I was never happy about going back to war against the Manties." He raised one hand in a placating gesture. "I understand your logic, and I can't disagree with it. Besides, you're the President. But I have to admit that I never liked the idea. And that Thunderbolt's success has exceeded my own expectations. So far, at least."

"Even after what happened—or didn't happen—at Trevor's Star?"

"Javier made the right decision on the basis of everything we knew," Theisman said firmly. "None of us fully appreciated just how tough Shannon's 'layered defense' was going to be against long-range Manticoran missile fire. If we'd been able to project probable losses during the approach phase as accurately then as we could now, then, yes, he should have gone ahead and pressed the attack. But he didn't know that at the time any more than the rest of us did."

"I see." Pritchart sipped coffee, and Theisman watched her with a carefully hidden smile. That was about as close as the President was ever going to allow herself to come to "pulling strings" on Javier Giscard's behalf, lover or no lover.

"And Lewis' projections?" she continued after a moment. "Do you feel confident about them, too?"

"As far as the numbers from our own side go, absolutely," he said. "Manpower's going to be a problem for about the next seven months. After that, the training programs Linda and Shannon have in place should be producing most of the personnel we need.

And a few months after that, we'll begin steadily mothballing the old-style wallers to crew the new construction as it comes out of the yards. We're still going to be stretched to come up with the officers we need—especially flag officers with experience—but we were able to build up a solid base between the Saint-Just cease-fire and Thunderbolt. I think we'll be all right on that side, too.

"As far as the industrial side goes, I realize the economic strain of our present building plans is going to be heavy. Rachel Hanriot's made that clear enough on behalf of Treasury, but I didn't need her to tell me, and I deeply regret having to impose it. Especially given the high price we've all paid to start turning the economy around. But we don't have a lot of choice, unless we end up successfully negotiating a peace settlement."

He raised his eyebrows questioningly, and she gave her head a quick, irritable shake.

"I don't know where we are on that," she admitted, manifestly unhappily. "I'd have thought even Elizabeth Winton would be willing to sit down and talk after you, Javier, and the rest of the Navy finished kicking *her* navy's ass so thoroughly! So far, though, nothing. I'm becoming more and more convinced that Arnold's been right about the Manties' new taste for imperialism from the very beginning . . . damn him."

Theisman started to say something, then stopped. This wasn't the time to suggest that the Queen of Manticore might have very good reasons to not see things exactly as Eloise Pritchart did. Or to reiterate his own deep distrust and suspicion of anything emerging from the mouth of Secretary of State Arnold Giancola.

"Well," he said instead, "in the absence of a negotiated settlement, we don't really have any choice but to press for an outright military victory."

"And you genuinely believe we can achieve that?"

Theisman snorted in harsh amusement at her tone.

"I wish you wouldn't sound quite so . . . dubious," he said. "You're the commander-in-chief, after all. Does terrible things for the uniformed personnel's morale when you sound like you can't quite believe we can win."

"After what they did to us in the last war, and especially Buttercup, it's hard not to feel a little doubtful, Tom," she said a bit apologetically.

"I suppose it is," he conceded. "But in this case, yes, I do believe we can defeat the Star Kingdom and its allies if we have to. I really need to take you out to Bolthole to actually see what we're doing there, and discuss everything Shannon Foraker is up to. The short version, though, is that we hurt the Manties badly in Thunderbolt. Not just in the ships we destroyed, but in the unfinished construction Admiral Griffith took out at Grendelsbane. We gutted their entire second-generation podnought building program, Eloise. They're basically having to lay down new vessels from scratch, and while their building rates are still faster than ours are, even at Bolthole, they aren't fast enough to offset the jump we've gotten in ships already under construction and nearing completion. Our technology still isn't as good as theirs is, but the tech information Erewhon handed over, and the sensor data we recorded during Thunderbolt—plus the captured hardware we've been able to take apart and examine—is helping a lot in that regard, as well."

"Erewhon." Pritchart shook her head with a sigh, her expression unhappy. "I really regret the position we put Erewhon in with Thunderbolt."

"Frankly, I don't think the Erewhonese are exactly ecstatic over it, themselves," Theisman said dryly. "And I know they didn't anticipate that they were going to hand over their tech manuals on Alliance hardware just in time for us to go back to war. On the other hand, they know why we did it," *why* you *did it, actually, Eloise*, he carefully did not say aloud, "and they wouldn't have broken with Manticore in the first place if they hadn't had some pretty serious reservations of their own about the Manties' new foreign policy. And since the shooting started, we've been scrupulous about respecting the limitations built into the terms of our treaty relationship."

Pritchart nodded. The Republic's treaty with the Republic of Erewhon was one of mutual defense, and her administration had very carefully informed Erewhon—and the Manticorans—that since Haven had elected to resume open hostilities without being physically attacked by Manticore, she had no intention of attempting to invoke the military terms of the treaty.

"In any case," Theisman continued, "they at least gave us a look inside the Manties' military hardware. What they had was dated, and I could wish it were more current, but it's been extraordinarily useful to Shannon, anyway.

"The upshot is that Shannon's already working out new doctrine and some new pieces of hardware, especially in the LAC programs and our system-defense control systems, based on the combination of our information from Erewhon, examination of captured and wrecked Manticoran hardware, and analysis of operations to date. At the beginning of Thunderbolt, we'd estimated that one of our pod superdreadnoughts probably had about forty percent as much combat power as a Manticoran or Grayson SD(P). That estimate looks like it was fairly accurate at the time, but I believe we're steadily moving the ratio in our favor."

"But the Manties have as much operational data as we do, don't they? Aren't they going to be improving their capabilities right along with ours?"

"Yes and no. Actually, except for what happened to Lester at Marsh, they didn't retain possession of a single star system where we engaged them, and none of Lester's modern hyper-capable types were taken intact. We, on the other hand, effectively destroyed virtually every one of their pickets we hit, so those pickets didn't have much opportunity to pass on any observations they might have made.

"In addition, we captured examples of a lot of their hardware. Their security protocols worked damned effectively on most of their classified mollycircs, and quite a bit of what we did get we can't really use yet. Shannon says it's a case of basic differences in the capabilities of our infrastructure. For all intents and purposes, we've got to build the tools, to build the tools, to build the tools we need to reproduce a lot of Manticore's cutting edge technology. But we've still picked up a lot, and, frankly, our starting point was so far behind theirs that our *relative* capabilities are climbing more rapidly than theirs are.

"As I say, we'd estimated pre-Thunderbolt that each of their modern wallers was about twice as combat-effective as one of ours. On the basis of changes we've already made in doctrine and tactics, and allowing for how much more capable our missile defenses turned out to be, we've upped that estimate to set one of their SD(P)s as equal to about one and a half of our podnoughts. On the basis of the current rate of change in our basic capabilities, within another eight months or a year, the ratio should drop from its original two-to-one to about one-point-three-to-one. Given the difference in the numbers of ships of the wall we can anticipate commissioning over the next T-year and a half or so, and especially bearing in mind how much more strategic depth we have, that equates to a solid military superiority on our part."

"But the Legislaturalists had a solid military superiority when they started this entire cycle of war," Pritchart pointed out. "And, like the one you're talking about, it depended on 'strategic depth' and offsetting the Manties' tech edge with numbers."

"Granted," Theisman acknowledged. "And I'll also grant you that the Manties aren't going to be letting any grass grow under them. They know as well as we do that their big equalizer has always been their superior technology, so they're going to be doing whatever they can do increase their tech edge. And as someone who had far more experience than I ever wanted working with the bits and pieces of assistance we were able to get from the Solarian League back in the bad old days under Pierre and Saint-Just, I sometimes suspect that even the Manties don't realize just how good their hardware really is. It's certainly better than anything the Sollies actually have deployed. Or *had* deployed as of two or three T-years ago, at least. And if NavInt's right, they haven't done a thing to change that situation since.

"But the bottom line, Eloise, is that they simply can't match or overcome our building edge over the next two T-years or so. Even then, the sheer numbers of hulls we can lay down and man—assuming the economy holds—should be great enough to allow us to more than maintain parity in newly commissioned units. But for those two years, at a bare minimum, they simply won't have the platforms to mount whatever new weapons or defenses they introduce. And one thing both we and the Manties learned the last time around is that strategic hesitation is deadly."

"What do you mean?"

"Eloise, no one else in the history of the galaxy has ever fought a war on the scale on which we and the Manties are operating. The Solarian League never had to; it was simply so big no one *could* fight it, and everyone knew it. But we and the Manties have hammered away at each other with navies with literally hundreds of ships of the wall for most of the last twenty T-years now. And the one thing the Manties made perfectly clear in the last war is that wars like this *can* be fought to a successful *military* conclusion. They couldn't do it until they managed to assemble their Eighth Fleet for 'Operation Buttercup,' but once they did, they drove us to the brink of military collapse in just a few months. So, if they won't negotiate, and if we have a time window of, say, two T-years in which *we* enjoy a potentially decisive advantage, then this is no time to be dancing around the edges."

He looked her straight in the eye, and his voice was deep and hard.

"If we can't achieve our war objectives and an acceptable peace before our advantage in combat power erodes out from under us, then it's time for us to use that advantage while we still have it and *force* them to admit defeat. Even if that requires us to dictate peace terms in Mount Royal Palace on Manticore itself."

Chapter One

The nursery was extraordinarily full.

Two of the three older girls—Rachel and Jeanette—were downstairs, hovering on the brink of adulthood, and Theresa was at boarding school on Manticore, but the remaining five Mayhew children, their nannies, and their personal armsmen made a respectable mob. Then there was Faith Katherine Honor Stephanie Miranda Harrington, Miss Harrington, heir to Harrington Steading, and her younger twin brother, James Andrew Benjamin, and *their* personal armsmen. And lest that not be enough bodies to crowd even a nursery this large, there was her own modest person—Admiral Lady Dame Honor Harrington, Steadholder and Duchess Harrington, and *her* personal armsman. Not to mention one obviously amused treecat.

Given the presence of seven children, the oldest barely twelve, four nannies, nine armsmen (Honor herself had gotten off with only Andrew LaFollet, but Faith was accompanied by two of her three personal armsmen), and one Steadholder, the decibel level was actually remarkably low, she reflected. Of course, all things were relative.

"Now, that is *enough*!" Gena Smith, the senior member of Protector's Palace's child-care staff, said firmly in the no-nonsense voice which had thwarted—more or less—the determination of the elder Mayhew daughters to grow up as cheerful barbarians. "What is Lady Harrington going to think of you?"

"It's too late to try to fool her about that now, Gigi," Honor

17

Mayhew, one of Honor's godchildren, said cheerfully. "She's known all of us since we were born!"

"But you can at least pretend you've been exposed to the rudiments of proper behavior," Gena said firmly, although the glare she bestowed upon her unrepentant charge was somewhat undermined by the twinkle which went with it. At twelve, the girl had her own bedroom, but she'd offered to spend the night with the littles under the circumstances, which was typical of her.

"Oh, she knows that," the younger Honor said soothingly now. "I'm sure she knows we're not *your* fault."

"Which is probably the best I can hope for," Gena said with a sigh.

"I'm not exactly unaware of the . . . challenge you face with this lot," Honor assured her. "These two, particularly," she added, giving her much younger twin siblings a very old-fashioned look. They only grinned back at her, at least as unrepentant as young Honor. "On the other hand," she continued, "I think between us we have them outnumbered. And they actually seem a bit less rowdy tonight."

"Well, of course—" Gena began, then stopped and shook her head. A flash of irritation showed briefly in the backs of her gray-blue eyes. "What I meant, My Lady, is that they're usually on their better behavior—they don't actually have a *best* behavior, you understand—when you're here."

Honor nodded in response to both the interrupted comment, and the one Gena had actually made. Her eyes met the younger woman's—at forty-eight T-years, Gena Smith was well into middle age for a pre-prolong Grayson woman, but that still made her over twelve T-years younger than Honor—for just a moment, and then the two of them returned their attention to the pajama-clad children.

Despite Gena's and Honor's comments, the three assistant nannies had sorted out their charges with the efficiency of long practice. Faith and James were out from under the eye of their own regular nanny, but they were remarkably obedient to the Palace's substitutes. No doubt because they were only too well aware that their armsmen would be reporting back to "Aunt Miranda," Honor thought dryly. Teeth had already been brushed, faces had already been washed, and all seven of them had been tucked into their beds while she and Gena were talking. Somehow they made it all seem much easier than Honor's own childhood memories of the handful *she'd* been.

"All right," she said to the room at large. "Who votes for what?"

"The Phoenix!" six-year-old Faith said immediately. "The Phoenix!"

"Yeah! I mean, yes, please!" seven-year-old Alexandra Mayhew seconded.

"But you've already heard that one," Honor pointed out. "Some of you," she glanced at her namesake, "more often than others."

The twelve-year-old Honor smiled. She really was an extraordinarily beautiful child, and for that matter, it probably wasn't fair to be thinking of her as a "child" these days, really, Honor reminded herself.

"I don't mind, Aunt Honor," she said. "You know you got me stuck on it early. Besides, Lawrence and Arabella haven't heard it yet."

She nodded at her two youngest siblings. At four and three, respectively, their graduation to the "big kids" section of the nursery was still relatively recent.

"I'd like to hear it again, too, Aunt Honor. Please," Bernard Raoul said quietly. He was a serious little boy, not surprisingly, perhaps, since he was also Heir Apparent to the Protectorship of the entire planet of Grayson, but his smile, when it appeared, could have lit up an auditorium. Now she saw just a flash of it as she looked down at him.

"Well, the vote seems fairly solid," she said after a moment. "Mistress Smith?"

"I suppose they've behaved themselves *fairly* well, all things considered. *This* time, at least," Gena said as she bestowed an ominous glower upon her charges, most of whom giggled.

"In that case," Honor said, and crossed to the old-fashioned bookcase between the two window seats on the nursery's eastern wall. Nimitz shifted his weight for balance on her shoulder as she leaned forward slightly, running a fingertip across the spines of the archaic books to the one she wanted, and took it from the shelf. That book was at least twice her own age, a gift from her to the Mayhew children, as the copy of it on her own shelf at home had been a gift from her Uncle

Jacques when *she* was a child. Of course, the story itself was far older even than that. She had two electronic copies of it as well—including one with the original Raysor illustrations—but there was something especially *right* about having it in printed form, and somehow it just kept turning up periodically in the small, specialty press houses that catered to people like her uncle and his SCA friends.

She crossed to the reclining armchair, as old-fashioned and anachronistic as the printed book in her hands itself, and Nimitz leapt lightly from her shoulder to the top of the padded chair back. He sank his claws into the upholstery, arranging himself comfortably, as Honor settled into the chair which had sat in the Mayhew nursery—reupholstered and even rebuilt at need—for almost seven hundred T-years.

The attentive eyes of the children watched her while she adjusted the chair to exactly the right angle, and she and the 'cat savored the bright, clean emotions washing out from them. No wonder treecats had always loved children, she thought. There was something so . . . marvelously whole about them. When they welcomed, they welcomed with all their hearts, and they loved as they trusted, without stint or limit. That was always a gift to be treasured.

Especially now.

She looked up as the veritable horde of armsmen withdrew. Colonel LaFollet, as the senior armsman present, watched with a faint twinkle of his own as the heavily armed, lethally trained bodyguards more or less tiptoed out of the nursery. He watched the nannies follow them, then held the door courteously for Gena and bowed her through it before he came briefly to attention, nodded to Honor, and stepped through it himself. She knew he would be standing outside it when she left, however long she stayed. It was his job, even here, at the very heart of Protector's Palace, where it seemed unlikely any desperate assassins lurked.

The door closed behind him, and she looked around at her audience in the big, suddenly much calmer and quieter room.

"Lawrence, Arabella," she said to the youngest Mayhews, "you haven't heard this book before, but I think you're old enough to enjoy it. It's a very special book. It was written long, long ago, before anyone had ever left Old Earth itself."

Lawrence's eyes widened just a bit. He was a precocious child, and he loved tales about the history of humankind's ancient homeworld.

"It's called *David and the Phoenix*," she went on, "and it's always been one of my very favorite stories. And my mother loved it when she was a little girl, too. You'll have to listen carefully. It's in Standard English, but some of the words have changed since it was written. If you hear one you don't understand, stop and ask me what it means. All right?"

Both toddlers nodded solemnly, and she nodded back. Then she opened the cover.

The smell of ancient ink and paper, so utterly out of place in the modern world, rose from the pages like some secret incense. She inhaled, drawing it deeply into her nostrils, remembering and treasuring memories of rainy Sphinx afternoons, cold Sphinx evenings, and the sense of utter security and peacefulness that was the monopoly of childhood.

"*David and the Phoenix*, by Edward Ormondroyd," she read. "Chapter One, In Which David Goes Mountain Climbing and a Mysterious Voice Is Overheard."

She glanced up, and her chocolate-dark, almond-shaped eyes smiled as the children settled more comfortably into their beds, watching her raptly.

"All the way there David had saved this moment for himself," she began, "struggling not to peek until the proper time came. When the car finally stopped, the rest of them got out stiffly and went into the new house. But David walked slowly into the back yard with his eyes fixed on the ground. For a whole minute he stood there, not daring to look up. Then he took a deep breath, clenched his hands tightly, and lifted his head.

"There it was!—as Dad had described it, but infinitely more grand. It swept upward from the valley floor, beautifully shaped and soaring, so tall that its misty blue peak could surely talk face-to-face with the stars. To David, who had never seen a mountain before, the sight was almost too much to bear. He felt so tight and shivery inside that he didn't know whether he wanted to laugh, or cry, or both. And the really wonderful thing about the Mountain was the way it *looked* at him. He was certain that it was smiling at him, like an old friend who had been waiting for years to see him again. And when he closed his eyes, he seemed to hear a voice which whispered, 'Come along, then, and climb.'"

She glanced up again, feeling the children folding themselves more closely about her as the ancient words rolled over them. She felt Nimitz, as well, sharing her own memories of her mother's voice reading the same story to her and memories of other mountains, even grander than the ancient David's, and rambles through them—memories he'd been there for—and savoring the new ones.

"It would be so easy to go!" she continued. "The back yard was hedged in (with part of the hedge growing right across the toes of the Mountain), but . . ."

"I imagine it's too much to hope they were all asleep?"

"You imagine correctly," Honor said dryly, stepping through the massive, inlaid doors of polished oak into the palatial chamber which the Palace guides modestly referred to as "the Library." "Not that you really expected them to be, now did you?"

"Of course not, but we neobarbarian planetary despots get used to demanding the impossible. And when we don't get it, we behead the unfortunate soul who disappointed us."

Benjamin IX, Planetary Protector of Grayson, grinned at her, standing with his back to the log fire crackling on the hearth behind him, and she shook her head.

"I knew that eventually all this absolute power would go to your head," she told him in a display of *lese majeste* which would have horrified a third of the planet's steadholders and infuriated another third.

"Oh, between us, Elaine and I keep him trimmed down to size, Honor," Katherine Mayhew, Benjamin's senior wife said.

"Well, us and the kids," Elaine Mayhew, Benjamin's junior wife corrected. "I understand," she continued with a cheerful smile, "that young children help keep parents younger."

"That which does not kill us makes us younger?" Benjamin misquoted.

"Something like that," Elaine replied. At thirty-seven T-years, she was almost twelve years younger than her husband and almost six years younger than her senior wife. Of course, she was almost a quarter T-century younger than Honor . . . who was one of the youngest-looking people in the room. Only the third and most junior of her personal armsmen, Spencer Hawke, and the towering young lieutenant commander in Grayson Navy uniform, looked younger than she did. Prolong did that for a person.

Her mouth tightened as the thought reminded her why they were all here, and Nimitz pressed his cheek against the side of her face with a soft, comforting croon. Benjamin's eyes narrowed, and she tasted his spike of recognition. Well, he'd always been an extraordinarily sharp fellow, and spending eight T-years as the father of a daughter who'd been adopted by a treecat had undoubtedly sensitized him.

She gave him another smile, then crossed to the young man in the naval uniform. He was a veritable giant for a Grayson—indeed, he was actually taller than Honor was—and although she was in civilian attire, he came to attention and bowed respectfully. She ignored the bow and enfolded him in a firm embrace. He stiffened for an instant—in surprise, not resistance—and then hugged her back, a bit awkwardly.

"Is there any new word, Carson?" she asked quietly, stepping back a half-pace and letting her hands slide down to rest on his forearms.

"No, My Lady," he said sadly. "Your Lady Mother is at the hospital right now." He smiled faintly. "I told her it wasn't necessary. It's not as if this falls into her area of specialization, and we all know there's really nothing to be done now except to wait. But she insisted."

"Howard's her friend, too," Honor said. She glanced at Andrew LaFollet. "Is Daddy with her, Andrew?"

"Yes, My Lady. Since Faith and James are safely tucked away here in the nursery, I sent Jeremiah to keep an eye on them." Honor cocked her head, and he shrugged slightly. "He wanted to go, My Lady."

"I see." She looked back at Carson Clinkscales and gave his forearms another little squeeze, then released them. "She knows there's nothing she can really do, Carson," she said. "But she'd never forgive herself if she weren't there for your aunts. By rights, I ought to be there, too."

"Honor," Benjamin said gently, "Howard is ninety-two years old, and he's touched a lot of lives in that much time—including mine. If everyone who 'ought to be there' really *were* there, there'd be no room for the patients. And he's been in the coma for almost three days now. If you were there, and if he knew you were there, he'd read you the riot act for neglecting everything else you ought to be doing."

"I know," she sighed. "I know. It's just—"

She stopped and shook her head with a slight grimace, and he nodded understandingly. But he didn't really understand, not completely, she thought. Despite the changes which had come to Grayson, his own thought processes and attitudes had been evolved in a pre-prolong society. To him, Howard Clinkscales was *old*; for Honor, Howard should have been less than middle-aged. Her own mother, who looked considerably younger than Katherine Mayhew, or even Elaine, and who'd carried Faith and James to term naturally, was twelve T-years years *older* than Howard. And if he was the first of her Grayson friends she was losing to old age so preposterously young, he wouldn't be the last. Gregory Paxton's health was failing steadily, as well. And even Benjamin and his wives showed the signs of premature aging she'd come to dread.

Her mind flashed back to the nursery and the book she'd been reading, with its tale of the immortal, ever-renewed Phoenix, and the memory was more bittersweet than usual as she saw the silver lightly threading the Protector's still-thick, dark hair.

"Your offspring and my beloved siblings did quite well, actually," she said, deliberately seeking a change of subject. "I'm always a bit surprised by how they settle down for reading. Especially with all the other more interactive avenues of amusement they have."

"It's not the same, Aunt Honor," one of the two young women sitting at the big refectory-style table to one side of the cavernous fireplace said. Honor looked at her, and the dark-haired young woman, who looked remarkably like a taller, more muscular version of Katherine Mayhew, reached up to rub the ears of the treecat stretched across the back of her chair.

"What do you mean, not the same, Rachel?" Honor asked.

"Listening to you read," Benjamin's oldest daughter replied. "I guess it's mostly because you're involved—we don't get to see enough of you here on Grayson—and you're, well, sort of larger than life for all the kids." No one else would have noticed the way the young woman colored very slightly, but Honor hid a smile as she tasted Rachel's own spike of adolescent admiration and embarrassment. "I know when Jeanette and I—" she nodded sideways at the slightly younger woman sitting beside her "—were younger, we always looked forward to seeing you. And Nimitz, of course."

The treecat on Honor's shoulder elevated his nose and flirted his tail in satisfaction at Rachel's acknowledgment of his own importance in the social hierarchy, and several people chuckled. Rachel's companion, Hipper, only heaved a sigh of long-suffering patience and closed his eyes wearily.

"She may be right, Honor," Elaine said. "Young Honor certainly volunteered suspiciously quickly to 'help keep an eye on the littles' this evening."

"Besides, Aunt Honor," Jeanette said in a softer voice (she was considerably shyer than her older sister), "you really do read awfully well." Honor raised an eyebrow, and Jeanette blushed far more obviously than Rachel had. But she also continued with stubborn diffidence. "I know I always really enjoyed listening to you. The characters all even sounded different from each other. Besides, there's more challenge in a book. Nobody just *gives* you the way the people and places look; you have to imagine them for yourselves, and you make that *fun*."

"Well, I'm glad you think so," Honor said after a moment, and Katherine snorted.

"She's not the only one who thinks so," she said, when Honor looked at her. "Most of the nannies have told me what a wonderful mother you'd make, if you weren't so busy off blowing up starships and planets and things."

"Me?" Honor blinked at her in surprise, and Katherine shook her head.

"You, Lady Harrington. In fact," she went on a bit more intently, "there's been some, um, discussion of your responsibility in that direction. Faith is a perfectly satisfactory heir for the moment, you understand, but no one in the Conclave of Steadholders really expects her to *remain* your heir."

"Cat," Benjamin said in an ever so slightly quelling tone.

"Oh, hush, Ben!" his wife replied tartly. "Everyone's been pussyfooting around the issue for a long time now, and you know it. Politically, it would be far better in almost every respect for Honor to produce an heir of her own."

"That's not going to be happening any time soon," Honor said firmly. "Not with everything I already have on my plate at the moment!"

"Time's slipping away, Honor," Katherine said with stubborn persistence. "And you're going back out into another war. Tester knows we'll all be praying for you to come back safely, but—"

She shrugged, and Honor was forced to concede her point. Still . . .

"As you say, Faith is a perfectly acceptable heir," she said. "And while I suppose I ought to be thinking in dynastic terms, it doesn't really come naturally to me."

"I hate to say it, Honor, but Cat may have a point from another perspective, as well," Benjamin said slowly. "Oh, there's no legal reason you need to produce an heir of your own body right this minute. Especially with, as you say, Faith acknowledged as your heir by everyone. But you're a prolong recipient. You say you're not used to thinking in dynastic terms, but what happens if you wait another twenty or thirty years and *then* have a child? Under Grayson law, that child would automatically supplant Faith, whatever special provisions the Conclave may have made in her favor when everyone thought you were dead. So there's Faith . . . who's spent thirty or forty years thinking of herself as the Harrington Heir Apparent and suddenly finds her nose put out of joint by a brand new infant nephew or niece."

Honor looked at him, and he sighed.

"I know Faith is a wonderful child and she loves you dearly, Honor. But this is Grayson. We've seen a thousand years of those dynastic politics you don't think in terms of, and there have been some really ugly incidents. And the ugliest ones of all have usually happened because the people they happened to were so sure they couldn't arise in *their* families. Besides, even if no overt problem crops up, would it really be fair to Faith to yank the succession out from under her like that? Unless you produce a child fairly soon, she's got to grow up thinking of herself as Miss Harrington, with all the trappings and importance of the job. You didn't do that, but she's in a totally different position, and it's going to be fairly central to her self-image, you know."

"Maybe so, but—"

"No buts, Honor. Not on this one," Benjamin said gently. "It *will* be. It has to be. I know it was a lot harder for Michael than he ever let on, and he never wanted the Protector's job in the first place. But he was in exactly the same position Faith is, and when Bernard Raoul came along and pushed him out of the succession, he was almost . . . lost for a while. He needed to redefine who he was and what he was doing with his life when he was suddenly no longer Lord Mayhew." The Protector shook his head. "I was discussing this with Howard just last month, and he said—"

It was Benjamin's turn to break off suddenly as Honor's face tightened in remembered pain.

"I'm sorry," he said after a moment, even more gently. "And I don't mean to be exerting any unfair pressure. But he was concerned about it. He loves Faith almost as much as he loves you, and he was worried about how she'd react. And," he smiled crookedly, "I think he was sort of hoping he'd have a chance to see your child."

"Benjamin, I—" Honor blinked rapidly, and Nimitz crooned soothingly in her ear.

"Don't," Benjamin said, and shook his head. "We don't need to be discussing this right now, and you don't need me reminding you that we're losing him. I wouldn't have brought it up at all, but I think maybe Cat was right to at least put the thought before you. Now we've done that, and you can think about it later. And as far as Howard himself is concerned, of course he loves you. He told me once that he thought of you very much as his own daughter."

"I'm going to miss him so much," she said sadly.

"Of course you are. So am I, you know," Benjamin reminded her with a bittersweet smile. "I've known him literally all my life. He's been an extra uncle, one I've loved almost as much as he sometimes exasperated me."

"And one whose death is going to make a hole in the Conclave," Katherine observed sadly.

"I've discussed my choice for his successor with the Standing Committee and the Chair of the Administration Committee," Honor said. She inhaled deeply, deliberately and gratefully turning to the change in subject. "I think it should go as smoothly as anything could, under the circumstances."

"And you're *not* supposed to discuss it with me, My Lady Steadholder," Benjamin pointed out.

"And I'm not supposed to discuss it with you," Honor conceded.

"Which is, if you don't mind my saying so, one of the stupider of Grayson's innumerable traditions."

"I suppose when you spend as long assembling them as we have, one or two suboptimal selections may make it through the filtering process." Benjamin shrugged. "Overall, they work pretty well for us, though. And the fact that you're not allowed to discuss it with me doesn't mean my various spies and agents don't know exactly who you're planning to nominate. Or that I don't heartily approve of your selection, for that matter."

"Well, since we've gotten all of that out of the way without ever transgressing, perhaps we could discuss some of the things we *are* allowed to talk to Honor about," Katherine suggested.

"Such as?" Her husband raised his eyebrows at her, and she gave him an exasperated look.

"Such as what the Admiralty is going to have her doing, for starters," she said.

"Oh. That."

Benjamin glanced at his elder daughters. Jeanette favored Elaine at least as strongly as Rachel favored Katherine, with her biological mother's fair coloring and blue eyes. At the moment, both young women seemed torn between attempting to appear invisible or mature and insightful, whichever was more likely to let them go on sitting exactly where they were.

"Sword rules apply, girls," he said. Both of them nodded solemnly, and he turned back to Honor. "What *are* they going to have you doing?"

"I can't really tell you for certain yet," Honor replied, watching the young women from the corner of one eye. Rachel had reached up to caress Hipper's ears again, and her expression was intent. Understandably, since she would be entering the Royal Manticoran Navy's Saganami Island academy in less than a month. Honor had delivered the traditional "Last View" address to the senior class two weeks before; the other forms' abbreviated wartime summer leaves would be up in ten days, and Rachel would be returning to Manticore aboard the *Paul Tankersley* to report to the newest class of snotties. Jeanette looked curious and sober, but she'd never been the navy-mad tomboy Rachel had.

"I'm not trying to be mysterious," Honor continued. "Things have been so crazy ever since I got back from Sidemore that it seems the Admiralty's strategic thinking changes on an almost daily basis. The numbers ONI is coming up with keep getting worse, not better, and they keep whittling away at what was supposed to be Eighth Fleet's order of battle." She shrugged with an alum-tart smile. "I suppose it's almost a tradition now that building up anything called 'Eighth Fleet' won't go smoothly."

"And you say *we* have some stupid traditions," Benjamin snorted.

"Well, it's not as if anyone *wants* it to be that way, Benjamin. But after the hammering we took in the opening phase, nobody's about to uncover Manticore, Grayson, or Trevor's Star. So anything Eighth Fleet gets is going to be what's left over after our minimum security requirements for those systems have been met. Which isn't going to be a lot. Not right at first, anyway. And to be totally fair, Eighth Fleet doesn't really exist yet. I'm Commanding Officer (*Designate*), Eighth Fleet. My staff and fleet HQ haven't even been formally activated yet."

"I know. And, to be honest, I was actually a bit surprised they made the announcement that Eighth Fleet would be reactivated as publicly as they did. Relieved, but surprised." Benjamin waved her into an armchair beside the hearth and seated himself facing her. His wives went over and sat beside their daughters, and Carson Clinkscales walked across to stand beside Honor's chair.

"I'm pleased at the evidence that the Admiralty is thinking in offensive terms," the Protector continued. "After the pounding Theisman gave us, it must have been dreadfully tempting to revert to a totally defensive stance."

"I'm sure it would have been for a lot of people," Honor said. "Not for Thomas Caparelli and Hamish Alexander, though." She shook her head again. "The difference between them and the Janacek Admiralty is like the difference between day and night."

"Which, if you'll forgive me, My Lady," Lieutenant Commander Clinkscales said, "may be because they can find their posteriors without approach radar."

"I think you could safely describe them as possessing that degree of native ability, Carson," she observed, and he blushed slightly.

"Sorry, My Lady," he said after a moment. "What I meant was that it was because Janacek and Chakrabarti *couldn't* find their backsides."

"Actually, that's a bit unfair to Chakrabarti, I think," Honor said. "But Janacek—and those idiots Jurgensen and Draskovic!" Her mouth tightened, and she shook her head. "In their cases, you certainly have a point. But *my* point was that Sir Thomas—and Earl White Haven—have been in this position before. They're not about to panic, and they know we're going to have to take the fight to the other side as soon and as hard as we can. We can't afford to leave the initiative completely in Thomas Theisman's hands. If we do that, he'll hand us our head within the next six months. At the outside, a T-year."

"Is it really that bad, My Lady?" Clinkscales asked quietly.

"Almost certainly," she replied, her soprano voice quiet against the background crackle of the flaming logs. "It's starting to look very much as if Admiral Givens' initial estimates may actually have been low."

"Low?" Benjamin frowned at her.

"I know. I think everyone—myself included—felt she was being too pessimistic in her original assumptions. It just didn't seem possible that the Republic could really have built a fleet the size of the one she was projecting. But that was because we all insisted on thinking in terms of ships built since Theisman overthrew Saint-Just."

"Well, of course we did. They couldn't possibly have had the technology to build the new types any sooner than that. Certainly not before Hamish hit them with Buttercup."

Honor's expression didn't flicker as Benjamin used the current First Lord of Admiralty's given name, but she was careful not to use it herself.

"No, they couldn't have," she agreed. "And that's the reason Earl White Haven, for one, was convinced Admiral Givens' estimates were too high. Unfortunately, he's had to change his mind in the last couple of weeks. I don't have the details yet, but according to his last letter, she's dug up some data that went back to before Jurgensen took over from her at ONI. Some anomalies her own analysts had turned up and been unable to explain at the time. Apparently, they suggest that the Peeps might have been stockpiling components even before Saint-Just was killed."

"Stockpiling? For that long?" Benjamin looked skeptical, and she shrugged.

"I haven't seen the data or the analysis myself, Benjamin. And

I may have it wrong. But that was my impression from the Earl's letter when I viewed it last night. I'm sure he'll have more to say to me about it when I get back to Manticore."

"I'm sure he will," Benjamin said slowly, frowning in manifest thought.

"And if Admiral Givens is right, My Lady?" Clinkscales asked quietly.

"If Admiral Givens is right, then we're looking at a serious numerical disadvantage," Honor said soberly. "And one which is going to get a lot worse before it gets better. The question, of course," she smiled without a trace of humor, "is whether or not the numbers are bad enough to offset our quality. And at the moment, considering the command team they've managed to put together, that's a very pointed question, indeed."

Chapter Two

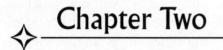

"Ah, there you are, Aldona! Come in. Find a seat."

Aldona Anisimovna nodded to her host with carefully metered deference and obeyed the smiling order. And it *was* an order, however pleasantly given. Albrecht Detweiler was, quite possibly, the wealthiest and most powerful single individual in the explored galaxy. There were entire star nations, and not just those full of neobarbs or stuck off in the back of beyond in the Shell, worth less than he was. Quite a few of them, in fact.

The door closed silently behind her. Despite the presence of over a dozen people, the combination office and library radiated a sense of spaciousness. As well it should, even if barely five percent of the population of Mesa even knew it existed. The percentage of people *off* Mesa who knew about it was, she devoutly hoped, considerably smaller than that.

It was also by far the most luxuriously and beautifully furnished "office" she'd ever been in, which was saying quite a lot for a full board member of Manpower Incorporated. The superb light sculptures in their tailored niches; the walls paneled in the exotic woods of at least a dozen different planets; the old-fashioned, priceless oil and watercolor paintings, some of them dating back all the way to pre-space days on Old Earth; the antique printed books; and the spectacular view across the Mendel Ocean's sugar-white beaches and sparkling blue water all came together to form an inevitably appropriate frame for the power and purpose concentrated in this meeting.

"I believe we're all here now," Detweiler observed as Anisimovna settled into one of the powered float chairs facing his desk, and the side conversations ended quickly. He smiled again and pressed a button on his desk panel, and the panoramic ocean view disappeared beyond an abruptly opaque wall of windows as he brought up the security systems which made it impossible for *any* surveillance device to snoop upon this particular meeting.

"I'm sure most of you have at least an idea of why I asked you to drop by the island today," Detweiler said, his smile fading into a purposeful expression. "Just in case I've overestimated the IQ of anyone present, however, the immediate cause for this little get-together is the recent plebiscite in the Talbott Cluster."

Faces tightened, and one could almost feel the combination of anger, tension, and—whether any of them would have admitted it or not—fear his words evoked. Detweiler certainly felt it, and he showed his teeth in what definitely was *not* another smile.

"I realize that for most Sollies, Manticore and Haven might as well be Shangri-La or Never-Neverland. They're off somewhere on the edge of the explored universe, full of belligerent neobarbs so primitive and bigoted they spend all their time killing one another. That, unfortunately, falls somewhat short of the truth, as all of us are rather painfully aware. What some of you may not realize, is that in many ways the situation is getting worse, not better, from our perspective."

He tipped back in his own chair and surveyed his guests. One or two of them looked a bit puzzled, as if they couldn't quite see why the situation was any worse than it had always been. After all, both the Star Kingdom of Manticore and the Republic of Haven had been the openly avowed mortal enemies of Manpower Incorporated and the genetic slave trade literally for centuries. From the viewpoint of Manpower and the Mesa System generally, the last twenty T-years of warfare between the Star Kingdom amd the Republic had been excellent news. At least it had distracted both of them, to greater or lesser extent, from their interference in Manpower's affairs.

"Aldona," he said after a moment, "suppose you and Isabel tell us about what happened at Congo."

"Certainly, Albrecht," Anisimovna said. She was rather pleased her voice sounded so calm and composed. She also managed to avoid breaking out into a nervous sweat, thanks to the last

twenty or so generations of genetic modifications to the Anisimov genome.

"As you know, Albrecht," she began briskly, trying not to think
about how many such reports had ended . . . badly in this office,
"and as some of the other members of the Board and Council
are aware, Congo was rather central to certain plans we had for
the Manties and Haven. The wormhole junction there offered
additional possibilities in that respect, as well as the more obvious, purely commercial opportunities. After discussions here on
Mesa, it was decided that the time to put our contingency plans
into effect was rapidly approaching, and—"

"Excuse me, Aldona," Jerome Sandusky interrupted. He looked at
her, but most of his attention was actually focused on Detweiler.
"We're all aware, in general terms, at least, of what happened at
Tiberian and Congo. In my own case, the fact that Congo's been
added to my bailiwick in Haven means I've become reasonably
familiar with previous operations there. But what I'm not quite
clear on is exactly why it seemed necessary or desirable to put
ourselves into a position where something like that could happen in the first place."

"The decision was made by the Strategy Committee, Jerome,"
Anisimovna said coolly, and he flushed ever so slightly. "As a
member of the Committee," *which you aren't,* she did not say
aloud, "I agreed with the logic, but as you know, the Committee's
discussions are privileged."

"In this instance, however, Aldona," Detweiler said easily, "I
believe we might make an exception. This is something all of
us need to be brought fully up to speed on, so go ahead and
answer Jerome's question for all of us." She looked at him, and
he nodded. "My authority," he added.

"Very well, Albrecht." Anisimovna returned her attention to
Sandusky. She spent a moment or two organizing her thoughts,
then leaned slightly forward in her chair, gray eyes intent.

"For most of the last two decades, the Manties and the Peeps
have been shooting at each other," she began. "From our perspective, that's been a good thing in many ways. They've always
hated us, and we've never been able to penetrate their military
or political establishments the way we have the League or most
other star nations. We've managed to . . . enlist certain individual
bureaucrats, diplomats, officers, and politicians, but never in

sufficient numbers to undermine their dogged devotion to the Cherwell Convention."

More than one of her listeners grimaced at mention of the Cherwell Convention, and Anisimovna smiled thinly.

"For the last seventy T-years, the one thing—the *only* thing—the Star Kingdom of Manticore and the People's Republic of Haven have agreed on is the suppression of the genetic slave trade. And let's be realistic—historically, their efforts have been much more effective than those of anyone else. We have zero market penetration in either of them, and although we've historically had major penetration in some areas of the Silesian Confederacy and Midgard, the Manties and the Peeps have made life hard on us even there. To be honest, it's really only since the two of them started concentrating on one another that we've been able to regain ground we'd been steadily losing in both of those areas. The Andermani Empire is another sore point, particularly since it happens to lie in such close proximity to the other two, but the Andies have never been as aggressive about attacking our interests outside their own territory.

"While the Manties and the Peeps were actively at war with one another, we managed to expand our influence and markets on the peripheries of their spheres. And their concentration on one another also made it easier for us to acquire a degree of penetration—of influence, not sales—which we'd never had before in both the Star Kingdom and the Republic themselves. Things, in other words, were looking up.

"Then along came the Manties' 'Operation Buttercup,' Pierre's assassination, the so-called 'Manpower Incident' on Old Earth, the cease-fire, and the overthrow of the Saint-Just version of the Committee of Public Safety. In combination, they produced three serious consequences for us."

She made a face and shrugged, then began ticking off points on her fingers as she summarized them.

"First, the end of the fighting would have been bad enough all by itself, given the way it was bound to free up their resources and attention for other concerns—like us. But, second, the overthrow of the Committee of Public Safety and the effective dismantlement of State Security hurt us badly in Haven. Not only did we lose the majority of the contacts we'd managed to make with the SS, but the new régime—Theisman, Pritchart, and their bunch—are almost fanatical in their hatred of everything we stand for. And, third, the 'Manpower Incident' happened before Theisman's coup, but its main effects weren't felt until afterward, when Zilwicki and Montaigne got back to Manticore with the records Zilwicki managed to hack. We were able to manage at least some damage control in the Star Kingdom, but let's not fool ourselves; we took a real body blow there, too. And the fact that that lunatic Montaigne has managed to pull us and our operations back into the limelight for the Manty public hasn't helped.

"Fortunately, our best and highest surviving contact in Manticore wasn't in Zilwicki's files and remained in place. She wasn't really what we could consider a reliable asset—she was using us as much as we were using her, and she definitely had her own agenda—but Descroix was willing to do what she could to mitigate Manty operations against us and assist with damage control domestically in the wake of the 'Manpower Incident' in return for our financial support and the intelligence we could provide her. Unfortunately, she was completely *un*willing to do the main thing we wanted out of her."

"Which was?" Sandusky prompted, as if he didn't already know the answer to his own question, when she paused.

"Which was to get rid of the damned cease-fire," Aldona said flatly. "We wanted Manticore and Haven shooting at each other again. To be frank, at that time, the Strategy Committee was actually more concerned about Haven than Manticore. Manticore has the bigger merchant fleet, and the stronger tradition of arrogating some sort of interstellar police power to itself, even to the extent of locking horns with the League. But the Republic is much larger, and the new régime there clearly has a 'crusading spirit,' whereas the High Ridge régime in Manticore was about as venal—and shortsighted—as we could have asked for. Unfortunately, neither side, each for its own reasons, wanted to resume hostilities. And initially, at least, it looked like something of a toss-up as to whether or not Theisman and Pritchart could make their new Constitution stand up. For at least a few years, they were going to be involved in what amounted to a civil war, even if they managed to win it in the end.

"About two T-years ago, however, it became evident they *were* going to win, and quite handily. In addition, one of the handful of contacts we'd managed to hang onto in the Republic—*your* contact, as a matter of fact, Jerome—informed us that the Havenite Navy was secretly in the process of some sort of major rebuilding program. The notion of a Theisman-Pritchart government, firmly in control of a star nation and an economy the size of the Republic, with a resurgent navy under its command, didn't make anyone on the Committee happy. Nor was anyone enthralled with what Montaigne and Zilwicki were up to in the Star Kingdom. You may recall the rather spectacular failure of our attempt to remove Montaigne by direct action. That was primarily the result of Zilwicki's active alliance with the Audubon Ballroom, and then Klaus Hauptman and his daughter climbed onto the bandwagon and began building actual light *warships* for those butchers."

She shook her head.

"So far, it was all straws in the wind, but it was pretty obvious which way the breeze was blowing in both star nations. And they *still* weren't shooting at each other.

"The only bright spot was the High Ridge Government's total diplomatic tone deafness. They might not want active military operations, but they didn't want a formal peace settlement, either, which produced steadily growing frustration in the Republic. The same source which had warned us about the existence of Bolthole—even though he didn't know exactly what was going on there—also kept us informed about Pritchart's rising anger and the public opinion which agreed with her. While we knew we couldn't get Descroix to actively seek to derail the negotiating process, we were able to feed her certain selected information which helped move her at least a bit in the direction we wanted. So the Committee saw a situation which was growing rapidly less stable and offered the possibility of producing the result we were after.

"That's where Verdant Vista entered the picture. We knew High Ridge had managed to seriously alienate several key allies, including the Republic of Erewhon and, we hoped, Grayson. We didn't have very high expectations where Grayson was concerned, but Erewhon seemed to offer possibilities. In addition, certain of our friends in the League—specifically, Technodyne Industries—*really* wanted access to the Manties' new technology, and Erewhon had that.

"So the idea was to use Verdant Vista to worry Erewhon. We knew the Cromarty Government had promised the Erewhonese the

Star Kingdom's assistance in their efforts to eject us from Congo. But we also knew the *High Ridge* Government was completely and totally—one might almost say vehemently—disinterested in the project. And we knew this was an area in which we could count on Descroix's support behind the scenes.

"With all that in mind, we abandoned our relatively low profile and started deliberately drawing attention to our presence there. We planted a few stories in the Erewhonese 'faxes about 'atrocities' on Verdant Vista, and we encouraged an upswing in 'piracy' in the area. The cruisers that were destroyed at Tiberian were part of that strategy. The idea was to draw the Erewhonese Navy into committing additional light units to piracy suppression in the vicinity, then to pounce on those units with modern Solarian heavy cruisers and wipe them out. Whether the Erewhonese decided we were directly involved in backing the 'pirates' or not, they were bound to become even more furious with the Star Kingdom when they started suffering losses among their warships as well as their merchant traffic. Given the peculiarities of the Erewhonese honor code, it was likely that if we continued to provoke them long enough, and if the Manties continued to ignore their demands for assistance, the Erewhonese would eventually withdraw from the Manticoran Alliance."

"Which would be good for us in exactly what way?" Sandusky asked, frowning intently as he followed her explanation.

"Erewhon's abandonment of the Alliance was bound to shake up even the Manticorans. The Manty woman-in-the-street seemed willing enough to go along with High Ridge as long as there was no clearly perceived external threat to the Star Kingdom's security. If, however, the Alliance seemed to be crumbling, still without any formal peace treaty, that was likely to change, hopefully in the direction of greater militancy directed towards the Republic. And, to be honest, although High Ridge's disinterest in suppressing slavery was good for us, we doubted that he'd be able to ignore the issue much longer, given the way the Winton dynasty's always hated us and how hard Montaigne, Zilwicki, Harrington, and people like the Hauptmans were all pushing it. So we were perfectly willing to see his government fall, especially if that contributed to the resumption of hostilities we wanted.

"From another perspective, once Erewhon withdrew from the Alliance, the Erewhonese were going to suddenly start feeling very lonely, especially if their one-time allies and the Republic *did* start shooting at each other again. Under those circumstances, it seemed likely they'd feel the need to bolster and maintain their own military, which would probably mean going back to the people who'd built all of their ships of the wall before they joined the alliance. Which happens to be our good friends at Technodyne. Which meant Technodyne would be able to get a direct look at the latest and best Manty war-fighting hardware. Whether or not the *League's* navy would be interested in it, Technodyne and the Mesan Navy certainly were, and getting access to it for ourselves and the system defense contingents of our friends in the region would have been a very good thing. That's why Technodyne was so cooperative about coming up with the Tiberian-based cruisers."

"But it didn't work out that way, did it, Aldona?" Detweiler asked. His tone was almost avuncular, but that didn't make Anisimovna feel one bit better. She started to reply, but someone else beat her to it.

"No, Mr. Detweiler, it didn't," Isabel Bardasano said.

The younger woman sat beside Anisimovna, and she met the Mesan Chairman of the Board's eyes levelly, with every appearance of complete equanimity. Which, Anisimovna thought, was probably accurate in her case. She envied Bardasano's composure, yet she was none too certain about the confidence, even arrogance, upon which that composure rested. At the moment, however, she was mostly grateful to Bardasano for intervening. And for reminding Detweiler that Anisimovna had not had primary, or at least solo, responsibility for the Verdant Vista operation.

"It should have," Bardasano continued. "Unfortunately, we hadn't counted on the Battle of Tiberian. Nor had we counted on the Stein Assassination, or on the fact that Elizabeth Winton would decide to send Anton Zilwicki, of all people, as her representative at the funeral on Erewhon. And we certainly hadn't counted on the interference of a Havenite spy and some sort of rogue operation by a Frontier Security governor!"

She shook her head, her expression disgusted.

"We got exactly the break with Manticore that we wanted. Unfortunately, instead of falling into Technodyne's arms, which is what we're almost certain the then current Erewhonese government would have done, left to its own devices, the Havenites and

Governor Barregos managed to convince them to run straight into the arms of the Republic of Haven. Worse, Ruth Winton was right there on the spot and actually managed to get the Star Kingdom, however marginally, involved in supporting what was effectively a *Havenite*-planned operation against Congo. That left the two of them standing as joint sponsors of the 'Torch' régime on Verdant Vista—a relationship which seems to be surviving so far despite the fact that they're shooting at each other everywhere else. And just to make the situation even better, we have strong indications that in the course of his own contributions to generating this fiasco, Zilwicki managed to get his hands on some sort of evidence which led to the disappearance of Countess North Hollow and the destruction of the North Hollow Files, which ultimately played its own part in the fall of the High Ridge Government and Descroix's complete loss of power."

"Speaking of Descroix...?" another of Detweiler's guests inquired.

"No longer a problem," Bardasano replied with a thin smile.

"Good."

"But eliminating her didn't eliminate the fallout from the entire Congo debacle," Sandusky pointed out.

"No, it didn't," Anisimovna agreed. "It comes under the heading of damage control, at best."

"Agreed," Detweiler said.

He sat back from his desk for a moment, surveying the people he'd assembled. They looked back, and he knew what they were seeing—the culmination of almost five centuries of steady genetic improvement. Much of the rest of the galaxy remained blissfully unaware that what the Ukrainian maniacs of Old Earth's Final War had failed to achieve with their "Scrags" had, in fact, *been* achieved on Mesa.

But Mesa had learned more than one lesson from the Slav Supremacists, including the need to be cautious. To build a position of security first, before trumpeting the fact of one's superiority to those who would justifiably see in one the hateful image of their future master.

"I didn't gather you all here just so we could recount our failures. Nor, for the record, do I believe that what happened to our Congo operations was the fault of anyone in this room or on the Strategy Committee. No one can allow for all the vagaries of blind chance bound to occur in a galaxy with this many inhabited worlds and competing power blocs.

"But the fact remains that we're entering a period of growing risk . . . and opportunity. The situation vis-à-vis Manticore and Haven is perhaps the most clear-cut, recognizable threat we face. At the moment, that threat is manageable, so long as we take steps to ensure it remains that way. The greater threat—and opportunity—we confront, however, is the fact that we are finally approaching the point towards which we and our ancestors have worked for so long. For now, that remains unrecognized by the vast majority of those who might oppose us. As we begin our final preparations, however, it becomes more and more likely our actual objectives will be recognized. That moment of recognition must be delayed as long as possible, and I believe one of the keys to doing that may be the fashion in which we manage the Manties and Peeps."

Tension had gathered perceptibly in the palatial office as he spoke. Now the big room was utterly silent as he swept his eyes slowly from face to face, searching for any signs of weakness, of wavering commitment. He found none, and he allowed his chair to come back fully upright.

"Fortunately for us, Haven and the Manties have managed to get themselves back into a shooting war despite the failure of our original plans for Erewhon. That's good. But the Manties are clearly intent on expanding into the Talbott Cluster, despite the distraction of the war, and that's bad. Bad for many reasons, but not least for how much closer to Mesa it will bring their advanced naval bases.

"Also on the deficit side of the ledger, we still haven't managed to obtain access to first-line Manticoran naval hardware. No matter how everything else works out, eventually we *are* going to find ourselves in open conflict with Manticore, unless we can somehow arrange for someone else to handle that chore for us. We'll continue to pursue the option of finding someone else to do the deed, and I'm sure we'd all find it extremely satisfying if we could, indeed, find a way to use Haven and Manticore to neutralize each other. I don't believe we can count on that, however, so it behooves us to continue planning for an ultimate direct confrontation. With that in mind, anything we can do to reduce Manticore's military, economic, and industrial power bases is eminently worthwhile. Which obviously includes keeping them from annexing the Cluster and all the industrial potential those planets represent.

"I happen to know the Strategy Committee is already working on a plan to at least destabilize and hopefully permanently derail the Talbott annexation. Personally, I give it no more than a thirty percent chance of succeeding, but I could be being unduly pessimistic. Aldona and Isabel will be our contacts for that particular operation, and I want it clearly understood by everyone in this room—whatever we may say or do for the consumption of others—that while I very much hope for their success, we must all be aware that that success is at best problematical. In other words, there will be no penalties and no retaliation if, through no fault of their own, this plan miscarries."

Anisimovna's expression didn't even flicker, despite the enormous sense of relief she felt at Detweiler's pronouncement. Of course, he hadn't said there would be no penalties if the plan miscarried and he decided the fault *was* theirs.

"While they deal with that aspect of the problem, Jerome," he continued, turning to Sandusky, "*you* will be polishing up the final details of our arrangement with Mannerheim. Make it very clear to President Hurskainen that it's almost certainly going to be up to him to provide the military muscle when the time comes for the open move to retake Congo." He grimaced. "We can't afford to postpone that particular necessity very long. We've got some time, but the last thing we need is for an entire planet of Ballroom fanatics to get loose in the galaxy. Especially not a planet which controls that particular wormhole junction."

"What about the indirect approach we've discussed?" Sandusky asked in a businesslike voice.

"We'll keep it in reserve," Detweiler directed. "It has a certain appeal on its own merits, but at the moment, Verdant Vista appears to be the only point over which the Manties and Havenites continue to find themselves sharing any common ground. Any move against this so-called 'monarchy' at this time would certainly be seen as our handiwork, however many cutouts we employed, and I don't want us to do anything which might push them closer together where we're concerned than they already are.

"Nonetheless, Isabel," he turned back to Bardasano, "we do need to keep the thought in mind. This is your particular specialty, and I want a detailed operational plan on my desk and ready for implementation before you and Aldona head out to meet with Verrochio. We'll call it . . . Operation Rat Poison."

An ugly ripple of amusement ran around the room, and he nodded in satisfaction.

"I've done the best preliminary groundwork I could for you and Aldona in Talbott," he continued to Bardasano. "Technodyne doesn't know everything we're up to, but they've agreed to at least listen to our proposition. I expect you'll probably be hearing from a Mr. Levakonic shortly, and everything I've been able to discover about him suggests he should be amenable. On the minus side, you're also going to have to deal with Kalokainos. The old man is bad enough, but Volkhart is an idiot. Unfortunately, Verrochio and Hongbo are firmly in Kalokainos' pocket, so we're going to have to at least go through the motions of 'consulting' with him. You may actually have to involve him in the initial strategy discussions, although I trust you'll be able to cut him out of the circuit fairly early. I've had our official representative in the area briefed to help you accomplish that—not fully, but in sufficient detail for him to understand what he has to do. He's supposed to be pretty good at this sort of thing."

"Who is it, Albrecht?" Anisimovna asked.

"His name is Ottweiler, Valery Ottweiler," Detweiler replied.

"I know him," she said, frowning thoughtfully. "And he really is good at this kind of thing. In fact, if it weren't for his genome, I'd say he should be brought fully inside."

"Are you suggesting probationer status for him?" Sandusky asked a bit sharply.

"I didn't say that, Jerome," Anisimovna returned coolly. She and Sandusky had crossed swords entirely too often in the past, and she wasn't certain whether he really opposed the notion or secretly hoped she would suggest it and be supported over his opposition. It was always risky to nominate a normal for probationer status, and he might be hoping this one would blow up, as others had, with the egg landing on *her* face this time.

"If this operation succeeds, and if he's as integral to its success as I expect him to be," she continued after a brief pause, "then it might be time for the *Council* to consider whether or not he should be offered that status. I don't personally know the man well enough to predict how he would react. But he does have a reputation for effectiveness, and he could be even more effective for us as a probationer brought more fully into the real picture."

"We'll cross that bridge when—and if—we come to it," Detweiler decreed. "In the meantime, you and Isabel undoubtedly have a lot of details to take care of before you depart. I'll be meeting with both of you—and with some of the rest of you—privately over the next few days. For now, though, I believe we're done, and dinner is waiting."

He started to push back from the desk, but Bardasano raised one hand in a respectful attention-requesting gesture. She was, by almost any conventional standard, the most junior individual in the room, but her professional competence—and ruthlessness—made her lack of conventional seniority meaningless, and Detweiler settled back.

"Yes, Isabel? You had a question?"

"Not about the Cluster," she said. "I do have one question concerning Rat Poison, however, and I thought I'd raise it while we were all here, since it may affect Jerome's planning, as well."

"And that question is?"

"As you know, most of our current scenarios for Rat Poison are built around the use of the new nanotech. We've run several test operations to be sure it works—the most prominent was the Hofschulte business on New Potsdam. As you also know," she didn't so much as glance at Sandusky, who had been responsible for that particular "test operation," "I had my doubts about the advisability of using the new technology in an assassination attempt which was bound to attract as much attention and comment as that one did. In this instance, it appears my concerns were misplaced, however, since there's no evidence anyone as much as suspects what really happened.

"The question in my mind, however, is whether or not we want to consider making additional use of the same technique in the interim. I can foresee several possible sets of circumstances where it could be very useful. In particular, according to Jerome's reports, our primary contact in the Havenite Department of State is almost certainly going to require a completely untraceable weapon sometime in the next few weeks or months."

"Well, *this* is an interesting change of mind," Sandusky remarked astringently.

"It isn't really a change of mind at all, Jerome," Bardasano said calmly. "My concern at the time was that someone would figure out how it was done, but the Andies have run every test they could think of on Hofschulte—or, rather, his cadaver—without, apparently, turning up a thing. If they haven't found anything after looking this long and this hard, then the R and D types may actually have known what they were talking about this time. Which," she added dryly, "always comes as a pleasant and unanticipated surprise for us unfortunate field grunts."

Several people, including Renzo Kyprianou, whose bio weapon research teams had developed the technology in question, laughed.

"If this technique works as well as it did in our tests, and really is this close to impossible to detect," she continued more seriously, "then it might be time for us to begin making judicious use of it in special cases." She shrugged. "Even if they figure out someone is deliberately triggering the attacks, there's not much they can do about it. Not, at least, without security arrangements which would effectively hamstring their own operations. And I can think of several prominent individuals in both Manticore and Haven whose sudden and possibly spectacular demises could be quite beneficial to us. Especially if we can convince both sides that the *other* one, not some third party, is responsible."

"I'll have to think about that," Detweiler said, after a moment. "I felt your original arguments for restraint had considerable merit. But what you've just suggested also has merit. Keeping something like this in reserve, as a total surprise, is always tempting. But if you keep it in reserve too long, then you never use it at all."

He pursed his lips for several seconds, then shrugged.

"Jerome, you and I will have to discuss this. Give some thought to the pros and cons and sit down with Isabel before she leaves. Work out a list of potential targets—not a big one, I don't want to flash this capability around any more obviously than we have to, however unlikely it is that someone will figure out how it works. At the very least, though, we can put the groundwork in place and have Renzo's people begin looking for the best . . . vehicles."

"Of course, Albrecht."

"Good!" Detweiler smacked both palms on his desktop and stood. "And on that note, let's get out of here. Evelina's brought in a brand new chef, and I think all of you are going to be amazed at what he can do with Old Earth rock lobster!"

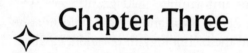

Chapter Three

The interior of Protector's Cathedral was like some huge, living jewel box.

Honor sat in the Stranger's Aisle to the left of the nave, immediately adjacent to the sanctuary. She, her parents and siblings, James MacGuiness, Nimitz, and Willard Neufsteiler, all of them in Harrington green, shared the Aisle's first pew with the Manticoran and Andermani ambassadors and consuls from each of the other members of the Manticoran Alliance. The two rows of pews behind them were solidly packed with officers in the uniform of the Protector's Own: Alfredo Yu, Warner Caslet, Cynthia Gonsalves, Harriet Benson-Dessouix and her husband Henri, Susan Phillips, and dozens of others who had escaped from the prison planet Hades with Honor. Their uniforms and the diplomats' off-world formal attire, in the styles of more than half a dozen different worlds, stood out sharply, but each of them also wore the dark, violet-black armbands or veils of Grayson-style mourning, as well.

That touch of darkness ran through the cathedral like a thread of sorrow, all the more obvious beside the rich, jewel-toned colors of formal Grayson attire, and Honor tasted its echo in the emotions surging about her. The emotional overtones of the Church of Humanity Unchained were always like some deep, satisfying well of renewal and faith, one she could physically experience thanks to her empathic link to Nimitz. But today there was that strand of sadness, flowing from every corner of the vast cathedral.

Brilliant pools of dense, colored sunlight poured down through the huge stained-glass windows of the eastern wall, and more spilled down like some chromatic waterfall through the enormous stained-glass skylight above the sanctuary. She tasted the grief reaching out from those deep, still pools of light and from the drifting, light-struck tendrils of incense on quiet feet of organ music. It came in different shapes and gradations, from people who had been personally touched by Howard Clinkscales to people who had known him only as a distant figure, yet it was also touched with a sense of celebration. A swelling faith that the man whose death they had come to mourn, and whose life they had come to celebrate, had met the Test of his life in triumph.

She gazed at the coffin, draped in both the planetary flag of Grayson and the steading flag of Harrington. The silver staff of Clinkscales' office as Harrington's regent and the sheathed sword he had carried as the commanding general of Planetary Security before the Mayhew Restoration lay crossed atop the flags, gleaming in the spill of light. So many years of service, she thought. So much capacity for growth and change. So much ability to give and so much kindness, hidden behind that crusty, curmudgeonly exterior he'd cultivated so assiduously. So much to miss.

The organ music swelled, then stopped, and a quiet stir ran through the cathedral as old-fashioned mechanical latches clacked loudly and its ancient, *bas-relief* doors swung ponderously open. For a moment there was complete and total silence, and then the organ reawoke in a surge of majestic power and the massed voices of the Protector's Cathedral Choir burst into soaring song.

The Cathedral Choir was universally regarded as the finest choir of the entire planet. That was saying quite a lot for a world which took its sacred music so seriously, but as its glorious voices rose in a hymn not of sorrow but of triumph, it demonstrated how amply it deserved its reputation. The torrent of music and trained voices poured over Honor in a magnificent tide which seemed to simultaneously focus and amplify the upwelling cyclone of the emotions all about her as the procession advanced down the cathedral's nave behind the crucifers and thurifers. The clergy and acolytes glittered in rich fabrics and embroidery, and Reverend Jeremiah Sullivan, resplendent in the embroidery and jewel-encrusted vestments of his high office, moved at the center of the procession, with the violet-black mourning stole around his neck like a slash of darkness.

They advanced steadily, majestically, through the storm of music and sunlight and the great, glowing dome of faith which Honor wished all of them could perceive as clearly as she herself did. It was at moments like this—vastly different though they were from the quieter, more introspective services of the faith in which she had been raised—that she felt closest to the heart and soul of Grayson. The people of her adopted planet were far from perfect, yet the bedrock strength of their thousand years of faith gave them a depth, a center, which very few other worlds could equal.

The procession reached the sanctuary, and its members dispersed with the solemn precision of an elite drill team. Reverend Sullivan stood motionless before the high altar, gazing at the mourning-draped cross, while the acolytes and assisting clergy flowed around him towards their places. He stood there until the hymn ended and the organ music faded once again to silence, then turned to face the filled cathedral, lifted both hands in a gesture of benediction, and raised his voice.

"And his lord said unto him," he said into that silence, "Well done, thou good and faithful servant: thou hast been faithful over a few things, I will make thee ruler over many things: enter thou into the joy of thy lord."

He stood for a long moment, hands still lifted, then lowered them and gazed out over the cathedral's packed pews.

"Brothers and Sisters in God," he said then, quietly, and yet in a voice which carried clearly in the cathedral's magnificent acoustics, "we are gathered today in the sight of the Tester, the Intercessor, and the Comforter to celebrate the life of Howard Samson Jonathan Clinkscales, beloved husband of Bethany, Rebecca, and Constance, father of Howard, Jessica, Marjorie, John, Angela, Barbara, and Marian, servant of the Sword, Regent of Harrington Steading, and always and in all ways the faithful servant of the Lord our God. I ask you now to join me in prayer, not to mourn his death, but to commemorate his triumphant completion of the Great Test of life as today he enters indeed into the joy of his Lord."

For all its rich pageantry and centuries of tradition, the liturgy of the Church of Humanity Unchained was remarkably simple. The funeral mass flowed smoothly, naturally, until, after the lesson and the gospel, it was time for the Memory. Every Grayson funeral had the Memory—the time set aside for every mourner to recall the life of the person they had lost and for any who so chose to share that memory with all the others. No one was ever forced to share a memory, but anyone who wished to was welcome to do so.

Reverend Sullivan seated himself on his throne, and silence fell once more over the cathedral until Benjamin Mayhew stood in the Protector's Box.

"I remember," he said quietly. "I remember the day—I was six, I think—when I fell out of the tallest tree in the Palace orchard. I broke my left arm in three places, and my left leg, as well. Howard was in command of Palace Security then, and he was the first to reach me. I was trying so hard not to cry, because big boys don't, and because a future Protector should never show weakness. And Howard radioed for a medical team and ordered me not to move until it got there, then sat down beside me in the mud, holding my good hand, and said 'Tears aren't weakness, My Lord. Sometimes they're just the Tester's way of washing out the hurt.'" Benjamin paused, then smiled. "I'll miss him," he said.

He sat once more, and Honor rose in the Stranger's Aisle.

"I remember," she said, her quiet soprano carrying clearly. "I remember the day I first met Howard, the day of the Maccabeus assassination attempt. He was—" she smiled in fond, bittersweet memory "—about as opposed to the notion of women in uniform and any alliance with the Star Kingdom as it was possible for someone to be, and there I was, the very personification of everything he'd opposed, with half my face covered up by a bandage. And he looked at me, and he was the very first person on Grayson who saw not a woman, but a Queen's officer. Someone he expected to do her duty the same way he would have expected himself to do his. Someone he grew and changed enough to accept not simply as his Steadholder, but also his friend, and in many ways, as his daughter. I'll miss him."

She sat once more, and Carson Clinkscales stood, towering over his aunts.

"I remember," he said. "I remember the day my father was killed in a training accident and Uncle Howard came to tell me. I was playing in the park with a dozen of my friends, and he found me and took me aside. I was only eight, and when he told me Father was dead, I thought the world had ended. But Uncle Howard held me while I cried. He let me cry myself completely out, until there were no tears left. And then he picked me up, put my head on his shoulder, and carried me in his arms all the way from the park home. It was over three kilometers, and Uncle Howard was already almost eighty years old, and I was always big for my age. But he walked the entire way, carried me up to my bedroom, and sat on my bed and held me until I drifted off to sleep." He shook his head, resting his right hand on the shoulder of his Aunt Bethany. "I never knew before that day how strong and patient, how loving, two arms could truly be, but I never forgot . . . and I never will. I'll miss him."

He sat, and an elderly man in the dress uniform of a Planetary Security brigadier rose.

"I remember," he said. "I remember the first day I reported for duty with Palace Security and they told me I was assigned to Captain Clinkscales' detachment." He shook his head with a grin. "Scared the tripes right out of me, I'll tell you! Howard was a marked man, even then, and he never did suffer fools gladly. But—"

At most Grayson funerals the Memory took perhaps twenty minutes. At Howard Clinkscales' funeral, it took three hours.

"It's always hard not to feel sorry for myself at a funeral," Allison Harrington said as she stood between the towering forms of her husband and her elder daughter. "God, I'm going to miss that old dinosaur!"

She sniffed and wiped her eye surreptitiously.

"We all are, Mother," Honor said, slipping an arm around her diminutive parent.

"Agreed," Alfred Harrington said, looking across at his daughter. "And his death is going to leave a real hole in the Steading."

"I know." Honor sighed. "Still, we all saw it coming, whether we wanted to talk about it or not, and Howard saw it more clearly than any of us. That's why he worked so hard getting Austen brought up to speed for the last three or four years."

She looked across the quiet, beautifully landscaped garden at a middle-aged—by pre-prolong standards—man with silvering, dark-brown hair and the craggy chin which seemed to mark most Clinkscales males. Like Howard himself, Austen Clinkscales was tall by Grayson standards, although far short of a giant like his younger cousin Carson.

"I think Austen is going to do just fine as regent," she said. "He reminds me a lot of his uncle, actually. He doesn't have as much experience, I suppose, but I think he's probably a bit more flexible than Howard was. And he's a good man."

"That he is," Alfred agreed.

"And he adores the kids," Allison said. "Especially Faith. Isn't it funny how all these firmly patriarchal Grayson males seem to go absolutely gooey inside when a little girl smiles at them?"

"You're a geneticist, love," Alfred said with a chuckle. "I'm sure you realized years ago that the species is hardwired to produce exactly that effect."

"Especially when the little girl in question is as cute as one of *my* daughters," Allison observed complacently.

"Somehow, Mother, I don't think anyone has applied the adjective 'cute' to me in quite a few years. I certainly *hope* not, at any rate."

"Oh, you hard-bitten naval officers are all alike!"

Honor started to respond, then stopped as Howard's three wives walked across the garden towards them. Carson and Austen Clinkscales followed them, and Bethany, the senior of the three, stopped in front of Honor.

"My Lady," she said quietly.

"Yes, Bethany?"

"You know our customs, My Lady," Bethany said. "Howard's body has already been reclaimed for our Garden of Memory. But he made an additional request."

"A request?" Honor repeated when she paused.

"Yes, My Lady." Bethany extended a small wooden box. It was unembellished by any carving or metalwork, but its hand-rubbed finish gleamed brilliantly in the sunlight. "He requested," she continued, "that a portion of his remains be given to you."

Honor's eyes widened, and she reached out to take the box.

"I'm deeply honored," she said, after a moment. "I never expected . . ."

"My Lady," Bethany said, looking her in the eyes, "as far as Howard—and my sisters and I—were concerned, you truly were the daughter you called yourself today. When you established the Harrington Garden for the armsmen who fell in your service, Howard was more pleased than he ever told you. We've always respected your integrity in refusing to profess faith in Father Church for political advantage, yet you've always demonstrated a personal sensitivity to and respect for our religion no Stead-holder could have bettered. I think Howard hoped that one day you would embrace Father Church, if you should decide it was truly what the Tester called you to do. But whether that day ever comes or not, he wanted to be a part of the Harrington Garden." She smiled mistily. "He said that maybe that way he could 'hold your place in line' until you catch up with him."

Honor blinked stinging eyes and smiled down at the shorter, older woman.

"If the day ever comes that I do join the Church of Humanity Unchained, it will be because of the example of people like you and Howard, Bethany," she said. "And whether that day ever comes or not, I will be honored and deeply, deeply pleased to do as Howard asked."

"Thank you, My Lady." Bethany and her sister wives curtsied formally, but Honor shook her head.

"No, thank *you*, Bethany," she said. "The Clinkscales Clan has served me personally and this Steading with a devotion and a skill far beyond anything I might reasonably have expected. My family and my people are deeply in your debt—in all of your debts—" she raised her eyes to look at Austen and Carson, as well, "and as Howard served me so well, and as Austen has agreed to serve me in his stead, so you've made yourselves family, not simply servants or even merely friends. My sword is your sword. Your battle is mine. Our joys and our sorrows are as one."

Bethany inhaled sharply, and Carson and Austen stiffened behind her.

"My Lady, I never—that is, Howard didn't make this request because—"

"Do you think I could not realize that?" Honor asked gently. She handed the wooden box to her mother and bent slightly to embrace her dead regent's widow, then kissed the older woman on the cheek.

"This is about service that went beyond any formal oath or obligation," she went on as she straightened once more. "It's about service that became love, and I should have done it long ago."

She looked at Carson again over his aunt's head, tasting his astonishment, and wondered if he'd been aware she even knew the formal phrases by which a Grayson steadholder created a legal familial relationship with another clan. The complex interweaving of clan networks had been integral to the Graysons' survival in their hostile planetary environment, and the creation of what equated to blood relationships between the great houses of the Steadholders and their closest allies and retainers had played a major role in forging those networks. In a sense, what Honor had done subordinated the Clinkscales Clan to the Harrington Clan, but it also bound Honor and her heirs personally to the defense and protection of Howard Clinkscales' descendants forever.

It was not a step to be taken lightly or impulsively, but Honor realized that her decision had been neither of those things. And that she truly ought to have done it much sooner, while Howard was still there to see it done. Well, no doubt he still could, from wherever he was at the moment, she thought fondly. And then her lips twitched as another thought struck her.

As Steadholder Harrington, she was the senior member of the Harrington Clan, which she suddenly realized, made her legally Carson's "Aunt Honor" under Grayson legal practice. And that meant . . .

Her lips twitched again, and she saw a sudden twinkle in Carson's eyes as the same realization hit him. They looked at each other, and then they began to chuckle. Honor felt her own chuckles segueing into full-bodied laughter, and gave Bethany a quick squeeze and stepped back.

"I'm sorry, Bethany!" she said. "I didn't mean to laugh. It's just that, I suddenly realized that—"

She broke off with another laugh, and Bethany shook her head with a fond smile.

"My Lady, I can think of many things that might have upset Howard. Having you laugh on the day of his funeral would never be one of them, though."

"That's a very good thing," Honor said with a smile, "because there's going to be more laughter before this is all over, you realize."

"My Lady?" Bethany looked at her quizzically.

"Of course there is," Honor said around another bubble of laughter of her own. "Faith and James were used to calling Howard 'Uncle Howard,' and I've heard them calling Austen 'uncle,' as well. But now *she's* going to be 'Aunt Faith' to him and Carson!" She shook her head. "We're never going to hear the end of *this*."

Chapter Four

"Welcome back, Your Grace."

"Thank you, Mercedes."

Honor followed Simon Mattingly through the private arrivals gate and held out her hand to the sturdy, plain-faced woman waiting for her in the Landing City VIP shuttle pad concourse. Mercedes Brigham still wore the commodore's uniform of her Manticoran rank rather than the rear admiral's star she would have been entitled to in Grayson's service. For that matter, she really ought to have traded in the double planets of her commodore's insignia even in the RMN. Honor knew perfectly well that Brigham had quietly made it clear to BuPers that she preferred her position as Honor's chief of staff, and promotion to rear admiral would have made her too senior for the slot. Honor had tried to convince her otherwise, though not as hard as she really felt she ought to have, but Mercedes had only grinned.

"If I really want command, Ma'am," she'd said, "all I have to do is go back to Grayson. At the moment, I think I'm more useful where I am. So unless you want to *fire* me . . ."

"And welcome back to you, too, Stinker," Brigham said now, reaching up to offer Nimitz her hand in turn. The treecat shook it solemnly, then flirted his tail and bleeked a laugh. Brigham chuckled, then turned back to Honor, her expression sympathetic.

"You look a bit frazzled, Your Grace."

"It's been a busy ten days," Honor conceded.

"Was it as hectic as you were afraid it would be?"

‹ At All Costs ›55

"No," Honor said. "Honestly, it wasn't. Not quite, at any rate. Austen's confirmation as regent went very smoothly. There was a little opposition, mostly from Mueller. I don't think the present Lord Mueller is quite as reconciled to his father's execution as he tries to make it seem, and he's starting to regain a little of his steading's old influence in the Opposition. But Benjamin, Owens, Yanakov, and Mackenzie steamrollered the nomination through."

"I assume," Brigham continued as LaFollet and Spencer Hawke came through the gate to hover watchfully at Honor's back and four more armsmen in Harrington green appeared, heavily laden with baggage, "that you had an opportunity to discuss the general situation with High Admiral Matthews?"

"I did. Not that either one of us was able to add a great deal to the other's understanding." Honor grimaced. "At the moment, the 'situation' at least has the advantage of a certain grim simplicity."

"The other side is still trying to complicate it, though, Your Grace," Brigham said. "Did you hear about the raid on Alizon?"

"Yes." Honor looked at her sharply. "The preliminary dispatch came in just before *Tankersley* broke Grayson orbit, but there weren't any details. How bad was it?"

"Nowhere near as bad as what McQueen did in their Operation Icarus," Brigham said quickly. "Not that it was exactly *good*, you understand. We lost a couple of our own freighters, and they blew the hell out of a respectable chunk of the asteroid extraction platforms and mining boats. But human casualties were very low and they never got close enough to hit the main industrial platforms. None of our people even got scratched, and the Alizonians only lost a half-dozen or so miners." She twitched one shoulder in a half-shrug. "Even that looks like it was an accident. From everything I've seen, they appear to have done their dead level best to play it according to the rules."

"They used LACs? No hyper-capable units?"

"Only LACs, Your Grace." If Brigham was surprised by Honor's questions, she showed no sign of it. "According to Alizon Defense Command, they lost between thirty and forty of them, too. All to the missile pods."

"Did our LACs engage at all?" Honor asked, and Brigham gave her a thin smile.

"By the strangest turn of fate, no, Your Grace. I know what you're thinking, and Alizon Defense Command thought the same thing. This was a probing attack, testing our defenses. If they'd wanted to do serious damage to the system infrastructure, they'd have attacked in much heavier strength. So when Defense Command realized we were up against a raid that probably wasn't even going to try to penetrate the inner defenses, not a serious assault on the system, all our *Shrikes* and *Ferrets* and—especially—*Katanas* stayed covert. So did the outer-system pods, for that matter. ONI gives us ninety percent-plus odds that the Peeps never even saw them."

"Good," Honor said, then nodded towards the concourse exit where the armored air limo in Harrington livery waited. Mattingly had already taken up his post beside it, and her entire party flowed into motion towards him.

"It's not very likely someone like Theisman isn't going to figure the LACs, at least, were there, anyway," she continued, "but at least he wasn't able to confirm it." She frowned thoughtfully. "Have you heard anything about Alizon's reaction to the attack?"

"Not officially." Brigham stood aside to let the baggage-toting armsmen load their burdens into the limo's luggage compartment. "We only got Defense Command's preliminary report five days ago. The Admiralty copied all of Admiral Simon's dispatches and after-action reports to us, but I haven't seen anything on the civilian side. According to certain sources of mine in Sir Thomas' shop, though, the Alizonians aren't what you might call pleased about it."

"As if that's a surprise," Honor snorted.

"Well, they did get the piss blown out of them the last time around, Your Grace," Brigham observed. "And after the way High Ridge and his bunch treated them, we've probably run our store of goodwill pretty close to rock bottom. Do you know Admiral Simon?"

"Not personally." Honor shook her head. "I know he's young for his rank, that he's a Saganami graduate, and that he's got a good reputation with us, as well as his own people. That's about it."

"Actually, that sums him up pretty well, except that I'd add that he's always been one of the stronger supporters of the Alliance. But even the dispatches from him I've seen make some pretty pointed references to how understrength the system defenses would have been against a *real* attack." She grimaced. "I'm guessing the civilians are going to be even more pointed about it, and I can't blame them. They're going to want some concrete demonstration of our willingness—and ability—to protect them from an Icarus repeat."

"Which is exactly why Theisman did it." Honor sighed. "I liked it so much better when Pierre and Saint-Just didn't trust their navy enough to let it do its job properly."

"At least we've managed to get back our own first team at Admiralty House," Brigham said encouragingly. "That's something."

"Quite a bit, actually," Honor agreed. "I'm looking forward to getting a firsthand brief from Sir Thomas."

"And Earl White Haven?"

Brigham's tone could not have been more natural, but Honor tasted the commodore's sudden spike of combined curiosity and concern.

"I'm sure we'll also discuss the situation," she replied after the briefest of pauses. "I know the Queen wants to see both of us tomorrow. I feel confident she's going to want a current briefing of her own, then, and it's pretty obvious Eighth Fleet is going to be a politically sensitive command, as well as a military one. I'm sure he'll have quite a bit to say in that regard as First Lord, probably both on and off the record. In fact, the Earl and Lady Emily have invited me to spend a few days as their guest at White Haven. Probably at least in part so that we can spend the time discussing all the ramifications."

"I see." Brigham gazed at her for a moment, then smiled. "It still seems odd to have him stuck on the civilian side instead of commanding a fleet, doesn't it?" She shook her head. "Still, I guess he's where we need him most right now. Ah, will you be taking any of the staff to White Haven with you, Your Grace?"

"Probably just Andrew, Spencer, and Simon," Honor said offhandedly. "Oh, and Mac. I'd like to take Miranda, as well, but I'm not going to pull her out of the Bay House for a stay this short. I need her staying on top of things right where she is."

"Of course, Your Grace," Brigham murmured, and gestured for Honor to enter the limo in front of her. "Please remember to give the Earl my respects."

✦   ✦   ✦

"Honor!"

Honor looked up quickly, with a huge smile, as the husky contralto called her name. The frail-looking, golden-haired woman in the life-support chair just inside the main entry of the Alexander family seat at White Haven smiled back, and her deep-green eyes gleamed with welcome.

"It's wonderful to see you back—you *and* Nimitz," the other woman continued. "How long can you say this time?"

"It's wonderful to see you, too, Emily," Honor said, striding quickly across the entry hall. She'd never been one to bestow easy public kisses, but she bent and kissed Emily Alexander's cheek. The older women reached up with her right arm—the only portion of her body below the neck that she could move at all—and laid the palm of her hand against Honor's cheek, in reply.

"Are you keeping her in shape, Sandra?" Honor asked the tallish, square-shouldered brunette standing beside the life-support chair.

"We try, Your Grace," Sandra Thurston, Lady Alexander's personal nurse, said and favored Honor with a welcoming smile. "I suspect seeing you again is going to do more for her than I ever could, though."

"Oh, nonsense!" Honor replied with a slight blush, then straightened to look at the man standing directly behind Lady Alexander's chair.

"It's good to see you again, too, Nico," she said.

"And you, Your Grace," White Haven's *majordomo* murmured with a slight bow. "Welcome back to White Haven."

"Thank you," Honor said, and smiled at him. The edge of defensive resentment Nico Havenhurst had felt the first time he saw her here had vanished, and he returned her smile, then he looked past her to the armsmen carrying in her baggage.

"If you'll excuse me, Your Grace, Milady," he said, with another small bow, this time to both women, "I'll attend to Her Grace's things." Emily nodded agreement, and he turned to Honor's armsmen. "I've arranged to lodge Her Grace in the Blue Suite, Colonel," he told LaFollet. "You and her other armsmen will be in the Bachelor's Wing. The billiard room is between that and the main house, directly adjacent to the only direct access stair to the Blue Suite, so I thought it might provide you with a relatively comfortable guardroom. I hope that's satisfactory?"

He looked innocently at Honor's senior personal armsman, and LaFollet gazed back for just an instant, then nodded.

"Perfectly," he replied. He looked at Honor's other two personal armsmen. "Simon, you and Spencer go ahead and get things organized. Then get some sleep. I'll cover things here through dinner, and you two lucky fellows will get the night shift."

"Rank, you see," Mattingly said to Hawke, "hath its privileges. *He* gets a good night's sleep."

"And well deserved it will be, too," LaFollet agreed equably as the youngest member of Honor's personal detachment grinned. "Now, move along." He made shooing motions with both hands. "There's a good lad," he added with a wicked grin.

"You know," Emily said as Honor's armed retainers trooped past her in Nico's wake, "I'd forgotten how much more . . . placid it is around here when your myrmidons are away."

"They do have a tendency to liven the place up, don't they," Honor said dryly, regarding LaFollet with an expression which combined amusement and resignation in near-equal measure. The armsman returned it with a look of total innocence, and she shook her head and turned back to Emily. "Mac went on to the Bay House to collect the mail, check in with Miranda, and get her report on things generally. He'll be arriving in another couple of hours."

"I know. He screened me from Landing with his schedule. Nico's already made arrangements for his arrival, too." Emily smiled crookedly. "One thing we've got plenty of in this rambling edifice is bedroom space."

Honor tasted the mingled affection, humor, and small, lingering trace of sorrow which accompanied Emily's last sentence and reached out again, almost involuntarily, to rest one hand on the other woman's shoulder. As always, the fragile delicacy of the invalid's flesh and bones under her hand was almost shocking, so totally at odds with the inner vitality of the woman trapped within it.

"I know," she said softly, and Emily reached up to lay her working hand briefly atop Honor's.

"Yes, I imagine you do," she said more briskly, still smiling. "And Hamish will be here shortly, as well. He screened to say he's been delayed by some Admiralty House business. Nothing critical, just details that have to be dealt with. And, yes, Nimitz," she said, looking directly at the 'cat on Honor's shoulder, "Samantha is just fine. I'm sure she'll be just as eager to see you as you are to see her when she and Hamish get here."

Nimitz rose higher, true-hands flashing, and Emily chuckled as she read the signs.

"Yes, I think you could say she's missed you as much as she would have missed celery. Possibly even a little more than that."

Nimitz bleeked with laughter, and Honor shook her head.

"You two are bad influences on each other," she observed severely.

"Nonsense. Both of us were completely beyond salvage before we ever met, Honor," Emily replied serenely.

"I'm sure." Honor glanced over her shoulder at LaFollet, and the colonel smiled faintly.

"If you'll pardon me for a moment, My Lady," he said, "I need to speak to the limo driver before he parks the car. With your permission?"

"Of course, Andrew," she said and watched fondly as he stepped back outside.

"Ah, I think I might just go and check with Tabitha about the supper menu, Milady," Thurston said to Emily. "You'll keep an eye on her till I get back, Your Grace?" she added innocently to Honor.

"Of course I will," Honor said gravely, and Thurston smiled and disappeared, leaving her alone with Emily and Nimitz.

"My goodness," Emily murmured as the door closed behind her. "She did that *very* neatly. And I didn't think anything could overcome that professional paranoia of his! For all he knows, assassins are lurking in the great hall right this moment."

"Andrew does more than simply protect me physically, Emily," Honor said. "He also does his best to let me cling to at least the illusion of a little bit of privacy." Her smile was more crooked than the one the artificial nerves in the left side of her face normally produced. "Of course, we both know it's *only* an illusion, but that doesn't make it any less important to me."

"No, I don't suppose it does," Emily said gently. "We Manticoran aristocrats think we live in fishbowls, but compared to you Grayson steadholders—" She shook her head. "I suppose it really is necessary, in your case, at least, given how many people seem to have tried to kill you over the years. But I often wonder how you can stand it without going mad."

"There are times I wonder, too," Honor admitted. "Mostly, though, it's my armsmen themselves who keep me sane. Graysons have had a thousand years to adjust to the peculiarities of their own traditions, and it's amazing how 'invisible' an armsman can make himself. But it's more than that, too. They just . . . become a part of you. I suppose it's like your relationship with Nico or Sandra, or mine with Mac, but with an added dimension. They know *everything* about me, Emily, and every single one of them will go to his grave without ever betraying a confidence of mine. That's what Grayson armsmen do."

"Then I suppose I envy you as much as I pity you," Emily said.

"You might want to keep some of that sympathy for yourself," Honor said. Emily arched an eyebrow, and Honor gave her another off-center smile. "If things go on as they have, you and Hamish are going to find my armsmen interfering in your lives almost as much as they do in the lives of my mother and father. Andrew will be as discreet about it as he possibly can, but it will happen."

Emily gazed at her for several seconds, then sighed.

"Yes," she said finally. "I can see that. In fact, I realized it while you were still in Sidemore. But I think I'm discovering that adjusting to the reality is a little more . . . complicated than I'd anticipated."

"I don't doubt it, and I'm sorry," Honor said softly. "You don't deserve all the complications I've inflicted on your life."

"Nonsense!" Emily shook her head firmly. "Just desserts don't come into it. Or, as Hamish has always been fond of saying—when he thinks I don't hear him, of course—shit happens."

Honor's mouth twitched, and Emily smiled at her as she smothered a giggle.

"You didn't plan any of this, Honor," Emily continued, "any more than Hamish did. In fact, if memory serves, the two of you were busy making everyone—Nimitz, Samantha, and myself included—thoroughly miserable because of your absolute determination *not* to 'inflict' any complications on my life. I may not like having to deal with all of them, but I don't regret any of them. You know that."

She looked Honor straight in the eye, and Honor nodded slowly. Emily was one of the small number of people who knew her empathic link with Nimitz was so deep, so intense, that she'd actually developed something very like the treecats' ability to sense the emotions of those about her. Which meant she did know Emily was being completely honest with her.

"Then Hamish and I are remarkably lucky people," she said. Emily made a small throwing away gesture with her mobile hand, and Honor inhaled a deep breath. "However, the question I'm sure Andrew stepped outside so I could ask you was whether it was genuine Admiralty business that detained Hamish, or simply good strategy on a more personal level."

"Both, I think," Emily said, green eyes twinkling. "Admiralty House has been keeping him late quite a bit these past few months," she went on more soberly, "and I don't doubt for a moment that he really is busy trying to club the latest batch of pseudogators to crawl out of the swamp. But it's also true we both thought it might be a bit more . . . politic if he stayed busy with routine matters while I got my friend Honor settled in here at White Haven instead of rushing home to greet you himself. Not," she added dryly, "that I don't expect his 'greeting' to be about as enthusiastic as you're likely to survive when he does get here."

Honor felt herself actually blushing, and Emily laughed delightedly.

"Oh, Honor! You really are so, so . . . so *Sphinxian!*"

"I can't help it," Honor protested. "I mean, Mother's from Beowulf, so I suppose I ought to be more, well, *liberated,* or whatever, but I'm not, all right?" She gave the older woman's shoulder a gently cautious shake. "You and Hamish may be from decadent old Manticore, but you're right, I *am* from Sphinx. And, just to make things worse, for the last eighteen T-years I've been from *Grayson,* too. Can you think of a planet less well suited to developing a sophisticated attitude about this sort of thing?"

"Actually, I'd think the Grayson element might help, really," Emily said, only half humorously. "I mean, they do have that tradition of multiple wives."

"That's multiple *wives,* Emily," Honor said dryly. "They're not so big on unmarried lovers. Especially when one of the lovers in question is married to someone else."

"I wonder if they might be just a bit more understanding than you think they would." Emily shook her head quickly, and continued before Honor could open her mouth. "I'm not suggesting you run home to find out, Honor! You're a steadholder. I understand that, and I understand you're not free to run the risks as Steadholder Harrington that you might run as simply Honor Harrington, just as you and Hamish can't openly display your feelings here in the Star Kingdom after the way those bastards tried to smear both of you last year. But I really do think you're both still being harder on yourselves for feelings neither of you sought than most other people would be."

"You're a remarkable woman, Emily Alexander," Honor said after a moment. "I see exactly why Hamish loves you as much as he does." She touched the older woman's cheek gently. "And I don't deserve to have you understand so deeply."

"You're not a very good judge of what you deserve, Honor," Emily said. "But," she went on more briskly, "before we get too maudlin, why don't we take ourselves off to the conservatory?" She grinned mischievously. "If we hurry, we can disappear before Colonel LaFollet comes back inside and see how long it takes him to find you again. Won't that be fun?"

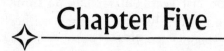

Chapter Five

"Mr. Secretary, Colonel Nesbitt is here for his three o'clock."

"Hm?" Secretary of State Arnold Giancola looked up from the correspondence on his display with a bemused expression. He gazed at his administrative assistant for a second or two, then blinked. "I'm sorry, Alicia. What did you say?"

Alicia Hampton suppressed a temptation to shake her head in fond exasperation. Arnold Giancola was by far the most satisfactory boss she'd ever had. He had a reputation for ambition, and she could believe it, but he was unfailingly courteous to his staffers, charismatic, and generally thoughtful. And he'd also become increasingly absentminded as the interstellar diplomatic situation darkened. He was working far too hard these days, and he'd taken to leaving the security systems in his office up all the time so he could be certain no one would interrupt him while he did it. Which only helped him forget things even more thoroughly.

"I said Colonel Nesbitt is here for his three o'clock, Sir," she repeated.

"Oh?" Giancola frowned, then, "Oh! Nesbitt. I'd forgotten all about him. Ask him to come in, please, Alicia!"

"Of course, Mr. Secretary." Alicia smiled at him and stepped back into the outer office.

"The Secretary will see you now, Colonel," she told the tallish, gray-eyed, broad shouldered man in civilian clothing.

"Thank you," Nesbitt said, pocketing the reader he'd been perusing while he waited for the appointed time.

"Oh, Colonel," she said quietly as he started to step past her, "please do remember that the Secretary's calendar is very tight. He has another appointment scheduled in twenty-five minutes." Nesbitt looked at her quizzically, and she smiled apologetically. "He's been a bit more absentminded and forgetful the last couple of days. *He's* likely to forget, and I don't want to cut you off before you're done when I announce his next visitor."

"Oh, I see!" Nesbitt's expression cleared, and he smiled back at her. "I'll try to keep him focused, Ms. Hampton. And he's lucky he's got someone like you looking after him."

"We all try, Colonel," Alicia said. "It would be a lot easier if he didn't drive himself as hard as he does."

Nesbitt smiled again, sympathetically, and walked past her into the inner office. He glanced casually at his wrist chrono as the doors closed behind him, and noted the inconspicuous green telltale on the instrument's face with satisfaction. That little device was of Solarian manufacture, not Havenite, and it confirmed that Giancola's security systems were all up and running.

"Mr. Secretary," he said, advancing across the deep carpet towards the half-hectare or so of desk behind which Giancola sat.

"Jean-Claude," Giancola said, in a brisk, no-nonsense tone which went very oddly with the preoccupied façade he was so careful to project for his staff . . . among other people. "Come in. Sit down. We haven't got much time."

"I know." Nesbitt seated himself in the indicated, comfortable chair, and crossed his legs. "Your charming assistant is rather concerned about you, you know, Mr. Secretary. She reminded me of the short window we have for this meeting because she was afraid you're getting absentminded enough you wouldn't remember."

"Good." Giancola smiled.

"Really?" Nesbitt cocked his head. "Actually, I'm wondering if it's really good tradecraft, if you don't mind my saying so."

"I don't mind your saying it, although that doesn't necessarily mean I agree with you. Why do you think it might not be?"

"Kevin Usher's no fool, whatever public image he chooses to project," Nesbitt said. "I don't know whether there's any truth to the rumors about his wife and Cachat—I think a lot of people wonder exactly what's going on there—but I do know the rumors about his drunkenness are just that: rumors. *Unsubstantiated* ones."

"And?" Giancola prompted just a bit impatiently. "It's not as if I hadn't figured that out for myself, Jean-Claude."

"And a man who's busy presenting that kind of false image to the rest of the universe is likely to wonder if someone else, especially someone who seems to have changed as much as you have, isn't doing the same thing. And if you are, he's going to wonder why."

"Oh." Giancola sat back, drumming lightly on his desktop with the fingers of one hand, then shrugged. "I see where you were going now. You may even have a point. On the other hand, it doesn't much matter *what* I do; Usher's going to think I'm up to something however I act. So I'm basically playing a shell game. I'm leaving my security systems up most of the time, no matter who I'm seeing, which means there's no way for him to tell whose conversations I *really* want to be certain he can't overhear. I'm sure *he* understands that; my little charade is to help explain to my staff and everyone else why I keep 'forgetting' to switch the jammers off. It isn't really directed at him at all, except, possibly, in a very secondary sort of way. I do like to spend the occasional minute thinking about how incredibly irritating he must find the entire thing, though."

"I see." Nesbitt regarded him narrowly, then shrugged. "If it amuses you, I don't imagine it's really going to do any harm. Personally, I'd find the entire thing much too exhausting to maintain, but that's up to you."

"If it starts getting tiring, I can always stop. Usher will probably find that even more irritating." Giancola smiled nastily. "But we're going to have to talk about that some other time. Right now, I need your report."

"Of course." Nesbitt folded his hands over his raised knee and tilted his head thoughtfully to one side. "I'm happy to say Grosclaude wasn't quite as clever as he thought," he said. "You're right—he did retain a complete file of the correspondence. *Both* sets of correspondence. Unfortunately for him, he knew he wouldn't be able to get the file off Manticore with him when he was expelled. They weren't going to be very concerned with observing all the niceties of diplomatic immunity after we'd just launched what amounted to a sneak attack against them, and

Manty surveillance is too good for him to get anything by it if they pulled out all the stops. And even if they didn't find it, there was always the possibility the security types waiting for him at our end might. So he piggybacked the information through the diplomatic bag several days before the balloon went up and had it remailed to a private account in Nouveau Paris after the bag got here."

"And?" Giancola said when he paused.

"And, also unfortunately for him, it was an account I already knew about. Courtesy of a few backdoors the new management still hasn't found yet, I was able to track the file to his account and also when he pulled it back out after his own arrival from Manticore and lodged it in the secure database of his attorney's law firm. Along with a cover letter directing that the file in question be sent to Kevin Usher's personal attention should anything . . . unfortunate happen to him."

"Damn." Giancola's mouth tightened. "I was afraid he'd done something like that."

"Only sensible thing for him to do," Nesbitt agreed. "Although, if he really knew what he was doing, he never would've used this sort of approach. He'd have buried it on an old-fashioned record chip under a mattress somewhere and used someone he'd never had any traceable relationship with before as his bagman. This way, he might as well have left me an engraved invitation."

"What do you mean?" Giancola asked intently.

"I mean that the central net is still riddled with StateSec backdoors, Mr. Secretary. To really nail them all shut, they'd have to slag the old system down and start from scratch. Oh," Nesbitt shrugged, "they actually did a fairly good job when LePic and Usher set things up over at Justice. I'd guess they probably managed to find and close a good ninety percent of them. But there were so many in place that they never had a prayer of getting all of them. I'm sure they're still looking, and of course not knowing for sure whether or not they've found *my* little keyholes does tend to make life a bit more exciting. There's always the chance they *have* found them and they're just sitting there, monitoring, letting me tie the noose around my own neck before they pounce."

"I hope you'll pardon me if I, for one, don't find the image particularly amusing," Giancola said tartly.

"I might as well find it amusing." Nesbitt shrugged again. "I'm taking every precaution I can think of, but if the precautions don't work, there's not much I can do about it. I guess it's the equivalent of your amusement at the notion of pissing Usher off with your silly little mind games."

Giancola looked at him steadily for a few seconds, then snorted.

"All right," he said briskly. "Let's cut to the chase. Should I assume from what you've said that you've got access to Yves' file at his attorney's?"

"Yes." Nesbitt smiled. "I can make the file—and his letter of instruction—disappear without a trace any time I want to."

"I'm sure you could," Giancola said with a slow smile of his own. "But if you've got the access to disappear it, then you've also got the access to *change* it, don't you?"

"Well, yes," Nesbitt said slowly, smile transforming into a slight, thoughtful frown. "Why?"

"I feel quite certain Yves would vastly prefer not to blow the whistle on our little . . . modifications. After all, if I go down, he goes down, and I rather suspect—given all the people who have been killed in the meantime—that Usher and Pritchart would make sure both of us went down rather messily. So what he's got is entirely in the nature of insurance, state's evidence he can use to bargain with if someone else figures out what the two of us did, not anything he really wants to use. Which means he's not going to do anything with it unless he starts to feel threatened. Or, of course, unless something really does happen to him."

"Which is essentially what you're thinking in terms of, no?" Nesbitt said.

"Unfortunately, yes," Giancola said, and Nesbitt was almost certain the regret in his voice was genuine. Not enough to dissuade him for a moment, but genuine. "But my point is that there's no need for us to hurry. We can take the time to make sure we do things right."

"Unless something happens to him which really is an accident," Nesbitt pointed out. "He could get run over by a ground car, you know, or break his neck skiing. He spends enough time doing *that* he could even die of sheer physical exhaustion. Hell, he could get hit by lightning! In which case his letter of instruction would be opened even though we—you—genuinely hadn't had a thing to do with it."

"Not very likely," Giancola replied. "I think the odds are fairly heavily in our favor in that respect. Still, you're right. It does behoove us to move expeditiously."

"Which I could do much better if you'd tell me exactly where we're moving to."

"Well, if Yves has gone to such lengths to be certain incriminating evidence against me will surface if something happens to him, then I think it's only fair for us to see to it that the incriminating evidence is there."

"What?" Nesbitt didn't raise his voice. Indeed, it went flatter. But there was no amusement at all in his suddenly intent gray eyes.

"Relax, Jean-Claude. I realize it sounds bizarre, but consider this scenario. Here you are, my senior internal security officer, responsible for finding leaks anywhere in the Department. Eventually, as you and I are both painfully aware, the current unpleasantness with Manticore is going to come to an end, one way or the other. When it does, there are going to be some very hard questions asked about the discrepancies between their version of our diplomatic correspondence and our own. Original documents are going to be compared by the victors, whoever they are, and neither side is going to be particularly amused by what they find. So, all things being equal, I think it would be a very good thing if *you*—efficient, hard-working person that you are—were the one who discovered that the documents had been tampered with from *our* end."

"I hesitate to suggest that you might be out of your ever loving mind, Mr. Secretary," Nesbitt said. "On the other hand, the possibility does present itself to my keen intellect."

"Don't worry, I'm not." Giancola leaned forward in his comfortable chair, his expression suddenly very intent. "The problem is that the documents *were* tampered with from our end. With access to both sets of originals, it wouldn't take Usher very long at all to prove that, and I'm confident the Manties could do it even more quickly. So our best defense is to make the discovery ourselves and be properly horrified to learn that my trusted colleague of many years, Yves Grosclaude, was responsible for the manipulation which led to the current, horrible bloodshed."

"And just how did he accomplish that?" Nesbitt asked in a fascinated tone.

"Why, by way of one of those StateSec backdoors you were just telling me about. After all, he was associated with the old Foreign Ministry's internal security services. Apparently, he was closer to StateSec than we ever suspected, and he used one of the old StateSec access programs to hack into my secure database and acquire copies of my personal and official encryption keys. That's how he was able to forge doctored versions of the correspondence and pass them off as genuine to the Manties."

"And the alterations in the Manties' notes?"

"He did that the way it was actually done," Giancola said with a smile. "He stole the Manticoran Foreign Office's encryption key from my secure database, as well."

"He did what?" Nesbitt asked very carefully.

"So, StateSec *did* manage to bury one or two skeletons in Nouveau Paris without your knowing about it, did they?" Giancola chuckled. "You know InSec and StateSec—all of the old régime's intelligence services, really, except possibly NavInt—were always more focused on political espionage than military intelligence. I think that's one reason Saint-Just was always so ready to embrace political operations, like that attempt to assassinate Elizabeth and Benjamin. And why, frankly, StateSec did such a piss-poor job on military intelligence all the way through the last war. They weren't very good at it because their institutional mindset just didn't work that way. But they were *quite* good at political and diplomatic espionage. I found some fascinating things in the Foreign Ministry archives when they were handed over to State after the Constitutional Convention. Including a few notes which suggest that Queen Elizabeth's father's grav-skiing 'accident' wasn't quite as accidental as everyone thought it was. Which, coupled with what happened in Yeltsin, might just help explain why she hates us with such outstanding virulence.

"At any rate, among StateSec's accomplishments was the corruption of one of Foreign Secretary Descroix's senior staffers. Someone senior enough, in fact, to have physical access to her official files."

"My God," Nesbitt said, finally startled out of his normal air of amused cynicism, "they actually stole Descroix's *encryption key?*"

"Not her personal key, no, but her departmental key. Which is another of the reasons I'm fairly confident the Manties would quickly figure out who did what if they got a chance to compare the raw originals. I'm going to be dreadfully embarrassed when I realize no one here in State realized we never saw Descroix's *personal* key on any of the correspondence. Of course, there was no reason why we should have felt unduly suspicious, since all of it had the official Manticoran Foreign Office codes, but still—"

He shrugged self-deprecatingly.

"So," Nesbitt sat back in his chair once more, drawing his normal persona back about himself, "Grosclaude stole both sets of keys from your database?"

"Exactly. It's going to be up to *you* to actually set up the access he would have used. On the other hand, you're also the efficient and dedicated security agent who will discover the security breach, so be sure you set it up in a way that makes discovering it plausible."

"I can do that," Nesbitt said thoughtfully. "It'll take some time, though. Especially to establish that all of this happened months ago."

"I assumed it would." Giancola nodded. "That's why I'm so pleased by the realization that Yves isn't going to be in any hurry to start blowing whistles. We've *got* some time to work with. But just to be on the safe side, we should probably deal with his insurance file first."

"Yes, tell me what you've got in mind for that, if you don't want me to simply make it go away."

"Two things," Giancola said. "First, we need a substitute letter of instruction to his attorney. One which has nothing at all to do with the contents of that particular file. Can you do that?"

"No problem," Nesbitt said, after a few seconds' thought. "He used a standard self-generated legal e-form for it. Probably didn't trust attorney-client privilege to hold if his lawyer knew what he had in mind ahead of time. Since no flesh-and-blood knows what *should* be in it, no one's going to ask any questions if I alter its content."

"Good. Go ahead and get that done immediately. And once we've defused that particular landmine, we need you to go into his existing file and make some judicious alterations. I don't want you to get rid of it entirely. I don't even want you to make it incriminate someone else. Instead, I want you to turn it into a forgery."

"Forgery?"

"Yes. It's going to have to be carefully done, but I want that file to prove Yves planned on setting *me* up as the fall guy for *his* manipulation of the notes. I want it to be good, but I want there to be a provable flaw in it, something a good security type like yourself can spot."

"You're figuring that if the fellow who really did it all also manufactured evidence that *you* were responsible for it, it will demonstrate that, in fact, you didn't have a thing to do with it," Nesbitt said slowly, gray eyes beginning to gleam.

"Exactly. The only way to 'prove' *I* didn't do it is to provide someone else who obviously did. And if the someone else who did it also manufactured evidence to implicate me in order to divert suspicion from himself, he obviously wouldn't have tried to divert it to someone who was really his accomplice and might have evidence of his own to prove *his* guilt as part of a deal with prosecutors."

"Neat," Nesbitt said after several moments of consideration. "Complicated. And I can see a half-dozen places right off the top of my head where the entire thing could go off the rails. But it's doable. It really is. And it's so damned Byzantine and filled with double-think and possible failure points that it would never have occurred to a professional like Usher—or me, for that matter. I think I can pull it all together for you, but putting all the pieces in place is going to take even longer than I'd thought. I don't like having that long for something to go wrong in."

"Not a problem," Giancola disagreed, waving one hand in a dismissive gesture. "As soon as you've dealt with the lawyer's instructions, Yves can go ahead and suffer that accident. It will have to be a *very* accidental accident, you understand?"

"That I can handle," Nesbitt said confidently.

"Then as soon as that's out of the way, you can move on to putting all of the other bits and pieces together. Once everything's been neatly tied to Yves, we can 'discover' the evidence anytime we want to. For that matter, we might even decide the thing to do is to steer Usher and his FIA to the evidence. Let *Kevin* turn it up. In fact, if I weren't afraid we'd be getting too fancy, I'd almost prefer for him to find Yves' evidence falsely implicating me and *accept* it initially, until State's own security types detected the fact that it was a forgery. Having him suspect me, or even formally accuse me, when I turn out to be totally innocent, would help me tilt the balance in the Cabinet against LePic."

He gazed thoughtfully at the ceiling for several heartbeats, then shook his head regretfully.

"No. We've got enough balls in the air without adding that one to it."

"You have no idea how glad I, as the wizard charged with conjuring all these minor miracles for you, am to hear you say that," Nesbitt said dryly.

"I'm always pleased when I'm able to make my associates happy," Giancola assured him. Then the Secretary of State's eyes narrowed once more. "But now that you're a happy wizard, do you really believe you can pull all of this off?"

"Yes. I'm not absolutely positive of it—not with it all coming at me cold, this way. But as I said, I think it's doable. I'm going to have to sit down and look at it very carefully, probably for several days, at least, before I can tell you more than that. At an absolute minimum, though, I'm certain I can disappear Grosclaude's evidence if it turns out we have to do that, instead. And I feel reasonably confident I can arrange the database hack you want and make it crystal-clear he was behind it. As for the rest, I'm going to have to see how it all comes together before I can tell you positively one way or the other."

"Take your time—within reason, of course." Giancola grimaced. "One thing I think we can count on is that this war isn't going to end tomorrow, or even next week. We've got time to do it right . . . and we'd damned well better not do it *wrong*."

Chapter Six

"That was delicious, Jackson," Honor sighed appreciatively as Jackson McGwire, White Haven's butler, oversaw the removal of the dessert dishes. Or, more precisely, of the dessert *dish*, singular, since the only one on the table was the one in front of Honor. "Please tell Tabitha that she outdid herself on the chocolate mousse."

"I'll be happy to, Your Grace," McGwire said, with a small half-bow and a twinkle. Honor's genetically modified metabolism's need for calories was phenomenal, and Tabitha Dupuy, White Haven's cook, and her staff had taken it as a personal challenge. So far, they had yet to repeat themselves with a single dessert offering, despite the recent frequency of her visits to the Alexander family's seat, and Honor and her hosts had a small betting pool going on how long they could keep it up.

Honor started to say something else, then paused as Nimitz sat up straighter in his treecat-sized highchair. He and Samantha, his mate, sat between their adopted humans, and now the male 'cat raised both true-hands to the top of his head, palms turned inward, raised first and second fingers on both hands signing the letter "U" and wiggling backward. From there, the right true-hand slid down, the palm facing his body, fingers extended and facing left, and moved from left to right. Then his true-hands crooked in the sign for the letter "C," with the tip of its thumb resting on the upturned first finger of his other true-hand before both true-hands came together in front of him, index fingers extended and held together, and moved across his body, fingers separating

74

and coming back together again as they traveled. And, finally, the second finger of his right true-hand touched his lips before the hand moved down and out a bit, while his thumb rubbed over the same finger.

"Of course, Nimitz," McGwire said with a smile. "I'll inform Ms. Dupuy personally."

"Please do," Honor reinforced, reaching out to rub the treecat's ears affectionately. "While I'm not a connoisseur of rabbit and celery stew, Stinker here certainly is. If *he* says it's delicious, Tabitha could probably get rich operating a treecat restaurant chain!"

"I'll certainly tell her that, too, Your Grace," McGwire assured her.

"I think that's probably all we'll need, Jackson," Hamish Alexander, Thirteenth Earl of White Haven, said from his place at the head of the table. "If we do discover we need anything—or if Her Grace should discover she has a hollow ankle somewhere that still needs filling—we'll buzz."

"Of course, Milord," McGwire replied with a smile, and followed the footman with the tray of dishes out of the dining room.

The dining room in question was one of the smaller ones White Haven boasted. The formal dining room was big enough for the massive parties a Manticoran aristocrat—even one with as little time for "social fripperies" as Hamish Alexander—was expected to host from time to time. Since he, Emily, and Honor were the only humans at the table, that cavernous chamber had not been called upon. Instead, Emily had directed that supper be served in the far tinier dining room off her personal suite. It was an intimate little room, built into the side of one of White Haven's older wings, with floor-to-ceiling windows which looked out over the landscaped east lawn, lovely under the light of Thorson, Manticore's single moon. The red ember of Phoenix, otherwise known as Manticore-A II, rested on the horizon, just above the tips of the Old Earth spruces fringing the lawn, and the gleaming gems of at least a dozen orbital platforms moved visibly against the stars. Emily and Hamish often dined there, because of its proximity to her rooms, but it was rare for them to invite anyone else to join them.

The door closed behind McGwire and the footman, and silence fell for a moment. Despite everything, Honor still felt a bit awkward, and she tasted a slight, answering spike of awkwardness from Hamish. The earl took a sip from his wine glass, and his wife smiled slightly. Emily was genuinely and affectionately amused, Honor knew, and that was important to her.

"Well," Hamish said after a moment, setting his glass down precisely, "I'd say Samantha was probably as happy to see Nimitz as Emily and I were to see you, Honor."

It was his turn to reach out and caress the ears of the small, dappled treecat sitting beside him. Nimitz's mate pressed back against his fingertips, and the loud buzz of her purr made the use of any signs totally unnecessary. Emily and Honor chuckled, and Nimitz bleeked a laugh of his own before he jumped lightly from his own highchair to join Samantha in hers. The two 'cats draped their prehensile tails about one another, and Nimitz's happy, bone-deep purr mingled with Samantha's.

"I think that's probably a safe statement, dear," Emily observed dryly.

"Actually," Honor said more seriously, "it's really hard on them to be separated." She shook her head. "I've come to suspect that one reason they're the only mated pair that ever both adopted humans is the separation factor. Treecats are literally almost a part of one another, especially mated pairs, and it's almost . . . physically painful for them to be apart from one another as much as these two have been since Samantha adopted Hamish."

"I know," Hamish sighed, looking at Honor, and she tasted the multiple layers of meaning in his tone. "Sometimes I'm afraid she'll come to regret having done it."

"Oh, no," Honor said, returning his gaze. "It's awkward, and neither one of them likes all the consequences, but 'cats don't look back over decisions of the heart, Hamish. As Emily pointed out to both of us once upon a time, they're remarkably sane in that respect."

"As well they should be," Emily pronounced. She looked back and forth between husband and Honor and started to say something, but Honor felt her change direction before she spoke. "On the other hand, it's not as if Samantha hasn't been able to find things to occupy her while the two of you were away, Honor."

"No?" Honor looked at Samantha, who returned her gaze and groomed her whiskers with an undeniable air of smugness.

"Oh, no. She and Dr. Arif formally opened the conference day before yesterday," Emily said.

"They did?" Honor sat a bit straighter, her eyes brightening. "How did it go?" she demanded eagerly.

"Well," Emily said with a fondly amused smile. "Very well, in fact. Of course, it was only the first day, Honor. You do understand that it's going to take a long time for them to make any real progress, don't you?"

"Of course I do." Honor shook her head, lips twitching as she tasted Emily's response to her own eagerness. "But the entire idea is incredibly exciting to a Sphinxian, especially one who's been adopted. After so many centuries when none of the experts could even agree on how intelligent the 'cats really were—or weren't—seeing them sit down with humans to formally discuss ways treecats can integrate themselves into human society as full partners is— Well," she shook her head again, "it's something there aren't really words to describe."

"And it was all your idea, wasn't it, love?" Hamish said to Samantha, reaching out to stroke her silken pelt.

"My impression is that Samantha has a rather forceful will," Emily observed dryly, and Honor laughed.

"From what the other 'cats have had to say since they learned to sign, that's probably as big an understatement as to say the Queen has a rather negative view of the Republic of Haven," she said.

"Which," Hamish said, his tone and his emotions both suddenly darker, "is apt, but not as amusing as it might have been a day or so ago."

"What do you mean?" Honor asked with abrupt anxiety, but Emily interrupted before he could reply.

"Now that is *enough*, Hamish," she said sternly. Her husband looked at her, and she waggled her right index finger in his direction. "We haven't seen Honor—*you* haven't seen her—for almost two weeks," she continued. "During that time, you've been wrestling with affairs at the Admiralty, and she's been dealing with the affairs of her Steading. Neither of you, however, is on duty tonight. You will not discuss the military situation, the diplomatic situation, or the domestic political situation—Manticoran *or* Grayson—tonight. Do I make myself sufficiently clear?"

"Yes," Hamish said after a moment, blue eyes smiling at her. "Yes, you do."

"Good. And don't forget, either of you, that my furry spies," she waved at the treecats, "will report faithfully to me if my instructions are violated."

"Traitors that they are," Hamish muttered with a grin.

"Treason, my dear, is often simply a matter of perspective." Emily told him, and her life-support chair moved silently back from the table on its counter-grav. "And now, why don't the two of you run on? I've had a long day, and you do have a lot of catching up to do. But no shoptalk!"

"No, Ma'am," Honor agreed meekly.

She and Hamish rose, and Hamish opened the door for Emily's chair. He bent and kissed his wife, and she reached up to run her working hand lightly over his dark hair. Then she was gone, and Hamish and Honor looked at one another.

"You know," Honor said very softly, "neither one of us deserves her."

"I don't know anyone who could," Hamish said simply.

He crossed the room to her, and she folded into his arms. Despite her own height, Hamish was slightly taller than she was, and his arms felt incredibly good about her. She leaned into his embrace, savoring the taste of his emotions, his welcome, and his love. The "mind-glow," treecats called it, and as she felt its bright power and savored once again the way the two of them fitted together on so very many levels, she knew exactly where the term had come from.

His mouth met hers, and her own arms went about him. Their lips clung together for what seemed a very long time, and then, reluctantly, she leaned back and looked across at him.

"I've missed you," she said quietly. "But you do realize that this is crazy?"

"Not crazy," he disagreed with a small, crooked smile. "Just . . . politically unwise."

"And arguably in violation of the Articles of War," Honor pointed out.

"Nonsense." He shook his head. "You know Article One-Nineteen only applies to personnel in the same direct chain of command."

"And you're First Lord and I'm a fleet commander designate."

"And the First Lord is a civilian, my dear." Hamish's mouth quirked in combined amusement and very real and bitter disappointment. "If I were First *Space* Lord, you might have a point. As it is, I couldn't legally give you a direct order even if I wanted to. Besides—"

A crisp, loud bleek interrupted him, and he looked down. Samantha returned his look sternly. Her right true-hand rose, its first two fingers closing onto her thumb in the sign for the letter "N," before both true-hands moved in front of her, right true hand in the palm-out sign for the letter "B" arcing from side to side in front of her to hit the back of her left true-hand, closed in the sign for the letter "S" before opening back into the sign for "N" and sliding down her left true-hand's fingers and palm.

"All right," Hamish said with a laugh. "All right! No more business, I swear."

Samantha sniffed, flirting her tail, and Honor echoed Hamish's laughed.

"Have you ever noticed how thoroughly our lives are managed for us?" she asked. "It was bad enough when it was just Nimitz. Then along came Mac, then Andrew, and Miranda, and Simon and Spencer, and Samantha. And now Emily."

"We're obviously outnumbered and outgunned," Hamish agreed. "In which case, it looks like our only real option is to surrender."

"Well, between them and Emily, Nico, Sandra, and Andrew have all conspired to see to it that no one is going to disturb us," Honor said gently, reaching out to cup the side of his face in her right palm. "And since they've all gone to such pains for us, I suppose we'd best be about it."

The buzz in her ear woke her.

Forty-five years of naval service had trained her to awaken instantly and fully alert but, this morning, her eyes opened slowly, luxuriously as Nimitz's gentle amusement filtered into her mind over their link. Hamish's body was warm, pressed against her spine, his left arm flung across her. She'd almost forgotten how comforting it could be to wake up that way, and she smiled as she roused further, tasting Hamish's sleeping mind-glow.

He was dreaming, and it was obviously a good dream. Honor had been surprised, although she realized she shouldn't have been,

when she discovered she could taste a sleeper's emotions as well
as those of someone who was awake. She couldn't actually tell
what Hamish was dreaming about, the way a treecat could have
done with another 'cat, but the way he stirred slightly, fingers of
his left hand tightening, suggested at least the subject.

Nimitz bleeked at her softly and leaned forward to touch her
nose with his own. Then he sat up, and his right true-hand formed
the sign for the letter "C" and touched his right shoulder, then
tapped the back of his left true-hand's wrist with the first finger
of his right true-hand.

Honor frowned, then twitched the muscles of her left eye
socket in the pattern which brought up the time/date display in
her artificial eye's field of view. The numbers obediently appeared,
and she sat up abruptly.

"Hmmm? Whazzat?" Hamish mutter-grumbled as she slid out
from under his arm and swung her feet onto the floor.

"Wake up!" she said, turning to bend back over him. His eyes
opened, and she tweaked the tip of his nose gently. "We're late!"
she continued.

"We can't be," Hamish protested, sitting up in bed himself.
His eyes lit as he completed the waking up process, and as she
tasted his emotions, she was abruptly reminded that she didn't
have a stitch on.

"Oh, yes we can be," she told him, and swatted his right hand
when he reached for her. "And despite all the lascivious things
going through your head right now, we don't have time to do
anything about them."

"Nico will get us up in plenty of time," Hamish objected.

"Unless, perhaps, somebody suggested to him that he shouldn't,"
Honor replied. His eyes widened suddenly, then narrowed, and
she nodded. "The same thought had occurred to me," she said.

"She did seem rather insistent on our staying away from shoptalk," Hamish conceded, climbing out of bed on the other side.
"On the other hand, she also knows we're both supposed to be
seeing Elizabeth this morning."

"Who happens to be her cousin and probably won't have her
beheaded if we happen to be late because she didn't happen to
wake us up in time," Honor pointed out. "Unfortunately for that
polite fiction all our henchmen are working so hard to maintain
for us, however, Nimitz says Andrew's sense of duty is about

to cause him to knock on your door. At which point it will be rather difficult to pretend I spent the night in the Blue Suite where I was supposed to be!"

"These contortions aren't really necessary, you know," Hamish said reasonably, watching her slip into the kimono which had somehow ended up on the floor. "As you just pointed out, all our people know what's really going on."

"Maybe. No, certainly. But it's going to make Andrew feel awkward the day he finally admits to both of us what he already knows."

"And what about you?" Hamish asked more gently, and she shrugged as she belted her sash.

"I don't really know," she admitted. She smiled. "Mind you, despite a few lingering spasms of guilt, I'm delighted with the way things are working out, so far, at least. And given the fact that I already know that he knows that I know that he knows—well, you get the picture. Given that, I really don't expect it to be particularly uncomfortable when the day finally comes. But I'm not quite sure." Her smile turned wry. "Like I told Emily, there's still a lot of Sphinx and Grayson in me, and the fact that my love-life's been remarkably similar to a nun's since Paul was killed doesn't really help."

"I can see that," he said, and she smiled again, pleased by the fact that neither of them felt awkward using Paul Tankersley's name. "Still," he continued, "you do realize that sooner or later this *is* going to come out?"

"At the moment," Honor scooped Nimitz up in her arms and held him, since her kimono lacked the specially padded shoulders built into her uniform tunics and Grayson-style civilian dress, "I'd prefer later, if you don't mind. I don't have any idea at all how Grayson is going to react when it finds out. And given what we all went through with the Opposition trying to insist we were already lovers when we weren't, I don't even want to think about what the political press would do if the word that now we are got out."

"Might be the best time," he suggested, climbing out of bed and pulling on his own robe as he escorted her to the bedroom door. "There's so much going on on the war front, and in Silesia and the Talbott Cluster, that it might even pass relatively unnoticed."

"And just what episode in our past suggests to you that *anything* about a relationship between you and me could 'pass relatively unnoticed'?" she inquired tartly.

"A point," he admitted, and drew her close to kiss her before she opened the door. "I tend to forget sometimes what good copy 'the Salamander' makes."

"That's one way to put it," she said, and poked him in the navel with two fingers, hard enough to make him "oof." Then she slipped through the door, with a cautious glance up and down the hall to assure herself LaFollet wasn't already on his way. "Now get yourself up and dressed," she told him sternly, and scurried down the hall to the discreet cross passage which connected the Blue Suite to the private family section of White Haven.

She let herself into the suite the back way, and Nimitz bleeked with laughter as the terminal on the table beside the bed which hadn't been slept in chimed gently.

"Shut up, Stinker!" she said, dumping him on the bed, and he laughed harder as she accepted the com call voice-only.

"Yes?" she said.

"We're running late, My Lady," Andrew LaFollet's voice said. He was too far away for her to actually taste his emotions, but she didn't need to in order to recognize the relief in his voice. "Ah, this is the third time I've screened you, My Lady," he added.

"Sorry," she replied. "I'll try to make up for the lost time."

"Of course, My Lady," he said, and she threw off her kimono once again and dashed for the shower.

"You look lovely this morning, Honor," Emily observed as Honor stepped into the sunlit dining room with LaFollet on her heels. She wore uniform today, complete with the Star of Grayson on its crimson ribbon, and "lovely" was not the precise adjective she would have chosen herself. "And so well rested," Emily continued with a certain gently malicious relish.

"Thank you," Honor said as LaFollet pulled her chair out for her and she seated herself. "Perhaps that's because I seem to have missed my wakeup call this morning."

"Goodness," Emily said placidly. "I wonder how that could have happened? Nico is usually so efficient about these things."

"Yes," Honor agreed affably. "For that matter, so is Mac . . . usually."

"Oh, well, don't feel too flustered," Emily told her. "I screened Mount Royal and spoke to Elizabeth. I told her you and Hamish both seemed to be running a bit late this morning, and she asked me to assure you that timing isn't that critical. She just requested we screen her again when you actually leave."

"I see." Honor regarded her across the table for a moment, then shook her head in surrender. "Why am I not surprised that you can snag even the Queen of Manticore in your nets?"

"You make me sound so devious, my dear," Emily reproved her gently.

"No, not devious—just . . . capable."

"I suppose I could accept that as a compliment, so I will," Emily said graciously. "Now eat."

Honor looked up as one of the White Haven servants entered the dining room with a tray of food. It was a fairly typical breakfast for someone with her enhanced metabolism—a thick stack of pancakes, eggs Benedict, tomato juice, croissants, melon, and a steaming carafe of hot chocolate—and her stomach rumbled happily at the sight. But then the tray was set before her, and she felt an abrupt stab of queasiness as the smell of the food hit her.

She grimaced, and Emily cocked an eyebrow at her.

"Are you all right, Honor?" she asked, with none of the teasing edge of banter of their earlier conversation.

"Fine, fine," Honor said, suppressing the flicker of almost-nausea firmly, and reached for her fork. "I'm just not as hungry as usual this morning. Possibly because despite your efforts to rearrange our schedule, I'm still feeling a little flustered at the notion of arriving late for a formal audience with my monarch."

"Only one of your monarchs," Emily pointed out.

"True," Honor conceded, and decided to start with the pancakes, whose aroma seemed more congenial than the scent of the eggs. Her stomach heaved rebelliously at the first bite, but it apparently decided to settle down quickly after she swallowed.

"Sorry I'm late," a deep voice said, and she and Emily looked up as Hamish Alexander stepped into the dining room. "I seem to have missed my wakeup call," he added, then blinked as both women burst into laughter.

Chapter Seven

The sting ships in Winton blue and silver which had escorted them from White Haven banked gently away to either side as the armored limousine in Harrington Steading livery came in across the sparkling waters of Jason Bay and crossed the threshold into Mount Royal Palace's defensive envelope. Honor suspected that very few citizens of Landing ever really considered the fact that Mount Royal was one of the most heavily defended pieces of dirt on any of the Star Kingdom's three inhabited planets. *She* was aware of it primarily because of the necessary interfacing between her own armsmen, the Queen's Own, and Palace Security, and even as a serving naval officer, she'd been astonished at the amount of firepower hidden away under the various innocuous-looking weather domes and secondary structures scattered over the immaculate grounds.

None of that firepower was directed at her, however, and she glanced at Hamish as Mattingly settled the limo lightly onto the semiprivate pad near the old-fashioned, squat spire of King Michael's Tower. Spencer Hawke opened the passenger door and stepped out first, sweeping the immediate area in the automatic threat search of a Grayson armsman even here. LaFollet followed him, and Honor watched her personal armsman give the uniformed Army captain waiting for them a sharp glance.

When no crazed assassins hurled themselves out of the shrubbery, LaFollet stepped to one side so she and Alexander could climb out of the vehicle. Hamish was in civilian court dress trimmed in the maroon and green of the earls of White Haven, as befitted the civilian head of the Admiralty on his way to a formal meeting with his monarch, but Honor was in mess dress uniform, complete with the archaic sword that demanded. In her case, the ancient weapon was no mere prop, either, and the jeweled hilt of the Harrington Sword glittered as she settled the scabbard at her side.

"Your Grace." The captain wore the griffin-headed shoulder patch of the Falcons End Rangers, the Griffin-recruited battalion of the Queen's Own, and saluted sharply, then turned to Alexander. "My Lord."

He saluted again, and Honor chuckled mentally, wondering exactly how the Palace Protocol Office had decided to resolve the question of precedence between them. Hamish was senior to her in Manticoran service, but although both of them were fleet admirals in Grayson sevice, *she* was senior to *him* in that navy.

"If you'd be so good as to follow me?" the captain requested without specifically addressing it to either of them, and the two of them fell into step behind him, trailed by LaFollet, Mattingly, and Hawke.

It was a relatively short walk, and one Honor had made before. The gardens about her were peaceful, drowsing in the sunlight which lay heavily across her shoulders. As a Sphinxian, Honor always found Landing's summer weather unnaturally warm, and the late morning sunlight was almost uncomfortably hot, despite her uniform's smart fabric. The scent of Old Earth roses and Manticoran crown blossom mingled in the still, humid air, and the buzz of Old Earth bees and Manticoran rainbow bugs was improbably loud in the quiet. It was hard to imagine a more placid, comforting setting . . . or one more totally at odds with the reality confronting the Star Kingdom and its allies.

They reached the tower, and the captain escorted them up the old-fashioned elevator. A lieutenant with the shoulder flash of the Copper Wall Battalion came to attention—and dropped one hand to the butt of her holstered pulser—as they approached the door outside which she stood.

"Her Grace, Duchess Harrington, and Earl White Haven to see Her Majesty," their escort announced. Quite unnecessarily, Honor felt certain.

The lieutenant keyed her com without removing her hand from her weapon.

"Her Grace, Duchess Harrington, and Earl White Haven to see Her Majesty," she repeated into the com, and listened a moment to her earbug, eyes still riveted to Honor and Hamish. Then she removed her hand from her pulser.

"Her Majesty is expecting you, Your Grace, My Lord," she said, and pressed the door button.

The door swung open, and Hamish stood back to allow Honor to precede him. She removed her uniform beret, tucked it properly under her left epaulette, and stepped through it.

"Honor!"

Queen Elizabeth III stood in front of the comfortable armchair from which she'd risen, holding out both hands with a huge smile of welcome. Her pleasure at seeing Honor again was like a crackling fire on an icy night, and Honor smiled back, reaching out to take Elizabeth's hands. The treecat on Elizabeth's shoulder flirted his tail, radiating his own pleasure, and bleeked a happy welcome to Nimitz and Samantha as the Queen turned to welcome Hamish, as well. Honor watched the three 'cats and felt an inner bubble of amusement at the contrast between today and her first, almost timorous visit to this room with its simple, comfortably-used furnishings and rust-red carpet.

"Sit down, both of you," Elizabeth commanded, pointing at a pair of chairs arranged around the coffee table. Honor obeyed, taking one of the chairs, and her mental antennae twitched as she noticed the white beret on the table.

"I realize we're running a bit behind schedule," Elizabeth continued as she seated herself once again, "but when Emily screened me, I was able to flip a couple of functions, so we've got time. Besides, I'm going to take the time for a personal visit with you before we get bogged down in all the formalities, no matter what my appointments secretary thinks." She grimaced. "Before things got rearranged, I'd allowed time for it between the audience and dinner, but we've squeezed this morning's briefing from the Admiralty into that slot, so there's not going to be long enough now."

"I'm sorry, Elizabeth," Honor said contritely.

"Don't be." Elizabeth waved the apology aside. "These formal receptions and dinners are important—I know that. And, to be perfectly frank, we need to show you off to the Allied ambassadors, Honor. Given what happened at Sidemore, most of our allies seem to regard you as something of a talisman." She smiled. "For that matter, so do I, I suppose. You do seem to keep doing three impossible things before breakfast every day for me, don't you, Your Grace?

"I've just been in the right place at the right time . . . and with the right people," Honor protested.

"I don't doubt it, although I suspect you personally have probably contributed a bit more to your string of successes than you're prepared to admit. But even at this level of diplomacy, Honor, it's still more of a game of perceptions than anything else. And what our Allies perceive right this minute is that you're the only Allied commander who won an unambiguous victory when the Peeps jumped us. They believe you're lucky, as well as good, and that gives you a stature in their eyes which I intend to capitalize upon to the maximum. The fact that it also gives me the opportunity to publicly thank someone who's done far more than most in the service of my kingdom, and who I happen to regard as a personal friend, is simply icing on my cake."

Honor felt her cheeks heat slightly, but she nodded.

"Good. Now," Elizabeth continued, sitting back in her chair with a broader smile, "there is one other small detail I wanted to deal with before the formal audience. Oh," she raised one hand and wiggled it back and forth in a dismissive gesture, "we'll have to cross the 't's and dot all the 'i's during the audience, but that's mostly for public consumption."

Honor regarded her monarch warily. Elizabeth Winton was a remarkably good card player, and her expression revealed only what she chose for it to reveal, but she couldn't conceal the anticipation bubbling within her from Honor. She was up to something, and Honor recognized that wicked zestfulness. She'd tasted it before when Elizabeth looked forward to opening the box of toys the Queen of Manticore got to bestow on people who had served her well. It was one of the perks of her office which Elizabeth most treasured, and she took almost childlike delight in exercising it when the opportunity arose.

"You needn't look so worried, Honor," the Queen scolded now. "This isn't going to hurt a bit, I promise."

"Of course, Your Majesty," Honor said even more warily, and Elizabeth chuckled. Then she leaned forward, scooped up the white beret on the coffee table, and flipped it across to Honor.

"Here," she said as Honor caught it reflexively. "I think this is yours."

Honor arched her eyebrows, then looked down at the beret in her hands. It looked exactly like the black one tucked under her epaulette, except for its color—the white color, reserved for the commander of a hyper-capable warship of the Royal Manticoran Navy. It was the emblem of a captain of a Queen's ship, a mistress after God, which *Admiral* Honor Harrington would never be again.

"I don't see exactly where you're going with this, Elizabeth," she said after a moment.

"Well, you've already got the Parliamentary Medal of Valor, a knighthood—although, now that I think about it, we're going to be promoting you to knight grand cross this afternoon, I believe—a duchy, a mansion, a baseball team—whatever *that* is—your own personal starship, a multibillion-dollar business empire, and a steading." Elizabeth shrugged. "With all that, deciding what to give you is getting a bit complicated. So I decided to give you back your white beret."

Honor frowned. In theory, she supposed, Elizabeth could issue whatever directives she wanted. She could permit Honor to wear the white beret even if she were no longer a ship's captain. She could even *order* Honor to wear it. But that wouldn't make it right. She opened her mouth, but before she could speak, Hamish put a hand on her knee.

"Wait," he said, then looked at Elizabeth. "I told you, didn't I?" he said to the Queen.

"Yes, you did. And I owe you five dollars." Elizabeth shook her head, grinning at Honor. "You really don't have a clue where I'm headed, do you?" she asked cheerfully.

"No, I don't," Honor admitted.

"Well, it happens that Admiral Massengale retired month before last," Elizabeth said slowly, watching Honor's expression carefully. Honor felt her eyes widen, and the Queen nodded. "Which means," Elizabeth continued, her voice much more serious, "that *Unconquered* needs a captain."

"Elizabeth, you can't," Honor protested. She shook her head. "I'm honored, flattered—delighted—you'd consider me, but there are too many people senior to me who deserve the berth at least as much as I do! You can't just jump me over their heads this way!"

"I can, I want to, and I have," Elizabeth told her flatly. "And, no, this isn't just politics, not a matter of waving my 'talisman' under everyone's noses. And, before you continue to protest, I remind you that the choice of *Unconquered*'s captain is not solely up to the Crown. I may get to make the final decision, but you know the tradition. I can choose only from the list of names submitted to me by the Navy. And *not*," she added, glancing at Hamish, "by the Admiralty. The list of candidates comes solely from the serving officers of the Queen's Navy. You know how it's generated, and you also have to know you were nominated for it after Cerberus."

"Well, yes, but—"

Honor broke off. HMS *Unconquered* was the oldest starship still in commission in the Royal Manticoran Navy. She had been commanded at the very beginning of her lengthy career by Edward Saganami when he was a commander, and her last commanding officer on active deployment had been Lieutenant Commander Ellen D'Orville. *Unconquered* was unique, the only ship to have been commanded by both of the Star Kingdom's greatest naval heroes, which was why she had been rescued from the breakers by the Royal Naval League after a century in reserve.

The League had organized a massive fund-raising project to repair and refurbish the ship, then convinced the Crown to return her to commissioned status as a combination memorial and living museum. Restored to her exact condition when she was Saganami's first cruiser command, she was maintained in permanent orbit around Manticore. Membership in her official "crew," which was maintained at the exact number of officers and ratings which had served under Saganami, was a high honor, reserved as a way of recognizing the achievements of the Navy's best and brightest. None of them actually served aboard her, because the tradition also required that they be personnel on the active duty list, and her captain, by long tradition, was an admiral. Nominated by majority vote by all of the Navy's serving officers, selected by the Queen from the list of elected candidates, *Unconquered*'s captain was the single serving flag officer of the Royal Manticoran Navy who was permitted to wear the white beret of a starship commander.

"I didn't put your name on the list, Honor," Elizabeth said quietly. "Your peers did that. And, while I might have been tempted to jump you to the top of the list if I'd had to, your name was already there."

"But—"

"No buts, Honor," Elizabeth said, shaking her head. "I have to admit this pleases me from an enormous number of perspectives. And, if I'm going to be honest, 'waving my talisman' *is* one of those perspectives. But much more important to me than that, it's an indication of the respect in which you are held by the officer corps of my Navy. If anyone in the galaxy is in a position to properly appreciate all you've done for me and for my Star Kingdom, it's that officer corps, and *they* saw fit to nominate you for this honor. You will not reject the judgment of *my* officer corps, Your Grace. Is that clear?"

Honor gazed at her, clutching the soft fabric of the beret, then, finally, nodded slowly.

"Good. And now, we've got about forty-five minutes before that audience, after which Willie will be turning up with Sir Thomas and Admiral Givens. We'll discuss all those depressing military details then. For now, I do intend to spend some time just visiting with you. Not with Admiral Harrington, not with Duchess Harrington, and not even with Steadholder Harrington. Just with you. All right?"

"Fine, Elizabeth," Honor said. "That's just fine."

"So the raid on Alizon didn't help a bit," Sir Thomas Caparelli said. He, Patricia Givens, Honor, Nimitz, Hamish, Samantha, Elizabeth, Ariel, and Lord William Alexander, the newly created Baron Grantville and Prime Minister of Manticore, sat around a conference table of brilliantly polished feran wood. Hamish, the Queen, and Baron Grantville still wore their formal court attire, but Caparelli and Givens, like Honor, were in mess dress uniform. Three sheathed swords lay across one end of the conference table, and a holographic star map was projected above it, spangled with the icons of friendly units and enemy units' reported positions.

There seemed to be considerably more of the latter than of the former, Honor noticed.

"We're badly strapped for deployable assets everywhere," the First Space Lord continued, turning back from the map to face the Queen. "Obviously, we're going to have to reinforce Alizon, if only to make our commitment to their defense clear, and that's going to stretch us even thinner, but there's no quick fix for that, Your Majesty. We're reactivating superdreadnoughts from the Reserve as quickly as we can, of course. They may be obsolete compared to the pod-layers, but *some* waller is better than *no* waller, and the Republic still has quite a few of the older ships in its own order of battle. But we're not going to be commissioning very many new ships in the foreseeable future. After what they did to Grendelsbane, we have only thirty-five SD(P)s under construction. They should be commissioning within the next six to ten months, but we won't see any more than that until the ships we're laying down right this minute commission. Which means our total available pod-laying wall will consist of no more than a hundred and ten units for at least another two T-years."

"Excuse me, Sir Thomas," Honor said, "but what about the Andermani?"

"Unfortunately, they don't have as many pod-layers as we'd estimated they might when it looked like they were going to be shooting at us," Caparelli said, and nodded to Givens. "Pat?"

"Essentially, Your Grace," Givens said, "the Andies were estimating the number they'd need if push came to shove between us on the basis that at least half our available strength would be required closer to home to keep an eye on Haven. They projected a total build of roughly a hundred and thirty SD(P)s, but they have only forty-two currently in commission. The other ninety are all under construction at various states of completion. Some of them won't be completed for at least another eighteen months."

"And even the ones they've completed are going to require fairly substantial refits before we can make best use of them," Hamish put in. Elizabeth cocked her head at him, and he shrugged. "Their multi-drive missiles are considerably cruder than ours. In fact, they're less sophisticated than the ones Haven is currently deploying. They're almost as big as Havenite three-drive missiles, but they incorporate only *two* drives. Tactically, they're a lot more

like the Mark 16s we're deploying aboard the new *Saganami*-Cs.
They've got heavier warheads than the Mark 16, but their range
is very similar. And because they're capacitor-fed, without the
Mark 16's fusion plant, their EW is less effective. They simply
can't match our birds' power budgets. And while their pods are
bigger than ours are, they actually carry fewer birds than the
Republic's currently do, which means their salvo density is thinner than ours, as well.

"We've put BuWeaps and BuShips on to the problem, and
Admiral Hemphill and Vice Admiral Toscarelli have come up
with a minimum-modification solution. They can't operate the
new fusion-powered MDMs from their pods, but we can load
their launcher cells with our own older-style, capacitor-fed three-
stage missiles. It won't give them any greater salvo density, and
the EW will still be less capable, but it will significantly improve
their range. It's going to require some modifications to their pods,
which they're going to be making at their end, but that part of
the process should be completed within the next sixty days. After
that, it's just a case of their building the new pods.

"The longer-range fix is to modify their existing SD(P)s to
accept the Keyhole platforms and fire our new 'flat-pack' pods
with the all-up fusion-powered birds. That's going to take considerably longer, because each ship will have to spend an absolute
minimum of ninety days in yard hands to carry out the modifications. Toscarelli's people have just about completed the blueprints
for the necessary alterations, and they've been working with the
Andies' architects to provide a fix which can be incorporated into
the ships still under construction. At best, though, that's going
to impose an additional delay on those units' completion."

"So," Caparelli said, "looking at every pod-laying waller we can
scrape up between us, Grayson, and the Andies, and including
all of the Andy SD(P)s currently in commission as fully effective
units, we have a total of two hundred and thirty-two. Assuming
our construction times hold up, and allowing for working up
time, we can have a total of just over four hundred within the
next eleven to eighteen months. We can add about a hundred
and sixty pod-laying battlecruisers to that total, but they can't
stand in the wall against proper superdreadnoughts. That's an
impressive number, but the Havenites have some pretty impressive numbers of their own."

"Yes," Elizabeth said, looking intently at Admiral Givens. "I saw a precis of your revised strength estimates last week, Admiral, but it didn't include the basis for your revisions. Is the situation really that bad?"

"That's impossible to say with certainty, Your Majesty," Givens replied. "I'm not trying to cover myself, and I stand by the numbers in the most recent report, but until the shooting's over, we can't do an actual nose count to prove it. I'm sorry it's taken this long to produce the report in the first place, but we still have a certain amount of reorganizing to do over at ONI."

Elizabeth grimaced, her eyes hard, at the oblique reference to Admiral Francis Jurgensen's disastrous tenure as Second Space Lord.

"Our human-intelligence sources in the Republic are considerably weaker than they used to be," the admiral continued. "Partly, that's due to the political changes there. Quite a few of the people supplying information to us were doing so because of their opposition to the old régime, and their motivation to continue to work with us largely disappeared along with Saint-Just. Others, who we'd managed to buy or suborn, lost their access when they were purged by the new management. And, unfortunately, under the Janacek Admiralty, ONI hadn't assigned a high priority to building new networks. In fairness, doing so under the new circumstances would have been difficult, time-consuming, and probably expensive."

Elizabeth's agate-hard eyes flickered, but she didn't seem disposed to entertain any excuses for the unfortunate Jurgensen's failures.

"At any rate," Givens went on, "there are serious holes in our information-gathering capabilities. And I have to admit that Pierre and Saint-Just managed to build this entire shipbuilding complex of theirs, wherever it is, on *my* watch, without my getting so much as a sniff of it. We're looking for it hard, scouting every system we can think of, but so far, we haven't found it. Which is more than mildly irritating, given the resources we're committing to the effort. On the other hand, the way they've spread out their building capacity since Theisman first went public about the Peep pod-layers, Bolthole is becoming steadily less of an absolutely critical node for them.

"But bearing in mind the limits on our intel ability, and

counting only the new ships we've actually observed, and making allowances for errors in post-battle reports, we're estimating that they must have a minimum of three hundred pod-layers currently in commission. We know they had at least two hundred old-style superdreadnoughts in service, as well, plus another hundred or so in reserve, but it's the pod-layers that pose the critical threat. If they do have three hundred in service at this time, then they have approximately one and a half times as many as we and the Graysons do. It drops to about one-point-three-to-one in their favor if we include all of the completed Andermani SD(P)s. By our best estimate of the differences between their current hardware and our own, that equates to near parity between the two sides, but they've got much more strategic depth than we do."

"That depth tips the strategic balance significantly in their favor, Your Majesty," Caparelli put in. "They can afford to concentrate their forces for offensive operations to a far greater extent than we can. We can't afford to allow them the opportunity to take out the industrial capacity here in the Star Kingdom or in Grayson, and that means we're forced to maintain sufficient strength in those systems to deter a serious attack. As Pat says, we don't even know where this 'Bolthole' of theirs is, so there's no way we could do the same thing to their infrastructure. We could hurt them badly in several places, if we uncovered enough to go after them, but without at least Bolthole's location, we can't *cripple* them the way they could cripple us."

"I understand," Elizabeth said, nodding, and reached out to scratch Ariel between the ears. "But you're estimating an enormous growth in their total numbers, Admiral Givens."

"Yes, Your Majesty, we are," Givens admitted bleakly. "The problem is that we've uncovered evidence that even before Theisman shot Saint-Just, they'd been stockpiling huge numbers of components. We'd picked up on that before Buttercup, but we'd never been able to figure out where they were going or why. Then, after the Cromarty Assassination and the cease-fire—" if Elizabeth's eyes had been hard before, they could have been used to cut diamonds now "—the Admiralty stopped worrying about it. We'd never been able to confirm it was happening in the first place, and it seemed irrelevant in light of our technical and tactical superiority.

"However, after examining the wreckage from Her Grace's victory at Sidemore, we've determined that even though the SD(P)s Haven deployed for the attack were new-build, new-design ships, they used existing, off-the-shelf components wherever possible. Obviously, many of their systems had to be new-construction, but the truth is that probably at least eighty-five percent of the design was based on existing hardware. Exactly what they appear to have been stockpiling. Our numbers for what they squirreled away are nowhere near as precise as I'd like, but allowing for a twenty-five percent overestimate, and assuming the stockpiled items represent only seventy percent of the new ships' total requirements, they could still have an additional four hundred to four hundred and fifty under construction at 'Bolthole' alone. And, of course, there's no way for us to estimate how far along in the construction process those ships might be."

Chill silence hovered in the conference room. Honor tasted the grim awareness of what those numbers meant radiating from her fellow naval officers. Elizabeth and the Prime Minister were deeply concerned, but the full impact didn't appear to have hit them yet.

"Excuse me, Pat," she said, after a moment, "but I noticed you said they could have that many ships under construction 'at Bolthole *alone*.'"

"Yes, I did, Your Grace." Givens nodded. "Obviously, until they announced the existence of their own pod-layers, all their construction was carried out under conditions of maximum secrecy—the entire rationale for Bolthole in the first place. But as soon as Theisman announced they had SD(P)s of their own, they began preparations to lay down additional units in other shipyards. Our estimate is that they're probably looking at longer construction times in the older yards, not to mention the fact that they had to set up all of the long-lead items and get organized before they could begin construction there at all. Nonetheless, we have indications from various sources that they have somewhere in the vicinity of an additional four hundred new units under construction at Nouveau Paris and two or three other of their central systems. That's the bad news. The *good* news is that although the Pritchart Administration authorized their construction the better part of a T-year ago, they only really hit their stride about four months ago. Which means it's going to take them at least another two and a half T-years to complete any of them. So they're not a factor in the immediate gap between our numbers and theirs."

"That may be, Pat," Hamish said, "but the thought of looking at twelve *hundred* SD(P)s in a couple of years doesn't exactly fill me with joyous enthusiasm."

"But, with all due respect, Admiral Givens," his brother said, "how realistic is your estimate in fiscal terms?" Givens looked at him, and Grantville smiled thinly. "As Duke Cromarty's Chancellor of the Exchequer I enjoyed quite a bit of experience of just how difficult it was for *us* to pay for hundreds of new superdreadnoughts, and the Havenite economy is still a long way from anything I'd call healthy. They may have laid down all the ships you're talking about, but will they be able to *sustain* the building program without an economic collapse?"

"That, Prime Minister, is outside my own area of expertise," Givens admitted. "The financial analysts attached to ONI believe they can, indeed, complete all or a high percentage of the total projected current program—or, rather, our estimate of what that program is. They're going to have to make some hard decisions about what *not* to build to pull it off, but they have many times the star systems we do. Despite our much higher per capita income, their *absolute* budgets are at least as big, or bigger, than our own, and their manpower costs are far lower. It's certainly possible that trying to complete this program would indeed lead to the economic collapse of the Republic. Which, on a long-term basis, could be good or bad from our perspective. My own feeling, however, is that we dare not count on that outcome. Especially not given how much of Havenite strategy under the Legislaturalist régime was based on seizing Manticore and our wormhole junction specifically as a revenue source. The new régime might well be willing to go deeply into debt if it believes that by doing so it can succeed where Harris, Pierre, and Saint-Just failed."

Baron Grantville nodded, but he clearly wasn't fully convinced, and Honor tasted his deep reservations about Givens' estimates.

"So what do we do?" Elizabeth asked simply after silence had lingered for several seconds.

"For the immediate future, we're effectively forced to stand primarily on the defensive," Hamish said. "I don't like it, and neither does Sir Thomas, but that's simply the reality we face. We're still working on ways in which we might be able to modify that defensive stance in order to put at least some pressure on Haven, and we'll be discussing those possibilities with Admiral Harrington and her staff over the next several days. Hopefully, we'll come up with something that will prevent the other side from retaining sole possession of the strategic initiative, but we'll probably still be forced to adopt a mainly reactive stance until our own new construction begins to come forward in large numbers."

Something else flickered behind his thoughts. Honor caught just a trace of it, too little to even begin to estimate what it was, but it seemed to carry a flavor of wariness and apprehensive disappointment. Whatever it was, no trace of it shadowed his voice as he continued.

"We're also engaged in a comprehensive evaluation of our building options. One of the very few things the Janacek Admiralty did right—by accident, I'm sure—was to leave Vice Admiral Toscarelli at BuShips. I doubt they would have done it if they'd realized what he was actually up to over there, although I may be doing Chakrabarti a disservice. He may have known *exactly* what Toscarelli was doing.

"At any rate, despite the official Janacek position that there was no need to build anything other than LACs and commerce-protection units, Toscarelli and his people managed to get the *Saganami-C* approved as a 'modification' of the existing *Saganami* design, rather than as a totally new class which represents as significant a tactical departure for cruisers as the *Medusa*-class represented for superdreadnoughts. He also managed to get the design for the new *Nike*-class battlecruisers and *Agamemnon*-class BC(P)s approved. We only have the lead ship of the *Nike*-class about to commission, and only six of the *Agamemnons*, but there are six more *Agamemnons* already in the pipeline. Almost more importantly, most of the construction kinks have been worked out of both designs, and they can be put into rapid series production quickly. Then there's the new *Medusa-B*-class SD(P). It was authorized by Chakrabarti solely as a paper study, but Toscarelli took it to the detailed blueprint stage. It's a significant improvement on the *Invictus* design, but we'd be looking at an additional delay of six to ten months to put a completely new design into production rather than simply building repeat *Invictus*-class ships."

"If we're looking at a two-year window of vulnerability," the Prime Minister asked, "why not consider building smaller units? I know we haven't built any dreadnoughts since before the first war, but given that we're talking about pod-laying designs, shouldn't it be possible to build an effective *DN*(P)? Units that size could be built much more rapidly, couldn't they?"

"Yes, and no, Prime Minister," Caparelli said formally. "Construction time on a dreadnought runs about eighty percent of the construction time on a *super*dreadnought. In theory, that means we could build one in about eighteen months rather than twenty-three. Unfortunately, we don't have a DN(P) *design*. We'd have to produce one from scratch, then get it into construction, with all the delays always attendant on the introduction of a completely new class. We'd probably be looking at a minimum of three T-years from the moment we began work to the moment we completed the first unit, which means it would take six months *longer* to build the first of the smaller ships. Thereafter, we could, indeed, build them faster, but if we're prepared to use dispersed yards and build 'Grayson-style,' we can build as many superdreadnoughts simultaneously as we can fund. So it doesn't seem to us over at Admiralty House that there's any advantage in designing a smaller, less capable unit when it would actually delay our building programs."

"There's no way we can speed construction?" Grantville asked. All of the uniformed officers—and his brother—looked at him, and he shrugged. "I'm sorry. I don't mean to question your professional judgment, but the Graysons managed to get their first SD(P) built in under fifteen months."

"Yes, they did," Hamish replied. "But to complete her to their new schedule, which had a little something to do with Honor's supposed execution, they pulled out all the stops. In fact, they diverted major components from older-style SDs to the new designs. The *Harrington*'s fusion plants, for instance—*all* of them were diverted from two of their *Steadholder Denevski*-class ships, which delayed *their* completion by almost eight months. We can't do that here because we don't have the new construction to divert components from. But that's pretty much what ONI is saying the Havenites have been doing with those stockpiled components Admiral Givens was just talking about."

"I understand," William said. He grimaced—in disappointment, not in anger—as Caparelli and his brother demolished his suggestions. "I hadn't considered the dreadnought notion from the aspect of design time," he added.

"We do have some additional potential force multipliers in the pipeline," Hamish said after a moment, with a slight edge of caution. "I've been very impressed with what Sonja Hemphill and Toscarelli have been coming up with ever since Sonja took over at BuWeaps."

He shook his head, his expression somewhat bemused, as if he couldn't quite believe what he was saying about the Admiral who had been his personal *bête noire* for literally decades.

"I don't want anybody counting on miracle weapons," he continued, the note of caution in his voice stronger than before. "Specifically, at this time, we don't see anything on the horizon that will equate to the sort of quantum leap in capabilities Ghost Rider and the MDM represented. It's always hard to project the impact of new technologies until you actually have them in hand, so I could be wrong about that, but I'd prefer to err on the side of caution at a time like this. And don't forget that any improvements we may make will be offset, at least to some extent, by *Havenite* improvements based on the examples of our own hardware they must have captured during their offensive and, I'm sure, ideas all their own. Their Admiral Foraker, for example, appears to be a fiendishly clever innovator. Having said all of that, however, Sonja and Toscarelli are looking at several developments which could have at least as significant an impact on our relative combat capabilities as the introduction of the Keyhole platforms."

"And while we're talking about things the Janacek Admiralty did right for the wrong reasons," Caparelli put in, "his mania for using LACs as a panacea has at least guaranteed that the LAC assembly line was in full swing when the penny dropped. We foresee no bottlenecks in LAC or missile pod production, including the new system-defense pods and setting up our own lines to produce the Graysons' Vipers. There may be some problems we haven't foreseen with the new munitions BuWeaps has in the pipeline, but production of our existing weapons should be ample for our needs. It's going to take us a while to build up to full speed for the system-defense units, but we can probably build LACs faster than we can train crews for them. They won't help us out a lot against an intact wall of battle, but they'll give us a high degree of scouting and rear area coverage which should at least allow us to economize on hyper-capable pickets."

"Which just about sums up the military side of our options," Hamish said, and Honor tasted another flash of that disappointment from him. This time there was an answering flicker, one of stubborn exasperation, from Elizabeth. And an echo of it from William Alexander, as well.

"Yes, I suppose it does," Elizabeth agreed, with a very slight but unmistakable note of finality. Then she glanced at her chrono.

"And it sums it up just in time," she said more briskly, with a wry grimace. "Honor, you and Willie and I—and you, Hamish—have a dinner appointment in the Crown Chancery in about twenty minutes. So," she smiled at Honor, "let's be about it, you three!"

Chapter Eight

"Anything from Admiral Duval, Serena?" Rear Admiral Oliver Diamato, Republic of Haven Navy, asked quietly.

"No, Sir." Commander Serena Taverner, his chief of staff shook her head.

"Good."

Diamato nodded to her, rose from his command chair, and crossed to the master plot on the battlecruiser *William T. Sherman*'s flag bridge. *Sherman* was no longer "his," and he'd already discovered just how much he missed the hands-on command of a ship. But at least the Octagon had let him keep her as his flagship.

He examined the plot carefully, hands folded behind him. By now, the posture was so familiar that it had become truly his, no longer an affectation deliberately copied from Captain Hall. He studied the icons, then nodded once in approval and turned away. This was the first time he'd served with Rear Admiral Harold Duval, CO of the 19th CLAC Division, and Duval had a reputation as a bit of a worrywort. Diamato had been half afraid he might come up with some last-minute alteration of the plan, but it seemed he'd been doing his superior an injustice, and that was good. He hated last-minute surprises.

Now he gazed at the pair of CLACs—RHNS *Skylark*, the flagship, and her sister *Peregrine*—his own squadron was escorting, then checked the time display ticking down in the corner of the plot. The combined force would translate out of hyper in another twenty-seven minutes, right on the hyper limit of the Zanzibar System's G4 primary.

After which, he thought, *things will get . . . interesting.*

"We have a hyper footprint, Ma'am."

Rear Admiral of the Green Dame Evelyn Padgorny looked up from her routine paperwork at her ops officer's announcement. Commander Thackeray stood in the flag briefing room's hatch, his voice a bit deeper than usual, and Padgorny cocked an eyebrow at him.

"I assume from the fact that you're telling me this that it isn't a *scheduled* footprint, Alvin," she said dryly.

"No, Ma'am. It isn't." Thackeray gave her a tight grin. "The outer reconnaissance platforms make it twelve units. At the moment it looks like a pair of either superdreadnoughts or their CLACs, with a battlecruiser squadron riding shotgun and a couple of light cruisers or big tin-cans for scouting."

"Another raid, then," she said.

"That's what it looks like to CIC and System Defense Command," Thackeray agreed. "The question, of course, is whether they *are* CLACs . . . or SD(P)s."

"You do have a way of cutting to the nub of a matter, don't you, Alvin?"

Padgorny smiled humorlessly, logged off her terminal, and stood. Thackeray stepped back to let her precede him through the hatch, then followed her across the deck to HMS *Prince Stephen*'s master plot. At least the plot's details were clear, she thought. The FTL links to the reconnaissance platforms planted around the system periphery were real-timing their take to *Prince Stephen*, and she pursed her lips thoughtfully as she studied the crimson icons.

Assuming they were, indeed, Havenite units—and Padgorny couldn't think of any reason for anyone else to be coming in without identifying themselves this way—Thackeray's question was well taken. *Prince Stephen* and the other four units of the understrength Thirty-First Battle Squadron weren't precisely cutting-edge. Although the oldest of Padgorny's ships was less than eight T-years old, none of them were pod-layers. All five were surrounded by shoals of missile pods, waiting to tractor themselves to their hulls upon command, but they weren't really optimized for pod-based combat. They simply lacked the sophistication of the fire control built into ships of the wall which had been intended from the outset for the new operational environment. *Prince Stephen* could "tow" as many as five or six hundred of the new pods, whose internal tractors glued them limpet-like to a ship's hull, but loading up with that many would seriously compromise her combat ability by blocking sensor and firing arcs. Worse, the maximum number of missiles she could actually simultaneously control effectively at range was no more than a hundred. One of the *Invictus*-class SD(P)s could control two or three times that many birds, even without the new Keyhole platforms, and she had to assume Peep pod-layers would also have several times the missile telemetry channels her ships had.

On the other hand, she reminded herself, *if these people really want to shoot at us, then they've got to come* to *us. Which means, in this case, not simply us, but all the* rest *of Zanzibar System Defense Command.*

Unless, of course, the Peeps in question were prepared to simply flail away at extreme range. It was unlikely they would choose to risk even accidentally violating the Eridani Edict, but they *were* Peeps, after all. The bastards hadn't been at all shy about killing thousands of Padgorny's fellow naval officers and ratings in their goddamned sneak attack, so they might not lose any sleep about the odd civilian mega-death or two, either.

"Any communication from them yet?"

"No, Ma'am," the com officer of the watch replied. "Of course, they've just come over the Alpha wall."

"Yes, they have," Padgorny agreed. "But by now, even the Peeps know our sensor platforms are out there and that they're FTL. Don't you suppose they might have figured out that a light-speed omnidirectional broadcast would be picked up and relayed to us?"

"Ah, yes, Ma'am," the hapless communications officer said. Obviously the Old Lady was *not* in a good mood, he noted.

"Sorry, Willoughby," Padgorny said a moment later, lips twitching in a wry smile. "Didn't mean to bite your head off."

"Yes, Ma'am," Lieutenant Willoughby said in a somewhat different tone, and returned her smile.

Padgorny nodded and turned away from him. She didn't really require any self-identifications from the intruders. The lack of any transmissions from them meant they had to be Peeps, since any Allied units most definitely would have identified themselves by now. So there was no point in taking out her frustration on Willoughby. Still, she would dearly love to know exactly what—

"LAC separation!" a voice announced. "We have LAC separation on Bogeys Alpha and Bravo! Estimate five hundred-plus inbound at six-eight-zero gravities!"

Well, it seemed that sometimes wishes came true. At least she knew, now, and it was unlikely the Peeps intended any Eridani violations if they were sending in LACs armed with short-ranged missiles.

"What about the battlecruisers?" she asked.

"They're maintaining constant decel with the CLACs, Ma'am," Thackeray replied. "Looks like this is more of a probe than a serious attack. The battlecruisers are hanging back to cover the CLACs while their birds are away."

Padgorny nodded in agreement with Thackeray's assessment.

"They're going to get hurt," another voice said, and Padgorny looked up as Commander Thomasina Hartnett, her chief of staff, arrived on the flag bridge. "Sorry I'm late, Ma'am," Hartnett continued with a grimace. "My pinnace was on final approach when these people turned up."

"Inconvenient of them," Padgorny replied with a thin smile, "but what can you expect out of Peeps?"

"Anything from Defense Command?" Hartnett asked Willoughby even as she accepted a memo board with a full situation update from Thackeray.

"Not after the initial alert, Ma'am," Willoughby said.

"Probably waiting to see whether or not they launched LACs," Padgorny said with a shrug, when Hartnett looked at her.

"Well, Ma'am," the chief of staff said, eyes scanning the memo board as she spoke, "I stand by my own initial assessment. These people are gonna get seriously hammered if they keep on coming in."

"A point which I suspect has occurred to them, as well," Padgorny said. "But it all depends on how deep in they want to get, Tommy."

"True, Ma'am." Hartnett nibbled on a thumbnail, eyes intent as she studied the master plot. "I really wish that bastard Theisman hadn't shot Saint-Just," she said, after a moment.

"Really?" Padgorny cocked her head inquiringly, and Hartnett shrugged.

"At least State Security kept their admirals looking over their shoulders all the time, Ma'am. They were too busy watching their own asses to think up inventive things to do to us. And they'd have thought two or three times about proposing probes like this one. They'd have been afraid they'd be expected to carry through with a serious attack."

"I don't know if it's really that much of an improvement," Padgorny objected in her best, approved devil's advocate tone. "McQueen did a number on us when she did carry through with 'a serious attack,' StateSec or no StateSec."

"Oh, she certainly did that," Hartnett agreed. "But that was a heavy-duty, full-press fleet operation. These people—" she jabbed an index finger at the plot's icons "—aren't here to *hurt* Zanzibar. They're here probing for information, and they're willing to take significant losses to get it. Which means they're planning on *doing* something with whatever info they can get, and, frankly, that could be a hell of a lot more dangerous to us than a serious attack on the system might have been."

Padgorny nodded thoughtfully. There was a new, tough-minded professionalism behind the Peeps' operations in this new and more dangerous war. The clumsy amateurism the previous régimes' civilian masters had imposed on their uniformed subordinates had disappeared, and it was painfully obvious the new management was working from a cohesive, carefully thought-out playbook. And Hartnett was right. Providing that sort of navy with the information needed to accurately assess just how threadbare the Alliance's defenses really were—everywhere, not just in Zanzibar—came under the heading of Really Bad Ideas.

"Well," she said after a moment, "in that case, I suppose we ought to get busy seeing these people off without giving them any better look at us than we can help."

"Yes, Ma'am," Hartnett agreed. "Flush the LACs?"

"Not all of them." Padgorny shook her head. "Let's keep at least one pulser up our sleeve. Alvin," she turned back to the ops officer, "launch just the in-system platforms. Have them form up on the squadron. We'll move out together."

"Aye, aye, Ma'am," Commander Thackeray acknowledged. "Should I inform System Defense that we're executing Hildebrandt?"

"Yes, of course you should." Padgorny grimaced. "I should have thought of it myself. In fact, before you pass the orders, contact System Defense. Inform them that I intend to put Hildebrandt into operation unless otherwise instructed."

"Yes, Ma'am."

Padgorny gave the expressionless operations officer a quick smile. The diplomatic management of allies had never been one of her own strong suits, and managing those allies had become both more important and much more difficult in the wake of the High Ridge Government's disastrous foreign policy. Stepping on the Zanzibaran System Navy's sensibilities by ignoring it in its own star system would have been less than brilliant. Especially after the system's industry and economy had been so brutally shattered by the Peeps "Operation Icarus" barely eight T-years ago. And extra especially, in the wake of the High Ridge Government's incredibly incompetent foreign policy, when the Treaty of Alliance specifically assigned command authority to the ZSN. Existing doctrine and previous discussions with the Zanzibarans made it obvious which system defense plan was called for, but that wasn't really the point . . . diplomatically speaking.

"Good catch, Ma'am," Hartnett said very quietly, cutting her eyes sideways to indicate Thackeray as the operations officer and Lieutenant Willoughby put the com call through to Zanzibar System Defense Command.

"Agreed," Padgorny replied, equally quietly, nodding her head. "Alvin does have his moments."

The admiral shoved her hands deep into her tunic's pockets, lower lip protruding slightly as she studied the plot, waiting for System Defense's response.

The Peeps were still boring steadily in, but there was plenty of time to show a little sensitivity to inter-allied coordination. Zanzibar was a G4, with a hyper limit of just over twenty light-minutes. The planet of the same name orbited its primary at just under eight light-minutes, which put it 12.3 light-minutes inside the limit, and most of the system's manufacturing and commercial infrastructure (rebuilt with the very latest technology and the aid of massive Manticoran loans and subsidies after Icarus) orbited the planet. The intruders were already inside both of the system's asteroid belts, and even if they hadn't been, Zanzibar's extraction industry was less centralized than most. There were very few belter nodes for them to hit, which meant any truly worthwhile targets had to be deep in-system.

They had arrived with a fairly low normal-space velocity—less than twelve hundred kilometers per second—and they were over two hundred and twenty million kilometers from any of those worthwhile targets. Even at their LACs' rate of acceleration, it would have taken them over two hours—132.84 minutes, to be precise—just to reach the planet, at which point their velocity would have been well over fifty-four thousand kilometers per second. And if they'd wanted a zero/zero intercept, flight time would have been roughly fifty-six minutes longer.

Of course, they weren't going to do either of those things. As Hartnett had observed, this was a probe, not a serious attack. They wouldn't commit that many LACs to a flight profile that would force them to enter the engagement envelope of Zanzibar's orbital defenses. Those tiny craft had nowhere near the firepower to tackle the orbital defenses, and there were six or seven thousand men and women aboard them. Sending them to their deaths for no meaningful return was something the Pierre régime or Saint-Just might have done. Theisman wouldn't. No, they were here to drag their coats behind them. To be just threatening enough to provoke the system's defenders into revealing at least a part of their capabilities. Even relatively tiny pieces of data could be combined, massaged by computers and human analysts, to reveal far more about the state of Zanzibar's defenses and, by implication, the status of the Alliance as a whole, than anyone wanted Theisman to know.

But probes of the defenses were precisely what System Defense Plan Hildebrandt was intended to prevent. With BS 31 and the inner-system LACs anyone but an idiot already knew were present advancing to meet them, the Peep LACs would be forced to withdraw without the defenders having revealed their full capabilities. Which—

"Excuse me, Admiral."

Padgorny turned her head and looked up, frowning slightly as Alvin Thackeray's tone registered.

"Yes?" she said.

"Ma'am, Admiral al-Bakr is on the com." Padgorny's eyebrows rose, and Thackeray gave a very slight shrug. "He says he's not prepared to authorize Hildebrandt, Ma'am."

Padgorny's raised eyebrows lowered, and her frown deepened.

"Did he say why not?" she asked, quite a bit more crisply than she'd intended to.

"He feels the Peeps' approach is too obvious," Thackeray said expressionlessly. "He thinks it may be a feint intended to draw us out of position."

Padgorny's lips compressed tightly, and the hands shoved into her tunic's pockets clenched into fists.

"A feint?" Commander Hartnett's voice was sharp as she asked the question Padgorny had kept herself from voicing. "And what does he think the system surveillance arrays are for?" she demanded.

"Calmly, Tommy," Padgorny said. The chief of staff looked at her, and the admiral let her eyes sweep around the flag bridge, reminding her of all the listening ears. Not that Padgorny didn't agree completely with Hartnett's response.

"Sorry, Ma'am," Hartnett said, after a moment. "But there's no way they're going to sneak another attack force into the system without our spotting a hyper footprint when they arrive, and the remote platforms have these people right under their eye. There's no way anyone else is lurking around out there to take advantage of any diversion the LACs might represent. This has to be exactly what Hildebrandt is supposed to stop."

"I'm inclined to think you're right," Padgorny replied. She was faintly surprised by how calm she managed to sound, and she looked past Thackeray to Willoughby.

"Please put the Admiral through to my display," she requested, striding across to her command chair and settling herself into it.

"Yes, Ma'am," Willoughby said, and Admiral Gammal al-Bakr's face appeared on the flatscreen display deployed from the left arm of Padgorny's command chair.

"Admiral al-Bakr," she said courteously.

"Admiral Padgorny," he responded. Al-Bakr wore the ZSN's visored cap, maroon tunic, and black trousers, with the doubled crescent moons of his rank glittering on his collar points. Like most Zanzibarans, he was dark-haired and eyed. He was also of medium height, with a lean, hawkish face and a neatly trimmed beard and mustache streaked with white around his lips.

"I understand you're opposed to the activation of Hildebrandt, Admiral?" Padgorny said as pleasantly as possible.

"I am," al-Bakr replied levelly. "I believe it's possible this attack represents a feint, intended to draw your units out of position and clear the way for a direct attack on the planet and its orbital installations."

"Sir," Padgorny said, after a brief pause, "we've detected no indications of any force waiting to exploit any diversion the LACs might manage to create. I feel confident your surveillance arrays would have detected any such force upon its arrival."

"They may have taken a page from Admiral Harrington's Sidemore tactics," al-Bakr countered. "They could very well have an entire task force waiting in hyper. If you activate Hildebrandt and move away from the planet, they could send a messenger into hyper to bring those reinforcements in at any point around the hyper-limit sphere of their choice."

Padgorny managed not to stare at him. It wasn't easy.

"Admiral," she said instead, controlling her tone carefully, "the incoming forces we know about are on Zanzibar's side of the primary. They're coming in on the shortest, least-time approach. If we move towards them, we'll remain between them and the inner system. Forces approaching from other directions will have much further to travel, and I think it's unlikely we could be drawn far enough out of position to prevent us from responding if and when they make their alpha translation and we detect their footprints."

And even if that weren't true, she thought, *why in the world would they be bothering with* diversions *if they have an all-up task force or fleet out there in the first place? If they've got that kind of firepower, they certainly don't need to "distract" a single understrength battle squadron!*

"Overall," al-Bakr said, "I agree that your assessment is logical. However, if you advance far enough from the planet under Hildebrandt, they could execute a polar translation and effectively cut in behind you. Particularly since your base velocity would be directly away from the planet at the moment they made translation."

Padgorny's jaw muscles tightened. What al-Bakr was suggesting was at least theoretically feasible. But it wouldn't be easy, and she couldn't conceive of any rational reason for the Peeps to attempt any such complicated maneuver.

"Sir," she said, "given the range of our MDMs, they would have to time things very, very carefully if they intended to remain outside our engagement envelope. Moreover, they would be attacking directly into your own orbital defenses and the fire of our inner-system defense pods. They would have to be present in overwhelming strength to crack those defenses, even without the presence of my own battle squadron. In my estimation, this represents another probing attack, precisely the scenario Hildebrandt is designed to defeat. They're looking for information on your star system's defensive capabilities for future reference. And if we don't execute Hildebrandt—don't move out to engage these LACs short of the inner-system—they'll be able to get much deeper in and get a far better look at those defenses."

"They can do that with recon drones, if they wish to," al-Bakr countered. "There's no need for them to risk their LACs doing the same job. So, with all due respect, Dame Evelyn, I believe the reason they *are* using LACs is specifically to draw you out of position."

"I doubt very much, Sir, that Peeps are going to be able to sneak recon drones deep enough in-system to obtain the sort of information they need without our detecting them. Their drones simply aren't as stealthy as ours, and their sensors aren't as good. They couldn't pick up our concealed units . . . unless those units go active. Which is why they're using LACs. They may well have a drone screen out, but they want us to engage the LACs—or at least move to do so—because their drones can't pick our units up unless and until we bring them on-line."

"Havenite technology has clearly improved greatly since the previous war, Admiral," al-Bakr said. "I believe it may be good enough to accomplish the task even if our defenses remain covert—or that *they* believe it is, at any rate. And it is, after all, their own assessment of their technology's capabilities which will govern their choice of tactics."

"Sir, I'm afraid I can't share your interpretation of their intentions." Padgorny kept both her tone and her expression as non-confrontational as she possibly could. "But whichever one of us is correct, we're faced with the fact that almost six hundred hostile LACs are headed in-system and accelerating at over six and a half KPS squared. And while they're already inside most of your asteroid industry, there are—" she checked the CIC sidebar on the main plot "—twenty-three of your extraction freighters directly in their path. In addition to one Manticoran, one Solarian, and two Andermani merchantmen. If we don't respond, most of those extraction vessels and at least one of the Andermani freighters will find themselves in the Peeps' attack range before they can reach the cover of your orbital defenses."

"I'm aware of the shipping movements, Admiral Padgorny," al-Bakr said a bit frostily. "This, after all, is not the first time the Peeps have visited this system," he added pointedly. "And I haven't said you can't engage these intruders. I've simply said that I won't authorize Hildebrandt. Your vessels, and the inner-system LACs, must remain in position to cover the planet and our most vital space infrastructure. I would point out to you that it was for precisely this sort of circumstance that the *outer*-system LACs and pods were deployed in the first place."

Padgorny discovered that her teeth ached from the force her jaw muscles were now exerting.

"Admiral al-Bakr," she said after a momemt, "at this time, we have no reason to believe the Peeps realize the outer-system defenses are present. If we use them against this attack, however, that will change. Which will provide their planners with valuable intelligence in the event that they do decide to execute a serious attack on Zanzibar in future. I strongly urge you to allow me to use Hildebrandt rather than reveal that capability."

"I'm afraid I can't do that," al-Bakr said flatly. "I realize you continue to have a great deal of faith in the superiority of our— and, particularly, your Star Kingdom's—technology over that of Haven. However, I—and my Caliph—are no longer in a position to place complete trust in that superiority, especially in light of the price the Caliphate has already paid. I believe it's probable Haven already knows from its own recon drones or other intelligence sources that we've been deploying LAC tenders and pods in the outer system. Which is one reason I believe this is a feint."

Padgorny tried hard not to goggle at him. If the Caliph and his military advisers thought anything of the sort, why the *hell* hadn't they said so sooner than *this*? From the hardening of his expression, she realized she hadn't fully succeeded in controlling her own.

"At any rate, Admiral Padgorny," his voice was flatter than before, "I am not prepared to further debate my decision as the commander of this star system's defenses. You will *not* execute Hildebrandt and uncover the inner-system. And you will use the outer-system defenses to deal with this attack. Is that understood?"

Padgorny inhaled deeply, nostrils flaring, and reminded herself diplomacy wasn't her forte.

"It is, Admiral al-Bakr," she said, her voice almost as flat as his. "For the record, however, I strongly dissent from your analysis of the situation and of the enemy's intentions. I wish for my objection to the orders you've just issued to be made part of the official record. And I will be reporting that objection to my own superiors in my next dispatch."

Their eyes locked in the com display. It was hard to say whose were harder, and tension hovered between them.

"Both your dissent and your objection are noted, Admiral," al-Bakr replied. "And, you are, of course, free to state whatever objections you choose to your superiors. Nonetheless, at this time, my orders stand."

"Very well, Admiral," Padgorny said coldly. "With your permission. Padgorny, clear."

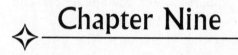

Chapter Nine

"You're kidding."

Commander Eric Hertz looked in disbelief at Captain Everard Broughton's face on his com screen.

"No," Broughton said with commendable restraint. "I am not kidding. Neither is Dame Evelyn."

"But there's no need," Hertz protested. "I thought the entire idea was for us to be a hole in space until they really *needed* us!"

"Plans, apparently, have changed."

Broughton turned away from Hertz to glare disgustedly at the tactical plot. The oncoming Havenite LACs had been inbound for almost thirty minutes. They were up to a velocity relative to the system primary of 12,788 kilometers per second, and they'd traveled over twelve million kilometers. They were also only about twenty minutes from bringing the closest extraction ships under long-range missile fire.

"Whatever we may think of it, we've got our orders," he said, turning back to his com pickup. "And under the circumstances, since there's no way you're going to be able to actually intercept them before they hit the extraction ships, we might as well go for the whole enchilada."

Hertz's expression tightened.

"What do you mean?" he asked in the tone of a man who suspected he'd already guessed.

"The only way we're going to be able to do anything to save the extraction ships is to use the pods," Broughton said bitterly.

"So since we're going to give away our presence, anyway, we might as well get the best return we can."

He looked across his command deck at his tactical officer.

"Activate the pods," he said. "Target the LACs with—" he glanced at the plot's data bars "—the gamma platforms that have the range. Then bring up the delta platforms and designate the CLACs for any of them that have the reach."

"Anything from the drone screen?" Oliver Diamato asked.

"Uh, no, Sir," Commander Robert Zucker, his ops officer said quickly, and looked a silent question at his admiral.

"There ought to be," Diamato said. "Look at it. The LACs are going to run right over those extraction ships. And it's going to take some sort of miracle for that merchantman to slip away. They've got to know we're here—for that matter, the fact that the extraction ships are scattering the way they are *proves* they know. So, where's the response? There ought to at least be a flock of Manty LACs coming out to meet us by now!"

"You think they're up to something sneaky, Sir?"

"I think there's a pretty good chance of it, yes," Diamato replied. "Manties can screw up just like anyone else, but counting on them to do that isn't exactly the smartest thing you can do."

He frowned at the master plot for a few more seconds, then wheeled around to face his communications officer.

"Get me a link to Admiral Duval."

"Yes, Sir."

Diamato crossed towards his command chair. He was just about to sit down in it when a strident alarm sounded.

"Missile launch!" a taut voice from CIC announced sharply. "Multiple hostile missile launches along the belt! Many missiles inbound at four-five-one KPS squared! Time to first impact four-zero-niner seconds!"

"Well, there they go," Hartnett observed bitterly as the firefly icons of multi-drive missiles suddenly speckled the master plot. They streaked across it, moving visibly even on the plot's scale, and the smaller, far more slowly moving light codes of LACs began to blossom as well, as the *Shrike* and *Ferret* squadrons lit off their impellers.

"Yes." Padgorny's single-syllable reply sounded as if she'd bitten it out of a sheet of hammered bronze. She found it difficult to believe just how angry she actually was, and she forced herself to lean back in her command chair and swallow all the *other* words she badly wanted to say.

"Broughton is targeting their CLACs with the delta platforms, Ma'am," Thackeray reported, and Padgorny nodded in acknowledgment. She hadn't specifically dictated targets, but she'd known Broughton would have to use at least some of the pods. His own LACs were much too far astern of the Peeps to overhaul them, after all. And he was right to go after the CLACs, as well. If they had to do this, then they might as well do it as effectively as possible. If he could pick off the CLACs, or even just hammer them badly enough to force them to withdraw into hyper, all the LACs the Peeps had committed to their probe would be doomed, whatever else happened. And killing a couple of the Peeps' superdreadnought-sized LAC carriers would be worthwhile in its own right.

"He's using the gamma platforms on the LACs," Hartnett observed. The chief of staff snorted. "I know it's the only way he can engage them short of the freighters, but his target solutions on them are going to be lousy at this range!"

"Better than he'd have on *our* LACs," Padgorny pointed out. "Their EW still leaves quite a bit to be desired."

Rear Admiral Diamato listened to the eruption of sharp, staccato combat chatter as the Manty missiles roared towards the task group.

The voices on the command circuits were harsh, strained, but not panicky. Communications discipline never really faltered, and the orders came crisply and quickly. He felt himself settling back into his command chair, nodding in satisfaction despite the suddenly altered tactical situation as he listened to his people responding to it. There was no need for him to give any orders; they were already doing exactly what they needed to do.

Captain Hall would be proud of them, he thought.

"Oh, shit," Captain Morton Schneider said almost conversationally as the sudden ugly rash of crimson missile icons erupted behind him. His LAC formation had been just about to reverse acceleration when the hundreds of impeller signatures sprang into malevolent life.

"Range is approximately five-one million klicks," Lieutenant Rothschild, his tactical officer reported in a hard-edged voice. "At constant acceleration on our part, actual flight distance will be five-seven-point-five million klicks. Flight time approximately eight-point-four minutes."

"Acknowledged," Schneider replied.

"We have LACs lighting off as well," Rothschild continued. "Estimate approximately fourteen hundred MDMs targeted on us. Looks like somewhere between four and five hundred of their LACs accelerating to come in behind them."

"They're not a threat . . . yet," Schneider said, concentrating on the far more immediate danger. "Formation Mike-Delta-One. And prepare to implement Zizka."

"Aye, Sir!"

The LAC formation altered abruptly, each tiny vessel accelerating on its own, carefully preplanned vector change. Zizka was new—a variant of the "Triple Ripple" the Fleet had employed so successfully against the Manties' LACs. It was wasteful, in some ways, but with that many Manty MDMs coming towards them, they needed the best defense they could get.

Not that circumstances were perfect for Zizka. With the hostile missiles already launched and incoming, there was less response time than the doctrine's formulators had hoped there would be, but Schneider's battle-hardened squadron commanders had learned their trade well. He watched his plot—necessarily far less detailed than that available in a larger, more capable warship—as his strike formation transformed itself into a defensive one, designed to provide the maximum number of clear sightlines for his units' sensors and flight paths for their counter-missiles.

"They're targeting the task group, too, Sir," the tac officer said. "Looks like they're concentrating on *Skylark* and *Peregrine*."

"Makes sense," Schneider grunted. "Kill the carriers, trap the LACs."

"And they're firing a *lot* of missiles, Sir," Rothschild said quietly.

"Launching counter-missiles!" Commander Zucker reported, and Diamato nodded.

The range was still long, but Republican warships carried a lot of counter-missiles these days. They had to, given their weapons' individually poorer capabilities. Now all eight of his battlecruisers, both the carriers, and his two light cruisers, were pumping out every CM they could. Targeting solutions were marginal, at best, at such a distance, but just over eight hundred MDMs were headed for the two CLACs, and any kills were better than none.

The counter-missiles streaked outward, and the EW platforms accompanying the attack missiles brought up their onboard systems. Jagged cascades of jamming erupted all across the wavefront of Manty missiles, blinding the counter-missiles' rudimentary seekers and seriously degrading even the performance of the starships' far more capable fire control. Then the platforms the Manties had designated "Dragon's Teeth" lit off, and the threat sources abruptly multiplied impossibly.

They must have deployed hundreds—thousands—of pods around the periphery, Diamato thought coldly. *That had to cost them a pretty credit. But I don't think they've got as many of them as they'd like to have.*

Sherman quivered as a second wave of counter-missiles erupted from her tubes. The Republican Navy had refitted its battlecruisers heavily, doubling their original number of counter-missile tubes at the expense of a sizable percentage of their energy armament. More energy weapons tonnage and volume had gone into additional telemetry links, and *Sherman* and her consorts were tossing canisters of counter-missiles out of their standard missile tubes, as well.

"First wave intercept in twenty-three seconds," Tactical announced tersely as yet a third wave of CMs launched.

"Jesus," somebody muttered behind Everard Broughton. It was hardly a professional comment, but it summed up the captain's own reaction quite nicely.

The heavily stealthed reconnaissance platforms which had been observing the Peeps since their arrival were close enough to see the individual counter-missiles being launched, and Broughton had never seen so many CMs from so few launch platforms.

"They've *got* to be cutting their own control links to the first wave," Lieutenant Commander Witcinski said quietly. Broughton looked at him, and the LAC tender *Marigold*'s captain grimaced. "They can't have clear transmission paths to them, Sir. Not with that many impeller wedges between them and the birds."

"They could be relaying through deployed platforms," Broughton countered, in the interest of considering all alternatives, not because he really disagreed with Witcinski.

"Then their platforms would have to be a lot more capable than anything they're supposed to be able to build, Sir," Witcinski returned, and Broughton nodded.

"Can't argue there, Sigismund," he conceded. "On the other hand, this looks like a straight evolution of the same basic missile defense doctrine they apparently employed at Sidemore. They're throwing everything they can at the birds, and it looks to me like they must have refitted heavily with additional counter-missile tubes and control links. It's the only way that few ships could produce that volume of defensive fire."

"I suppose it makes sense, especially if they can't deploy their version of the MDM aboard something as small as a battlecruiser," Witcinski said.

"And it's going to play hell with our calculations of the necessary salvo density for effective system defense," Broughton agreed.

Morton Schneider watched the Manticoran missiles knife towards his LACs like so many space-going sharks. A blizzard of counter-missiles raced to meet them, but the attack missiles' accompanying electronics warfare platforms were far too capable. CM after CM lost its target, wandering hopelessly off course. The first wave intercept killed only twenty of the incoming MDMs. The second wave of counter-missiles did better—over a hundred and fifty of the Manticoran missiles disappeared—but that left over twelve hundred, and he wasn't going to have time for more than another two or three CM launches. Only, if he took those launches, there wouldn't be time for Zizka, and in the face of that massive missile storm . . .

"Implement Zizka now!" he snapped.

"Aye, Sir. Implementing Zizka," Rothschild replied instantly, and smacked the heel of his hand down on the big, red button beside his tactical panel.

Two hundred *Cimeterre*-class LACs launched their full missile loads. Six thousand far-shorter ranged missiles, launched in three slightly staggered waves, went streaking to meet the incoming Manticoran MDMs, and Broughton watched his display narrowly as they spread apart, each bird positioning itself precisely to play its part in the "Triple Ripple." Designed to knock back the sensors and EW of Manty LACs, it ought to do a real number on missile sensors which *had* to be pointed directly towards their target at this point.

The lead wave of his missiles was almost into position when the MDMs abruptly changed heading. Schneider's jaw muscles clenched painfully as the attack missiles' vectors changed. Half of them were "climbing" sharply, while the other half "dove" equally sharply, and he swallowed a venomous oath as he realized what they were doing.

So one of their pickets who saw the Ripple did *get home,* he thought. *And the bastards decided to do something about it. Worse, they figured out the possibilities for missile defense and did something about* them, *too.*

The maneuver had to be the result of a preprogrammed attack profile. There was far too little time for whoever had fired them to change profiles that quickly on the fly. But whoever had done the preprogramming had timed it well. The change in attitude interposed the floors and roofs of the MDMs' impeller wedges between them and the *Cimeterres'* missiles just as the powerful, dirty warheads of the Republican missiles began to detonate. The solid wall of blast fronts and EMP which was supposed to blind and burn out the Manticoran missiles' seekers wasted itself against sensors which couldn't even see it.

All three Zizka waves detonated, and the flood of attack missiles which had parted around the Triple Ripple's roadblock altered heading once more. Their noses swung back towards their targets, and there wasn't time for another counter-missile launch.

Laser heads began to detonate in deadly sequence. X-ray lasers, designed to engage superdreadnoughts, ripped and tore at mere LACs, and space was abruptly ugly with broken and dying craft. Light attack craft shattered, vomiting hull splinters and bodies. Fusion bottles flashed like funeral pyres, and a tsunami of fire washed over Schneider's formation.

The evasion maneuver programmed into the Manticoran missiles as a counter to the Triple Ripple had blunted the defensive maneuver, but it had also broken the attack missiles' locks on their designated targets. They had to reacquire on their own, without guidance from the ships which had launched them, and their onboard targeting systems were far less capable than the fire control of their motherships.

Twelve hundred missiles reached attack range, but over half of them never managed to relocate a target before their overtake velocity carried them clear past the Havenite LACs. Of the five hundred-plus which *did* see a target, the vast majority concentrated on the most exposed, clearly visible targets. "Only" one hundred and seventy-five of Schneider's LACs were actually attacked. Of that number, seventeen survived.

"Well, that sucks," Lieutenant Janice Kent observed.

The youthful, dark-haired lieutenant was the tactical officer aboard HMS *Ice Pick*, the command LAC of Captain Broughton's strike. Commander Hertz, *Ice Pick*'s commanding officer and Broughton's COLAC, glanced sideways at her.

"It's an almost thity percent kill of their entire formation," he pointed out, and she made a face.

"Sure it is, Skip," she agreed. "But it's less than a *ten* percent kill *ratio* for the launch as a whole. Against targets we're supposed to be killing with a single hit each."

"True," Hertz conceded. "But I'll bet you it came as a nasty surprise to them. And at least we know the pop-up maneuver works. Not well, maybe, but well enough to get at least some hits through."

"And now they know we know," Kent said. "Which means they're going to be thinking of another new wrinkle of their own."

"If you can't take a joke, you shouldn't have joined," Hertz told her, and she chuckled sourly.

Oliver Diamato watched his plot as the counter-missiles tore into the cloud of attacking missiles. Despite their relatively poor targeting solutions and limited tracking capability, the sheer mass of Republican CMs had to have some effect, and dozens of Manticoran missiles began to disappear.

Unfortunately, there were *hundreds* of them.

Next time, a distant corner of Diamato's brain thought, *we hold some of the LACs back. We need their point defense.*

The second and third waves of counter-missiles killed still more of the attackers, but the Manticoran electronic warfare platforms were fully active, now, and intercept accuracy plummeted.

The torrent of MDMs slammed across the outer and middle intercept zones, and shipboard point defense laser clusters began to fire. Broadside energy weapons joined them, blazing away in defiant fury as the heavy warheads thundered down upon them.

Everard Broughton had fired eight hundred and thirty missiles at Diamato's squadron and the CLACs he was escorting. Counter-missiles killed two hundred and eleven of them. The close-in energy weapons killed another two hundred and six. Of the remaining four hundred and thirteen, fifty-one were EW platforms, and another hundred and six were defeated by Republican ECM and simply lost lock and wandered off course until they self-destructed at the end of their run.

But that meant that two hundred and fifty-six reached attack range and detonated.

The long range had aided the Republic's defenses by giving them longer tracking time and a deeper engagement envelope. The capability of Manticoran EW had gone a long way towards offsetting that, but nothing the Manticorans could do could magically erase the fire control problems inherent in targeting a maneuvering starship at a range of almost three light-minutes. Every one of the attack missiles had been initially targeted upon one of the CLACs, but a third even of those which reached attack range had lost their original targets and took whatever they could find in replacement.

Some of them reacquired one or the other of the CLACs. Others didn't.

William T. Sherman staggered as a dozen X-ray lasers gouged at her. Half of them wasted their fury against her impeller wedge, and her sidewalls caught at the other half-dozen, bending and deflecting them. Only two actually struck the ship, but they blasted deep into her, shattering her relatively light armor with contemptuous ease.

"Heavy damage starboard forward! Grasers Three and Five are gone—heavy casualties on both mounts! Missile One, Three, and Seven are out of the net! We have a breach in the core hull between Frame Sixty and Frame Seventy!"

Diamato heard the damage reports, but his eyes were riveted to the icons of RHNS *Skylark* and *Peregrine* as the full brunt of the Manticoran attack slammed down upon them.

Skylark heaved as the X-ray lasers blasted into her. Over half the total surviving laser heads went after her, and the big ship shuddered in agony as laser after laser ripped into her. The carrier division's flagship was big—bigger than most superdreadnoughts—but she *wasn't* a superdreadnought. She was a CLAC, her flanks studded with launch bays which simply could not be as massively armored as a superdreadnought's hull. Her *core* hull, wrapped around her fusion plants, her magazines, her life-support and other critical systems, could be and was, but it lacked the layer upon layer of defenses built into the outer structure of a ship of the wall.

Hull plating shattered. Glowing splinters—some bigger than one of her own LACs—flew like sparks from some hideous forge. Counter-missile tubes and point defense stations were blasted away, along with their crews, and the stilettos of bomb-pumped fury tore deeper and deeper into her.

Diamato would never know exactly how many of them stabbed into her, but, in the end, it was one too many.

Her entire forward impeller room exploded in a chain reaction of arcing capacitors. Her wedge faltered, letting still more lasers through to rend and tear, and power surges blew through her systems like demons.

One of them reached her inertial compensator. It failed, and the two hundred-plus gravities of acceleration from her still-active after impeller ring killed every man and woman aboard her in the fleeting seconds before it broke her back. The white-hot flare of her failing fusion bottles simply punctuated her destruction.

The light cruiser *Phantom* went with her, victim of at least three MDMs intended for her betters, and *Peregrine* was severely damaged. All of Diamato's battlecruisers took at least some damage of their own, but *Peregrine* was far more badly hit.

"She's down two alphas and five betas out of her after ring, Sir," Zucker reported. "Half her starboard bays are out of action, and she's lost at least thirty percent of her missile defense. Her starboard sidewall's down to about forty percent, and Captain Joubert reports very heavy casualties."

"Thank you, Robert," Diamato said, projecting a calm he was far from feeling.

He looked back at his master plot. With Duval—and *Skylark*—dead, the full responsibility of command had just landed squarely on his shoulders, and he forced himself to draw a deep breath. As Captain Hall had once said, there was always time to think. Maybe not a lot, but there was always *some* time . . . or else you were already so screwed it didn't matter *what* you did.

His mouth quirked mordantly at the thought, and his brain began sorting through the situation.

Sherman was hurt, but still combat capable . . . except for the minor fact that he couldn't see anything to engage other than the Manty LACs who were far, far out of his range. And while it seemed likely that the torrent of missiles which had ravaged the task group had come from independently deployed pods, it was entirely possible they hadn't. There might well be *Manty* battlecruisers—or even a couple of ships of the wall—out here. A couple of old-style wallers, without onboard MDM capability, would make mincemeat out of his remaining strength without breaking a sweat, and if there were even a single pod-layer in range . . .

Captain Schneider's LACs were shaking back down into formation, he saw, and made his decision. The Republic's FTL communications ability continued to lag far behind that of the Manticorans, despite the tech windfall from Erewhon. It was better than it had been, and there were promises of better still, but the new Havenite systems were more massive than their Manty counterparts, and they were difficult to refit to an existing ship's impeller nodes. New-build ships would come from the yards with vastly improved capabilities, but older ships—like *Sherman*—remained far more limited. Still, what Diamato had was going to be enough for what he had to do.

"We've got to get *Peregrine* clear, Serena," he said flatly. "Instruct Captain Joubert to translate out immediately. He's to take his ship to the Alpha rendezvous and wait for us there. If he hasn't seen any of us within forty-eight hours of his own arrival, he's to return independently to base. Instruct *Specter* to escort *Peregrine*."

"Yes, Sir," Commander Taverner said quietly, and Diamato's mouth twitched in a bitter almost-smile at the chief of staff's tone. Detaching *Peregrine* meant Diamato was writing off *all* of his LACs, but the rear admiral had no choice. The ship was simply too badly damaged, and the Republic couldn't afford for him to lose her as he'd already lost *Skylark*.

"Send a message to Captain Schneider," Diamato continued, turning to Communications. "Inform him that Plan Zulu-Three is in effect."

"Aye, Sir."

Diamato sat back in his command chair, watching his plot with hard blue eyes, as his orders went out. *Peregrine*'s icon turned away, accompanied by the surviving light cruiser, and disappeared into the concealing safety of hyper-space.

At least I got her safely out of here, he thought. He knew his bitter self-recrimination was undeserved. He and Harold Duval had done exactly what their orders had specified, and the people who'd written those orders had known something like this might happen. The entire point of the attack had been to discover how the Manties' system defense doctrine was evolving, and in the callous calculus of war, the price the Republic had paid to achieve that goal was not excessive. Or, at least, it was far lower than the price the same sort of defenses might have exacted against a heavier, serious attack in force which didn't know about them.

But that made him feel no better about *Skylark*'s destruction. Even with her LACs away, there had been over three thousand men and women aboard that ship, and not one of them had survived. That was a bitter price, excessive or not. And it did not include the sixty-five hundred Republican naval personnel aboard the task group's LACs. Too many of them were already dead, more of them were going to die, and Oliver Diamato had just ordered the only ship which could have recovered their LACs out of the system.

He watched the impeller signatures of Schneider's LACs breaking down into three- and four-squadron formations, scattering on individual evasion courses. This, too, had been planned for, however little anyone had actually expected the plan to be needed. Under Zulu-Three, Schneider's units would make for half a dozen widely separated rendezvous beyond the hyper limit, where Diamato's battlecruisers would recover as many of their crewmen as possible.

It was going to be tight, and difficult. The odds were that Schneider's escape courses would take his LACs into the reach of still more of the deployed system defense pods. It was possible *none* of his ships would survive to reach a rendezvous, or that the Manties would manage to deduce the rendezvous locations and get something into position to interdict them. Or that the faster, more capable Manty LACs would intercept the *Cimeterres* short of the limit.

But Oliver Diamato was grimly determined that anyone who *did* reach one of the rendezvous points would find someone waiting there to take him home.

"All right," he said. "Take us into hyper. Astrogation, start your update on the Zulu-Three positions."

Chapter Ten

"Everyone is here now, Your Grace."

Honor looked up from the report she'd been reading. James MacGuiness stood in the open door of her Jason Bay mansion's office, and she shook her head wryly at his expression and the taste of his emotions.

"You needn't sound quite so disapproving, Mac," she said. "I'm not really overworking myself, you know."

"That depends on your definition of overwork, doesn't it, Your Grace?" he responded. "I've certainly seen you work harder and on less sleep. But I don't recall ever having seen you with a stomach bug that's lasted as long as this one. Neither," he added pointedly, "does Miranda."

"Mac," she said patiently to the man who had once been her steward and remained her keeper, "it's not that bad. It's just a little stomach upset. For that matter, maybe it's nerves." Her lips twitched. "It's not like my new assignment is stress free, you know!"

"No, Ma'am, it isn't." Honor's eyes narrowed as MacGuiness reverted to the old, military form of address. He was careful not to use it these days, for the most part. "But I've seen you under stress before," he continued. "After you were wounded on Grayson, for example. Or after the duel. And with all due respect, Ma'am," he said very seriously, "*nerves* have never put you off your feed the way you've been lately."

Honor regarded him thoughtfully for several seconds, then sighed.

"You win, Mac," she surrendered. "Call Doctor Frazier. Ask her if she can see me Monday, all right?"

"Perfectly, Your Grace," he said, rationing himself to only the slightest flicker of satisfaction.

"Good," she told him, "because I'm going to be up pretty late, and I don't want you hovering disapprovingly outside the door. We've got a perfectly capable staff who can feed us and bring us things to drink if we need them, and you can take yourself off to bed at your usual time. Is that understood?"

"Perfectly, Your Grace," he repeated with a slight smile, and she chuckled.

"In that case, Mr. MacGuiness, would you be so good as to ask my guests to join me?"

"Of course, Your Grace."

He bowed slightly and withdrew, and Honor climbed out of her chair, walked to the opened crystoplast wall, and stepped out onto the office balcony.

Jason Bay gleamed before her under the light of Thorson. The moon's disk drifted in and out of breaks in the thin, high overcast, a brisk breeze pushed waves across the bay, and the lights of Landing glittered in sprawling heaps across the water. She felt the wind pressing against her and smelled salt, and longed suddenly for her sailboat. She could almost feel the spokes of the wheel pressing against her palms, the spray on her cheeks, the simple pleasure of watching the sharp-edged sails stealing the wind's power. Moonlight, stars, and freedom from care and responsibility all beckoned to her, and she smiled wistfully. Then she turned her back on the night-struck bay's seduction and stepped back into her office as MacGuiness ushered in her visitors.

A brown-haired officer in the uniform of a rear admiral led the procession, followed by a tall, youngish-looking captain of the list, Mercedes Brigham, and the other key members of the staff Honor was profoundly grateful she'd managed to retain intact from Task Force Thirty-Four.

"Alistair," she said, stepping forward with a warm smile as she offered the flag officer her hand. "It's good to see you again. Mercedes told me you'd gotten in this morning."

"It's good to see you, too," Alistair McKeon said, squeezing her hand with an even bigger smile. "Nice to know you were satisfied enough to want me again, for that matter!"

"Always, Alistair. Always."

"That's what I like to hear," he said, looking around the office. "Where's your furry little shadow?"

"Nimitz is visiting Samantha at White Haven," she said.

"Oh. At White Haven, eh?" He looked at her, gray eyes glinting. "I hear it's nice up north this time of year."

"Yes, it is." She gripped his hand for a moment longer, then looked at the dark-haired, improbably handsome captain who had accompanied him.

"Rafe." She held out her hand to him in turn, and he shook it firmly.

"Your Grace," he said, inclining his head.

"I'm sorry about *Werewolf*," she said in a quieter tone.

"I won't pretend I'm not going to miss her, Your Grace," Captain Rafe Cardones replied. "But a brand new *Invictus*-class superdreadnought is nothing to sneeze at when you haven't been on the list any longer than I have. And another stint as *your* flag captain isn't going to hurt my résumé any."

"Well, that's going to depend on just how well we all do, isn't it?" she responded, then looked at Brigham and the other staffers.

Captain Andrea Jaruwalski, her operations officer, was as composed-looking as ever, but Honor tasted the combination of anticipation, eagerness, and trepidation behind Jaruwalski's hawklike profile. George Reynolds, her staff intelligence officer, promoted to full commander from lieutenant commander after Sidemore, wasn't quite as good at concealing all of the questions bubbling through his active brain. Her staff astrogator, Lieutenant Commander Theophile Kgari, also recently promoted, followed Reynolds through the door. Kgari was only a second-generation Manticoran, and his complexion was as dark as Honor's friend Michelle Henke's. Timothy Meares, Honor's flag lieutenant, brought up the rear, and his fair hair and gray-green eyes might have been specifically designed to contrast with Kgari's dark coloring.

"All right, people," she invited, gesturing at the comfortable armchairs scattered around the large office, "find seats. We've got a lot to talk about."

Her subordinates obeyed, settling quickly into place. Honor took one last look through the opened crystoplast wall, then pressed the button that closed the sliding panels. Another command rendered the outer surface opaque, and a third activated the anti-snooping systems installed throughout the mansion and its grounds.

"First," she began, turning her own chair to face them all, "I want to say that I asked the Admiralty to let me keep all of you because of how satisfied I am with your performance at Sidemore. I couldn't have asked for better from you there . . . but it looks like I may have to in our new assignment."

She tasted the way nerves tightened after her last sentence, and she smiled without any humor at all.

"The bottom line is that Eighth Fleet is something of a paper hexapuma at the moment. The Admiralty doesn't have the ships to make it anything but a shadow of what it was under Admiral White Haven. Your battle squadron, Alistair—all six ships worth of it—will constitute our entire 'wall of battle' for at least the immediate future."

"Excuse me?" McKeon blinked. "Our *entire* wall?"

"That's what I said," Honor replied grimly. "Not only that, but any additional wallers we receive for the next few months will almost certainly be old-style, pre-pod ships from the Reserve."

"Your Grace," Mercedes Brigham said quietly, "that's not a 'fleet'; it's a task force. Or maybe only a task *group*."

"It's a little better than that, Mercedes," Honor said. "For example, we'll have two full squadrons of CLACs under Alice Truman. That's over a quarter of the total we have in commission, including—" she smiled at Cardones "—*Werewolf*. And they're giving us all of the Manticoran pod-battlecruisers. We'll have first call on additional *Agamemnons* as they commission, as well. And we should be seeing the majority of the *Saganami-C*s, as well."

"Excuse me, Your Grace," Jaruwalski said slowly, "but that sounds like a peculiar force mix, if you'll pardon my saying so. My impression from the *media* reports, at least, was that Eighth Fleet was being reactivated as our primary offensive command, just as it was during Operation Buttercup. But you're talking about primarily light units, aren't you?"

"That's exactly what I'm talking about," Honor confirmed. She drew a deep breath and leaned back in her chair.

"The other day, the Queen referred to me as her 'lucky talisman,'" she said, with a slight grimace. "I might quibble with the accuracy of that label, on several levels, but thanks to the media coverage of Sidemore, there's some truth to it. At least in terms of public perception. At the moment, Admiralty House is rather hoping the Havenites will read those reports at face value.

"The truth is that the deployment cupboard is bare, people. We're scraping the bottom of the barrel just to maintain the fleets we've got to have to cover our critical core systems. We simply can't reduce them any further, even with all of the system-defense pods and other fortifications we can put into position. But bad as the situation is, it's going to get worse before it gets better. We'll get to the exact figures ONI is projecting shortly, but what matters for our purposes right this minute is that the Havenites' wall of battle is already bigger than ours is, and it's going to grow *faster* than ours is for at least the next two T-years.

"Which means that, if they're prepared to take the losses, they probably have—or shortly will have—the combat power they need to hammer Manticore or Grayson."

Her office was deathly still and silent.

"Needless to say, all of that is highly classified information," she continued after a moment. "We don't know if the Republic is as well aware of those numbers as we are, but we have to assume they are. After all, our prewar strength was pretty much a matter of public record; theirs wasn't, so they started with an intelligence advantage. However, we're hoping they won't want to take such massive losses if they can possibly avoid it. And the job of Eighth Fleet, at this moment, is to persuade them to disperse as much of their fleet strength as possible, so that it won't be available for offensive operations."

"So they're giving us units optimized for raiding operations," McKeon said.

"Exactly." Honor nodded. "The idea is for us to wreak a fair amount of havoc in the Republic's rear areas. They can't have built up and maintained a fleet the size of their present navy without having weakened themselves *somewhere*. For example, ONI's best estimate, from all the intelligence sources we still have in the Republic, is that one thing they did was to scrap all the old battleships the Old Regime was using for rear-area defense. Even if they hadn't needed the manpower anywhere else, those ships would have been sitting ducks for MDMs and LACs, so it would make a lot of sense to retire them. But it's unlikely they've been able to replace them out of new construction, either. It's more probable they're relying on light units and, possibly, LACs of their own for normal security. Undoubtedly, they also hope the damage they did to us in their opening operation knocked back our offensive capability badly enough we won't be in any position to take advantage of the weakness of their secondary systems' defenses. Our job is to convince them they're wrong."

"And they gave *you* Eighth Fleet, and played up its role as our 'primary offensive force,' to help convince them of that," McKeon said. Honor looked at him, and he shrugged. "It's not that hard to figure out, Honor. If the Admiralty gave you the assignment after Sidemore, then clearly it regards Eighth Fleet as a critical command which it will reinforce as rapidly as possible. Which means the Peeps are going to have to assume that whatever we do to them with raids will only grow steadily in intensity and weight. Right?"

"Something along those lines," she said. "And, as much as possible, they'll be right. It's just that the degree to which anyone *can* reinforce us is going to be limited."

She let her chair come fully upright once again, laying her folded forearms on her desk and leaning forward over them.

"So, that's the bottom line, people. We'll have essentially a free hand in selecting our objectives and timing our operations. We'll base out of Trevor's Star, so we can also serve as a ready reinforcement to Admiral Kuzak's Third Fleet. And we'll do everything we can to convince the media—and the Republic—we have a lot more tonnage and firepower than we actually do."

"Sounds . . . interesting," McKeon said.

"Oh, it'll be '*interesting*,' all right," she said grimly. "And now, the floor is open for suggestions about ways to make it even more interesting for the Republic than it is for us."

"Have you got a minute, Tony?"

Sir Anthony Langtry, Foreign Secretary of the Star Kingdom of Manticore, looked up in faint surprise as the Earl of White Haven poked his head into Langtry's private office.

"I suppose I do," the Foreign Secretary said mildly. He watched quizzically as White Haven stepped fully into the office, treecat on his shoulder, then pointed at a chair and cocked his head. "May I ask just how you got through the dragon's den without tripping any alarms?"

White Haven chuckled as he took the indicated chair and lifted Samantha down into his lap. Early morning sunlight poured in through the office windows to his left, splashing over his chair, and Samantha buzzed in pleasure as its warmth soaked into her.

"It's not really all that hard," the earl said, stroking the 'cat's silken pelt. "I just walked into the outer office, told Istvan you were expecting me this morning, and that there was no need to announce me."

"Interesting." Langtry tilted his chair back. "Particularly since Istvan's been with me for over ten T-years, and he happens to be the person who keeps my schedule. Ah, I *wasn't* expecting you, was I?"

"No," White Haven said, much more seriously. "A point, judging from Istvan's expression, of which he was quite well aware."

"I thought I wasn't." Langtry regarded his unexpected visitor thoughtfully. "As it happens, there's nothing else on my calendar just at the moment—except, of course," he added a bit pointedly, "for this position paper I'm *supposed* to be studying before I meet with the Andermani ambassador for lunch. So I suppose Istvan may have decided to humor you. And now that he has, why are you here?"

"For a private conversation."

"It wouldn't be a bit more of an end run than just a get together of two old friends, now would it?" Langtry asked.

"As a matter of fact, it is," White Haven admitted, now without a trace of humor, and the treecat in his lap sat up to regard Langtry with grass-green eyes.

"Hamish, it's not going to do any good," the Foreign Secretary said.

"Tony, she's *got* to at least get them talking again."

"Then I suggest you convince *her* of that. Or at least your brother." Langtry regarded White Haven very levelly. "He *is* the Prime Minister, you know."

"I certainly do. But on this particular point, he's almost as . . . focused, let's say, as Elizabeth herself. He knows how I feel. He disagrees with me. And, as you say, he is the Prime Minister."

"As it happens," Langtry said slowly, "I find myself substantially in agreement with him and the Queen on this one, Hamish."

"But—"

"Hamish, there's not really anything substantively new in any of Pritchart's so-called proposals. She's still flatly denying her government falsified our diplomatic exchanges. She's still asserting that she attacked us because of High Ridge's refusal to negotiate in good faith, and that our publication of our 'forged' diplomatic traffic indicates that the leopard—that's us, Hamish, in case you hadn't noticed—hasn't changed its spots just because of his fall from power. And she's insisting the plebiscites to be held on the previously occupied Havenite planets be conducted under *her* exclusive supervision. Where's anything new in any of that?"

"What's 'new' is that she's proposed a cessation of hostilities while we negotiate on the basis of her most recent round of proposals," White Haven said sharply. "Trust me. We need that cessation a lot worse than they do right now!"

"Why?" Langtry demanded bluntly. "Unless you've forgotten, we had a cease-fire in place—as far as *we* knew, anyway—the *last* time the Peeps launched a sneak attack on us. You are familiar with the old proverb that goes 'Fool me once, shame on you; fool me twice, shame on *me*,' aren't you?"

"Of course I am. But do you really think she's going to make that sort of proposal just so she can violate the cease-fire a second time? The whole point of the squabbling over who forged whose diplomatic correspondence is that she's trying to convince her own public, the rest of the galaxy, and possibly even a significant portion of our public opinion, that *we* were the ones who violated the accepted standards of diplomacy. That she attacked us only because we'd demonstrated we couldn't be trusted. If she offers to sit down and talk with us, then attacks us a second time while the talks are still in progress, she gives us the perfect opportunity to demonstrate that she's the one whose interstellar word can't be trusted."

"You could be right," Langtry acknowledged. "At the same time, she can always officially announce she's breaking off talks before she hits us again. And if she's careful to observe all the diplomatic niceties this time around, wouldn't that tend to strengthen her claim that she tried to observe them the last time?"

"That's so Machiavellian it makes my head hurt just thinking about it," White Haven complained. "Given the military situation, why should she try anything that complex?"

"How the hell should I know?" Langtry demanded testily. "All I can tell you is that she's already acted in ways that are at least that 'Machiavellian.' And as far as the military situation is concerned, I can actually see some logic from her side in calling a *temporary* halt to the war."

"I know," White Haven said wearily. He shook his head, sitting back and cradling Samantha against his chest. "I've had exactly the same conversation with Willie."

"Well, he has a point. At the moment, according to your own analysts, we've still got something close to effective military parity. But that balance is going to shift steadily in their favor over the next year or so. Wouldn't it make sense for them to use diplomacy to neutralize our military forces without firing another shot until they've built their own up to a point which gives them a decisive superiority?"

"Of course it would. And I'm not trying to suggest the Peeps are the most trustworthy people in the explored galaxy. Or, for that matter, even that Pritchart is remotely interested in negotiating in ultimate good faith. It may be significant that she's at least offering the possibility of third-party monitoring of the plebiscites on the disputed planets, but I'll freely acknowledge that even that could be nothing more than window dressing. But the point is that if they hit us again as hard as they did the last time, if they go for a single vulnerable point and they're willing to take the losses, they can punch right through us tomorrow. Give me eight months—six; hell, give me *four* months!—and I'll make the price they'd pay for an attack like that so high even Oscar Saint-Just would've hesitated to pay it! *That's* what negotiating with them can buy us. The time to get our feet back under us."

"Hamish, it's not going to happen," Langtry said, shaking his head. "It's not going to happen for a lot of reasons. Because we can't trust them after they've already lied so comprehensively. Because even the reports from Admiral Givens admit that at this moment we can't be certain a cease-fire would help us militarily more than it would help them. Because the fact that they're offering it in the first place suggests it *would* help them militarily, at least in their opinion, more than it would help us. Because we're not going to allow them to rehabilitate themselves diplomatically and take back any of the moral high ground in interstellar public opinion. And, frankly, because the Queen hates their guts with a pure, burning passion. If you want her to sit down and talk with these people, after everything that's happened, then you've got to be able to demonstrate that it will provide us with a significant advantage without improving the Peeps' position simultaneously. And the truth is, Hamish, that you can't demonstrate that."

"No," White Haven admitted after a moment, his voice and expression both weary. "No, I can't. To be perfectly honest, there's a part of me which genuinely believes they mean it. That the demands they're still making are really pretty damned minimal, given the fact that they currently occupy all the planets in question. But I can't prove they are. And I can't prove that my awareness of our own weaknesses isn't causing me to overestimate how valuable a few months of relative operational inactivity would be for us."

"I know." Langtry regarded him with something almost like compassion. "And I also know," he added in an oddly gentle tone, "that Duchess Harrington continues to believe the Peeps' current leadership—or at least some elements of it—can be trusted to keep its word."

Samantha's ears twitched, and White Haven looked up quickly, eyes narrowed, at the reference to Honor, but Langtry only looked back levelly.

"As it happens," the Foreign Secretary continued, "I, also, have a very lively respect for Duchess Harrington's judgment. And I realize the two of you—and Emily, of course—have become close allies, politically, as well as militarily. But in this particular instance, I think I have to agree with the Queen and Willie that she's wrong. The Peeps' actions aren't those of the honorable people she thinks they are. There could be a lot of extenuating circumstances which account for that, but it's true. And we have to make our decisions based on their demonstrated behavior, not on what we think their internal character is really like."

White Haven started to reply, then clamped his jaw tightly. Whether he liked it or not, everything Langtry had just said made sense. It all hung together, and the Foreign Secretary was certainly right about the Havenites' demonstrated behavior.

And Langtry's tactful suggestion that he might be allowing Honor's view of Thomas Theisman—who, after all, was only one man—to influence his own analysis of the situation could well have merit. He didn't think he was, but it wasn't impossible.

He drew a deep breath, ran his hand gently down Samantha's spine, and forced his jaw muscles to relax. It really was possible he was being influenced by the fact that the woman he loved—*one* of the women he loved—found her view so profoundly at odds with that of virtually everyone else in the current government. She didn't make a point of her disagreement, but she didn't back away from it, either. The Queen, and his own brother, for that matter, knew exactly what she thought. Which was one of the reasons they didn't discuss that particular aspect of the war with her at the moment.

And, he admitted to himself, *it's the reason* you *haven't told her about Pritchart's "new" proposals, either, Hamish.*

"All right, Tony," he said finally. "Maybe you're all right and I'm wrong. And maybe I am reacting this way because I'm too well aware of where we're in trouble and not aware of where *they* might be, or think they are. At any rate, I've given it my best shot with Willie and Elizabeth, and now even with you."

"You have that," Langtry agreed wryly. "Emphatically, one might almost say."

"All right, all right!" White Haven repeated, this time with a hint of a smile. "I'll go away and leave you in peace."

He stood, lifting Samantha back to his shoulder, and started for the door. But he stopped, just short of it, and looked back.

"It all makes sense the way you interpret it. And Elizabeth, and Willie," he said. "And you may all be right. But I can't help thinking, Tony—what if you're not? What if *I'm* not? What if this isn't just a chance to buy time to organize our defenses, but a genuine opportunity to end the war without anyone else getting killed?"

"In that case, a lot of people are going to be killed who wouldn't have to be," Langtry said levelly. "But all any of us can do is the best we can do and hope at the end of the day we can live with our choices."

"I know," Hamish Alexander said softly. "I know."

"We're ready for you now, Your Grace."

Honor switched off her pad, rose from the comfortable chair in the private waiting room, scooped Nimitz up from the chair beside her, and followed the nurse. Andrew LaFollet trailed along behind her, and she hid a smile as she remembered his expression the first time he'd accompanied her on a visit to her physician and she'd innocently invited him to accompany her into the examination room. She hadn't done that to him again, but she tasted his own memory of the event as he followed her down the hallway. And, to be honest, she was tempted to do it again this time, since it was only too obvious LaFollet strongly supported MacGuiness' insistence on this nonsense.

"Through here, Your Grace," the nurse said. He opened the exam room's door, and Honor glanced mischievously at LaFollet, who returned her gaze stoically, then looked at the nurse.

"Thank you. Ah, would it be all right if my armsman stands in the hall here?" she asked him.

"Quite all right, Your Grace," the nurse assured her. "We're aware of the Grayson security requirements."

"Good," she said, and smiled at LaFollet. "This shouldn't take too long, Andrew," she told him. "Of course, if you'd like to—"

She gestured at the examination room, one eyebrow arched, and treasured his long-suffering expression.

"That's all right, My Lady. I'll be fine right here," he assured her.

Honor checked the time again, and Nimitz bleeked a question as she frowned.

"Sorry, Stinker," she said, reaching out to scratch his chest as he reclined comfortably beside her on the examining table. "Just wondering what's become of Doctor Frazier."

Nimitz flipped his shoulders in an unmistakable shrug, and she chuckled. But she didn't stop wondering.

Both her parents were physicians, and she'd spent enough time undergoing repairs to be more familiar with the medical profession than most. There was a rhythm and a timing to examinations, and a routine physical shouldn't be taking this long. Doctor Frazier's nurse had run all the diagnostics and departed with the results almost ninety minutes ago. Frazier should have evaluated them and put in her own appearance within fifteen or twenty minutes at the outside.

"Wait here, Stinker."

Honor climbed down off the examining table, opened the door, and stuck her head out into the hall. LaFollet started to turn towards the door as it opened, then stopped, facing rigidly away from it.

"Oh, don't be silly, Andrew!" she scolded fondly. "I'm perfectly decent."

He turned his head, and his mouth twitched, hovering on the edge of a smile, as he took in her uniform trousers and blouse.

"Yes, My Lady?"

"I'm just wondering where Doctor Frazier is."

"Do you want me to go check, My Lady?"

"No, no." She shook her head. "I just wanted to poke my head out and look around. I'm sure she'll get here as soon as possible. I wonder what's holding her up, though."

"If you'd like—" LaFollet began, then broke off as Doctor Frazier came briskly down the hall with a memo board tucked firmly under her left arm.

Janet Frazier was trim, slender, auburn haired, and a good twenty-five centimeters shorter than Honor. She moved with a brisk confidence and habitually exuded the sense of authority which was one of the hallmarks of a good physician. She looked just as composed as usual, but both of Honor's eyebrows rose as she tasted the doctor's actual emotions. Consternation predominated, mingled with something very much like apprehension-flavored amusement.

"Your Grace," Frazier said. "I apologize for the delay. I had to, ah, recheck some test results and do a little research."

"I beg your pardon?" Honor said.

"Why don't we step back into the exam room, Your Grace?"

Honor obeyed the polite command. She stepped back up onto the stool, and parked herself on the edge of the padded table. Nimitz took one look at Frazier, then sat up beside Honor, ears cocked. The raised diagnostic sensors just cleared the top of Honor's head as she sat down, and Frazier tossed her memo board onto the polished top of a low cabinet and folded her arms across her chest.

"Your Grace," she said after a moment, "I'm pretty sure I have a surprise for you. The nausea you've been experiencing?"

She paused, and Honor nodded.

"It's morning sickness, Your Grace."

Honor blinked. For a long moment, perhaps five seconds, she had absolutely no idea what Frazier was talking about. Then it registered, and she sat bolt upright. In fact, she sat up so quickly she bashed the top of her head on one of the sensors.

Not that she even noticed the impact.

"That's ridiculous!" she snapped. "Impossible!"

"Your Grace, I checked the results three times," Frazier said. "Trust me. You *are* pregnant."

"But—But . . . I *can't* be!" Honor shook her head, thoughts skittering like a treecat kitten on ice. "I can't be," she repeated. "On more levels than you can possibly imagine, Doctor, I *can't* be."

"Your Grace," Frazier said, "I'm not in any position to comment on exactly how much opportunity you've had to *become* pregnant. But I can tell you, without any doubt whatsoever, that you are."

Honor's head spun. Frazier couldn't be right—she just *couldn't*.

"But . . . but my implant," she protested.

"I thought about that as soon as I saw the initial result," Frazier admitted. "That's one reason I checked it three times."

Honor stared at her. All active-duty female naval personnel eligible for shipboard duty were required to maintain current contraceptive implants as insurance against accidental pregnancy. The Navy provided a perfectly adequate implant good for one T-year, renewable with each annual physical, as part of its basic medical care, but anyone who wanted to pay for her own implant could do so, as long as it met the minimum one-year require-ment of the Service and was kept current. Without that implant, she was restricted to dirt-side duty, safely away from the risk of accidental radiation exposures. Given her own career plans, Honor had opted for a ten-year implant. It could have been deactivated at any time, in the unlikely event her plans had changed, and it was simply one less detail to bother about.

"I'm not positive yet, Your Grace," Frazier continued, "but I think I *may* have figured out what happened. To the implant, I mean."

Honor shook her head and settled back down on the edge of the examining table. Nimitz flowed into her lap, leaning back against her, and she wrapped her arms tightly about his soft, comforting warmth and rested her chin on the top of his head.

"If you have *any* idea how it happened, it's more than I have," she said.

"I think it's a data entry error, Your Grace."

"A *data entry* error?"

"Yes." Frazier sighed. "This probably wouldn't have happened if Doctor McKinsey hadn't been called back to Beowulf, Your Grace. Unfortunately, he was, and I've been your personal physician only since your return from Cerberus. And your file was delivered to me from Bassingford when I first saw you."

Honor nodded.

"Apparently what happened was that when the Peeps announced your 'execution,' the Navy removed your files from the medical center's active database. After all, you were dead. So, when you turned up alive again, they had to reactivate your records. And I'm guessing there was some glitch, because according to your file, your implant was renewed *after* your return from Cerberus."

"After my return?" Honor shook her head vigorously. "Certainly not!"

"Oh, I'm well aware of that, Your Grace," Frazier said. "In fact, this is at least partly my fault. I didn't do a complete enough review of your records, or I might have realized the date indicated for your implant renewal was flatly impossible."

"But how could someone have screwed it up?" Honor demanded. Her brain, she realized, was not functioning especially well at the moment.

"My best guess?" Frazier said. "It looks to me as if when your records were reactivated all entries specific to Navy-monitored requirements—like the requirement that your contraceptive implant be current—were somehow reset to the date they were reactivated. Which means that so far as I knew from my records, which were based on Bassingford's, your implant should have been good for another three and a half T-years. Which, obviously, it wasn't."

Honor closed her eyes.

"I realize the timing on this is . . . awkward, Your Grace," Frazier said. "There are, of course, several options available to us. Which one you choose is up to you, but at least it's very early in the pregnancy. There's time to decide what you want to do."

"Doctor," Honor said, without opening her eyes, "I'm due to deploy to Trevor's Star in less than two weeks."

"Oh."

Honor opened her eyes at last, and smiled crookedly at Frazier's expression.

"That does put rather a tighter time constraint on it, doesn't it?" the doctor continued.

"You might put it that way . . . assuming you're given to understatement."

"Well, in that case, Your Grace," Frazier said, "and speaking as your physician, I think you'd better inform the father as quickly as you can."

Chapter Eleven

"My Lady?"

Honor twitched in her comfortable limousine seat and looked up.

Nimitz was curled tightly in her lap, pressing against her while he radiated comfort. The 'cat clearly didn't understand all of the reasons behind her consternation and anxiety, but his loving concern and support poured into her, and she treasured them. Unfortunately, Nimitz couldn't begin to resolve all of the potentially disastrous consequences which might stem from her condition.

"Yes, Spencer?" she said, looking at the fair-haired armsman who'd spoken.

"We just received a com call from the spaceport, My Lady," he said respectfully. Her youngest armsman obviously also realized something was wrong, but he didn't know what, and his tone was cautious. "The *Tankersley* just made orbit," he continued.

"She did?" Honor sat straighter, her chocolate-dark eyes brightening suddenly. "She's early."

"Yes, My Lady."

"Thank you, Spencer. Simon," she leaned forward, looking past Hawke to the armsman in the pilot's place, "contact the escort and turn us around. We're going to the spaceport to pick up my parents."

"Now, then, Honor Stephanie Harrington," Allison Harrington said sternly, "what in the world has your panties in such a knot?"

Honor, Nimitz, and her parents were alone together for the first time since their arrival. Allison and Alfred Harrington sat in Honor's office while she stood facing the crystoplast wall, arms crossed, with Nimitz on her shoulder, but she had no attention to spare for her favorite view of Jason Bay. The twins had been handed off to Jennifer LaFollet, Allison's Grayson-born personal maid, and Lindsey Phillips, their Manticoran nanny, after properly affectionate greetings, but Honor had tasted her mother's concern as Allison watched her with Faith and James. She'd often thought Allison had a lot in common with treecats, and her ability to read her daughter's mood and body language so acutely was one of the reasons.

"What makes you think anything has my underwear tangled, Mother?" Honor replied now, turning back from the bay to face her. She unfolded her arms and reached up to scratch Nimitz's chin soothingly with her right hand.

"Oh, please, Honor!" Allison rolled her eyes, then waved at Nimitz. "That furry little henchman of yours is as tightly wired as I've ever seen him. Certainly since the day the two of you snuck off for that first trip to his home range which I'm sure you both continue to fondly imagine your father and I knew nothing about." Honor's eyes widened, and Allison snorted. "And as for you, young lady! I've never seen you as skittish around the kids as you were this afternoon. So, what is it?"

"Oh, nothing much." Honor's voice wavered slightly around the edges, undermining her attempt at nonchalance. "I just got a little . . . unexpected medical news this morning."

She looked back out at the bay, then faced her mother's eyes.

"I'm pregnant, Momma," she said quietly.

For a moment, Allison—and Honor's father—both seemed as totally clueless as she'd felt when Frazier informed *her*. Both of them recovered from the instant of total noncomprehension much more quickly than she had, however. Probably, she thought, with a flicker of half-bitter amusement, because they weren't the ones who were pregnant!

The quick, bright flare of their emotions once the news truly registered upon them was too powerful and complex for her to sort out clearly. Astonishment. Consternation. A bright flash of joy, especially from her mother. A sudden surge of concern, tenderness. Protectiveness, especially from her father. And wrapped around all of it an abrupt spike of concern as their reaction to the news took them to the place it had already taken her.

"Hamish?" her mother said, and Honor nodded, feeling her eyes brim with tears. She'd never discussed her relationship with Hamish with her parents, but both of them were highly intelligent and knew her altogether too well.

"Yes," she said, and Allison opened her arms. Honor stepped into her embrace, hugging her mother's small, immensely comforting form tightly, and her father reached out to stroke her hair as he'd done when she was a very small girl.

"Oh, my," Allison sighed. Then she shook her head ruefully. "You simply can't do *anything* the easy way, can you, dear?"

"Apparently not," Honor agreed with a slightly watery chuckle.

"The timing could have been better." Her father's observation was totally unnecessary, but she chuckled again at the dry, tender amusement in his tone. "What about your implant?" he asked after a moment.

"Ran out," she said. She gave her mother another squeeze, then stood back and shrugged. "We haven't had time to figure out exactly *how* it happened, but there was a glitch in my records. Neither Doctor Frazier nor I realized that it had run out months ago."

"*Honor*," Allison said reproachfully. "Your parents are both doctors. How often have you heard us say it's the patient's responsibility, as well as the physician's, to keep track of things like that?"

"I know, Mother. I know." Honor shook her head. "Believe me, you can't scold me for that any harder than I've already scolded myself. But there was just so much going on . . ."

"Yes, there was." Allison touched her forearm remorsefully. "And you don't need my scolding you about it on top of everything else, either. I suppose it's just the shock of discovering I'm about to be a grandmother."

"Are you, Allison?" Alfred Harrington asked gently, and his wife's head snapped around abruptly. Allison Chou Harrington was a Beowulfer by birth. More than that, she was a daughter of one of the great medical "dynasties" of Beowulf. For her, the termination of a pregnancy was unthinkable, except under the most unusual possible circumstances. Something out of the barbaric era before medicine had made so many alternatives available.

She started to open her mouth, then visibly stopped herself, and Honor could actually feel her throttling her immediate, instinctive protest. Then she inhaled sharply and turned back to her daughter.

"Am I, Honor?" she asked quietly, and Honor felt a deep, sudden surge of love as Allison asked the question without a trace of pressure either way.

"I don't know," Honor said, after a moment. Despite all Allison could do, hurt flickered in her eyes, and Honor shook her head quickly. "I'm not going to have it terminated, Mother," she said. "But I may not be able to acknowledge the child."

Allison frowned.

"I realize this could be very awkward for you, Honor. Both personally and politically. But you and Hamish have responsibilities."

"I'm fully aware of that, Mother," Honor replied, just a bit more sharply than she'd intended to. She heard her own tone, and made a small, quick gesture of apology. "I'm aware," she continued, her voice calmer than it had been. "And I intend to meet them. But I've got to consider all of the possible consequences, not just for the child, or for me and Hamish, or for . . . anyone else, on a personal level. And it may be that placing the child for adoption would be the best alternative."

She met her mother's gaze steadily as she said the last sentence, and Allison looked back for a long, still moment. Then she shook her head.

"That's the last thing in the universe you want to do, isn't it, Honor?" she said very, very softly.

"Yes," Honor admitted, equally softly. She inhaled deeply. "Yes, it is," she said more briskly, "but I may not have a choice."

"The one thing you can't do," her father said, "is decide too quickly. If you make the wrong decision here, it will haunt you. You know that."

"Yes, I do. But it's a decision I can't take too long making, either. I'm due to deploy in two weeks, Daddy, and not aboard a passenger ship. Even if Regs didn't completely prohibit shipboard pregnancies, it would be criminally negligent to take a fetus into that sort of environment."

"Even so, there's no *medical* reason you have to rush things," he argued gently. "You've already ruled out simply terminating the pregnancy. Obviously, that means tubing or a surrogacy. And if you're going to have the child tubed, you're talking about a routine out-patient procedure. Your mother's a geneticist, not an OB, but *she* could perform the procedure in a half-hour."

"You're right," Honor said. "I am going to have to have her—or him—tubed. And," her voice wavered again, very slightly, as she looked at her mother, "you were right, too, all those years ago, when you told me I'd understand why you didn't have *me* tubed when it was my turn. I don't want to. God, how I don't want to!" She pressed a palm gently to her flat, firm belly and blinked hard. "But I simply don't have that option."

"No, I don't suppose you do," Allison said. She reached up to touch her daughter's cheek. "I wish you did, but you don't."

"But, if I have the child tubed, I have to tell Hamish before I make that decision," Honor said. "It's my body, but it's *our* child. And the longer that I—that *we*—delay in making our final decision, the harder it's going to get, for both of us."

"That's true." Allison looked at her thoughtfully. "You're thinking about Emily, aren't you?"

"Yes," Honor sighed. "Oh, the political consequences if this were to get out don't bear thinking on. Not right now, not when things are still so up in the air, and when Hamish is First Lord and I'm a designated fleet commander. And especially not after what High Ridge and his cronies tried to do to us. But it's Emily I'm most concerned about."

"From what I've seen of Earl White Haven," Allison said slowly, "and from what I *know* of you, Honor Harrington, I don't imagine the two of you have been sneaking around behind her back."

"Of course we haven't. Even if we'd wanted to, we'd never have been able to get away with it!" Honor's chuckle carried a slightly bitter edge. "What with my armsmen, the newsies watching every move either one of us make, and the White Haven staff's devotion to Emily, if she hadn't been in on it from the start, we'd've been tripped up the first time we kissed each other."

"Which," her mother observed with a slight, devilish twinkle, "you've obviously done."

"Obviously," Honor agreed repressively.

"In that case, while this may come as a surprise to her, it's a consequence of something she's tacitly approved," Allison pointed out.

"That may be true, but she had every right to expect Hamish and me to be responsible enough not to let something like this happen. She had no reason to anticipate that the fact that he and I are lovers would become public knowledge, which is exactly what will happen if the two of us acknowledge this child. Worse than that, I don't have the least idea how she'll react on a personal emotional level to the fact that Hamish and I are going to have a child."

"Are you sure you're not borrowing trouble, Honor?" her father asked. She looked at him, and he shrugged. "They've been married longer than you've been alive," he pointed out, "and they've never had a child. Did Emily even want children?"

"I haven't really discussed it with her," Honor admitted. "She's a wonderful person, but we're all still feeling our way into this relationship. She's a lot more Beowulfan—" she smiled at her mother "—about this than *I* am, and she's the one who took the initiative in resolving how Hamish and I felt about one another. But there are still some things we simply haven't discussed, either because we haven't had enough time for it yet, or because we might have felt . . . awkward."

"And does this come under the heading of 'not enough time' or 'I'd feel awkward as hell'?" Allison asked.

"The latter, I'm afraid."

Honor folded her arms once more, and Nimitz shifted his weight on her shoulder as she leaned back, propping herself against the edge of her desk.

"I think Emily probably did want children, at least once," she said slowly. "I think she'd have made a wonderful mother, and I think it would have been incredibly good for her to have a child to invest herself in. And I think she and Hamish fully intended to produce children—and an heir to White Haven—when they married."

"Then why didn't they?" Allison asked, frowning thoughtfully as she listened intently to her daughter. "I'm not asking you to violate any confidences, Honor, but that sounds rather unlikely in a lot of ways. While I realize the nature and extent of her injuries would make a normal pregnancy impossible, they could easily have had a child fertilized *in vitro* and tubed, or used a surrogate. And they're obviously well provided with staff; finding caregivers couldn't have been a problem."

"I'm not positive, but I *think* I know," Honor said. "Mind you, this is all speculation on my part, since we've never discussed it."

"So speculate," her father said.

"All right. You know, obviously, that just like me, Emily doesn't regenerate?" She paused, and both of her parents nodded just a bit impatiently for her to continue. "Well, I think she's afraid any child of hers would inherit the same inability."

"What?"

Allison blinked. She looked at her daughter for several seconds, then shook herself.

"That's ridiculous," she said. "Even if it weren't, look at you! God knows I wish you'd been a bit more careful about getting bits and pieces of yourself shot off, but regen or not, *you're* still fully functional. Are you telling me she's afraid a child of hers would not simply be unable to regenerate but experience the same sort of catastrophic damage *she* did?"

"I know it sounds irrational," Honor said. "But I think that's what it is. I know, from something Hamish once said, that they were waiting to have children until his schedule was a bit less hectic. He was working himself almost as hard at the time of her accident as he is now, and both of them wanted to be available as full-time parents. So I'm guessing whatever changed their plans is related to what happened to her. I suppose it's possible she felt her injuries would prevent her from being a 'proper mother,' but, as you just said, she has to've known she and Hamish could still have provided the best child care on Manticore. And on the one or two occasions when the subject of regeneration has come up—most people are pretty careful not to discuss it around her—what I've 'tasted' of her emotions strongly suggests she's not as completely rational about what happened to her as most people assume she is from how well she copes with it."

"It's certainly possible," Alfred Harrington said before Allison could respond. His wife and daughter both looked at him. "I've seen a lot of serious neural damage," he said, with massive understatement. "Admittedly, very little of it's been as severe as what happened to Lady Emily. I haven't reviewed her case file, obviously, but the fact that she survived at all is clearly a not so minor medical miracle. And even people with far less severe impairment than she's suffered often experience difficulty adjusting to it. You've done far better in that regard than many do, Honor," he added, gesturing at her artificial arm, "but I strongly suspect that even you have the odd moment when you're less than totally reconciled to what's happened to you."

"I don't know if I'd say I wasn't 'reconciled,' to it," Honor replied after a moment. "I *will* say there are times I deeply and intensely regret it, though. And times I still experience the 'phantom pain' you warned me I would."

"But you aren't trapped inside a totally nonresponsive body," Alfred pointed out. "Emily is, and she's been that way for over sixty T-years. She's learned to compensate, as much as anyone possibly can, and to get on with her life, but the fact that she's had to accept her impairment doesn't mean it's stopped hurting— especially for someone who was as physically active as she was before the accident. I think the thought of even the remotest possibility of her seeing someone else she loved in the same situation, rational or not, would terrify her. So, if she's managed to fixate on the possibility of her passing her inability to regenerate on to her children, she could, indeed, have simply closed off all consideration of *having* children in her own mind."

"That's exactly what I think she's done," Honor said. "And if she has, if Hamish and I have a child, I think we may rip her wounds wide open. I don't want to do that to her. In fact, I'll do anything to keep from doing that to her."

"I'm not at all sure you have that choice, Honor," Allison said with a certain implacable gentleness. Honor looked at her, and her mother's expression was an odd blend of serenity and sternness.

"I'm not speaking just as your mother," Allison continue. "I'm also a physician, and not just any physician. I'm a geneticist—a *Beowulf* geneticist—and Emily Alexander is Hamish Alexander's wife. She may have decided to force the issue of the way you and Hamish feel about one another, and she may have decided to embrace both of you. For that, I respect and honor her. But that doesn't change the fact that she's his wife, and as her husband he has a deep-seated moral obligation to tell her about this, just as you have a deep-seated moral obligation to tell *him*. You may want to 'spare her,' Honor, but I don't think you have the right to. And even if you tried to, what would happen if she later discovered what you hadn't told her? What would happen to her trust in you—and Hamish?"

Honor stared at Allison, and Nimitz rose on her shoulder, wrapping his tail protectively about her throat. She felt him pressing against her, radiating his support . . . and his agreement with what he read in her mother's emotions. And the hell of it was that *Honor* could read those emotions herself. And that she knew her mother was right.

"I don't know how to do this," she admitted after a moment.

"I don't either," Allison said, "but I do know how you should *start*. And so do you." Honor looked at her, and Allison snorted. "Go find Hamish and tell *him*. I know both of you may have believed your implant would prevent this from happening, but it takes two, and he shares responsibility. Don't you try to take all of this on *your* shoulders, Honor Harrington. Just this once, spread some of it around where it belongs."

"Pregnant?"

Hamish stared at Honor. They were in his Admiralty House office, the one place whose security she could be sure of, yet which was neither her Landing mansion nor White Haven. He'd seemed just a bit baffled when she screened him and requested a few minutes of his time on undisclosed "official business," but he'd cleared the last half-hour of his day's schedule for her.

Now she sat stiffly upright, facing him with Nimitz in her arms. Samantha's head had come up, the instant Honor and her mate entered the office; now she leapt from her perch behind Hamish's desk onto the back of his chair and sat upright, bracing herself with a light true-hand on the top of his head.

"Yes," Honor said, watching him closely and tasting his emotions even more intently. "I found out from Dr. Frazier just before lunch. My implant's expiration date was incorrectly entered in my Bassingford records when they reactivated my medical file. Dr. Frazier checked the test results three times." She shook her head. "There's no question, Hamish."

He sat absolutely motionless, radiating shock. But then, like a slow-motion recording of an opening flower, other emotions began to blossom. Surprise. Disbelief, fading quickly into an incredible melange of feelings so intense, so strong, she couldn't even begin to untangle them. His arctic blue eyes glowed, and he rose from his chair and crossed quickly to her. She started to stand, but he dropped to one knee in front of her chair before she could and captured both of her hands in his while the wild, vaulting tide of emotions cascaded through him.

"I never—" He stopped and shook his head. "I never expected, never thought..."

"Me either," she said, freeing her organic hand from his and running it across his hair. She blinked misty eyes as an unmistakable strand of joy soared to the top of his swirling emotional tide. But then she made herself sit back.

"I never expected this, Hamish," she said quietly, "but now that it's happened, we have some decisions to make."

"Yes." He stood slowly, then sank into an armchair, facing hers, and nodded. "Yes, we do," he agreed, and although the glowing ribbon of joy remained, she tasted anxiety and sudden concern rising to the surface beside it.

Samantha hopped down from his desk and pattered across the floor. She leapt up into Honor's chair long enough to rub cheeks with Nimitz, then leapt across to sink down in Hamish's lap, and his hands stroked her silken pelt slowly, reflexively. Just, Honor discovered, as her own hands were doing with Nimitz.

"Your command," he said. "Emily."

"And the media," Honor said, and grimaced. "My mother asked me why I couldn't do anything the easy way. I wish I had an answer for her."

"Because you're the Salamander," he said, his mouth twisting wryly. "Although, just between the two of us, I wish you could jump into a few less fires, at least where your personal life is involved."

"Unfortunately, we're in this one together, love."

"Yes, we are." He smiled a bit more whimsically. "I'm tempted to take the coward's way out and tell you that since you're the one who's pregnant, we'll do whatever you think is best. But you didn't get pregnant all by yourself, and it strikes me that a father shouldn't begin his duties by trying to shirk them. By the same token, you have had at least a little bit longer to think about this. So, having said that, *do* you have a strong feeling for what we ought to do?"

"Well, I'd thought the best place to begin would be to ask you whether or not you wanted to be a father," she said with a smile of her own. "Fortunately, you've already answered that one. So the next step is for us to decide how we tell Emily." Her smile disappeared. "Frankly, I don't have any idea at all how she's likely to react to this news, and I desperately want to avoid hurting her, Hamish. But I think my mother was right. We don't have the moral right to 'protect' her from something like this. Besides," her mouth tightened, "remember what an ungodly mess we made trying to 'protect her' before."

"You're right," he said. "And so is your mother. And I'm not sure how she'll respond, either. I know she wanted children when we married, and I know she changed her mind after the accident. Her mother had something to do with that, I think."

His expression took on a certain bleakness, and Honor tasted a cold, bitter strand of long-held, steely anger.

"Emily's mother didn't take what happened well," he said quietly. "At first, she wanted us to move heaven and earth to save her daughter's life. Later, when she realized how badly Emily had been damaged, and that it was permanent, she changed. I can't really fault her for not reacting well, at least initially. *I* didn't handle it very well—no, that's not fair; I completely, one hundred percent screwed up—when I finally accepted that I couldn't make her well again.

"But Emily's mother never did get herself back on track. For her, it was a quality-of-life issue, and she actually told me once—not in Emily's hearing, thank God!—that it would have been far kinder of me to simply let her die than to 'heartlessly condemn her to such a horrible life as a pathetic, helpless cripple out of pure selfishness.'"

Honor's jaw clenched. Emily's mother might never have said it where her daughter could hear, but Honor had discovered for herself just how observant Emily was, and how acutely and accurately she read the people around her. There was no way Emily Alexander could have been unaware of her mother's feelings.

"I don't think Emily ever saw herself as a helpless victim," Hamish continued, speaking slowly as he looked for exactly the right words. "I'm not trying to say she was a paragon of total courage, who never felt sorry for herself, never asked 'Why me?' There've been times, I know, when she's had to fight incredible bouts of depression. But she never saw herself as *helpless*, never saw herself as a mere, passive survivor. She was always her own person, always determined to go right on being *her*, no matter what happened.

"But I think...I think that despite that, a part of her saw herself through her mother's eyes. Or, maybe what she saw wasn't so much *her*, as some other victim. Someone else in the same condition, without the combination of support team and sheer guts and integrity that got her through it. Someone else who might agree with her mother that a life like hers wasn't worth living."

"You're talking about her children."

"Yes. No." He shrugged. "I don't know that she ever actually thought it out, or that it ever reached that level in her conscious thought. But I know she started shying away from the notion of having children, even after her physicians pointed out to her that there was no reason, given the state of modern medicine, why she couldn't still have them. And I know it started after her mother's attitude became obvious to those about her. And," he frowned, "I know I never pushed her about it. Never tried to work through it with her. I simply went along with what I believed her wishes to be, without examining for myself—or pushing her into examining for *herself*—whether or not they truly were her wishes."

"Well, I think we're all going to have to find out," Honor said softly.

Chapter Twelve

"So, what do you two have on your minds?"

Emily Alexander looked back and forth between Honor and her husband, one eyebrow arched. She sat in her favorite nook in the White Haven atrium Hamish had built for her years before, gazing at them speculatively across the constantly rippling surface of a crystal-clear *koi* pond. Honor could taste her curiosity, and with it a faint edge of amusement, and her own lips twitched as she realized how much she and Hamish must resemble a pair of truant schoolchildren, standing before their instructor with their 'cats on their shoulders to own up to their misdeeds.

But the temptation to smile disappeared as Honor reflected on what they were here to "own up to," and she inhaled deeply.

"Emily," Hamish said, "Honor and I have something we need to tell you. I hope it won't distress you, or cause you any pain, but it's something you have to know about."

"My, that sounds ominous," she said lightly, with a smile. But Emily Alexander had been the Star Kingdom's leading actress before her accident. Her expression might have fooled others, yet Honor tasted the sudden throat-tightening surge of anxiety behind it, and she felt herself shaking her head—hard—before she even realized she was going to speak.

"No, Emily!" she said sharply. "It's not that." Emily looked at her, green eyes suddenly vulnerable, and Honor shook her head even harder. "Hamish and I both love you," she heard herself say with a fierce intensity which surprised even her. "Nothing can change that. And nothing between me and Hamish could ever change the way he feels about *you*."

Emily looked at her for two or three more seconds, then nodded slowly. Not just in acceptance of Honor's reassurances, but in admission. Strong as she was, confident as she was in herself, she could never quite forget that Honor was all of the things, physically, that she could no longer be. There was always that tiny edge of fear she couldn't quite crush that the sheer vibrancy and physical health radiating from Honor would, indeed, change the way Hamish felt about her.

"Honor is right," Hamish told her softly, crossing to sit on an ornamental stone bench beside her life-support chair. He reached out and captured her one working hand in both of his, lifting it to press a kiss onto its back. "In an odd sort of way," he continued, gazing into her eyes and reaching out to cup the side of her face with his right hand, "you've become the center for both our lives. Maybe we've both simply been too contaminated by our Grayson experiences, but somehow the *three* of us have become a unit, and neither Honor nor I would ever change that, even if we could."

He paused for a moment, and she closed her eyes, pressing her cheek into his palm.

"But," he continued, after a moment, "we're both more than a little concerned about how you're going to react to the news we *do* have for you, love."

"In that case," she said, with something very like her normal tartness, "perhaps the two of you should stop trying to prepare me for it and go ahead and tell me what it is."

"You're right," he agreed. "So, to cut straight to the conclusion, there was a screwup with Honor's medical records. Both of us thought her contraceptive implant was current. It wasn't."

Emily looked at him. Then her eyes darted to Honor, opening very wide, and Honor nodded slowly.

"I'm pregnant, Emily," she said quietly. "Hamish and I never thought this was going to happen. Unfortunately, it has. And because it has, we—all three of us, not just Hamish and me—have to decide what *we're* going to do about it."

"Pregnant?" Emily repeated, and the sudden torrent of her emotions surged over Honor like an avalanche. "You're *pregnant!*"

"Yes." Honor crossed to Emily and sank to her knees, facing the older woman, and Nimitz and Samantha crooned softly, comfortingly. She started to say something more, then stopped, forcing herself to wait while Emily fought her way through her own emotional tumult.

"My God," Emily said after a moment. "Pregnant." She shook her head. "Somehow, this is one possibility that never occurred to me." Her voice quivered, and her working hand tightened on Hamish's left hand as she blinked hard. "How . . . how far along are you?"

"Only a few weeks," Honor said quietly. "And I'm third-generation prolong, not first- or second-generation, so we're looking at a regular nine-month pregnancy. Or we would be, at least, if I had the option of carrying the child to term normally."

"Oh, God." Emily tugged her hand out of Hamish's grasp and reached out to Honor. "Oh, no." She shook her head, green eyes welling with tears. "Honor, if something happens to you *now*—!"

"I'd like to say nothing will," Honor said gently, taking Emily's hand and pressing it to her own cheek as the confusion of Emily's initial response focused itself down into a single, overriding emotion. Concern. Concern not over the consequences of the pregnancy for her, or even for the three of them, but for Honor's safety, redoubled and concentrated by the fact of her pregnancy.

"I'd like to say nothing will," Honor repeated, "but I can't, because it could. A lot of people are going to be hurt or killed before this war is over, Emily. And a lot of babies are going to be born because of people's fears of what may happen to them, or to the people they love. All of which mixes into the concern Hamish and I feel over how *you* may feel about this."

The last sentence came out as a question, and Emily shook her head.

"I don't *know* how I feel about it," she said with an honesty which was almost physically painful for Honor. "I'd like to say that all I feel is happy for you—and for Hamish. But I'm only human." Her lower lip quivered ever so slightly. "Knowing you can give Hamish the physical intimacy I can't hurts badly enough sometimes all by itself, Honor. I don't blame you for it; I don't blame Hamish for it. I don't even blame God for it, very much, anymore. But it does hurt, and I'd be lying if I told you it didn't."

A tear trickled down Honor's cheek as she tasted Emily's determination to be totally candid, not just with Honor and Hamish, but with herself. Perhaps to be *totally* candid with herself for the very first time.

"I look at you, Honor," she said, green eyes glistening, "and

I remember. I remember what it was like to have two legs that worked. To be able to stand on my own. To be able to move. To be able to *feel* anything—anything at all—below my shoulders. To be able to breathe by myself."

She looked away and drew a deep, shuddering breath.

"Did Hamish ever tell you just how bad the damage was, Honor?" she asked.

"We've discussed it . . . some," Honor said with an odd serenity, returning candor for candor, and reached out to wipe a tear from Emily's cheek with her thumb. "Not in great detail."

"It wasn't just my spine that was smashed in that accident," Emily said, still looking away from Honor. "They repaired everything they could, but there was an enormous amount of damage that couldn't be fixed. Or that there was no point in fixing, anyway, because I haven't felt anything except my right hand—anything at all, Honor—below my shoulders in sixty T-years. Nothing."

She looked back at Honor again.

"I can't survive outside this chair. Can't even breathe on my own. And there you are. So healthy, so *fit*. And so beautiful, though I doubt you actually realize it. Everything I once was, you *are*, and, oh, God, Honor, there are times I resent it so. When it *hurts* so much."

She stopped for a moment, blinking, then smiled tremulously.

"But you aren't me. You're someone else entirely. A rather wonderful someone else, actually. When I first realized—when you first told me—how you and Hamish truly felt about one another, it was hard. I realized, intellectually, at least, that it wasn't your fault, and I recognized how dreadfully the two of you had hurt yourselves in order to avoid hurting *me*. And because of that, and because of the political consequences if the world had believed the Opposition's smear campaign, I made the decision—the *intellectual* decision—to accept what couldn't be changed and try to minimize the consequences.

"It was only later, when I'd come to truly know you, that I realized emotionally, deep down inside, that you truly are a part of Hamish, and so a part of *me*, as well. But that still doesn't make you me. And the hurt I still feel sometimes when I look at you standing beside Hamish, where I used to be able to stand, or think about you in his bed, where I used to be, is so much less important than who you *are* and what you mean to Hamish . . . and to me.

"And now this." She shook her head. "Now, whether you meant to or not, you've moved still further beyond me. Moved to do something else I used to be able to see myself doing. A baby, Honor." She blinked again. "You're going to have a *baby*—Hamish's baby. And that hurts, hurts so terribly . . . and feels so wonderful."

A glow of joy flowed out of her, like sunlight through the chinks between thunderheads. It wasn't really *happiness*—not yet. There was too much jagged-edged hurt and a lingering resentment which knew it was both unreasonable and irrational. But it was joy, and within it Honor sensed the capacity to *become* happiness.

"Hamish and I have discussed this," Honor told her, meeting her gaze steadily. "We both want the child. But even more, we want to avoid hurting or distressing you. Among the philanthropies Willard is overseeing for me from Grayson I've got at least three orphanages and two adoption affiliates, one on Grayson, and one here in the Star Kingdom. We can place this child for adoption, Emily. We can guarantee that she—or he—will have loving, supportive parents."

"No, you can't," Emily said. "Can't place it for adoption, I mean. I know you could find loving parents. But I couldn't ask you to give up your child. And if something does happen to you, I couldn't ask Hamish to give up the only part of you that he—*we*—could keep."

"So," Honor paused and drew a deep breath. "So you want us to keep the baby?"

"Of course I do!" Emily looked at her. "I'm not saying I don't have mixed feelings, because I do. You know that, if anyone does. But mixed feelings can get themselves unmixed, and even if they couldn't, how could I possibly ask you to give up your *child* just to spare my feelings?"

Honor closed her eyes, pressing Emily's hand more firmly against her cheek, and, to her surprise, Emily chuckled.

"Of course," she went on, her voice and the glow of her emotions both much closer to normal, "now that I've gotten past my initial surprise, I can see where this could pose a few problems. I don't suppose the two of you are hoping I can help solve them . . . again?"

"Actually," Honor said, raising her head and smiling a bit mistily at Emily, "that's exactly what we're hoping."

✧   ✧   ✧

"All right, let's look at the problem and our options for dealing with it," Emily said much later that evening, after the supper dishes had been cleared away and the three humans and two treecats were alone once more. She'd regained most of her emotional balance, and Honor treasured the serenity flowing from her.

"First, Honor's—*our*—giving up this child is *not* an option," Emily continued. "Second, Honor's carrying the child to term naturally is also not an option. Third, the potential political consequences of our acknowledging the pregnancy at this particular point in time would be . . . difficult. Both here, in the Star Kingdom, and on Grayson. Fourth," she looked back and forth between her husband and Honor, "however we resolve the problems, *I* want and intend to be involved in raising this child. So, with option number one already settled, what about the second one?"

"Under normal circumstances," Honor said, "and bearing in mind that Mother is from Beowulf, the solution would be simple. She'd become my surrogate, but I'm afraid that won't work here."

"Why not?" Emily asked, cocking her head. Honor looked at her, and Emily flipped her hand in the gesture she used for a shrug. "It just seems like such a good idea from so many perspectives, I'm wondering if we're thinking about the same difficulties."

"It would be a wonderful idea," Honor agreed, just a trifle sadly. "Mother's always had easy pregnancies, and the twins are just old enough now that she's started missing having a toddler around. And I can't think of anyone who would be a better surrogate. But legally, this child will replace Faith in the Harrington succession, and eventually I'm going to have to acknowledge that publicly, which presents all sorts of problems in using Mother as my surrogate. If she's visibly pregnant, the assumption on Grayson will be—unless we tell them to the contrary—that Father is the father."

She paused and chuckled wryly.

"'Father is the father,'" she repeated. "Does that sound as odd to you as it does to me?"

"It does sound a bit peculiar," Hamish conceded. "But you were saying?"

"I was saying that everyone will assume the child is Mother's, and she's much too visible to be pregnant without *someone's* noticing. Which means that either we tell everyone, including the Conclave of Steadholders, who the actual biological parents are, or else we have to lie."

She shook her head, all humor fled.

"I won't do that. I can't. Not only would it be wrong, but it would be politically disastrous for me when the truth finally did come out. It would be far better, in terms of Grayson perceptions and politics, for me to go ahead and acknowledge Hamish as the child's father right now, despite all the potential adverse reaction, than to be caught lying about the paternity of my child before her birth. And," she looked back and forth between Emily and Hamish, "maybe I've been a Grayson too long myself, but I'd agree with them."

"But eventually you're going to have to tell them what happened, and when," Emily pointed out.

"I'm willing to stand on my legal and moral right to privacy," Honor replied. "I'm not saying my Graysons will be *happy* about it when the truth comes out, however we handle it, but they'll accept that I had the right to not tell them something at all much better than they will my having lied about it."

"Don't you have an obligation as Steadholder Harrington to inform the Conclave of the birth of any heir to the Steading?" Hamish asked, frowning intently.

"Not precisely."

Honor reached out and handed Nimitz a stick of celery. The 'cat broke it neatly in half and passed one piece on to his mate, and she watched the two of them chew blissfully—and messily—for a second. Then she looked back up at Hamish and Emily.

"My obligation, legally, is to inform the Sword and the Church," she said. "Technically, it could be argued that I'm not under any obligation to inform anyone at all until such time as a child is actually born. Trust me," she smiled a bit bleakly, "I've done some research this afternoon. But, while the law specifies that the *birth* of an heir has to be reported to, and acknowledged by, the Protector and the Church, the practice has always been that they're to be informed when the pregnancy is confirmed. So, the two people on Grayson I *have* to tell about this, legally speaking, are Benjamin and Reverend Sullivan. I'm sure Benjamin would respect my confidence, and the Reverend's vows would require him to treat it as privileged information, like something revealed under the seal of the confessional, at least until the child is actually born."

"At which point?" Emily asked.

"At which point your guess is as good as mine as to exactly what happens," Honor admitted. "I can't see any way it would be possible to conceal the child's birth even if I wanted to. And, to be honest, I *don't* want to, for a lot of reasons. I think the best we can do, really, is to buy nine months for the political climate to change before I go public."

"We could always consider placing the embryo in cryo until the 'political climate' *has* changed," Hamish said slowly.

"No, we couldn't," his wife said flatly. He looked at her, and she shook her head firmly. "Honor is going into combat very soon now, Hamish. It's possible, however much we'd all like to pretend it isn't, that this time she could be killed." Her voice wavered slightly, and she looked across the table at Honor. "If God is actually listening to me, that's not going to happen, but sometimes I think He's lost my com combination. And, if that happens, we are *not* going to have deprived her of a single moment she might have had holding her child in her arms first."

Honor's eyes burned, and Emily smiled at her. But then the older woman shook her head again.

"Even if that weren't a consideration," she continued, "it would still be the wrong thing to do. If something does happen to Honor, the exact circumstances of the child's paternity will be in question. I realize genetic testing would confirm that the child is Honor's and yours, Hamish, but if Honor were killed—if she weren't around to confirm the circumstances under which conception occurred—there would always be someone who'd accuse us of some sort of Machiavellian plot to 'steal' Harrington."

"There are procedures for a posthumous declaration of paternity," Honor pointed out.

"We're not talking about what's legal or illegal," Emily replied. "We're talking about public perceptions, and on a planet which, if you'll forgive me, is still coming to grips with the implications of modern technology. Specifically, of modern medical technology."

"That's true enough," Honor acknowledged. "My parents and I are working on that, but sometimes it seems to me that at least half the people on Grayson still consider what we can do black magic." She shook her head. "And in some ways, it actually got worse when Mother came up with the nanites for the stillbirth defect."

"I heard about that," Emily said, "but I've never understood why any *woman* would be opposed to it. A way to eliminate all those spontaneous abortions and stillbirths?" It was her turn to shake her head. "Of course, no one's ever explained to me exactly how it works, either," she admitted.

"It's not an ideal solution," Honor said. "She's still working on a way to actually *repair* the defect in a way she's certain won't introduce additional problems of its own. In the meantime, the nanites she came up with are more of a brute force approach. They're engineered to invade the ovaries and identify the ova which carry an X-chromosome with the defect. Once they've identified an ovum with one of the damaged chromosomes, they destroy it. Since all of a woman's ova are already formed, Mother can eliminate any woman's damaged chromosomes completely with a single treatment. But there's a lot of resistance to using it. Some of it's from the more conservative elements of the population, who think that she's mucking about with God's plan—and a *lot* of whom are afraid that altering the ratio of male births to female births will bring chaos to their existing society. Another chunk of resistance, I think, comes from women who are afraid that *all* of their ova are affected, and that the nanites would render them completely sterile. And others just seem to find the entire concept creepy, or distasteful. But I think a lot of it comes from the point you've already raised, Emily—from the people who really do think of it as if it were black magic. They don't actually understand *any* of the new medical technology, really, and some of them are at least as frightened by it as grateful that it's become available."

"Precisely," Emily said, nodding vigorously, "and it's that portion of the population least comfortable with modern medicine which would be played upon by anyone who wanted to make trouble.

"Why should anyone *want* to make trouble?" Hamish asked almost plaintively, and Honor and Emily turned almost identical pitying looks upon him. Then they looked at each other, and Emily snorted.

"Frightening, isn't it?" she asked Honor. "And hard to believe he's a senior member of the Queen's Cabinet."

"Oh, I don't know," Honor replied with a crooked smile. "He's probably not any more totally incompetent where politics are concerned than I was when they first sent me to Yeltsin."

"But with so much less excuse," Emily said, eyes twinkling.

"Not really," Honor, chuckling wickedly as Hamish leaned back, raising one eyebrow, and folded his arms in resignation. "After all, he suffers from at least one physical handicap."

"Which one?" Emily asked, then shook her head quickly. "Oh, I know! You mean that 'Y' chromosome of his?"

"That's the one," Honor agreed, and both of them laughed.

"Very funny," Hamish said. "And now, if the two of you are done cackling, how about answering my question?"

"It's not so much why we can think of anyone wanting to make trouble," Honor said much more seriously, "as our responsibility to recognize that someone *could* want to. Human nature being human nature, some idiot who disapproves of all the changes on Grayson—and don't fool yourself; there are still a lot of them, even if they are a distinct minority—is likely to fasten on it out of simple delusional paranoia. And don't forget Mueller and Burdette, or the current Grayson Opposition. They'd probably see forcing Benjamin to expend political capital defending you as worthwhile in its own right." She shrugged. "It might be unlikely to create serious problems, but Emily's right. The potential's always there, and on the level of a Steadholdership, *any* problem can become a serious one."

"So what you're saying is that we really have no more than nine months before we *have* to go public," he said.

"I think that's exactly what I'm saying," she acknowledged. "I can stand on my right to refuse to declare the child's paternity even after her birth, which would probably work out fairly well on Manticore. It won't play on Grayson, though. Or, at least, not very well. But I'm going to have to acknowledge the birth itself as soon as it occurs."

"That's true," Emily agreed. "But every month we can buy before you have to go public would be very much worthwhile. It would give the political situation time to stabilize, and put some more time between the Opposition smear campaign and the moment of truth. Not that it's not still going to be messy, you understand."

"Oh, believe me, even a political incompetent like me understands that, Emily," Hamish said wryly.

"So what I think we're really saying here," Emily said after a moment, looking back and forth between Honor and Hamish once more, "is that our only real option is to have the child tubed under conditions of medical confidentiality and hope that by the time she—or he—is born, the political and military situation will have changed enough for the fact of her birth to generate somewhat less of a firestorm."

"I'm afraid so," Honor replied.

"Well, in that case," Emily said with a whimsical smile of her own, "I think Hamish and I had better spend the next few months learning how to be salamanders, too."

Chapter Thirteen

"Very well, Your Grace," the efficient young staffer at the other end of the com link said, scanning the e-form on her own display. "We can schedule the procedure for Wednesday afternoon, if that's convenient."

"Wednesday would be fine," Honor replied. "In fact, given my schedule, I really need to take care of it as soon as possible."

"I understand." The other woman paused with a slight frown. "I notice you've listed your mother as our alternate contact." Her voice ended on a slightly rising note, and Honor very carefully didn't grimace.

"That's correct," she said, her own voice completely level. Yet something about her tone made the staffer look up. If she'd felt any temptation to fish for additional information, it evaporated quickly as she met Honor's gaze.

"In that case, Your Grace, I'll put you down for . . . fourteen-thirty."

"Thank you. I'll be there."

"I don't think I've ever seen the Steadholder quite like this," Spencer Hawke said quietly.

He and Simon Mattingly stood against one wall of the palatial gymnasium under Honor's Jason Bay mansion, watching her work out.

Her normal routine had been somewhat altered. As usual, she'd spent an hour working out with the Harrington Sword. Grand Master Thomas Dunlevy had come out of retirement last year to help program her training remote, and the ringing clash of the remote's blunt-edged training blade against the razor-sharp Harrington Sword had sent its harsh music through the gym. But the Steadholder had donned much heavier practice armor than usual, and she'd had Mattingly step down the remote's reaction speed. It was also a Monday, and usually on Mondays she put on her *coup de vitesse* training *gi* and pads and worked out full-contact against the training remote or Colonel LaFollet. But today, instead, she'd contented herself with the stretching exercises and training *katas*. And as if that weren't enough, she'd sent LaFollet himself away without her. Neither she nor the colonel had discussed exactly what it was he was doing today, but Mattingly and Hawke both knew it had something to do with the rather peculiar travel agenda Lady Harrington had laid out for LaFollet the evening before.

All of that was odd enough, yet it wasn't what had prompted Hawke's remark. There was a . . . distracted edge to her. She lacked that complete and total focus on whatever the task in hand happened to be which was usually so much a part of her. And she seemed both excited and apprehensive, which was very much not like her.

Mattingly glanced at the younger armsman. Hawke had not yet been briefed on the details of the aforementioned peculiar travel agenda. For that matter, Mattingly hadn't been *fully* briefed on it, himself, but he believed in being prepared. So he'd done a little research of his own on this "Briarwood Center" the Steadholder was intent upon visiting so privately.

"I've seen her in moods like this one," he said after a moment. "Not often, but once or twice. Thank God it's not as bad as the one she was in before they sent us to Marsh!"

"Amen," Hawke said with soft fervency, and remembered anger flickered in the backs of his usually mild eyes. Mattingly wasn't surprised to see it, but he was glad. He'd chosen that particular example deliberately, given what Hawke was going to inevitably figure out for himself tomorrow.

"She's got a lot on her mind," he continued quietly, watching the Steadholder flow gracefully through her katas. She was almost ten T-years older than he was, but she looked half his age. He'd become as accustomed to that as anyone could, who'd grown to adulthood on a planet without prolong, but he was finding it increasingly difficult to match her flexibility and speed.

No, he corrected himself. *Not* "match them"; *I never did manage that. But it's getting harder just to stay in shouting distance.*

"I know she does," Hawke replied to his last remark, and cocked his head. "But this isn't just about her navy job."

"No, it isn't," Mattingly agreed. "There are some . . . personal issues involved, as well."

Hawke's eyes turned instantly opaque, and his expression blanked. It was a professional armsman's reaction which Mattingly found a bit amusing, under the circumstances. He couldn't really fault the younger man for probing for information—armsmen all too often found that their primaries had neglected to mention some vitally important bit of information because it hadn't seemed important to them. Or because they didn't *want* to share it. Or even sometimes, as happened much too frequently for Mattingly's peace of mind in the Steadholder's case, because they'd simply decided to subordinate security requirements to . . . other considerations.

But it was a mark of Hawke's relative youthfulness that he should go into immediate "the-Steadholder's-private-life-is-none-of-my-business" mode the instant he began to suspect where his probing might lead him.

"She's not going to tell you about them, you know," Mattingly said conversationally, his tone almost teasing, as the Steadholder finished her *katas*.

He watched her alertly, even here, wondering if she was going to head straight for the showers, but instead, she crossed to the indoor shooting range at the far end of the gymnasium. He'd already checked the range before the Steadholder ever entered the gym, and there were no other entrances to it, so he didn't try to intercept her at the range door. Instead, he jerked his head at Hawke, and the two of them walked over to flank the door, watching through the soundproof armorplast with one eye while they kept most of their attention focused on the only access routes.

"There's no reason she ought to tell me about them," Hawke said, just a bit stiffly. "She's my Steadholder. If she wants me to know something, she'll tell me."

"Oh, nonsense!" Mattingly snorted. He felt a small flicker of surprise when the Steadholder didn't put on her ear protectors, but his incipient twinge of concern vanished when he realized she didn't have her .45 at the shooting line. Unlike that thunderous, anachronistic, propellant-spewing monster, pulsers were relatively quiet.

Satisfied that his charge wasn't going to hammer her unprotected eardrums with gunfire, he looked back at Hawke. Who was regarding him with a moderately outraged expression.

"Spencer," he said, "Colonel LaFollet didn't handpick you for the Steadholder's personal detail because you're an idiot. You know—or you damned well *ought* to know, by now—that no primary ever tells his armsmen everything they need to know. And, frankly, the Steadholder's worse than most in that regard. She's better than she was, but, Tester—the things she *used* to do without even mentioning them to us ahead of time!"

He shook his head.

"The thing you have to understand, Spencer, is that there's the Job, and then there's everything else. The Job is to see to it that that lady in there stays alive, period. No ifs, no ands, and no buts. We do whatever it takes—*whatever* it takes—to see to it that she does. And it's our privilege to do that, because there are steadholders, and there are steadholders, and I tell you frankly that one like *her* comes along *maybe* once or twice in a generation. If we're lucky. And, yes, although I'm not going to tell her, I'd do the Job anyway, because I love her.

"But every so often, and more often in her case than in most, the Job and who the person we're protecting *is* run into one another head on. The Steadholder takes risks. Some of them are manageable, or at least reasonably so, like her hang-gliding and her sailboats. But she's also a naval officer, and a steadholder in the old sense—the kind who used to lead his personal troops from the front rank—so there are always going to be risks we can't protect her from, however hard we try. And as you may recall, those same risks have killed quite a few of her armsmen along the way.

"And there's another factor involved, where she's concerned. She wasn't born a steadholder. In a lot of ways, I think that's the secret of her strength *as* a steadholder; she doesn't think like someone who knew from the time he learned to walk that he was going to be one. That's probably a very good thing, over all, but it also means she didn't grow up with the mindset. It simply doesn't occur to her—or, sometimes it does occur to her and she simply chooses to ignore the fact—that she *has* to keep us informed if we're going to do the Job. And since she doesn't, every one of us—like every armsman who ever was—spends an awful lot of time trying to figure out what it is she isn't telling us about this time."

He grimaced wryly.

"And, of course, we spend most of the rest of our time keeping our big mouths shut about the things we have figured out. Especially the ones she didn't tell us about. You know, the things she knows that we know that she knows that we know but none of us ever discuss with her."

"Oh." Hawke frowned. "So you're saying I'm *supposed* to pry into her personal life?"

"We *are* her personal life," Mattingly said flatly. "We're as much her family as her mother and father, as Faith and James. Except that we're the *expendable* part of her family . . . and everyone knows and accepts that. Except her."

His own frown mingled affection, respect, and exasperation as he looked through the armorplast at his Steadholder. Hawke looked as well, and Mattingly felt the younger man twitch in something very like shock as the Steadholder calmly removed the very tip of her left index finger.

"Haven't seen this one before?" Mattingly asked.

"I've seen it before," Hawke replied. "Just not very often. And it . . . bothers me. You know, I keep forgetting her arm's artificial."

"Yeah, and her father's a seriously paranoid individual, Tester bless him!" Mattingly said. "Although," they watched with half their attention as the Steadholder flexed her left hand and the truncated index finger locked into a rigidly extended position, "that particular hideout weapon of hers is something of a case in point for what I was saying earlier. She didn't even tell me or the Colonel about it until after we were sent to Marsh."

"I know." Hawke chuckled. "I was there when we all found out, remember?"

On the other side of the armorplast, the Steadholder pointed her finger down-range, and a hyper-velocity pulser dart shrieked

dead center through the ten-ring of a combat target. She hadn't
even raised her hand, and as they watched, she actually turned
her head away, not even looking at the targets as they popped
out of their holographic concealment . . . and the pulser darts
continue to rip their chests apart.

"How does she *do* that?" Hawke demanded. "Look at that!
She's got her eyes *closed*!"

"Yes, she does," Mattingly agreed with a smile. "The Colonel
finally broke down and asked her. It's fairly simple, really. There's
a concealed camera in the cuticle of the finger, and when she
activates the pulser, the camera feed links directly to her artificial eye. It projects a window with a crosshair, and since the
camera is exactly aligned with the bore of the pulser, the dart
will automatically hit anything she sees in the window." He shook
his head, still smiling. "She's always been a really good 'point-
and-shoot' shooter, but it got even worse when her father had
her arm designed."

"You can say that again," Hawke said with feeling.

"And a damned good thing, too." Mattingly turned away from
the armorplast. "They say the Tester is especially demanding when
He Tests those He loves best. Which tells me that He loves the
Steadholder a lot."

Hawke nodded, turning away from the armorplast himself
and frowning as he considered everything Mattingly had said to
him. After several moments, he looked back across at the older
armsman.

"So what is it she's not telling us?"

"Excuse me?" Mattingly frowned at him.

"So what is it she's not telling us?" Hawke repeated. "You
said it's an armsman's responsibility to know all those things his
primary doesn't tell him about. So tell me."

"Tell you something the Steadholder *hasn't* told you?" Mattingly's
frown became a wicked grin. "I'd never dream of doing such a
thing!"

"But you just said—"

"I said it's an armsman's responsibility to *find out* about the
things he needs to know. At the moment, the Colonel and I—older
and wiser, not to say sneakier, heads that we are—have already
found out. Now, young Spencer, as part of your own ongoing
education and training, it's your job to figure it out for yourself.

And, I might add, without stepping on your sword in front of the Steadholder by admitting that you have."

"That's dumb!" Hawke protested.

"No, Spencer, it isn't," Mattingly said, much more seriously. "Finding out for yourself is something you're going to have to do. And for quite a long time. Unlike the Colonel or me, you've got prolong. You're going to be with the Steadholder probably for decades, and you need to figure out the sorts of things she isn't going to tell you. And just as importantly, you need to learn how to leave her her privacy even as you invade it."

Hawke looked at him, and Mattingly smiled with more than a trace of sadness.

"She *has* no privacy, Spencer. Not anymore. And like I just said, she didn't grow up a steadholder. Someone who's born to the job never really has privacy in the first place. He doesn't miss what he never had, or not as much, at any rate. But she did have it, and she gave it away when she accepted her steadholdership. I don't think she's ever admitted to anyone just how much that cost her. So if we can play the game, let her cling to at least the illusion that she still has some privacy, then that's part of what it means to be an armsman. And however silly, however 'dumb,' that might sometimes seem, it isn't. Not at all. In fact, playing that game with her has been one of the greatest privileges of my service as her personal armsman."

"Were you able to catch up with Duchess Harrington, Adam?"

"Yes, Sir. Sort of."

Admiral Sir Thomas Caparelli looked up from the report in front of him and quirked an eyebrow at the tallish, fair-haired senior-grade captain.

"Would you care to explain that somewhat cryptic utterance?" he inquired of his chief of staff.

"I spoke to Her Grace, Sir," Captain Dryslar replied. "Unfortunately, I didn't catch up with her until just after eleven. She had a working lunch scheduled with some of Admiral Hemphill's people, and immediately after that she has a doctor's appointment. She said she could reschedule the doctor's appointment if it was an emergency, but that she'd really prefer not to."

"Doctor?" Caparelli's eyes narrowed, and he sat up straighter. "Is there a health problem I ought to know about?"

"Not so far as I'm aware, Sir," Dryslar said carefully.

"Meaning? Don't make me pull it out of you one syllable at a time, Adam!"

"Sorry, Sir. I did ask Her Grace where her appointment was, in case we needed to reach her. She said it was at Briarwood Center."

Caparelli had opened his mouth. Now it closed again, and both eyebrows rose in obvious startlement.

"Briarwood?" he repeated after a moment.

"Yes, Sir."

"I see. Well, in that case, we can certainly reschedule my meeting with her. Please screen her back and see if she'll be available tomorrow. No, wait. Make it Friday."

"Yes, Sir."

Dryslar left the office, closing the door behind him, and Caparelli sat for several seconds, gazing at nothing in particular while he contemplated the potential complications of Admiral Harrington's afternoon appointment. He considered screening her himself, personally, but only very briefly. If there was anything she wanted to discuss with him, she had his com combination, and there were certain things of which the First Space Lord did not want to take official cognizance unless he had to.

"My Lady, I really don't think the Queen—or Protector Benjamin—is going to be very happy about this."

Colonel Andrew LaFollet's voice was in diffident mode, but there was something undeniably mulish about his gray eyes, and Honor turned to look at him sternly.

"Her Majesty—and the Protector—aren't going to hear about it from *me*, Andrew. Did you have some other possible informant— excuse me, *reporter*—in mind to carry them the news?"

"My Lady, sooner or later, they're going to find out," LaFollet replied, standing his ground. "I'm your armsman. I understand the need for confidentiality, and you know perfectly well what that means, just as you know all the rest of the detail will keep their mouths shut. But they're not exactly without sources of their own, and when they find out about this little escapade, they are *not* going to be amused. For that matter," he added, his face even more expressionless, "I rather doubt the Earl or Lady White Haven would be very pleased about it if they knew just how uncovered you are right now."

Honor had already opened her mouth, but she swallowed what she'd been about to say and looked at him narrowly. It was the first time LaFollet had come that close to openly acknowledging her relationship with Hamish. And, whether she wanted to admit it or not herself, her personal armsman had a point.

She glanced out the one-way window of the air limo. Over the years, she'd become accustomed to the routine security arrangements which attached to her persona as steadholder and duchess. She still didn't like them, and she never would, yet after so long she felt undeniably . . . naked when she looked out and saw the empty chunks of air where the sting ships ought to be. And ridiculous as it often still seemed to her, she'd learned the hard way that figures as public as she'd become attracted the lunatic fringe. Not to mention the fact that over the years she'd acquired quite a few enemies who would have been less than brokenhearted should something permanent happen to her. Which was one reason LaFollet and Simon Mattingly were the only two survivors of her original personal armsmen. And which was also why "not amused" was an awfully pale description of Benjamin Mayhew's probable reaction to what she was doing this afternoon. Elizabeth might cut her a little more slack, but even she would have a few choice things to say when she found out Honor had ditched all of her standard security arrangements except for the close-in cover of her personal three-man detachment.

Unfortunately, she didn't have much of a choice, and she was grateful to Lieutenant Commander Hennessy, Admiral Hemphill's chief of staff and representative at the meeting she'd just left, for covering for her. Hennessy hadn't asked LaFollet why it would be necessary for Duchess Harrington's official limousine—and sting ship escort—to return to the Bay House without her. He'd simply run interference for her, as she'd requested, which had allowed her, LaFollet, Mattingly, and Hawke to get to the parking garage and this waiting, anonymous limousine unobserved.

"I know all of you will keep your mouths closed, Andrew," she said after a moment, and her tone was an apology. "I guess I'm just a little more worried about this than I'm willing to admit." Nimitz crooned to her, and she stroked his spine. "It's . . . complicated."

"My Lady," LaFollet said gently, " 'complicated' isn't exactly the word I'd choose. It's a bit too . . . mild. And I'm not trying to complicate things any more badly than they already are. But I wouldn't be doing my job if I didn't point out that, however valid your reasons, gadding about Landing with only the three of us isn't exactly the safest thing you could be doing."

"No, it isn't. On the other hand, I've got quite a bit of faith in your ability to look after me if anything goes wrong. And I'm not exactly helpless myself, you know. All of which is beside the point. Arriving at Briarwood in an official car, complete with escort and the whole brass band, wouldn't exactly contribute to the low profile I'm trying to maintain."

"No, My Lady." LaFollet didn't—quite—sigh, but Honor tasted his resignation. "Only, if you insist on doing it this way," he went on, "you're going to follow *my* orders while we're out here on our own. Agreed, My Lady?"

She looked at him for a few seconds, and he gazed back levelly, gray eyes unflinching while she tasted the adamantine determination behind them.

"All right, Andrew," she surrendered. "You're in charge . . . this time."

To his credit, LaFollet didn't even say "good."

The limo pulled directly into the Briarwood Center's hundred and third-floor parking garage. Simon Mattingly settled it into the designated stall, and Spencer Hawk climbed out of the front seat and rapidly—but thoroughly—swept the area. It was deserted, as Honor had anticipated at this time of day, and LaFollet allowed her to get out of the vehicle herself.

Her armsmen fell into formation about her and she settled Nimitz on her shoulder as they crossed the garage for the quick lift shaft trip to the Center. It wasn't easy for a uniformed admiral of the Royal Manticoran Navy, escorted by three uniformed body-guards, to pass unnoticed anywhere, but confidentiality was often something Briarwood had to take into consideration. The Center was accustomed to providing for it without drawing attention to the fact, and the lift deposited Honor and her party, exactly at the appointed time, outside a discreetly private waiting room.

The woman at the arrivals desk looked up with a pleasant smile as the door closed behind them.

"Good afternoon, Your Grace."

"Good afternoon," Honor replied with a smile of her own. One, she discovered, which covered a higher degree of nervousness than she'd expected. Routine medical procedure or not, there was an undeniable flutter of anxiety in the pit of her stomach. *Or,* she thought, *perhaps someplace a bit lower.*

"If you'd care to have a seat, Dr. Illescue will be with you in just a few moments."

"Thank you."

Honor settled into one of the comfortable chairs, and her dark eyes gleamed with amusement as she and Nimitz tasted the outwardly unflappable receptionist's emotions as her three arms-men positioned themselves with silent, well-practiced efficiency to cover the waiting room.

She'd been waiting for less than five minutes when Dr. Franz Illescue walked in.

"Your Grace," he said, greeting her with a slight bow.

"Doctor."

Illescue was on the short side, dark haired, and slightly built, with a closely trimmed beard. He exuded the comforting professionalism of an excellent "bedside manner," she thought, with the critical appreciation of the child of two physicians, but carefully hidden curiosity bubbled behind his brown eyes. And there were other emotions along with the curiosity, including a thread of something almost like . . . hostility. She wondered where that came from, since she'd never met the man before in her life, but he seemed to have it well under control. Which didn't really surprise her. Franz Illescue was Briarwood's senior physician, and he hadn't drawn her appointment by random chance.

"If you'll come with me, Your Grace," he invited now, then frowned as her armsmen fell into their normal triangular pattern about her. That thread of almost-hostility strengthened abruptly, and his eyes narrowed.

"Is there a problem, Doctor?" she asked mildly.

"If you'll forgive my saying so, Your Grace," he replied, "we're not really comfortable with guns here in Briarwood."

"I can appreciate that," she said. "Unfortunately, I'm not entirely free to make my own decisions where security matters are concerned."

Illescue looked at her, and she frowned herself, mildly, as she tasted more than a little skepticism. She couldn't fault his unhappiness at having his medical facility invaded by armed, obviously protective bodyguards, but she didn't care at all for the undertone of something very like contempt she tasted along with the skepticism. Not contempt for her armsmen, but for the insecurity—or egotism—behind her obvious need for such an ostentatious display of her own self-importance.

"I hope it won't disrupt your normal routine, Doctor," she allowed the very slightest hint of frost into her voice, "but I genuinely have no choice under Grayson law. I believe you were informed of my security requirements when I scheduled the appointment. If it's a problem, we can always leave."

"No, of course it isn't, Your Grace," he said quickly, despite a flicker of intense annoyance. "Will you require one of them in the treatment room?"

"I believe we can dispense with that particular requirement, as long as we're allowed to post them outside the room," Honor said gravely, unable to completely suppress her inner amusement as his carefully hidden annoyance flared still higher briefly.

"I don't believe that will be a problem," he told her, and she followed him from the waiting room.

"Are you all right, My Lady?"

Honor grimaced, torn between amusement and affectionate annoyance at LaFollet's tone. She'd often thought Grayson attitudes towards sex and procreation were oddly skewed. On the one hand, no properly brought up Grayson male would even have contemplated discussing such a subject with a woman to whom he was not married. On the other hand, given the Grayson population's thousand-year struggle to survive, not even the most properly reared male could grow up on the planet without becoming fully informed on all the "female" details which went with it.

"It's an outpatient procedure, Andrew," she said, after a moment, shifting on the limousine's luxurious seat. "That doesn't necessarily mean there's no discomfort, even with quick-heal."

"No, My Lady. Of course not," he said just a bit hastily. She looked at him levelly, and after a moment, he grinned wryly.

"Sorry, My Lady. I don't mean to hover. It's just, well . . ."

He shrugged and flipped both hands, palms uppermost.

"I know, Andrew." She smiled at him, and Nimitz bleeked in amusement from her lap. "And I really am just fine."

He nodded, and she looked back out the window. Nimitz rose

in her lap, careful about where he let his weight fall, and leaned against her, pressing his muzzle very gently against her cheek. His buzzing purr vibrated into her comfortingly, and she let his love and support flow through her. At the moment, she needed them badly.

The realization surprised her, yet it was true. Her mind kept returning to that tiny embryo, floating now in the replication tube. Such a minute bit of tissue . . . and yet, how enormous that unborn child loomed in her own heart. She felt hollow, as if she had been emptied of something unutterably precious. Intellectually, she knew her child was far safer where she—or he—was, yet her emotions were something else. A part of her felt as if she'd abandoned her baby, left it in a coldly sterile, antiseptic storage box, like some bit of inconvenient luggage.

She hugged Nimitz gently, wishing with all her heart that Hamish could have accompanied her to Briarwood. He'd wanted to. In fact, he'd tried to insist on coming, until she'd pointed out that his presence would tend to somewhat undermine her insistence on asserting her privacy right to not disclose the father's identity. Bad enough if someone had spotted her and her detail at the Star Kingdom's premier fertility and reproductive center without seeing her there in company with the First Lord of Admiralty. And yet, at this moment, she longed to feel his arms about her.

Well, she'd feel them this evening, she told herself. And, at least as importantly, she would feel Emily's support. Perhaps she'd been an adoptive Grayson too long, she thought, her lips twitching in a smile of mingled tenderness and amusement. She wondered how many other Manticorans would have found the thought of spending an intimate evening in the company of the wife of the father of her unborn child *comforting*, yet that was the only word she could think of to describe it.

And she didn't really care how bizarre it might once have seemed to her pre-Grayson self.

Chapter Fourteen

"Well, well, well...*there* you are," Jean-Claude Nesbitt murmured.

He studied the lines of alphanumeric text on his display for several seconds, then frowned thoughtfully and began very carefully copying the critical passages of the document for safekeeping. He made certain he had everything he needed, then closed the file and withdrew from the "secure" memory bank as tracelessly as he had entered it.

He punched up another file, running down the checklist he'd assembled over the last three arduous weeks. Putting it together would have been a full-time job under almost any circumstances. Given the fact that he couldn't afford to let any of his erstwhile subordinates guess he was working on a completely private black project of his own, it had become a monumental pain in the neck. But unless he was very mistaken, he had all the pieces he needed now.

He reached the end of the list, grunted in satisfaction, and then closed that file, as well. It wasn't easy. In fact, it was extraordinarily tempting to move ahead quickly now that he'd completed the preparatory groundwork. But it was late, he was tired, and he'd seen entirely too many fatigue-induced errors in his time. Besides, Giancola's instructions to replace Grosclaude's letter of instruction to his attorneys had been carried out over two months ago. Even if something happened to Grosclaude before the colonel got around to completing the rest of the project, he was covered. So best to take things slowly and cautiously.

He powered down his console, nodded to his own reflection in the blank display, and pushed back his chair. Time for bed, he thought, but first, a well-earned nightcap.

"Are you really serious about this, Boss?" Special Senior Inspector Abrioux asked quizzically.

"And just what about my clearly phrased directive makes you think I might not be?" Kevin Usher, Director of the Federal Investigative Agency of the Republic of Haven inquired.

Usher was a huge, powerfully built man. Danielle Abrioux, on the other hand, was delicately petite. Like Usher, she'd come up through the Resistance before joining the FIA, and if she looked like a slender, brown-haired child, appearances could be deceiving. She was a very *dangerous* "child" . . . as the shades of over a dozen assassinated InSec and StateSec officials—and far more currently carnate inmates of the Republic's penal systems—would have vehemently attested. At the moment, she was perched on the corner of Usher's desk, sipping coffee, and a matching coffee mug sat on his blotter, because Abrioux was one of his most trusted investigators. She knew all about his alleged drunkenness, and it was a relief to be able to abandon the charade during their meetings.

"Boss," she said now, her tone just a bit plaintive, "you know you've got a screwy sense of humor. Just look at what you put Ginny and Victor through, for God's sake! So, yeah, when you call me in for something like this, I've got to wonder whether or not you're trying to see if my leg will come off if you pull it hard enough."

"My sense of humor isn't the least bit screwy," he said with dignity. "Everyone *else's* sense of humor is. But in this particular instance, I'm serious as a heart attack, Danny."

"My God." Abrioux lowered her coffee cup, her smile fading. "You really *are*, aren't you?"

"I am, and I wish to hell I wasn't."

Abrioux felt her stomach congealing into a lump of frozen lead. She set her coffee cup down and pushed the saucer away from her.

"Let me get this straight, Kevin," she said very quietly. "You're telling me you think we may have gone back to war against the Manties not because *they* altered our diplomatic traffic, but because *we* did?"

"Yes." Usher's always deep voice sounded like a gravel crusher, and he inhaled deeply. "I'm not saying I'm convinced that's what happened, but I'm afraid it *may* be, Danny."

"Why?" she demanded.

"Partly because of Wilhelm's reports." Usher tipped back in his float chair. "We lost a lot of our best conduits when we took down Saint-Just's organization, but he's still got a few sources in place inside the Manty Foreign Office. Not as highly placed as they were, but high enough to have access to the sorts of insider shop talk permanent assistant undersecretaries get to hear. And according to them, everyone—*everyone*, from the top down—is convinced we did it."

"That may not indicate anything," Abrioux countered. "Putting something like this together successfully would have required very tight security. Not only that, but it would have been put together by the High Ridge Government, not the current one. So anyone who'd been in on it would probably be out of office by now, anyway."

"Agreed. But the people who are so thoroughly convinced *we're* the heavies of this particular piece are the people who *replaced* High Ridge's cronies. Every other bit of gossip Wilhelm's sources have given us only confirms the utter contempt they have for their immediate predecessors. If there were even the tiniest sniff of a possibility that anyone in the High Ridge crowd had been responsible for this, *someone* would have picked up on it by now. You know as well as I do there are always conspiracy theorists hiding in the woodwork, Danny. Combine that with the blinding rage most of Manticore feels for anyone remotely associated with the High Ridge Government, and one of those theorists would certainly have pounced on any possibility, even if it was only as one of those shivery 'no-shit' urban legends to share over a coffee break. And no one's dropped a single word about it. Not one."

"Hmmm . . . ." Abrioux plucked at her lower lip, then shrugged. "Maybe. But I've gotta tell you, Boss, it sounds mighty flimsy."

"I said that was part of the reason," Usher reminded her. "There are other factors—straws in the wind, you might say. One is how well I know the players on our side."

"Boss, I hate Giancola's guts myself. And I wouldn't be too surprised at anything he did. But much as I might like him as the baddie for this one, I think you're reaching. First of all, he's smart. He has to know that sooner or later whoever wins this war's going to get her hands on the other side's diplomatic archives. Second, however much I may despise and distrust him, I don't see even him as deliberately starting a war just to serve his own personal political ambitions. Especially not when there's no way to be sure we're going to *win* the damned thing. And, third, how the hell could he have pulled it off without *someone* else at State realizing he'd altered the original notes?"

"I never said he was stupid," Usher said mildly. "And taking your first and second points together, I also never said he deliberately set out to start a war. If my more paranoid suspicions are on track, what he wanted was to create a crisis he could then successfully 'resolve' as a demonstration of his own competence and tough-mindedness to strengthen his hand when *he* runs for the presidency a few years down the road. If he'd managed to pull off what I think he was after, there wouldn't have been a war, and neither side would have access to the other's archives. At the very least, it would probably have been decades before anyone had a chance to compare originals."

"Maybe so, but there's still the question of how he could have pulled it off." Abrioux shook her head. "Somehow he'd have had to alter at least the Manty originals after they were received and logged in. And given what the Manties have published as their version of *our* correspondence, he would have had to alter that from the version the President and the rest of the Cabinet had seen before it was sent, as well."

"Altering the outgoing correspondence wouldn't have been difficult," Usher responded. "He has personal, direct access to the traffic. He's the Secretary of State, after all! And he also has access to the State Department's internal recordkeeping, chip-shredding, and security systems. And, yes," he waved one hand, cutting off her interruption, "I know he still should have stubbed his toe after the Manties published their version of the documents. After all, our 'Special Envoy' also had access to the documents actually delivered to Manticore. He must know whether or not what they've published matches the notes he actually delivered. And Mr. Grosclaude hasn't said a word to indicate they did. Which means that either the documents they're publishing are, indeed, false, or . . ."

"Or else Grosclaude was in on it, too." Abrioux's dark eyes narrowed thoughtfully, and Usher nodded.

"Exactly. And Yves Grosclaude and Arnold Giancola go way back together. It's only reasonable that the Secretary of State would have picked a special envoy in whom he had complete faith, of course. But what, exactly, did he have faith Grosclaude would do for him?"

"Jesus." Abrioux rubbed her forearms as if she'd felt a sudden chill. But then she frowned again.

"Okay, granted he could have altered the outgoing correspondence, and, assuming Grosclaude really was willing to put it all on the line for him, he could have gotten away with that part of it. But what about the *Manty* notes? Surely they all carried the proper authentication codes!"

"Which is why I called you in," Usher said grimly. "I've had to be very circumspect, but last week I finally got my own hands on a copy of one of the original Manty notes."

"Wait a minute." Abrioux looked at him with the beginning of genuine alarm. "*Got your hands* on a copy? Why the hell didn't you just ask for one? As I recall, you and the President are supposed to be on pretty good terms, Boss. So exactly whose back are we sneaking around behind *this* time?"

"Oh, be serious, Danny!" Usher snorted explosively. "Eloise—and LePic and Tom Theisman—are all absolutely dead serious about the 'rule of law.' Well, so am I. But we're not really there yet. And think about the military and diplomatic implications of what we're talking about here. If I asked Eloise for access to the original diplomatic correspondence, I'd have to tell her why I wanted it. She probably trusts me—and *distrusts* Giancola—enough to give me the access. But then she has to take official cognizance of what I suspect. So does she just quietly give me the access I'm not supposed to have without State's knowledge and approval or the congressional oversight the Constitution mandates, or does she order LePic to begin a full-press covert investigation? And what happens if and when word leaks that one of our own Cabinet secretaries may actually have created a completely falsified diplomatic exchange which prompted us to go back to war against Manticore? At the very least, it would probably cripple her administration, and the possibilities go steadily downhill from there. At the moment, exactly two people know what I suspect, and we're both in this office right now. And until I'm in a position to tell Eloise something definitive, one way or the other, this stays a completely unofficial, unacknowledged, totally 'black' investigation. Is that clearly understood?"

"Yes, Sir," Abrioux said with unwonted formality. His hard eyes held hers for several seconds, and then he grimaced in satisfaction.

"Didn't mean to sound hard-assed about it," he said, "but this is one operation we literally cannot afford to have go public until we've dotted all the i's and crossed all the t's."

"I see you haven't lost your gift for understatement, Boss," Abrioux said dryly. "But you were about to say something about the Manty authentication codes?"

"I was about to say that the fact the dispatches did carry proper Manty authentication actually tends to reinforce my original suspicions."

Abrioux looked confused, and he chuckled. It was a remarkably humorless sound.

"There are a lot of things I'm officially not supposed to know about, Danny," he said. "In particular, the President—and Congress—were remarkably clear about the cast-iron firewall they want between our domestic police agencies and our espionage activities. Hard to blame them, with InSec and StateSec's horrible examples. And, in principle, I couldn't agree with them more. That's why I'm being so careful to establish the official precedent of respecting that firewall. Whoever takes over this chair after me is going to be stuck with it, and rightly so. But given the incredibly tangled can of worms StateSec left us with, it's literally impossible to draw those neat dividing lines this soon. So I've got my *unofficial* and personal feelers spread as wide as I can get them, which is how I came across an interesting tidbit of information."

"Which was?" she demanded just a bit testily as he paused.

"Which was that shortly before Citizen Chairman Saint-Just had that unfortunate encounter with a pulser dart, StateSec actually managed to steal the Manties' Foreign Office key. Not the Foreign Secretary herself's, but they did get the *departmental* key."

"You're joking!"

"No, I'm not." He shook his head. "I'm just guessing, since I don't have access to the full case files on the operation, but I suspect StateSec had planted someone on Descroix years ago. God knows she was twisty enough she might actually have knowingly allowed them to, if she thought it might give her some advantage. New Kiev might be an idiot, but she's a principled idiot, and I doubt they could have gotten anyone deeply enough into her confidence to have the necessary access. But when High Ridge shuffled his Cabinet after accepting the cease-fire, whoever they already had in place on Descroix managed to get them a physical copy of the key."

"Which made it the current key," Abrioux said.

"Exactly. They changed keys when Descroix took over from New Kiev. And if Giancola had the right contacts, he could have found out we had the key. You know we've still got open back doors all through our security systems, Danny. There's no telling who he might know who might have had that information or been able to hack it for him."

"But you haven't established that someone *did*, have you, Boss?"

"No. Not yet. That's one of the entertaining little chores I had in mind to drop on *you*."

"Golly gee, thanks," she said, and her forehead creased in thought.

"Even if I manage to establish that," she went on after a moment, "the mere fact he had access to the key wouldn't prove he actually did anything with it."

"It might. Or, at least, it would be highly suggestive. Enough so for me to feel confident about showing probable cause."

"How?"

"Because the *only* key the original diplomatic note I saw carried was the one we've managed to compromise," Usher said grimly. "It's not unheard of for a note, even a high-level one, not to carry the Foreign Secretary's personal key, but it *is* unusual. So suppose we're able to establish that Giancola had, in his possession, the general key. And suppose we go back and examine all of the disputed correspondence and we find that *none* of the Manty originals carried Descroix's personal key?"

"Probable cause out the ying-yang," Abrioux said softly.

"Bingo." Usher raised his coffee cup in ironic salute, took a sip, and then smiled thinly at her.

"So, Special Senior Inspector Abrioux, just how do you plan to begin your totally unauthorized, off-the-record, rogue investigation?"

Chapter Fifteen

"Well, it's about time," Mercedes Brigham said with profound satisfaction as the superdreadnought *Imperator* grew steadily through the pinnace's viewport. "I was beginning to think we'd *never* get this fleet activated!"

Brigham sat beside Honor, next to the hatch, and Honor nodded in silent agreement with her chief of staff as she studied the ponderous mountain of battle steel drifting against the stars, glittering with the brilliant pinpricks of its own riding lights. HMS *Imperator* was a far cry from Honor's last flagship. The better part of two megatons larger, massively armored, without the hatch-studded flanks of a CLAC. One of the new *Invictus*-class ships, *Imperator* was one of the dozen or so most powerful warships in existence. Unfortunately, her class was also far smaller than originally projected, thanks to all the incomplete *Invictuses* which had been destroyed in their building slips in Grendelsbane.

The other five units of her squadron—two more *Invictus*-class ships, and three of the older but still formidable *Medusa*-class SD(P)s—orbited San Martin in company with the fleet flagship. Just beyond *Imperator*, she saw HMS *Intransigent*, Alistair McKeon's squadron flagship, and she smiled fondly at the sight. If anyone deserved a flag, it was certainly Alistair, she thought. And she couldn't think of anyone she would rather have watching her back.

Her pinnace decelerated to a halt relative to *Imperator*, then rolled on its gyros as the superdreadnought's boat bay tractors locked on. They drew the small craft steadily in, then deposited it with scarcely a tremor in the docking arms. The boarding tube ran out to mate with the hatch collar, and the service umbilicals extended themselves and locked into the proper receptacles aboard the pinnace as Honor gazed through the transparent armorplast of the boat bay gallery at the waiting side party.

"Good seal," the flight engineer informed the flight deck crew, studying her panel.

"Crack the hatch," the pilot replied, and the hatch slid open.

Brigham climbed out of her seat, moved into the aisle, then stood waiting while Honor got up, lifted Nimitz to her shoulder, and started for the hatch. The Royal Manticoran Navy's tradition that the most senior officer boarded last and disembarked first was ironclad . . . for most people, at least, she thought with a slight grimace. As usual, things weren't quite that simple for Steadholder Harrington, but she'd won at least one concession from LaFollet. She got to swim the tube first, *then* her armsmen broke into the traditional disembarkment queue.

She tasted Nimitz's excitement and anticipation, like an echo of her own, as she swept gracefully through the tube's zero gravity. She caught the grab bar at the far end and swung through the interface with the ship's gravity with the smoothness of decades of experience. She landed in precisely the right spot, just outside the painted line on the deck which indicated the official beginning of HMS *Imperator*.

"Eighth Fleet, designate, arriving!" the intercom announced as the electronic bosun's pipes began to wail, and the side party snapped stiffly to attention, Marines presenting their bayoneted pulse rifles with parade ground precision.

"Permission to come aboard, Ma'am?" Honor requested formally of the senior-grade lieutenant with the brassard of the boat bay officer of the deck.

"Permission granted, Ma'am," the lieutenant replied, saluting crisply, and Honor returned the salute then stepped past her, down the avenue between the rows of side boys to where Rafael Cardones stood waiting.

"Welcome aboard, Your Grace," he said, reaching out to shake her hand as the bosun's pipes sounded again for Mercedes Brigham behind her.

"Thank you, Captain," she said, observing the formalities, but her eyes gleamed. Rafael Cardones had changed in a great many ways from the youngster she'd first met, but she could still taste his little-boy excitement and pride in his new command, and he grinned as he glanced at her own white beret.

"Congratulations, 'Captain' Harrington." It was the first time he'd seen her since she'd been formally named *Unconquered*'s CO. "It seems we both have new ships, Your Grace."

"I suppose we do," she agreed, glancing around the spacious, spotless boat bay. "And yours looks beautiful, Rafe," she added in a softer voice, and his teeth flashed in a broad smile.

"Not as nimble as *Werewolf* or a battlecruiser, Ma'am," he said, "but she's still got that new-air car smell. Among other things."

"So I understand," she agreed, turning to stand beside him and watch the arrival of the remainder of her staff. It took a while, and—not for the first time—she thought the Navy could have gotten things done more quickly if it wasn't quite so enamored of proper procedures, formalities, and traditions. Of course, then it wouldn't have *been* the Navy.

"Would you care to be shown to your quarters, Ma'am?" Cardones asked after everyone had joined her.

"I would like to see them," Honor replied, "but we might as well get the rest of the official business out of the way first. Are all of the squadron commanders aboard?"

"Admiral Henke is still in transit, Ma'am," he said. "Her ETA is about six minutes. She sent her apologies, but she was delayed aboard Admiral Kuzak's flagship."

"Well, I don't imagine I'll have her shot just yet," Honor said judiciously. "But if she's that close to arriving, would you object to waiting for her here and going up to Flag Bridge together after she arrives?"

"Of course not, Ma'am," Cardones replied. "In fact, if you wouldn't mind, we might use that time introducing you to some of my own senior officers."

"I'd appreciate that," she said, and he turned to the officers standing behind him.

"This is Commander Hirshfield, my XO," he said, indicating a tall, slender, red-haired officer who extended her right hand. Hirshfield's blue eyes were frankly curious as she met Honor's gaze, but her handclasp was firm and Honor liked the taste of tough, professional competence the other woman exuded.

"Commander," she said.

"Welcome aboard, Your Grace," Hirshfield replied. "If there's anything you need, just let me know."

Honor nodded, and Cardones turned to the next officer in line.

"Commander Yolanda Harriman, Your Grace. My Tactical Officer."

"Commander." Honor shook the proffered hand firmly. Harriman, despite her surname, obviously had at least as much Old Earth Oriental in her genotype as Honor herself. The tactical officer was dark-eyed and dark-haired, with eyes so brown they were almost black and a delicate sandalwood complexion. She also radiated a certain subtle ferocity. That was the only word Honor could come up with. This was obviously a woman who had found her proper niche.

"Welcome aboard, Your Grace," Harriman said, smiling with perfect white teeth. "If the newsies know what they're talking about, I'm sure you'll be able to scare up enough action to keep us all busy."

"It seems likely," Honor agreed mildly. "Not that you want to believe everything you read in the 'faxes."

"No, Ma'am. Of course not," Harriman said, but her eyes dropped to the medal ribbons on Honor's chest, and Honor felt a slight twinge of alarm. The last thing she wanted in a tactical officer was someone who still believed in glory. She started to say something else, then stopped, smiled again, and turned her head as Cardones indicated the next officer in the queue.

"Commander Thompson, my Engineer," he said. Thompson was red-haired and wiry, and Honor's smile grew much broader as she saw him.

"Well, well, Glenn!" she said. "It's been quite a while, hasn't it?"

"Yes, Your Grace, it has," he agreed, and Cardones raised one eyebrow inquiringly.

"Glenn made his snotty cruise aboard *Hawkwing* a few more years ago than either of us would like to remember, Captain," Honor explained. "At the time," she continued with a wicked twinkle, "he was the despair of Lieutenant Hunter, our Engineer. Apparently he's managed to sort out the widgets from the gizmos since then."

"Almost, Your Grace," Thompson said with a slightly worried

expression. "I still get them confused once in a while, but, for-tunately, I've got really good assistants to keep me straight."

Honor chuckled and touched him lightly on the shoulder, then turned to the lieutenant commander standing beside him.

"Commander Neukirch, our Astrogator."

"Commander."

Honor shook the offered hand. Neukirch was probably in her mid-thirties. It was often difficult to tell, especially without knowing which generation of prolong therapy someone had received. In Neukirch's case it was rendered more difficult because she was one of the minority of female Manticoran officers who had chosen to completely depilate her head. The severe style contrasted with her sensual lips and exotically planed features, and her eyes—a curiously neutral shade of gray—studied Honor almost warily.

Honor held her hand a moment longer than she had held Hirshfield's or Thompson's, and her own eyes narrowed as she tasted the other woman's emotions. There was a peculiar combina-tion of apprehension, or perhaps anxiety, coupled with an oddly focused, burning sense of anticipation and curiosity.

"Have we met, Commander?" Honor asked.

"Uh, no, Your Grace," she said hastily. She seemed to hesitate, then smiled tautly. "You did meet my father once, though. The same time Glenn did."

Honor frowned, then her eyes widened.

"Yes, Your Grace," Neukirch said more naturally. "Father stayed in the Star Kingdom after Casimir."

"And took Dr. Neukirch's surname," Honor said, nodding.

"Yes, Your Grace. He's spoken of you often over the years. When he heard *Imperator* was going to be your flagship, he asked me to remember him to you and to extend his thanks once more."

"Tell him I'm honored he remembered," Honor said, "and that while I appreciate his thanks, they aren't necessary. It's obvious," she smiled at the younger woman, "that he—and you—have amply repaid me and the Star Kingdom."

Neukirch's face blossomed in a huge smile of pleasure, and Honor turned to the next officer in the queue, who wore the uniform of the Royal Manticoran Marines.

"Major Lorenzetti, commanding our Marine detachment," Cardones said.

"Major." Honor shook Lorenzetti's hand, liking what she saw and what she tasted of his mind-glow. Lorenzetti was a typical Marine, who reminded her strongly of Tomas Ramirez. He was much shorter and nowhere near as broad, built on merely mortal lines, but he had that same no-nonsense tenacity.

"Major," she acknowledged, and he surprised her by bending over her hand. His lips just brushed its back in a formal Grayson-style greeting, and then he straightened.

"Your Grace." His voice was deep and resonant, and he smiled at her. "Since I appear to be one of the minority of officers in the ship who hasn't already met you, Your Grace, perhaps I should point out that I spent two T-years in the Masada Contingent. They weren't the most pleasant tour I ever pulled, but after seeing that planet—and comparing it to Grayson—I can only say that if anyone's navy ever needed its sorry ass kicked, it was Masada's."

"The Major, as you can see, like all Marines, is particularly eloquent," Cardones said dryly, and Honor chuckled.

"So I noticed," she said. "Although, on balance, I'd have to agree with his sentiments. When were you there, Major?"

"I transferred back to Fleet duty last year, Your Grace," Lorenzetti said in a much more serious tone.

"I've often considered visiting Masada myself. Colonel LaFollet here—" she gestured at her senior armsman "—doesn't seem to feel that would be the smartest decision I ever made, however."

"On balance," Lorenzetti replied, deliberately using her own choice of phrase, "I'd have to agree with him, Your Grace. Things have improved a lot just in the time since I was first stationed there, but there's still a nasty underground ticking away. And, with all due respect, you're probably one of the three or four people they'd most like to assassinate. The real fanatics would pull out all the stops if they knew *you* were coming."

"I know," she sighed, then smiled at the Marine and turned to the final officer awaiting introduction.

"Commander Morrison, Your Grace. Our surgeon," Cardones said, and Honor gripped the slender, fair-haired lieutenant commander's hand. Morrison was probably the oldest of Cardones' officers, and she felt . . . solid. There was something profoundly reassuring about her calm assurance and confidence in her own competence.

"Dr. Morrison," she murmured, and the physician smiled and bobbed her head.

"I'm pleased to meet all of you," Honor continued, meeting their combined gaze. "I know there's something of a tradition of rivalry between a flagship's officers and the admiral's staff, and up to a point, that's probably not a bad thing. However, it's been my experience that the flagship's personnel are just as vital as the staff if a squadron or a task force is going to operate smoothly. Commodore Brigham here," she waved Brigham forward, "and I have discussed that very consideration, and if any difficulties do arise, I want them resolved as expeditiously as possible. I think you'll find Commodore Brigham is much more interested in results than in assigning blame when problems do arise."

Everyone smiled and nodded with murmurs of understanding. Well, of course they did, given that any admiral's suggestion carried the force of a direct decree from God aboard her flagship . . . however stupid it might be. In this case, however, Honor tasted genuine agreement behind the proper formula, which gave her a pronounced sense of satisfaction.

"Excuse me, Captain," the BBOD said, interrupting diffidently, "but Admiral Henke's pinnace is on final."

"Thank you," Cardones responded, and Honor turned to watch the side party reassemble itself smoothly.

The newly arrived pinnace settled into the docking arms, the tube ran out, and the green light indicating a good seal blinked to life over the inboard end.

"BatCruRon Eighty-One, arriving!" the intercom announced, and a moment later an ebony-skinned woman in the uniform of a rear admiral swung herself lithely out of the tube into the twitter of pipes.

"Permission to come aboard, Ma'am?" she requested of the BBOD in a husky, almost furry-sounding contralto.

"Permission granted, Ma'am," the lieutenant replied, exchanging salutes, and the new arrival stepped forward quickly.

"Welcome aboard, Ma'am," Cardones said, shaking her hand.

"Thank you, Rafe," she said with a smile, which grew considerably broader when she turned to Honor.

"It's good to see you back in uniform, Your Grace," she said, gripping Honor's hand firmly, then nodded to LaFollet. "And I see you've brought along your baseball fanatic."

"Nonsense," Honor said airily. "By Grayson standards, he's a mere dilettante. Now, Simon, here—he's a *real* fan. Unlike myself, of course."

"Oh, of course!" Henke chuckled.

"I believe all of the squadron COs are aboard now, Your Grace," Cardones said.

"So we should get out of your boat bay crew's way and take ourselves off to Flag Bridge," Honor agreed.

"Attention on deck," Vice Admiral Alice Truman, as the senior officer present, said as Honor stepped through the flag briefing room's hatch, and the officers who had been seated around the large conference table rose.

"As you were, Ladies and Gentlemen," Honor said briskly, striding into the compartment and crossing to the head of the table. She seated herself and laid her white beret neatly in front of her.

Henke, Cardones, and her staff followed her, and as they found their chairs and the other officers settled back into their places, she let her eyes run around the table.

It was as near to a hand-picked command team as anyone was likely to be able to come under the current circumstances. Alice Truman, Alistair McKeon, and Michelle Henke—commanding her carriers, her "wall of battle" (such as it was, and what there was of it), and her most powerful battlecruiser squadron, respectively— were all known quantities. Vice Admiral Samuel Miklós commanded the second of Eighth Fleet's two CLAC squadrons—Truman herself commanded the other, as well as the entire carrier force—and Rear Admiral Matsuzawa Hirotaka commanded Honor's second battlecruiser squadron. Rear Admiral Winston Bradshaw and Commodore Charise Fanaafi commanded her two heavy cruiser squadrons, and Commodore Mary Lou Moreau commanded her attached flotilla of light cruisers, while Captain Josephus Hastings was present as her senior destroyer captain.

She knew Matsuzawa and Moreau personally, although not well; Miklós, Bradshaw, Fanaafi, and Hastings were complete newcomers to her command team, but all of them had excellent records. Perhaps even more importantly, given the nature of their mission, all of them had already demonstrated flexibility, adaptiveness, and the ability to display intelligent initiative.

"It's good to see all of you gathered in one place at last," she said, after a moment. "And, as Commodore Brigham commented as we docked with *Imperator*, it's about time. Eighth Fleet is officially activated as of twelve hundred hours, Zulu, today."

No one actually moved, but it was as if an invisible stir had run around the compartment.

"We can anticipate the arrival of the remaining units of our initial order of battle over the next three weeks," she continued levelly. "We're all aware of how tightly the Navy is stretched at the moment, so we won't dwell on that just now. I met with Admiral Caparelli immediately before my departure for Trevor's Star, however, and he emphasized to me once again the importance of beginning active operations as quickly as possible.

"Commodore Brigham, Captain Jaruwalski, and I have given considerable thought to the most appropriate initial targets for our attention. This isn't simply a military operation. Or, rather, it's a military operation with a political dimension of which we must be well aware. Specifically, we want the Havenites to divert forces to provide rear security against our raids. That means balancing vulnerability of target against economic and industrial value, but it also requires us to think about which target systems are most likely to generate political pressure to divert enemy strike forces to *defensive* employment.

"I'm confident we can find such targets, but accomplishing our objective is almost certainly going to require us to operate widely dispersed attack forces, at least in our initial operations. That means we're going to be relying very heavily on the judgment and ability of our junior flag officers—more heavily than we'd originally anticipated. I know the quality of my squadron commanders, but I'm less familiar with your divisional commanders, and, unfortunately, the pressure to begin operations is going to sharply restrict the time we have to get to know one another through exercises. Which means, of course, that I'm going to be relying heavily on all of you to provide the insight about your subordinates which I won't have time to develop for myself."

Several heads nodded, and every expression was sober and intent.

"In just a moment, Commodore Brigham and Commander Reynolds will brief all of us on current intelligence, enemy strength appreciations, and the parameters the Admiralty's set forth for our target selection criteria. Afterwards, I'll ask all of you to return to your flagships and bring your own staffs up to speed. Get them started brainstorming. This evening, I'd like all of you—and your chiefs of staff and operations officers—to join me for dinner."

McKeon, Truman, and Henke looked at one another expressionlessly, and Honor smiled.

"Bring your appetites," she said, "because I think you'll find the food quite good. But plan on staying out late, Ladies and Gentlemen. It's going to be a working dinner. Probably the first of many."

"Could I have a minute?"

Honor turned her head to look at Michelle Henke, and her eyebrows rose as she tasted the edge of apprehension and frustration behind the question. The other flag officers were flowing through the briefing room hatch, and she glanced at Brigham. She flipped her eyes to one side, and the chief of staff caught the silent order and discreetly urged her other staffers towards the hatch as well.

"Of course you can have a minute, Mike," Honor said, turning back to Henke. "Why?"

She allowed a touch of concern to soften her own voice. Henke was one of the people who'd realized long since that Honor could actually feel the emotions of people around her, so there was no point pretending she didn't know her friend was concerned about something. Henke's lips twitched in a brief smile of half-amused recognition, but the smile barely touched her eyes.

"Something came to my attention the other day," she said quietly. "Specifically, the circumstances which led to my being given the Eighty-First."

There was something oddly formal about her tone, and Honor frowned slightly.

"What about it?"

"According to my sources, I got the command because you specifically asked for it for me," Henke said, and looked at her steadily.

Honor looked back, and tried not to sigh. She'd hoped Henke wouldn't hear about that. Not that there'd ever been much realistic chance she wouldn't.

"That's not exactly how it happened, Mike," she said after a moment.

"Honor, let's not quibble over words like 'exactly.' *Did* you pull strings to get me the command?"

Honor gazed at her for a moment longer, then glanced around the compartment. Everyone had departed except Andrew LaFollet and Mercedes Brigham.

"Mercedes, Andrew," she said, "could you give us a minute, please?"

"Of course, My Lady," LaFollet replied, and he and the chief of staff stepped outside. Honor waited until the hatch slid closed behind them, then turned back to Henke.

"All right, Mike," she sighed. "Just how difficult do you intend to be about this?"

"Honor," Henke began, "you know how hard I've fought against playing the patronage game. It's important to me that—"

"Michelle Henke," Honor interrupted, "in this particular regard, you are the most stubborn, stiffnecked, prickly, hyper-sensitive person I've ever met. And I remind you that I know my own parents, Nimitz, and your cousin Elizabeth, so you're in some pretty select company for stubbornness."

"It's not a joke," Henke said, almost angrily, and Honor shook her head.

"No, it's not," she said. "And by this stage in your career, Mike, it's gone a long way past funny, too." Henke's eyes widened at the sudden severity of Honor's tone, and Honor grimaced. "Have you ever seen the 'Confidential Notes' section of your personnel jacket?" she asked.

"Of course not." Henke looked surprised by the apparent *non sequitur*. "That's why it's marked 'Confidential,' isn't it?"

"Yes, it is. And I'm not surprised it's never even occurred to you to bend the rules in this particular regard. But, if you *had* read it, you'd discover that BuPers has noted this particular phobia of yours. There's a specific notation, Mike, which says—and I paraphrase—'This officer is of superior quality but not prepared for accelerated promotion.'"

Something like hurt flickered in Henke's eyes, and Honor snorted in exasperation.

"You're not listening to what I said, Mike. It doesn't say 'not qualified'; it says 'not *prepared*.' As in 'not prepared to accept.'

Everyone knows you're the Queen's first cousin. Everyone knows you've always stomped all over anything which even *looked* like preferential treatment. We *understand* that, Mike. What *you* don't seem to understand is that a flag officer's chair would have been pulled out for you at least four or five T-years before it was if BuPers hadn't realized you would have *thought* it was because of who you're related to. *And* that you're so stubborn you'd probably have resigned your commission rather than accept 'preferential treatment.'"

"That's ridiculous," Henke protested.

"No, it isn't. What's ridiculous is that you've managed to slow your career and to deprive the Star Kingdom of the full value of your skills and talents because in this one regard you—you, Mike Henke, Ms. I-Know-What-I'm-Doing, Brash-and-Confident—suffer from a serious self-confidence crisis. Well, as it happens, I'm not prepared to put up with that sort of silliness any longer."

"Honor, you can't—"

"I not only can, I *have*," Honor said flatly. "Look at the record, Mike. Of our graduating class, thirty percent have attained at least junior flag rank; another forty percent are captains, over half of them senior-grade; and fifteen percent are dead or medically retired. Are you seriously going to tell me that if you were another officer, evaluating your record and your performance, you wouldn't rate your command ability as being in the top thirty percent of our classmates? You do remember some of the idiots who graduated at the same time we did, don't you?"

Henke's lips twitched at the acid tone in which Honor delivered her last sentence, but she also shook her head.

"I'm not saying I'm not qualified to be a commodore, or even a rear admiral. What bothers me is that I just got command of the one and only squadron of pod-laying battlecruisers in the entire Royal Navy. If you aren't aware of how cutthroat competition for this slot was, I certainly am."

"Of course I'm aware. And before you go any further, I should point out to you that I was promised that squadron for Eighth Fleet *before* I submitted my list of requested squadron commanders. I was getting those ships whether I got you or not, and when I asked for you and Hirotaka, you were senior. Which is why *Admiral Cortez* suggested you for the Eighty-First when I inquired as to whether or not your services were available. And before you say it, I'm quite certain that one reason he made the suggestion was the fact that he knew about our friendship. But you know as well as I do that Sir Lucian is not exactly in the habit of suggesting incompetent officers for critical slots just to curry favor with politically important people."

Honor folded her arms, and Nimitz rose high on her shoulder, cocking his head at Henke.

"Bottom-line time, Mike. Yes, you could say I 'pulled strings' to get you assigned to Eighth Fleet, knowing it would probably mean you got the Eighty-First. And, yes, I did it on purpose, and I'd do it again. But if you think for one single moment that I would have requested *anyone* for this command if I didn't believe she was the very best person available for it, regardless of friendship, then you don't know me as well as you think you do. Or, for that matter, as well as *I* think you do, when you aren't bending over backward to make sure no one does you 'any favors.'"

Henke looked at her, and Honor tasted that stubborn sense of integrity and the need to prove she merited any promotion that came her way warring with her intellectual recognition that everything Honor had just said was the simple truth. Then, finally, the other woman sighed.

"All right, Honor. You win. I'm still not entirely comfortable with it, you understand. But I have to admit I really, really don't want to give it up, however I got it."

"Fine. I can live with that," Honor told her with a smile. "And if *you* still entertain any doubts about it, then I suggest you use those doubts as a self-motivator to go out and prove to both of us that you really do deserve it."

Chapter Sixteen

"Lady Harrington is here, Milady."

"Thank you, Sandy." Emily Alexander looked up at her nurse's announcement. Her life-support chair was parked in her favorite niche in her atrium, and she tapped the save key with her right index finger, saving the HD script she'd been annotating. "Please ask her to join me," she said.

"Of course, Milady."

Thurston bowed slightly and withdrew. A few moments later, she returned, followed by Dr. Allison Harrington.

Not for the first time, Emily felt a certain amusement at the thought that such a tiny mother could have produced a daughter Honor's size. There was something undeniably feline about Allison Harrington, she thought. Something poised, perpetually balanced and faintly amused by the world about her. Not *detached*—never that—but comfortable enough with who *she* was to let the rest of the world be whatever it needed to be. She didn't really look that much like Honor, and yet no one could ever mistake her for anyone but Honor's mother. It was the eyes, Emily thought. The one feature which was exactly identical in both mother and daughter.

"Good afternoon, Lady Harrington," Emily said as Thurston smiled and withdrew, leaving them alone together, and Allison rolled those almond-shaped eyes very much as Honor might have.

"Please, Lady Alexander," she said. Emily cocked an eyebrow, and Allison snorted. "I'm from Beowulf, Milady," she said, "and

I married a yeoman. Until my daughter fell into bad company, it never occurred to me I might be even remotely associated with the Manticoran aristocracy, far less the Grayson version. If you insist on using titles, I'd much prefer 'Doctor,' since that's at least a title I earned on my own. Under the circumstances, however, if it's all the same to you, I'd prefer simply Allison."

"I see where Honor gets it from," Emily said with a faint smile. "But if you'd prefer to ignore aristocratic titles, that's certainly all right with me. After all," her smile broadened, "as the mother of a duchess and a steadholder, you outrank me rather substantially."

"Bullshit," Allison said pithily, and Emily chuckled.

"All right, Allison. You win. And in that case, I'm Emily, not 'Milady.' "

"Fine." Allison shook her head, her expression almost bemused for a moment. "I suppose any parent always wants her daughter to do well and succeed, but I sometimes think I must have dropped Honor on her head when she was a baby. The girl has an absolute compulsion to overachieve, however inconvenient it may be for her father and me."

"And you're inordinately proud of her, too," Emily observed.

"Well, of course I am. At least, when I'm not spending my time sitting up at night worrying over what sort of insane risk she's going to run next."

Allison's tone was light, amused, but there was a sudden flash of darker emotion in those chocolate eyes, and Emily felt her own smile waver.

"She does tend to make the people who love her worry," she said quietly. "I'll be honest, Allison. I was never so glad of anything as I was when the Queen asked Hamish to take over at the Admiralty. I know he hated it, but having both of them out in space, waiting to be shot at, would be even worse."

"I know." Allison seated herself on a stone bench—the one Honor usually used when she joined Emily in the atrium—and met Emily's eyes steadily. "I realize the timing on this entire situation is as 'interesting,' in the Chinese sense of the word, as anything else Honor's ever gotten herself into. And I obviously don't know you very well . . . yet. But I hope you won't mind my saying that in many ways, Hamish and you are the best thing that's happened to Honor at least since Paul Tankersley was killed.

I hope it's a good thing for you, too, but I'm selfish enough to be happy for her anyway."

"She's very young, isn't she?" Emily replied obliquely, and Allison smiled.

"I'm sure she doesn't see it that way at her age, but in a lot of ways, you're right. And she's very Sphinxian, too. I, on the other hand, am an experienced old lady from the decadent world of Beowulf. By way of Grayson these days, of all bizarre places."

"I know. On the other hand, I won't pretend it was easy for me. Certainly not at first. But there's a quality, a magnetism, about your daughter, Allison. Charisma, I suppose you'd have to call it, although she never seems to realize she's got it. You don't meet very many people who do have it, actually. And she's just as striking physically. Most of the professional dancers I knew back when I was still acting would have killed to be able to move the way she does. In fact," she smiled, "if I weren't stuck in this chair, I suspect I'd be just as physically attracted to her as Hamish is." That wasn't an admission Emily would have made even to most members of her own social class, but as Allison had just pointed out, she *was* from Beowulf. "Even without that, though, she's an incredibly lovable person, in her own way. And so damned determined to never put herself first that sometimes you just want to strangle her."

"She gets it from her father," Allison said cheerfully. "All that altruism." She shook her head. "My own philosophy's much more hedonistic than hers."

"I'm sure." Emily smiled. "Which undoubtedly explains, in some convoluted fashion, what brings you to White Haven this afternoon?"

"Well, even a card-carrying hedonist is usually willing to exert herself at least a little for her first grandchild."

Allison watched her hostess closely, but Emily's smile didn't waver.

"Somehow, I'm not surprised to hear that," she said. "But while we're on the subject, what's your *official* reason for being here? Just so we can keep our stories straight, you understand."

"Oh, *officially* I'm here for Doctor Arif. She's drafted me for her commission, as a representative of the medical profession who's as close to an expert on treecats as she can find. I kicked and screamed about how busy I am on Grayson, but it didn't do me much good. And, actually, it's fascinating watching Samantha and the other memory singers working with her to demonstrate their value. At the very least, it's going to revolutionize psychotherapy here in the Star Kingdom, and I think the implications for law enforcement may be at least equally significant. But for the official record, I'm here to talk to you—and Hamish, when he gets home this evening—about your experiences with Samantha for a paper I'm putting together. I'm supposed to present it to the commission next Wednesday."

"I see. And the real reason?"

"And the real reason is to talk to you about something else entirely," Allison said, her voice suddenly softer. Emily looked at her, and Allison shook her head.

"I'm not going to ask you how you feel about my daughter and your husband. First of all, that's not really any of my business. More importantly, even before I met you, I knew you were a strong-minded woman, not the sort to meekly acquiesce in anything against your will. But Honor didn't have time to complete all the arrangements with Briarwood before she had to deploy to Trevor's Star. Since I'm the official contact, with power of attorney to make medical decisions in her absence, I'm tidying up those loose ends for her. To be perfectly honest, Emily, this is something which I believe *you* ought to be allowed to do. And something which, under any other circumstances, I think Honor herself would have insisted you should."

Emily's eyes misted over, and she felt her lips tremble. Then she inhaled deeply.

"I wish I could," she said quietly. "More than I can ever tell you."

"My own personality, oddly enough for someone from Beowulf, is firmly monogamous," Allison said in a lighter tone. "I suppose it's part of my own rebellion against the mores of my birth world. But in your position," the lightness faded, "I know how badly *I'd* want to be making those decisions, discharging those responsibilities. And because of that, and because Honor feels exactly the same way, I'm here to ask you and Hamish to assist me with the environmental recordings."

Emily's eyebrows rose. One of the things about artificial gestation which the medical profession had learned the hard way was the necessity of providing the developing fetus with the physical and aural stimulation the child would have received in its mother's womb. Heartbeat, random environmental sounds, movement, and—most importantly of all, in many ways—the sound of its mother's voice.

"Honor and I have made selections from several of her letters to me and to her father," Allison continued. "She's also found time to record several hours of poetry and a few of her favorite childhood stories. And she insisted that my voice, and her father's, should also be included. Just as she very, very much wants her child to hear the voices of its father . . . and both its mothers."

Emily's expression froze. She looked at Allison for several seconds, unable to speak, and Allison smiled gently.

"She's told me in general terms how you reacted to the news of her pregnancy, Emily. And she's almost as much from Grayson as Manticore these days. Sometimes I don't think even she realizes how true that really is. But she's seen the strength of Grayson family structure, how nurturing it is, and she wants that for her—for *your*—child. And she loves you. She doesn't want it only for the child's sake; she wants it for your sake, as well."

"And she told Hamish they didn't deserve *me*," Emily said finally, her voice husky. "Of course we'll help with the recordings, Allison. Thank you."

"I'd say you were welcome, if there were any reason to thank me," Allison replied. "And on a lighter note, I trust you're prepared to come up with some reason for *me* to be spending inordinate amounts of time visiting you." Emily felt her eyebrows rising again, and Allison chuckled. "I intend to be a very involved grandmother, which means you're going to be seeing a lot of me over the next several decades."

Emily laughed.

"Oh, I'm sure we'll be able to come up with something. By now, devising plausible pretexts is getting to be second nature."

Allison started to reply, then paused, her expression suddenly pensive. Several seconds passed, and Emily frowned, wondering what direction the other woman's thoughts had gone.

"Actually," Allison said slowly, at last, "I think there might be a completely legitimate reason. One I hadn't really intended to suggest."

"That sounds faintly ominous," Emily said.

"Not ominous, I hope. But maybe a little . . . intrusive."

"*Definitely* ominous," Emily said as lightly as possible. "Given that you're the mother of the mother of my husband's child, anything that strikes you as being more intrusive than that is probably fairly terrifying."

"I wouldn't choose that precise adjective," Allison said seriously, "but I'm afraid it is going to be rather personal. And if you'd prefer not to discuss it, that's entirely your decision. But given what's happened accidentally between Hamish and Honor, Emily, I can't help wondering why you've never considered the possibility of having a child of your own."

Emily's heart seemed to stop. It couldn't, of course. Her life-support chair's hardware wouldn't let it, any more than it would let her stop breathing. But despite her brutally damaged nervous system, she felt for just a moment as if someone had just punched her in the pit of the stomach.

She stared at Allison, shocked, unable to speak, and Allison reached out and laid her own hand atop Emily's right hand.

"This is coming from me, not Honor," she said quietly. "Honor would never dream of intruding on you the way I just have. Partly, that's because she loves you and recognizes how much emotional stress she's already accidentally inflicted upon you. And partly, it's because she's so much younger than you—which I'm certainly not. And partly because she's not a physician. We've talked, especially since she found out she was pregnant, of course, but she hasn't betrayed any of your confidences to me, and I'd never ask her to. Still, I'm sure you must realize that as a doctor, and especially as a geneticist, I'm very well aware of all the reproductive options which have been available to you. And that, Emily, suggests to me that you must have some deeply personal reason for not availing yourself of them.

"That's your decision, of course. But Honor's told me how you responded to the discovery that *she's* going to have a child. And I've just seen how you reacted to the awareness that you're also going to be that child's other mother. So I'm wondering why someone who so clearly recognizes how *Honor* must feel, and who so obviously wants and needs to be a part of that, has never had a child of her own."

A part of Emily Alexander wanted to scream at Allison Harrington. To tell her that however *curious* she might be, it was none of her damned business. But she didn't. The combination of gentle, very personal compassion and professional detachment in Allison's eyes and voice stopped her.

Not that anything could have made the topic any less painful.

"I have my reasons," she said finally, her voice far more clipped and harder-edged than usual.

"I'm certain you do. You're a strong, smart, competent person. People like you don't turn their backs on something so obviously important to them without reasons. The thing I'm wondering, though, is whether they're as valid as you may think they are."

"It's not something I decided lightly," Emily said harshly.

"Emily," Allison's voice was gently chiding, "no woman can have gone through everything you've survived without realizing that the mere fact a decision wasn't made lightly doesn't necessarily make it a good one. I'm a doctor. I specialize in genetic disease and repair—too often after the fact, even today—and my husband's one of the Star Kingdom's three top neurosurgeons. The sort they send the 'Omigod!' cases to. If he'd been in civilian practice when you were hurt, he'd probably have been one of *your* doctors. Do you have any idea how much carnage, how many shattered lives and broken bodies, the two of us have seen? Between us, we've been practicing medicine for well over a century, Emily. If there are two people in the entire Star Kingdom who know exactly what you, your family, and all the people who care about you have been through, it's us."

Emily's lips trembled, and her single working hand clenched into a fist under Allison's fingers. She was shocked—physically shocked—at the abrupt realization that she desperately wanted to open her heart to Allison. By the discovery that she *needed* to know Allison did, indeed, understand the savagery with which the physical damage to her body had smashed far more than mere muscle and sinew.

And yet . . . and yet something held her back. Her own version of Honor's stubbornness and pride, her need to fight her own battles. As Allison had said, Emily Alexander was an extraordinarily intelligent woman. She'd had half a century in her life-support chair to realize just how foolish it was to insist on facing down all of her own demons, all her own challenges, unassisted. More than that, she knew she hadn't. That Hamish was there for her. That except for one brief period of weakness, which he bitterly regretted, he'd *always* been there for her, and she'd always relied upon him. But that was different. She couldn't have defined exactly how, yet she knew it was.

"Emily," Allison said again, quietly, as the silence stretched out between them, "you aren't as unique as you may think you are. Oh, the injuries you've survived probably *are*. At least, I can't think of another case in my own or Alfred's experience in which someone survived physical damage as extreme as it clearly was in yours. But people who are as badly injured as you were take damage in a lot of ways. Obviously, I've never had access to any of your case history. And I've never probed Honor for information about it—not that she'd have given it to me, even if I had. But I have to ask you. Like Honor, you don't regenerate. Is that the reason? Are you afraid a child of yours might share that inability?"

"I . . ." Emily's voice rasped, and she stopped and cleared her throat.

"That's . . . a part of it," she said finally, distantly amazed she could admit even that much to Allison. "I suppose I've always known it's not entirely . . . rational. As you say," her mouth twisted in a bitter smile, "the fact that someone has reasons for her decisions doesn't necessarily make those reasons valid."

"Did you ever discuss the question with a good geneticist?" Allison's gentle voice was completely devoid of any shadow of judgment.

"No." Emily looked away. "No, not really. I *consulted* several of them. But I suppose, if I were honest, I'd have to admit I was just going through the motions. For me, perhaps for Hamish. I don't know." She looked back at Allison, green eyes brimming with tears. "I talked to them. They talked to *me*. And they kept reassuring me, telling me it wouldn't happen. And that even if somehow I did pass on my 'curse,' it was absurd to think any child of mine would ever be injured the way I was. And none of it mattered. Not one bit of it." She stared into Allison's eyes and forced herself to admit to someone else what she had never until this moment fully admitted to herself. "I was too frightened to be rational."

She hovered on the brink of telling Allison why. Of telling her what she'd overheard her own mother saying. Of admitting how deep that wound had cut, even though her intellect had fiercely rejected the searing hurt. But she couldn't. Even now, she couldn't expose that jagged scar. Not yet.

"If that's the only way in which you reacted 'irrationally' after what happened to you, then you're some sort of superwoman," Allison said dryly. "My God, woman! Your life was *destroyed*. You've rebuilt a new one, a deeply productive one, without ever surrendering. You're entitled to not be strong about everything every instant. And you have the right to admit that it hurts, and that things frighten you. Someday you need to sit down with Honor and let her tell you about the things she carried around inside for far too long. The things she didn't share even with me. They've left scars—I'm sure you've seen some of them—and she'd be the very first person to say that everything that happened to her was small beer compared to what happened to *you*.

"But I think perhaps it's time you revisited that decision of yours. Perhaps enough time's finally passed that you *can* think about it rationally . . . if you want to."

"I think . . . I think, perhaps, I do," Emily said, very slowly, astonished at the words coming out of her own mouth. And even more astonished to realize how true they were.

"I think I do," she repeated, "but that doesn't magically dispel the things that frighten me."

"Maybe not, but then again," Allison grinned suddenly, "that's *my* job."

"Your job?" Emily looked at her, and Allison nodded.

"You know what Honor's been through in terms of physical injury. Nothing that's happened to her was as severe as what happened to you, but it was more than enough to make her worry about passing her inability to regenerate on to her children. Fortunately for her, her mother happens—if I may be pardoned for blowing my own horn—to be one of the Star Kingdom's leading geneticists. I made identifying the gene group which prevents her from regenerating a personal project, and I found it years ago. The problem child is a dominant, unfortunately, but it's not associated with the locked sequences of the Meyerdahl modifications—if it were, Alfred wouldn't regenerate either, and he does—so it's not automatically selected for at fertilization. Once I'd determined that, I also determined that she carries it only on the chromosome she received from her father, and I've done a scan on her child. As a result of which, I was able to reassure her that she hasn't passed it along to him."

"*Him?*" Despite her own whiplashing emotions, Emily fastened on the personal pronoun.

"Oh, crap!" Allison shook her head, her expression suddenly disgusted. "Forget you heard that," she commanded. "Honor doesn't want to know yet. Which, if you'll pardon my saying so, is fairly silly. *I* always wanted to know as soon as possible."

"Him," Emily repeated. Then she smiled. "Well, once Grayson gets over the fact that he's illegitimate, *they'll* probably be pleased!"

"Bunch of stuck-in-the-mud patriarchal male chauvinists, the lot of them. It pisses me off to think how frigging *delighted* they're all going to be," Allison muttered, and Emily surprised herself with a genuine laugh.

"That's better!" Allison approved with a smile. "But my point is that even with Hamish and Honor's genetic material colliding as accidentally as it did in this case, his Y-chromosome's done the trick quite neatly. Mother Nature didn't even need my intervention."

"Not in *her* case," Emily agreed, and Allison snorted.

"Oh, for goodness sakes, Emily! This isn't the *dark* ages, you know. I haven't looked at your chart yet, for obvious reasons, but I will be frankly astonished if the problem is anywhere near as complicated as you seem to believe it is. Since we already know Hamish's genotype is perfectly capable of regenerating, and since we already know he and Honor can produce a child equally capable of regenerating, it's probably as simple as selecting the sperm with the genes we need. If it's not, then I feel quite certain I can repair the problem before fertilization. In fact, I could *probably* repair it *after* fertilization, although I'd hesitate to promise that without a careful examination of you both."

"You sound . . . remarkably confident," Emily said slowly.

"I sound—?" Allison paused, looking at Emily with an expression of almost comical surprise. Then she cleared her throat.

"Ah, Emily. Although I haven't reviewed any of your files, I know you spent quite some time on Beowulf after the accident. And I believe Dr. Kleinman is Beowulf-trained. He graduated from Johns Hopkins, Beowulf, didn't he?"

"I think so, yes."

"Then it would be fair to say you've been exposed to the Beowulf medical establishment in all its smug, not to say narcissistic, tradition-encrusted glory?"

"To some extent," Emily said, puzzled by the curious bite in Allison's tone.

"And do you happen to know what my maiden name was?"

"Chou, wasn't it?" Emily's puzzlement was, if anything, deeper than ever.

"Well, yes. Except that if I'd stayed on Beowulf, I'd have been known by my *entire* maiden name . . . whether I particularly wanted to be or not. Which, as it happens, I didn't."

"Why not?" Emily asked, when she paused.

"Because my full family name is Benton-Ramirez y Chou," Allison said, and Emily's eyes widened.

Of all the medical "dynasties" of Beowulf, acknowledged throughout explored space as the preeminent queen of the life-sciences, the Benton-Ramirez and Chou families stood at the very pinnacle. They *were* Beowulf, with a multigenerational commitment to the field of genetic medicine which stretched back to well before Old Earth's Final War. George Benton and Sebastiana Ramirez y Moyano had actually led the Beowulf teams to Old Earth to battle the hideous consequences of the Final War's bioweapons, and Chou Keng-ju had led the bioethics fight against Leonard Detweiler and the other "progressive eugenics" advocates six centuries ago. Among the many jewels in the crown of their families' achievements since was a leading role in the development of the prolong process itself. And—

"Well," she said, mildly, after a moment, "at least I finally understand exactly where Honor's rather . . . volcanic attitude towards the genetic slave trade and Manpower comes from, don't I?"

"You might say she imbibed it with her mother's milk," Allison agreed. "Bad science, no doubt, but I *did* breast-feed, and having a direct ancestor's signature on the Cherwell Convention didn't hurt, I suppose." She smiled thinly. "My point, however, is that if I come across as sounding just a bit breezily confident, I come by it honestly. I can't give you an absolute, categorical assurance that you and Hamish could produce a biological child who will regenerate. The probability that you *couldn't*, especially with my intervention, is so vanishingly small I literally couldn't quantify it, but it does exist. What I *can* guarantee you, however, is that with my intervention you *won't* produce a child who *can't* regenerate."

She looked straight into Emily's eyes again.

"So tell me, Emily. With that guarantee, do you want a child of your own, or not?"

"Mr. Secretary, you have a com call from Colonel Nesbitt," Alicia Hampton said from Arnold Giancola's display.

"Ah?" Giancola gave her his best absentminded smile, then shook himself visibly. "I mean, by all means put it through, Alicia. Thank you."

"You're welcome, Sir," she said with a slight, fond smile of her own, and her face disappeared from his display. A moment later, Jean-Claude Nesbitt's face replaced it.

"Good afternoon, Mr. Secretary," he said courteously.

"Colonel," Giancola nodded. "What can I do for you this afternoon?"

"It isn't really anything especially important, Sir. I'm just screening you to let you know I'm about to begin the regular quarterly security review." Giancola's expression never changed, but he felt his stomach muscles tense. "I know it's a pain," Nesbitt continued, "but your personal staff is going to have to be vetted again, as well. Under the circumstances, I thought I'd give you a heads-up so we could try to avoid any scheduling conflicts that might interfere with your planned workload."

"I appreciate that, Colonel," Giancola said, and a particularly attentive observer might have noticed that his eyes narrowed ever so slightly as they met Nesbitt's on the display. "But if you're quite satisfied with your own arrangements, I feel confident we could accommodate our schedule to yours. If you'll contact Ms. Hampton when you're ready to begin, we'll be at your disposal for you to proceed any time you're ready."

"Thank you, Mr. Secretary. I understand," Nesbitt said with a respectful nod. "And I appreciate your readiness to cooperate."

"One can never be too careful where security matters are concerned, Colonel," Giancola said seriously. "Was there anything else we needed to discuss?"

"No, Mr. Secretary. Thank you. I have everything I need."

"In that case, Colonel, good day," Giancola said, and cut the circuit.

✧   ✧   ✧

Yves Grosclaude leaned back in the comfortable flight couch and wished his mind were as comfortable as his body as his air car sliced through the night shrouded mountains on autopilot.

None of this was supposed to have happened. *None* of it. He'd agreed with Giancola that it was time to take a firmer line with the Manties, and God knew they'd certainly managed to stiffen that ninny Pritchart's spine! But who would ever have expected her to do something like *this?* And now that she had, what the *hell* did they do about it?

He frowned, worrying at one thumbnail with his teeth, wondering how Giancola could remain—or, at least, appear to remain—so unconcerned. He supposed that after this long without detection, he should be feeling less worried, himself. After all, if anyone was going to suspect something, certainly they should have done so by now, right?

But it didn't work that way. Whether anyone suspected now or not, eventually they would, and there was no statute of limitations on treason.

He drew a deep breath and forced his hand back down into his lap. There was nothing to do about it right now, and if the war lasted long enough, and if Giancola played his political cards astutely enough, it was entirely possible that *President* Giancola would be in a position to quash any unfortunate investigations after the fighting finally ended.

And if he couldn't, at least Grosclaude had tucked away the vital evidence he could undoubtedly trade to the prosecution for at least limited immunity.

That, he knew, was all he could realistically do to disaster-proof his own position. In the meantime, he'd just have to keep his head down and concentrate on being as innocent and aboveboard as possible. It wasn't easy, but he hoped this ski trip would help. It ought to at least let him burn off some of his accumulated nervous energy!

He chuckled at the thought and made himself stretch and yawn, then settled more firmly into the couch. His flight plan was just about to take him through the Arsenault Gorge, one of the most spectacular mountain passes on Haven. It was a huge, axe-blow of a chasm through the Blanchard Mountains, with sheer cliffs towering vertically for as much as two hundred and fifty meters in some places. It was quite a tourist attraction, and Grsoclaude himself loved it. He always programmed his flight path to take him through it, despite the need to slow down around its hairpin bends.

Now the autopilot dipped the air car slightly, dropping a bit lower to give him a better view, and he felt a familiar stir of enjoyment as the rocky, tree-crowned cliffs loomed up on either side of his prow.

And at that moment, something very peculiar happened.

Yves Grosclaude felt something almost like a mental tickle. As if someone were running a finger down his spine, except that it was behind his eyes somewhere. He started to frown, but then the frown vanished into another expression entirely.

He'd never noticed the almost microscopic capsule which had somehow found its way into the yogurt he'd enjoyed with his supper two nights ago. He hadn't been looking for anything of the sort, never suspected anything like it was remotely possible.

Nor was it . . . for the Republic's tech base. That capsule's contents had been well beyond the capability of Haven's own scientists, and as the capsule itself disintegrated in his digestive tract, submicroscopic virus-based nanotech had infiltrated his bloodstream. They'd traveled to his brain, seeking very specifically targeted sections of it, and then waited.

For this specific moment.

Yves Grosclaude jerked in his seat as the tiny invaders executed their programmed instructions. They did no physical damage at all; they simply invaded his body's "operating system" and overwrote it with instructions of their own.

He watched helplessly, screaming in the silence of his mind, as his hands switched off the autopilot. They settled on the stick and throttle, and his eyes bulged in silent horror as his right hand wrenched the stick suddenly to the right even as his left rammed the throttle to the wall.

The vehicle was still accelerating when it struck a vertical cliff face head-on at well over eight hundred kilometers per hour.

Chapter Seventeen

"All right, Kevin. What's all the mystery this time?"

President Eloise Pritchart's striking, topaz-colored eyes tracked slowly from the FIA director's face to that of the petite, dark-haired woman with him. Presidential Security was never happy when she met alone with anyone, even in her private office, out from under their protective oversight, although at least in this case the person she was meeting with was their ultimate boss. Which, she thought, had undoubtedly helped with Kevin's insistence that this meeting had to be completely off the record. Her personal detachment had made no more than *pro forma* protests before withdrawing and shutting down the various covert surveillance systems which normally let them discreetly monitor while remaining out of sight but ready to respond instantly. And Kevin's position meant they probably really had turned them off this time, which meant she was enjoying a novel sense of freedom for at least the next little bit.

Of course, she was always more than a bit nervous about anything *Kevin* wanted kept black.

"Thank you for clearing the time for us," Usher said, and Pritchart's eyebrows rose at his unwontedly formal—and somber—tone. "This, by the way," he indicated her other visitor, "is Special Senior Inspector Danielle Abrioux. Danny is one of my top troubleshooters."

"And why am I seeing the two of you without the additional presence of the Attorney General?" Pritchart leaned back in her comfortable chair. "If I remember correctly, Denis is not simply your direct superior, but also a member of my Cabinet."

"Yes, he is," Usher agreed. "On the other hand, much as I like Denis, and as much as I respect him, he's very much a connect-all-the-dots, follow procedure kind of guy."

"Which is why *he's* Attorney General, and why the wild cowboy, seat-of-the-pants kind of guy works for him. Correct?"

"Granted. In this case, however, I think you need to know about this before we decide exactly how to bring him into it officially. His principles are just as cast-in-battle-steel as Tom Theisman's. And in this particular instance, his own dislikes and distrust might push him into a more . . . confrontational stance than we can afford at this particular moment."

"Kevin," Pritchart said, with very little humor, "you're starting to really worry me. What the *hell* is all this about?"

The woman with him—Abrioux, Pritchart reminded herself—looked decidedly nervous as the President glared at the FIA Director. Usher, however, only settled deeper into his chair, herculean shoulders tensing as if under a massive weight.

"It's about the diplomatic correspondence the Manties altered," he said.

"What about it?"

"Actually, what I ought to have said," Usher replied, "is that it's about the diplomatic correspondence the Manties are *alleged* to have altered."

For an instant, Pritchart felt only puzzled by his choice of words. Then an icy dagger seemed to run down her spine.

"What do you mean 'alleged'?" she demanded harshly. "I saw the originals. I *know* they were altered."

"Oh, they certainly were," Usher agreed grimly. "Unfortunately, I've begun to have some serious questions about just who did the altering."

"My God." Pritchart knew her face had gone white. "Please, Kevin. *Please* don't tell me what it sounds like you're about to tell me."

"I'm sorry, Eloise," he said gently. "At first, I thought it was just because of how much I disliked Giancola. It seemed preposterous, even for him. And, for that matter, it seemed outright impossible. But I couldn't shake the suspicion. I kept picking at it. And a few weeks ago, I put Danny here on it, very, very quietly. It's not only possible, I'm pretty damn sure it happened."

"Sweet Jesus." Pritchart stared at him, more flattened—more horrified—than she'd been even by the knowledge that Oscar Saint-Just fully intended to have Javier Giscard shot. In which case, he would inevitably have discovered just how *she* had been covering for Javier for so long.

"How could he possibly have done such a thing?" she asked finally. "Not *why* did he do it—if he did—but *how*?"

"Assuming the right accomplice in the right position, and assuming the sheer big brass balls to try it in the first place, it really wouldn't have been all that technically difficult to make the substitutions," Usher said. "I'd pretty much worked out how he could have done it before I ever brought Danny into it, and she's pretty much confirmed that it could have been—and almost certainly was—done that way. She can give you the technical details, if you want them. Basically, though, he could send *out* whatever version of your agreed-upon diplomatic notes he wanted to. After all, he's Secretary of State. And as long as the fellow playing mailman for him didn't blow the whistle on them, there'd be no way for anyone at this end to know he'd departed from the planned script. And we've also figured out how he could have had access to the Manties' Foreign Office validation key, which would have let him change the *incoming* correspondence, as well."

"That—" Pritchart paused and drew a deep breath. "That doesn't sound good, Kevin. Especially given how black you wanted this meeting. If you've figured all that out, and you're not ready to seek an indictment or make open accusations, then there's got to be a boot in the works somewhere. Right?"

"Right," he said grimly, and waved one hand at Abrioux. "Danny?" he invited.

"Madam President," Abrioux said, her expression more than a little nervous, "I wasn't too sure Kevin—the Director, I mean— hadn't stripped a gear when he sprang all of this on me. I've known him a long time, though, and he *is* my boss, so I had to take the possibility seriously. And the more I looked into it, the more I realized it really could have been done exactly the way he'd hypothesized. But the key element, as he and I both recognized from the beginning, was that Giancola couldn't have acted alone, couldn't have done it all by simply manipulating the electronic message traffic. He had to have at least one flesh- and-blood accomplice. Someone who could cover for him at the other end and conceal the true content of our actual outgoing correspondence *and* the Manties' incoming traffic from anyone else in the Republic.

"And as soon as we'd come to that conclusion, it was obvious who his accomplice—if he'd had one—had to have been: Yves Grosclaude."

"Our 'Special Representative,'" Pritchart said, nodding her head grimly.

"Exactly." Abrioux nodded back. "The fact that he had an accomplice was, frankly, the one real chink I could see in his armor. I'm sure there has to be other physical evidence, but we're up against the need to show probable cause before we can go looking for it. If I could pull Grosclaude in and sweat him a little, put a little pressure on him, he might give Giancola up. Or, he might at least provide me with *something* concrete to lend at least some credence to the rather preposterous scenario the Director had come up with. On the other hand, I needed to approach him a bit cautiously, hopefully without Giancola figuring out I was interested in him at all.

"Unfortunately, either I wasn't cautious enough, or else Giancola's had his own plans for Grosclaude all along."

"Meaning what?" Pritchart demanded when she paused with a chagrined expression.

"Meaning Mr. Grosclaude was killed in a single-air car accident four nights ago," Usher said flatly.

"Oh, *shit*," Pritchart said with soft yet deadly feeling. "An *air car* accident?"

"I know. I know!" Usher shook his head. "It's like some sort of bad joke, isn't it? After all the inconvenient people StateSec disappeared in mysterious one-air car accidents, this is going to be just peachy keen when we have to go public, isn't it?"

"Unless we can prove it wasn't one," Pritchart said, eyes slitted in intense thought. "Before, it was always the state claiming it had been an accident. If we claim it *wasn't* an accident—and if we can prove it—we might actually turn that around and use it in our favor."

"If there *is* any way to turn this 'in our favor' you may have a point," Usher said. "Honestly, though, the more I've looked at this thing, the less sure I've become there is such a way. And even if there is, I'm afraid that so far it doesn't look as if we're going to be able to prove any such thing."

"Why not?"

"I've tapped very quietly into the investigation of his death, Madam President," Abrioux replied for Usher. "I've kept my interest in it entirely black, which has required calling in quite a few old markers. But the crash investigation team has been through the wreckage of his air car—which, by the way, was reduced to very small pieces—very, very carefully without finding any indication of any sort of mechanical or electronic sabotage. The black boxes came through more or less intact, and they all agree that for some unknown reason, Grosclaude suddenly disengaged his autopilot, put the throttle right through the gate, and flew straight into a near vertical cliff. He impacted at a speed somewhere around Mach one."

"He did *what*?" Pritchart sat up straight and frowned at the senior inspector.

"There's no question, Madam President. And there's also no explanation. That's one reason the Director and I didn't come to you sooner; we kept hoping we'd find *something* significantly bogus. But the weather was clear, visibility was good, and there was no other traffic on or near his flight path at the time; the crash team's pulled the air traffic satellite records to confirm that. There's no sign anyone tampered with his vehicle in any way, and there's absolutely no indication of any external factor which could have inspired him to do what he did. At the moment, to be perfectly honest, the crash team is leaning towards the theory that it was a suicide."

"Oh, that's just wonderful!" Pritchart snarled, fear and the sudden cold suspicion that she'd gone back to war because of a lie driving her into an uncharacteristically savage fury. "So now we're not even claiming it was an 'accident.' Now we're going to tell the galaxy our suspect fucking committed suicide! *That's* going to give us a lot more credibility when we try to pin anything on him!"

"I suppose it's possible it really *was* suicide," Usher pointed out. Pritchart glared at him, and he shrugged. "Just playing devil's advocate, Eloise. But it really is possible, you know. An awful lot of people have been killed since the shooting started again, and more are going to *be* killed, whatever else happens. If he was involved in anything with Giancola, he might well have been feeling a lot of guilt over all those deaths. Or, conversely, he may have wanted to come forward but been afraid Giancola would eliminate him if he tried. In that case, he might have seen this as his only way out."

"And if you believe that fairy tale for a moment, I've got some bottom land I want to sell you," Pritchart said caustically. "Just don't ask me what it's on the bottom *of*."

"I didn't say I believed it," Usher responded mildly. "I just said it's possible, and it is."

"Bullshit," Pritchart said bluntly. "Much as I'd like to believe you're completely off the beam with this one, Kevin, you're not. God knows it would be better if you were, but Grosclaude's death—especially this way, at this time—is just too damned coincidental. And too damned convenient for Giancola. No." She shook her head. "I don't know *how* he did it, but somehow he got to Grosclaude."

"So you believe he did alter the correspondence?"

"I don't want to," she admitted heavily, "but you said it would take big brass balls. Well, that's one thing Arnold has. And he's not overly burdened with scruples, either. Certainly not burdened enough to offset his ambition. I doubt he wanted it to go this far, but..."

She shook her head again.

"There is one odd thing about Grosclaude's death, Madam President," Abrioux said after a moment.

The President's topaz eyes swung back to the senior inspector, and she twitched the fingers of one hand in a "tell me" gesture.

"Given the... peculiar circumstances of the 'accident,'" Abrioux said, "the crash team's lead investigator requested a complete toxicology screen and blood workup as part of the autopsy. Given the nature of the impact, the doctors didn't have a whole lot to work with, you understand. There was more than enough to make a genetic identification of the remains they could find, but nowhere near what they needed for any sort of regular autopsy.

"The medical examiner, however, did note that there appeared to be 'unidentifiable organic traces and DNA markers' in one of the blood samples."

"Meaning what?" Pritchart's expression was intent.

"Meaning we don't know what the hell what," Usher replied. "When he says 'unidentifiable,' that's exactly what he means. All the organic elements he's picked up on could be explained away by a simple case of the flu, except that there's no indication of it in any of the other samples. If you really want to wade through his report, I can get you a copy of it, but I doubt it will mean anything more to you than it did to me. The key element, though, seems to be the DNA he turned up. There's been some speculation in Solarian medical literature for a while now about the possibility of viral nanotech."

"Are they *insane*?" Pritchart demanded incredulously. "Didn't those lunatics learn *anything* from the Final War?"

"I don't know. It's not my field, by two or three light-years. But *apparently* the people doing the speculating believe it should be at least theoretically possible to control their viruses and prevent unwanted mutations. After all, we've managed the same sort of thing with nanotech for centuries now."

"Because the damned things don't have DNA and don't reproduce even in medical applications!" Pritchart said snappishly.

"I didn't say I thought it was a good idea, Eloise," Usher said. "I just said there's been some Solly speculation about the possibilities. As far as I'm aware, and I've done some judicious research on the subject since Danny brought me the blood workup results, it's all purely theoretical at the moment. And even if the *Sollies* can do it, there's no one here in the Republic who could. So assuming these highly ambiguous results—found, I remind you, in only one of the blood samples—mean Grosclaude was murdered using that sort of technology, where the hell did *Giancola* get access to it?"

"You're just full of sunshine this evening, aren't you?"

"If a shit storm's on the horizon, it's good to know far enough ahead you can at least bring along an umbrella," Usher said philosophically, and she grimaced at him. Then she sat thinking hard for several endless seconds.

"All right, Kevin," she said finally. "You've had longer to think about this than I have, and I doubt very much, knowing you, that you asked for this meeting without at least some idea of how we might proceed."

"As I see it," Usher said after a moment, "there are four basic dimensions to this problem. First, there's the war itself and just why in hell we're fighting the damned thing. Second, there's the constitutional implications of treason on this level by a cabinet secretary. Not to mention the fact that I'm not even certain what he did—assuming we're right, and he did actually do it—falls under the Constitution's definition of 'treason' in the first place. Abuse of office, conspiracy, malfeasance, high crimes and misdemeanors; I'm sure we could get him on any of those. But treason is a rather specific crime. Third, after the constitutional aspects, there are the purely political ones. Not in terms of interstellar diplomacy and wars, but in terms of whether or not our system is strong enough yet to survive something like this. And, of course, the question of just how effective your administration can be if it turns out one of your own cabinet secretaries manipulated us into going to war. And, fourth, there's the question of just how we proceed with this investigation, bearing all those other aspects of this particular can of worms in mind."

He looked at the President, one eyebrow raised, and she nodded in glum agreement with his analysis.

"I'm not in any sort of position to comment on the first point," he said then. "That's your bailiwick—yours and Admiral Theisman's. On the constitutional implications, Denis would probably be a much better authority than me. My gut reaction is that the Constitution probably gives us the scope we need to carry out an investigation and, if it turns out the bastard did it, to bring the hammer of God down on him with a vengeance. However, that brings us to the political aspects. Specifically, I'm worried as hell that we haven't had the Constitution back up and running long enough to weather this kind of crisis."

He met the President's eyes, his strong-featured face as grim as she recalled ever having seen it.

"I've played fast and loose around the margins more than once, Eloise. You know that. In fact, I'm pretty sure it's one of the reasons you wanted me for this job. But I really do believe in the Constitution. I believe the only cure, the only preventative, for the sorts of outright insanity the Republic's been prey to is a powerful consensus on the absolute sanctity of the rule of law. If we pursue this, then it's more than possible, in my estimation, that we could wind up pulling the pillars of the temple down on our own heads.

"If we're going to accuse Arnold Giancola of what I'm almost certain he did, we've got to have proof. Not suspicions, however profound. Not hypotheses, however convincing. *Proof.* Without that, he and his partisans—and he has a lot of them, as we all know—are going to scream we're simply pulling a StateSec. We're concocting ludicrous charges against a political adversary as a pretext for purging your opposition. Anyone who actually knows you would realize how preposterous that was, but by the time the spin masters on both sides get done with it, no one outside your immediate circle is going to be sure of that. Which means we might just find Giancola and his supporters seeking to topple your administration on the basis that *they're* the ones protecting the Constitution from abuse and manipulation. And if he can generate enough confusion, drum up enough support, the consequences for everything we've been trying to accomplish could be very, very ugly."

"It's probably even worse than you're thinking," Pritchart said unhappily. "This war's incredibly popular at the moment. I hadn't realized how much public opinion wants to get our own back against the Manties for the way they kicked our ass in the last round. And at the moment, there's absolutely no question in Congress that the *Manties* manipulated the diplomatic exchanges. Why should there be? I personally certified that there wasn't!

"So what happens if I suddenly go before Congress and announce that *we're* the guilty parties after all? Suppose I tell the Senate's Foreign Affairs Committee we went back to war—with Congress' enthusiastic support—on the basis of a lie told not by the Manties, but by our own Secretary of State?"

"I have absolutely no idea," Usher admitted frankly. Abrioux shook her head, as well. Unlike Usher, however, her expression was that of someone who was entirely certain she was involved with something way, way above her pay grade.

"The first thing that's going to happen," Pritchart told him with absolute certainty, "is that they're going to refuse to believe it. Even with the sort of proof you've already pointed out we need, it would take time—probably quite a bit of it—to convince a majority of Congress of what really happened. And that assumes a majority of Congress is willing to be open-minded enough to even entertain the possibility. Don't forget how many friends Arnold has over there.

"But even if Congress buys our version of it, we're *winning* the damned war. At least, that's the way it looks right now, and Congress as a whole is absolutely convinced we are. So even if it turns out the shooting started because one of our own cabinet officers deliberately manipulated, falsified, and forged diplomatic notes, there's going to be a sizable number of senators and representatives who don't *care*. What they're going to see is that *this* time it's the Manties on the ropes, and there's no way in hell they're going to be willing for us to drop an e-mail to Elizabeth Winton saying 'Oops. Sorry about the misunderstanding. Let's all make nice now.' Especially not if that means—as it damned well ought to, if Arnold's done what you—*we*—think he has—that the Republic publicly acknowledges its war guilt. And if we make what we believe happened public knowledge, we've *got* to acknowledge our guilt if we're ever going to convince the rest of the galaxy we're not still the *People's* Republic of Haven."

Her beautiful face was drawn, her topaz eyes shadowed, and Usher nodded slowly.

"I knew it was going to be a shit bucket, whatever happened," he said. "I didn't follow through to realize just how bad it really would be, though."

"It's not your job to worry about the political consequences. It's mine. And if you can come up with concrete proof—proof I can take in front of a judge, proof I could lay in front of an interstellar arbitration panel, or use to convince even our Congress—then I've got no option but to make that proof public and try to survive whatever the political, diplomatic, and constitutional consequences may be. If you give me that proof, then I will by God do it, too."

"Eloise—"

"No, Kevin. This isn't something we can avoid, or dance around. We can't afford to open it up in public at all without proof. But if that proof exists, we can't afford *not* to open it up. Sooner or later, if it really happened, and if there's proof it did, then it's going to become public knowledge whatever we do. And I won't—I *can't*—let the Constitution prove to be something built on foundations of sand. If we're ever going to put the old power games behind us once and for all, then you're right, it has to be done on the basis of the rule of law. And that means we have to follow the law wherever it leads us, whether we want to go there or not."

"All right, Madam President," Usher said with unusual formality, his eyes dark with mingled concern and respect. "That's your call. Whatever you decide, however you decide to handle it, you know I'll back your decision."

"Yes, I do," she said softly, topaz eyes softening.

"But that brings us to the final consideration. And, frankly, to the reason I did an end run around Denis for this meeting. You say we need proof. I don't know for a fact we're going to be able to find it, even if I'm a hundred percent correct in my suspicions. But before I can find it, if it exists at all, we need to decide how I'm going to go about *looking* for it. Under a strict interpretation of the law, I need to inform the Attorney General of my suspicions. He, in turn, needs to inform you, and *you* need to inform the Foreign Affairs and Judicial Oversight Committees of both houses, at the very least, because of their oversight role. And there are probably at least a couple of other committees which also ought to be brought on-line. Plus, an official investigation ought to be opened by the Attorney General, through the FIA, under a finding of probable cause from a magistrate. Unfortunately, all of that requires bringing dozens, almost certainly hundreds, of other people into the investigation.

"If we do that, it's going to leak. At the very least, word of it will get to Giancola from one of his friends. More probably, it'll hit the info boards within a matter of hours. In which case—"

He shrugged, and Pritchart bit her lip and nodded.

"The worst of all worlds," she acknowledged. "Especially if Arnold decides his best defense is to mount a strong offense before the investigation really gets rolling."

"And particularly if he decides not to restrict himself to due process when he does," Usher pointed out.

"Absolutely."

She drummed nervously on her desktop with her fingertips, then shook herself.

"I notice you said all of that was what would follow from a strict interpretation of the law. I'm almost afraid to ask this. No, I *am* afraid to ask it." She grimaced. "Unfortunately, I don't have much of an option. So, tell me, Kevin. Just how *un*-strict do you suggest we be?"

"Believe it or not, Eloise, I wish to hell we could do this one one hundred percent by The Book. If we don't, and if the wheels come off, it's going to be at least as bad as anything you've just described. In fact, it's probably going to be worse.

"Even so," he continued implacably, "I don't see any way we can. You're going to have to decide who else you can trust to bring in on this. I think you're going to *have* to tell Theisman, and God knows how he's going to react. And even though I'm the one who deliberately cut him out of the loop for this meeting, I really want to bring Denis in on it. Not only does he have both a right and a constitutional responsibility to know what we're doing, but if he *doesn't* know, we're a lot more likely to have someone step on his own reproductive equipment if I'm running some sort of clandestine op he doesn't know about. Especially if he finds out I'm up to *something* without knowing what that 'something' is.

"But after you've decided who else needs to know, everything else has to be blacker than black until we either have the proof in hand or know with absolute certainty where that proof is and how to get our hands on it. I don't like it, it's dangerous, but it's the *least* dangerous option I see under the circumstances."

"I wish you were wrong. Dear *God*, how I wish you were wrong."

Pritchart closed her eyes for a moment, rubbing her forehead, then exhaled noisily.

"Unfortunately, you aren't," she said. "All right. I hereby authorize you to pursue your black investigation. But be very, very careful, Kevin. This one could destroy everything you and I—and Tom Theisman and Javier—have fought for for decades. I'll have to think long and hard about who else to tell, and how, but at least if someone has to be finding our way through the minefield, I'm glad it's you."

"Gee, thanks." Usher made a face, and the President chuckled. There wasn't much humor in the sound, but perhaps it was at least a beginning.

"How are you going to start?" she asked.

"With Danny here." Usher nodded at the senior inspector. "She's already on board, and she's already black. I'll just keep her that way. However," he looked Pritchart straight in the eyes, "before she makes a single additional move, I want a presidential pardon, signed and in her hand, for any laws she happens to break doing what we're asking her to do."

"You always were loyal to your people in the Resistance," Pritchart said with a smile, and looked at Abrioux. "As a matter of fact, Inspector Abrioux, so was I." She looked back at Kevin. "The senior inspector will have her letter of pardon within the hour," she promised.

"Good. And as far as where we begin, Danny is going to have to put together her own team, one we can cut completely out of normal Agency operations. I think she's already got the people she wants in mind, and I'm pretty sure I can do a little creative paperwork on their assignments to make them available to her. And once that's out of the way, we'll probably start by putting the entire life of the late Yves Grosclaude under an electron microscope. If he really was Giancola's accomplice, and the fact that he's dead would seem to suggest very strongly that he was, then he may have been careless and left us something. For that matter, he may have had an insurance file stashed away somewhere. We're not going to get any legal search warrants without proving probable cause, which we've just agreed we can't do without going public, but if Danny and her people can figure out where what we need is, I can probably finagle some semiplausible way to get possession of it in a way which won't irreparably taint it in an evidentiary sense."

Pritchart's nostrils flared, and he shrugged again.

"I'm going to have to do some dancing in the shadows to make this one work, Eloise. You know I am."

"Then I probably need a pardon for you, too," she said.

"No, you specifically *don't* need a pardon for me," he disagreed. "I'm the cutout. The rogue, working without any authorization from you because of my personal antipathy for Secretary Giancola."

"Kevin—" she began in automatic protest, but he shook his head.

"You've got to have deniability on this one," he said flatly. "If news of what we're doing leaks and we haven't found the proof we need, you're going to need someone to throw off the sleigh. If you don't have it, the consequences are going to be worse than our having gone public from the get-go would have been. And I'm the only logical candidate."

She looked at him, seeing her fellow revolutionary, her longtime friend and sometime lover, and she wanted desperately to disagree with him. She wanted it as badly as she'd ever wanted anything in her life. But—

"You're right," President Eloise Pritchart said. She hesitated only a heartbeat longer, then nodded sharply.

"Do it," she said.

Chapter Eighteen

"Well, Chief," Captain Scotty Tremaine said, "what do you think?"

"Me, Sir?" Chief Warrant Officer Sir Horace Harkness shook his head. "I think the rest of the Navy got itself reamed a new one while we were off at Marsh. And I think they expect *us* to do something about it now."

"Chief, that is *so* cynical of you." Captain Tremaine shook his head with a lopsided smile.

"No, Sir. Not cynical, just experienced. Look at it. Everywhere we've been with the Old Lady, we've kicked ass and taken names. And the minute those assholes working for High Ridge send us off to the back of beyond, what happens? And who do they always send in to do the dirtiest jobs after it all hits the fan? The Old Lady. And us, of course," Harkness added with becoming modesty.

Tremaine's smile grew wider, but he really couldn't argue with Harkness' analysis. And everything he'd seen so far, especially in the classified situation reports and ONI analyses to which his rank allowed him access, suggested things were even worse than the warrant officer knew.

"I'm sure Duchess Harrington is vastly relieved to know you're along, Chief," he said. "In the meantime, we've got an entire squadron of carriers waiting for us to whip their LAC groups into shape. Now, Her Grace hasn't seen fit to tell me *exactly* what we're going to be doing, but from the force mix I've seen and a few things Admiral Truman's let drop, it's not going to be picketing the approaches to the home system. So I was thinking it's time you and I spent a few productive afternoons thinking up particularly evil training scenarios for those poor souls entrusted to our care."

"Actually, Sir," Harkness said with a grin of his own, "I've already been giving some thought to that. You want to get Lieutenant Chernitskaya in on this?"

"Of course I do. She's our tac officer, after all. And it distresses me to see such innocence and lack of guile in an officer of her seniority and native talent. It's time we began initiating her into the true deviousness of our profession."

"Officers really have a way with words, don't they, Sir?"

"We try, Chief. We try."

"So you're fairly satisfied with the Cutworm target list, Ma'am?"

"As satisfied as I can be, Andrea," Honor agreed, sitting back from the table and wiping her lips on a napkin. The scattered remains of lunch lay on the table between her, Jaruwalski, Brigham, Alice Truman, and Samuel Miklós, and she looked up with a smile as James MacGuiness refilled her cocoa mug and handed Nimitz a fresh stick of celery.

"I don't like spreading our forces this thinly," she continued more seriously, looking back at her subordinates as MacGuiness silently withdrew from the dining cabin of *Imperator*'s enormous admiral's quarters. "But we've *got* to get this op moving. We've been sitting here for over three weeks since we finally activated the command, and we *still* don't have our entire assigned order of battle. Part of me wants to go right on waiting until we do, so we'd have the strength to hit better-defended targets, but we can't. And given the pressure to move, it's probably as good a distribution as we could hope to come up with."

"That's true enough, Honor," Truman agreed, "although I don't think I'm any crazier than you are over the notion of splitting up into such small penny packets. On the other hand, we ought to catch them fairly unprepared."

"I know." Honor sipped cocoa, letting her mind run back over the framework of the operation which had been assigned the randomly generated codename of "Cutworm." It was a silly name, but no sillier than "Operation Buttercup" had been. And unlike some navies—including, apparently, the Havenite fleet, upon occasion—the Royal Manticoran Navy had a pretty good track record for selecting operational designators which didn't give clues as to what those operations were intended to do.

"To be honest," she said finally, lowering her mug, "I think part of what I'm suffering from is opening-night jitters. But all of us need to remember that Thomas Theisman and Lester Tourville, at least, have frighteningly steep learning curves. The fact that we're almost certain to get away with it the first time around is really, really going to ... irritate them. Which means they're going to devote some serious effort to figuring out what to do about us before we come calling the next time."

"Agreed, Your Grace," Miklós said. "Still, their options are going to be constrained by the availability of forces, unless they do exactly what we want them to do in the first place, and divert rear area security detachments from their frontline formations. In which case, we'll have achieved our primary objective."

"Which will no doubt be very satisfying to our next of kin," Truman observed dryly, and a chuckle ran around the table.

"All right," Honor said, sitting a bit more upright in her chair, "given the target list Andrea and Mercedes have come up with, how soon do you two—" she looked at Truman and Miklós "—think we can be ready to move."

"That depends partly on how ready the screen and Alistair are," Truman, as the senior of the two vice admirals, replied after a moment. "Speaking purely for the carriers, I think ... another week. Miklós?"

She glanced at the other CLAC squadron commander and cocked one eyebrow.

"About that," he agreed. "We could go sooner if *Unicorn* and *Sprite* had gotten here on schedule. But—"

He shrugged, and everyone at the table understood his wry expression perfectly.

"They're not really fully up to standard yet, but they're coming along well. I'd be happier with more time for exercises, of course. Any flag officer always is. But, to be perfectly honest, the way we're breaking the formations up pretty much precludes the need for training above the divisional level. And we're hitting them deep enough we'll have another nine days to drill *en route*."

"That's what I was thinking." Truman nodded. "And on that

basis, I think we're in pretty good shape. But if you don't mind, Sam, I've got some training scenarios I'd like to upload to your carriers, as well." Miklós looked faintly curious, and she gave him a rather nasty grin. "It would appear our good Captain Tremaine has pretty accurately deduced what we're going to be doing. He and Chief Harkness have put together some simulator packages built around individual LAC groups."

"Scotty and Harkness?" Brigham laughed. "Why do I find that particular combination of authors just a bit ominous, Ma'am?"

"Because you know them?" Honor suggested.

"Probably," Truman agreed. "On the other hand, Lieutenant Chernitskaya, Scotty's tac officer seems to have made quite a few contributions of her own. I think you'd like her, Honor. She's . . . devious."

"Chernitskaya?" Jaruwalski repeated. "Any relation to Admiral Chernitsky?"

"His granddaughter," Truman said.

"Viktor Chernitsky?" Honor asked.

"Yes. Did you know him?"

"We only met once, after he'd retired. Admiral Courvoisier once told me, though, that he thought Viktor Chernitsky might have been the greatest strategist he'd ever known. He always said it was a great pity Chernitsky was too old for prolong by the time it got to the Star Kingdom."

"I don't know about strategy, but if there's a gene for sneaky *tactics*, I think he passed that one on," Truman said.

"I'm always looking for new sims," Miklós said. "Mind telling me what's so special about these, though?"

"Mostly the op force. The bad guys in these simulations are about as sneaky as they get, and Scotty and his minions have consistently integrated ONI's most pessimistic assumptions about the Peeps' current hardware, as well. Somewhere—" Truman smiled at Honor "—he seems to have come up with the notion that the best simulations put you up against enemies who are better than anyone you're actually likely to meet."

"Makes sense to me," Miklós said. "But you said it was *mainly* the op force?"

"The other part is that Scotty seems to have visualized what we're going to be doing more clearly than most of the other COLACs. His sims are almost all built around raids and how the bad guys might respond. No one's given him any official briefings all the others didn't get, but he's clearly figured out what these operations are going to entail."

"Then by all means let's get them as widely distributed as we can," Honor decided.

"Yes, Ma'am," Jaruwalski acknowledged, making a note in her memo pad.

"And while she's doing that, Mercedes," Honor decided, "you and I are going to hop one of the shuttle flights back to Manticore. We can make the round-trip in thirty-six hours, even allowing for time at the Admiralty, and I want to touch base with Sir Thomas one last time before we actually kick off."

"Of course, Your Grace," Mercedes murmured, and Honor tasted her chief of staff's carefully concealed fond amusement. Obviously, Mercedes realized she was also looking forward to "touching base" with Hamish Alexander, as well as his First Space Lord. While Brigham clearly continued to nurse some serious reservations about the wisdom of the entire affair—Honor managed not to wince at her own unintentional *double entendre*—she'd apparently come to the conclusion that it had been good for Honor, at least in a personal sense.

On the other hand, she didn't know about certain rapidly approaching *consequences* of their relationship.

"While we're there," Honor continued serenely, "I'll inform Sir Thomas that, barring any unforeseen eventualities, we'll be launching Operation Cutworm in approximately seven days from now."

"All of that sounds excellent, Honor," Sir Thomas Caparelli said. He was tipped back in his chair behind the desk in his Admiralty House office, where Honor and Mercedes Brigham had just finished a final briefing on Cutworm.

"I'm sorry it's taken us so long to get organized, Sir Thomas," Honor said.

"Not your fault." He shook his head quickly. "After episodes like that fiasco in Zanzibar, and the pressure of the Alizon raid, we've been forced to do more redeploying of assets than anyone here at the Admiralty ever wanted to. The delays in building up your order of battle have been entirely our fault, not yours."

"I know. But at the same time, I also know how badly we need to do something to keep them from launching more attacks like the one on Zanzibar."

"We do. But you were absolutely right when you pointed out that attacking in insufficient strength would be worse than useless." He sighed. "I just wish it didn't feel so much like 'insufficient strength' is all we've got."

"We'll just have to maximize the edges we have," Honor replied. She glanced at Brigham for a moment, then went on. "Mercedes and I haven't mentioned anything about the new targeting systems in our staff sessions, Sir Thomas. We don't like to think about losing people or having them captured, but it can happen, and we decided to restrict that information as tightly as possible. But the last time I spoke to Commander Hennessy, he indicated that Admiral Hemphill's people were planning an all up test over in Gryphon space. Do we have the test results yet?"

"Yes, we do." Caparelli nodded. "I've only seen the preliminary report so far, not the details, but I understand it looked promising. Very promising. No one's talking about deploying it tomorrow, but it's beginning to look like it should be available, at least in small numbers, sometime in the next three to four months."

"That quickly?" Honor smiled. "If it lives up to Hennessy's billing, the Havenites are going to hate that. May I also ask how we're coming on the Andermani refits?"

"That's a bit less cheerful," Caparelli replied. "It's not coming along as well as I'd hoped. It's going to take at least a few weeks more than Admiral Hemphill's original projections suggested to get their pod-layers refitted with our old-style MDMs, and the Keyhole modifications to the later ships are going to take even longer. The good news is that we'll probably get a bigger 'python lump' of them delivered in a single shot. Of course," he grimaced, "Silesia's drawing a lot of the Andies' attention just now. Ours, too, for that matter."

"I haven't been following the reports on Silesia as closely as I should have," Honor admitted. "Still, the last I heard, things seems to be going fairly well."

"Compared to the cesspool the Confederacy used to be? Certainly. Compared to any halfway honestly governed section of the galaxy, though, it's entirely too interesting for my taste. Admiral Sarnow has his hands full, believe me."

"What do you mean?" Honor asked, just a trifle anxiously. Mark

Sarnow was an old friend, and she would have thought he was an almost perfect choice for the new Silesia Station's CO.

"Oh, it's nothing he isn't going to be able to deal with eventually," Caparelli said reassuringly. "But some of the old Silesian administrators obviously didn't really believe us when we told them it wasn't going to go right on being business as usual. And although most of the appointive system governors were simply retired as part of the annexation deal, almost a quarter of the governors were 'freely elected' by their citizens."

"Trust me, Sir Thomas," Honor said dryly, "there was nothing 'free' about an old-style Silesian election. The winning candidate paid cash on the barrel head for every one of those votes."

"I know, I know. But we can't simply go in and depose elected governors, however they got themselves elected in the first place, without excellent justifying cause. Some of them are stupid enough to think that will let them get away with running things the old way, and, unfortunately, several of the stupid variety had their local Confederacy Navy command structure firmly in their pockets under the previous régime. There's been a lot of passive resistance to Admiral Sarnow's instructions to decommission so many of their older units, obsolescent pieces of junk or not. And there's been even more resistance and obstructionism to his policy of completely reshuffling the star systems' command staffs. He's made a couple of salutary examples which seem to be convincing all but the most brain-dead we mean business, but unfortunately, we can't account for almost thirty percent of the Confeds' official ship list."

"Thirty *percent*, Sir?" Surprise startled the question out of Mercedes Brigham, despite her relative lack of seniority, and Caparelli chuckled with very little humor.

"It's nowhere near as bad as that sounds, Commodore," he reassured her. "At least half—more probably two-thirds—of the ships we can't account for were long gone before we ever came along. Hell, one of the more audacious system governors and his local naval commander were listing an entire squadron of battlecruisers—eight ships, and the next best thing to twenty thousand personnel—as present on active duty when they didn't even exist! The two of them, and maybe a half dozen other officers they needed to maintain the charade, were pocketing the nonexistent crews' salaries, not to mention every penny that was supposedly being spent on ammunition, reactor mass, maintenance, etc."

He shook his head, obviously bemused by anything which could operate on that sort of basis and still call itself a "navy."

"Still," he continued after a moment, his voice a bit bleaker, "some of those ships really did disappear, crew and all. I suspect that more than a few of the ones that did were already doing a little freelance piracy on the side, and I'm quite certain a lot of them think they can get away with doing it full-time, given how distracted we are by the Peeps. Which means, of course, that the very ship types Sarnow needs to chase them down are also the ones *Eighth Fleet* needs for operations like Cutworm. And then, of course, there's always Talbott."

"Are the reports about terrorist operations accurate, Sir?" Honor asked quietly.

"I think they've probably been sensationalized a bit by the media, and so far they're highly localized, but, yes. There've been some ugly incidents, especially in the Split System. Admiral Khumalo isn't exactly the sharpest stylus in the box, either, I'm afraid. Not a bad administrator, under most circumstances, but not really the right man to have on the spot when there's blood in the streets. Fortunately, Baroness Medusa is quite the opposite."

"I remember her from Basilisk," Honor agreed with a nod.

"Experience dealing with occasionally murderous aborigines is probably standing her in pretty good stead just at the moment," Caparelli said with an alum-tart smile. "Still, whatever I may think of Khumalo, it's hard to fault him for the way he keeps screaming for more ships. His area of responsibility's actually considerably larger than Sarnow's, and he's spread awfully thin. Unfortunately, there's only so much butter for our bread. We've had to send him at least a few modern ships, but overall, he's just going to have to make do with what he has. And *we're* just going to have to hope the situation there doesn't get any worse."

Honor nodded again. That seemed to describe the only thing they could hope for in quite a few places, at the moment, she reflected.

"Well, Sir Thomas," she said after a moment, climbing out of her chair and lifting Nimitz onto her shoulder, "we'll just have to do what we can to reduce pressure here closer to home."

"Yes, we will." He rose behind his desk. "And at least it looks like you've got a good command team to do the reducing with."

"That I do. If we don't manage to pull it off, it's not going to be *their* fault."

Late afternoon sunlight lay heavy and golden on the emerald green lawns of White Haven as Honor's armored limousine settled on the parking apron. The sting ships lifted away, and she climbed out of the car and stood for a moment, filling her lungs with the crisp northern air while her eyes devoured the towering, ancient trees.

Breeze moved through the swaying branches and plucked at her hair with tiny, gentle hands, and a deep, unabashedly sensual pleasure seemed to purr in her bones and muscles. Part of it was the reaction she always had after spending time on shipboard. The artificiality of her normal working environment was an inescapable fact of her life, but she'd been born and raised in the wilderness of Sphinx. She was as much a child of mountain forests and the vibrant, sometimes wild energy of sailboats on Sphinx's deep, cold oceans, as an officer of the Queen's Navy. It was an odd, sometimes painful, dichotomy which made her appreciate both her worlds even more deeply.

Yet there was more to it than that this time. She felt Nimitz at the back of her mind, savoring her sense of . . . content. That was the word, she decided, reaching up to rub the 'cat's ears gently. In the deepest sense of the word, "home," for her, had always been her parents' house on Sphinx. The house Stephanie Harrington's parents had built so many centuries before, which had sheltered so many generations of her family. Harrington House on Grayson was also "home" these days, in another sense, of course. And she supposed her Manticoran mansion on Jason Bay was, too, although somehow it still seemed more her "house" than truly home. Perhaps that was why she'd gone along with MacGuiness and Miranda—and her mother—when they insisted on rechristening that "Harrington House" as simply "the Bay House" to distinguish it from her home on Grayson.

But this, she thought, letting the quiet sounds of stirring wind, birds, and flowing water sweep through her, *this* had also become home. Certainly more than Jason Bay. More even than

Harrington House on Grayson. Possibly as much so as the house in which she'd quite literally been born. Not because of the welcoming tranquility of the grounds, the sense of being welcomed and enveloped by the ancient house and its lovingly maintained grounds, although she certainly felt that, as well. But what made this truly home were the people who lived here.

Her three-man detail fell into formation about her even here as she headed up the graveled path. The door opened as they approached, and her heart leapt as Hamish Alexander stepped out of it. Nimitz's purr buzzed in her ear, rich with loving amusement as he tasted and shared her brilliant flash of joy, and then a float chair drifted smoothly and silently out of the door behind Hamish.

Samantha lay curled up on Emily's chest like a long, sinuous question mark, her chin resting on Emily's right shoulder, and Nimitz's purr abruptly redoubled. Honor laughed, but she couldn't really fault his reaction. Not when her own sense of homecoming had just redoubled, as well.

"Welcome home," Emily said softly, almost as if she'd been reading Honor's mind, as Honor climbed the steps.

"I can't believe how good it feels to be here," Honor replied, and then her eyes widened in surprise as Hamish put his arms around her. She stiffened for just an instant, in startlement, not resistance, looking over his shoulder at Emily. They had always been so careful to never openly embrace one another in front of her armsmen or the White Haven staff. In front of *anyone*, actually. And perhaps especially, by unspoken agreement, in front of Emily.

But as Honor looked at Emily, tasting her emotions, she realized they needn't have worried. There was still that thread of bittersweetness, that descant of sorrowful regret for all Emily had lost, but there was also a sense of intense . . . satisfaction. A welcoming happiness that echoed Hamish's own with a joy all Emily's own.

Honor's stiffness vanished. Her eyes prickled, and she let her cheek rest on Hamish's broad shoulder, hugging him with her left arm while she reached her right hand past him to Emily.

"It ought to feel good here," Emily said gently. "It's where you belong."

✦   ✦   ✦

Honor looked narrowly back and forth between Hamish and Emily as they escorted her into the house. Now that the initial emotional high of homecoming had started to ebb just a bit, she realized there was something else going on under the surface of their emotions.

Nimitz sensed it, too. He had leapt lightly from Honor's shoulder to Emily's float chair, joining Samantha, but now he looked up at his person, and she tasted his own curiosity.

They're up to something, she thought. *They've got some sort of surprise in store for me.*

She started to say something, then stopped. Whatever they had in mind, they were obviously looking forward to it with anticipation, and she wasn't about to do anything to spoil their surprise. And it *was* a surprise when they walked into Emily's atrium and found both her parents waiting for them.

"Mother? Daddy?" Honor stopped dead in the doorway when she saw them. "What are *you* doing here?"

"Always the diplomat," Allison Harrington said mournfully, shaking her head. "No soft soap from this girl. Brisk, business-like, and straight to the point. Always makes you feel so *welcome,* doesn't she Alfred?"

"I think someone needs a spanking," her husband said tranquilly. "And not our daughter."

"Ooooooh! *Promise?*" Allison demanded, smiling at him wickedly.

"*Mother!*" Honor protested with a laugh.

"What?" Allison asked innocently.

"Filial piety precludes my answering that question the way it really deserves," Honor said repressively. "So, if you don't mind, and to return to my original question. What *are* you doing here? Not that I'm not delighted to see you both, of course. But having the entire Harrington family at White Haven at the same time doesn't exactly come under the heading of a discreetly low profile, now does it?"

She glanced at Hamish and Emily as she spoke, but neither of them seemed particularly worried. In fact, they seemed inordinately pleased.

"So you really were surprised," Emily said with immense satisfaction, confirming Honor's impression. "Good! You have no idea how difficult it can be to try to surprise someone who's an empath!"

"I'd figured out you were up to *something*," Honor told her, "but it never occurred to me that Mom and Dad might be sitting in here waiting for us. Which, if no one especially minds," she added pointedly, "brings me back to my original question. Again."

She swept the entire quartet—and the two obviously amused treecats, as well—with a demanding gaze, and Emily laughed. Laughed, Honor realized, around a bubble of intense joy. One which included her happiness at seeing Honor again, but which also partook of something else—something at least as powerful and even deeper.

"No one could possibly object to their presence," Emily said. "After all, it's a matter of public record that I invited *you* to dinner—I thought it was rather clever of me to time the invitation for a moment when I knew you'd be in Tom Caparelli's office and then go through the switchboard. And it's perfectly reasonable, when I invite a friend to supper, for me to invite her parents, as well. Especially," her voice softened, "when one of those parents is my newest physician."

"Physician?" Honor repeated.

"Yes." Emily smiled with a curious serenity. One that felt somehow more . . . whole in some indefinable fashion. "Your mother and I had a very interesting discussion when she told me you wanted my voice, as well as Hamish's, for the Briarwood recordings. The fact that you did meant a lot to me. But, in some ways, what your mother had to say meant even more. Hamish and I have an appointment of our own over there next week."

It took Honor an instant to realize what Emily had just said. Then the implications shot home.

"*Emily!*" Somehow, Honor found herself on her knees beside the float chair, holding Emily's right hand to her cheek with both of her own hands. The tears which had prickled at the backs of her eyes when Hamish and Emily welcomed her "home" spilled free, and Emily blinked her own eyes hard.

"That's wonderful!" Honor said. "Oh, Emily! I wanted to suggest the same thing so badly, but—"

"But you thought I wasn't ready for the notion," Emily interrupted, the force of her happiness at Honor's instant and obvious joy at the news flooding through the younger woman. "Well, *I* thought I wasn't, as far as that goes. That was before I discovered where you get your stubbornness, of course."

"I am not, and never have been, *stubborn*," Allison said with enormous dignity. "Determined, forceful, a compassionate healer—*always* a compassionate healer. Clearly committed. Insightful. Blessed with a unique ability to visualize the most successful possible outcome in any given situation. Always forging ahead in pursuit of—"

"Definitely a spanking," Alfred decided.

"Bully." Allison smacked him gently on the shoulder. "Bounder. *Cad!*"

"'Stubborn' is a remarkably pale word to describe my esteemed female parent," Honor said, sitting back on her heels to look deeply into Emily's eyes, and wondering just how . . . forceful her mother's "suggestions" might have been. "I've often thought 'obstinate' would be a better fit."

"I imagine that's part of what makes her such a successful physician," Emily replied, her happiness and deep satisfaction an unspoken answer to the question Honor hadn't asked.

"Yes, it is," Honor agreed. "But this is really what *you* want? Truly?"

"More truly than you can possibly imagine," Emily said softly.

" . . . so I called Briarwood and made the appointment," Emily said much later, as all five of them sat in her private dining salon looking out into the embers of sunset as they sipped after-dinner coffee or chocolate.

"Who's your doctor?" Honor asked.

"Illescue," Allison replied for Emily, and grimaced when Honor looked at her. "I really would have preferred Womack or Stilson, but it was probably inevitable that Illescue would assign himself. And I have to admit, he's very good at what he does."

"Mother," Honor said in a semi-accusing tone, "when I met Dr. Illescue, I had the distinct impression I wasn't exactly his favorite person in the entire galaxy. Which I found peculiar, since I'd never met the man before. Is there something you'd like to tell me? Something which, perhaps, you might have told me *before* I went to Briarwood myself?"

"Don't look at me, dear," Allison said, and jabbed her husband in the ribs with a knuckle. "This overgrown adolescent is probably responsible for any slight hostility you might have detected."

"Meaning what?"

"Meaning the two of them were at medical school together on Beowulf, and they didn't exactly see eye to eye."

"Daddy?" Honor leveled her gaze on her father, who shrugged.

"It wasn't *my* fault," he assured her. "You know what an invariably easy-going, pleasant sort I am."

"I also know where I get my temper," Honor told him tartly.

"Never laid a finger on him," Alfred Harrington said virtuously. "I was tempted a time or two, I'll admit. It's hard to imagine someone who could have been a bigger snot than Franz Illescue at twenty-five. He comes from one of the best medical families here in the Star Kingdom—his family's been physicians ever since the Plague Years—and he wasn't about to let a mere yeoman from Sphinx forget about it. Especially not a yeoman who was being sent to med school by the Navy. He was one of those people who thought the only reason people joined the Navy was because they couldn't get jobs in the 'real world.' I understand he's mellowed a bit with time, but the two of us were like a leaking hydrogen canister and a spark when we were younger."

"Tell her *everything*, Alfred," Allison admonished.

"Oh, well, there was one other *minor* matter," Alfred said. "He'd asked your mother out once or twice before I came along."

"Once or twice!" Allison snorted. "He'd been just a *bit* more persistent than that. I think he was trophy hunting—he always did think of himself as quite the ladies' man."

"Maybe he was," Alfred acknowledged. "But if so, at least he had impeccable taste, Alley. You have to admit that."

"Such a *sweet* man," Allison said, patting his cheek, and looked at Emily. "You see why I keep him?"

"Does all that history mean you're going to have a problem working with him, Mother?" Honor asked with an edge of seriousness after the chuckles had subsided.

"I've worked with him before," Allison told her calmly. "He's grown up quite a bit over the last half-century. And, as I say, he really is very good in his area. He wouldn't be Briarwood's senior partner if he wasn't. Given what the two of us do, it was inevitable we'd wind up at least consulting from time to time, and both of us recognized that long ago. So while I'd really prefer one of the other docs, I don't foresee any difficulty working with Franz."

"Good." Honor shook her head with a crooked smile. "The things one finds out about one's parents. And here for all these years I thought *I* was bad about picking up feuds."

"Well, you've refined an inherited ability to a truly rarefied height," her mother said, "but I suppose you did come by it honestly in the beginning."

"Imperator, this is India-Papa-One-One, requesting approach instructions."

"India-Papa-One-One, *Imperator* Flight Ops. Be advised our approach pattern is currently full. Please stand by."

"Flight Ops, India-Papa-One-One. Understand approach pattern is currently full. However, be advised that I have Eighth Fleet flag on board."

There was a moment of silence, and the pinnace's pilot grinned at his copilot.

"Ah, India-Papa-One-One, *Imperator* Flight Ops." The controller aboard the flagship sounded suddenly much brisker. "Come to approach vector Able-Charlie. You are cleared for immediate approach to Boat Bay Alpha."

"Thank you, Flight Ops. India-Papa-One-One copies approach vector Able-Charlie for immediate approach to Bay Alpha," the pinnace pilot acknowledged, without allowing even a trace of satisfaction to show.

"How was your visit to the Admiralty, Ma'am?"

"Good, Rafe." Honor looked at her flag captain as the two of them, accompanied by Nimitz, Mercedes Brigham, her three armsmen, and Timothy Meares rode the lift car from the boat bay towards Flag Bridge. "That's not to say everything Sir Thomas had to tell me was something I wanted to hear, but at least we're all on the same page. And," her mouth tightened slightly, "it's more important than ever that we get Cutworm launched successfully."

"Everything's ready, Ma'am," Cardones told her soberly.

"I expected it would be." Honor brought up the time display

in her artificial eye, then looked over her shoulder at her flag lieutenant.

"Tim, general signal to all flag officers. They're all invited to supper. We should just about have time for that before we all pull out."

Chapter Nineteen

"Alpha translation in seventeen minutes, Ma'am," Lieutenant Weissmuller said.

"Understood," Lieutenant Commander Estwicke acknowledged, and turned to her com officer. "Pass the final readiness signal to *Skirmisher*."

"Aye, aye, Ma'am," Lieutenant Wilson acknowledged, and Estwicke nodded to her executive officer.

"Bring the ship to general quarters, Jethro."

"Yes, Ma'am." Lieutenant Jethro Stanton replied, and pressed the GQ button on his console. Alarms blared throughout the ship, although they were scarcely needed. HMS *Ambuscade*'s crew had closed up to their action stations over half an hour ago, taking their time, making certain they'd done it right.

Readiness reports flowed back to the bridge steadily, and Stanton listened carefully, watching the icons in his display's sidebar blink from amber to a steady, burning red.

"All battle stations report manned and ready, Skipper," he reported formally as the last symbol turned red.

"Very good." Estwicke swiveled her chair to face Lieutenant Emily Harcourt, her tactical officer. "Stand by to deploy the remotes."

"Unidentified hyper footprint! Correction—*two* hyper footprints! Range four-six-point-five light-minutes! Bearing one-seven-three by oh-niner-two!"

Captain Heinrich Beauchamp looked up sharply, swiveling his

chair to face the petty officer. The twin, rapidly strobing blood-red icons of unknown hyper translations glared in the depths of the master plot, and the chief of the watch was leaning forward over the shoulder of one of the other sensor techs, watching her display as she worked to refine the data.

"What do we have so far, Lowell?" Beauchamp asked the petty officer who'd made the initial report.

"Not a lot, Sir," the noncom said unhappily. "That far out, we don't have any of the FTL platforms close enough for a good look, and the sub-light—"

He broke off as the crimson icons vanished as abruptly as they had appeared.

"Did they translate out?" Beauchamp demanded.

"Don't think so, Sir," Petty Officer Lowell replied.

"Definitely not, Sir," Chief Torricelli said, looking up from where he'd been watching the sensor tech work the contacts. "Whatever they are, they've gone into stealth."

"Damn," Beauchamp muttered. He let his chair swing back and forth in a tight arc for a few seconds, then shook his head. "All right, Chief. How much did we get?"

"Not much, Sir," Torricelli admitted. "We only had them on sensors for about eight minutes, and like Lowell says, that's an awful long way out for any kind of detail. Best I can tell you is they weren't anything really big. Might've been a pair of light cruisers, but it looked more like destroyers, from the little we got."

"If that's all we've got, it's all we've got," Beauchamp said, more philosophically than he really felt, and punched the com stud on the arm of his bridge chair.

"System HQ, Commander Tucker," a voice responded in his earbug.

"George, it's Heinrich," Beauchamp said. "I know the Commodore just turned in, but you might want to wake him."

"This better be good," Tucker replied. "He was dead tired before I managed to chase him off to bed."

"I know. But we just picked up two unidentified hyper footprints—destroyer or light cruiser range. We had them on sensors for a bit less than eight minutes, then lost them. Our best estimate is that they're still out there, just in stealth."

"Shit." There was silence for several seconds, then Beauchamp heard Tucker inhale deeply. "Not good, Heinrich. I guess I really will have to wake him back up."

"Good light-speed telemetry on the arrays, Skipper," Lieutenant Harcourt reported, studying the readings coming back over the whisker lasers. "Deployment profiles look optimal."

"*Skirmisher* reports good deployment as well, Ma'am," Wilson added from Communications.

"Good," Estwicke replied to both officers simultaneously. "Any sign they got a hard read on us, Emily?"

"Impossible to say, Ma'am," Harcourt replied in the respectfully formal tone she kept for those rare special occasions when her commanding officer asked a silly question. "We didn't pick up any active sensors, of course. But there's no way of knowing whether or not we came out close enough to one of their platforms for it to get a good read on passives."

"Understood." Estwicke's wry smile acknowledged the ever so proper smack on the wrist the tac officer had just given her.

"I haven't picked up any grav-pulse transmissions," Harcourt added. "Anything they did get on us, aside from our footprint itself, has to be coming in light-speed. So whatever it might be, they won't have it for another twenty-five minutes or so."

"By which time we'll have cut even the laser links and be very tiny needles in a very large haystack," Estwicke said with a nod of satisfaction.

"Exactly, Skip," Harcourt agreed. Then she cocked her head. "By the way, Skipper, there's something I've always meant to ask."

"And what might that be?"

"What the hell *is* a 'haystack,' anyway?"

"I don't like this, George," Commodore Tom Milligan said. "I don't like it a bit."

The Commanding Officer, Hera System Command, and his chief of staff were hunched over the latest report from the Hera System's sensor arrays.

"I don't either, Sir," Commander Tucker agreed. The chief of staff's face was tight with worry, but far less exhausted-looking than Milligan's. Then again, he was sleeping better than Milligan was.

Probably, he thought, *because the ultimate responsibility is his, not mine.*

"Those damned ships have been hanging around for two frigging days," Milligan continued harshly.

"We *think* they have, Sir," Tucker amended conscientiously.

"Oh, of course." Milligan's irony was withering, although Tucker knew it wasn't actually directed at him. He was simply unfortunate enough to be in range. "Well, I *think* they're hanging around for a reason," the commodore continued in slightly less sarcastic tones. "And I don't like these readings, either."

He tapped another paragraph of the report, and Tucker nodded silently.

"They aren't very strong, Sir," he pointed out after a moment. Milligan looked at him, and the commander shrugged slightly. "I wish they were a little stronger. Maybe then we could at least have gotten a directional bearing for the LAC sweeps."

The chief of staff wasn't happy about how much wear and tear they'd put on their LAC personnel. The LACs were the only search platforms they had with a chance of running down something as elusive—and fast—as a stealthed Manty destroyer. Unfortunately, they didn't have very many of them, and as the last two days had demonstrated, even their chance was a piss poor one without at least *some* sort of sensor clue to give them an edge.

"Wouldn't have mattered much if we had," Milligan said moodily. "Our birds are too slow to run them down before they could break back across the limit and translate out. Besides, we may not know where they are, but we sure as hell know *what* they are."

Tucker nodded again, not even tempted to play devil's advocate this time. The only thing those transmissions could be were scraps of backscatter from Manticoran directional FTL transmissions. Which, of course, meant the ships which had deployed the recon platforms producing them were still in the system receiving their reports . . . somewhere.

Or at least *one* of them was, anyway.

"Well," Milligan said again, bracing both hands on the tabletop and straightening his back, "I can only think of one reason for them to be hanging around this way."

"I'm afraid I agree, Sir." Tucker smiled without humor. "Which isn't to say I wouldn't like to discover that all they're doing is screwing with our minds."

"Just trying to convince us they have something nastier in mind, you mean?" Milligan snorted. "That *would* be better than what I'm pretty sure they're really up to. Unfortunately, I don't think we're going to be that lucky."

"Me either," Tucker admitted.

"And I don't much like what their damned sensor arrays are telling them, either," Milligan continued more heavily. "Damn. Who would've expected the bastards *here*?"

That, Tucker thought, was a very good question. The Hera System was just over sixty light-years from Trevor's Star . . . and barely thirty light-years from the Haven System itself. That was closer to the capital system than the Manties had ever come, even during Operation Buttercup, but Hera was scarcely a major bastion like the Lovat System. It was important, true, but clearly a second-tier system: a significant industrial node, but not vital enough to demand a heavy fleet presence for its security. Especially not when it was only four days from the capital itself, which meant it could be quickly reinforced in the unlikely event that the Manties managed to mount a second Buttercup.

Except that wasn't what was going to happen.

"We've sent for help, Sir," Tucker said after a moment. "And we've brought the local defenses to Condition Two. I wish there were something more we could do, but I don't think there is."

"No, there isn't," Milligan agreed. "It's just—"

"Excuse me, Sir." Both officers turned to face the office door as the duty communications tech appeared in it. "Sorry to disturb you," the young woman continued, her face tight with worry, "but Perimeter Watch just picked up unidentified hyper footprints."

"How many?" Milligan demanded sharply.

"It looks like at least six ships of the wall, split into two groups, Sir," the com tech said. "They're coming in on converging courses, and Captain Beauchamp estimates they're accompanied by six additional cruiser-range vessels."

Milligan's jaw tightened. Six wallers—even six *old-style* wallers— would go through his "System Command" like a pulser dart through butter. And if they were coming in separated but on converging courses, they undoubtedly meant to pincer any defensive forces between them. However unnecessary that particular refinement might actually be.

"Very well," he said after a moment. "Instruct Captain Beauchamp to keep us informed. Then transmit a general signal to all units. Set Condition One. After that, inform Captain Sherwell that the staff and I will be joining him aboard the flagship directly. He's to immediately begin and expedite preparations for getting underway. And—" he glanced at Tucker "—inform Governor Shelton that I'll be speaking to him shortly."

"Yes, Sir." The communications tech braced briefly to attention and disappeared.

"Sir," Tucker said very quietly, "if this really is six wallers, we're not going to stop them."

"No," Milligan said bleakly. "But if they're doing what I think they are, we couldn't avoid action with them even if we tried."

Tucker started to open his mouth, then changed his mind and nodded, instead.

"Get with Stiller," Milligan continued. "I want an immediate evacuation of the entire orbital infrastructure. I'll get Shelton to confirm that when I speak to him."

"And our civilian shipping, Sir?"

"Anything that's hyper-capable and can reach the hyper limit before the Manties can bring it into range, runs for it. Get that order out immediately. Anything in their way, tries to evade, but I don't want any more dead heroes than I can help. If a ship's crew is ordered to abandon or, God help us, simply fired on, I want them to take to the boats *immediately*."

"Yes, Sir."

"As for the system defense units, we'll just have to do our best. Maybe," Milligan showed his teeth in a rictuslike caricature of a smile, "we can at least scratch their paint."

"*Unidentified hyper footprints!* Many unidentified footprints at eighteen light-minutes, bearing oh-niner-oh by oh-three-three!"

Rear Admiral Everette Beach, CO, Gaston System Command, wheeled towards his operations officer, blue eyes widening in disbelief.

"How many? What class?" he barked.

"We can't say yet, Sir," the ops officer replied. "Looks like a couple of ships of the wall—might be CLACs, instead—with at least a dozen battlecruisers or cruisers. Probably at least a couple of destroyers, as well. And—" she turned to look Beach straight in the eye, and her voice harshened almost accusingly "—we've got a single destroyer-range impeller signature already in-system and moving to meet them."

Beach's jaw tightened, and anger sparkled in his eyes. But angry as he was at Commander Inchman, he knew even more of his anger was directed at himself. Inchman had tried to convince him that the "sensor ghost" the arrays had picked up two days ago was really there, but Beach had disagreed. Oh, it had *looked* like a hyper footprint, but almost a full light-hour beyond the system hyper limit? At that range, given the rudimentary state of Gaston's sensor net, it could have been almost anything. And whatever it was, it had vanished within minutes of appearing in the first place.

Sure it did, he thought harshly. *And you were so damned sure Inchman was wrong about its simply going into stealth, weren't you Everette? You* stupid *shit. You've been whining to the Octagon ever since you took over here that you needed a better sensor net. Well, genius, why didn't you at least pay attention to what you* had?

"You were right," he made himself say, a little surprised his voice sounded so close to normal. "They *were* scouting us."

Inchman didn't reply. Not that he'd really expected her to. But he'd owed her that apology, and assuming he survived, he'd have to make it official in his after-action report. The one he'd no doubt have plenty of time to write after the board of inquiry beached him.

"Signal to all units," he continued, "Condition Red-Three. Axis of threat is oh-niner-oh, oh-three-three. All merchant shipping to immediately get underway. Order the industrial platforms to commence evacuation at once."

"Yes, Sir."

"Right on the tick, Your Grace," Mercedes Brigham observed with immense satisfaction as Commander Estwicke's *Ambuscade* accelerated steadily towards rendezvous with *Imperator*. "And exactly where she's supposed to be," the chief of staff continued, watching the destroyer's icon on the huge plot on *Imperator's* flag bridge.

"So far, so good," Honor agreed. She stood beside the admiral's command chair, watching the plot as *Ambuscade's* fresh tac data started coming in. Commander Daniels' *Skirmisher* had delivered the basic take from the two destroyers' heavily stealthed arrays six hours ago, at the prearranged rendezvous, but Estwicke had remained behind to make sure there'd been no important changes after *Skirmisher*'s departure. Now Honor gazed intently at the star system's schematic while a skinsuited Nimitz perched on the chair's back. She felt him at the back of her mind, sharing her tension as he had so many times before, and she reached out to him with a quick mental caress.

"I hope the other groups' timing is as good," Andrea Jaruwalski said from Honor's other side, and Honor glanced at her. "I know it doesn't really matter all that much in the greater scheme of things, Your Grace," the ops officer said with a crooked smile, "but this is opening night, so to speak. I want our audience to appreciate all the trouble we've gone to in order to impress them."

"Oh, I imagine they'll get the message," Honor said with a half-smile of her own. She could taste Jaruwalski's excitement and anticipation, and the information from her scouting destroyers' spy mission strongly suggested that Hera was going to prove a case of severe overkill. No wonder the captain was confident of success.

So was Honor. In fact, she'd suspected from the beginning that they were bringing along more firepower than was going to be required. But Hera was the closest of their targeted systems to Nouveau Paris, and this was the only attack going in without any carrier support at all. So she'd brought along Alistair McKeon's entire squadron . . . in no small part to make the point to Thomas Theisman that the Alliance could—and would—operate even its most modern superdreadnoughts aggressively this deep behind the front line systems. But, unlike Jaruwalski, Honor wasn't really looking forward to what they were about to do.

Or to killing all the men and women who were about to die.

"*Ambuscade*'s upload is complete, Captain Jaruwalski," one of the ops officer's plotting team's petty officers announced.

"What does it show?" Jaruwalski asked, as she and Honor both moved closer to the plot.

"CIC sees no changes from *Skirmisher*'s data, Ma'am. It still looks like two battleships, four battlecruisers or big heavy cruisers, and less than a hundred LACs."

"I still find that hard to believe," Jaruwalski muttered, then grimaced as Honor cocked a sardonic eyebrow at her. "Sorry, Your Grace. I don't mean to suggest Daniels and Estwicke didn't do a good job. I'm just surprised their system picket is that light, even this close to Nouveau Paris."

Honor shrugged, never taking her gaze from the icons of the ships trapped between her own incoming forces. *Skirmisher*'s report had allowed her to plot her own alpha translations perfectly, and the defenders found themselves caught squarely between the two prongs of her attack.

They'd obviously realized the system was being probed and brought their mobile units—such as they were—to a high state of readiness, because they were already underway. In fact, they were accelerating hard, almost directly towards her flagship and its division mate, HMS *Intolerant*. Clearly their commander had realized she could never get outside the attackers' MDM envelope and had elected to attempt to stay as far away as possible from the four SDs of McKeon's first and third divisions. The defenders' outclassed, obsolescent ships and sparse LAC force stood no chance of survival against a pair of *Invictus*-class superdreadnoughts, but they probably had a marginally better chance of inflicting at least some damage on her single division before they died.

"They can't be strong everywhere, Andrea," she said after a moment. "That's the whole point behind Cutworm. And don't forget that *Ambuscade* and *Skirmisher* probably didn't get reliable reads on any system-defense pods they may have deployed."

"Agreed." Jaruwalski nodded. "Still, they're hanging all but naked. And I've got to say, I didn't expect to see *any* battleships still in commission."

"I didn't either. On the other hand, this is an awful long way from the front. I suppose if they've got one or two left, it makes more sense to use them here than somewhere more likely to be attacked. Of course," Honor's smile was knife-blade thin, "they're going to be reevaluating where attacks are 'likely' very shortly now."

"It's confirmed, Sir." Captain Beauchamp's expression was grim on the com screen connecting Milligan's flag bridge to the system's planet-side Defense Headquarters. "Bogey Alpha is two superdreadnoughts and three big heavy cruisers—they look like the new *Saganami-C*s. Bogey Beta is four SDs and three light cruisers. From the emissions signatures, two of Beta's wallers are *Medusa*-class SD(P)s. We don't have positive IDs on Beta's other SD, or on either of Alpha's, but all three of them are even bigger than a *Medusa*."

"*Invictuses*," Tucker said bitterly. "They've got to be."

"Here?" Milligan shook his head. "According to NavInt, they can't have more than a handful of them. Why in God's name would they send three of them this deep into the Republic to hit a target as secondary as Hera?"

"At a guess, Sir, they're sending a message," Tucker replied. Milligan looked at him, and the chief of staff waved one hand at the ominous light codes in the plot. "We've all been assuming they'd have no choice but to pull in their horns and fort up after Thunderbolt, and especially after Grendelsbane." He shrugged. "Well, Sir, I'd say they intend to suggest we were mistaken."

"Harper."

"Yes, Your Grace?"

"Record a message for the system commander."

"Of course, Your Grace." If Lieutenant Brantley thought there was anything odd about sending a message to the commander of a naval force one intended to destroy momentarily, no sign of it showed in his voice or expression.

"Live mike, Ma'am," he said after a moment, and Honor looked directly into her pick up.

"This is Admiral Honor Harrington, Royal Manticoran Navy," she said levelly. "By this time, you must be aware of the disparity of combat power between your forces and mine. I am here to destroy the industrial infrastructure in this star system, and I *will* do so, however regretfully. I have no interest in killing anyone when that can be avoided, however. I submit to you that the forces under your command, even assuming—as I do—that they're backed by a substantial number of previously deployed missile pods, can't hope to seriously damage my own units. Your vessels, on the other hand, are little more than targets. Courage alone cannot substitute for tactical inferiority on this scale. You are already inside my powered missile envelope; you won't survive to bring *us* into *your* shipboard range. Nor will your LACs survive to reach attack range of us."

She paused for just a moment, then continued in that same level, measured voice.

"It's obvious from your maneuvers to this point that you're prepared to do your duty in defense of this star system, however hopeless you must know that defense to be. I respect that, but I also implore you not to throw away the lives of the men and women under your command. If you continue to close, I *will* fire on you. If, however, you choose to abandon ship and scuttle at this time, I will not fire upon your small craft or life pods. Nor will I fire upon your LACs if you order them to withdraw and stand down. I'm not asking you to surrender your vessels to me; I'm simply asking you to allow your personnel to live.

"Harrington, clear."

"Clean recording, Your Grace," Brantley said, after replaying it to be certain.

"Then send it," she said.

"Do you think it will do any good, Ma'am?" Mercedes Brigham asked, leaning close to Honor's command chair and speaking quietly into her ear.

"I don't know," Honor replied bleakly, rubbing Nimitz's ears as he curled in her lap. "I like to think *I'd* be rational enough to abandon in her shoes, but, to be completely honest, I'm not certain I would. I just know I don't want to slaughter people who can't even shoot back."

" . . . asking you to allow your personnel to live. Harrington, clear."

Tom Milligan watched the message from the tall, level-voiced, exotically attractive woman in the black-and-gold uniform and white beret silently, his eyes hard. There was no doubt in his mind that Harrington—*God, it would be* Harrington, *wouldn't it?*—had summarized his command's chances of survival with agonizing accuracy.

Of course, she did wait until—as she herself just pointed out— she'd trapped us into entering her missile envelope, whether we'd wanted to or not, didn't she? Obviously, however concerned she may be with sparing people's lives, she's not especially concerned about what's likely to happen to my career!

He surprised himself with a chuckle, but it was short-lived.

"Sir?"

He turned his head. Commander Tucker stood beside his bridge chair, where he'd viewed the message along with his commodore, and his expression was profoundly unhappy.

"Yes, George?" Milligan asked, his voice remarkably calm.

"Sir, she may be right about our relative combat power. But we can't just blow up our own ships!"

"Even if she's going to do it for us sometime in the next ten or fifteen minutes?"

Milligan nodded his head at the implacably advancing icons in the plot. Harrington's converging superdreadnought divisions were already up to a velocity of over twelve thousand kilometers per second, forging straight ahead, like twin daggers plunged directly into the heart of the Hera System. He felt a spike of pure, burning rage at the complete—and completely *justified*—confidence of their unwavering approach.

Harrington. "The Salamander" herself, coming straight down his throat with a pair of SD(P)s while four more came right up his backside, and armed with the advantage of detailed tactical scans of the star system and his own defensive forces. No *wonder* she was "confident!"

"But, Sir—!" Tucker protested, and Milligan smiled grimly.

"George, for what it matters—and, at this particular moment, it doesn't matter a whole hell of a lot—my career crashlanded the instant those ships came over the hyper wall. I realize that, unlike the previous management, Admiral Theisman's unlikely to have me shot for something that obviously wasn't my fault, but someone's still going to have to carry the can for this one, and I'm elected. Under the circumstances, it's not going to make things much worse for me personally if I do what she's suggesting. And, in case you've forgotten, there are over six thousand people aboard these two obsolete, piece-of-crap battleships, alone. I'm not sure I'd take a lot of consolation from the knowledge that I got them killed for absolutely no return. In fact, what I most regret right now, is that I didn't simply order them all to turn tail and run from the outset."

"You couldn't do that, Sir."

"I could have, and I damned well should have! Not that it would've done much good, given her approach vectors, although at least the *LACs* might have been able to stay away from her," Milligan said with quiet, intense bitterness. Then he inhaled deeply.

"Inform Captain Beauchamp that he's to coordinate the missile pod engagement from dirt-side," he said flatly. "Then instruct the LAC crews to return immediately to their launch platforms.

They're to abandon and evacuate to the planetary surface, and the platform skippers are to set their demolition charges and accompany them."

Tucker was staring at him in something like shock, but Milligan continued steadily.

"In the meantime, I'll contact Admiral Harrington. I'll accept her offer on behalf of our mobile units, and we'll abandon ship."

"*Sir!*"

"God *damn* it, George!" Milligan grated. "I am *not* going to get thousands of people killed for nothing! I won't *do* it. We'll take our best shot with the missile pods, but those ships—" he jabbed his finger at the hostile icons "—can kill anything we have from outside any range where we can even shoot back. Our 'main combatants' don't have MDMs, and our LACs are *Cimeterres*, not frigging *Shrikes*. They'd never live to reach their own range of superdreadnoughts without MDM support to cover their approach. We're fucked, and nothing we can do can change that. Do you understand me?"

"Yes, Sir," Tucker said finally, slowly, and turned away.

"Communications," Milligan said heavily, "raise Admiral Harrington for me."

"There they go, Your Grace," Andrea Jaruwalski said, and Honor nodded. Her remote sensor arrays were close enough to see the drive signatures of the Havenite warships' small craft. Individual life pods were much harder to detect, even at that range and even with Manticoran sensors, but their beacons showed as a fine green haze of diamond dust glittering around the warship icons, and the ships themselves had struck their wedges five minutes earlier.

"That isn't a happy man over there," Mercedes Brigham murmured, and Honor looked at her.

"I've been in his shoes, Mercedes. When I ordered Alistair to surrender *his* ship. It isn't easy, however hopeless the situation might be. Milligan showed a lot of moral courage when he accepted my offer, although I doubt most of his critics will see it that way."

"From his tone, I think he agrees with you, Ma'am."

Honor snorted softly at Brigham's understatement. Milligan had actually thanked her for offering an out which would spare his people's lives, but he'd looked—and sounded—like a man chewing ground glass.

"I noticed he didn't say anything about any missile pods, Your Grace," Jaruwalski observed quietly.

"No, he didn't, did he?" Honor looked at her ops officer. Jaruwalski was as professionally focused as ever, but Honor tasted something very like frustration under the younger woman's surface. That wasn't exactly the right word for the emotion, but it came close. Andrea Jaruwalski was no more enamored of killing people just to kill them than Honor was, but the tactician in her couldn't help . . . regretting the lost opportunity to carry through with their neatly planned mousetrap and finish off the enemy ships herself.

"I didn't *ask* him to stand down the pods, either, Andrea," Honor continued. "Mostly because I knew he'd refuse, just as you or I would have in his position. If I'd made the stand down of *all* of his defenses a precondition for my offer, he would have rejected it."

"It might have been worth a try, anyway, Your Grace." Jaruwalski's tone was mostly humorous, but she grimaced and gestured at one of the secondary plots. "We're beginning to pick up active targeting emissions. A lot of them."

"As expected." Honor examined the indicated plot. "Actually," she said after a moment, "there aren't as many as I'd expected. I wonder if that means they're as light on pods as they were on ships?"

"We can hope, Ma'am," Brigham said. "Of course—"

"There go the scuttling charges, Captain Jaruwalski!"

Honor and both her staffers turned towards the main plot once more. The range was still long enough that in the visual display, the brief, bright stars which once had been warships of the Republic of Haven were little more than short-lived, brilliant pinpricks. The presentation in the plot was even less dramatic than that. Seven crimson icons simply blinked once, and disappeared.

The bright ruby light chips representing the Hera System's LACs were still there, but they continued to accelerate steadily *away* from Honor's ships, obviously bound—as Commodore Milligan had promised—for their base platforms.

"You think they'll turn around if their missile pods get lucky,

Ma'am?" Brigham asked softly, gazing at the retiring light attack craft.

"That's hard to say." Honor considered the question for a few seconds, then shrugged. "Their pods would have to get awfully lucky to make any difference. If those were *Shrikes* or *Ferrets*, it might be different, but they aren't."

"*Missile launch!*" a Plotting rating announced suddenly. "Multiple missile launches! Time to impact four-point-six minutes!"

"Captain Beauchamp has launched, Commodore!"

Tom Milligan looked up at the announcement. He'd been staring moodily and silently out the pinnace's viewport, gazing out into the endless emptiness which had swallowed up the dispersing plasma of his command. Now he shoved himself out of his seat and stepped quickly to the cramped command deck's hatch.

A pinnace's sensor capability wasn't particularly good at the best of times, and the display was far too small to show much detail, but he could see the wavefront of Beauchamp's outgoing missiles. He'd been surprised when Harrington hadn't tried to insist that he agree to stand them down, as well. In her place, he certainly would have at least made the attempt. Unless, of course, her scouting destroyers had managed to tell her just how threadbare *all* of Hera's defenses were.

"Estimate eleven hundred—I say again, one-one-zero-zero—inbound," Plotting reported. "Target is Second Division."

"Makes sense," Brigham said quietly. "We're closer to most of their platforms, and two superdreadnoughts have to have less missile defense than four of them."

Honor didn't respond. In fact, she was almost certain her chief of staff didn't even realize she'd spoken aloud.

The tornado of multi-drive missiles howled towards them, and whoever had programmed their launch times and accelerations had done her job well. Despite how widely separated many of the launching pods were, their coordination was flawless. *All* of those missiles would arrive on target simultaneously as a single, tightly focused hammer blow.

The quiet murmur of voices behind her grew louder, more clipped and intense, as Jaruwalski's plotting parties and tactical crews concentrated on their tasks. Not that there was a great deal for them to actually *do* at this moment. Everything an admiral's staff could do for a situation like this had to happen earlier, in the planning and training stages, when the crews of the individual ships of the admiral's command were learning what was expected of them, and how to perform it.

As *Imperator*, *Intolerant*, and their screening heavy cruisers were performing it now.

As little as five or six T-years earlier, that many missiles, fired at a mere pair of superdreadnoughts, would have been both enormous and deadly. Today, it was different. In an era of pod-laying ships of the wall, missile densities like that had become something defense planners had to take into the routine calculations.

Doctrine and hardware had required major modifications, and the modifying process was an ongoing one. The Mark 31 counter-missiles Honor's ships were firing represented significant improvements even over the Mark 30 counter-missiles her command had used as recently as the Battle of Sidemore, only months before. Their insanely powerful wedges were capable of sustaining accelerations of up to 130,000 gravities for as much as seventy-five seconds, which gave them a powered range from rest of almost 3.6 million kilometers.

Kill numbers at such extreme ranges were problematical, to say the least, and the incoming Havenite missiles were equipped with the very best penetration aids and EW systems Shannon Foraker could build into them. That made them much, much better than anything the People's Navy had possessed during the First Havenite War, but BuShips and BuWeaps hadn't precisely been letting grass grow under their feet, either, Honor thought grimly. Her ships mounted at least three times as many counter-missile launchers as ships of their classes had mounted before the advent of pod-based combat.

Their telemetry and control links had been increased by an even higher factor, and each of her ships had deployed additional Mark 20 electronics platforms at the ends of dedicated tractor beams. Nicknamed "Keyhole" by the Navy, the Mark 20 wasn't a traditional tethered decoy, or even an additional sensor platform or Ghost Rider EW platform. *These* platforms were placed much further from the ships which had launched them, and they had only one function—to serve as fire control telemetry relays.

They extended well beyond the boundaries of their motherships' impeller wedges, like an old-style wet-navy submarine's periscope, and they gave the tactical crews aboard those ships the ability to look "down" past the blinding interference of their own outgoing counter-missiles' wedges.

To a civilian, that might have sounded like a small thing, but the implications were huge. The Keyhole platforms were massive and expensive, but they allowed a ship to control multiple counter-missiles for each dedicated shipboard fire control "slot." And they also allowed counter-missile launches to be much more tightly spaced, which added significant depth to the antimissile engagement envelope.

And as a final refinement, the grav-pulse com-equipped reconnaissance arrays deployed in a shell three and a half million kilometers out watched the incoming missiles' EW with eagle eyes, and their FTL data streams provided the missile defense crews aboard Honor's ships a priceless nine-second advantage. Although the missile controllers and their AIs were still limited to light-speed telemetry links, they were able to refine and update targeting solutions with much greater speed and precision than had ever been possible before.

Shannon Foraker had been forced to rely on mass and sheer numbers, to build a wall in space using thousands of weapons whose individual accuracy was very low. Manticore had approached the problem from a different direction, relying on its technological advantages and superior technique.

The first counter-missile launch killed only a hundred and six of the incoming MDMs. The second, intercepting them less than ten seconds later killed another hundred. But the *third* launch, with almost twenty seconds for its controllers to react, killed three hundred.

Tom Milligan turned away from the pinnace's tiny display without a word. He returned to his seat, staring out the viewport once again, and his expression was bleak.

One hit, he thought. *Surely one frigging hit wasn't too much to ask for!*

But the Republic hadn't gotten it. Only forty of Beauchamp's MDMs had broken through the Manties' counter-missiles, and the point defense laser clusters—whose numbers also seemed to have been hugely increased—had blasted those threadbare survivors out of existence well short of attack range.

We knew they were improving their antimissile doctrine, but nothing I ever saw suggested that they'd improved it this much! And it's going to play hell with our system defense doctrine.

Hera's defenses had been weak, even by the existing standards of the Republican Navy. He should have had at least three times the missile pods he'd actually been able to deploy, and they ought to have been backed up by a much stronger LAC force, at a bare minimum. But given what he'd just seen, even the defensive strength he ought to have had wouldn't have stopped Harrington.

I've never failed this completely at anything before in my life, he thought bitterly. *At least I didn't get all of my people killed for nothing, but just at the moment, that's pretty cold comfort.*

He stared broodingly into the endless ebon infinity of space. It looked so peaceful out there, so calm. And that cold, merciless vista was infinitely preferable to what was about to happen closer to the life-giving beacon of the star called Hera.

"That's the last of them, Your Grace," Jaruwalski said. "They may have some additional pods squirreled away, but if they could have reached us with more of them, they would have. Anything else they throw our way will be lighter, easier to handle."

Honor didn't respond for several seconds. She was gazing into her plot, her eyes picking out the icons of orbital factories, extraction facilities, power satellites, warehouses. By the standards of a wealthy star system like the Manticore home system, or of a major transportation node, like one of the Junction's termini, Hera's orbital and deep-space facilities might seem sparse, but they still represented decades of investment. They were where people worked, what powered over half the star system's economy. They represented literally billions of dollars of investment, and even more earning potential, all in a star nation struggling doggedly to overcome more than a century of ongoing economic disaster.

And she was here to destroy them. *All* of them.

"One of the platforms in planetary orbit just blew up, Ma'am," Brigham reported. Honor looked at her, and the chief of staff pointed into the plot, indicating the icon of the platform in question.

"That one," she said. "According to CIC, it was one of the LAC basing platforms, so it looks like they're making good on Milligan's stand down order."

"Yes, it does." Honor's chocolate eyes were sad, and her fingers caressed Nimitz's silken coat while she drew strength from the bright, fierce power of his support and love, but her voice was calm, unshadowed.

"All right, Mercedes, Andrea," she said after a moment, turning her command chair to face them. "We came to wreck this system's space-going economy, and it would appear the way is clear. So let's be about it."

Chapter Twenty

"What the hell *are* those things?" Rear Admiral Beach murmured. Behind him, he could hear the disciplined bedlam as his communications staff coordinated the evacuation of Gaston's deep-space industrial infrastructure, but his attention was focused on two of the tentatively identified Manty battlecruisers.

"They've got to be battlecruisers," Commander Myron Randall, his chief of staff, replied.

"I know that," Beach said, just a bit impatiently. "But look at the tonnage estimates. According to CIC, these things mass dammed close to two million tons. That's a big dammed battlecruiser, Myron!"

"The Graysons' *Courvoisier IIs* mass over a million tons," Randall pointed out.

"Which is still considerably smaller than these are." Beach shook his head. "I'll bet you this is the *Manties'* version of a pod-laying battlecruiser."

"Wonderful," Randall muttered.

"Well," Beach said, glancing at the shoals of LACs which had launched themselves from the incoming CLACs, "how much worse can it get, Myron? We've got three hundred *Cimeterres*, the missile pods, and four battlecruisers. I don't think the fact that they've brought along some of their newer toys is going to make a lot of difference in the long run."

"Message from Admiral Henke, Ma'am."

"Put it on my tertiary display," Dame Alice Truman replied,

and a moment later Michelle Henke's ebony face appeared on the tiny flatscreen by Truman's knee.

"Mike," the vice admiral greeted her.

"Admiral," Henke responded.

"To what do I owe the honor?"

"We've been going over the fresh data from *Intruder's* platforms over here, Ma'am. Have your people noticed that odd little cluster of blips they're picking up in Charlie-Two-Seven now that they've gone active?"

"Just a minute, Mike." Truman looked up from the display, and beckoned to her chief of staff. Captain Goodrick crossed to her immediately, and she waved him forward into the field of her own com pickup. "Would you repeat that for Wraith, Mike?"

"Have your people noticed that cluster of blips in Charlie-Two-Seven?" Henke asked, after nodding a welcome to Goodrick.

"You mean the ones just to system north of the refitting platform?" She nodded again, and he shrugged. "We've seen them, but so far we've put them down as just orbital clutter. You know how sloppy a lot of civilian facilities are about disposing of their trash."

"Tell me about it," Henke said sourly. "In this case, though, I don't think that's what it is." Goodrick raised his eyebrows, and she grimaced. "The arrays aren't getting very clear returns off of them. In fact, it looks to us over here as if that could be because we're not supposed to."

"Low-signature platforms?" Truman asked.

"Definitely a possibility," Henke agreed. "Especially if you look at how they're distributed. Captain LaCosta's tactical section agrees with us that they *look* like what could be missile pods dispersed just widely enough to clear their birds' impeller wedges when they launch."

Goodrick was leaning over a secondary display, reexamining the sensor data for himself. Now he looked up and nodded to Truman.

"I think Admiral Henke has a point, Ma'am," he said. "As a matter of fact, it looks to me like what we're seeing here could be just a portion of the entire pattern. I'd say there's a good chance they've got a lot more of them than we've actually picked up."

"Well, we expected something like it," Truman observed. She considered for a moment, then shrugged. "I don't think it really changes anything, Wraith. But launch an additional shell of arrays and pass the word to Scotty. I want them sweeping the space in front of him like a fine tooth comb, and I want him tied directly into their take."

"Yes, Ma'am. I'll get right on it."

Goodrick began issuing orders, and Truman nodded to Henke over the com.

"Good catch, Mike. Aside from that, how are things looking from your side?"

"Nominal, so far." Henke's smile was unpleasant. "I know it's on a lot smaller scale, but I think we're about to get a tiny bit of our own back for Grendelsbane."

"That's what we came for," Truman agreed, and leaned back in her command chair, studying the plot.

Given Eighth Fleet's command structure, she was actually wearing three separate "hats." She was Honor's second-in-command and carrier commander; the commanding officer of CLAC Squadron Three; and the CO of CarRon 3's first division, the carriers *Werewolf* and *Chimera*. Of course, two of those three slots weren't especially relevant just now, she thought, watching *Werewolf*'s and *Chimera*'s LACs moving steadily away from their carriers. And, speaking as the commander of the first division—and the senior officer of the Gaston attack force—things seemed to be going quite well at the moment.

Knock on wood, she reminded herself. *Knock on wood.*

"They're coming right in on us, Sir," Commander Inchman said flatly.

"But they aren't closing into standard missile range, are they, Sandra?" Beach observed, standing at her shoulder and looking down at the icons on her plot.

"Their hyper-capable units aren't, Sir; it looks like they're decelerating to rest relative to the planet at about one light-minute. But their LACs are still boring straight in."

"And if anyone thinks they're going to leave *our* hyper-capable units intact to shoot at their LACs, they're dreaming," Myron Randall muttered from behind the rear admiral.

"Probably not," Beach agreed grimly, and Randall colored slightly. Obviously, he hadn't realized he'd spoken loudly enough for his admiral to overhear.

"On the other hand," Beach continued, "they are going to come into range of our missile pods." He showed his teeth in what only the most myopic might have called a smile. "Pity they didn't wait another couple of months."

"You've got that right, Sir," Inchman agreed, her voice harsh with angry frustration.

"Maybe, and maybe not, Sandra." Beach put his hand on her shoulder and squeezed gently. "Odds are Supply would've been sending us their regrets again."

He understood Inchman's frustration—and anger—perfectly. The additional pods they'd been promised would have increased their long-range missile power hugely. Then again, they'd been "promised" for quite some time.

"I know, Sir. It's just—" Inchman bit off what she'd been about to say, and Beach sighed.

"They're shipping them to the front line systems as quickly as they can, Sandra. Someone's got to suck hind teat when quantities are limited. And to be fair, if you'd been in charge of prioritizing deliveries, would *you* have predicted an attack on Gaston, of all damned places?"

"No, Sir," she admitted.

"So we do the best we can with what we've got," Beach said as philosophically as he could. He looked over his shoulder at Randall.

"How long until we can get underway, Myron?"

"Another twelve minutes," Randall said, after checking his chrono quickly. "Captain Steigert's engineers are doing their best, but—"

"Understood." Beach gave a bitter chuckle, and squeezed Inchman's shoulder again. "If I'd listened to Sandra, at least I'd have had our impellers at a higher state of readiness."

He brooded down at the ops officer's plot, then drew a deep breath and turned away.

"They'll be in range to engage us in another thirty-five minutes, even if we just sit here in orbit. To be honest, if I thought it would do any good, I'd order all of our hyper-capable units to just bug out."

Randall looked at him with an expression which mingled surprise and disapproval, and Beach snorted.

"Of course I would, Myron! It might not be particularly glorious, but if those *are* pod-laying battlecruisers out there—and their deceleration profile certainly suggests they are—then we're truly and royally screwed. Dying gloriously sounds good in bad historical novels. Speaking for myself, I think doing it in real life when you don't have to is fucking stupid, and it irritates the hell out of me that we don't appear to have any choice."

He couldn't quite keep the bitterness out of his voice, but he drew another breath and gave himself a mental shake.

"Since we can't avoid action with them, and since we can't match their engagement range, I want all of our ships moved around to the far side of the planet. We'll keep it between us and them as long as we can."

Randall looked vaguely rebellious. He didn't say anything, but Beach read his thoughts without much difficulty.

"No, it's not particularly glorious. And I doubt it's going to make a lot of difference in the end, for that matter. But if whoever's in command over there is feeling particularly stupid, he may send in his LACs to flush us out of cover. If he does, we might actually manage to pick a few of them off. Even if he doesn't, he'll have to maneuver his MDM-capable units to clear the planet if he wants a shot at us. For that matter, he may decline to fire from extended range at us at all, if we're close enough to the planet."

"I think the Admiral has a point, Myron," Inchman said. Both men looked at her, and she shrugged. "Given all the other irons the Manties have in the fire right now, they certainly aren't going to court a violation of the Eridani Edict, and even *their* MDMs' targeting discrimination is pretty shaky at long range. This is our best chance to at least draw them into a range where we'll get to shoot back."

"They're pulling back behind the planet, Ma'am," Commander Oliver Manfredi said.

"Not very obliging of them," Michelle Henke observed dryly, and Manfredi chuckled without much humor.

Henke smiled and tipped back in her command chair, steepling her fingers under her chin in a posture she'd seen Honor assume scores of times. She couldn't say the Peep CO's choice of tactics was totally unexpected, but that didn't make it any more welcome.

"All right, Oliver," she told her golden-haired chief of staff after a moment. "Make sure Dame Alice has that information, and inform her that unless she disapproves my actions, I intend to execute Grand Divide."

"Aye, Ma'am," Manfredi replied.

The chief of staff's own smile creased his classically chiseled features and showed perfect white teeth, and Henke suppressed a mental laugh as he turned towards Lieutenant Kaminski, her communications officer. It wasn't anything Manfredi had done; it was simply the way he looked. He was as competent as he was decorative, but he really ought to have been on Truman's staff, not Henke's. For some reason, Alice Truman always seemed to have an executive officer, or a chief of staff, or a flag captain who was as golden-haired and blue-eyed as she was.

But not this time, Henke thought with amused satisfaction. *This time, I've got him . . . not to mention the rest of my "harem."*

It was harder not to laugh this time. Unlike her friend Honor, Henke had always enjoyed an . . . energetic love-life, although she'd never allowed it to spill over on to her professional life. This time, though, it had been Honor's turn to twit *her* from the moment Henke had invited her to dinner aboard *Ajax* and she'd laid eyes on Henke's assembled staff. Manfredi was certainly the most gorgeous of her staffers, but every single one of them was male, and there wasn't a homely one in the bunch.

She pushed the thought aside and straightened in her chair. Grand Divide was the approach she'd worked out with her staff to deal with a situation like this one. It wasn't a perfect solution, but that was because there *weren't* any "perfect solutions." It was just the best available.

She glanced at the master plot, watching the projected vectors of her ships begin to shift. She had only four of her six battle-cruisers actually under her own command—her third division, HMS *Hector* and HMS *Achilles*—had been attached to Samuel Miklós' force for the attack on Tambourin, which left her only *Agamemnon*, *Ajax* (her own flagship), and the second division's *Priam* and *Patrocles*. They had four of the *Edward Saganami*-class heavy cruisers in support, including Henke's old ship, the *Saganami* herself, but none of them were equipped to fire internally launched MDMs. On the other hand, they did have several dozen of the new-style missile pods tractored to their hulls.

Now *Agamemnon* and *Ajax*, accompanied by two of the heavy cruisers, began to angle away from *Priam*, *Patrocles*, and the other two heavy cruisers. By spreading her forces, she ought to be able to bring the defenders' starships under fire with at least one of them. After all, the opposition commander couldn't keep the planet between her ships and *everybody*. But it meant Henke would probably be able to engage with only half her total platforms. Worse, it meant her two attack groups were moving steadily out of mutual support range for missile defense.

If the destroyers which had scouted the system had detected larger numbers of deployed missile pods, Henke would never have dared put Grand Divide into action. Even against the number of pods the destroyers *had* detected, she was risking significant damage. But they couldn't take out the system's industrial base without going in close, not when virtually all of it orbited the system's inhabited planet. Which meant the defending ships *had* to be neutralized first.

Well, at least it should be interesting, she told herself.

"They *are* splitting up, Sir," Inchman reported. Her in-system sensor platforms had the Manticoran units under observation, and she indicated the changing vector analyses under the icons of the two diverging cruiser forces. "CIC is designating this force Alpha and this one Beta."

"They're going to pincer us," Beach grunted. "About what I expected. Too bad they didn't just go ahead and send in the LACs as beaters."

"But look at this, Sir," Randall said, indicating the red arrows of projected vectors. "They may be going to try to open clear lines of sight to us, but on their current headings, the range will be less than seven million klicks."

"So they are a little nervous about Eridani violations," Beach observed, and smiled humorlessly. "On the other hand, our ships' best powered envelope from rest is under *two* million. Not a huge improvement."

"Except that we haven't fired any of our orbital pods yet, Sir," Inchman pointed out. "And the closer they come before we do, the better our firing solutions are going to be."

"True." Beach nodded and frowned thoughtfully down at the plot. "I know doctrine says to kill the CLACs as our first priority in a situation like this one," he said, after a moment, "but they aren't being obliging enough to bring *them* in closer. If we had more pods, if we could get a better salvo density, it might still make sense to go after them, first. Under the circumstances, though, I think we'll hold our fire as long as we can, then concentrate it all on Alpha. Run your firing solutions accordingly, Sandra."

"Yes, Sir."

"And while we're waiting, Myron," Beach turned to the chief of staff, "tell the LACs to continue to fall back. If they can, I want them drifting towards system east."

"You want them in position to hit Alpha if the pods actually get through, Sir?"

"Exactly."

"What about *us*, Sir?" Randall waved one hand at the icons representing Beach's battlecruisers.

"It's tempting, but it wouldn't work." Beach shook his head. "We're too far away. Even at our best acceleration, it would take us over an hour to get into our range of them. Unless the pods and the LACs do a hell of a lot better than I expect, they'd pick us off with MDMs before we ever reached them. Worse, as soon as we left the planetary shadow, *Beta* would nail us." He shook his head again. "No. We stay put, using the planet for cover against Beta. If we can hammer Alpha, so much the better, but we can't afford to get out into deeper water against sharks like these."

"That's a pretty cool customer over there, Ma'am," Commander Manfredi said.

"That it is, Oliver," Henke agreed. "I don't think it's going to do her a lot of good in the end, though. She's obviously decided to play it all the way out, but she's holding a losing hand."

She swivelled her command chair to face Lieutenant Commander Stackpole, her operations officer.

"John, I think she's going to hold fire on her pods to the last possible minute. I know I would, in her place. And notice the way her LACs are shifting oh so casually over to flank our vector."

"You think he's going to concentrate on us and ignore the carriers, Ma'am?"

"It's what I'd do. She can't possibly hope to kill *them*, anyway, and she's not going to beat off our attack. So the only thing left for her to do is to inflict whatever losses she realistically can. Which means us."

Stackpole considered it for a moment. Although he was physically attractive—taller than Honor and almost as dark as Henke herself, with high cheekbones and a powerful nose—he was nowhere near as decorative as Manfredi's holo-star good looks. He was probably, however, even better at his job.

"You're thinking about the pods, aren't you, Ma'am?"

"I am."

"Well," he said thoughtfully, "we've still only picked up a couple of hundred of them. With hard locks, I mean. CIC's projecting general zones for about twice that many, but we don't have anything we could use for reliable targeting information on them. We could kill most of those we've actually found with proximity warheads, but they're all awfully close to the planet, Ma'am."

"Too close," Henke agreed. "Especially for MDMs at this range. We might have a nasty accident, and Duchess Harrington wouldn't like that."

"No, Ma'am, she wouldn't," Stackpole agreed with feeling.

Honor had made it abundantly, one might almost say painfully, clear that she would not be amused by anything which might be remotely construed as a violation of the Eridani Edict's prohibitions, even by accident. And if smacking an inhabited planet, however accidentally, with a ninety-five-ton missile moving at fifty percent of light-speed couldn't be construed as using a "weapon of mass destruction" against it, very few things could be.

"I think we've still got to find a way to make them use them at longer-range, though," Henke said. "Albert."

"Yes, Ma'am?" Lieutenant Kaminski replied.

"Message to Admiral Truman. My compliments, and I would appreciate it if she could order the LACs to go after the pods."

"Yes, Ma'am."

"Antonio."

"Yes, Ma'am?" Lieutenant Commander Braga, her astrogator, responded.

"Compute us a new course. I want to end up in the same spots, but assuming the Admiral agrees to let the LAC jockeys kill pods for us, I want to reduce our acceleration to give them more time."

"Yes, Ma'am. How *much* more time?"

✧   ✧   ✧

"They've reduced their acceleration, Sir."

Beach swung his command chair to face Commander Inchman.

"By how much?"

"Almost fifty percent," Inchman replied.

"And their LACs?"

"Changing course and coming straight in on the planet, Sir." It was apparent from Inchman's tone that she'd anticipated her admiral's second question, and Beach nodded unhappily.

"So they aren't going to reach their originally projected firing points until *after* the LACs' get close enough to start killing pods," he said.

"No, sir, they aren't. And," Inchman turned her head to meet Beach's eyes, "if they're close enough to kill pods, they're also close enough to kill all our orbital platforms on their side of the planet."

"Are the LACs on profile for a zero-zero approach?"

"Yes, Sir. They'll hit turnover on their current profile in about twenty minutes."

"Crap." Beach drummed on the arm of his command chair for a moment, then shrugged.

"So much for using the *Cimeterres* against Alpha. Contact Captain Abercrombie. Order him to reverse course and engage the Manties' LACs."

"Aye, Sir."

"At least they'll meet far enough from their battlecruisers and cruisers to be out of standard shipboard weapons range," Commander Randall observed quietly.

"That should help some," Beach agreed, although both of them knew it wouldn't make a great deal of difference. Gaston System Command had three hundred and twenty *Cimeterre*-class LACs. The Manty attack force had just over two hundred *Shrike* and *Ferret*-class LACs, and they knew about the "Triple Ripple" by now. Given the difference in the basic capabilities of the two sides, Beach's LACs were about to face a painful exchange rate.

In theory, Beach could have moved his battlecruisers out to support them, since the Manty LACs would have to enter the reach of his own shorter-ranged shipboard missiles. But that would have required him to come out from behind the planet and expose his ships to MDM fire.

He couldn't do that. And so he sat in his command chair, watching the plot, as his *Cimeterres* swept around and headed directly towards their much more dangerous foes.

"Vector change!" Lieutenant Veronika Chernitskaya announced. "Their LACs are coming back around, Skipper."

"They have to protect their pods, Vicki," Captain Tremaine replied philosophically. "Frankly, I'm a bit surprised they didn't make the move sooner."

"Probably didn't like the odds, Skip," Chief Harkness replied from HMLAC *Dacoit*'s engineering station. "Might've taken whoever's in command a few minutes to decide he had to bite the bullet and do it anyway."

Tremaine nodded, but his attention was focused on *Dacoit*'s plot as the tight formation of Havenite LACs accelerated towards his own formation at almost seven hundred gravities. Numerically, the odds were better than three-to-two in the Havenites' favor; in terms of actual combat power, they weren't even close. Examination of the Havenite light attack craft captured at the Battle of Sidemore made it clear the *Cimeterres* carried more missiles than even a *Ferret*, but those missiles were much less capable than those in Tremaine's LACs' magazines. And the Havenites had nothing remotely comparable to the massive grasers built into his *Shrikes*.

Of course, it didn't take weapons that powerful just to kill another LAC. *Anything* would kill a LAC . . . assuming it could score a hit in the first place. But the Havenites' sidewalls and EW were both far inferior to their Manticoran counterparts, and none of the *Cimeterres* at Sidemore had mounted a bow or stern wall at all. Worse, from the Havenites' perspective—though they might not realize it yet—six of Tremaine's squadrons were Grayson *Katanas*.

Designed specifically as "space superiority" LACs, the *Katanas* were the Alliance's conceptual equivalent of the *Cimeterre* itself. Unlike the *Cimeterre*, however, the *Katana* incorporated all of the Alliance's tech advantages. It was smaller than its Havenite rival—and also faster, more maneuverable, far better protected, with enormously superior electronic warfare capabilities and the

LAC-sized version of the new bow wall "buckler," and equipped with what were for all intents and purposes a trio of superdreadnought point defense laser clusters, in addition to the Graysondesigned Viper anti-LAC missile.

The Viper was about two-thirds the size of a standard LAC missile, but it was quite different. It carried a much smaller warhead, without the multiple lasing rods of a conventional warhead, in order to incorporate significantly better seekers and an enhanced AI. And it also was designed for engagements at much shorter ranges. Engagements in which massive acceleration, agility, and the ability to reach targets quickly were vastly more important than endurance. Which was why the Viper used the same drive systems as the Mark 31 counter-missile.

"Central, Dagger One," he said to *Dacoit*'s com system. A tone sounded in his earbug as the AI which had replaced the regular communications officer aboard the highly automated LACs routed his transmission to Commander Crispus Dillinger, the senior *Katana* Squadron CO.

"Dagger One, Ramrod," Tremaine said, identifying himself as the Third Carrier Squadron's COLAC.

"Ramrod, Dagger One," Dillinger's voice came back instantly.

"They're coming to meet us after all, Chris. I think it's time your people took center stage. We'll go with Bushwhack Three."

"Ramrod, Dagger One copies Bushwhack Three."

"Go get them," Tremaine replied. "Ramrod, clear."

Captain Boniface Abercrombie watched the Manticoran LACs on the plot of his command LAC. He didn't much care for the odds. The *Cimeterre* was a pure attrition unit, designed to overpower the individual superiority of its Manty opponents by means of massive numerical superiority. Abercrombie knew Admiral Foraker and her staff were working furiously to improve the *Cimeterre*'s capabilities in the Republic's second-generation light attack craft, but the limitations of their tech base, even with the rumored upgrades from the Erewhonese, meant her teams simply couldn't match the Manties' capabilities.

Current doctrine called for engaging Manty LACs at minimum odds of four-to-one. Even at that level, Republican casualties would probably be heavy in a straight-up fight. It was hard to say for certain, because the only LAC-on-LAC engagements so far had been dominated by the Republic's surprise "Triple Ripple" tactic. But the MDM missile profiles employed against Captain Schneider at Zanzibar were chilling proof the Manties knew all about the Ripple. They'd undoubtedly adjusted their LAC tactics even more than their MDM doctrine, and Abercrombie didn't look forward to being the first Republican COLAC to discover exactly how they had.

Unfortunately, it appeared he didn't have any choice.

"Stand by for Zizka," he said tautly. Lieutenant Banacek, his tactical officer, looked at him, and he shrugged. "I don't know if they're going to give us the opportunity to use it, but if they do, I want it ready."

"Yes, Sir," Banacek acknowledged.

"It's more likely we'll be looking at a close-in dogfight," Abercrombie continued. "I want squadron discipline maintained. They're going to have the range advantage, and our point defense is going to have to carry the load until we get close enough to hurt them."

"Understood, Sir." There was the slightest edge of a tremor in Banacek's voice, but her gray eyes were steady, and Abercrombie gave her a tight smile of approval.

"Range four-point-six-eight million klicks. Closing velocity one-two-thousand KPS."

Commander Crispus Dillinger, call sign "Dagger One," grunted in acknowledgment of Lieutenant Gilmore's report while his brain whirred steadily, balancing variables and possibilities.

At their closing velocity, the missile geometry extended their powered missile envelope at launch by almost five hundred thousand kilometers from the 3.6 million kilometers the Viper could attain from rest. Which meant they'd be in extreme range in another thirty-five seconds.

He wondered why the Peeps hadn't fired yet. The one drawback of the Viper was that its maximum range was little more than half that of a more conventional anti-ship missile. In theory, that had given the Peeps almost three minutes in which they could have fired upon their opponents without taking return fire. From the *Katanas*, at least; if they'd opened fire from that far out, the *Ferrets* backing the Dagger squadrons would have replied in kind.

Probably holding their own birds as long as we'll let them, he thought. *All the indications are that their accuracy sucks compared to ours, and their tac crews have to baby them more on the way in, so they've got to worry more about light-speed transmission lags. They'll want to get to as short a range as they can in order to maximize their hit probabilities. And they may think they can get away with that damned EMP maneuver of theirs. If they do, it's time we . . . disabused them of the notion.*

"All Daggers, Dagger One," he said over the net. "Bushwhack Three is confirmed. Repeat, Bravo-Whiskey-Three is confirmed. Stand by to initiate launch sequence on command."

Acknowledgments came back from his squadron commanders, and he felt himself settling deeper into his flight couch as the range flashed downwards. Then he nodded sharply to Gilmore.

"Initiate!" she said sharply. "Repeat, *initiate!*"

"Missile separation!" Lieutenant Banacek called out. "Multiple missile separations. Flight time . . . *seventy-five seconds?*"

Disbelief burned in her voice as her computers reported the enormous acceleration rate of the incoming missiles, and Boniface Abercrombie didn't blame her a bit.

"Christ," somebody whispered, and Abercrombie felt his own jaw tighten.

"So that's their answer to the Ripple," his XO said quietly, bitterly.

"That's got to be *Katanas* launching," Abercrombie replied, almost calmly. He'd wondered what the infernally inventive Graysons had come up with. NavInt had managed to confirm that they had, indeed, developed a dedicated space control LAC, but no one in the Republic had had any idea exactly what they'd done.

Until now.

"They can't sustain that kind of accel for long," the XO said. "It's got to be some adaptation of a counter-missile."

Abercrombie nodded, never taking his eyes from the plot.

"They'll be short-legged," he agreed. "But they're going to be a real bitch to stop. Worse, they're launching staggered."

It was the XO's turn to nod. He and Abercrombie had discussed it often enough, and it seemed the Manties—or Graysons, as the case might be—had come up with the same solution to the Ripple as they had. They weren't going to let their onboard sensors be blinded again; that part had been a no-brainer, once the Manties realized what had been done to them. Nor were they going to expose their decoys and EW platforms any sooner than they must, and it was a given that they'd have spread their remote recon platforms as widely as possible in order to get them outside the Ripple's area of effect.

And now they'd taken Zizka out of the equation, as well, by the simplest expedient of all. They knew Republican missile defense doctrine, especially for LACs, relied more on mass and volume than individual accuracy, so they'd realized it was less the *density* of a missile salvo than its *duration* which really mattered. At any sort of extended range, Abercrombie's LACs had no choice but to attempt to saturate the incoming missile patterns rather than attempting to pick off individual threats, the way Manty missile-defense crews would have. So it wasn't really necessary for the Manties to achieve the sort of precise time-on-target concentrations which would have been used to saturate more sophisticated defenses. Or, to put it another way, Abercrombie's defenses were too crude to be significantly degraded by that sort of sophistication.

So the Manties had staggered their launches, spreading them out in time, and seeded their attack birds with their damnably effective EW platforms. Coupled with the impossibly high speed of the attack missiles themselves, those decoys and jammers were going to degrade point defense kill probabilities catastrophically. And by stretching out their launch envelope, by creating what was effectively a missile *stream*, rather than a single, crushing hammer blow, they'd made it impossible for a single Ripple launch to kill more than a fraction of their total attack. Worse, the LACs who'd launched the Ripple could no more see through it than vessels on the other side could, and Abercrombie couldn't afford to further hamstring his missile defense by providing the enemy with the opportunity to effectively attack "out of the sun."

A part of him cried out to issue orders, enforce his will on the engagement, do *something* to give his people a better chance. But there was no time for that, no last-minute adjustments that would have any impact on what was unfolding. For all intents and purposes, he was a passenger now, waiting to see how well his battle plan worked.

He didn't entertain very high hopes in that regard.

✧   ✧   ✧

Commander Dillinger's missiles streaked towards the Havenite LACs.

It was the first time they'd ever been used against live targets, and even Dillinger was a bit surprised by how well they performed. Their AIs were better than those of any previous missile remotely close to their size, and those AIs had been carefully optimized to go after small, fast, *fragile* targets. They were far more capable of independent engagements, with less need for telemetry links to the vessels which had launched them. After all, LAC EW—or, at least, the Havenite version of it—was much less capable than that of a starship. There was less need for fire control officers to correct for the sort of sophisticated razzle-dazzle larger ships could perform, and their shorter powered envelope meant the Vipers' sensors had a much better look at their target when they were launched.

In effect, they were launch-and-forget weapons, which saw to their own midcourse corrections, and the *Katanas* were free to maneuver, and to employ all of their fire control links for counter-missiles, once they'd gotten the Vipers away.

And it was obvious the Peeps hadn't had a clue that they were going to face attack missiles whose acceleration had just been increased by forty-two percent. The incoming Vipers were actually over thirty percent faster than the counter-missiles trying to kill them.

Boniface Abercrombie listened to the combat chatter, jaw clamped as he heard the consternation—in all too many cases the outright panic—of missile-defense crews who'd suddenly discovered all of their defensive programs' threat parameters were out of date. He turned his head, watching Banacek working frantically, trying to update her tracking and threat prioritization in the seventy-odd seconds she had.

Then he looked away. Not even Shannon Foraker could have pulled that one off, he thought grimly.

Each *Katana* fired twenty-five Vipers.

The six Dagger squadrons between them put eighteen hundred of them into space over a thirty-second window, and they scorched through the shell of Havenite counter-missiles like white-hot awls.

Some of them were killed.

A few of the counter-missiles—a very few—managed to discriminate between real threats and the false targets of the Dragon's Teeth platforms. Managed to see through the blinding strobes of jamming. Managed to steer themselves and their wedges into the path of the preposterously fleet attackers. But they were the exception. Most of the kills were attained only because even against an attack like this, Shannon Foraker's layered defense was at least partially effective. There were simply so many counter-missiles that blind chance meant some of them had to find and kill Vipers.

Under the circumstances, *any* kills were an impressive achievement . . . but the counter-missiles managed to actually stop less than three hundred.

Laser clusters began to fire as the Vipers scorched in, clearly visible to fire control at last as they broke clear of the blinding interference of outgoing counter-missile wedges. The missile-defense crews were highly trained, highly disciplined. A substantial percentage were veterans of the bloody multisided civil war Thomas Theisman had fought against breakaway adherents of the old régime. Even now, very few of them panicked, and they stood to their stations, firing steadily, doing their best.

But their best wasn't good enough. Their fire control software simply wasn't up to the challenge, couldn't react quickly enough, to missiles capable of that sort of acceleration. Not at such short range, not without more time to adjust.

Vipers broke past the last, desperate shield of laser fire, and warheads began to detonate.

"Oh my God," Sandra Inchman whispered, her face white as her surveillance platforms showed *Cimeterre* after *Cimeterre* disappearing from her plot. They went not by ones or twos, but by tens.

Captain Abercrombie's was one of the first to die, but he'd kept his tactical uplink on-line to the very end. Inchman could scarcely believe the acceleration numbers, yet she had no choice *but* to believe as the brutally efficient massacre wiped away the Gaston System's total LAC force in less than three minutes.

Everette Beach sat frozen in his command chair. His swarthy face was the color of cold gravy, and his hands were pincers clamped on the armrests of his chair.

"I can't—" Commander Randall paused and cleared his throat. "I can't believe that," he said.

"Believe it," Beach rasped. He closed his eyes for a moment, then thrust himself up out of the chair.

"I knew we were going to lose them," he said flatly. "But I never would have sent them in if I'd even guessed they wouldn't kill a single Manty."

Some of Abercrombie's *Cimeterres* had gotten off their own offensive launches, but they'd achieved nothing. At their slower acceleration rate, it had taken them nine seconds longer to reach their targets, and most of the ships which had launched them were already dead by the time they did. Even the handful of *Cimeterres* which hadn't already been destroyed had had little or no attention to spare for the attack profile updates Republican missiles needed so much more badly than Manty missiles did, anyway. The tactical crews which would normally have provided those updates had been too distracted by the threat they'd faced . . . and too busy dying.

Superior Manty EW, sidewalls, point defense, and maneuverability had done the rest.

"You couldn't have known, Sir," Inchman said quietly.

"No. No, I couldn't have. And just at the moment, that's remarkably cold comfort, Sandra."

He gave her a tight smile, trying to take the sting from his response to her effort to comfort him, and she managed to smile back, briefly.

"What now, Sir?" Randall asked in a low voice.

"First, we make sure all of the tactical details on what they just did to Abercrombie get recorded in the secure database dirtside. The next poor son-of-a-bitch some stupid fucking admiral sends in against Manty LACs needs to at least know what he's getting into. And after that—"

He turned to look at his chief of staff.

"After that, it's our turn."

Chapter Twenty-One

"Good evening, Senator."

Arnold Giancola pressed the hold key on the document viewer in his lap as one of his bodyguards opened the limousine door.

"Good evening, Giuseppe," Senator Jason Giancola said, nodding courteously to the security man as he slid in through the opened door to join his older brother in the luxurious passenger compartment.

Giuseppe Lauder closed the door behind him, gave the immediate vicinity a quick scan, then waved to the chase car and climbed into the front passenger seat beside the driver.

"Central, State One is departing for the Octagon," he said into his boom mike.

"Central copies, Giuseppe. State One departing the Residence for the Octagon at . . . eighteen-thirty-one hours."

The response wasn't exactly by The Book, but Camille Begin had the Central Dispatch watch this evening, and she and Lauder had worked together for over three years.

"Confirm, Central," Lauder said. He nodded to the driver, and the limo and its chase car lifted quietly into the evening.

"Just what's this 'emergency meeting' all about, Arnold?" Jason Giancola asked.

"You're asking me?" Arnold replied. "You're the one on the Naval Oversight Committee, Jason! And—" he smiled without much humor "—our good friend Thomas Theisman seems to've lost my personal com combination these days."

"Because he hates your guts," the younger Giancola said seriously. Arnold cocked an eyebrow at him, and Jason frowned. "I know you're the brains, Arnold. I've never pretended you weren't. But I'm telling you, that man is dangerous."

"I never thought he wasn't," Arnold said mildly. "On the other hand, he believes passionately in due process. Until—and unless—I do something illegal, he's not going to take the law into his own hands, however much he and I may...disagree."

"Maybe not," Jason conceded. "But getting back to my original question, I don't know any more about this meeting than you do. Except for the fact that I got *my* invitation as the ranking minority member of the Naval Committee. So whatever it is, it sounds like it's got a military dimension."

"What doesn't, these days?" Arnold said philosophically.

"Not much."

Jason glanced up to be certain the partition between the passenger compartment and the driver's compartment was closed, and that the privacy light on the intercom was illuminated. Then he looked very intently at his older brother.

"I don't know everything you've been doing, Arnold. But I do have my own sources, and according to one of them, someone inside the FIA is showing an awful lot of interest in Yves Grosclaude. I'm not going to ask you to tell me anything you don't want me to know, but the source who handed me that seems to think the interest in question has something to do with *you*, as well. Which, to be honest, is one reason I mentioned the fact that Theisman doesn't like you very much."

"Interest in Yves?"

Arnold blinked mildly at the Senator, his expression only moderately curious. After all, it wasn't as if Jason's warning was the first he'd heard about it. Jean-Claude Nesbitt had informed him four days ago that someone else had finally quietly—and quite illegally—accessed Grosclaude's documentary file. The information had produced a slight adrenaline jag, but mostly, what he'd felt was something very like relief.

"I don't have the least idea why anyone should be officially interested in Yves, Jason," he said after a moment, his gaze candid. "And if someone is, I don't see how it could possibly concern me."

❖   ❖   ❖

His name was Axel Lacroix, and he was twenty-six T-years old. His family had been Dolists for three generations, until the First Manticoran War. He'd been only a child when that war began, but he'd grown to young adulthood against its backdrop. He'd seen his family move off the BLS at last, seen his parents regain their self-respect, despite the oppressive grip of the Committee of Public Safety and State Security. He'd seen the changes beginning in the educational system, seen the even greater changes his younger siblings had faced when they entered school. And he'd seen the restoration of the Constitution and the concepts of personal responsibility . . . and liberty.

He'd been too young to serve in the First War, and he knew his parents really would have preferred for him to remain a civilian. But he owed a debt for all of those changes, and so when the fighting resumed, he'd enlisted in the Republican Marines.

Because of his occupation—he was a trained shipyard worker—his induction had been delayed, but orders to report for duty had finally been delivered to his modest apartment the day before.

He couldn't say the prospect didn't worry him. It did. He wasn't an idiot, after all. But he also had no regrets. He'd spent most of yesterday with his family, and today it had been time for the "going away party" his buddies and fellow workers at the yard had put together for him. The alcohol had flowed freely, there'd been laughter, and some tears, but no one had really been surprised. And since he was under orders to report the next day, he'd decided it was time for him to turn in early and sleep off as much of the conviviality as he could.

"You're sure you're okay to drive, Axel?" Angelo Goldbach asked as they walked across the parking garage.

"Of course I am," Axel replied. "It's not very far, anyway."

"I could run you home," Angelo offered.

"Don't be silly. I'm fine, I tell you. Besides, if you did, we'd probably sit up late drinking, and I need the sleep. And Georgina would hunt me down and hurt me if I kept you out all night again."

"If you're sure," Angelo said.

They reached Angelo's parking stall, and he stood looking at his friend for a moment, then swept him into a quick, rough embrace.

"You watch your ass, Axel," he said, standing back and shaking Lacroix gently by the shoulders.

"Damn straight," Lacroix said jauntily, a little embarrassed by Goldbach's intensity. He smacked his friend on the upper arm, watched Goldbach climb into his car and pull out of the parking stall, then continued to his own vehicle.

The runabout wasn't very new, but personal vehicles of any sort were still relatively rare, especially here in the capital city, where most people relied on mass transit. For Lacroix, though, the slightly battered, jaunty little sports air car had always symbolized his and his family's success in proving they were more than simply one more clan of Dolist drones. Besides—he grinned as he unlocked the door and settled into the front seat—it might be old, but it was still fast, nimble, and downright *fun* to fly.

"Five minutes, Mr. Secretary."

"Thank you," Arnold Giancola acknowledged Giuseppe Lauder's warning and began sliding his document viewer and sheafs of record chips into his briefcase.

"Well, Jason," he said with a smile, "I imagine we'll be finding out shortly what all the mystery is about. And just between the two of us—"

"*Ten o'clock!*"

Giancola's head snapped up at Lauder's sudden shout. The limousine swerved wildly, yanking hard to the right, and the Secretary of State's head whipped around to the left.

He just had time to see the runabout coming.

"With your permission, Madam President, I'll have Admiral Lewis go ahead and begin the briefing," Secretary of War Thomas Theisman said.

Eloise Pritchart looked at him, then glanced at the two empty chairs at the conference table.

"I realize the situation is serious," she said, after a moment. "But I think we might give the Secretary of State a *few* more minutes."

There might have been just the tiniest hint of a reprimand in her voice, although only someone who knew her well would have recognized it as such. Theisman did, and he bobbed his head very slightly in acknowledgment. One or two of the other people seated around the table seemed to have some difficulty suppressing smiles as they observed the byplay. But Secretary of Technology Henrietta Barloi, one of Giancola's staunchest allies in the Cabinet, was not among them.

"I certainly agree, Madam President," she said frostily. "In fact—"

"Excuse me, Ma'am."

Pritchart turned her head, eyebrows rising in mild surprise at the interruption. Sheila Thiessen, the senior member of her security detachment, was a past mistress at being totally unobtrusive at high level, sensitive meetings. She also possessed a formidable degree of self-control—what Kevin Usher called a "poker face"—which made her present stunned expression almost frightening.

"Yes, Sheila?" Pritchart's voice was sharper than usual, sharper than she'd intended it to be. "What is it?"

"There's been an accident, Madam President. Secretary Giancola's limousine's been involved in a mid-air."

"*What?*" Pritchart stared at Thiessen. Shock seemed to paralyze her vocal cords for a moment, then she shook herself. "How bad is it? Was the Secretary injured?"

"I . . . don't have the details yet," Thiessen said, brushing her unobtrusive earbug with a fingertip as if to indicate the source of what she did know. "But it doesn't sound good." She cleared her throat. "The preliminary message said there appear to have been no survivors, Ma'am."

"Jesus. I did *not* need this on top of everything else."

Thomas Theisman leaned back in his chair, rubbing both eyes with the heels of his hands. The emergency meeting had been hastily adjourned while the President dealt with the stunning news that her Secretary of State and his brother were both dead. Theisman couldn't fault her priorities, especially not in light of the inevitable time delays in the transmission of any messages or orders over interstellar distances. It wasn't as if responding to what had prompted the meeting in the first place was as time-critical as dealing with the immediate consequences of what promised to be a fundamental shift in the Republic's domestic politics.

But now that everyone who needed to be informed had been told and Pritchart had released her official statement (which dutifully expressed her profound regrets over the unexpected demise of her valued colleague and longtime friend), the President and her closest advisers and allies—Theisman himself, Denis LePic, Rachel Hanriot, Kevin Usher, and Wilhelm Trajan—had assembled in the Secretary of War's Octagon office.

"Oh, we didn't need it in more ways than you know, Tom," Pritchart said wearily. The last three hours had been a hectic whirl, and even she looked a little frazzled around the edges.

"Especially not combined with the news of the Manties' raids," Hanriot said sourly. "What's that old saying about when it rains it pours?"

"I expect public opinion isn't going to take kindly to the news the Manties just bloodied our nose," Theisman agreed. "On the other hand, it's possible what happened to Giancola will actually distract the newsies. And let's be honest here—I don't think anyone in this room is especially going to miss him."

"You might be surprised." Pritchart's tone was bleak, and Theisman frowned at her.

"What do you mean, Eloise? You've been sounding semi-cryptic all evening."

"I know. I know!"

The President shook her head. But instead of explaining immediately, she looked at Usher.

"Have you heard from Abrioux, Kevin?"

"Yes, I have." Usher's voice was deeper than usual. "All the preliminary indications are that it was a genuine accident."

Theisman looked back and forth between the President and the FIA Director.

"And just why shouldn't it have been a 'genuine accident'?" he asked. "I admit I detested the man, but I promise I didn't have him killed!"

Nobody smiled, and his frown deepened.

"How did it happen?" Pritchart asked Usher. "I mean, a traffic *accident* less than five minutes from the Octagon!"

"According to the forensics team's preliminary, the other driver—an Axel Lacroix," Usher said, consulting his memo pad's display "—was well over the legal limit for blood-alcohol. Basically, he was simply flying on manual, rather than under traffic control, and he failed to yield and broadsided Giancola's limo at a high rate of speed."

"Flying on manual?" LePic repeated. "If his blood-alcohol was so high, why was he on manual?"

"We'll have to wait for the tech teams to complete their examination of the wreckage, but Lacroix was driving an older model runabout. Right off the top of my head, I'd guess the internal sensors weren't working properly. Hell, I suppose it's even possible he deliberately disconnected the safety overrides. It's against the law, of course, but a lot of people used to do it simply because traffic control was so spotty they didn't trust it in an emergency. At any rate, for some reason the overrides which should have locked someone in his condition out of manual control didn't do it."

"Oh, how perfectly fucking wonderful," Pritchart said bitterly, and Theisman leaned forward, both palms flat on his desk.

"All right," he said, his voice the flat, no-nonsense one of a flag officer accustomed to command, "suppose you just explain to me what the hell is going on here?"

If anyone in that room—with the possible exception of Hanriot—found his tone an inappropriate one in which to address the President of the Republic, they didn't say so.

"Tom," Pritchart said instead, her voice very serious, "this is going to open an incredible can of worms."

Theisman looked like a man in serious danger of spontaneously exploding, and she went on in the same flat, hard tone.

"Kevin's been conducting a black investigation of Giancola for almost a month now. Denis has known about it from the beginning, but I didn't tell *you* about it because, frankly, you're an even worse actor than Denis. You already hated Giancola, and I was afraid you'd have a hard time not making him suspicious that something was going on. I'd intended to bring you fully on board as soon as Kevin's team had anything concrete to report."

"Investigating him over what?" Theisman's eyes were intent, as were Trajan's. Hanriot's expression still showed more puzzlement than anything else, but alarm was beginning to show, as well.

"Investigating the possibility that *he* falsified our diplomatic correspondence, not the Manties," Pritchart sighed.

"That he *what?*" Theisman erupted to his feet. Trajan didn't even move, as if astonishment had frozen him, and Hanriot jerked back as if Pritchart had slapped her.

"Kevin," Pritchart said harshly. "Tell them."

All eyes swivelled to the FIA chief, and he sighed.

"It all started when I began asking myself a few questions I couldn't answer," he said. "And when I started trying to *find* the answers, it turned out that—"

"—so we finally hacked into Grosclaude's attorney's files four days ago," Usher concluded, several minutes later. "And when we did, we found Grosclaude had apparently tucked away evidence which incontrovertibly proved Giancola was responsible for altering both our own outgoing diplomatic correspondence and the incoming notes from the Manties."

"Let me get this straight," Theisman said in a dangerously calm voice. "You found this file *four days ago*, and this is the very first I'm hearing about it?"

"First," Pritchart said crisply, "you're the Secretary of *War*, Tom Theisman. You are not the Attorney General, you aren't a judge or magistrate, and you had no pressing 'need to know' until we'd been able to confirm things one way or the other."

Steely topaz eyes met angry eyes of brown, and it was the brown ones which looked away.

"Second," the President said slightly more mildly, "as I've already mentioned, your thespian abilities leave something to be desired in a politician operating at your level.

"Third, despite the fact that I very unofficially authorized Kevin's investigation, it's been totally black and, to be perfectly honest, operating outside the law. You wouldn't have been very happy to hear about that. And even if *you'd* been prepared to sing joyous hosannas, there was the minor problem that the only evidence we had was illegally obtained.

"And, fourth—" She gestured at Usher.

"And, fourth," Usher took over, "the evidence in the files was clearly fabricated."

"Fabricated?"

Any number of people would have been prepared to testify that Thomas Theisman was a tough-minded individual, but he was beginning to sound undeniably shellshocked.

"There are at least three significant internal inconsistencies," Usher said. "They aren't at all obvious on a first read-through, but they become quite apparent when you analyze the entire file carefully."

"So Giancola *didn't* do it?"

"On the basis of the documentary evidence we currently possess, no," Usher said. "In fact, on the basis of the evidence, it looks very much as if *Grosclaude* did it and intended to frame Giancola if and when his actions were discovered."

"Why do I seem to hear a 'but' hovering in the background?"

"Because I'm pretty sure that somehow or other it was actually Giancola who fabricated the files we found and then planted them on Grosclaude. After having him murdered."

"In an 'air car accident,'" Theisman said.

"There seem to be a lot of those going around," Usher agreed with mordant humor.

"So you see our problem, Tom? And you, Rachel?" Pritchart said. "The only 'evidence' we've actually been able to turn up—illegally—is demonstrably falsified. Apparently, it was intended to implicate Giancola, which would undoubtedly be construed by a lot of people, especially his allies and supporters, as proof he was actually innocent. However, we have the fact that the person who supposedly falsified it was killed in what Kevin and I both consider to be a highly suspicious 'accident.' And now, unfortunately, our only other suspect has just been killed in yet *another* air car accident. Bearing in mind just how fond of similar 'accidents' both the Legislaturalists and StateSec were, how do you suppose public opinion—or Congress—is going to react if we lay this whole—What did you call it, Kevin? Oh, yes. If we lay this whole 'shit sandwich' out on the public information boards?"

"But if he did do it, then our entire justification for going back to war disappears." Theisman shook his head, his expression haunted.

"Yes, it does," Pritchart said unflinchingly. "I could argue—convincingly, I think—that what the High Ridge Government actually did do would have justified our threatening to use force, or actually using it, to compel the Manties to negotiate in good faith. Unfortunately, that isn't what we did. We used force because we appeared to have evidence they were negotiating in *bad* faith, and we published the diplomatic correspondence *they'd* falsified to prove our point.

"And that, however much we may regret it, and however we

got there, is the point we have to begin from now. We're in a war. A popular war, with powerful political support. And all we have is a theory, evidence we can't use (and which was probably manufactured), and two dead governmental officials, who we'll never be able to convince the public died in genuine accidents. And on top of that, we've got the news of these raids by Harrington."

She shook her head.

"How bad *were* the raids?" Hanriot asked. Theisman looked at her, and the Treasury Secretary grimaced. "Look, part of this is probably a case of my looking for anything to distract me from this little vest pocket nuke Eloise and Kevin have just dropped on us. On the other hand, I really do need to know—both as the head of the Treasury Department and if I'm going to be able to offer any opinion on how news of them would combine with all the rest of this."

"Um." Theisman frowned, then shrugged. "All right, I see your point, Rachel."

He tipped his chair back again, clearly marshaling his thoughts.

"To put it bluntly," he said, after a moment, "Harrington just gave us an object lesson in how rear area raids ought to be conducted. She hit Gaston, Tambourin, Squalus, Hera, and Hallman, and there's not a damned bit of orbital industry left in any of them."

"You're joking." Hanriot sounded shocked.

"No," Theisman said in a tone of massive self-restraint, "I'm not. They took out everything. And, in the process, they also destroyed our defensive forces in all five systems."

"How much did you lose?" Pritchart asked.

"Two battleships, seven battlecruisers, four old cruisers, three destroyers, and over a thousand LACs," Theisman said flatly. "And before anyone says anything else," he continued, "as depressing as those numbers are, remember the pickets were spread across five separate star systems. None of the system commanders had anything like the forces he would've required to stand off an attack planned this carefully and executed in such force. And all of that is a direct consequence of the deployment patterns *I* authorized."

"But if they took out *everything*," Hanriot said, "then the economic consequences are—"

"The economic damage is going to be bad," Theisman said. "But in the final analysis, all five of the systems were effectively noncontributors to the war effort. And, for that matter, to the economy as a whole."

Hanriot started to bristle, but Theisman shook his head.

"Rachel, that's based on your own department's analysis. Remember the one you and Tony Nesbitt put together before Thunderbolt?"

Hanriot settled back in her chair and nodded slowly. After two T-years of hard, unremitting labor, her analysts, in conjunction with Nesbitt's Commerce Department, had completed the first really honest, comprehensive survey of the Republic's economic status in better than a century barely six months before the shooting had started back up.

"All these systems were listed in the 'break even' category," the Secretary of War continued. "At best, they were second-tier systems, and Gaston and Hallman, in particular, had been money-losing propositions under the Legislaturalists. That was turning around, but they were still barely contributing to our positive cash flow. The destruction in the star systems is going to have a net negative effect, I'm sure—your analysts will be able to evaluate that better than I'm in any position to do—because the damage to the local civilian infrastructure means we'll be forced to commit federal relief funds and resources on an emergency basis. But none of them were particularly critical. Which is, frankly, the reason they weren't more heavily defended. We can't be strong everywhere, and the systems we've left most weakly covered are the ones we can most readily survive losing."

"Granted," Pritchart said after a moment. "But what we can afford in cold-blooded economic and industrial terms and what we can afford in terms of public opinion may not be exactly the same thing."

"They almost certainly aren't the same thing, and the Manties clearly understand that," Theisman replied. "Whoever selected their targets did a damned good job. Harrington was able to use relatively limited forces and still attain crushing local superiority. She took virtually no losses of her own, cost us sixteen hyper-capable units in addition to all those LACs, and scored the Manties' first clear-cut *offensive* victory of the war. And, to be perfectly honest, the fact that they did it under Honor Harrington's command is also going to have an impact. She's something of our own personal bogeyman, after all.

"So, completely exclusive of any *physical* damage she's done to us," he continued, "this is inevitably going to have an impact in Congress. I've already got the General Staff considering how we're going to respond when the senators and representatives from every system which hasn't been raided yet start demanding we strengthen *their* covering forces."

"I'm afraid you're absolutely right about what they're going to demand," Pritchart said. "And it's going to be hard to explain why they can't have it."

"No," Theisman disagreed. "It's going to be very easy to explain we can't possibly be strong everywhere, and especially not without frittering away our offensive capability, exactly as the Manties want us to do. What's going to be hard is convincing frightened men and women to *listen* to the explanation."

"Not just members of Congress, either," LePic said heavily. "It's going to be just as hard to explain to the general public."

"Actually," Pritchart said, "I'm less concerned about explaining that to them, or even explaining how we 'let this happen,' than I am about the impact on public support for the war. It isn't going to undermine it—not at this point, at least. What it's going to do is further inflame public opinion."

"I admit it *could* have that effect," Trajan said, "but—"

"No, Wilhelm. She's right," Hanriot interrupted. "Public opinion has been riding a sustained emotional high since Thunderbolt. As far as the woman in the street's concerned, we cleaned the Manties' clock everywhere except at Sidemore, and there's a tremendous feeling of satisfaction, of having rehabilitated ourselves as a major military power. I think it would be impossible to overestimate the degree to which our sense of national pride has rebounded with the restoration of the Constitution, the turnaround in the economy, and now the successful reconquest of the occupied systems, coupled with the enormous losses we've inflicted on the Manties' navy. So far, this has got to have been the most popular war in our history.

"And what's happened now?" She shrugged. "The Manties have punched us back. They've hurt us, and they've demonstrated that they may be able to do it again. But our actual naval losses, however painful they may be, are literally nothing compared to the losses *we* inflicted on *them* in Thunderbolt. So what's going to happen, at least in the short term, is that public opinion's going to demand we go out and whack the Manties back, harder, to demonstrate to them that they don't want to piss us off. There's going to be some panic, some shouting about reinforcing to protect our more vulnerable star systems, but mostly, people are going to figure the best way to do that is to finish Manticore off, once and for all."

"I'm afraid Rachel's right, Wilhelm," Pritchart said. "And that's one reason I wish to *hell* Arnold hadn't gotten his goddamned traitorous ass killed this evening. If I'm ever going to go public with all this, this would be the best time to do it—now, immediately. The longer we wait, the more suspect the theory's going to look for anyone who's not already inclined to believe it. But there's absolutely nothing concrete we can give the newsies, Congress, or anybody else, only theories and suspicions we can't prove. If I did what I really ought to do—ordered a standstill of our own forces, told the Manties what we think happened, and asked for an immediate cease-fire—I'd probably be impeached, even assuming anyone in Congress, or any of Arnold's allies in the Cabinet, were prepared to believe us for a moment. And, frankly, I don't know if the Constitution could survive the kind of dogfight this would turn into."

Silence hung heavily in the office for at least two minutes. Then Theisman shook himself.

"Bottom line time, Madam President," he said. "As I see it, we have two options. One is to do what you 'really ought to do' on the basis of what we *think* happened. The other is to vigorously pursue military victory, or at least our efforts to attain a sufficiently powerful position of military advantage to *force* the Manties to accept our original, fairly limited objectives. What I don't think we can do is try to accomplish both of those at once."

"Not without some sort of proof of what happened," Hanriot agreed.

"At the moment, I think it's entirely possible we'll *never* have that sort of proof," Usher cautioned. "These are awfully muddy waters, and the only two people who really knew what happened—Grosclaude and Giancola—are both dead."

"Sooner or later we're going to have to get to the bottom of it, and it's going to have to be done publicly," Pritchart said. "There's no other way for an open society which believes in the rule of law to handle it. And if we don't do it now, then when we finally get around to it, all of us—and especially me, as President—are going to be castigated for delaying open disclosure. Our personal reputations, and quite possibly everything we've accomplished, are going to come under attack, and a lot of it's going to be vicious and ugly. And, to be perfectly honest, we'll deserve it."

She looked around the office, her shoulders squared.

"Unfortunately," she said into the silence, "at this moment, I don't see any choice. Kevin, keep looking. Find us *something*. But until he does," she swept the office once again with her eyes, "I see no option but to keep our suspicions to ourselves and get on with winning my goddamned war."

Chapter Twenty-Two

"All right," Admiral Marquette said. "What do we actually know?"

"We're still getting the details, Sir," Rear Admiral Lewis told the Chief of the Naval Staff and Thomas Theisman's immediate uniformed subordinate. "We know there's still a lot to come, but so far, it looks like most of what we don't already have is only going to be variations on the same theme."

"And those variations are?" Marquette prompted when Lewis paused.

"I'm sorry, Arnaud," Vice Admiral Trenis said, "but I thought Admiral Theisman was going to join us today."

"And you're wondering why I'm not waiting for him." Marquette smiled thinly. "I'm afraid that's one point about which not even you and Victor have a 'need to know,' Linda. Let's just say something else has come up which requires the attention of the Secretary and certain other members of the Cabinet. And when they get done with that meeting," he added a bit more pointedly, "they're going to want analysis and, if possible, recommendations from us. So, let's get to it, shall we?"

"Of course, Sir," Trenis said, and nodded to Lewis. "Victor?"

"Yes, Ma'am."

Lewis tapped his memo pad to life, glanced at it—more out of habit than need, Marquette suspected—and then looked back up at his two superiors.

"I think probably our initial evaluation of why they hit the targets they hit was on the money," he said. "All five systems have enough population to give them several representatives in the lower house, plus, of course, their senators. If the object is to create political pressure to disperse our forces, that would obviously have been a factor in their thinking, and my people are confident it was.

"Economically, as I'm sure we're all already aware, the elimination of their industrial bases will have only a minor direct impact on our ability to sustain our war effort. The indirect economic implications are something else, of course, and I expect Secretary Hanriot and Secretary Nesbitt are going to be less than happy dealing with the civilian fallout."

"How complete was the destruction, Victor?" Marquette asked. "Was it is bad as the initial reports indicated?"

"Worse, Sir," Lewis said glumly. Marquette arched an eyebrow, and the rear admiral gave an unhappy shrug.

"Our own raids have been primarily probes for information, Sir—reconnaissances in force, for all intents and purposes. We've used light units, primarily LACs, and we've settled for picking off individual industrial lobes that we could get to without taking on really heavy forces. And, of course, the Manties don't have anywhere near as many systems to protect as we do. That means the ones they do have to cover are generally picketed much more heavily than anything except our truly critical ones.

"Harrington's target selection was different. She wasn't after information; she was here to deliver a message. She picked star systems which weren't heavily defended, and she attacked them with much heavier forces. She not only brought along the firepower she needed to destroy all of our defensive units, she also brought along enough she was able to spread out, take her time, and destroy effectively every single orbital platform in each of the systems she hit. Asteroid extraction centers, foundries, power satellites, communications satellites, navigation satellites, construction platforms, freight platforms, warehouses—*all* of it, Sir. Gone."

"And that was part of her 'message,' as you put it?"

"Yes, Sir. It was a statement of the level of 'scorched earth' policy the Manties are prepared to embrace. It was also a statement that they intend to operate as aggressively as possible within the limitations of their force availability. Please note, for example, that they committed both *Invictus*-class superdreadnoughts and what appears to be their complete current inventory of *Agamemnon*-class pod battlecruisers. And they weren't particularly shy about showing us just what the *Katanas* and those frigging awful missiles of theirs could do, either."

"In other words, they're prepared to pull out all the stops."

"Yes, Sir. And they're also prepared to let some of their technical cats out of the bag. They're not trying to maintain operational security, which is an indication of how important they believe their raids to be. This is the first team they're sending in, Admiral. The fact that Harrington is in command of it would be a strong enough indication of that, but the force mix they're employing confirms it, in my opinion."

"And mine," Marquette agreed. Trenis nodded as well, but then she tapped a forefinger on the conference table.

"There's another message in what they've done, this far, at least, Arnaud," she said.

"I'm certain there are quite a few," the chief of staff said dryly. "Which one did you intend to point out?"

"The casualty figures," she said flatly. "I know we took virtually one hundred percent casualties in our LAC groups in Gaston, Tambourin, Squalus, and Hallman. And our shipboard casualties were almost as bad—not surprisingly, I suppose, when they destroyed every single ship they managed to bring into range. But in Hera, Harrington herself gave Milligan the option of saving his people's lives. And they didn't kill or even injure a single civilian when they took out the infrastructure in that system, or anywhere else."

"That was partly because they had the *time*, Ma'am," Lewis pointed out. "They had complete control of the star systems, and they could afford to give our civilians time to evacuate."

"Agreed. But Harrington didn't have to let Milligan stand down his forces. And they would have been justified, under accepted interstellar law, in simply giving us 'a reasonable time' to evacuate, which would have been a lot shorter than the time they actually gave us." She shook her head. "No, I think part of it was the Manties' way—or, at least, Harrington's way—of telling us that if *we* show restraint—whenever we can, at least—they'll do the same."

"You may have a point," Marquette said. "Certainly Harrington's record, despite that ridiculous 'murder conviction' the

Legislaturalists cooked up after Basilisk, would lead us to expect that out of her. But I think she may also be being a bit subtler than some of our analysts would have expected out of her."

"Subtler?"

"Yes. Think about the other side of her 'message' to Milligan. 'Our technical superiority is so great we could kill you anytime we want to, but because we're nice guys, we're not going to today. All you have to do is blow up your *own* ships and get out of our way.'"

Marquette's irony was withering, and Trenis frowned.

"You're seeing it as an attack on our people's confidence and morale."

"At least in part. Mind you, from what we know of Harrington, I'm sure she was delighted to not kill anyone she didn't have to. But she apparently also believes in killing as many birds with each stone as she can."

Trenis nodded silently for a moment, then looked almost diffidently at the chief of staff.

"May I ask if a Board's going to be convened on Milligan's actions?"

"I think you can confidently assume one is," Marquette said a bit grimly. "And I'm not at all sure how it's going to come out, but if I had to place a bet, it wouldn't be on a happy outcome. The fact is that Milligan showed good sense in not getting his people killed for nothing. Unfortunately, that psychological warfare element I just mentioned has to be considered as well. I suspect any Board's going to find he acted appropriately . . . and that he's going to be beached anyway, as a sort of object lesson. It's not fair, but we have to consider the morale of the Service as a whole."

"I agree that we do, Sir," Trenis said after a moment. "On the other hand, we've gone to some lengths to convince our people they won't get shot as an example to others if they get caught in the gears through no fault of their own. And, frankly, that's exactly what happened to Tom Milligan. He couldn't run, he couldn't bring the enemy into his weapons' range, and the force mix *we'd* assigned him was hopelessly inadequate even to stand off modern Manty LACs, much less SD(P)s. If we hammer him for his actions, then we tell people we expect them to do the same thing Admiral Beach did, and that we'll hammer *them* if they don't."

"Um." Marquette pursed his lips, then shrugged. "I said I wasn't sure how it's going to come out, and what you've just said is the main reason I'm not. As for Beach, he wasn't given the same option Harrington gave Milligan, so it's not exactly as if he rejected the opportunity to save his people's lives. And from what we've been able to piece together about his tactics, they were about as good as someone in a position that hopeless could have come up with."

"I wasn't criticizing him, Sir. As a matter of fact, Everette and I knew one another for almost fifteen T-years. I'm just not sure most of our people would appreciate the difference between the options he and Milligan had, and I don't want to create a situation in which our flag officers and captains start to think we expect them to go down, every beam firing, no matter how hopeless the situation." Trenis' expression was grim. "I lost too many friends, saw too many good ships blown out of space, because their COs knew that was *exactly* what the Committee expected out of them."

Marquette considered her thoughtfully. Linda Trenis wasn't simply one of the new Republican Navy's senior admirals. As the head of the Bureau of Planning, she was responsible for the formulation and implementation of doctrine and training standards. As such, the concerns she was expressing fell squarely and correctly within her purview.

"Very well, Linda. Your concern is noted, and I'll make certain it's taken into consideration whenever the Board on Hera is impaneled. For what it's worth, I agree that the points you've raised are entirely valid. The problem's going to be exactly where we balance them against the need to maintain the most aggressive mental and psychological stance we can."

Trenis nodded, and Marquette turned back to Victor Lewis.

"As *you* just pointed out, Victor, they did show us their best where their combat hardware is concerned. What did we learn in the process?"

"Not as much as I'd have liked, Sir," Lewis said frankly. "Especially not given the price we paid for the info we did get. There are a few things we know now that we didn't know then, though.

"The one drawback to Milligan's acceptance of Harrington's terms, from our perspective over at Operational Research, is that her SD(P)s were never forced to fire. As such, we weren't able to get any sort of feel for how the *Invictuses'* armaments may vary from their *Medusa/Harrington* ships. The one thing that does stand out from the visual scans some of our recon platforms got and transmitted down to the planet before Harrington wiped them out is that the reports that the *Invictus* mounts no broadside missile tubes appears to be accurate. We're not certain why. We've had to make the same decision primarily because our missiles are so damned big, compared to theirs, that we really can't afford the mass penalty for launchers big enough to handle them in ships already designed to deploy pods. All the indications from captured hardware and what we've gotten from Erewhon are that the Manties don't suffer from that particular problem, or not, at least, to anything like the same degree, so there's obviously a different basis for the design philosophy.

"In the case of Gaston, we got a *lot* of sensor information on the Grayson *Katanas*. I'm having all of it sent directly to Admiral Foraker at Bolthole for her teams' consideration, although my initial take on it is that most of it indicates the *Katana* is built around more of that damned Manticoran miniaturization tech we can't match yet. Certainly, they're very small units, with extremely high acceleration rates. They appear to have all the *Shrike's* defensive capabilities, and whatever the hell they call that new missile of theirs. On the other hand, they never fired a shot in energy range, so we're not sure what they carry there. Even bearing in mind that we're talking about a Manty-derived design, there can't be a lot of room for the kind of energy armament the *Shrike* hauls around with it.

"The real bad news seems to be those missiles. They obviously can't have the sort of range our *Cimeterres'* missiles do, but they're incredibly fast. At the very minimum, we're going to have to completely overhaul our missile defense software to deal with their speed and maneuverability, and their sensor and tracking ability appear to have significantly improved, as well. The fact that the Manties obviously know about the Triple Ripple, and have adapted their tactics to defeat it, further complicates the situation. Frankly, at least until the next-generation LACs start coming out of Bolthole, I don't think our LACs are going to be able to encounter Manty units—or, at least, *Katanas*—with any realistic hope of victory."

"My initial feeling was that Victor was being unduly pessimistic,

Sir," Trenis put in. "Having had a better look at the raw data, though, I no longer think that. My own feeling, at this time, is that we need to restrict the *Cimeterres* essentially to the anti-missile role. If they have to mix it up with Manty or Grayson LACs, they're really going to need to do it from within our own starships' engagement envelope. They're going to need the support that badly."

"Wonderful," Marquette muttered sourly. Then he shrugged. "On the other hand, we never did see the *Cimeterre* as anything except a way to blunt *Manty* LAC attacks. Certainly they've been useful in other roles, but no one on our side is likely to confuse them with a main combatant. Actually, I'm more interested in what we know about their *Agamemnons*."

"First of all, Sir, they're big," Lewis said. "Our best estimate from Admiral Beach's tactical take is that they're somewhere around one-point-seven to one-point-eight megatons. That makes them about twice the size of their previous battlecruiser classes.

"Secondly, they don't appear to deploy the same number of pods per salvo as we've seen out of their SD(P)s. Manty pods are damnably hard sensor targets, but it looks like they were only rolling four pods at a time. However—" he looked up and met Marquette's eyes "—the pods they were rolling apparently carried fourteen missiles each."

"*Fourteen?*"

"That's correct, Sir. So their four-pod salvos were effectively rolling almost as many missiles as their SD(P)s' *six*-pod salvos."

"How in God's name did they cram that many missiles into a single pod?" Marquette demanded.

"I know I'm in charge of NavInt, Sir, but that's a question I just can't answer. Not yet. We do know they've gone to a fusion plant, instead of capacitors, in their current-generation MDMs. All indications, however, were that they were sticking with about the same number of birds per pod and simply reducing the size of each pod, to get more combat endurance rather than greater salvo density. That doesn't seem to be what they've done *here*, though, and so far, we don't have a clue how you could possibly stuff that many missiles—even if they are fusion-powered—into battlecruiser-sized pods. Some of my people are suggesting that we must be looking at an entirely new missile, but if we are, they managed to keep its development completely black. Which, unfortunately, wouldn't exactly be a first. Say what you will about the Manties, they're clearly aware of the importance of their tech advantage, and they're very good at maintaining security on their R and D programs."

"Fourteen birds," Marquette muttered, shaking his head. "Jesus. If they *do* start packing their SD(P)s' pods that full, proportionately, we're going to be in even more trouble in a long-range duel."

"Agreed," Trenis said. "On the other hand, they appear to have concluded that sixty-missile salvos are about the max for their fire control. For the moment, at least."

"Sure," Marquette snorted. "Until they get around to upgrading *it!*"

He frowned down at the tabletop, considering what he'd been told so far, then inhaled deeply.

"All right. Whatever else we may think about Admiral Beach's tactics, or the casualties he suffered, we're damned lucky we got all the tactical info that we did. And we wouldn't have, if he'd declined to fight. Another point," he looked up at Trenis, "to be considered when the Board sits on Milligan's actions.

"I can tell from what you've already said," he returned his attention to Lewis, "that Admiral Theisman and I are going to want to sit down and spend some time with your detailed, written report. And, as you've already observed, it's imperative we get all of this information to Admiral Foraker as soon as possible.

"However, I want you personally, Victor, to concentrate on something else."

"Sir?"

"There's going to be hell to pay in Congress when news of this is confirmed. People are going to be screaming for additional protection for *their* constituents, and it's going to be damned hard to tell them no. By the same token, if we're looking at an increased technological inferiority, it's going to be more imperative than ever that we keep our combat power concentrated. I can't begin to predict how that's all going to play out—politics, thank God, aren't part of my turf! But I do know, from the brief conversations I've had so far with the Secretary, that he's going to want some sort of prediction of where they're likely to do this to us next."

"Sir," Lewis said, his expression troubled, "I don't see any way to do that. There are literally dozens of places they could hit us the way they did here. We've got maybe twenty-five or thirty first-tier systems, and that many again secondary or tertiary systems. Without completely dispersing our fleet strength, we can't begin to cover that broad an area against attacks in the strength these demonstrated. And I'm afraid tea leaf-readers have at least as good a chance as my analysts do of predicting *which* of them we need to cover. For that matter, if they scout aggressively enough, they'll be able to tell where we've beefed up the defenses and simply go someplace else. What they did with their stealthed destroyers and FTL arrays this time around is proof enough of that."

"I assure you, I'm already painfully aware of the points you just raised," Marquette said grimly. "I'm also aware that I'm asking you to do something which is quite possibly impossible. I don't have any choice but to ask you, however, and *you* don't have any choice but to figure out how to do it anyway. There *has* to be some sort of underlying pattern to their target selection. I can't believe someone like Harrington is just reaching into a hat and pulling out names at random. For that matter, the spacing on this cluster of raids demonstrates she isn't. So try to get inside her head. Run it through the computers, kick it around, try to get some sort of feel for what kind of tendencies or inclinations may be pushing her choices."

"We can do that, Sir—run it through the computers and kick it around, I mean. Whether or not we can get 'inside her head' is something else entirely. And, Sir, I'm afraid that even if that's possible, we're going to need a bigger sample of her target selections before any pattern begins to suggest itself. In other words, I don't think I'll be able to give you any sort of prediction until after she's hit us again, possibly more than once."

"Understood," Marquette said in a heavy voice. "Do your best. No one's going to expect miracles out of you, but we need your very best on it. If we can guess right, even once, and smack her with heavier forces than she anticipates—maybe even mousetrap one of her raiding forces—we may be able to make them reconsider this entire strategy."

Chapter Twenty-Three

"That's the last of them, Your Grace."

"Everyone?"

"Yes, Ma'am." Mercedes Brigham smiled hugely at Honor. "According to the preliminary reports, we didn't lose *anyone* on combat ops."

"That's . . . hard to believe," Honor said. She reached up to gently caress Nimitz's ears and shook her head. "Mind you, I'm delighted to hear it. I just didn't expect it."

"Good planning, good target selection, detailed preattack reconnaissance, FTL sensor capability, overwhelming force advantage at the point of contact, and *Katanas* to smack hell out of their piece-of-crap LACs." Brigham shrugged. "Ma'am, we were playing with our deck, and they didn't even get to cut the cards, much less shuffle."

"Not this time," Honor agreed. "I suspect they're going to make it a priority to see to it we don't do that to them again, though."

"Which was the entire point of the exercise, wasn't it, Your Grace?"

Brigham grinned at her. Nimitz bleeked in amusement, echoing the chief of staff's cheerfulness, and Honor was forced to smile back at her.

"Yes, Mercedes. Yes, it was," she agreed. "And I rather suspect the Admiralty's going to be pleased with us."

"I'm sure they are," Brigham said a bit less jubilantly. "And they're also going to want us to go out and do it again, as soon as we can."

"Of course they are, although I'm sure we'll have at least a couple of weeks to plan."

"I'd like to have more time, Your Grace," Brigham's tone was downright sober this time. Honor looked at her a little quizzically, and the chief of staff shrugged. "Part of the reason it went so well this time was that you, Andrea, Admiral Truman and Admiral McKeon, and I had so much time to kick it around. There was time to look at the best current intelligence data, to model the attacks, to think about where their rear area coverage was going to be weakest. With less time, we're more likely to miss something and stub our toes."

"It's always that way, isn't it?" Honor's smile was a bit more crooked than the artificial nerves in the left side of her face could normally account for. "Remember what Clausewitz said."

"Which quote this time?"

"'Everything in war is very simple, but the simplest thing is difficult.'"

"Well, he got that one right, Your Grace."

"He got quite a few of them right, actually. Especially for a theorist who never exercised high command himself. Of course, he got some of them *wrong*, too. In this case, though, I think we'll probably be okay for at least Cutworm II. Especially if any of our additional units have reported in while we were away."

"That *would* be nice, wouldn't it? Care to place any small wagers on whether or not they have?"

"Not particularly." Honor shook her head, her smile tarter than ever. "We should know in the next few hours, one way or the other. In the meantime, Tim," she looked over her shoulder at her flag lieutenant, "please have Harper make a general signal. I'd like all flag officers to repair aboard the flagship, with their senior staffers, by fourteen-thirty hours. I want them prepared to discuss each system, including analysis of damage inflicted, and any observations on the Havenites' system defense doctrine. I also want discussion of how well our current doctrine and hardware worked and any suggestions for how we might make further improvements. And tell them to plan on staying for dinner."

"Yes, Ma'am." Lieutenant Meares grinned. "By this time, they all know what *that* means!"

"Lieutenant, I have no idea what you're talking about," Honor said sternly, almond eyes twinkling, then made a shooing motion with one hand. "Now run along and see to it before something nasty happens to you."

"On my way, Ma'am, and—" Meares paused in the day cabin hatch just long enough to give her another grin "—shaking in abject terror."

He disappeared, and Honor looked at Brigham.

"Is it my imagination, or does the staff seem to be getting just a bit uppity these days?"

"Oh, *definitely* your imagination, Your Grace."

"I thought it was."

"Okay," Solomon Hayes said, "what's so important?"

He sat in an expensive Landing restaurant, looking out through its two hundredth-floor's crystoplast wall across the waters of Jason Bay. The sun was just dipping below the horizon, turning the wrinkled blue sheet of water bloody and painting the clouds in crimson, purple, and vermilion.

The food was almost good enough to justify its priciness, and the view, he admitted, was spectacular. And not just where the scenery was concerned. The exquisitely attired woman seated across the table from him looked as if she'd probably profited from more than a bit of biosculpt, and the flowing mass of beautiful red hair spilling down her back spoke directly to Hayes' smattering of ancient Irish genes.

She was also immoderately wealthy, with powerful political connections. Most of which, he conceded, could probably be construed as liabilities, just at the moment. Still, she'd been an important inside source during the High Ridge years, and she continued to offer an insight into the inner workings of the currently gelded Conservative Association.

"So direct and to the point," she said now, pouting slightly. "You might at least pretend I'm more than just a newsy's source, Solomon."

"My dear Countess," Hayes replied, leering at her only half-professionally, "I believe I've amply demonstrated in other environs that you're much more than just a source. In fact, I do hope you haven't made other plans for the evening?"

"Bertram has, but since he didn't discuss them with me—and since I believe they include a pair of barely legal-age girls—I felt free to reserve my own evening for other . . . activities. Did you have something in mind?"

She smiled, and Hayes smiled back.

"As a matter of fact, I do. Something involving a friend's yacht, moonlight, champagne, silk sheets, and a few other things like that."

"My goodness, you *do* know how to compensate an informant for her news, don't you?" There was an ever so faint steeliness in the glorious blue eyes across the table from him.

"I try," he said, not attempting to deny the implication. There wasn't much point, after all. Besides, Countess Fairburn had used him at least as much as he'd ever used her. That little matter of the supposed Harrington-White Haven love affair came to mind, among others.

"And you succeed nicely," she told him, sipping wine. Then she smiled. "And since you've taken such pains to arrange a pleasant evening, why don't we go ahead and get the sordid details out of the way now?"

"I think that would be an excellent idea," he agreed. "The best reason to put business before pleasure is to dispose of the former early so you can concentrate on the latter properly."

"I see why you've done so well working with words," she said, setting the wine glass down. "Very well. It's actually a fairly small tidbit, in some ways, but I'll confess that I take a certain amount of pleasure in being able to pass it along to you. After all, there's not much point pretending I'm not a rather vengeful sort at heart."

She smiled again, and this time there was no humor at all in the expression.

"That sounds a bit ominous," he said lightly, watching her warily.

"Oh, I suppose it will be . . . for some. And after that unfortunate little fiasco last year, I'm sure you'll want to check it out independently before you do anything with it." Hayes' eyes had narrowed at the "fiasco" reference, and she chuckled. "It just happens to have come to my attention," she said, "that the heroic Duchess Harrington, before her departure for Trevor's Star, stopped by the Briarwood Reproduction Center."

Hayes blinked.

"Briarwood?" he repeated after a moment.

"Precisely. Now, I suppose it's possible she was there to consult with the doctors because of some fertility problem. That seems a bit unlikely, given her profession and current duties, however. And even if it didn't, according to a little bird who sang into my ear, she was there for a routine outpatient procedure. The tubing of a fetus, I believe."

Hayes looked at her, his eyes narrower than ever, and she smiled back sweetly.

"How good a source is your 'little bird'?" he asked.

"Quite good, actually."

"And he—or she—says this is *Harrington's* child?"

"I can't imagine any other reason for *her* to have outpatient surgery, can you?"

"Not at Briarwood," Hayes conceded. "Not unless, for some bizarre reason, she was *trying* to get pregnant at this moment." He thought some more. "Do you happen to know who the *father* is?"

"No."

For just a moment, something ugly flashed in the countess' eyes. Disappointment, Hayes realized. He knew who she *wanted* the father to be, but *she* knew equally well that after the way Emily Alexander had rabbit-punched the attempt to link her husband and "the Salamander," he wasn't about to leap to any conclusions that couldn't be firmly substantiated. Not in this case, at least, no matter how sharp a personal ax he had to grind. Or perhaps *because of* how very personal this particular ax was.

"Pity," he said, picking up his own wine and sipping thoughtfully.

"I do have three other bits of information," Fairburn said. "Straws in the wind, one might say."

"Which are?"

"First, Harrington's declined to declare paternity. She didn't simply ask Briarwood to maintain confidentiality; she didn't tell them. Secondly, and not surprisingly, I suppose, she's designated her mother, Dr. Harrington, to act in *loco parentis* for her child while she's away or if anything . . . unfortunate should happen to her. And third—*third*, dear Solomon, Dr. Harrington is also the physician of record for one Emily Alexander, who has mysteriously decided, after sixty or seventy years in a life-support chair, that the time has come for her and her husband to become parents, as well."

Hayes blinked again. He was sure he could have come up with half a dozen explanations for the coincidences Fairburn had just listed without even trying. But that didn't matter. His instincts told him that, motivated by vengefulness or not, the countess had zeroed in on what was actually going on. Especially in light of Harrington's refusal to declare paternity even to Briarwood's medical staff.

"Those are interesting straws, Elfrieda," he conceded after several seconds. "And I do have my own ways of confirming your information—not that I believe for a moment that it isn't accurate." *This time*, he didn't add, although he was certain she heard it anyway. "I imagine you'd like me to maintain confidentiality about your own part in bringing this to my attention?"

"I'm afraid so," she sighed with what he realized was genuine regret. "A part of me would dearly love to let that lowborn upstart bitch know *precisely* who blew the whistle on her. Given the current . . . unfortunate political climate and the disgusting way the proles are fawning all over her, however, it probably wouldn't be very wise to make myself a target for retaliation. Bertram wouldn't thank me for it, either."

"I thought as much," Hayes said, projecting as much sympathy as he could. "So I'll be very careful to document any hard facts I use without mentioning your name."

"Such a dear, cautious man!" Countess Fairburn cooed.

"I try, Elfrieda. I try."

"Honor!"

Sir Thomas Caparelli came to his feet, stepping out from behind his desk and smiling broadly as he reached out to grip Honor's hand firmly.

"It's *good* to see you," he said, and Honor smiled as she tasted the personal warmth behind his greeting. "And you, of course, Nimitz," Caparelli continued, nodding to the treecat on Honor's shoulder. "And you, Commodore," he added with a smile as he released Honor's hand to shake Mercedes Brigham's.

"I see you have your priorities in proper order, Sir Thomas," Brigham murmured, responding to the twinkle in the First Space Lord's eye.

"Well, Her Grace and Nimitz do rather come as a unit, Commodore."

"That they do, Sir."

"Sit down. Sit down, both of you—well, all three of you!" he invited, waving at the comfortable chairs in the conversational nook around his splendid office's coffee-table. Two carafes—one of coffee, and one of hot chocolate—steamed on the coffee-table in question, which also offered cups and saucers, a plate of fresh croissants, and a fresh head of celery.

Honor and Brigham obeyed, and Nimitz slithered down into Honor's lap, eyeing the celery with cheerful greediness. Honor chuckled and gave him a gentle smack, and he rolled over onto his back, grabbing her wrist with true-hands and hand-feet and wrestling with it cheerfully.

"And this," Caparelli observed with a chuckle, "represents Sphinx's native sentient species?"

"Some 'cats tend to revert to kittenhood more readily than others, Sir Thomas," Honor told him, swatting at Nimitz with her free hand while he purred happily.

"I'm glad he likes you," Caparelli said. "I've seen pictures of what those claws of his can do." He shook his head. "Personally, I've always wondered how something that short can do so much damage."

"That's probably because, like most people, you think of treecat claws the way you do of terrestrial cats' claws. In fact, they aren't at all the same. Stinker?"

Nimitz released her wrist and forearm and sat up in her lap. He extended one true-hand—long, wiry fingers slightly crooked—and unsheathed his needle-pointed claws. Caparelli leaned closer, his expression fascinated, and Nimitz held them up where he could see them clearly.

"If you'll notice," Honor said, "his claws are much broader at the base than those of a terrestrial cat. When people call them 'scimitar-shaped,' it's literally descriptive, except that the wrong side is edged. And they retract into some fairly specialized, cartilage-lined receptacles, because they're actually more like a terrestrial shark's tooth than anything someone from Old Earth would call a 'claw.' The actual composition of the claw itself is more like stone than it is like horn, cartilage, or bone, and this curved inner section is at least as sharp as most flaked obsidian knives. It's true they aren't very long, but for all intents and purposes, he's got scalpel blades on each finger that are the next best thing to a centimeter and a half in length. That's why a 'cat in a true killing rage looks so much like a berserk buzz saw. Each individual cut isn't that deep, but with all six limbs going at once in repeated slashes, well—"

She shrugged, and Caparelli shuddered slightly at the image her words had evoked.

"I never realized just how formidable those weapons were," he confessed.

"Well, Sir Thomas," Honor said cheerfully, "if you want something to give you real nightmares, you might consider that hexapumas—which, you know, are just a *little* bigger—have exactly the same sort of claws. Of course, *their* claws tend to be eight or nine centimeters long. Which is why we Sphinxians never go into the bush unarmed."

"Your Grace," Caparelli said, "if *I* were a Sphinxian and knew about hexapuma claws, I wouldn't go into the bush *at all!*"

"We do lose the occasional tourist," she said, straight-faced.

"No doubt," he said dryly, leaning forward and personally pouring coffee for Brigham and chocolate for Honor. He waved at the croissants and celery, and settled back in his own chair with a cup and saucer while they helped themselves.

"I've got a formal meeting set up for tomorrow afternoon," he told them more seriously. "I'll have several people there—including Hamish, Honor—and I hope you and Commodore Brigham will be prepared to give us a comprehensive brief and answer any questions about Cutworm."

He raised one eyebrow interrogatively, and Honor nodded.

"Good. In the meantime, I just wanted to say the preliminary read on Cutworm indicates that it did exactly what we had in mind. Good work. Especially pulling it off without any losses of your own. Whether or not it has the long term effect we hoped for remains to be seen, but no one else could have done the job better. Or, for that matter, as well, probably."

"Thank you, Sir Thomas," Honor murmured, tasting the sincerity behind his words.

"We've managed to scare up a few more units for you, as well," Caparelli continued. "Not as many as I'd like, or anywhere near as many as we'd originally scheduled, although some of them will be a bit newer than projected, to compensate. What we have been able to dig up will be waiting for you when you get back to Eighth Fleet. The main problem, as I'm sure you've guessed, is the need to cover Zanzibar and Alizon. Especially Zanzibar, since the Peeps got such a good look at our defensive deployments there. To be honest, your success in Cutworm is actually going to make that particular problem worse. The logic, I'm sure, is going to run something like 'If Harrington can do that to *them*, then *they* could do it to *us*.' And the hell of it, of course, is that they're right. Even if they weren't, the political realities of the Alliance would require us to respond to their concerns."

Honor frowned very slightly, and he shook his head.

"One of the reasons those realities are real, Honor, is that they ought to be. High Ridge's total incompetence makes the situation even worse, I agree. But it doesn't change the fact that those two systems are our allies; that they're currently the most exposed—and most attractive—secondary targets available to the Peeps; and that they have a moral right to demand, and receive, adequate protection. I don't like what it does to my deployable fleet strength, but I can't pretend they don't have that right."

"Maybe so, Sir," Brigham said diffidently, "but Admiral al-Bakr's decisions when the Peeps probed Zanzibar didn't help any."

"No, they didn't," Caparelli agreed in a tone whose very neutrality was a gentle rebuke. "That, however, is now atmosphere out the airlock, Commodore. We have to deal with the situation as it exists. And while I know it wasn't your intent, we can't afford to lend any credence to the attitude which unfortunately exists among some of our own personnel. Things are thorny enough already without suggesting to the Zanzibarans that we believe they're incompetents or cowards who jump at shadows."

"No, Sir. Of course not," Brigham agreed.

"Leaving that aside, however," Caparelli continued, turning back to Honor, "the newsies are already playing this one up as our first offensive victory of the war, which means you now hold title to both our defensive and offensive accomplishments. I'm afraid your reputation's been even further enhanced."

"That's ridiculous," Honor half-muttered. She shook her head irritably. "'Offensive victory,' indeed! Those poor Havenite picket forces were so outclassed it was like . . . like feeding baby chicks to near-sharks!"

"Of course it was." Caparelli shook his own head—in his case, more in amusement than anything else. "That's the way it's supposed to be, whenever we can arrange it. On the other hand, your accomplishments—and especially the way you allowed Milligan to scuttle his own ships—is the kind of copy the newsfaxes dream of. They can't quite seem to decide whether to play you as the elegant, chivalrous corsair or the tough-as-nails, blood-and-guts warhorse. Hamish mentioned a couple of wet-navy types from Old Earth. Someone named Raphael Semmes and someone else named Bill Halsey. Although he did comment that you had marginally better tactical sense than Semmes and better strategic sense than Halsey."

"Oh, he did, did he?" Honor's eyes gleamed ominously, and Caparelli chuckled.

"Somehow I suspect he was looking forward to having me tell you that. Still, however . . . irksome you may find it, don't expect anybody in the Government or the Navy to try to put the brakes on it. Frankly, we need all the good press—and all the morale-boosting stories—we can get. Anything that simultaneously helps our morale and hurts the Peeps' morale is much too valuable for us to even consider not using."

"In that respect, Sir Thomas," Brigham said, "I think what the *Katanas* and *Agamemnons* did to them ought to have a definite morale-hurting effect. For that matter, I suspect it's going to make them reconsider their estimates of relative combat effectiveness across the board."

"I hope you're right, Commodore. And I also have to admit that what I've seen in the preliminary reports makes *me* feel better about the relative effectiveness of the new ships and hardware. But the fact of the matter is that we don't have very many of them. In fact, that's one reason we gave such a high percentage of the ones we do have to Eighth Fleet. We want the Peeps to see them being used—to throw them right into Theisman's face in hopes he'll be so impressed by their effectiveness he won't realize how few of them we actually have."

"And just how likely does ONI think that is, Sir?" Honor asked neutrally. In her own mind, she already knew, and Caparelli smiled wryly at her.

"About as likely as *you* think it is," he said. "On the other hand, when the . . . water is this deep, Your Grace, you reach for *anything* that might help you keep your head above the surface."

Chapter Twenty-Four

"Welcome home, Honor." Emily Alexander smiled broadly from her life-support chair as Honor stepped through the White Haven door. "I seem to be saying that a lot. I'm only sorry I don't get to say it more often."

"I'm afraid White Haven isn't as convenient to Admiralty House as Jason Bay, Emily. Besides, I have to keep reminding myself a certain degree of discretion is indicated. Otherwise," Honor bent to kiss Emily's cheek, "I'd be out here every minute I was on the planet."

"Hmmm. I suppose that *could* be called indiscreet."

"Tell me about it. Miranda and Mac have certainly done their best—in, of course, their own exquisitely tactful fashions—to make the point."

"Do they disapprove?"

Emily frowned slightly, and Honor tasted the older woman's ambiguous emotions. For all her natural graciousness and kindness, and for all the deep and mutual devotion between her and her servants, she was a product of the Manticoran aristocracy. For her, servants could become friends, literally members of her family, but they were always *servants*. It might be important to her that her servants think well of her, but whether they did or not would never be allowed to affect her decisions, and that little, naturally aristocratic corner of her couldn't help feeling it would be presumptuous for any servant to actually judge her actions.

"No, they don't."

Honor straightened with a smile. Emily might be a natural

born aristocratic, but Honor Harrington certainly wasn't. She wasn't about to let other people's opinions dictate her decisions, either, but for quite different reasons. And for her, people like Miranda LaFollet and James MacGuiness would never be "servants," even if they were her employees. Retainers, perhaps, but never servants. Even leaving aside the fact that both of them were millionaires in their own rights, she thought with a mental chuckle.

"They don't disapprove at all of my doing what my heart requires, to borrow a phrase from the bad novelists. They just worry about what could happen if the newsies get hold of this . . . relationship." She grimaced. "They had an entirely too up close and personal look at what the 'faxes put us through last time, and they worry about me. Can't imagine why."

"Of course you can't." Emily's incipient frown turned into a smile once more.

"Actually, what I mind the most about this whole clandestine thing, in a lot of ways," Honor said with a grimace, "is that I see so little of Miranda these days. She's still officially my 'maid' as far as Grayson is concerned, but she's effectively my chief of staff, especially here on Manticore. So I end up leaving her home to tend to business, and it would look a bit odd if I started dragging her out here to visit 'friends.' Of course, on Grayson, under similar circumstances—although I admit that the mind boggles at the concept of 'similar circumstances' there—I'd be leaving *Mac* home to tend to business and dragging *Miranda* around with me." She shook her head. "It's a lot less complicated being a commoner, you know."

"Cling to your illusions if you must," Emily replied. "Given your rank, little things like your military reputation, and the fact that you're probably one of the dozen wealthiest people in the entire Star Kingdom, I doubt very much that your life could ever be uncomplicated again."

"Oh, thank you for that douche of reality!"

"You're welcome."

"This is your wakeup call, Admiral Harrington."

Honor twitched as the deep, soft voice spoke into her ear, and her sleeping mind snuggled closer to the bright, caressing mind-glow behind the words. Perhaps that was why she didn't awaken the way she normally did—quickly, completely, senses coming immediately alert.

"This is your *wake*up call," the voice repeated with a chuckle, and Honor's eyes snapped open—very quickly indeed, this time—as she tasted Hamish's intent. Quick as she was, she wasn't *quite* quick enough, and ruthless fingers danced up her ribs to her armpits, despicably exploiting the secret she had guarded for so many decades.

"*Hamish!*" she half-shrieked as he tickled her mercilessly. Her upper arms clamped tight to her rib cage, trapping his hands, but his fingers went right on moving, and she writhed. Both of them were perfectly well aware she could have broken both his arms anytime she chose to, but he continued his attack with the fearlessness of someone prepared to take unscrupulous advantage of the knowledge that she loved him.

She flung herself out of bed, whipping around to face him, and he propped himself on one elbow, stretched sensually, and grinned wickedly at her. Nor was his the only amusement in the bedroom; Nimitz and Samantha sat side-by-side on the headboard, bleeking with laughter.

"I see you're awake," Hamish said cheerfully.

"And *you*, Earl White Haven, are a dead man," she told him with a glower.

"I'm not afraid of you." He elevated his nose with a sniff. "Emily will protect me."

"Not when I tell her why you have to die. When I explain, she'll help me hide the body."

"You know, she might, at that."

"Darn right she might."

"Well, it was probably worth it anyway to wake up to a sight like this," he said, blue eyes gleaming, and Honor actually felt herself blushing as she glanced down at her nude state. The taste of the treecats' amusement at her reaction only made her blush more rosily, and she shook her fist.

"I think," she said ominously, "that *all* of you need to be seen to. Especially *you*, My Lord Earl. To think, I trusted you enough to actually admit I'm ticklish. The sheer treachery of your actions takes my breath away."

"Of course it does." He sat up and swung his own legs over the side of the bed. "Which is undoubtedly the reason you shared your deep, dark secret in the first place. You must have known any decent tactician would take advantage of it when the critical nature of his mission required it."

"Definitely seen to." She smiled sweetly. "You know, I was talking it over with Andrew just the other day, and he mentioned to me that it's never too late to take up a new form of exercise. Take you, for example, Hamish. I realize that at your advanced and decrepit age you may think you're too old to learn new tricks, but you *are* a prolong recipient, and I saw you on the handball court just a couple of months ago. I think you'd be a fine prospect."

"Prospect for what?" he asked warily.

"Why, for taking up *coup de vitesse*, of course." She widened her eyes innocently. "Think how much it would increase your self-confidence, not to mention how good it is as a systemic exercise."

"You, young lady, are out of your mind if you think I'm going to let you get me onto the mat as your punching bag." He snorted. "I might—*might*, I say—be prepared to take up Grayson-style fencing. I was always pretty good with foil and epee. At least I *was*, many, many years ago, when I was at the Island. But that brutal, sweaty hand-to-hand business of yours isn't my style at all." He shook his head. "Oh, no—self-defense is *your* forte, not mine. If we should ever happen to encounter a mugger who somehow penetrates the protection of those three Rottweilers of yours, I'll be perfectly happy to hold your coat while *you* mop up the pavement with him. Heck, I'll even buy you a bonbon and a cup of hot chocolate afterward."

Honor chuckled, trying to picture a Grayson male, however enlightened, suggesting anything of the sort to *any* woman, be she ever so well-trained in self-defense.

"Well," she said, after a moment, checking the date/time display in her artificial eye, "we're both going to need to brush up on our self-defense skills if we don't get ourselves down to breakfast pretty quickly."

"Hey, don't blame me! I've been *trying* to get you up! And, I warn you, I fully intend to tell Emily that when we're late to breakfast."

"God, there're no *limits* to your treachery," Honor said, snatching up her kimono and sliding into it. "If only I'd known ahead of time!"

"Sure, sure." He stood and stretched luxuriously. "And speaking of treachery . . ."

Honor frowned. He was up to *something*, she could taste it. But—

Hamish smiled sweetly at her, and then, with absolutely no warning, dashed for the bathroom.

"Hamish, don't you *dare*—!"

She was too late. The master bath's palatial shower's door clicked shut, and she slid to a halt as he smiled at her through it.

"Looks like *I* get the first shower," he said complacently. "Unless, of course, you'd care to . . . ?"

He flipped the shower door open, just a crack, and Honor laughed and let the kimono slip back off her shoulders to the floor.

They were, indeed, late to breakfast.

Given the fact that Andrew LaFollet and her other armsmen knew exactly why Honor had been to Briarwood, the colonel had clearly decided there was no longer any point in pretending he didn't also know exactly what was going on. Hamish's reaction the first time he'd opened the door of *his* suite and found LaFollet standing guard outside it had not been one of unalloyed amusement. He'd had the good sense not to make an issue of it, however, and it was certainly much more convenient for Honor to no longer have to go scurrying through the back hallways every morning.

There were, however, some things not even an armsman could protect a steadholder from, and she and Hamish peeked through the dining room door cautiously when they finally got there.

Emily sat in her life-support chair, parked in her normal place, with a steaming cup of coffee in front of her. But she looked up quickly at their arrival, and Honor's smile disappeared instantly.

Nimitz jerked upright on her shoulder, and Samantha did the same on Hamish's, as both treecats tasted what Honor already had. Hamish couldn't, but the quickness and unanimity of the other three's reaction wasn't lost upon him.

"Emily?" Honor stepped quickly through the door, her voice concerned, all humor in abeyance. "What is it?"

"It's—" Emily started to speak quickly, then stopped herself.

"It's not good," she said after a moment, the words coming less rapidly, sounding much more like *her*. "I'm afraid," she showed her teeth in a humorless smile, "we're not quite as finished with the newsies as we'd hoped."

Honor moved across to Emily's chair, her appetite disappearing, despite her enhanced metabolism. She pulled back one of the dining room chairs, turning it to face Emily, and sank into it. Nimitz slid down into her lap, gazing at Emily as intensely—and anxiously—as Honor herself, and she felt Hamish stepping up close behind her even before his hand came down on her shoulder.

"It leaked," she said flatly.

"I think you could say that," Emily agreed with poison-dry humor. Her right hand flipped a 'fax viewer onto the table. "You remember our good friend Solomon Hayes, I'm sure."

The sinking sensation in Honor's midsection intensified abruptly. She glanced up over her shoulder at Hamish, then drew the viewer in front of her and keyed it.

She wasn't at all surprised when it lit with the current day's *Landing Tattler*. Nor was she surprised that the display was centered on Solomon Hayes' gossip column. It wasn't the first time she'd found herself the object of Hayes' interest, and white-hot anger glowed as she remembered the smear campaign High Ridge and his cronies had used Hayes to open.

Her eyes ran down the text, and her lips tightened. Normally, Hayes touched on several victims in each of his maliciously barbed columns. And he was also normally careful to couch his accusations and veiled insinuations sufficiently obliquely to avoid anything which might be actionable under the Star Kingdom's stringent libel laws.

This time, the entire column was devoted to only a single topic, and there was nothing oblique about it at all. Especially not about its three concluding paragraphs.

" . . . to sources at Briarwood," she read, "Duchess Harrington was attended by Dr. Illescue, Briarwood's senior physician, who personally oversaw the tubing of her son seven weeks ago. Despite all inquiries, it was impossible to determine who the father might be. Indeed, sources indicate the Duchess has specifically declined to declare paternity.

"That, of course, is her unquestioned legal and moral right. Nonetheless, those of us in the press must inevitably find ourselves speculating on her reasons for availing herself of that right. Certainly it's only natural for a military woman, facing all the risks of naval combat, to be concerned about the future. To assure herself and her loved ones of a child. Still, one must wonder just why she felt it necessary to proceed in that perfectly reasonable project with such secrecy. One might almost say clandestinely.

"And yet another, clearly coincidental yet interesting, tidbit has come to our attention. We feel confident that all of Lady Emily Alexander's myriad fans and well-wishers will be delighted to learn that Countess White Haven has also availed herself of Briarwood's services. According to the same sources, her child will be born within less than two months of Duchess Harrington's.'"

"That son-of-a-*bitch*," Hamish hissed behind her as he read it over her shoulder. "That goddamned, *worthless*, cowardly, *mealy-mouthed* piece of—"

He chopped himself off with a physical effort Honor could literally feel, and walked across to sit on Emily's other side.

"I wonder who his 'sources' might be?" Honor mused in a tone whose lightness fooled no one.

"Actually," Emily said, "you might not want to leap to any conclusions in that regard." Honor look at her, and Emily snorted. "It doesn't take an empath to guess which road you're headed down, Honor, given what your parents had to say about their history with Illescue. And you might even be right. But I've had a little longer to think about this than you two have, and there are several rather odd things about this particular column."

"Beside the fact that this time he laid his sights on just one target—well, *two* targets?" Hamish put in.

"As a matter of fact, yes. The biggest difference between this one and his usual style is that he's very specific. He gives the exact day you were actually at the Center, Honor. And he also gives the correct date for our second child's birth. He wouldn't do that unless he was entirely confident of his facts, knowing what the three of us would do to him in court if he didn't have them right. But he specifically mentions Dr. Illescue by name, and if Illescue *were* his source, he wouldn't have provided that particular snippet of information. There's no reason he has to, and the one thing he's never done is give up his sources."

"That's because half the time he doesn't *have* any sources," Honor half-snarled.

"That's not really fair," Emily observed. "Solomon Hayes is a loathsome, disgusting, toadlike gigolo who homes in on vicious gossip and rumors like a near-buzzard homing in on carrion. Three-quarters of his 'news' comes from bored, wealthy women with the moral fiber of Old Earth alley cats in heat, at least half of whom have scores of their own to settle. But he usually does have a source. The thing that lets him survive is that *most* of the time there's at least a core of truth to the rumors he spreads. Distorted, exaggerated, or deliberately twisted, perhaps, but still there. That's what made him so damnably effective when High Ridge and North Hollow used him against you before. Salaciousness has always sold 'faxes, and a lot of people take Hayes lightly because of that. But the truth is, he's actually a very dangerous enemy, with much more power than many people assume, precisely because he does have that reputation for knowing what secrets he's spilling so gleefully."

Her tone was almost dispassionate, but it wouldn't have fooled anyone who could see the fire in her green eyes.

"You may be right," Hamish said after a moment. "No, scratch that. You're almost certainly right—you usually are about things like this, love. Unfortunately, that doesn't give me any ideas about what to do about this. Aside from hiring an assassin, at least."

"If we want to go that route, we don't need any assassins," Honor said grimly.

"Somehow, I suspect challenging him to a duel and then shooting him smartly between the eyes, however satisfying, might not be precisely the best way to handle the situation," Emily said dryly. "Not that we couldn't make a tidy fortune selling tickets to the event."

"Ha! The instant you challenge him, he'll emigrate to Beowulf!" Hamish growled. "They don't allow duels there."

"I think perhaps we can leave that pleasant fantasy out of our considerations?" Emily suggested just a bit tartly, and her husband muttered something she chose to take as agreement.

"The thing that bothers *me* the most," Honor said, her eyes troubled, "is how explicitly he's linked you and me, Emily. Well," she smiled almost naturally, "that and the fact that I didn't really want to know whether it was a boy or girl just yet."

"The question in my mind," Emily said thoughtfully, "is whether he genuinely believes Hamish is also the father of your child,

Honor, or if he included the linkage only as a way to remind his readership about his earlier allegations about the two of you. Does he know something, or is he simply using innuendo to take a swipe at the three of us because of what we did to him last time around?"

"I think he either knows, or strongly suspects," Honor said. Then she shook her head. "No, I think it has to be 'strongly suspects.' The only way he could *know* would be if he'd somehow managed to obtain a genetic comparison of the child and Hamish, and if Illescue *isn't* his source, then I don't see any way he could have done that."

"That's a good point," Hamish agreed. "And I'm inclined to agree with you. Which leads to another point." He grimaced unhappily. "You've been spending an awful lot of time at White Haven whenever you're on-planet, Honor. It's not going to take a hyper-physicist to figure that out. And the fact that we were accused of being lovers when we weren't isn't going to help us very much now that we *are*. So whether *he* openly suggests I'm the father or not, the suggestion's going to be out there very soon, if it isn't already."

"I suppose I could try staying away," Honor said slowly, her expression much unhappier than his had been.

"No, you certainly can't," Emily said tartly, and shook her head. "You two should never be allowed out in a social situation without a keeper!" Both of them looked at her, and she snorted derisively. "If you suddenly stop visiting your friend Emily after Hayes' little bombshell, the only conclusion anyone is going to be able to draw is the correct one—which is the last thing you want at this particular moment, don't you agree, Honor?"

"Well, yes, but—"

"But me no buts," Emily interrupted. "Besides, in the final analysis, since we've always intended to eventually admit Hamish's paternity, we can't stand up and call Hayes a liar. He's a cretin, a sneak, and a treacherous little worm, but *this* time, at least, the one thing he isn't is a liar. If we call him one now, it's going to create all sorts of problems when we finally come forward. And unless we're prepared to do that, suddenly changing your habits would be the same thing as admitting he's hit the nail on the head . . . and that you're trying to pretend he hasn't."

"So what *do* we do?" Honor demanded.

"Nothing," Emily said flatly. The other two looked at her incredulously, and she flipped her working hand in her shrug equivalent. "I didn't say I liked the idea. It's just that the best of the several bad options available to us is simply to ignore it. Honor's going to be going back off-world tomorrow, and the sort of newsy who'd be interested in following up on a story like this is going to find it pretty hard to get to her when she's back with Eighth Fleet. And much as I hate playing on the 'poor invalid' stereotype, it does offer *me* a certain amount of protection from the same sort of intrusiveness. Which means the only one who's likely to be stalked over this is you, Hamish."

"Gee, thanks for the warning," he said glumly.

"You're a politician now, not a mere admiral," his wife told him. "That makes you fair game, and by now you ought to have at least some notion of how the rules work."

"No comment?"

"That will probably work for anything from your official press secretaries. After all, even if Hayes is right, it's a personal matter, not something government spokespeople should waste time and effort on. It won't work for *you*, though. If someone manages to corner you in a personal interview, you're going to have to come up with something better, or you might just as well go ahead and tell them you're the father."

"And your suggestion is?"

"I think your response ought to be that if, in fact, Duchess Harrington is having a child tubed, and if she's declined—at this time—to disclose that child's paternity, that's certainly her right, and you have no intention of speculating about it."

"And if they ask me point-blank if *I'm* the father?" Hamish waved one hand in a gesture of intense frustration. "Damn it, I *am* the father, and accident or not, I'm proud to be!"

"I know you are, sweetheart," Emily said softly, eyes luminous as she laid her working hand on his forearm. "And if they do ask you point-blank, the one thing you *can't* do is lie. So my suggestion would be that you laugh."

"*Laugh?*"

"As naturally as you possibly can," she agreed. "I know your thespian skills leave a bit to be desired, dear, but I'll help you practice in front of a mirror."

There was actually a twinkle in her eye, and he made a face at her.

"But," she continued more seriously, "that really is your best response. Laugh. And if they continue to press, simply repeat that you have no intention of speculating, and that you believe Honor's obvious wishes in this matter ought to be respected by everyone. *You*, at any rate, intend to respect them just as thoroughly as you would if you *were* the father."

"And you really think this is going to work?" he asked skeptically.

"I never said that," Emily replied. "I just said it was our best option."

Chapter Twenty-Five

"Do you want me to do anything about this . . . *person* while you're away, My Lady?"

Miranda LaFollet sat at her desk in her Jason Bay office, and when Honor poked her head in the open doorway, her "maid" held up a 'fax viewer between thumb and forefinger with the expression of someone who'd just found a dead mouse in her soup.

"And just what did you have it in mind to do about Mr. Hayes?" Honor inquired mildly. "This isn't Grayson, you know, Miranda."

"Oh, I certainly do, My Lady." Miranda's mouth twisted in distaste, and Farragut, her treecat, made a soft hissing sound from the perch beside her chair. "Freedom of the press is a wonderful thing, My Lady. We have it on Grayson, too, you know. But this Hayes person wouldn't care at all for what his brand of 'journalism' would get him back home."

"Sounds like a very free press to me," Honor observed. "Not that I don't think Mr. Hayes would look ever so much better with a couple of broken legs. Unfortunately, if that were a practical solution to the problem, I'd already have taken care of it myself."

"There's always Micah," Miranda pointed out. Micah LaFollet, her youngest brother, had just turned twenty-six. Young enough for third-generation prolong and blessed with adequate diet and medical care since childhood, he towered more than fourteen centimeters taller than his eldest brother, Andrew. Despite his formidable height (he was actually five centimeters taller than Honor herself), he looked much younger than his age to Grayson eyes, but he was already in the final stages of armsman training, and he had a pronounced case of hero worship where Honor was concerned.

"No, there *isn't* always Micah," Honor scolded. "He's not an armsman yet, and he's overly enthusiastic. Besides, assault with violence is a felony here in the Star Kingdom, and unlike your older brother, *he* doesn't have any sort of diplomatic immunity."

"Well, then surely there's something *Richard* could do about him." Miranda kept her tone light, trying to pretend she was no more than half-serious, but Honor tasted the white-hot rage just below the younger woman's surface.

"Miranda," she said, stepping fully into the office, "I truly, truly appreciate how angry you. How much you—and Andrew, and Simon, and Micah, and Spencer, and Mac—all want to protect me from this. But you can't do it. And while Richard's a very good attorney, Solomon Hayes has spent decades figuring out exactly how close he can sail to outright libel without quite crossing the line into something actionable."

"But, My Lady," Miranda protested, abandoning her pretense of humor, "word of this is going to get home to Grayson. It's not going to matter much to *our* steaders, but that midden-toad Mueller and his loathsome bunch are going to try as hard as they can to hurt you with it where the conservatives are concerned."

"I know," Honor sighed. "But there's not anything I can do about it at this point. I'm getting out of town and away from the newsies myself by going back to the Fleet, but I've sent letters to Benjamin and Austen, warning them about what's coming. That's about all I can do at this point."

Miranda looked rebellious, and Honor smiled at her.

"It's not like I've never had anyone taking shots at me in the 'faxes before," she pointed out. "And so far, I've managed to survive, however little I've enjoyed the experience, sometimes. And..."

She paused for a moment, then shrugged.

"And," she confessed, "I'm not being *quite* as blasé about this entire thing as you seem to be assuming. Trust me, Mr. Hayes is going to come to regret this particular...endeavor."

"My Lady?" Miranda perked up noticeably, and there was a

slight edge to her voice. An edge accompanied by the sort of look a Grayson nanny might employ when not one of her charges seemed to know *anything* about how that dead sandfrog had miraculously materialized in the nursery air purifier.

"Well," Honor said, "I just *happened* to run into Stacey Hauptman at lunch yesterday, and somehow or other the conversation turned to journalism. And it seems Stacey has been considering venturing into that area for some time. She told me she thinks she might begin by buying the *Landing Tattler*—just to get her toes wet, you know. Sort of explore the possibilities. And I think she might also have said something about making it her business to—how *did* she put it? Oh, yes. Making it her business to 'clean up the professionalism of Manticoran journalism generally.'"

"My *Lady*," Miranda said in quite a different tone, her gray eyes twinkling suddenly. "Oh, that's *evil!*" she continued with deep satisfaction.

"*I* never suggested that she take any action whatsoever," Honor said virtuously, "and no one could possibly accuse me or any of my retainers of taking any sort of action, either. I will confess, however, that I find the prospect of Stacey Hauptman taking personal aim at Mr. Hayes . . . profoundly satisfying. It won't do much to undo what he's already done, but I feel fairly confident we won't be hearing from him a third time."

"And you were just suggesting the *Grayson* press might incorporate a few journalistic constraints."

"Even in the Star Kingdom, Miranda, private citizens—as opposed to governmental agencies or public bodies—are permitted to make their displeasure known, so long as they violate no laws or civil rights. Which, I assure you, Stacey has no intention of doing. Or, now that I think about it, any *need* to do."

"Oh, of *course* not, My Lady!"

"I want to know who leaked this, and I want to know yesterday."

Dr. Franz Illescue's voice was flat, almost calm, with a lack of emphasis and exclamation points which rang alarm bells in every member of the Briarwood Reproduction Center's senior staff.

"But, Doctor," Julia Isher, Briarwood's business manager, said cautiously, "so far, we don't really have any evidence it was one of our people who was responsible."

"Don't be stupid, Julia. And let's not pretend *I* am, either," Illescue said in that same almost-calm tone, and Isher winced.

Franz Illescue could be an unmitigated pain in the ass, and despite the very nearly half century he'd spent getting the worst of his natural aristocratic arrogance knocked out of him, there would always be that core of implicit superiority. That unassailable knowledge that he was, by the inevitable process of birth and the natural working of the universe, inherently better than anyone around him. Despite that, however—or possibly even because of it—he was normally very careful to observe the rules of courtesy with the "little people" with whom he came into contact. On the rare occasions when he wasn't, it was a very, very bad sign, indeed.

"One of 'our people,' as you put it, most definitely *was* responsible," he continued after a heartbeat or two. "Whether someone deliberately sold the information to this . . . this . . . *individual* Hayes or not, that information *had* to come from someone inside the Center. Someone with access to our confidential records. Someone who, if he or she didn't deliberately sell the information was still criminally—and I use the adverb advisedly, in light of our confidentiality agreements with our patients—negligent. Someone who either gossiped about it where he or she shouldn't have or allowed someone else unauthorized access. In either case, I want his—or her—ass. I want it broiled, on a silver platter, with a nice side of fried potatoes, and I intend to see to it that whoever it was never works in this field—or any other branch of the medical profession—in the Star Kingdom again."

More than one of the staffers seated around the huge table blanched visibly. Illescue had *still* to raise his voice, but the temperature in the conference room seemed to hover within a degree or two of absolute zero Kelvin. Some of those staffers, like Isher herself, had been with Illescue for twenty T-years or more, and they had *never* seen him this incandescently angry.

"Doctor," Isher said, after a moment, "I've already initiated a review of everyone who had access to Duchess Harrington's records. I assure you we're doing everything we possibly can to determine how that information got out of our files and into Mr. Hayes' hands. But so far our security people, some of whom are very well versed in forensic cybernetics, are coming up completely blank. I asked Tajman Meyers—" Meyers was the Center's head of security, who was absent from this meeting only because he was out personally heading the investigation "—if we need to bring in someone else, like the Landing PD. He says our people are probably as good as most of the LCPD's investigators, but he also agrees that if you want to bring in a completely outside team, he'll cooperate fully."

She met Illescue's hooded, basilisk gaze levelly.

"The truth of the matter is, though, Sir, that we may never be able to identify the individual responsible. As you say, it could have been a case of idle gossip. Or, of course, although I don't like to think any of our people would violate our trust that way, someone could have deliberately handed the information over. In either case, however, my personal feeling is that it was almost certainly done verbally, with no written or electronic record. Which doesn't leave us very much in the way of clues."

Illescue looked at her, eyes cold, his normal, reassuring physician's personality noticeably in abeyance. The fact that he knew she was right only made him still angrier.

"I want a list of every name of every member of our staff who had access to both Duchess Harrington and Countess White Haven's files," he said, after a moment. "*Everyone*—physicians, nurses, technicians, clerical staff. As a general rule, I don't much care for witch hunts, but I'm going to make an exception in this case." He looked around the conference room and showed his teeth in an expression no one would ever mistake for a smile. "To be perfectly honest, I'm looking *forward* to it."

"Jesus, Julia," Martijn Knippschd muttered softly as he walked down the hall beside her, "I've never seen him *that* mad!" He shook his head. "I mean, this is terrible, sure. I agree, and not just because of the way it violates Duchess Harrington's confidentiality. It leaves us covered with crap here at the Center, too. But, let's face it—this really isn't the first time we've had an information leak. And that talk of his about 'witch hunts'—!"

"It isn't just talk, Marty," Isher said, equally quietly. "He means it. And if he does find out who's responsible..."

She shrugged, her expression bleak, and Knippschd shook his head.

"I believe you. I just don't understand *why*."

Isher looked at him for a moment, clearly considering whether or not to say something more. Dr. Martijn Knippschd was, in many ways, her equivalent on the medical support side of Briarwood's operations. He wasn't one of the Center's partners, but he was directly responsible for overseeing the labs' physical operation and directing the technicians who worked in them. And unless something very unexpected happened, he *would* be Briarwood's newest junior partner within the next three T-years.

"It's . . . personal this time," she said finally. "Dr. Illescue has something of a history with the Harringtons."

"I had the impression he'd never met the Duchess before she became a patient," Knippschd objected.

"I didn't say he had a history with *her*, Marty. He has one with her *parents*, and it's personal, not professional. I'm not going to go into any details, but suffice it to say that if there are any two physicians in the entire Star Kingdom who he'd crawl across ground glass to avoid giving a reason to fault his professional conduct, it's Alfred and Allison Harrington. Worse, I think he's afraid they may believe he let the information out himself."

"That's preposterous!" Knippschd was genuinely angry. "He can be a royal pain, but I've *never* met a physician who takes his professional, ethical responsibilities more seriously than he does!"

"I agree," Isher said mildly. "And I didn't say *I* think the Harringtons are going to believe anything of the sort. What I said was that *he's* afraid they may. And that, Marty, is why I am delighted that I, for one, am *not* the person who actually did spill the beans to Solomon Hayes."

The two of them walked along in silence for another few moments, and then Isher chuckled humorlessly.

"What?" Knippschd asked.

"I was just thinking. He says he wants whoever it is broiled, right?" Knippschd nodded, and she shrugged. "Well, I wonder if he'd let *me* at least light the fire for him when the time comes?"

"We're coming up on her now, Your Grace," the pinnace pilot announced over the intercom. "She's at your ten o'clock, low."

Honor leaned close enough to the pinnace viewport that the tip of her nose almost touched the armorplast. She was on the starboard side of the small craft, seated just forward of the variable geometry wings, and she peered still further forward as the sleek, white spindle of a starship came into view.

A missile barge hung close beside it in orbit, which gave her a sense of perspective, something to relate the new ship's size to, and that perspective made her look just a bit odd to experienced eyes. She was obviously a battlecruiser, yet she was larger than any battlecruiser Honor had ever seen. The *Agamemnons*, like Michelle Henke's *Achilles*, massed almost 1.75 million tons, but this ship was more than a half-million tons heavier still. And where the *Agamemnons* were a pod-laying design, this one most definitely was not.

She stepped up the magnification of her artificial eye, zooming in on the hull number just aft of the forward impeller ring. BC-762, it said, and under that, the name: *Nike*.

She tasted the name in the depths of her mind, and her feelings were mixed as she gazed at the splendid new ship. This *Nike*'s predecessor had been listed for disposal by the Janacek Admiralty in order to free the name for this new class' lead ship. The sudden eruption of renewed hostilities had saved BC-413 from the breakers, but the name had already been reassigned, so 413 had been renamed *Hancock Station*. If they'd had to rename her, Honor couldn't really fault the choice, but as that *Nike*'s first captain, she would always think of the older ship as the rightful holder of that name.

And yet, despite her manifold disagreements with the late Edward Janacek and her bitter opposition to so many of his disastrous policies at Admiralty House, she had to admit that this time he might have gotten it right. *Nike* was the proudest ship name in the Royal Manticoran Navy. There was *always* a *Nike*, and she was *always* a battlecruiser. And when she was commissioned, she was always the newest, most powerful battlecruiser in the fleet.

Yet the old *Nike*—*Hancock Station*—was at best obsolescent, despite the fact that she was barely sixteen T-years old. She'd been worked hard during those sixteen years, but it was the changes in weapons and tactics, especially in missile warfare, not senility, which had relegated her to the second rank of effectiveness. In an age of multi-drive missiles, the traditional battlecruiser's niche had altered dramatically, and BC-413 was simply out of date.

Battlecruisers were designed to run down and destroy enemy

cruisers, or to raid and run. The ideal commerce protectors, and, conversely, the ideal commerce destroyers. Traditionally, especially in Manticoran service, they weren't intended to stand in the wall of battle, because their relatively light armor and "cruiser style" construction could never stand the pounding superdreadnoughts were expected to endure. They were intended to run away from wallers—to be able to destroy anything lighter than them, and to outrun anything heavier.

Yet the sheer reach of the MDM made staying out of effective range far more difficult than it had ever been before, and the emphasis on long-range missile combat required denser salvos and greater magazine space. For a time, it had seemed the battlecruiser had simply become obsolete, as the battleship had before it, and that it would vanish just as completely from the order of battle of first-class navies. But the type—or, at least, the role it filled—was just too valuable to be allowed to disappear, and improvements in compensator efficiency and other aspects of military technology had allowed a transformation.

The Graysons had led the way toward one possible iteration of the type, with their *Courvoisier II*-class of pod-layers. The RMN's *Agamemnons* were the Manticoran version of the same design concept, as the *Blücher*-class was for the Andermani, and that approach clearly offered significant advantages over the older designs.

But the BC(P) wasn't really completely satisfactory. Although it could produce a very heavy volume of fire, its endurance at maximum-rate fire was limited, and the type's hollow core design came at a greater cost in structural integrity than the same concept did in a bigger, far more strongly built superdreadnought. So Vice Admiral Toscarelli's BuShips had sought another approach at the same time it was designing the new *Edward Saganami-C*-class heavy cruisers.

Nike was the result: a 2.5 million-ton "battlecruiser," almost three times the size of Honor's old ship, but with an acceleration rate thirty percent greater. The old *Nike* had mounted eighteen lasers, sixteen grasers, fifty-two missile tubes, and thirty-two counter-missile tubes and point defense clusters. The new *Nike* mounted no lasers, thirty-two grasers—eight of them as chase weapons, fifty missile tubes (none of them chasers), and thirty counter-missile tubes and laser clusters. The old *Nike* had carried a ship's company of over two thousand; the new *Nike's* complement was only seven hundred and fifty. And the new *Nike* was armed with the Mark 16 dual-drive missile. With the "off-bore" launch capability the RMN had developed, she could bring both broadsides' missile tubes to bear on the same target, giving her fifty birds per salvo, as opposed to the older ship's twenty-two. And whereas the old *Nike's* maximum powered missile range from rest had been just over six million kilometers, the new *Nike's* missiles had a maximum powered endurance of over *twenty-nine* million.

She couldn't fire the all-up, three-stage MDMs the *Courvoisiers* and *Agamemnons* could handle, so her tactical flexibility was marginally less, and her warheads were slightly lighter, but an *Agamemnon* rolling pods at her maximum rate would shoot herself dry in just over fourteen minutes, whereas *Nike* carried sufficient ammunition for almost forty minutes, and she carried fifty percent more counter-missiles, as well. For that matter, although the *Courvosiers* did, in fact, carry the three-stage weapons, the RMN had chosen to load the *Agamemnons'* pods with Mark 16s. BuWeaps had gone ahead and produced the standard pods, as well, but Admiralty House had decided the salvo density the Mark 16 permitted was more important than the bigger missiles' greater powered envelope.

Personally, Honor was convinced that this *Nike* represented the pattern for true battlecruisers of the future, and she deeply regretted the fact that although the Janacek Admiralty had authorized her construction, they had seen her as a single-ship testbed. The Navy desperately needed as many *Nikes* as it could get, and what it had was exactly one. Which was *all* it would have for at least another full T-year.

But at least Honor had the only one of her there was, and—she smiled at her reflection in the armorplast—she'd convinced Admiral Cortez to give her to a captain who was almost as competent as he was . . . irritating.

"Do you want another pass on her, Your Grace?" the pilot inquired, and Honor pressed the intercom key on the arm of her chair.

"No, thank you, Chief. I've seen enough. Head straight on to the flagship; Captain Cardones is expecting me in time for lunch."

"Aye, aye, Ma'am."

The pinnace turned away, and Honor leaned back in her seat as her mind reached out to the future.

"Dr. Illescue! Dr. Illescue, would you care to comment on the press accounts of Duchess Harrington's pregnancy?"

Franz Illescue walked stolidly across the Briarwood lobby, ignoring the shouted questions.

"Dr. Illescue, are you prepared to confirm that Earl White Haven is the father of Duchess Harrington's child?"

"Dr. Illescue! Isn't it true *Prince Michael* is the child's father?"

"Are you prepared to categorically deny that the father is Baron Grantville or Benjamin Mayhew?"

"Dr. Illescue—!"

The lift doors cut off the hullabaloo, and Illescue keyed his personal com with an almost savage thumb jab.

"Security, Meyers," a voice responded instantly.

"Tajman, this is Dr. Illescue." The fury seething in Illescue's normally controlled baritone was almost palpable. "Will you please explain to me what the *hell* that . . . that three-ring circus in our lobby is about?"

"I'm sorry, Sir," Meyers said. "I wasn't aware you were coming in through the public entrance, or I would have at least warned your driver. They descended on us right after lunch, and so far, they haven't committed any privacy violations. According to SOP, I can't bar them from the public area of the facility until they do."

"Well, as it happens, I *wrote* the damned SOP," Illescue half-snarled, "and as of now, you can bar those jackals from *any* part of this facility until Hell's a hockey rink! Is that perfectly clear?!"

"Uh, yes, Sir. I'll get on it right away, Sir."

"Thank you." Illescue's voice was marginally closer to normal as he broke the circuit and inhaled deeply.

He leaned back against the wall of the lift car and rubbed his face wearily.

He and Meyers were no closer to finding the leak than they'd been when they began, and the story was ballooning totally out of control. Not that he'd ever had much hope of controlling it in the first place. The press was working itself up to a feeding frenzy, and the most preposterous speculation imaginable—as the shouted question in the lobby indicated—had become rampant. At least he'd spoken to both Doctors Harrington, unpleasant though it had been, and he felt reasonably confident neither of them thought it had been *his* doing, but that didn't make him feel much better. Even though he was prepared to dislike Duchess Harrington because of her parentage, she was a patient. She had a legal and moral right to privacy, to trust that doctor-patient confidentiality would not be violated, and it had been. It was almost like a form of rape, even if the assault was nonphysical, and he would have been coldly, bitterly furious in *any* patient's case. In this instance, given the prominence of the patient in question and the way that prominence was goading the newsies' speculations, his emotions went far beyond fury.

Franz Illescue was not a man with much use for the custom of dueling, even if it was legal. But in this case, if he could find out who was responsible, he was prepared to make an exception.

"Welcome back," Michelle Henke said with a smile as Andrew LaFollet peeled off at her day cabin's hatch and Honor and Nimitz stepped through it.

"Thanks." Honor crossed the cabin and flopped onto Henke's couch far more inelegantly than she would ever have considered if anyone else had been present.

"I trust Diego did the honors properly?" Henke asked lightly. Captain Diego Mikhailov was *Ajax*'s captain. "I told him you wanted it kept low key."

"He kept it as low key as my faithful minion outside the hatch there would permit," Honor replied. "I like him," she added.

"He's a likeable sort. And good at his job. Not to mention smart enough to realize how harried and hunted you must feel right now. He understands exactly why he's not invited to dinner tonight. In fact, he commented to me that you must be delighted to be back aboard ship."

"As a matter of fact, I've seldom been happier to find myself confined aboard ship in my entire life," Honor admitted as she rested her head on one couch arm, closed her eyes, and stretched out with Nimitz on her chest.

"That's because the worst that can happen *here* is that you get blown up," Henke said dryly. She crossed to the wet bar, opened a small refrigerator, and produced a pair of chilled bottles of Old

Tilman. Honor chuckled appreciatively, although her amusement was clearly less than complete, and Henke grinned as she opened the beer bottles.

"I told Clarissa I'd buzz for her if we decided we needed her," she continued, holding out one of the bottles to Honor. "Here." Honor cracked one eye and looked up, and Henke waggled the bottle at her. "You look like you need this."

"What I *need* is about fifteen minutes—no, *ten* minutes would do nicely, actually—alone with Mr. Hayes," Honor said balefully. She accepted the bottle and swallowed a mouthful of cold beer. "I'd feel ever so much better afterward."

"At least until they came to put you in jail."

"True. The courts *are* tacky about things like that, aren't they?"

"Unfortunately." Henke swallowed some of her own beer, leaning back in an armchair facing Honor's couch, and rested one heel on the expensive coffee table on the thick, even more expensive carpet between the two of them.

Honor smiled at her and looked around curously. It was the first time she'd visited Henke aboard *Ajax*, and although Henke's day cabin was substantially smaller than her own lordly flag quarters aboard *Imperator*, it was still large and comfortable indeed by the standards of most battlecruisers. *Ajax*'s total complement was under six hundred, including Marines, and her designers, faced with all that space, had obviously felt someone as lordly as a flag officer deserved the very best. The deep pile carpet was a dark crimson, which Honor knew Henke would never have chosen for herself and undoubtedly intended to change at the earliest possible moment, but the paneled bulkheads, indirect lighting, and holosculptures gave it an air of almost sinfully welcoming comfort.

Best of all, it was totally empty except for Henke, Honor, and Nimitz.

"Feeling better?" Henke asked after a moment.

"Some." Honor closed her eyes again and rolled the chilled beer bottle across her forehead. "Quite a bit, actually," she went on, after a moment. "The mind-glows out here are a lot easier on Nimitz and me."

"There must be times when being an empath is a complete and total pain," Henke said.

"You have no idea," Honor agreed, opening her eyes once more and sitting up a bit. "To be perfectly honest, Mike, that's one reason I was so happy *you* invited *me* to dinner tonight. All my staffers are firmly in my corner, but if I'd stayed home aboard the flagship, I'd almost have had to host a formal dinner on my first night back. Eating alone with my oldest friend is an awfully much more attractive proposition. Thanks."

"Hey, it's what friends are for!" Henke said, more lightly than she felt and trying not to show how touched she was.

"Well, the company's good," Honor said with a crooked smile. "But I suppose if I'm going to be *completely* honest, the *real* attraction is Chief Arbuckle's paprikash."

"I'll see to it that Clarissa gives Mac the recipe," Henke said dryly.

"Attention on deck!"

The Eighth Fleet's flag officers, their senior staffers, and their flag captains rose as Honor, Rafael Cardones, Mercedes Brigham, and Andrea Jaruwalski entered the compartment. Simon Mattingly and Spencer Hawke parked themselves against the bulkhead just outside the compartment, flanking the hatch, and Andrew LaFollet followed the naval officers in. He took his customary, inconspicuous place against the bulkhead behind Honor's chair, and level gray eyes swept the entire briefing room with instinct-level, microscopic attention to detail.

"Be seated, Ladies and Gentlemen," Honor said, striding to her own place.

MacGuiness had contrived a proper perch for Nimitz, bracketed to the back of her chair, and the treecat gave a buzzing purr as he arranged himself upon it. Honor smiled as she tasted his approval of the new arrangements, then seated herself and looked out at her command team.

The senior divisional commanders were present this time, as well, and they were no longer such unknown quantities. There were a few about whom she nursed some minor concerns, but by and large she was supremely confident in the temper of her weapon. Whether it would be enough for the tasks demanded of it was more than she could say, but if it failed, it would not be because of any fault in the quality of the men and women of whom it was composed.

"As you all know," she said after a moment, "we've actually received a few reinforcements. Not as many as we were slated to—other commitments, unfortunately, are drawing off units which otherwise would have been earmarked for us. Nonetheless, we have more striking power than we had last time. And," this time, the wolf at her core showed in her smile, "we're still getting the opportunity to show the Havenites our newest and best."

Several other people smiled, as well, and Honor looked at Michelle Henke.

"I'm sure you were less than pleased when Captain Shelburne reported *Hector*'s engineering casualty, Admiral Henke. I trust, however, that the replacement I've managed to arrange for you until *Hector* can get that beta node replaced is satisfactory?"

"Well, Your Grace," Henke replied judiciously, "I suppose, under the circumstances, I'll just have to make do."

This time, the people who'd smiled laughed out loud, and Honor shook her head.

"I'm sure you'll manage somehow, Admiral," she told Henke. Then she looked at the other officers again.

"In most ways, this meeting is something of a formality," she told them. "You've all done well in training and preparing your commands for Cutworm II. You've all had time to study our objectives. And I'm confident all of us are well aware of the importance of this operation."

She paused to let that sink in.

"Cutworm II is both more ambitious and less ambitious than our first attacks were," she continued after a moment. "It's more ambitious primarily in terms of timing and how deep we're penetrating to hit Chantilly and Des Moines. Since all of our task forces will have different transit times, and since I've decided to once more orchestrate our strikes to hit our targets simultaneously, Admiral Truman and Admiral Miklós will depart immediately after this meeting. Admiral McKeon will depart for Fordyce the day after tomorrow, and Admiral Matsuzawa and I will depart for Augusta four days after that.

"Remember, hitting our assigned objectives—hard—is critically important, but bringing your ships and your people home is equally so. It seems unlikely the Republic will have been able to adjust its defensive stance significantly in the last three weeks. Nonetheless, it isn't impossible, so be alert. We're more likely to see changes in doctrine and tactical approaches than we are to see significant redeployment of covering forces. Eventually, obviously, we hope that's going to change, but simple message transit times are going to preclude their having done it yet. Hopefully," she smiled again, "our modest efforts over the next two weeks will provide additional encouragement for their efforts.

"In just a moment, Captain Jaruwalski will run through the entire ops schedule one last time. Afterward, I want to go over the plan individually with each task force commander. If any questions or suggestions have occurred to *any* of you since our last meeting, that will be the time to bring them forward."

She paused a second time, then nodded to Jaruwalski.

"Andrea," she invited, and sat back in her own chair to listen as the ops officer activated the holo display above the conference table.

"Your guests are here, Reverend."

Reverend Jeremiah Sullivan, First Elder of the Church of Humanity Unchained, nodded in response to his secretary's announcement and turned away from the picture window of his large, comfortable office in Mayhew Cathedral.

"Thank you, Matthew. If you'd be good enough to show them in, please."

"Of course, Your Grace."

Brother Matthew bowed slightly, and withdrew. He was back a moment later, accompanied by half a dozen men. Most were of at least middle years. The sole exception was a very young man, indeed, for the office he held. Obviously a prolong recipient, but less than thirty-five T-years old.

He was also the evident leader of the delegation.

"Reverend," he murmured, bending to kiss the ring Sullivan held out to him. "Thank you for seeing us."

"I could hardly say no to a request from such distinguished visitors, Steadholder Mueller," Sullivan said easily. Mueller smiled and stepped aside, and Sullivan extended his ring hand to the next steadholder in line.

Mueller's smile became just a trifle fixed as he watched. It was certainly correct etiquette for visitors, however exalted their rank, to kiss the Reverend's ring of office. But it was *customary* in cases like this morning's meeting for the Reverend to settle for receiving the courtesy from the senior member of the delegation.

All five of Mueller's fellows kissed the ring in turn, and Sullivan waved a graceful hand at the half-circle of chairs arranged before his desk to await them.

"Please, My Lords. Be seated," he invited, and waited courteously until all of them had settled before seating himself behind the desk once more with an attentive expression on his strong, fierce-nosed face.

"And now, Lord Mueller, how may Father Church serve the people of Grayson?"

"Actually, Your Grace, we're not quite sure," Mueller replied with an air of candor. "In fact, we're here more to consult than for anything else."

"Consult, My Lord?" Sullivan arched one eyebrow, his bald scalp gleaming in the morning sunlight pouring in through the hermetically sealed window behind him. "About what?"

"About—" Mueller started impatiently, then made himself stop.

"About the Manticoran news reports concerning Steadholder Harrington, Your Grace," he said after a moment, his tone and expression once more controlled.

"Ah!" Sullivan nodded. "You're referring to that person Hayes' column about Lady Harrington?"

"Well, to that, and to all the other commentary and speculation he seems to have generated in the Manticoran press," Mueller agreed, and produced a grimace of distaste.

"Obviously, I find the original story and its thinly veiled innuendos an unconscionable invasion of the Steadholder's private life. The sort of thing, I'm afraid, one might expect from such a thoroughly . . . secular society. Nonetheless, the story's been printed, and widely commented upon, in the Star Kingdom, and it's already starting to make its way through our own news media here in Yeltsin."

"So I'd observed," Sullivan agreed almost placidly.

"I'm sure," Mueller said, his tone more pointed, "you must find that fact as deplorable as I do, Your Grace."

"I find it inevitable, My Lord," Sullivan said in a tone of mild correction, and shrugged. "Steadholder Harrington is one of our most popular public figures, as all of us are perfectly well aware.

This sort of speculation about her is bound to create a great deal of public comment."

Despite his formidable self-control, Mueller's eyes flickered as Sullivan referred to Harrington's popularity. He really did look a great deal like a much younger edition of his deceased father, Sullivan mused. It was unfortunate the resemblance went so much deeper than the surface.

"Comment is one thing, Your Grace," Mueller said now, a bit sharply. "The *sort* of comment we're observing, however, is something else entirely."

The other members of the Conclave of Steadholders' delegation looked uncomfortable, but none disagreed with their spokesman. In fact, Sullivan saw, most seemed firmly in agreement. Not surprisingly, given that they'd more or less nominated themselves for their present mission.

"In what specific way, My Lord?" the Reverend inquired, still mildly, after a moment.

"Your Grace, you're obviously aware Steadholder Harrington's declined to reveal the paternity of her child," Mueller said. "Moreover, as I'm sure you're also aware, the Steadholder isn't married. So, I'm very much afraid, that her son—the son, I remind you, who ought to replace Lady Harrington's sister in the succession of her Steading—is illegitimate. Not to put too fine a point upon it, Your Grace, this boy will be not simply a bastard, but a bastard whose father is a total unknown."

"I might point out," Sullivan replied tranquilly, "that Manticoran practices are somewhat different from our own. Specifically, Manticoran law doesn't recognize the concept of 'bastardy' at all. I believe one of their more respected jurists once said there are no illegitimate children, only illegitimate parents. Personally, I find myself in agreement with him."

"We're not talking about Manticoran law, Your Grace," Mueller said flatly. "We're talking about *Grayson* law. About Lady Harrington's responsibility, as a Steadholder, to keep the Conclave of Steadholders informed about the birth of an heir to her Steading. About the fact that she hasn't bothered to marry this boy's father, or even to inform us as to who that father is!" He shook his head. "I believe, however great her services to Grayson, we have legitimate cause to be concerned when she so clearly chooses to flaunt the law of *our* planet and of Father Church."

"Excuse me, My Lord, but precisely how has she done that?"

Mueller stared at the Reverend in consternation for at least three seconds. Then he shook himself.

"My Lord, as I'm sure you're perfectly well aware, I, as a steadholder, am required by law to inform my fellow steadholders of the prospective birth of any heir to my steading. I'm also required to provide proof that the heir in question is my child and the legitimate inheritor of my title and my responsibilities. Surely you aren't suggesting that simply because Lady Harrington wasn't born on Grayson she's somehow exempt from the obligations binding upon every *other* steadholder?"

It was obvious from his manner that Mueller very much hoped Sullivan *would* make such an argument. As his father before him—although, so far, at least, without crossing the line into active treason (*so far as anyone* knows, *at any rate*, Sullivan told himself tartly)—Travis Mueller had found his natural home in the ranks of the Opposition. And in the Opposition's eyes, Honor Harrington represented everything they detested about the "Mayhew Restoration's" "secularization" of their society. The unassailable position Steadholder Harrington held in the hearts of the majority of Graysons was gall-bitter on their tongues, and Sullivan could almost physically taste the eagerness with which they anticipated this opportunity to discredit her.

Not that the unfortunately large number of people who'd attempted the same task before them had enjoyed much luck, he reflected.

"First of all, My Lord," he said after a moment, "I'd recommend you consult a good constitutional scholar, since you appear to be laboring under a misapprehension. Your responsibility as a steadholder is to inform myself, as the steward of Father Church, and the Protector, as Father Church's champion and the guardian of secular matters here on Grayson. It is not to inform the Conclave as a body."

Mueller's eyes first widened, then narrowed, and he flushed slightly.

"I'll grant you, My Lord," Sullivan continued imperturbably, "that, traditionally, that's included a notification of the Conclave as a whole. However, the Conclave's responsibility to examine and prove the chain of succession actually begins only after the birth of the heir in question. And, although I realize you weren't aware of it, Lady Harrington informed Protector Benjamin and myself almost two full months ago that she was pregnant. So I assure you all of her constitutional obligations have been faithfully discharged."

"It hasn't simply been *traditional* to notify the Conclave, Your Grace," Mueller said sharply. "For generations, it's had the force of law. And that notification is supposed to be given well before the actual birth of the child in question!"

"Quite a few erroneous practices had the 'force of law' prior to the reestablishment of the correct provisions of our *written* Constitution, My Lord." For the first time, there was a very definite iciness in Reverend Sullivan's voice. "Those errors are still in the process of correction. They are, however, *being* corrected."

Mueller started to reply angrily, then clamped his jaw and visibly made himself reassert control of his temper.

"Your Grace, I suppose you're technically correct about the letter of the written law," he said, after several moments, speaking very carefully. "Personally, I disagree with your interpretation. You are, however, as you pointed out a short time ago, Father Church's steward. I will, therefore, not contest your interpretation at this time, although I reserve the right to do so without prejudice at another time and in another forum.

"Nonetheless, the fact remains that Steadholder Harrington isn't married; that *our* law, unlike that of the Star Kingdom of Manticore, clearly does recognize the concept of bastardy and regards it as a bar to inheritance; and that we don't even know who the father of this child *is*."

"No, Lady Harrington isn't married," Sullivan agreed. "And, you're quite correct that Grayson law, as presently written, does recognize bastardy and the disabilities and limitations which normally attach to it. However, it's incorrect to say that we—in the legal sense of Father Church and the Sword—don't know who the father of Lady Harrington's son is."

"You *know* who the father is?" Mueller demanded.

"Of course I do, as does the Protector," Sullivan said. *For that matter,* he thought, *everyone on the entire planet knows, whether they're prepared to admit it or not.*

"Even so," Mueller said after a brief pause, "the child is clearly still a bastard. As such, he must be unacceptable as the heir to a steading." ₄

His voice was flat, hard, and Sullivan nodded mentally. Mueller had finally and unambiguously thrown down his gauntlet. Whether or not a majority of the Conclave of Steadholders would agree with him and sustain his position was another matter. It was possible a majority would, but even if—as Sullivan thought was far more likely—the majority didn't agree with him, he would gleefully take advantage of the opportunity to do all he could to blacken Honor Harrington's reputation in the eyes of Grayson's more conservative citizens.

"It occurred to me, when Lady Harrington first informed me she was pregnant," the Reverend said mildly after a long, thoughtful moment, "that a view such as that might present itself. Accordingly, I asked my staff to conduct a brief historical review."

"Historical?" Mueller repeated, against his will, when Sullivan deliberately paused and waited.

"Yes, historical."

The Reverend opened a desk drawer and withdrew a fat, old-fashioned hard-copy folder. He laid it on the blotter, opened it, glanced at the top sheet of paper, and then looked back at Mueller.

"It would appear that in 3112, nine hundred and ten T-years ago, Steadholder Berilynko had no legitimate male children, only daughters. The Conclave of Steadholders of that time therefore accepted the eldest of his several illegitimate sons as his heir. In 3120, Steadholder Elway had no legitimate male children, only daughters. The Conclave of Steadholders of that time therefore accepted the eldest of his several illegitimate sons as his heir. In 3140, Steadholder Ames had no legitimate male children, only daughters. The Conclave of Steadholders of that time therefore accepted the eldest of his several illegitimate sons as his heir. In 3142, Steadholder Sutherland had no legitimate male children, only daughters. The Conclave of Steadholders of that time therefore accepted the eldest of his several illegitimate sons as his heir. In 3146, Steadholder Kimbrell had no legitimate male children, only daughters. The Conclave of Steadholders of that time therefore accepted the eldest of his reportedly thirty-six illegitimate sons as his heir. In 3160, Steadholder Denevski had no legitimate male children, only daughters. The Conclave of Steadholders of that time therefore accepted the eldest of his illegitimate sons as his heir. In 3163—"

The Reverend paused, looked up with a hard little smile, and closed the folder once more.

"I trust you'll observe, My Lords, that in a period of less than seventy years from the founding of Grayson, when there were less than twenty-five steadings on the entire planet, no less than six steadholderships had passed through illegitimate—*bastard*—children. Passed, mind you, in instances in which there were clearly recognized, legitimate *female* children. We have nine hundred and forty-two years of history on this planet. Would you care to estimate how many more times over that millennium steadholderships have passed under similar circumstances?" He tapped the thick folder on his desk. "I can almost guarantee you that whatever total you guess will be too low."

Silence hovered in his office, and his old-fashioned chair creaked as he sat back in it and folded his hands atop the folder.

"So what we seem to have here, My Lords, is that although the stigma of bastardy legally bars one from the line of succession of a steadholdership, we've ignored that bar scores of times in the past. The most recent instance of which, I might point out, came in Howell Steading less than twenty T-years ago. Of course, in all the prior instances of our having ignored the law, the bastards in question were the children of *male* steadholders. In fact, in the vast majority of the cases, there was no way for anyone to prove those steadholders were actually even the fathers of the children in question. However, in the case of a *female* steadholder, when the fact that she's the mother of the child in question can be scientifically demonstrated beyond question or doubt, *suddenly* bastardy becomes an insurmountable bar which can't possibly be set aside or ignored. I'm curious, My Lords. Why is that?"

Four of the Reverend's visitors looked away, unable—or unwilling—to meet his fiery, challenging eye. Mueller only flushed darker, jaw muscles ridging, as he glared back. And Jasper Taylor, Steadholder Canseco, looked just as stubbornly angry as Mueller.

"Very well, My Lords," Sullivan said finally, his voice hard-edged with something far more like contempt than these men were accustomed to hearing, "your ... concerns are noted. I will, however, inform you, that neither Father Church nor the Sword questions the propriety of this child's inheriting Steadholder Harrington's titles and dignities."

"That, of course, is your privilege and right, Your Grace," Mueller grated. "Nonetheless, as is also well established in both our Faith and our secular law, a man has both the right and the responsibility to contend for what he believes God's Test requires of him, whatever the Sacristy and Sword may say."

"Indeed he does," Sullivan agreed, "and I would never for a moment consider denying you that right, My Lord. But before you take your stand before God and man, it might, perhaps, be prudent of you to be certain of your ground. Specifically, this child will *not* be illegitimate."

"I beg your *pardon*?" Mueller jerked upright in his chair, and the other steadholders with him looked equally confused.

"I said, this child won't be illegitimate," Sullivan repeated coldly. "Surely that should satisfy even you, My Lord."

"You're God's steward on Grayson, Your Grace," Mueller shot back, "but not God Himself. It's been well established, in both Church and civil law, that no Reverend—not even the entire Sacristy in assembly—can make falsehood true simply by saying something is so."

"Indeed I cannot," Sullivan said icily. "Nonetheless, this child will not be illegitimate. You will not be given the opportunity you so obviously desire to use Lady Harrington's child as a weapon against her. Father Church won't permit it. *I* won't permit it."

He smiled once again, his eyes frozen agate-hard.

"I trust that is sufficiently clear, My Lord?"

Chapter Twenty-Six

"Ma'am, I hate to disturb you, but I think you'd better see this."

Rear Admiral Jennifer Bellefeuille, the Republican Navy's senior officer in the Chantilly System, turned towards the dining cabin hatch with a scowl that was angry, despite her best effort to control her temper.

"What is it, Leonardo?" She tried to keep herself from chopping the words off in small, icy chips, but it was more than she could manage.

"Admiral, Mr. Bellefeuille, I apologize for breaking in on your dinner, but I think this is urgent."

Commander Ericsson, Bellefeuille's operations officer, held out a message board to his admiral. She managed to not—quite—snatch it out of his hand, and glared at the display. Then, abruptly, her angry expression smoothed into something very different.

"This is confirmed?" she asked crisply, looking back up at Ericsson.

"Yes, Ma'am. I had Perimeter Tracking doublecheck before I broke in on you." He smiled apologetically. "I know how much you and your family have been looking forward to this visit, Admiral. I really wish I hadn't had to disturb you on your very first evening."

"I wish you hadn't had to, too," Bellefeuille said, her own smile thin. "For a lot of reasons." She glanced at the message board again, then set it down on the table. "Ivan's seen a copy of this, as well?"

343

"Yes, Ma'am. And I also routed a copy to Governor Sebastian's office."

"Thank you." This time Bellefeuille's smile was warmer, though it still seemed strained, a bit taut. "I don't think there's much we can do about it right now. If they get clumsy and we get a solid read on them, I'd love to nail them. I'm not going to try holding my breath until we do, though, and I don't want to give away anything we don't have to. So tell Ivan to activate Smoke and Mirrors. I want everything we've got brought to immediate readiness, but no one moves, and we shut down the Mirror Box platforms right now. And I want all of our stealth-capable units except the destroyers into stealth now. They stay there until I tell them differently."

"Yes, Ma'am. Anything else?"

"Not right now, Leonardo. Thank you."

Commander Ericsson smiled, nodded once again to his admiral and her family, and withdrew.

"Jennifer?"

The Chantilly System commander looked up. She realized she'd been settling into what her mother used to call "a brown study," but the sound of her name pulled her back out of it abruptly. Her husband looked back at her, waiting patiently despite the concern in the back of his deep, brown eyes.

"I'm sorry, Russ," she said quietly. "I know you and the kids just got here, and I've really been looking forward to this visit. But it appears the Manties didn't get the memo about your trip."

Russell Bellefeuille's lips quirked very slightly at her feeble attempt at humor, but their children, Diana and Matthew, didn't even try to conceal their worry.

"Can you tell us about it?" Russell asked. His tone said he'd understand if she couldn't, and she smiled at him, far more warmly, while she wondered how many other spouses could have honestly said the same in his position.

Russell Bellefeuille had spent thirty T-years fighting a hopeless struggle against the "democratized" Legislaturalist educational system. Fortunately, he and his wife had been born and raised in the Suarez System, and Suarez had been added to the People's Republic only thirty-six years before the outbreak of the first war with Manticore, so at least he hadn't had to deal with the entrenched, massively intrusive bureaucracy of places like

Nouveau Paris. He'd had enough slack to get away with actually *teaching* his students something, and although—like his wife—he'd hated and despised the People's Republic of Rob Pierre and State Security, he'd finally seen the idea that schools were *supposed* to teach students take root once more.

Along the way, he'd found the time and patience to marry a serving naval officer, despite all of the dislocation a military career imposed on anyone's personal life . . . and the very real risk involved in marrying an officer while Oscar Saint-Just's State Security was shooting entire families under his infamous policy of "collective responsibility." And in the middle of all that, he'd somehow managed to raise two teenaged children, with only occasional visits from their mother, and done a damned good job.

"There's not much to tell . . . yet," she said. "Perimeter Tracking's detected what's probably a pair of hyper footprints well out from the system primary. It may be nothing."

"Or it may be Manty scout ships, like I saw on the boards about Gaston and Hera," Diana said tautly. At seventeen, she was the older of Bellefeuille's children, with her mother's dark hair coloring and gray-green eyes. She also had her mother's sharp-edged, adrenal personality, and at the moment Bellefeuille wished she'd inherited more of her father's equanimity.

"Yes, it may," Bellefeuille said as calmly as she could. "In fact, I think it probably is."

"*Here?*" Technically, Matthew wasn't quite a teenager yet. One reason for this trip to Chantilly had been to celebrate his thirteenth birthday, and at the moment, he looked and sounded very young—and frightened—indeed. "The Manties are coming *here*, Mom?"

"Probably," Bellefeuille repeated.

"But—"

"That's enough, Matt," Russell said quietly. The boy looked at him, as if he couldn't believe he could be so blasé about it. But then he saw his father's eyes, and his mouth shut with an almost audible click.

"Better," Russell said, reaching out to ruffle his hair gently, the way he had when Matthew had been much younger. Then he turned back to his wife.

"All I really know is what I've read in the 'faxes and on the boards," he told her. "Is this as bad as I think it is?"

"It's not good," she told him honestly. "Just *how* not-good, I don't know yet. We probably won't, for at least a couple of days."

"But you expect them to attack?"

"Yes." She sighed. "I wish now you hadn't come."

"I don't," he said softly, and her eyes prickled as he looked steadily at her across the table. Then he reached for his fork and glanced at their children. "I think we should go ahead and finish eating before we pester your mother with any more questions," he told them.

"There's another one, Sir," Chief Sullivan said flatly.

"Did we get a locus on it?" Lieutenant Commander Krenckel asked.

"I wish, Sir," Sullivan replied in disgusted tones. He looked up from his display, and his expression was a mixture of frustration and apology. "Whatever it is—and between you and me, Sir, it's got to be a stealthed Manty recon platform—it's moving like a bat out of hell. I wish to hell I knew how they got these kinds of acceleration levels and endurance numbers on their platforms!"

"NavInt says they've probably put micro fusion plants on them."

Sullivan blinked.

"Fusion plants? On something this small?"

"That's what they say." Krenckel shrugged. "I haven't seen any raw data on captured hardware or anything to support it, but it comes out of Bolthole. And if anyone knows what they're up to, it's got to be Admiral Foraker and her teams."

"Well, isn't *that* just peachy," Sullivan muttered, then grimaced. "Sorry, Sir."

"You're not saying anything I haven't thought, Chief," Krenckel said dryly. "Still, it'd make sense out of how small they've managed to make their MDMs. Not to mention the hellacious power levels their remote EW platforms pump."

"Yeah, it would," Sullivan agreed. Then he seemed to give himself a mental shake. "But what I was saying, Sir—all we're getting is the back scatter, and their directional transmission capability's better than ours. The best read we've gotten was an accident—one of our own platforms just happened to wander into their transmission path—and we haven't gotten what we need for a good crosscut bearing for any of them. Even if we did, by the time we could vector anything out there, the platform would be long gone. It'd have to see us coming, and it can pull a hell of a lot more accel than any LAC we might send after it."

"Then we're just going to have to hope we do get a cross bearing, I guess," Krenckel said.

"Yes, Sir."

Sullivan turned back to his display, bending once more to the wearisome task of listening for the tiny spies flitting about the Augusta System. Personally, he figured the effort was as pointless as it was exhausting. They knew the bastards were out there; they knew they weren't going to be able to run down any of the platforms, even if they spotted them; and they knew those platforms wouldn't be there if Hell itself wasn't coming to dinner.

Still, he supposed he might as well waste his time doing this as anything else.

"Commander Estwicke's data is coming in now, Your Grace."

"Thank you, Andrea."

Honor nodded to her ops officer, then turned back to the com.

"You heard, Rafe?"

"Yes, Ma'am. Yolanda's already looking at the preliminaries. So far, it seems to be about what we expected."

"Then it probably is. But remember, surprise—"

"Is usually what happens when someone misinterprets something he's seen all along," Cardones finished for her. She closed her mouth, then chuckled.

"I think I may have spent too many years at the Island."

"No, Ma'am. You've always been a teacher."

Honor was a little surprised by the flicker of embarrassment she felt at the sincerity in Cardones' tone.

"Well, I had some pretty good teachers of my own," she said, after a moment. "Admiral Courvoisier, Captain Bachfisch, Mark Sarnow. I guess once you get stuck in the pattern, it's hard to break."

"If it's all the same to you, Ma'am, I think we'd all just as soon you didn't try."

"I'll . . . bear that in mind, Captain Cardones."

"Good. And now, if you don't mind, Your Grace, we've both got some tactical information to look over. So," he grinned broadly at her, "let's be about it."

"Tell the Admiral we've got a major hyper translation."

Commander Ivan deCastro, Rear Admiral Bellefeuille's chief of staff, hoped he looked calmer than he felt as he gazed into the display at Commander Ericsson.

"How big is it, Leonardo?" he asked.

"At least thirteen footprints," Ericsson said grimly. "It may be fourteen. We're working to refine the numbers."

"Not good," deCastro said, and Ericsson snorted.

"I see you subscribe to the theory understatement can be its own form of emphasis."

"When it's all you've got, you might as well be witty, I suppose." DeCastro produced a wan smile. Then he squared his shoulders. "All right, I'll tell her. At least she's got her family dirt-side now, not on the flagship."

"I know." For just a moment, Ericsson's expression was haunted. "Christ, that's got to be hard. Knowing your kids are down there. That they know exactly what's happening."

"It's a bastard, all right," deCastro agreed. "Get me those refined numbers as soon as you can."

"*How* big a force did you say?"

Governor Joona Poykkonen's face was gray on Rear Admiral Baptiste Bressand's com. Not that Bressand blamed him a bit. The rear admiral intended to do his best to defend Augusta, but after he had—and after the wreckage had dissipated—Poykkonen was going to have to deal with what the frigging Manties were about to do to his star system.

"Perimeter Tracking makes it four superdreadnoughts, four battlecruisers, and seven heavy and light cruisers," Bressand repeated. "It's possible one or more of the superdreadnoughts could be a carrier, but so far the emissions signatures are consistent with *Invictus* and *Medusa*-class SD(P)s. If I had to guess, I'd guess we're up against the same force that hit Hera."

"*Harrington* is here?" Poykkonen's face got a little grayer, if that was possible.

"Honor Harrington is not the devil herself," Bressand said

testily. "So far as I'm aware, she hasn't even made any *deals* with the devil—assuming the devil exists. Which I don't."

"I'm sorry, Baptiste." Poykkonen shook his head like a man trying to shake water out of his ears and managed an apologetic smile. "It's just, well . . . Oh, hell! You *know* what it is."

"Yes." Bressand sighed. "Yes, Joona, I know what it is."

"Do you intend to fight her?" Poykkonen asked quietly after a moment.

"I've got some orders around here somewhere that say something about my being the Augusta System's naval commander. If memory serves, they also say something about defending my station against attack."

"I know they do." Poykkonen's tone told Bressand his feeble attempt at humor had failed. "But that doesn't change the fact that you've got one old-style superdreadnought, six battlecruisers, and a couple of hundred LACs. That's not enough to stop her, and you know it."

"So what do I do, Joona?" Bressand sat back and raised one hand, palm uppermost. "Do I lie down and play dead? Do I just let her—or whoever's in command over there—waltz right in and blow this system's economy and industrial base to hell? We've got pods on tow, we've got the system defense pods already deployed, and if they don't have any CLACs of their own, then at least they don't have any of those damned *Katanas* to throw at us. I sent off a dispatch boat to Haven as soon as we realized they were scouting the system. A relief force is probably already on its way. If I can just delay these people until it gets here, we may be able to save at least some of your star system for you, after all."

"We're thirty light-years from the capital, Baptiste. That's four days' transit for a task force and your message can't reach the Octagon until sometime later today. Do you really think you can stand off a force this size for four frigging *days*?"

"Probably not," Bressand said bleakly. "But that doesn't mean I don't have to try." The two friends looked at one another for a moment, and then Bressand cleared his throat. "In case we don't get another chance to talk, Joona, take care of yourself."

"I will," the Governor promised softly. "And if you don't mind, I'm going to ask that God you don't believe in to look after you."

❖   ❖   ❖

"They're here, Ma'am," Commander Alan McGwire said. "Perimeter Tracking makes it at least six of the wall—some of them might be carriers, of course—ten cruisers, and at least three destroyers."

Commodore Desiree Carmouche, CO of the 117th Heavy Cruiser Squadron and the Republic of Haven Navy's senior officer in the Fordyce System, looked at her chief of staff and shook her head.

"Bit of overkill there, wouldn't you say?" she observed with ironic bitterness.

"I'm guessing their intelligence appreciation was off," McGwire replied. "Up until Thunderbolt, we had a much heavier system defense force stationed here." He shrugged. "Without an actual recon before they dropped their damned destroyers and stealthed arrays in on us, they had no way of knowing the system picket had been so reduced."

"For what I'm sure seemed like a perfectly good goddamned reason at the time," Carmouche grated. She glared at the plot for several seconds, eyes fiery as she studied the blood-red rash of incoming enemy warships and the seven threadbare green icons of her own understrength squadron, and then her shoulders sagged visibly.

"There's nothing we can do to stop them, Alan," she said heavily.

"No, Ma'am, there isn't," he agreed softly. "Petra's already passed the word to Governor Dahlberg."

Commander Petra Nielsen was Carmouche's operations officer, and the commodore nodded in understanding and approval.

"I've been on the horn with Captain Watson, myself," McGwire continued. Captain Diego Watson commanded the Fordyce LAC groups. "He says his people are prepared to engage."

"In which case I might as well simply shoot them myself." Carmouche turned away from the plot at last. "For Christ's sake, Diego has less than a hundred and fifty *Cimeterres*! If I commit him against these people, they'll blow him out of space before he even gets into his missile range of them. And just what the hell does he imagine he'd accomplish against *superdreadnoughts* even if he got into range in the first place?"

"Of course he wouldn't accomplish anything, Ma'am. But what did you expect him to say?"

"That he was ready to go in." Carmouche sighed, then shook her head wearily. "And I suppose the rest of our magnificent 'task force' is equally ready to get itself killed for absolutely nothing?"

"They are if you ask them to, Ma'am," McGwire said softly, and she looked at him sharply. He met her eyes steadily, and after a moment, she nodded.

"It does come down to that, doesn't it?" She inhaled deeply. "Well, Alan, as it happens, I'm not prepared to get all those people killed pointlessly. Have Communications pass the evacuation order for all of the civilian platforms, as well as the Fleet yard and repair station. If these are the same people who hit us last month, they're probably going to be careful about inflicting civilian casualties. But they might not be the same ones, so let's not take any chances."

"Aye, Ma'am," McGwire said formally.

"Then turn the Squadron around. We've got time to get out of the system before the Manties can range on us, but only if we start now. Any civilian starships who can evade are to do the same thing, but if the Manties bring them into range and order them to halt, they are to obey immediately. Make certain that's clearly understood."

"And the LACs, Ma'am?" McGwire's voice was completely nonjudgmental as Carmouche announced her intention of abandoning the star system to the enemy.

"They're to return to base immediately, and those bases' personnel are to be evacuated dirt-side as rapidly as possible. After which they'll blow their fusion plants," she replied flatly. "I wish we had the personnel lift to pick up Diego's crews in passing, but we don't. And I very much doubt the Manties brought along transports to haul prisoners home with them, anyway."

"That would require a bit of gall, Ma'am," McGwire agreed. "On the other hand, look how close to Haven they're operating. I'm afraid gall is one thing they obviously aren't short on."

"Well, *this* is an anticlimax," Alistair McKeon observed to his chief of staff.

"ONI can't get it right all the time, Sir," Commander Orndorff said. "The last time we looked, there was a sizable picket here. Obviously, times have changed." She shrugged philosophically. She was a substantial woman, who produced a substantial shrug, and the treecat on her shoulder flirted his tail in agreement with his person's observation.

"As if *you* know anything about intelligence appreciations!" McKeon told the 'cat.

"Banshee made it all the way through the Crusher with me, Sir," Orndorff pointed out. "You might be surprised what he picked up along the way."

"I might at that," McKeon agreed, chuckling as he remembered the first treecat *he'd* ever met. Then he shook himself.

"All right, CIC is confident about its tracking data?" he asked.

"Yes, Sir," another voice said. It belonged to Commander Alekan Slowacki, McKeon's ops officer and a relative newcomer to his command team. Now Slowacki gestured at the master plot's display of the Fordyce System, indicating a small cluster of red dots accelerating rapidly towards the hyper limit.

"That's all seven of the heavy cruisers *Venturer*'s arrays picked up, Sir," he continued. "And this," he pointed to another swarm of ruby light chips, "is over a hundred LACs returning to base." He shook his head. "Their system commander, whoever he is, hasn't commed us to announce he's standing down, but he's obviously intelligent enough to know what would happen if he didn't."

"And their missile pods?"

"No word on those, Sir. Probably the reason the system CO hasn't contacted you directly," Slowacki said. "He's not prepared to stand *them* down, as well, and he's afraid you might insist he do so."

"Damned straight I would," McKeon half growled. Then he shook his head. "Not that I'd be inclined to commit any atrocities if he declined. Mind you, it'd be tempting, but Duchess Harrington would feed me to Nimitz, one bite at a time, if I did anything like that!"

"That's probably an understatement, Sir," Orndorff said with a ghost of a smile.

"Whatever." McKeon brooded over the plot for several more seconds, then nodded decisively.

"Okay. They're abandoning the system—or, at least, they aren't going to defend it with anything except the pods—and according to *Venturer* and *Mandrake*, they don't have more than a hundred or so of those. I'm going to assume they have at least twice as many as we've actually found, however. And if they don't want to get their LACs killed, I don't see any reason we should get *ours* killed, either. Contact Admiral Corsini. I want only the *Katanas* deployed, strictly in the missile defense role. We'll take *Intransigent* and *Elizabeth* in, covered by Gottmeyer's cruisers and the *Katanas*. Corsini is to retain Atchison's cruiser division and the destroyers as a screen for the carriers and stay outside the hyper limit. If any unpleasant strangers appear, she's to immediately withdraw and return directly to Trevor's Star."

"We could probably sweep up the pieces faster with a couple of LAC groups, Sir," Orndorff pointed out in a diplomatic tone, and McKeon nodded.

"Yes, we could. On the other hand, a couple of SD(P)s can wipe out every significant platform out there in less than fifteen minutes if we have to. I'm not going to send in the LACs while holding the wallers out of missile range, and if I'm going to take the division in anyway, there's no point exposing *Shrikes* and *Ferrets* to potential lucky hits from the pods. If it takes us a little longer to do the job this way, so be it."

"Aye, aye, Sir," Orndorff said, and waved Slowacki towards the flag bridge's com section.

Captain Arakel Hovanian, acting commodore of the 93rd Destroyer Squadron, Republican Navy, glared at the master plot showing the icons of four CLACs, four battlecruisers, and seven destroyers and light cruisers sweeping inward from the hyper limit of the Des Moines System.

"Sir, Governor Bruckheimer is on the com," Commander Ellen Stokley, the skipper of the destroyer RHNS *Racer* and Hovanian's flag captain said quietly.

"Switch it to my display," Hovanian directed, and the small com flatscreen filled with the image of Governor Arnold Bruckheimer as the commodore slid into his command chair.

"Commodore Hovanian," the Governor said without preamble. "What the hell are you still doing here?"

"I beg your pardon?" Hovanian's eyes narrowed in surprise.

"I asked you what the hell you're still doing here," Bruckheimer repeated flatly. "Aside from the very high probability of getting yourself and all of your personnel killed, that is?"

"Governor, I'm responsible for the defense of this system, and—"

"And if you try to defend it, you're going to fail," Bruckheimer interrupted brusquely. "I can still read a tactical plot, you know."

Hovanian had opened his mouth to reply hotly, but he closed it again with a click at the reminder that Bruckheimer was a retired admiral.

"Better," Bruckheimer said a bit more conversationally. Then he cocked his head to one side, his eyes compassionate. "Commodore—Arakel—you just got dropped straight into the crapper through absolutely no fault of your own. If they'd waited another three weeks, we'd have had some significant reinforcements waiting for them. But they didn't, and you don't have a single capital ship under your command. There are exactly twenty-six *Cimeterres* in this entire star system; I know even better than you just how thin our missile pods are stretched; and you've got less than half your own squadron present for duty. There's no way you're going to stop this with three destroyers, and," Bruckheimer's voice hardened around the edges once more, "if you try—and survive the experience—I will personally see you court-martialed. Do I make myself clear?"

"Yes, Sir," Hovanian said after a long, still moment. "Yes, Sir. You do."

"Good." Bruckheimer ran the fingers of his right hand through his hair and grimaced. "We're going to have to come up with some sort of response to this strategy of theirs, but I'm damned if I know what the Octagon's going to do about it. In the meantime, get your people out of here before they all get killed."

"Aye, Sir," Hovanian said. He nodded to Stokely, who began issuing the necessary orders, then looked back at Bruckheimer. "And . . . thank you, Sir," he said to the man who had just saved his life.

"I wonder what other systems they're hitting today?" Admiral Bressand said.

"Maybe they aren't hitting *any* other systems, Sir," Commander Claudette Guyard, his chief of staff said.

"Oh, please, Claudette!" Bressand shook his head.

"I didn't say I thought they weren't, Sir. I just pointed out a possibility."

"Theoretically, *anything* is possible," Bressand said. "Some things, however, are more likely—or, conversely, *less* likely—than others."

"True, but—"

Guyard paused as Lieutenant Commander Krenckel appeared quietly at her elbow.

"Yes, Ludwig?" she said.

"We've confirmed it," Bressand's ops officer said. "Assuming they haven't decided to try to spoof our identification for some reason, two of those ships are definitely a pair of the *Invictuses* that hit Hera. I'm guessing one of them is the Manties' Eighth Fleet's flagship."

"Which means we probably *are* about to play host to 'the Salamander' herself," Guyard observed. "*There's* an honor—you should pardon the pun—I could have done without."

"You and me both," Bressand said, remembering his conversation with Poykkonen. "Not that it's going to take any tactical genius to kick the crap out of us with this kind of force imbalance."

"Maybe not, Sir," Krenckel said. "On the other hand, there's a sort of backhanded compliment in getting pounded by the other side's best."

"Did I ever mention that you're a very strange man, Ludwig?" Guyard asked.

Chapter Twenty-Seven

"It looks like we caught them with their pants down, doesn't it?" Vice Admiral Dame Alice Truman observed as her Task Force Eighty-One accelerated steadily in-system towards Vespasien, the inhabited planet of the Chantilly System.

"Yes, it does," Michelle Henke agreed from the vice admiral's com. "Of course, I have this sneaky suspicion that it's *supposed* to look that way."

"Why, Admiral Henke! I hadn't realized you had such a broad streak of paranoia."

"It comes from associating with people like you and Her Grace," Henke said dryly. Then she continued more seriously. "As Honor keeps pointing out, the Peeps aren't stupid. And this time around, they don't have political masters insisting they act as if they were. They haven't had time to reinforce heavily, but Chantilly is a jucier target than Gaston was. It should have been more heavily defended to begin with, and they sure as hell had more hyper-capable units in-system than the three destroyers our arrays have picked up. Which suggests to my naturally suspicious mind that as soon as they realized we'd inserted those arrays, they went to full-court stealth on their main combatants."

"It's what I'd do," Truman agreed. She drummed lightly on the arm of her command chair for a few moments, then shrugged. "Our arrays are good, but their stealth systems have gotten a lot better, and any star system represents a huge volume. If you were going to hide *your* defensive task force, where would you put it?"

"It's got to be close enough to protect the near-planet plat-forms," Henke replied. "Ninety percent of the system's industry's concentrated there, so there's no point deploying to defend any other area. *Greyhound* and *Whippet* swept the entire volume on this side of Vespasien very carefully, though. Even assuming they were stealthed, our arrays probably would have spotted them. But they have to base their deployment plans on the probability that we'll go for a least-time approach and figure they'll adjust if we do something else, instead. So, if *I* were looking for a good hiding place, I'd probably put my units on this side of the primary, but inside Vespasien's orbit. Far enough in-system the other side's remotes would have to do a fly-by on the planet, and all of the bunches and bunches of recon platforms of my own I'd have concentrated covering the inner system, before they could see me. But close enough so I could build an intercept vector headed out to meet an attack short of the planet."

"More or less what I was thinking," Truman murmured.

"To be perfectly honest, I'm less concerned about their war-ships than I am about their predeployed pods," Henke said. "They didn't have a huge number of them in Gaston, but that's the most cost-effective area-denial system they've got. And we found out in Gaston that they're a lot harder to spot than we thought they'd be. It's pretty obvious—assuming we're right about where their starships are—that whoever's in command here's a pretty cool customer. Sneaky, too. I don't like to think about what someone like that could do with a big enough stack of system defense pods if she put her mind to it."

"Do you think their scouts spotted us, Ivan?"

"It's too soon to say, Ma'am," Commander deCastro replied. "If they got close enough, if they looked in the right direction—if they got lucky—then, yes. They probably know exactly where we are. But nothing Leonardo's sensor crews have picked up sug-gests they did."

And we both know it's not going to make a lot of difference, either way, he thought, looking affectionately at his admiral.

"I guess it's just the principle of the thing," Admiral Bellefeuille said whimsically, as if she'd heard what he carefully hadn't said. "Whether it does any good or not, knowing we managed to at least surprise them would do wonders for my own morale."

"Well, in that case, let's assume they're surprised until and unless we know differently, Ma'am."

"So I want you to take point, Captain," Michelle Henke said.

"I'm honored," the tall, gangly man at the other end of the com link drawled in a maddening aristocratic accent. "Be interestin' t' see how well she does in her first action, too."

"She's got a lot to live up to," Henke said.

"That she does," Captain (senior grade) Michael Oversteegen agreed. "In fact, I believe someone may have mentioned t' me in passin' that the last *Nike*'s first captain and XO had a little somethin' t' do with that."

"We tried, Captain. We tried."

Despite Oversteegen's sometimes infuriating mannerisms and sublime—one might reasonably say arrogant—self-confidence, Henke had always rather liked him. The differences between their families' political backgrounds only made that liking even more ironic, as had the fact that their fathers had loathed one another cordially. But not even the Earl of Gold Peak had ever questioned *Michael* Oversteegen's competence or nerve, and she was glad he was senior to Captain Franklin Hanover, *Hector*'s CO. She liked Hanover, and he was a good, solid man. But he wasn't Michael Oversteegen, and Oversteegen's seniority gave him command of Henke's third division. If ever there'd been a case of the right man in the right place, this was it, and she watched *Nike* and *Hector* crack on a few more gravities of acceleration.

Winston Bradshaw and his two *Saganami*-class cruisers—HMS *Edward Saganami* and HMS *Quentin Saint-James*—closed up on Truman's carriers, while Henke herself, with *Ajax*, *Agamemnon*, and the light cruisers *Amun*, *Anhur*, and *Bastet* followed in Oversteegen's wake. She didn't want the interval between her own ships and Oversteegen's division to get too great, but she wanted at least a few more seconds to react to any traps or ambushes Oversteegen might trip. And she wanted to be sure she kept her ships and the four squadrons of *Katanas* providing her close cover between Oversteegen and the two hundred-plus Peep LACs shadowing the Manticoran ships.

She looked at the tiny icons of the LACs on her plot, and

once again, she was tempted to roll pods. The small vessels were well within her powered missile envelope, but far enough out accuracy would be even lower than usual against LACs, and *Agamemnons* weren't wallers. They had to watch their ammunition consumption carefully.

"I don't think they do know where we are, Ma'am," deCastro said. "It looks like they may suspect, though. And I'd say it's pretty definite that someone's figured out we're pretending we're a hole in space *somewhere.*"

"Pity," Bellefeuille a replied. "I'd hoped they'd keep coming all fat and happy. Anyone care to speculate on whether or not they've deployed additional recon drones?"

"Anythin' on the drones yet, Joel?"

"Not yet, Sir. Betty is still steering them into position," Commander Joel Blumenthal said from the small com display connecting Oversteegen to *Nike*'s backup bridge.

Joel Blumenthal had moved up from tactical officer to exec when Captain Oversteegen had to give up HMS *Gauntlet* in order to assume command of *Nike*. Linda Watson, Oversteegen's XO in *Gauntlet* had no longer been available, since she'd received a long overdue promotion of her own to captain and taken over his old ship. And, despite some people's possible qualms, Oversteegen had brought along the newly promoted Lieutenant Commander Betty Gohr to replace Blumenthal as *Nike*'s brand spanking new tactical officer. Competition for any slot on *Nike*'s command deck had been fierce, but Michael Oversteegen had a knack for getting the bridge crew he wanted.

Which probably, Blumenthal reflected, had something to do with the results he consistently produced.

"I believe Admiral Henke's correctly deduced the other side's most probable position," Oversteegen said now, tipping back in his command chair with a thoughtful expression. "The question in my mind is precisely what they hope t' accomplish."

"I imagine not getting shot at for as long as possible is pretty high on their list, Sir," Blumenthal said dryly, and Oversteegen gave one of the explosive snorts he used instead of a chuckle.

"No doubt it is," he said after a moment. "At th' same time, if that was all they wanted, th' simplest thing for them t' have done would be t' have simply decamped. No." He shook his head. "They've got somethin' more than that in mind."

He pondered for a few more moments, then looked at Lieutenant Commander Gohr.

"Have we confirmed *Greyhound* and *Whippet*'s numbers on the pods they did detect, Betty?"

"No, Sir." Gohr looked up from her own console and half-turned to face her CO. "But as Commander Sturgis pointed out, his platforms had a very difficult time picking them up in the first place on passives," she reminded him. "It's probably not too surprising there's a discrepancy."

"Perhaps not. But are our numbers high compared t' his, or low?"

"Low, Sir. We seem to be coming in at least twenty-five percent lower than his original numbers overall."

"That's what I thought," Oversteegen said softly, and Blumenthal's com image gave him a sharp look. One that turned suddenly speculative.

"Precisely," Oversteegen said, then looked at his communications section. "Lieutenant Pattison, I believe I need t' speak t' Admiral Henke again. Would you be so kind as t' see if she's prepared t' take my call?"

"I think Oversteegen's onto something, Ma'am," Michelle Henke told Dame Alice Truman.

"But how could they have moved them without Sturgis' arrays seeing them?" Truman's question was thoughtful, not dismissive.

"Very carefully," Henke replied dryly. Truman made a face, and Henke chuckled humorlessly.

"Seriously, Ma'am," she went on, after a moment, "think about it. Whoever this is, she's cool enough, and she's thought far enough ahead, to get her mobile units—aside from her LACs—into stealth before our arrays found her. Personally, I'm betting she did it as soon as her sensors picked up *Greyhound* and *Whippet*'s hyper footprints. And I'm also betting she'd already decided what she was going to do with her pods if it came to it. So what she's probably been doing is quietly using some of that near-planet 'merchant traffic' Sturgis reported to pick up and drop off previously deployed pods. If she did, I think we need to rethink our recon doctrine."

"Go ahead and park one or two in close and just let them sit?"

"Yes, Ma'am."

Henke didn't mention that she'd already suggested that modification only to have the Powers That Were at Admiralty House shoot it down. They were concerned that a stationary platform would be more readily tracked down, especially since it would be inside most of the system's defenders' surveillance platforms, which would give them a far better chance of detecting the array's directional transmissions and triangulating on their source. Having the arrays localized and destroyed would have been bad enough, but the present generation of recon drones had *all* the Ghost Rider bells and whistles, including the very latest grav-pulse coms and several other goodies Erewhon had never had to turn over to Haven in the first place. The possibility that one of them might be disabled without being destroyed, while slight, did exist, and Admiralty House strongly objected to the notion of handing the Star Kingdom's latest and best hardware to the other side for examination.

"I think you were probably right all along, Mike," Truman said after a moment. "Certainly, if they did what Oversteegen thinks they did, having a couple of platforms—or even just one—keeping a close, permanent eye on near-planet space would probably've caught them at it."

"Maybe. The question, though, Ma'am, is what we do about it," Henke pointed out.

"Well, I see two possibilities. First, we send in the LACs. That means radically slowing your ships' approach while Scotty and his LAC jockeys get themselves organized and catch up with you. Second, we go right on doing what we're doing. Which do you vote for?"

"A variant of Option Two," Henke said without any appreciable hesitation. "I don't want to waste any more time than we have to, since we don't know where any response force they've sent for is coming from, or exactly how long it's going to take to get here. What I propose is that I send the *Katanas* ahead to catch up with Oversteegen. Hopefully, the bad guys won't have guessed we've taken a page from their own missile-defense doctrine, but whether they have or not, forty-eight *Katanas* should help out quite a bit."

"I don't know, Mike," Truman said dubiously. "Scotty would only need a couple of hours more than Oversteegen to get there, and *Shrikes* and *Ferrets* are a lot harder targets for their fire control than battlecruisers."

"And a lot easier to kill if they get hit," Henke pointed out. "Besides, we're already inside their powered missile envelope, if they're where we think they are. At the moment, they're not firing because we're still closing, and they're willing to wait until we give them better firing solutions. But if we suddenly break off, they're going to fire anyway, well before we could get a LAC strike in close enough to start killing platforms. Since we've already stepped into their parlor, I think our best chance is to just keep going, offer Oversteegen as the most attractive target, and back him up with the best missile-defense capability we can."

Truman thought some more. Then she nodded, once, sharply. "All right, Mike. Do it."

"They've definitely figured out roughly what we're doing with our main combatants, Ma'am," Leonardo Ericsson said. He tapped the projected vectors CIC was throwing into the master plot. "Look at this."

The four squadrons of LACs which had been glued tightly to the second Manty battlecruiser division were accelerating away from it, closing rapidly on the *lead* division. At the same time, some of the near-planet sensor platforms were beginning to pick up the shadowy ghosts of Manticoran recon drones. They weren't finding many of them, but that didn't mean they weren't there; the drones were hellishly difficult sensor targets at the best of times. The limited number they were actually seeing suggested there was probably a solid shell of them, spreading out in front of the oncoming Manty starships, and CIC was doing its best to project where that shell was in three-dimensional space. The tracking crews' hard data was limited, but Bellefeuille felt confident they'd gotten it effectively correct, and the shell they were projecting was aligned all too closely upon her own ships' positions.

"So," she said flatly, "the question is whether we fire now, when it's pretty clear they haven't quite locked in our positions, or wait a little longer in hopes of improving our firing solutions. Opinions, anyone?" She looked up from the plot. "Ivan?"

"Wait," Commander deCastro said, quickly and positively. She cocked an eyebrow, and he shrugged. "We're so outgunned that one good shot is all we're likely to get, Ma'am," he pointed out. "That being the case, I'd like it to be as effective as we can make it. That's what Smoke and Mirrors was all about to start with."

"I see. Leonardo?" she looked at her ops officer.

"Normally, I'd tend to agree with Ivan," Ericsson said after a moment. "But I don't like this." He indicated the steadily accelerating icons of the enemy LACs once more. "They've been careful to keep them between our known LAC concentrations and the rest of their ships. To me, that suggests they're probably *Katanas* in the escort role. But now they're sending them in along with their probe, and I'm wondering if they've evolved something like our LAC fleet missile-defense doctrine. If they have, then the people we're going to have the improved firing solutions on are also going to've significantly improved their defenses by the time we finally fire."

"On the other hand, Ma'am," deCastro pointed out, "the closer they get to *us*, the further they are from their main body. And if they are a sizable chunk of the Manties' *Katana* force, mousetrapping them now might be the best thing we could do. Especially since they also seem to've completely missed Mirror Box."

Jennifer Bellefeuille nodded slowly, and her senior staffers waited. She always invited opinions, careful to avail herself of the best advice available, and she always made the final decision herself.

"We wait," she said. "Not as long as you'd probably like, Ivan, but long enough for our solutions to tighten up. I think we'll wait until their *Katanas*—and I think you're right about what they are, Leonardo—are about ten minutes from matching vectors with their battlecruisers. I'd actually have liked to catch them close enough to engage our missiles with their counter-missiles but still too far out to use their laser clusters, but that's not going to work, given the geometry. I think we'll go with a staggered launch, though."

"Staggered, Ma'am?" Ericsson repeated.

"The first one to concentrate on their battlecruisers," she said, with a thin smile. "I'll want it heavy enough to get their attention pretty emphatically, too. Particularly, I'd like their *Katanas* to commit as many as possible of their counter-missiles to stopping the first wave."

Her thin smile grew vicious, and her staffers found themselves returning it slowly.

"Dagger One, Ramrod."

"Ramrod, Dagger One," Commander Dillinger replied. "Go."

Dillinger and his *Katanas* were over five million kilometers in front of Scotty Tremaine's command LAC and the rest of the carrier division's strike, but there was no perceptible delay in their grav-pulse FTL conversation.

"I'm getting that uncomfortable feeling between my shoulder blades, Crispus," Tremaine continued more informally. "I don't know why, but I've got the feeling there's something nasty waiting out here."

"Ah, Ramrod," Dillinger said with a smile, "I'm afraid I didn't quite copy that threat analysis. Could you repeat all after 'something.'"

"Dagger One, you're a smart ass," Tremaine told him. Then his tone sobered. "Seriously, Crispus. Watch your six. I don't like how conspicuous these people's inactivity has been. I don't know exactly what they're up to, but they're up to *something*. That much I am confident of."

"Ramrod, I hear you," Dillinger responded, his smile fading. "So far, though, I haven't seen a thing you haven't."

"I know." Tremaine frowned as he gazed at his own plot aboard *Dacoit*. "That's what worries me. Ramrod, clear."

"Another ten minutes, I think," Jennifer Bellefeuille said quietly.

She stood beside Commander Ericsson, gazing into the master plot of RHNS *Cyrus*, her battlecruiser flagship, at the icons of the oncoming warships. Even a few years before, she knew, the Manties would already have localized her own ships, opened fire, and almost certainly destroyed them by now. But one of the Manty drones had passed within less than ten light-seconds of her flagship and simply continued on its way, which made it obvious the improvements in the Republic's stealth systems were giving the enemy's sensors a hard time. The fact that none of her starships had their wedges up and that all of them had gone to total emissions control undoubtedly helped, but even so, she felt the tension prickling sharper in her palms. *Cyrus* and her consorts were barely one light-minute from Vespasien, and the Manties were clearly looking for them hard.

But they haven't found *us yet*, she reminded herself. *So it's time to give them something else to think about before they do.*

"Initiate Decoy," she said.

"Aye, Ma'am," Ericsson said, and nodded to the com officer. "Send 'Initiate Decoy.' "

"I have something, Sir!" Lieutenant Commander Gohr said sharply. "The Gamma-Three array is picking up what looks like stealthed impeller wedges. Bearing three-four-niner, zero-zero-niner from the ship, range approximately five-six-point-eight million klicks!"

Michael Oversteegen punched a command into the small-scale plot deployed from the arm of his command chair, and his eyes narrowed as the display zoomed in on the indicated datum.

Nike and *Hector* were still 20,589,000 kilometers from Vespasien, but their velocity was down to a mere 5,265 KPS as they continued to decelerate at a steady 5.31 KPS². Their present flight profile would bring them to a halt, relative to the system primary, one light-minute short of the planet. That was close enough to bring all the near-planet orbital infrastructure into sufficiently short range to avoid any embarrassing accidents . . . like unintentional missile strikes on an inhabited world. But it was also far enough out to keep him at least *two* light-minutes from his own estimate of the enemy's closest probable position.

Commander Dillinger's *Katanas* were continuing to close from astern. Their higher acceleration rate meant they'd been able to attain a higher base velocity before they began decelerating towards a rendezvous, and their current velocity was 6,197 KPS. Their vectors would merge with *Nike*'s in another ten minutes, at which point they would both be down to a velocity of 2,079 KPS and less than four hundred thousand kilometers from their planned zero-zero point—or about 18,400,000 kilometers from Vespasien.

The new emission signatures Gohr had picked up were just over two light-minutes inside Vespasien's orbit. Assuming the ships responsible for the signatures had pods of multi-drive missiles, that would put his ships inside their effective range, but far enough out for Havenite accuracy to be very, very poor.

"Move the platforms closer, Betty," he said, after a moment. "And don't forget t' watch the other approaches, as well."

"Yes, Sir."

Jennifer Bellefeuille watched her own plot, gray-green eyes slitted in concentration. It was impossible to tell whether or not the Manties had bitten, but the decoy emissions looked very convincing to her own recon platforms. She didn't have much faith in their ability to fool the Manties for long, but if CIC's projection of their recon shell's probable deployment was correct, it would take them precious minutes to get even one of *their* drones close enough to realize the units they were picking up were actually the recon variant of the *Cimeterre*. There were eight of them out there, each with a standard tethered decoy tractored to it, and their only job was to "leak" enough of an impeller signature to keep the Manties looking in *their* direction just a little longer.

"Dagger Flight will match vectors with us in about six minutes, Sir," Lieutenant Commander Gohr announced.

"Very good. Anythin' more on those impeller signatures?"

"Not a lot, Sir. But the arrays are closing in, and so far it looks like a half-dozen or so point sources. Maybe a few more."

"I see." Michael Oversteegen grimaced. Over the years, he'd learned to trust his instincts, and those instincts told him something wasn't quite right. He looked back down at Blumenthal's face on the com screen deployed from his command chair.

"Why d'you suppose these fellows are just sittin' there, Joe?"

Blumenthal frowned. He gazed down into his own plot for a second or two, then looked back up.

"If they're planning to let us continue to close, which seems to be what they've been doing so far, then they're probably waiting until they're *sure* they've been detected," he said, in the tone of a man who wondered if he'd just been asked a trick question.

"Unless they're complete and total idiots, like my beloved cousin, Countess Fraser," Oversteegen replied, "they've got t' have a pretty shrewd notion we've already picked them up. One thing Commander Sturgis was able t' positively confirm is that the space around Vespasien is crawlin' with Havenite reconnaissance assets. D'you seriously think we managed t' get that many of our own

drones right past the planet without any of those assets noticin'
as they went by?"

"Well, no, Sir. Of course, they *are* very stealthy."

"Yes, they are," Oversteegen agreed dryly. "But good as our
stealth technology is, it's not yet perfect. And, much as it pains
me t' admit it, between what they got from the Erewhonese and
what they've probably managed t' pick up on their own from
examinin' captured hardware, our cloak of invisibility's probably
just a tad thinner than any of us would like t' think. I'm not
sayin' they can get solid lockups on our platforms. But when we
operate this many of them, in such close proximity and so deep
into the other side's sensor envelope, they're bound t' pick up at
least *some* of them. And if they've managed t' do that, any tac
officer worth his salt should be able t' project our basic deployment pattern. In which case, they damned well ought t' know
that if they're sittin' there with active impeller wedges, we're *goin'*
t' have picked them up by now."

"Put that way, Sir, you may have a point," Blumenthal conceded.
"At the same time, they may be waiting until our platforms go
active and they *know* we've got them."

"Maybe so, but why put themselves that far from the planet?"
Oversteegen asked. "It puts Vespasien outside their best MDM
envelope by a considerable margin, which means *they're* riskin' an
accidental hit on the planet if they engage us. They didn't have
t' let us this close t' the planet in the first place. They ought t'
be at least a light-minute closer, and if they aren't, then they
ought t' still be lyin' doggo." He shook his head. "No, they've
got somethin' else in mind."

He brooded down at the plot for a few more seconds, then
looked up at Gohr.

"Launch another shell," he said. "I want t' sweep this area
again."

He tapped a command into his armrest alphanumeric pad,
highlighting the indicated volume of space on Gohr's larger
plot.

"Sir, I can recall the Beta platforms to cover that volume," she
pointed out.

"I'm certain you could," he agreed pleasantly. "Unfortunately,
that would require at least twenty minutes, and I want it swept
now."

"Yes, Sir."

Gohr beckoned to her assistant, and the two of them began punching in commands to deploy the specified drone shell to cover the area to system north of Vespasien once again.

"Crap," Leonardo Ericsson muttered as the fresh drones began deploying from the outsized Manty battlecruiser.

"So they didn't buy the decoys after all," deCastro said.

"No." Bellefeuille shook her head. "They bought them—for a little while, at least. But whoever that is over there, she's a suspicious one. So she's doublechecking the 'clear areas' just in case."

"Well, they're going to pick us up, emissions control or no emissions control, in about another seven minutes, Ma'am," Ericsson pointed out. "These two, especially, are coming straight down our throats."

He tapped two light codes on his display, and this time Bellefeuille nodded.

"Yes, they are. And they're about where we wanted them anyway." She straightened, inhaled deeply, and nodded to deCastro.

"It's time," she said.

"Missile launch!" Betty Gohr barked suddenly. "*Multiple* missile launches!"

Oversteegen looked up sharply as the deadly, blood-red icons appeared on the master plot.

"Range at launch eight-five-point-two light-seconds," Gohr said flatly. "Time to attack range six-point-one-three minutes!"

Jennifer Bellefeuille and her staff had devised the operational plan she'd dubbed "Smoke and Mirrors" in response to the Manticorans' first set of raids. Although Chantilly had been assigned a substantially heavier system defense force than Gaston or Hera to begin with, she'd known it was grossly insufficient to hold off attacks in such strength using any conventional defensive plan, so she'd had to go outside the box.

Her six heavily refitted *Warlord*-class battlecruisers and three *Trojan*-class destroyers were the only hyper-capable combatants she had, but she also had almost six hundred *Cimeterres* and almost a thousand system-defense missile pods to back them up. And she also had two hundred and forty standard MDM pods to go with it.

The problem was that although the system-defense pods' out-sized, over-powered birds could actually slightly exceed Manticoran MDMs' acceleration rates, her standard pods' missiles couldn't quite match them, and neither of them were as accurate as Manty missiles. In addition, what had happened in Gaston demonstrated that her LACs simply could not mix it up with *Katanas*—on Manty terms, at least—and win. So she'd had to get creative if she wanted to do any good.

The instant Perimeter Tracking picked up evidence the Man-ties were scouting Chantilly, her battlecruisers, already in their preselected positions, had gone to stealth and strict emissions control under the Smoke and Mirrors operational plan. In addi-tion, two-thirds of her total LAC strength had gone to immedi-ate readiness, but been restricted to its bases. She'd continued to operate two hundred LACs normally, making certain the Man-ties saw them, but four hundred additional *Cimeterres,* based on Vespasien's main space station and a dozen other innocuous orbital platforms, outwardly indistinguishable from any freight-handling facility, had stayed completely covert.

Now, like any good magician, Bellefeuille began her stage show by fixing her audience's attention firmly on the distraction she *wanted* it to see.

"Estimate nineteen hundred incoming," Lieutenant Commander Gohr announced.

"Understood. Lieutenant Pattison, request Dagger One t' expe-dite his arrival, if you please."

Michael Oversteegen's voice was as calm and drawling as ever as he watched the cyclone of missiles tear through space towards his command.

"Defense Plan Alpha," he continued, and HMS *Nike* and HMS *Hector* altered course. They rolled up on their sides to turn the bellies of their wedges towards the incoming fire while Keyhole platforms deployed far beyond the boundaries of their protec-tive sidewalls, and counter-missile defense solutions were already cycling.

"Looks like you had a point, Sir," Blumenthal observed quietly.

"Those—" he jabbed a hand at his own plot's icons representing the elusive impeller signatures "—have to be decoys."

Oversteegen nodded. The missiles coming at *Nike* and *Hector* had been launched from a point in space *this* side of Vespasien and just under one light-minute "north" of it . . . the next best thing to four light-minutes away from Blumenthal's decoys.

"Obviously they wanted t' get us in as close as they could before launchin', so they kept us lookin' somewhere they weren't," he agreed. But even as he spoke, something continued to bother him.

"All Daggers, Dagger One!" Commander Dillinger snapped. "Flyswatter. I say again, Flyswatter!"

The forty-eight *Katanas* of Dagger Flight changed acceleration in almost instant response. One moment they were decelerating at seven hundred gravities, sixty thousand kilometers astern of *Nike* and slowing neatly towards rendezvous; the next, they were *accelerating* at the same seven hundred gravities as they charged to catch up with and pass the battlecruisers. Although they were smaller and far frailer than any battlecruiser, they were also much more difficult targets for long-range missile fire, and they raced towards the enemy to place their own defensive missile launchers between the incoming MDMs and their targets.

"The *Katanas* are moving to intercept, Ma'am," Ericsson announced, and Rear Admiral Bellefeuille jerked her head in combined acknowledgment and approval. The possibility of *Cyrus'* surviving the next half-hour or so was remote, but she'd actually managed to put that out of her mind as she concentrated on the task in hand.

"Remind the Mirror Box platforms that they do *not* launch without my specific order," she said.

"Aye, Ma'am."

"Damn," Michelle Henke said, far more mildly than she felt. The fact that her instincts had been correct didn't make her feel much better as she watched the massive missile launch sweeping towards *Nike* and *Hector*.

"Take us to maximum acceleration," she told Stackpole. "Close us up on Oversteegen and prepare to support his missile defenses."

"Aye, aye, Ma'am!" her ops officer said crisply. "But it's going to be awfully long range for our CMs," he pointed out. "And we're really too far out to coordinate with *Nike* and *Hector*. Even with FTL telemetry, we're simply too far away to data share effectively."

"I understand that, John. But, worst case, any attack bird we kill is simply one Oversteegen would have nailed anyway. And if we take out one he would have missed . . ."

"Yes, Ma'am."

Stackpole began issuing orders, and Henke turned back to her own display. The ops officer was certainly correct about the dispersal problem, she thought. Her own battlecruiser division was two and a half million kilometers behind Oversteegen. She had the reach—barely, with the new extended-range counter-missiles—to bolster his defensive umbrella, but her support would be far less effective from this far out. Still, something about the attack pattern—

"There aren't enough birds," Oliver Manfredi said suddenly. She looked up, turning towards the chief of staff, and Manfredi shook his golden head. "There's less than two thousand in the salvo, Ma'am. That's less than three hundred of their standard pods. So where are the others?"

Henke looked at him for perhaps three seconds, then spun her chair to face Lieutenant Kaminski.

"Get me an immediate priority link to Captain Oversteegen!"

"Aye, aye, Ma'am," the communications officer replied instantly.

"Weapons free!" Commander Dillinger snapped, and the *Katanas* of Dagger Flight began punching counter-missiles at the incoming fire.

Dillinger didn't really like to think about just how expensive each of his LACs' "counter-missiles" actually was. The systems built into the Viper for its anti-LAC role meant it cost twice as much as the standard extended-range Mark 31 CM on which it was based. But the Viper retained the Mark 31's basic drive system, and a counter-missile's impeller wedge was what it used to "sweep up" attack missiles. Which meant the Viper was still perfectly capable of being used defensively, and earmarking a percentage of them for missile defense, rather than using magazine space on dedicated Mark 31s which couldn't be used in the anti-shipping role, simplified their ammunition requirements and gave them a potentially useful cushion both offensively and defensively.

Now the Vipers bored out of their launch tubes, streaking to meet the incoming missiles, and Dillinger smiled nastily. He was willing to bet the Peeps had never seen *LACs* kill missiles at this range!

"You were right, Ma'am," deCastro said. "They do use those things for counter-missiles, too."

"Made sense," Bellefeuille said almost absently, watching her plot. "The signatures Admiral Beach recorded at Gaston made it pretty clear they were basically the same missile body and drive package, after all."

"And it's a reasonable decision from the viewpoint of ammo supply, too," Ericsson agreed, then showed his teeth. "Of course, sometimes even the most reasonable decisions can bite you right on the ass."

"Especially if someone else helps it do it," deCastro said with a tight, answering grin.

"Tactical," Michael Oversteegen said suddenly. "Have the near-planet pods we've located launched?"

"Sir?" Lieutenant Commander Gohr sounded startled. It took her a fraction of a second to shake her mind loose from the anti-missile engagement as the steady vibration of counter-missile launches shook *Nike*. The first wave of Vipers from Dagger Flight was beginning to rip holes in the Havenite salvo, and her own missile defense section was running at full stretch, analyzing the attack missiles' EW patterns. But then she stabbed a quick look at a secondary plot, and Oversteegen saw her twitch upright in her chair as the data registered.

"No, Sir," she said, turning her head to look directly at him. "*None* of this fire's coming from Vespasien orbit!"

"That's what I thought," he said grimly. "Com, get me Dagger One."

"Sir," Lieutenant Pattison said, "you have an immediate priority signal from Admiral Henke."

"Put it through, Jayne—and get me Dagger One!"

"Aye, aye, Sir."

Michelle Henke's face appeared on Oversteegen's display, her expression tense.

"Michael, I'm looking at the missile density, and—"

"And it's too low," Oversteegen broke in. "We've just confirmed the near-planet platforms haven't launched a single bird." A window opened in the corner of his display, showing Crispus Dillinger's face. "And now, I've got t' go," Oversteegen told his admiral, and punched the button that brought Dillinger to the center of the display.

"Yes, Sir?" Dillinger said.

"There's somethin' peculiar about their attack pattern, Commander," Oversteegen said quickly. "They're only using a fraction of their total missile power—and everything they're actually firin' is coming from further away, with what have t' be poorer targetin' solutions."

"Sir?" Dillinger looked puzzled, and Oversteegen shook his head impatiently.

"They're tryin' t' distract us—and quite possibly t' lure us into expendin' counter-missiles before their real attack."

"But—"

"This isn't a debatin' society, Commander," Oversteegen said. "Abort your missile defense of this division—*now!*"

Crispus Dillinger looked at the face on his communications display with something very like incredulity. The man had to be insane! There were almost a thousand missiles tearing down on each of his ships, and he wanted Dillinger to *stop* defending them?!

But—

"All Daggers," he said harshly, "Dagger One. Abort Flyswatter. Repeat, *abort* Flyswatter. Missile Defense Alpha is now in effect."

"Well, it was nice while it lasted," Jennifer Bellefeuille said as the torrent of counter-missiles pouring from the *Katanas* slowed abruptly to a trickle. She looked at Ericsson. "Estimates on their expenditure, Leonardo?"

"Assuming they have the same basic magazine space as the Manty missile LACs we were able to inspect after Thunderbolt, and that these things are basically the same size as their standard counter-missiles, that has to be at least fifty percent of their total loadout, Ma'am. Possibly as high as sixty, if they've committed additional volume and mass to more point defense clusters, as well."

"And they did a real number on our missiles with them, too," deCastro pointed out. "Their kill percentages are damned close to twice what *Cimeterres* would have managed, even at much shorter ranges."

"True." Bellefeuille nodded. "On the other hand, there are less than fifty of them, and if Leonardo's right, they don't have a lot of missiles left."

She gazed at the plot a second or two longer, then nodded again, crisply.

"Initiate Phase Two, Leonardo."

HMS *Nike* twisted sinuously as the depleted missile storm tore down upon her and her division mate.

The *Katanas* had thinned it considerably before Oversteegen ordered them to stand down. Of the nineteen hundred missiles which had launched, the LACs had killed seven hundred. The battlecruisers' counter-missiles killed two hundred and sixty, and another hundred and fifty or so simply lost lock and wandered off on their own. Three hundred and twelve more locked onto the Ghost Rider decoys *Nike* and *Hector* had deployed, and another sixty looped suddenly back towards the *Katanas*, only to be ripped apart by the LACs' point defense clusters.

But that left four hundred and seventy-eight, and as they streamed past the *Katanas*, the battlecruisers were on their own.

Oversteegen watched them come, absolutely motionless in his command chair, narrow eyes very still. Thirty point defense laser clusters studded each of *Nike*'s flanks. They were individually more powerful than any past Manticoran battlecruiser had ever mounted, with fourteen emitters per cluster, each capable of cycling at one shot every sixteen seconds. That came to one shot every 1.2 seconds per cluster, but that was only twenty-five per broadside per second, and these were *MDMs*. They had traveled over twenty-five million kilometers to reach their targets, their closing speed was almost 173,000 KPS—fifty-eight percent of the speed of light—and they had a standoff attack range of 30,000 kilometers.

They crossed the inner perimeter of the counter-missile interception zone, losing another hundred and seventeen in the process. Of the three hundred and sixty-one survivors, fifty-eight were electronic warfare platforms, which meant "only" three hundred and three missiles—barely fifteen percent of the original launch—actually attacked.

The space about *Nike* and *Hector* was hideous with incandescent eruptions of fury, and bomb-pumped lasers ripped and gouged at their targets. But these battlecruisers had been designed and built to face exactly this sort of attack. Their sidewalls—especially *Nike*'s—were far tougher and more powerful than any previous battlecruisers had mounted, and both of them were equipped with the RMN's bow and stern walls. The fact that they'd been able to keep their wedges turned towards the incoming fire even while they engaged it with their own counter-missiles presented additional targeting problems for the Havenite missiles' onboard systems. Instead of the broadside aspect ships were normally forced to show attack missiles' sensors, all *these* missiles saw was the wedge itself. But no sensor could penetrate a military-grade impeller wedge, which made it impossible for them to absolutely localize their targets. They could predict the volume in which their target must lay, but not precisely where *within* that volume to find it.

And that was why *Nike* and *Hector* survived. The missiles' sensors *could* have seen through the battlecruisers' sidewalls, but the sidewalls were turned away from them. Most of them streaked "above" and "below" the Manticoran battlecruisers, fighting for a "look-down" shot, while others crossed the Manticorans' bows or sterns, trying for "up-the-kilt" or "down-the-throat" shots. Tough as *Nike*'s passive defenses were, they were no match for the raw power of the Havenite lasers, but the very speed which made MDMs such difficult targets for short-range point defense fire worked against them now. They simply didn't have time to find their targets and fire in the fleeting fragment of a second they took to cross the Manticoran ships' tracks.

"No damage, Sir!" Lieutenant Commander Gohr announced jubilantly. "None!"

"Well done, Guns," Oversteegen replied.

"Captain Hanover reports one hit forward on *Hector*, Sir,"

Lieutenant Pattison reported. "No casualties, but she's lost one graser and a laser cluster."

"Good," Oversteegen said. "In that case, let's—"

"Missile launch!" Gohr said suddenly. "Multiple launches! Sir, I have LAC separation from in-system platforms!"

Oversteegen's eyes flew to the main plot, and his jaw tightened as threat sources exploded across it. A fresh wave of MDMs had abruptly appeared, launched from the same spot as the first salvo. But this one was considerably more massive. The next best thing to six thousand missile icons spangled the display, streaking towards his ships—and also Dillinger's LACs and Michelle Henke's division—and Gohr was right about the LAC launches, as well. The two hundred Task Force 81 had already known about went suddenly to full acceleration, charging towards the Manticorans, but twice that many more were erupting into space, turning towards Dillinger's *Katanas* and the battlecruisers behind them.

Oversteegen glared at the innocent icons of the near-planet missile pods Gohr's sensor crews had managed to locate. They hadn't launched yet, but they would, he knew. They were waiting, until their missiles could join the missile storm coming in from further out. Their lower base velocities when they arrived would make them easier targets, but it would also give them better shots at his sidewalls, and there were probably at least another two or three thousand missiles aboard them. The tactician in him cried out to hit them with proximity-fused warheads, to kill them before they fired. But they were too close to Vespasien. There was too big a chance a faulty firing solution would hit the planet itself or kill one of the unarmed civilian platforms and everyone aboard it.

No. They were simply going to have to take it, and his expression was bleak as he watched the attack come in. It was unlikely that even this would destroy his ship. The one mistake whoever had planned the attack had made was in his targeting selection. He ought to have directed all of that fire at no more than one or two targets, not spread it among so many. But it was hard to fault him for that, when he probably hadn't realized just how tough the battlecruisers he faced truly were. And if he wasn't going to kill them, that didn't mean he wasn't going to *hurt* them badly. Which didn't even consider what was going to happen to

Dillinger's *Katanas* after they'd been mousetrapped into expending so many of their missiles against the first wave of MDMs.

For just a moment, behind the armor of his eyes, Michael Oversteegen felt a fleeting glow of admiration for his opponent. Whoever he was, he'd made maximum use of his limited resources, and Task Force 81's lead elements were about to get hammered.

But the moment passed, and Oversteegen straightened in his command chair.

"Defense plan Alpha-Three," he said calmly.

Chapter Twenty-Eight

"Reverend Sullivan." Robert Telmachi, Archbishop of Manticore, walked across his spacious, sunlit office to shake hands as the bald, fierce-nosed visitor was ushered into it.

"This is an honor," Telmachi continued. "And, if I may say so, a meeting I've hoped for for quite some time."

"Thank you, Archbishop." The head of the Church of Humanity Unchained shook the offered hand firmly. "I, too, have looked forward to meeting you. Monsignor Davidson has been most satisfactory as your representative on Grayson, but given the intimacy of our two star nations' political relationship . . ."

He smiled, and Telmachi nodded with a smile of his own.

"Precisely," he said, escorting his guest towards an inviting conversational nook arranged in the office's huge, floor-to-ceiling bay window. "Of course," he continued, his smile broadening as they sat, "I don't have quite as much authority in the Star Kingdom's spiritual matters as you do in the Protectorate's."

"You might be surprised," Sullivan said wryly. "Our doctrine of the Test makes for a certain spiritual obstreperousness."

"But obstreperousness can be a good thing, as long as you learn to pay attention to its causes," Telmachi replied. "We found that out the hard way in my own Church. In fact, I believe we'd begun discovering it well before your own ancestors departed for Grayson."

"As did we, with those lunatics on Masada," Sullivan said more grimly.

"Every Faith has its moments of lunacy, Reverend." Telmachi

shook his head sadly. "The Inquisition, the Islamic terrorist movement, the New Athens Jihad, your own Faithful. . . . Extremism is no one's monopoly when faith turns to fanaticism."

"But no one faith has a monopoly on *resisting* fanaticism, either," Sullivan replied. "A point certain of my own predecessors have had difficulty remembering on Grayson, given Father Church's monopoly—" he reused the word deliberately "—on spiritual authority there."

"Perhaps," Telmachi said. "Yet I think no one could accuse you or Reverend Hanks of that. I've deeply admired the way both of you have grappled with the huge changes your society has faced in the wake of your alliance with the Star Kingdom."

"You mean, in the wake of our having been exposed to an entire galaxy of dangerous, if not downright heretical, notions about radical things like women's rights," Sullivan corrected with an easy chuckle.

"Well, of course I did. But I'm far too diplomatic to ever say so."

Both men laughed, but then Telmachi sat back in his chair, crossed his legs, and looked at his visitor thoughtfully.

"Your Grace, I'm truly delighted to meet you, and I see you're just as engaging in person as Monsignor Davidson's reports indicated. But I'm also aware this is the first time in the history of Grayson any Reverend has ever left the planet for any reason. I've issued all the expected press statements and news releases, and I've arranged to attend the meetings with representatives of all of our major religions and denominations which you requested. But I must confess I wasn't very surprised when your staff contacted mine to suggest a private preliminary meeting between the two of us."

"You weren't?" Sullivan asked, leaning back in his own chair.

"No. Monsignor Davidson is, as I'm sure you've discovered, as intelligent as he is charming. From certain questions which you'd asked him, he concluded you were particularly interested in establishing direct contact with me. He did not, however, suggest a reason for your interest, although I may have drawn a few conclusions of my own."

Sullivan looked out the window, at the sky-piercing towers of the City of Landing. It was a fascinatingly alien sight for any Grayson. Landing had been built by a counter-gravity civilization, on a planet whose environment had welcomed mankind, rather than attempting to repel the audacious invader. Its buildings towered far higher than any Grayson structure, and there wasn't a single environmental dome in sight. All that unobstructed sky was enough to make any Grayson nervous, especially when he watched the branches of the city greenbelts' trees dance in the brisk morning breeze. The Reverend felt almost undressed, and his hand twitched as he suppressed the reflex to reach for the breath mask normally cased on the right side of his belt. The fact that airborne dust on Manticore didn't represent a dangerous toxic threat was something his intellect had accepted more readily than his emotions. And yet, as he looked at the moving air cars, the pedestrians, the sidewalk cafes he could see from where he sat, he saw much the same people, however bizarrely some of them were dressed, as he might have seen at home.

He turned to gaze at the Archbishop once more, and there, too, he found the alien mingled with the utterly familiar. He recognized Telmachi's personal faith, and his genuine welcome, and Sullivan had deliberately immersed himself in studies of comparative theology since Grayson had been wrenched into the galactic mainstream. He saw in Telmachi the current heir to an apostolic succession stretching clear back to the dawn—the source—of their shared faith in God. And yet, Telmachi's spiritual authority was far less than his own. *His* Church had seen its uncontested primacy broken long before Man ever left Old Earth, and it had come to terms with that. It had evolved, survived, reached out to the stars along with a multiplicity of other religious beliefs and ways of thought which would have been totally bewildering to any Grayson. In many ways, he knew, Telmachi was far more . . . cosmopolitan than he himself was, but was that strength, or was it weakness? And in Telmachi, did Sullivan see the Reverends of Grayson's future?

That lay in God's hands, the Reverend told himself. One of the cardinal elements of the New Way, perhaps *the* cardinal element, was the belief that the book was never closed, never ended. God was infinite; Man's understanding was not. And so, there would always be more for Man to learn, more for God to teach him, and as the doctrine of the Test taught, it was best to pay attention to one's lessons, whatever the form in which they might come.

Like his visit here, today.

"Actually, Archbishop," he said, "you're right. I see Monsignor Davidson's description of your own intelligence was accurate. I do have many pressing and completely valid reasons, as Father Church's spiritual head, for meeting with as many Manticoran religious leaders as possible. For almost a thousand years, Grayson has been effectively a theocracy—a *closed* theocracy. Given our doctrines, our people have tended, by and large, to see the opening of the doors of our temple, as it were, as yet another of God's Tests. There's been some friction, but less, I suspect, than there would have been on almost any other planet under similar circumstances.

"Still, as we've become more and more integrally involved with the Star Kingdom on a secular level, the influx of foreigners with their very foreign belief structures has swelled steadily. I see no reason to believe that tendency will reverse itself, and so I think it's probably past time Father Church reached out his hand to the Star Kingdom's religious leadership. There will undoubtedly be misunderstandings, or at least points of difference, but we must embrace the religious toleration which has always been a part of the Manticoran tradition. To that end, my visit to Manticore will have great significance for Father Church's members back home on Grayson.

"Yet, while all of that is true, the reason I specifically asked to meet with you had less to do with the fact that you are, whether you choose to admit it or not, what I suppose I might think of as the senior member of the Manticoran religious establishment, than it did with a pastoral concern."

"Pastoral." Telmachi smiled. "Let me see," he murmured. "Now, what could it possibly be about? Hmmm. . . . Could it be something to do with Steadholder Harrington and certain members of my own flock?"

"Monsignor Davidson didn't do you justice, Your Grace," Sullivan said with an answering smile.

"It wasn't very difficult to guess, Your Grace," Telmachi replied. "Especially not in light of Dame Honor's stature on Grayson and the rather poisonous commentary of one of our less than scintillating examples of journalistic professionalism. Of course, the fact that she's neither Catholic nor a member of the Church of Humanity Unchained does leave both of us in rather a gray area where she's concerned."

"She may not be a daughter of Father Church," Sullivan said quietly, his eyes level, "but of my own experience, I can tell you she is most certainly a daughter of God. I'll be honest with you and admit that nothing would give me greater joy than to have her embrace Father Church, but this is one woman for whose soul I feel no concern at all."

"That accords well with my own impression of her," Telmachi said seriously. "I believe she's a Third Stellar?"

"She is. Which presents me with something of a problem, since the Third Stellars appear to have no organized hierarchy in the sense your Church or mine does."

"The Third Stellars are actually rather like I suppose the Church of Humanity might have turned out without a firmly established hierarchy," Telmachi said. "When the representatives of all their congregations meet for their General Convocation every three T-years, they elect a leadership for the Convocation, and also the membership of a Coordinating Committee to function between Convocations, but each congregation—and each individual member of each congregation—is personally responsible for his or her relationship with God. I'm on quite good terms with several of their clergy, and one of them compared their General Convocation to an exercise in herding treecats."

Sullivan chuckled at the image, and Telmachi nodded.

"They agree about a great many core doctrines and issues, but beyond those central areas of agreement, there's room for an enormous diversity."

"I'd gathered that impression from my own conversations with Lady Harrington and her parents," Sullivan agreed. "And I believe you're probably correct—the . . . individualism the Third Stellars encourage does have many resonances with our own doctrine. Indeed, I've often thought that was one of the reasons Lady Harrington's been so comfortable with Father Church, despite our inevitable differences.

"However, the problem to which I referred was my inability to identify some one individual member of the Third Stellar clergy with whom to discuss my concerns. My impression of their doctrine is that it is extremely . . . inclusive, but I must confess I'm less familiar with it than I could wish."

"If your concerns are what I suspect they are, Your Grace," Telmachi said, "I think you don't need to worry. However, I'd be very happy to suggest two or three of their theologians with whom you might discuss your thoughts."

"I would deeply appreciate that," Sullivan said, bending his head in an abbreviated bow of thanks. "But that, of course, brings me to the reason I specifically needed to meet with you."

"Reverend," Telmachi said with another chuckle, "*Mother* Church has learned a few lessons of her own over the millennia. I don't believe there will be any problems."

"So, *here* you are," Dr. Allison Harrington said severely. "And just what made you think you were going to be allowed to stay at a *hotel*, if I may ask?"

"The Royal Arms Hilton is scarcely a mere 'hotel,' My Lady," Jeremiah Sullivan replied mildly as he stepped past a solemn Harrington armsman into the foyer of Honor's Jason Bay mansion. He smiled, then bent over her hand and kissed it in approved Grayson style.

"*Piffle!*" she shot back. "I'll bet it was really just that you planned on stealing the towels. Or one of those cute little bathrobes of theirs."

The armsman seemed to cringe slightly, obviously awaiting the thunderbolt, but Sullivan only smiled more broadly as her eyes twinkled at him.

"It was the soap, actually, My Lady," he said solemnly.

"I knew it!"

She gurgled a laugh and tucked her arm through his as she escorted him into the house.

"It's good to see you," she said more seriously. "And while I'm sure you really would have been perfectly comfortable at the Royal Arms, Honor and Benjamin would both have wanted my scalp if I'd let you stay there. Besides, I wouldn't have been that happy about it myself."

"Thank you," he said.

"Nonsense." She squeezed his arm tighter, and the laughter in her eyes was momentarily quenched. "I still remember how comforting you were when we all thought Honor was dead."

"As I remember the day you explained to me why our birthrate has always been so skewed," he replied. "*And* the day you and your team made your nanites available."

"Yes. Well, now that we've both congratulated one another on what splendid people we are," Allison said, "what *really* brings you to Manticore?"

"Why, what makes you think I might have any sort of ulterior motivation?" Sullivan fenced, accepting the change of subject with a smile.

"The fact that I have a functional brain," she replied tartly. He looked at her, and she snorted. "In a thousand years, not one Reverend has ever left the planet. Not one. Now, three weeks after that poisonous toad Hayes' articles must have reached Grayson, here you are. Allowing a week or so for travel time, you must have set some sort of galactic record for arranging this 'state visit' of yours!"

"I do hope," Sullivan said a bit plaintively, "that my Machiavellian schemes aren't going to be this transparent to *every* Manticoran I meet."

"Most Manticorans don't know you as well as I've come to," Allison assured him comfortably. "And most other Manticorans wouldn't begin to understand how damaging something like this could be to a political figure like Honor on Grayson. Or," she smiled warmly at him again, "how deeply you care about my daughter."

He inclined his head slightly, and she nodded.

"I thought so. You've come to straighten out the children's problems, haven't you?"

He burst out laughing, and she paused, turning to smile up at him until he shook his head.

"My Lady, all of the 'children' involved, including your daughter, are quite a few T-years older than I am!"

"Chronologically, perhaps. In other ways?" She shrugged. "And whatever your comparative ages may be, they *definitely* need straightening out. Which *is* why you're here, isn't it?"

"Yes, Allison," he admitted, surrendering at last. "I do intend to accomplish a few other things while I'm here, but, yes. Mostly, I came to straighten out the children's problems."

Chapter Twenty-Nine

"Tell me you've got some good news for a change, Armand," Thomas Theisman said moodily as the naval Chief of Staff stepped into his office with a memo board clasped under his left arm.

"The only 'good' news I've got is a follow up report that Belle-feuille survived after all," Admiral Marquette replied.

"She did?" Theisman perked up just a bit, and Marquette nodded.

"She and her entire staff got off *Cyrus* before the scuttling charges blew. We lost a lot of good people, but not her, thank God."

"Absolutely," Theisman agreed fervently.

Of the four star systems Harrington had hit this time around, only Chantilly had mounted any effective resistance. Not for want of trying, he reminded himself grimly. Rear Admiral Bressand had done his best in Augusta, but he'd been totally outclassed and outgunned . . . and not as cunning as Jennifer Bellefeuille. Harrington's pod-layers had reduced his hyper-capable combatants to scrap metal in return for minor, if any, damage. And when his LACs had closed with suicidal gallantry, they had discovered that the Manties' counter-missile tubes, at least aboard their newer construction, were perfectly capable of launching the "dogfighting" missiles they'd developed for their damned *Katanas*.

It had been a massacre, and not one for which he could blame Bressand. A part of him would have liked to, and he could actually make a case for it, if he really tried. After all, Bressand could have exercised his discretion and declined to engage such a massively superior force. But the reason that force had been so superior to his was that his own superiors—headed by one Thomas Theisman—had failed to adequately support him.

Bressand had done his job with what he had, and, like Bellefeuille in Chantilly, he'd obviously hoped to inflict at least attritional damage on the raiders. And that, Theisman reminded himself, was probably a direct consequence of the staff analysis he'd ordered shared with all of his system commanders. Given the numerical advantage the Republic enjoyed—or shortly would enjoy—even an unfavorable exchange rate was ultimately in Haven's favor. He'd ordered that analysis disseminated because it was true, yet it had been much easier to accept its truth before so many thousands of Navy men and women had died in Augusta.

"Do we have a better read on the damage Bellefeuille managed to inflict?" he asked Marquette, resolutely turning his mind away from Bressand.

"We hurt their LACs pretty badly, relatively speaking," Marquette said. Then he grimaced. "I can't believe I just said that. Bellefeuille took out about seventy of their LACs, including fifty or so of their *Katanas*, in return for just over *five hundred* of our own. As exchange rates go, that sucks, but it's the equivalent of about three quarters of one of their LAC groups, and much as I hate to say it, we can replace our personnel and materiel losses more easily than they can.

"On the starship side, we didn't do as well. Mostly because those damned new battlecruisers of theirs are a hell of a lot tougher than a battlecruiser has any right being. We hammered one of their pod-layers pretty badly—her wedge strength was down, and she was venting a lot of atmosphere by the end. Bellefeuille's other main target—that big-assed 'battlecruiser' that just has to be this new *Nike* we've been hearing rumors about—got off with what was probably only minor damage."

Marquette shook his head, his expression rueful.

"That's a very tough ship, Tom. And they appear to have armed her with that new, smaller MDM NavInt's also been hearing about. By the way, that's how the staff weenies figure they've managed to cram so many missiles into their battlecruiser pod-layers' pods. They're using pods big enough to fire all-up missiles, but loading them with these smaller ones. It costs them something in total powered envelope, but it also increases their throw weight, and accuracy at extreme range's so poor the heavier fire more than compensates across the *effective* envelope. And the reports that they're somehow firing both broadsides simultaneously from their more conventionally armed ships—and doing it while they're rolled on their sides relative to their targets, to boot—seem to be confirmed."

"Wonderful." Theisman turned his chair to gaze out the window behind his desk at the massive towers of the city of Nouveau Paris, all of them freshly refurbished and properly maintained for the first time in his memory. Clean windows glittered in the slanting rays of the westering sun, air cars and air buses moved steadily in the traffic lanes, and the walkways and pedestrian slideways were crowded with busy, purposeful people. It was a scene of rebirth and revitalization—of rediscovery—of which he rarely tired, but today, his expression was profoundly unhappy.

"How are we going to respond, Tom?" Marquette asked quietly after a moment, and Theisman's expression turned unhappier still. He stared out the window into the sunset for several more seconds, then turned back to face the Chief of Staff.

"We've got two options—well, three, I suppose. We could do nothing, which wouldn't exactly sit well with Congress or the public at large. We could immediately launch a general offensive, which *might* succeed, but probably wouldn't—at least until we've got more of the new construction up to speed and ready for action—and which definitely would entail heavy casualties. Or we dust off the contingency plans for Operation Gobi and hand it to Lester."

"Of the three, my gut reaction is to favor Gobi," Marquette said. "Especially given the intelligence we've managed to gather and the operational data Diamato brought back."

"I think I agree with you, but that doesn't make me extraordinarily happy. It's going to divert us and disperse at least a sizable fraction of the striking force we've been working so hard to build up. Worse, it's going to take at least three weeks or a month for Lester to get it up and running. If the Manties stick to their apparent operational tempo, that means they'll hit us again at least once while we're hitting them."

"We could have him try something a little more extemporaneous." Marquette didn't seem especially pleased by his own suggestion, but he continued anyway. "He's got Second Fleet's core organization just about set up, and he's got a nucleus of experienced units to go with the new ones. He could probably slice off a battle squadron or two for a quick-and-dirty, off-the-cuff job if we told him to."

"No." Theisman shook his head firmly. "If we hand him Gobi—and I think we're going to have to—he gets time to set it up right. I saw too many operations fucked up when the old management decided to improvise and demand miracles. I won't send our people in without adequate time to prepare unless there's absolutely no other alternative."

"Yes, Sir," Marquette said quietly, and Theisman smiled almost apologetically at him.

"Sorry. Didn't mean to sound like I was biting your head off. I think maybe I'm using you to rehearse what I'm going to wind up saying in front of the Naval Committee when *it* wants to know why we haven't already kicked the Manties' asses."

"I suppose it shouldn't really have come as a surprise that a genuine representative government's no more immune to the 'But what have you done for me *recently*?' syndrome than the Legislaturalists were," Marquette said sourly.

"No, it shouldn't have. But it's still a lot more satisfying to work for. And at least we don't have to worry about being shot, just fired."

"True."

Marquette stood for a moment, rubbing his chin thoughtfully, then cocked his head.

"Actually, Tom," he said slowly, "there may be a *fourth* option. Or, at least, one we could try in conjunction with Gobi."

"Really?" Theisman regarded him quizzically.

"Well, Lewis and Linda have handed me their tea leaf-readers' best guess as to the most threatened systems. Their report is full of qualifiers, of course. Not so much because they're try-ing to cover their asses, as because they really don't have a good predictive model. They're having to use more intuition and old fashioned WAGs than number-crunching at this point, and they don't like it. Despite that, though, I think they're on to something."

"Tell me more," Theisman commanded, and pointed at one of the chairs facing his desk.

"Basically," Marquette said, sitting obediently, "they tried looking at the problem through Manty eyes. They figure the Manties are looking for targets they can anticipate will be fairly lightly defended, but which have enough population and representation to generate a lot of political pressure. They're also hitting systems with a civilian economy which may not be contributing very much to the war effort, but which is large enough to require the federal government to undertake a substantial diversion of emergency assistance when it's destroyed. And it's also pretty clear that they want to impress us with their aggressiveness. That's why they're operating so deep. Well, that and because the deeper they get, the further away from the 'frontline' systems, the less likely we are to have heavy defensive forces in position to intercept them. So that means we should be looking at deep penetration targets, not frontier raids."

"All of that sounds reasonable," Theisman said after considering it. "Logical, anyway. Of course, logic is only as good as its basic assumptions."

"Agreed. But it's worth noting that two of the systems they predicted might be hit were Des Moines and Fordyce."

"They were?" Theisman sat a bit straighter, and Marquette nodded.

"And Chantilly was on their secondary list of less likely targets."

"That *is* interesting. On the other hand, how many *other* systems were on their lists?"

"Ten on the primary list and fifteen on the secondary."

"So they hit three out of a total of twenty-five. Twelve percent."

"Which is a hell of a lot better than nothing," Marquette pointed out.

"Oh, no question. But we could fritter away an awful lot of strength trying to cover a list of systems that long without being strong enough in any one place to make a difference."

"That wasn't really what I had in mind."

"Then tell me what you *did* have in mind."

"You and I—and our analysts, for that matter—agree that these raids represent what's basically a strategy of weakness. They're trying to hurt us and throw us off balance for a minimal investment in forces and minimal losses of their own. So I would submit that we don't really have to stop them dead everywhere;

we just have to hammer them really hard once or twice. Hurt them proportionately worse than they're hurting us."

"All right." Theisman nodded. "I'm in agreement so far."

"Well, Javier's doing a lot of expansion work, too, if not as much as Lester. He's been discussing training missions and simulations to fit his new units into existing battle squadrons and task group organizations, and he'd really like a chance to try some of his task force and task group commanders in independent command before it's a life-or-death situation. What if we were to take, say, three or four—maybe a half-dozen—of those task groups and pull them back from the front? We're not going to be committing them to offensive action anytime soon, and it's obvious the Manties aren't going to launch any frontal assaults when they're running this sensitive about losses. So it wouldn't weaken our offensive stance, and it would give us some powerful forces close to likely targets, plus an opportunity to test and refine our new tactical doctrines."

"Ummm . . . ." Theisman gazed into space, the fingers of his right hand drumming lightly on his blotter. He stayed that way for quite some time, then refocused on Marquette.

"I think this has . . . possibilities," he said. "I should've thought of a similar approach on my own, but I guess I've been too fixated on maintaining concentration instead of swanning around in understrength detachments the way we used to operate. There are still some risks involved, though. Strategy of weakness or no, this is clearly their first team we're talking about. If it weren't, Harrington wouldn't be in command of it. So it's not something we want to throw green units in front of."

"I was figuring we'd use detachments working up a relatively smaller percentage of new units," Marquette replied. "And, while I'm thinking about it, I think it would be a very good idea to put Javier himself in position to cover the system we think is most likely to be hit."

"Now *that* is a very good notion." Theisman nodded enthusiastically. "He's still kicking himself over Trevor's Star, and pointing out to him that he's being wise with the benefit of hindsight doesn't seem to help much. It'd make a lot of sense for him to be involved in training his own squadrons, and if he just happened to kick the ass of a Manty raid . . ."

"That's what I was thinking," Marquette agreed. "It would do a world of good for his confidence, and the shot in the arm it would provide for public and fleet morale wouldn't be anything to sneer at, either."

"And if we get some of Shannon's new goodies deployed to help him out, things could get hot enough for even 'the Salamander' to think twice about climbing back into the oven again," Theisman said.

He thought about it again for several seconds, then nodded once more.

"Sit down with Linda. Draft me a preliminary plan for it by tomorrow afternoon."

Chapter Thirty

"Excuse me, Your Grace."

Honor paused in her conversation with Mercedes Brigham, Alice Truman, Alistair McKeon, and Samuel Miklós, and one eyebrow rose in surprise. It was very unlike James MacGuiness to insert himself into a serious meeting like this. He was a past master at unobtrusively refilling coffee and cocoa cups, sliding food in front of people when they started looking peaked, and otherwise keeping them provided with whatever they needed. But the key word was "unobtrusively." Most of the time, people never even realized he'd been there until he was already gone.

That was her first thought. Her second was more concerned as she tasted his emotions.

"What is it, Mac?" she asked as Nimitz sat upright on the back of her chair and pricked his ears at the man who still insisted on functioning as Honor's steward.

"You have a personal message, Your Grace. From your mother." Honor stiffened, eyes darkening with concern. "I have no idea what it's about," he continued quickly, "but it came up in the standard mailbag from Jason Bay. If it were really bad news, I'm sure it would have been delivered by special courier. For that matter, Miranda would have dropped me a line about it, as well."

"You're right, of course, Mac," she said, smiling in thanks for his reassurance.

"On the other hand, Your Grace," he said, "it does carry a priority code. I really think you ought to view it as soon as possible."

"I see."

MacGuiness bobbed his head and withdrew, and Honor frowned thoughtfully for a moment. Then she shook herself and returned her attention to her guests.

"I think we're just about at a decent stopping point, anyway, aren't we?" she said.

"I think so," Truman agreed. "We need to spend a little more time kicking around what happened at Chantilly, but we can do that later. I'd never heard of this Admiral Bellefeuille until she screened me after the shooting was over to thank us for arranging the full evacuation of the civilian platforms before we blew them. She was floating around in a pinnace—or maybe even a life pod—for most of that time, I understand. But I think we need to bring her name to ONI's attention. This woman is *sneaky*, Honor. She reminds me a lot of what you've said about Shannon Foraker, and if she'd had better information on our defensive capabilities, we'd have gotten hurt a lot worse."

"It was bad enough, anyway," McKeon growled, shaking his head. "*Hector*'s going to be out of action for at least three months."

"I know, I know," Truman sighed. "But at least Hanover's personnel casualties were light. To be perfectly honest, I'm more distressed by what happened to my *Katanas*. We managed a four- or five-to-one exchange rate even after Bellefeuille tricked us into firing off so many of their missiles, but that's pretty cold comfort. And," she looked at Honor, "Scotty blames himself."

"That's ridiculous," McKeon said sharply.

"I agree entirely," Truman replied. "The deployment decision was mine—not his, not Mike Henke's, but mine. Given what I knew at the time, I'd do the same thing again, too. But Scotty seems to think he should have argued with me, although exactly what form of clairvoyance was supposed to tell him this was coming eludes me."

"And how is Mike taking it?" Honor asked quietly.

"Better than I was afraid she might, actually," Truman said. "She's not happy about it, and especially not about the fact that she was the one who suggested using *Hector* and *Nike* as her point. But the truth is that she was right. *Hector* may have gotten hammered, but her core hull was never penetrated, and she and *Nike* stood up to missile attack even better than BuShips predicted they might. And if Dillinger hadn't used up so many of his Vipers defending Oversteegen's division, he'd have made out much better against the Peep LACs. I think she's drawn the right conclusions."

Honor nodded. She knew both Truman and McKeon well enough to be confident they understood why she was concerned without getting any more specific.

"I hope you and she both have," she said aloud, smiling wryly at Truman. "The two of you are developing a nasty habit of always finding the feistiest system defense forces! I'd appreciate it if you'd cut that out."

"Hey, you're the one assigning the targets," Truman shot back. "Well, you and Mercedes here."

"Don't blame me!" Brigham protested. "*My* idea of how to assign the task forces was to pull system names out of a hat. For some reason, neither Andrea nor Her Grace thought that was a wonderful idea."

"Nonsense," Honor said as the other admirals laughed. "What I said was that it didn't seem very professional and it wouldn't do very much for the public's confidence in the Navy if we did it that way and word got out."

"As long as it works as well as it seems to be working so far, I don't think they'd have any problems," McKeon said, and Truman and Miklós nodded in agreement.

"Then let's keep it that way, shall we?" Honor replied. "And on that note, I think we should probably adjourn and let me find out what's on Mother's mind. Alice, could you have dinner with me this evening? And invite Mike and Oversteegen along? For that matter, bring Scotty and Harkness, too; I haven't seen either of them in a while, and their perspective on something like this is almost always worth getting. Let's go over it with all of them in person. As you say, we need to get a better feel for what Bellefeuille did to us, and I'd like to give Mike and Oversteegen, especially, a chance to talk out their own reactions to it."

"I think that would be a good idea," Truman agreed.

"In that case, people, let's be about it."

"Hello, Honor," Allison Harrington said, and smiled from Honor's display. "We got the news about your return this morning—Hamish screened from Admiralty House to tell us you and Nimitz are back safe and sound. Obviously, we're all delighted to hear that . . . some even more than others."

She smiled again, wickedly, but then her expression grew more serious.

"I'm sure you have all sorts of Navy things you need to attend to, but I think it would be a very good idea if you could come home for a day or two. Soon."

Honor felt herself tightening internally. Nothing about her mother's expression suggested anything terrible, but she was a little surprised to realize how much it bothered her to be unable to taste Allison's emotions from the recorded message. Had she become that reliant upon her odd empathic capabilities?

"There are several reasons I feel that way, dear," Allison continued. "Among them, the fact that Reverend Sullivan's extended his visit to the Star Kingdom. They were going to put him up at the Royal Arms, but I put a stop to that, and he's been comfortably ensconced here at the Bay House. I'm sure that one reason he's stayed over longer than he originally planned was to see you before he returns to Grayson. So take care of anything you really need to deal with, and then hop one of the shuttle flights home as soon as you can. We're all really eager to see you. I love you. Bye!"

The display blanked, and Honor frowned. A lifetime's instincts told her there was more to her mother's request than a simple desire for her to have dinner with Sullivan before the Reverend went home. Not that that wouldn't have been a perfectly valid consideration. It just wasn't the only thing on her mother's mind, and she wondered exactly what sort of devious scheme was revolving inside that agile brain.

Unfortunately, there was only one way to find out, and she punched a button on her com.

"Admiral's Quarters, MacGuiness speaking," a voice said.

"Mac, please check my calendar with Mercedes. You and she both know what I'm doing better than I do, anyway. I need to clear a couple of days, the sooner the better, for a quick hop back to Manticore."

"I thought you might, Ma'am." Even across the voice-only circuit, Honor could almost feel his satisfaction. "I've already checked. I believe that if you shift a few of your meetings—and possibly combine the meetings you'd scheduled with the division and squadron commanders into a single session—you could be on the evening shuttle flight tomorrow. Would that be satisfactory?"

"And have you already discussed your proposed agenda with my chief of staff, O Puppetmaster?"

"Not in any specific detail, Ma'am." MacGuiness' dignified response was somewhat flawed by the chuckle lurking in its depths.

"Well, do so."

"Of course, Your Grace."

"There's the limo, My Lady."

Honor turned her head, looking in the indicated direction, and saw Jeremiah Tennard, the senior of Faith's personal armsmen, standing beside the door of one of the VIP lounge's private air car stages.

"So I see, Andrew," she said, and chuckled. "I wonder how Mother pried him loose from fending off assassination attempts on Faith to send him after us?"

"Actually," Andrew LaFollet said seriously, "we have a very good team in place at the house. Especially since Captain Zilwicki upgraded our electronic systems for us. He's not really running any risks leaving her uncovered, My Lady. You know I wouldn't tolerate that, don't you?"

"Andrew, it was a *joke*," she said, turning back to him. "I didn't—"

She stopped speaking as she tasted her personal armsman's emotions. No one, looking at his expression, could doubt for a moment the earnest seriousness of his response to her question. She, however, had certain additional advantages, and her eyes narrowed.

"All right," she told him. "You got me. For a minute, there, I actually thought you were serious."

"My Lady," he said in shocked tones, "I'm *always* serious!"

"You, Andrew LaFollet," she said severely, "have been hanging around with Nimitz entirely too long. His questionable excuse for a sense of humor seems to have infected you."

Nimitz bleeked a laugh on her shoulder, and his hands flashed.

The first two fingers of his right true-hand closed onto his thumb. Then the hand rolled over, palm downward, and folded into the sign for the letter "N" and jerked slightly downward. Next, it rose to his temple, curled into the closed fist sign for the letter "E," and moved forward. Both true-hands folded their fingers over in the palm-up sign for the letter "A," then swung inward and down twice, ending palm-down. The right hand extended all three long, wiry fingers, while the left hand extended only two, signing the number five in one of the compromises forced upon the treecats by the fact that they had fewer digits than humans did. Next, both true-hands rose, slightly bent, fingertips just touching his chest, and the right hand flicked back slightly before turning to form a palm-out "A" that moved slightly to his right. Then the two opened fingers of the letter "P" circled his face before the right true-hand touched its fingers to his chin, then dropped into the palm of his left true-hand. The bent second finger of his right true-hand tapped behind his ear, then fell to meet his left true-hand as he linked the thumb and first fingers of both hands before raising both hands to the corners of his mouth in the "H" sign.

"So there was no need for you to infect him, since he already had a good sense of humor?" Honor said.

Nimitz nodded and raised his right true-hand, palm-in, to press his forefinger to his forehead, then twisted it into a palm out position before it closed into the upright, thumb-extended fist of the letter "A." Then he held up two fingers and patted the thigh of his right leg with his right true-hand formed into the extended forefinger and thumb of an "L."

"Oh, for a 'two-legs' is it?" she demanded, and he nodded again, even more complacently, while she shook her head. "You're riding for a fall there, Stinker. Besides, I *know* your sense of humor, and I don't think the sign for 'good' means quite what you think it does."

The 'cat only looked away, flirting his tail airily, and LaFollet chuckled.

"Don't take that as a compliment," Honor told him darkly. "Not until you've discussed some of his ideas of what constitutes a joke with the Harrington House staff, at any rate."

"Oh, I have, My Lady!" LaFollet assured her. "My favorite was the one with the stuffed treecat and the cultivator."

"Stuffed treecat?" Honor's eyebrows arched, and he chuckled again.

"They were using the robotic cultivators to trench for the new irrigation system," the armsman explained. "So Nimitz and Farragut kidnapped one of the lifesized stuffed treecats from Faith's bedroom."

"They didn't—" Honor began, dark eyes starting to laugh, and LaFollet nodded.

"Oh, but they did, My Lady. They used those sharp little claws of theirs to . . . disconnect the front and back ends, then burrowed down on either side of the trench and left the tail sticking up on one side and one poor, pathetic true-hand poking up on the other. The assistant gardener almost died on the spot when he found it."

"Stinker," Honor said, as severely as a sudden attack of giggles would permit, "when they finally come for you with pitchforks, *I'm* not going to protect you from the mob. I hope you realize that right now."

Nimitz sniffed, elevating his muzzle. Timothy Meares had hopped the same shuttle flight back to Manticore with his Admiral, and he laughed out loud. Honor gave him a glare and shook her head at him.

"A proper flag lieutenant does *not* encourage his Admiral's 'cat in the ways of evil, Lieutenant Meares!"

"Of course not, Ma'am!" Meares agreed, eyes twinkling. "I'm shocked that you should think I would even consider doing such a thing!"

"Sure you are," Honor growled. Then she smiled at him as Tennard started across the lounge towards them. "As Andrew says, our ride is here, Tim. Can we drop you anywhere?"

"No, thanks, Ma'am. I'll catch a cab. I need to do a little shopping before I head home to surprise Mom and Dad."

"All right, then you'd best be about it," she said, and he smiled back at her, saluted, and trotted off just as Tennard reached them.

"My Lady, Colonel." The armsman bowed to Honor in greeting.

"Jeremiah." Honor nodded back. "It's good to see you."

"And you, My Lady. We've missed you—all of us. Especially Faith, I think."

"How is she?" Honor asked.

"Excited about her new nephew," Tennard replied, with a smile.

"Is she really?"

"Really, My Lady," Tennard said, reassuringly. "Don't forget, she's seen what Bernard Raoul has to put up with, and she's a smart child. She's already figured out that she's been getting off light where her own security detachment is concerned, compared to most steadholders' heirs, and I don't think she really wants to have to put up with any more of us armsmen than she has to. At this particular point in her life, avoiding that is a lot more important than being Steadholder Harrington could ever be."

"Good," Honor sighed. Then she smiled. "And I suppose you're here to ferry me off to meet the Reverend at the house?"

"To meet the Reverend, yes, My Lady. But not at the Bay House. You and your parents are having dinner at White Haven this evening, and he's joining you there."

"He's what?" Honor blinked, but Tennard only shrugged.

"That's the itinerary I was given, My Lady. If *you* want to argue with your Lady Mother about it, you go right ahead. *I* have better sense."

"Mother's been a terrible influence on all of you armsmen," Honor said. "I don't remember you being this uppity before she got hold of you!"

"It's all purely self-defense, My Lady, I promise," Tennard said earnestly, and she laughed.

"*That* I can believe. All right. If it's White Haven, it's White Haven. Let's get this cavalcade in the air."

"What the—?!" Timothy Meares jerked back as he opened the air cab door and got hit in the face with an eye-stinging spray of moisture.

"Oh, shit!" a voice said, and he blinked his burning eyes, then found himself glaring somewhat blearily at the cabby on the other side of the opened partition between the cockpit and the passenger compartment. She was an attractive, if not spectacular, blonde, and she held a bottle of commercial air freshener in one hand, still pointed almost directly at Meares. She also wore an expression of almost comical dismay.

"I'm so *sorry*, Lieutenant!" she said quickly. "I didn't see you coming, and my last fare was a smoker." She shook her head in angry disgust. "Big sign, right there," she jabbed her head at the "No Smoking In This Vehicle" notice on the partition, "and the jerk sits right down and lights up. A *cigar*, of all damned things. And not a very expensive one, from the stink!"

The air freshener's scent was almost overpowering, but as it began to dissipate, Meares could smell the tobacco reek to which she'd referred. And, he admitted, it really was pretty bad.

"So I was just turning around to spritz some of this stuff—" she waved the air freshener "—and you opened the door, and, well . . ."

Her voice trailed off, and her expression was such a mixture of dismay and apology that Meares had to laugh.

"Hey, I've had worse happen, okay?" he said, wiping the last film of air freshener off his face. "And you're right. It is pretty ripe back here. So I'll just stand back and let you spray away to your heart's content."

"Oh, gee, thanks!" she said, and applied the air freshener industriously for several seconds. Then she sniffed critically.

"That's about as good as it's going to get, I'm afraid," she said. "You still want a ride? Or do you want to wait for something that smells a little fresher?"

"This smells just fine to me," Meares said, and climbed into the cab.

"Where to?" she asked.

"I need to do some shopping, so let's hit Yardman's first."

"You got it," she agreed, and the cab whined away towards the capital's best known shopping tower.

Behind it, a nondescript man watched it with carefully incurious eyes, then turned and walked away.

"Hello, Nico," Honor said as Nico Havenhurst opened the front door for her. "You seem to have quite a mob out here this evening."

"Oh, it's been more crowded than this upon occasion, Your Grace," Havenhurst said, stepping back with a welcoming smile. "Not in the last few decades, you understand, but—"

He shrugged, and Honor chuckled. Then she stepped past him into the entrance hall, and paused in mid-stride. Emily, Hamish, and her parents were there. So was Reverend Sullivan, but Honor had expected that. What she hadn't expected was the distinguished, dark-haired man in the episcopal purple cassock and glittering pectoral cross. She recognized him almost instantly, although they'd never met, and she wondered what Archbishop Telmachi was doing at White Haven.

Surprise kept her focused on him for at least a few heartbeats. Long enough for her feet to get reorganized and resume carrying her forward. She'd just noticed the younger man standing at Telmachi's elbow and recognized him as Father O'Donnell, Emily and Hamish's parish priest, when the mingled flow of the welcoming committee's emotions swept over her.

There were too many individual sources for her to analyze their feelings clearly, but Hamish and Emily's strands stood out more clearly than those of anyone else, including her parents. She felt herself reaching out for them, as automatically as breathing, and then both eyebrows rose as she tasted the mingled love, determination, apprehension, and almost giddy anticipation rising off of them like smoke.

Obviously, she'd been right to suspect her mother was up to something. But what?

"Hello, Honor," Emily said calmly, reaching out her hand. "It's good to see you home."

The meal, as always, was delicious, although Honor decided Mistress Thorne could have taught Tabitha DuPuy a thing or two about poaching salmon. The company had also been convivial, and Honor was pleased by the genuine friendship and mutual admiration she tasted between Sullivan and Telmachi. The Star Kingdom was legally nondenominational, with a specific constitutional bar against any state religion. Despite that, the Archbishop of Manticore was recognized as the "dean" of the Manticoran religious community, and she was glad he and Sullivan had hit it off so well.

But despite that, and despite her happiness at being home, she found it increasingly difficult not to select someone at random to strangle as supper went on and on and the strange combination of the Alexanders' emotions—and her parents', and even *Sullivan's*, now that she thought about it—continued to swirl about her. She still didn't have a clue what they were all so . . . energized about, which was maddening enough. But what made it even more maddening was her absolute confidence that it all focused on *her*, somehow.

At last, finally, the dessert dishes were cleared away, the servants withdrew, and the Alexanders and their guests were left alone around the huge table. It was the first time Honor had ever eaten in White Haven's formal dining salon, and despite its low ceiling and ancient wood paneling, she found it just a bit overpowering. Possibly because it was half the size of a basketball court, or seemed that way, at least, after the more intimate quarters in which she, Hamish, and Emily normally dined.

"Well," her mother said brightly as the door to the serving pantry closed, "here we all are at last!"

"Yes," Honor said, handing a last celery stalk to Nimitz, "here we are, indeed, Mother. The question in my mind—and it does appear to be in *my* mind, alone, since everyone else at this table obviously already knows the answer—is *why* we're all here."

"Goodness!" Allison said placidly, and shook her head. "Such youthful impetuosity! And in front of such distinguished guests, too."

"I might point out that the guests in question are *Hamish and Emily's*, not yours, Mother," Honor replied. "Except, of course, that whenever someone is pulling the strings and you're present, I never have to look very far for the puppetmaster."

"Honor Stephanie Harrington!" Allison shook her head mournfully. "Such an undutiful child, too. How could you possibly think of me in that way?"

"Sixty years of experience," the undutiful child in question responded. "And now, if someone could possibly answer my question?"

"Actually, Honor," Hamish said, and his voice—and emotions— were far more serious than her mother's droll tone, "the person 'pulling the strings,' inasmuch as anyone is, isn't your mother. It's Reverend Sullivan."

"Reverend Sullivan?" Honor looked at the Grayson primate in surprise, and he nodded back gravely, although there was a twinkle in his dark eyes and she clearly tasted the affectionate amusement behind it.

"And just which strings are being pulled?" she asked more warily, looking back at Hamish and Emily.

"What it comes down to, Honor," Emily said, "is that, just as we'd feared, the news about your pregnancy—and mine—has gotten back to Grayson. It's already started to die down a bit here in the Star Kingdom, actually. Especially," a bubble of pure, malicious delight danced in her mind-glow, "since the *Landing Tattler*'s new management discovered certain irregularities in Solomon Hayes' financial records and let him go. I believe he's currently discussing those irregularities with the LCPD and the Exchequer.

"But," the brief flicker of amusement faded, "the situation on Grayson was about what you and I had feared it might be. In fact, a delegation of Steadholders called on the Reverend to discuss their . . . concerns."

Her mouth tightened bleakly for a moment, then she flipped her right hand in a shrug.

"Needless to say, Reverend Sullivan supported your position strongly," Honor glanced at Sullivan, who bent his head gravely in response to the gratitude in her eyes, "but it was clear some of them—especially Steadholder Mueller, I understand—are prepared to use this situation to attack you as publicly as possible. So the Reverend decided to take matters into his own hands, pastorally speaking."

Emily paused, and Reverend Sullivan looked at Honor.

"In some ways, My Lady," he said, "I suppose my decision to involve myself in such a deeply personal matter must be considered intrusive, especially since none of you are communicants of the Church of Humanity Unchained, and I hope I haven't offended by doing so. I might argue that my position as Reverend and First Elder and head of the Sacristy, and the constitutional obligations of those offices, give me a *responsibility* to involve myself, but that would be less than fully honest of me. The truth is," he looked directly into her eyes, and she tasted his utter sincerity, "that my own heart would have driven me to speak, were I Reverend or not. You, as a person, not simply as Steadholder Harrington, are important to far too many people on Grayson, myself included, for me to do otherwise."

"Reverend, I—" Honor paused and cleared her throat. "I can think of many things people could do which I might find offensive. Having you take a hand to help in a situation like this certainly isn't one of them."

"Thank you. I hope you'll still feel that way in a few minutes."

Despite the ominous words, there was a very faint gleam in his eye, and Honor frowned in puzzlement.

"The thing is, Honor," Emily continued, reclaiming her attention, "the Reverend's come up with a solution for all our problems. Every one of them."

"He's what?" Both of Honor's eyebrows rose, and she looked back and forth between Sullivan, Hamish and Emily, and her parents. "That's . . . hard to believe."

"Not really," Emily said, with a sudden, huge smile and a matching internal swell of delight. "You see, Honor, all you have to do is answer one question."

"One question?"

Honor blinked as her eyes prickled suddenly and unexpectedly. She didn't even know why—just that the joy inside Emily had reached out and blended with a matching tide of joyous anticipation from Hamish into something so strong, so exuberant and yet so intensely focused on *her*, that her own emotions literally couldn't help responding to it.

"Yes," Emily said softly. "Honor, will you marry Hamish and me?"

For an instant that seemed an eternity Honor simply stared at her. Then it penetrated, and she jerked upright in her comfortable chair.

"*Marry* you?" Her voice trembled. "Marry both of you? Are . . . are you serious?"

"Of course we are," Hamish said quietly, while Samantha purred from the high chair beside him as if the bones were about to vibrate right out of her body. "And if anyone can be certain of that," he added, "you can."

"But . . . but . . ." Honor looked at Archbishop Telmachi and Father O'Donnell, finally understanding why they were both here. "But I thought your marriage vows made that impossible," she said hoarsely.

"If I may, My Lord?" Telmachi said gently, looking at Hamish, and Hamish nodded.

"Your Grace," the Archbishop continued, turning to Honor, "Mother Church has learned a great deal over the millennia. Many things about human beings and their spiritual needs never change, and God, of course, is always constant. But the context in which those humans confront their spiritual needs *does* change. The rules evolved to handle those needs in a preindustrial, pre-space civilization simply cannot be applied to the galaxy in which we live today, any more than could the one-time religious ratification of slavery, or of the denial of the rights of women, or the prohibition of women in the priesthood, or the marriage of priests.

"Hamish and Emily chose to wed monogamously. The Church didn't require that of them, for we've learned that what truly matters is the love between partners, the union which makes it a true marriage, and not simply a convenience of the flesh. But that was their decision, and at the time, I believe it was the proper one for them. Certainly, anyone looking at them or speaking with them today, after all their marriage has endured, can still see the love and mutual commitment they share.

"But we live in an era of prolong, when men and women live literally for centuries. Just as Mother Church was eventually forced to deal with the tangled problems of genetic engineering and of cloning, she's been forced to acknowledge that when individuals live that long, the likelihood that even binding decisions must be revisited increases sharply.

"The Church doesn't look lightly upon the modification of wedding vows. Marriage is a solemn and a holy state, a sacrament ordained by God. But ours is a loving and an understanding God, and such a God wouldn't punish people to whom He's given the joyous gift of a love as deep as that which binds you, Hamish, and Emily together by forcing you to remain apart. And because the Church believes that, the Church has made provision for the modification of those vows, so long as all parties are in agreement and there's no coercion, no betrayal. I've spoken with Hamish and Emily. I have no question in my mind that they would welcome you into their marriage with unqualified joy. The only question which must be answered before I grant the necessary dispensation is whether or not that's what *you* most truly and deeply desire."

"I—" Honor's vision wavered, and she blinked back tears. "Of course it's what I desire," she said huskily. "Of course it is! I just never thought, never expected—"

"Forgive me for suggesting it, dear," her mother said gently, rising from her chair to fold her arms about her seated daughter, "but sometimes, much as I love you, you can be just a tiny bit slow."

Honor gurgled with tearful laughter and hugged her mother tightly.

"I know. I know! If I'd ever thought for a minute—" She broke off and looked at Hamish and Emily through her tears. "Of course I'll marry you, both of you! My God, of course I will!"

"Good," Reverend Sullivan said, and smiled when Honor turned to look at him. "It just happens that Robert, here," he waved one hand at Telmachi, "has already granted the necessary dispensation, contingent upon your acceptance of the idea. And it also just happens that Father O'Donnell, here, has brought along his prayerbook and a special license, and that I happen to know the Alexander family chapel just happens to have been given a most thorough cleaning this morning. *And* it just so happens that at this particular moment there's a representative of Father Church here on Manticore to serve as the temporal witness required for any steadholder's marriage. So since the bride's family," he bowed to include Nimitz and Samantha in that family, "are present, I don't really see any reason why we couldn't get this little formality out of the way tonight."

"*Tonight?*" Honor stared at him.

"Indeed," he replied calmly. "Unless, of course, you had other plans?"

"Of course I had—!"

Honor chopped herself off, torn between laughter, more tears, and a sense of the entire universe whirling further and further out of control.

"What?" her mother demanded, still hugging her. "You want a big fancy, formal wedding? Piffle! You can always have that later, if you really feel the need, but all that hoopla isn't what makes a marriage—or even a wedding. And even if it were, I'd think having the Archbishop *and* the Reverend assist in the ceremony should satisfy even the highest social stickler!"

"It isn't *that*, and you know it!" Honor half laughed, giving her mother a shake. "It's just all moving so quickly. I hadn't even considered it ten minutes ago, and now—!"

"Well, it's something you *ought* to have considered long ago, My Lady," Sullivan said with twinkle-eyed severity. "After all, you *are* a Grayson. And if you think I'm going to permit you and this man—" he jabbed a finger at Hamish "—to spend one more night cavorting in sin, then you have another think coming."

He waved the jabbing finger at Honor, smiling as she simultaneously laughed and blushed.

"All right. All right! You win, all of you. But before we get to the 'I do's,' we've got to get Miranda and Mac out here. I can't get married without them!"

"Now that," Allison congratulated her, "is the first reasonable objection you've raised all night. And, as the Reverend is fond of saying, it just so *happens* I sent Jeremiah back to fetch them—and Farragut and the twins—about the time we sat down to dinner. They should be here in—" she checked her chrono "—another thirty minutes or so. So," she cupped Honor's face between her hands, and her own smile was just a little misty, "why don't you and I spend the time between now and then making you even more beautiful, love?"

Chapter Thirty-One

Admiral Lady Dame Honor Alexander-Harrington, Duchess and Steadholder Harrington (and possibly—Hamish wasn't certain exactly how it would work out—Countess White Haven), walked across the shuttle pad lounge in a euphoric haze.

Being married was going to take some getting used to. This floating feeling of joy and relaxation—the knowledge that she'd truly come home at last—was worth any price, yet she already foresaw all sorts of problems on Grayson, once news of the marriage became public. Grayson conventions denoting marital status all assumed the husband's surname would be adopted by all of his wives. But those same conventions had also always assumed any steadholder would be male, and she had a pretty shrewd notion the Conclave of Steadholders wouldn't take kindly to the notion of changing the Harrington Dynasty to the Alexander Dynasty in the very first generation of the Steading. Plus, of course, the fact that they were going to have to deal with the fact that the Steadholder was the *junior* wife of a man who stood completely outside the succession.

Personally, she was rather looking forward to watching her fellow steadholders work their way through the problems. It would do their residually patriarchal little hearts good, she thought as she counted noses in her travel party. Then she frowned, as she came up a nose short.

"Wasn't Tim supposed to hop back up with us?" she asked MacGuiness.

"Yes, he was, My Lady." MacGuiness shook his head with an

408

irritated expression. "But he screened last night, and I forgot to tell you. He'll be catching the next shuttle flight back. Something about his younger sister's birthday, I believe. Technically, he's got another thirty-six hours before he's due to report back aboard, so I told him I didn't think there'd be any problem."

"Oh." Honor rubbed the tip of her nose for a moment, then shrugged. "You were right, of course. And goodness knows a birthday party's more important—and probably a lot more fun—than riding back to the flagship with a stodgy old flag officer."

"Nonsense, My Lady," MacGuiness said with an absolutely straight face. "I'm sure he doesn't think of you as old."

"And you, Mac, may not *get* a lot older," she told him with a smile.

"I'm terrified, Your Grace," he said sedately.

"You did *what*?" Michelle Henke asked, staring at Honor.

"I said that while I was back on Manticore and didn't have anything better to do, I went ahead and got married," Honor repeated with a huge smile. "It . . . seemed like the thing to do."

She shrugged, and Nimitz bleeked with laughter on her shoulder as the two of them enjoyed Henke's poleaxed mind-glow.

"But . . . but . . . but—"

"Mike, you sound like one of those antique motorboats Uncle Jacques and his SCA buddies play with."

Henke closed her mouth, and her stunned expression began to transform itself into one of outrage.

"You *married* Hamish Alexander—and his wife—and you didn't even invite me?!"

"Mike, *I* almost didn't get invited," Honor said. "Reverend Sullivan, Archbishop Telmachi, my mother, Hamish and Emily—I think about thirty percent of the entire population of Manticore!—knew about it before anybody bothered to tell *me*. And when the *Reverend* suggests you get married right now instead of—how did he put it? Oh, yes—instead of continuing to 'cavort in sin' with your intended groom, it takes more intestinal fortitude than I just discovered I have to say no."

"Yeah, *sure* you don't." Henke eyed her narrowly. "I've known treecats—hell, I've known *boulders*—less stubborn then you are, Honor Harrington. No way in the world did anyone hold a pulser to your head and *make* you do this!"

"Well, that's true," Honor admitted. "In fact, I'm a more than a little ticked off with myself for not having thought of this and proposed it myself months ago. It's just, after the High Ridge smear campaign, it never occurred to me."

"Even if it had," Henke said shrewdly, "you wouldn't have suggested it. You'd have just sat on it and hoped the idea occurred to *Emily.*"

"You might be right," Honor said, after a moment. "I hadn't really thought about that while I was busy kicking myself for being so slow."

"Honor, you're my best friend in the universe, but I've got to tell you, you've got one blind spot about two kilometers wide. It's funny, given that you're also the only functional two-foot empath I know, but it's true. You are constitutionally incapable of suggesting anything that will get you what you want if it might step on someone else. And you're *so* incapable of it, that you go into some sort of immediate internal denial where the very possibility of suggesting it is concerned."

"I do not!"

"You do so." Henke looked at Nimitz. "Doesn't she, Stinker?"

Nimitz looked down at Henke from Honor's shoulder for a moment, and then nodded firmly.

"See? Even your furry minion knows it. Which is one reason this marriage of yours is going to be so good for you. Somehow, I don't see Hamish and Emily Alexander—or Hamish and Emily Alexander-Harrington, I suppose now—letting you get away with that anymore."

Honor considered protesting further, but she didn't. And one reason she didn't, she admitted to herself, was that she wasn't positive she *could,* and be honest. The notion certainly bore thinking on, at any rate.

"Whatever," she said, instead, smiling at Henke. "But the main thing is that, aside from Mac and my armsmen, you're the only one in the Fleet who knows. I'm going to tell Alice and Alistair, as well, but no one else. Not for a while."

"Marriage licenses and wedding certificates are public records, Honor," Henke pointed out. "You can't keep this one quiet for long."

"Longer than you might think," Honor replied with an urchin-like grin. "Since I'm Steadholder Harrington, and a steadholder outranks a duchess or an earl, the license and certificate are both being filed on Steadholder Harrington's planet of residence. In the Public Records Office of Harrington Steading, as a matter of fact. Reverend Sullivan offered to take care of it for me."

"Well, wasn't that nice of him," Henke said with a matching grin. "I don't suppose they're likely to get temporarily misfiled, are they?"

"No, they aren't," Honor said, more seriously. "They're important official documents, so we're not going to be playing any games with them. But we're also not going to mention to anyone that they're there, and while the records are public, they have to be requested, so we'll know if anyone accesses them." She shrugged. "We couldn't keep it secret forever, even if we wanted to, which we don't. This will just buy a little more time."

"But why buy it in the first place?" Henke frowned. "Like Emily said, this solves all your problems. Except, of course, for the people who're going to suggest that the fact that you're marrying them now probably proves Hayes was right with his original rumors about you and Hamish."

"The main reason is my command and Hamish's position at the Admiralty," Honor admitted. "Hamish's theory is that since the First Lord, unlike the First *Space* Lord, is a civilian without any authority to issue orders to uniformed personnel, he's not in my direct chain of command, and so there's been no official prohibition against our . . . involvement from the start. Unfortunately, that's currently just *his* opinion. Before we go public, we want to be certain the courts are going to agree with him."

"And if they don't?" Henke frowned again. Rules-lawyering was very unlike the Honor Harrington she'd always known.

"And if they don't, the solution's relatively simple. I resign my Manticoran commission, and High Admiral Matthews makes Admiral Steadholder Harrington available to the Alliance to command Eighth Fleet. *That* we know would be legal, since there's no similar prohibition in Grayson service. But it would be complicated and an obvious case of finding a way to technically comply with the law, and we'd all prefer to simply find out that what we're doing is legal in the first place under the Star Kingdom's Articles of War."

"And how long will it take for you to determine whether or not it is?"

"Not too long, I hope. I've got Richard Maxwell working on it now, and he feels confident he can have a definitive opinion for us within a month or so. Which is actually moving at light-speed for the legal system, you know. In the meantime, we've got to get Cutworm III organized and launched, and no one at Admiralty House or here in the Fleet needs to be worrying about something like this while we're planning an op."

"I don't suppose I can argue about that," Henke said. "Personally, given who you and Hamish are—not to mention Emily—I figure you could probably get away with just about anything short of murder!"

"Maybe we could," Honor said with a frown of her own, "but that's one game I *really* don't want to start playing."

"Honor, you've *earned* a little slack, a little special consideration," Henke told her quietly.

"Some people may think so. And, in some respects, I suppose I do, too," Honor said slowly. "But the minute I begin demanding some sort of free pass, I turn into someone I don't want to be."

"Yes, I guess you would," Henke said, shaking her head with a slight, rueful smile. "Which is probably one reason everyone else would be so willing to give it to you. Oh, well." She shook herself. "I guess we'll just have to put up with you the way you are."

"And don't forget to *write* this time!"

"*Mom!*" Lieutenant Timothy Meares protested. "I *always* write! You know I do!"

"But not *often* enough," she said firmly, with an impish smile, as she banked into the final approach to Landing Field's parking bays.

"All right. All right," he sighed, giving in with a smile of his own. "I'll try to write more often. Assuming the Admiral gives me the free time."

"Don't you go blaming *your* slackness on Duchess Harrington," his mother scolded. "She doesn't keep you *that* busy."

"Yes, she does," Meares objected in tones of profound innocence. "I swear she does!"

"Then you won't mind me dropping her a little note of my own to ask her not to overwork my baby boy that way?"

"Don't you dare!" Meares protested with a laugh.

"That's what I thought," his mother said complacently. "Mothers know these things, you know."

"And they fight dirty, too."

"Of course they do. They're *mothers*."

The air car settled into the designated parking bay, and she turned to look at him, her expression suddenly much more serious.

"Your father and I are very proud of you, Tim," she said quietly. "And we worry about you. I know—I know!" She raised one hand when he started to protest. "You're safer on the flagship than you would be almost anywhere else. But a lot of mothers and fathers who thought their children were safe before the Peeps started shooting again found out they were wrong. We're not lying awake at night, unable to sleep. But we do worry, because we love you. So . . . be careful, all right?"

"I promise, Mom," he said, and kissed her cheek. Then he climbed out of the car, collected his single light bag, and waved goodbye.

His mother watched him step onto the pedestrian slideway. She watched him until he disappeared into the crowd, then lifted the air car into the exit traffic lanes and headed home.

She never noticed the nondescript man who also watched her son head for the departure concourse.

"I wish we were getting a few reinforcements, Ma'am," Rafael Cardones said as he, Simon Mattingly, and Honor and Nimitz walked down the passage away from the flag briefing room where the first preliminary meeting for Cutworm III had just broken up.

"So do I," Honor replied. "But realistically, it's only been three months since we activated Eighth Fleet. It's going to be at least a few more months before we start seeing anything else, I'm afraid."

"Three months." Cardones shook his head. "It doesn't seem anywhere near that long, somehow, Ma'am."

"That's because of how much more intense the operational pace has been this time around," Honor said with a shrug. "For us, at least. Time is probably dragging for the folks in Home Fleet and Third Fleet." It was her turn to shake her head. "I was always fortunate, as a captain. Except possibly for Hancock Station, I never got anchored to one of the major defensive fleets and had to sit around cooling my heels for months at a time with nothing but simulations to keep my people sharp."

"No, you didn't," Cardones said dryly. "If I recall correctly, Your Grace, you were generally too busy getting the crap shot out of your ship to worry about something like that."

"Picky, picky, picky," Honor said, and the flag captain chuckled. "At least it kept my people from getting *bored*," she added, and he laughed harder.

Honor smiled, and the four of them stepped through the hatch onto *Imperator*'s flag bridge.

It was fairly late in the shipboard day, and the watch was at a minimum. Mattingly peeled off, just inside the hatch, and Honor and Cardones crossed the spacious command deck to stand on its far side, gazing into the main visual display. The endless depths of space lay before them, crystal clear and sooty black, spangled with stars.

"Beautiful, isn't it, Ma'am?" Cardones asked quietly.

"And it looks so peaceful," Honor agreed.

"Too bad looks can be so deceiving," her flag captain said.

"I know what you mean. But let's not get too moody. It's always been 'deceiving,' you know. Think about what each of those tiny little, cool-looking stars is like when you get close to it. Not so 'peaceful' then, is it?"

"You do have an interesting perspective on things, sometimes, Your Grace," Cardones observed.

"Do I?"

Honor turned her head as the hatch opened again and Timothy Meares walked through it, carrying his memo board under his arm. The flag lieutenant had stayed behind to tidy up his notes of the session.

"If my perspective seems odd," she continued, turning back to Cardones, "it's only because—"

Her voice chopped off as abruptly as a guillotine blade, and she whirled back towards the hatch even as Nimitz catapulted off her shoulder with a bloodcurdling, tearing-canvas snarl. Cardones' jaw dropped, and he started to turn himself, but he was far too slow.

"Simon!" Honor shouted, even as her right hand flashed up,

caught Cardones by the front of his tunic, and flung him towards the floor with all the brutal power of her genetically engineered heavy-world musculature.

The armsman's head snapped up, but he lacked Honor's empathic sense. He couldn't taste what she tasted—couldn't recognize the sudden, surging horror radiating from Timothy Meares as the young man abruptly found his body responding to the orders of someone—or *something*—else.

It wasn't Mattingly's fault. Timothy Meares was part of his Steadholder's official family. He was her aide, her student, almost an adoptive son. He'd been alone in her company literally thousands of times, and Mattingly *knew* he was no threat. And so, he was totally unprepared when Meares' right hand reached out casually—so casually—in passing . . . and snaked Mattingly's pulser out of his holster.

The armsman reacted almost instantly. Despite the totality of his surprise, his own arm lashed out, seeking to recapture the weapon, or at least immobilize it. But "almost instantly" wasn't quite good enough, and the pulser snarled.

"*Simon!*"

This time it was no shout. Honor screamed her armsman's name in useless protest as the burst of heavy-caliber darts ripped into his abdomen and tracked upward into his chest. His uniform tunic, like Honor's, which had been modified to resist Nimitz's claws, was made of antiballistic fabric, but it wasn't designed to resist military-grade pulser fire at point-blank range, and Mattingly went down in an explosion of blood.

Honor felt the agony of his death, but there was no time to grieve. And agonizing as what had just happened to Mattingly was, it was actually *less* agonizing than what she tasted from Timothy Meares. His horror, shock, disbelief and guilt as *his* hand killed a man who'd been his friend was like some horrifying shroud. She could feel him screaming in protest, fighting with desperate futility, as his arm came up, sweeping around the bridge, holding down the stud on the stolen pulser.

A hurricane of darts shrieked across Flag Bridge. Two Plotting ratings went down, one of them screaming horribly. The Communications section exploded as the darts chewed their way through displays, consoles, chair backs. The deadly muzzle tracked onward, slicing the bandsaw of hyper-velocity darts across Andrea

Jaruwalski's unmanned station and killing the Tactical quarter-master of the watch. And yet, even as the carnage mounted, Honor knew it was all incidental. She knew her horrified flag lieutenant's actual target.

Nimitz hit the back of a command chair, bounding towards Meares, but the cyclone of darts slammed into the chair. They missed the 'cat, but the chair literally exploded under him, and not even *his* reflexes could keep him from falling to the deck. He landed with his feet under him, already prepared to bound upward once again, but he'd lost too much time. He couldn't possibly reach the flag lieutenant before the pulser in Meares' hand found Honor.

Honor felt it coming. Felt the useless denial screaming in Timothy Meares' mind. Knew the flag lieutenant literally could not resist whatever hideous compulsion had seized him. Knew he would rather have died himself than do what he'd just done. What he was *about* to do.

She didn't think about it, not consciously. She simply reacted, just as she'd reacted by throwing Rafael Cardones out of the line of fire. Reacted with the trained instincts of over forty years of practice in the martial arts, and with the muscle memory she'd drilled into herself on the firing range under her Jason Bay mansion.

Her artificial left hand flexed oddly. It rose before her, forefinger rigid, and in the instant before Timothy Meares' fire reached her, the tip of that forefinger exploded as a five-dart burst of pulser fire ripped across the flag bridge and the flag lieutenant's head erupted in a ghastly spray of gray, red, and pulverized white bone.

Chapter Thirty-Two

"Your Grace, Captain Mandel is here," James MacGuiness said quietly.

Honor looked up from her console with a feeling of guilty relief. She'd gotten only a few hours of fitful sleep in the twenty-one hours since the massacre on her flag bridge, and she was still dealing with personal letters to the families of the dead. The message she'd already composed for Simon Mattingly's family had been bad enough; the one she was recording now, for Timothy Meares' parents, was far worse.

MacGuiness stood in the open hatch of the office workspace attached to her day cabin, and his expression was as haggard as she felt. Simon Mattingly had been his friend for over sixteen T-years, and Timothy Meares had been like a younger brother. Eighth Fleet's entire command structure was stunned by what had happened, but for some, Honor thought, it was far more personal than for others.

"Show the Captain in, please, Mac."

"Yes, Ma'am."

MacGuiness disappeared, and Honor saved what she'd already recorded for Timothy's parents. As she did, her eyes fell on the black glove on her left hand—the glove concealing the tattered last joint of her index finger—and she felt once again the terrible, tearing grief there'd been no time to feel then as she shot down all of the potential and youthful exuberance of the flag lieutenant who'd meant so much to her.

A throat cleared itself, and she looked up once more.

"Captain Mandel, Your Grace," the burly, broad-shouldered officer just inside the hatch, black beret tucked under his left epaulet and spine ramrod straight, said gruffly. He and the slightly taller, slender woman beside him both wore the insignia of the Office of Naval Intelligence. "And this," Mandel indicated his companion, "is Commander Simon."

"Come in, Captain, Commander." Honor pointed at the chairs in front of her desk. "Be seated."

"Thank you, Your Grace," Mandel said. Simon—Honor felt herself flinch inside as the commander's last name lacerated her sense of loss—said nothing, only smiled politely and waited a moment until Mandel had seated himself. Then she sat, as well, economically and neatly.

Honor regarded them thoughtfully, tasting their emotions. They were an interesting contrast, she decided.

Mandel's emotions were just as hard-edged as his physical appearance. He radiated bulldog toughness, but there was no sense of flexibility or give. Focused, intense, determined . . . all of those applied, yet she had the sense that he was a blunt instrument. A hammer, not a scalpel.

But Simon, now. Simon's emotions were very different from her outward appearance. She looked almost colorless—fair-haired, with a complexion almost as pale as Honor's own and curiously washed out looking blue eyes—and her body language appeared diffident, almost timid. But under that surface was a poised, 'cat-like huntress. An agile mind, coupled with intense curiosity and an odd combination of a puzzlesolver's abstract concentration and a crusader's zeal.

Of the two, Honor decided, Simon was definitely the more dangerous.

"Now, Captain," she said, after a moment, folding her hands atop her blotter, "what can I do for you and the Commander?"

"Obviously, Your Grace, everyone at Admiralty House—and in the Government at large, for that matter—takes a very grave view of what's happened," Mandel said. "Admiral Givens will be personally reviewing all our reports, and I've been instructed to inform you that Her Majesty will also be receiving them."

Honor nodded silently when he paused.

"Commander Simon is attached to counterintelligence," Mandel continued. "My own specialty is CID, however, which means I'll be functioning as the lead investigator."

"Criminal Investigation Division is taking the lead?" Honor managed to keep the surprise out of her voice, but her eyes sharpened.

"Well, clearly what's happened here represents a serious security breach," Mandel replied. "The Commander has an obvious responsibility to determine how the penetration occurred. However, in a case like this, it's usually most efficient to allow an experienced criminal investigator to go over the ground first. We know what to look for, and we can often identify the points at which the perpetrator began acting abnormally." He shrugged. "With that to direct them to the point at which he was first recruited, the counterintelligence types can hit the ground running."

"Perpetrator," Honor repeated, and to her own ears her voice was oddly flattened.

"Yes, Your Grace." Mandel radiated puzzlement at her comment, and she smiled thinly.

"Lieutenant Meares," she said quietly, "was a member of my staff for almost a full T-year. He was a diligent, responsible, conscientious young man. Had he lived, he would, I feel no doubt, have attained senior rank and discharged it well. He won't do that now, because *I* killed him. I would greatly appreciate it, Captain, if you could find some word other than *'perpetrator'* with which to describe him."

Mandel looked at her, and something clicked into place behind his eyes. She could feel it, taste his sense of "Oh, *that's* what it was!" as he recognized—or thought he did—what he was dealing with.

"Your Grace," he said compassionately, "it's not unusual, especially this soon after something like this, for it to be difficult to accept that someone we knew and liked, trusted, wasn't exactly what we thought he was. I'm sure you feel responsible for the death of the 'conscientious young man' you killed. But you killed him in self-defense, and the fact that you had to demonstrates that he wasn't who or what you thought he was."

Honor's eyes narrowed, and she heard Nimitz's soft, sibilant hiss.

"Captain Mandel," she said even more quietly, "did you or did you not read my own report about what happened here?"

"Of course, Your Grace. I have a copy of it here." He tapped the microcomputer cased at his belt.

"In that case, you ought to be aware that Lieutenant Meares was not responsible for his actions," she said flatly. "He wasn't the 'perpetrator' of this crime, Captain; he was its first victim."

"Your Grace," Mandel said in patient tones, "I did, indeed, read your report. It was well written, concise, and to the point. However, you're a combat officer. You command ships and lead fleets in battle, and the entire Star Kingdom knows how well you do it. But you aren't a criminal investigator. I am, and while I don't doubt a single factual observation from your report, I'm afraid your conclusion that Lieutenant Meares was under some form of compulsion simply doesn't make sense. It's just not supported by the evidence."

"I beg your pardon?" Honor asked, almost conversationally, and a slight tic began at the right corner of her mouth.

"Your Grace," Mandel probably wasn't even aware of his own sense of patient, confident superiority in his area of expertise, but *Honor* certainly was, "you stated in your report that Lieutenant Meares was attempting to resist some sort of compulsion the entire time he was killing people, including your own armsman. But I'm afraid that statement is in error—a conclusion I base on two main points of observation and logic.

"First, I've reviewed the flag bridge visual records of the incident, and there's absolutely no sign of hesitation on his part. Secondly, for him to have been operating under compulsion would have required major personality adjustment, were he, in fact, the person you believed him to be.

"It's not at all unusual, when something as violent and totally unexpected as this incident occurs, for someone involved in it to be mistaken in his observations. And that, I'm afraid, is even more common when the observer doesn't want—for perfectly understandable, very human reasons—to believe what's happening or why. The visual records, however, are immune to that sort of subjectivity, and they reveal nothing but purposeful, intentional, controlled, *unhesitating* action on Lieutenant Meares' part.

"And as far as personality adjustment is concerned, it's simply not possible. Lieutenant Meares, like all Queen's officers, had received the standard anti-drug and anti-conditioning protocols. It wouldn't have been flatly impossible for those safeguards to be broken or evaded, but it would have been difficult. And even without them, adjustment takes *time*, Your Grace. Quite a lot of it. And we can account for almost every instant of Lieutenant Meares' time over the past T-year. Certainly, there's no unaccounted for period long enough for him to have been involuntarily adjusted to carry out an action like this one."

The CID captain shook his head, his expression sad.

"No, Your Grace. I know you want to believe the best of an officer to whom you were so attached. But the only explanation for what happened here is that he was, and had for some time, been an agent for Peep intelligence."

"That's preposterous," Honor said flatly. Mandel's face stiffened, his feeling of professional superiority segueing into beginning anger, and Honor leaned forward in her chair. "If, in fact, Lieutenant Meares—Timothy—" she used the dead officer's first name deliberately, "had been a Havenite agent, he would have been far more valuable as a spy than as an assassin. As my flag lieutenant, he had access to virtually *all* of Eighth Fleet's most secure and sensitive data. He would have been a priceless intelligence asset, and they would never have thrown that away in an attempt like this.

"In addition, Captain, I didn't state in my report that I believed him to have been under compulsion; I stated that he *was* under compulsion. That was not interpretation. It was an observed fact."

"With all due respect, Your Grace," Mandel said stiffly, "my own analysis of the visual records doesn't support that conclusion."

"My *observation*," Honor stressed the noun deliberately, "didn't rely upon visual analysis."

"Feelings and instinct are a poor basis for a criminal investigation, Your Grace," Mandel said even more stiffly. "I've been doing this for almost fifty T-years. And, as I explained on the basis of that experience, it's normal for emotions to cloud one's interpretation of events like this one."

"Captain," the muscle tic at the corner of Honor's mouth was more pronounced, "you're aware of the fact that I've been adopted by a treecat?"

"Of course, Your Grace." Mandel was obviously trying to sit on his temper, but his voice came out just a bit too clipped. "Everyone is aware of that."

"And you're aware that treecats are empaths and telepaths?"

"I've read some articles to that effect," Mandel said, and Honor felt her own temper click a notch higher at the dismissiveness in his emotions. Clearly, the captain was one of those people who continued, despite the evidence, to reject the notion that 'cats were fully sentient beings.

"They are, in fact, telepathic and empathic, and also highly intelligent," she told him. "And *because* they are, Nimitz was able to sense what Lieutenant Meares was feeling in the last few moments of his life."

She considered—briefly—telling Mandel she'd sensed those emotions herself, personally and directly, but rejected the temptation immediately. If he was sufficiently closed-minded to reject all the recent scientific evidence of treecat intelligence and capabilities, he would undoubtedly consider any *human* who claimed the same empathic ability was obviously insane.

"Nimitz knows, Captain Mandel. He doesn't suspect, and he doesn't think, he *knows* Timothy was trying desperately *not* to do what he was doing. That he was horrified by his own actions but couldn't stop them. And that, I submit to you, is the exact definition of someone acting under compulsion."

Mandel looked at her, and she tasted his incredulity that anyone could possibly expect him to allow the supposed observations of an animal, be it ever so clever, to influence the direction of his investigation.

"Your Grace," he said finally, "I'm attempting to make full allowance for your obvious close emotional attachment to Lieutenant Meares, but I must disagree with your conclusions. As far as his value as an intelligence asset is concerned, I will, of course, defer to the judgment of Commander Simon's people in counterintelligence. From my own perspective, however, and given how successful Eighth Fleet's operations have been, it seems obvious you'd make a perfect target for an assassination. We know the Peeps are fond of assassination as a technique, and your death would have been a major blow to the Star Kingdom's morale. In my own judgment, it seems likely Peep intelligence felt that killing you would be even more valuable than whatever sensitive data Lieutenant Meares might have been in position to give them.

"As far as your treecat's 'observations' are concerned, I'm

afraid I can't allow them to overrule my own analysis of the visual records, which aren't subject to emotional overtones or subjectivity. And those records show absolutely no sign of hesitation on Lieutenant Meares' part from the instant he seized your armsman's weapon.

"And, finally, as I've already pointed out," he concluded with dangerous, pointed patience, "there simply hasn't been an unaccounted for block of the lieutenant's time long enough for him to have been adjusted."

"Captain," Honor said, "should I conclude, from what you've just said, that you don't believe a treecat's empathic sense is a valid guide to the emotional state of humans in his presence?"

"I'm not sufficiently versed in the literature on the subject to have an opinion, Your Grace," he said, but she tasted the truth behind the meaningless qualification.

"No, you don't believe it," she said flatly, and his eyes flickered. "Nor," Honor continued, "is your mind even remotely open to the possibility that Timothy Meares was acting against his will. Which means, Captain Mandel, that you're completely useless for this investigation."

Mandel reared back in his chair, eyes wide with shock, and Honor smiled thinly.

"You're relieved of authority for this investigation, Captain," she told him softly.

"You can't do that, Your Grace!" he objected hotly. "This is an ONI investigation. It falls outside your chain of command!"

"*Captain*," Honor emphasized his rank coldly, "you do *not* want to get into a pissing contest with me. Trust me on that. I said you're relieved, and you are relieved. I will inform all Eighth Fleet personnel that you have no authority, and instruct them not to cooperate with your investigation in any way. And if you choose not to accept my decision, I will personally return to Manticore to discuss it with Admiral Givens, Admiral Caparelli, Earl White Haven, and—if necessary—with the Queen herself. Are you reading me clearly on this, *Captain*?"

Mandel stared at her, then seemed to deflate in his chair. He didn't say a word, and as she tasted his emotions, she knew he literally couldn't.

She held him for a moment longer with icy brown eyes, then turned her attention to Commander Simon. The commander was almost as stunned as Mandel, but she was already beginning to come to grips with it.

"Commander Simon."

"Yes, Your Grace?" Simon had a pleasant mezzosoprano much warmer than her washed out coloring, Honor noticed.

"On my authority, you'll assume lead responsibility for this investigation until and unless Admiral Givens assigns a replacement for Captain Mandel."

"Your Grace," Simon said carefully, "I'm not certain you have the authority in my chain of command to give that order."

"Then I suggest you accept it provisionally, under protest, if you must, until the situation is clarified by someone you know *is* in your chain of command," Honor said coldly. "Because unless you do, this investigation will go nowhere until such time as an entire new team is sent out from Manticore. I will *not* have Captain Mandel in charge of it. Is that clear?"

"Yes, Your Grace," Simon said quickly.

"Very well then, Commander. Let's be about it." •

Chapter Thirty-Three

"So we've been rethinking our previous target selection criteria and force levels," Andrea Jaruwalski said, looking around the flag briefing room.

All of Eighth Fleet's division commanders attended electronically, each with his or her own individual quadrant of the huge holo display hovering above the conference table. The squadron and task force commanders, and Scotty Tremaine as Eighth Fleet's senior COLAC, were physically present, and even now, almost three full days after the flag bridge massacre, Honor could taste the residual shock, the stunned desire to disbelieve what had happened, hovering in the compartment like smoke.

"At this point," Jaruwalski continued, seeking her own escape from personal grief in brisk professionalism, "Commander Reynolds and I are in agreement with Her Grace. The Peeps have to have begun putting in place some response to Cutworm I and Cutworm II. What that response may be, we can't predict. Obviously, we all know what we'd like it to be. However, even if we've succeeded completely in convincing them to do what the Admiralty wants, it's still a situation with a definite downside for us here in Eighth Fleet. Specifically, the targets are going to get tougher. Whether it's simply improved doctrine—more of what we saw at Chantilly—or an actual redeployment of assets, they're going to do their best to ensure that we don't have any more cakewalks.

"Bearing that in mind, we're reducing our objectives list for Cutworm III to only two star systems: Lorn and Solon. Admiral

Truman will command the attack on Lorn; Her Grace will command the attack on Solon. We'll be assigning one carrier squadron to each attack, and splitting the heavy cruisers and battlecruisers just about down the middle."

She paused, looking up and sweeping the faces of her audience, corporeal and electronic, then continued.

"Even without any precautionary redeployment on the Peeps' part, both these targets would almost certainly be more heavily defended then our previous objectives. Lorn, in particular, is a relatively important secondary naval shipyard. It's not a building yard, but a satellite yard that handles a lot of refit activity, although it's really geared to working on units below the wall. Also, we know from prior intelligence that Lorn is fairly heavily involved in construction of the Peeps' new LACs. Because of that, we anticipate that the likelihood of encountering at least light and medium combatants in some numbers is relatively high.

"Solon is less directly involved in the construction or maintenance of Peep naval units. It is, however, substantially more heavily populated than any of the systems we've hit so far. According to the last census data available to us, the system population is over two billion, and its economy was one of the relatively few bright spots for the Peeps even before the Pierre Coup. This makes it particularly valuable from our perspective, since a successful attack on it is certain to generate powerful political pressure for Theisman and his staff to deploy additional heavy units for home defense. In addition, the severity of the economic damage inflicted by the destruction of this system's industrial infrastructure will be truly significant. All of which, again, suggests the system will be more heavily defended than the more lightly populated systems we've attacked so far."

She paused once again, glancing over the notes on her individual display, then looked up once more.

"That completes the overview, Your Grace. Would you care to entertain discussion of the points already raised, or would you prefer for me to begin the point-by-point operational brief?"

"I think we'll begin by seeing if anyone has anything she wants to add to what you've already said," Honor replied.

It was her turn to look around the faces, physical and electronic, and she smiled, despite her fatigue and her aching awareness of the empty spots behind her which should have been filled by Simon Mattingly and Timothy Meares.

"Who'd like to start the ball rolling?" she asked.

The intercom buzzer sounded shockingly loud in the stillness.

Honor sat up quickly, brushing her right hand across her eyes, and grimaced as she brought up the time display in her left eye. She'd been stretched out on the couch for barely fifty minutes, and the small amount of sleep she'd gotten made her feel even worse than she had before she collapsed onto it.

The intercom buzzed again, and she shoved herself to her feet and stalked across to it.

"Mac," she said, with unaccustomed ire, "I thought I *told* you—"

"I'm sorry, Ma'am," MacGuiness interrupted. "I know you didn't want to be disturbed before supper. But there's someone here you should see."

"Mac," she said again, without her previous atypical heat, but wearily, "unless it's some sort of an emergency, I really don't want to see anyone. Can't Mercedes handle whatever it is?"

"I'm afraid not, Ma'am," MacGuiness replied. "He's come directly from Admiralty House specifically to speak to *you.*"

"Oh."

Honor made her spine straighten and inhaled deeply. There'd been just enough time for her blistering comments on Mandel to reach Admiralty House and draw a response, and the fact that they'd sent someone out to deliver that response in person suggested that Admiral Givens and the Judge Advocate General might not have been too delighted by her actions.

Well, that's just too bad, she thought grimly. *I'm a full admiral, a fleet commander, a duchess, and a steadholder. This investigation is too important to be sandbagged at the outset by someone too closed minded to even consider the blindingly obvious, and this time around, the Powers That Be are* damned *well going to pay attention to me!*

The anger in her own thoughts surprised her, just a bit, and she wondered—not for the first time—how much of it stemmed from her own feeling of guilt. But that didn't really matter. Not when she _knew_ she was right about whatever had been done to Timothy Meares.

"Very well, Mac," she said, after a moment, "give me two minutes, then send him in."

"Yes, Ma'am."

Honor keyed off the intercom, picked up her uniform tunic and slipped it back on, sealed it, and glanced into a bulkhead mirror. She shrugged her shoulders to settle the tunic perfectly in place, and ran her right hand lightly over her hair. That hair fell halfway to her waist when it was unbound, these days, but its tightly coiled braids hadn't slipped during her all too brief nap, and she nodded in approval. The slight tightness around her eyes might have told someone who knew her very well how weary she actually was, but there was no fault to find in her outward appearance.

She glanced at Nimitz, but the 'cat was draped over his sleeping perch, still sound asleep. She sensed him in the back of her mind, just as she knew he was always at least peripherally aware of her, even when his sleep was deepest, but she didn't wake him. He was as exhausted as she was, and he, too, was still dealing with his grief for two people who had been close personal friends.

Simon Mattingly's funeral had helped . . . some. There'd been at least a little catharsis in it, but at the same time it had only made her more aware of how far he'd come from his native world to die. She'd borrowed Brother Hendricks, the chaplain attached to one of the Grayson LAC groups assigned to Alice Truman's carrier squadron, to perform the ceremony. She'd known from agonizing personal experience that the Grayson tradition was that an armsman was buried where he fell, and Andrew LaFollet and Spencer Hawke had stood ramrod straight at her back throughout the brief military funeral ceremony. And then they, Alistair McKeon, Michelle Henke, and James MacGuiness had carried the Harrington Steading flag-draped coffin to the waiting airlock.

The two armsmen had stood rigidly at attention at her back once again as the airlock's inner hatch closed. And then Brother Hendricks had spoken quietly.

"Unto Almighty God we commend the soul of our brother departed, and we commit his body to the endless sea of space, in sure and certain hope of the Resurrection unto eternal life, through the Intercessor, our Lord Jesus Christ, at whose coming in glorious Majesty to judge the universe, it shall give up its dead, and the corruptible bodies of those who sleep in Him shall be changed, and made like unto His glorious body, according to the mighty workings whereby He is able to subdue all things unto Himself. Amen."

Honor had reached out as he spoke, and at the final word, she'd pressed the button beside the hatch that expelled Simon Mattingly's coffin. The coffin's small reaction drive had activated as soon as it was clear of the ship, turning the coffin, aligning it perfectly with the distant fusion furnace of Trevor's Star, and she'd felt her own heart go with it.

Perhaps she'd be able, in time, to find the comfort in the ancient words of farewell. And certainly, if there'd ever been a man who had met the Test of his life, that man had been Simon Mattingly. But, oh, she *missed* him so.

She drew a deep breath, crossed to her desk, seated herself behind it, switched on her terminal, and pretended to be studying the document upon it, then waited.

Precisely one hundred and twenty seconds from the moment she'd given him the instruction, MacGuiness opened the cabin hatch.

"Your Grace," he said, "your visitor is here."

There was something peculiar about his voice, and something even odder about his emotions, and Honor looked up sharply.

"Hello, Honor," her visitor said, and she shot up out of her chair.

"*Hamish!*"

She never clearly remembered stepping around her desk. She just was, and then she walked straight into his arms.

She heard a thump behind her as Samantha vaulted from Hamish's shoulder and flowed across the carpet. She tasted Nimitz's awakening and sudden delight as his mate's mind-glow reached out to him, and then Hamish's arms were about her, and hers were about him.

"Hamish," she repeated more quietly, almost wonderingly, letting her head rest on his shoulder.

"'Salamander,' indeed." Hamish's deep voice was more than a little frayed around the edges, and his arms tightened. "Damn it, woman—can't you go *anywhere* without somebody trying to kill you?!"

"I'm sorry," she said, never opening her eyes as she tasted his very real worry. "I'm sorry, but no one could have seen this one coming."

"I know, I know." He sighed, and his embrace loosened at last.

He put his hands on her upper arms, holding her back at arm's length, and looked deeply into her eyes. He lacked her own empathic abilities, but once again, she tasted that echo of a treecat bonding between them, and she knew she could no more conceal her innermost feelings from him than he could conceal his from her.

"Poor Honor," he said, after a moment. "Love, when we got the initial dispatches, Emily and I—" He broke off, shaking his head firmly. "Let's just say we didn't take it well. I wanted to come straight out here personally, but I was afraid of the attention I might have drawn. But then you fired Mandel, and I decided the hell with the attention I might attract. I know you, Honor. You wouldn't have brought the hammer down that hard on him unless he was a complete and utter idiot and you felt an overriding urgency to get someone competent to replace him, or unless you were really, really hurting. In either case, I needed to be here."

"I suppose it was a bit of each," she admitted, stepping back and linking her arm through his. She urged him across the cabin, and the two of them sat side by side on the couch, leaning comfortably against one another.

"I *am* hurting, badly," she said quietly. "Not just over Simon. Not even *mostly* over him, in some ways. Tim—"

She broke off, biting her lip, her vision misting, remembering how vehemently she had rejected Mercedes Brigham's suggestion that perhaps she should be thinking about filling the hole in her staff Meares death had left. But no admiral was *required* to have a flag lieutenant, and Honor refused to replace him. It might not be the most rational decision she'd ever made, but she had no intention of changing her mind.

"I'm hurting," she repeated. "And I will be, for a long time. But I honestly believe that it was mostly because Mandel was such a square peg in a round hole."

"From the tone of your dispatches—and, frankly, *his* report to Pat Givens—I sort of figured it was something like that," he said.

"Although, I understand Mandel really does have a reputation as an effective investigator."

"I don't doubt he does," she said. "In fact, to be scrupulously fair, which I really don't want to, I imagine he really is very good at what he does . . . under more normal circumstances. But in this instance, he's simply not the man for the job. Maybe he's *too* experienced. It's like . . . like he's got some sort of tunnel vision. He knows what he knows, and he's going to focus in on that and get the job done without any distractions from amateurs who don't know their ass from their elbow about criminal investigations."

Hamish quirked one eyebrow at her language.

"You *are* pissed," he observed.

"Frustrated," she corrected. "Well, and maybe pissed off *because* he made me so frustrated. But he wouldn't believe me when I told him Tim was being compelled somehow, and he wasn't ready to believe Nimitz was smart enough to recognize what was going on—assuming a 'cat really had any sort of telempathic ability in the first place—or to tell anyone anything sensible if he could recognize it."

"Jesus, he managed to step on *all* your sore toes, didn't he?"

"Just about," she admitted, smiling faintly at the humor in his voice. "But he was so fixated on the notion that my sense of guilt was *making* me believe the best about Tim that he wasn't paying any attention to what I was telling him about what really happened. And he wasn't about to change his mind, either. I could tell."

She tapped her temple with her right forefinger, grimacing wryly, and he nodded.

"I figured that was what it was. And I imagine from what you're saying you weren't about to tell him *you'd* sensed what was happening?"

Honor simply snorted, and he chuckled without much humor.

"Frankly, I'm just as glad you didn't. I'd like you to go on holding that little ability in reserve for as long as you can. Let people think Nimitz is the one doing the sensing. It never hurts to be *under*estimated in some ways."

"I know. Not to mention the fact that I don't want people to think I'm some sort of mind-reading, privacy-invading freak."

"Um."

Hamish gazed into space for a few moments, then looked back at her.

"I don't doubt a single thing you've said," he told her, "but I've got to tell you, I viewed the same footage from the bridge visuals." His face tightened. "It scared the *shit* out of me, too, even though I knew you hadn't been hurt before they ever showed it to me."

He shook his head, jaw muscles bunching for a second, and she slipped her arm around him and squeezed tightly.

"But the point I was going to make," he continued more normally after a couple of heartbeats, "was that watching what happened, I can see why someone who didn't realize how you can get inside somebody else's head would discount the possibility that Lieutenant Meares was trying to stop himself. He moved so *fast*, Honor. So smoothly. As if he'd not only planned out what he was going to do, but actually rehearsed it ahead of time. I don't know if you really realize sometimes just how fast your own reflexes are, but you killed him just fractions of a second before *he* would have killed *you*. And I don't think anyone else could have done it, trick finger or not."

Honor looked down at her gloved left hand.

"I know it was fast," she said. "If I'd had even a fraction of a second more warning—if I'd been able to do more than just shout Simon's name—we might . . ."

She stopped and made herself inhale.

"I'll always wonder if it would have been better *not* to shout," she said, admitting to Hamish what she wasn't certain she would have been able to admit only to herself. "Did I distract him? Did I make him look at me, in exactly the wrong direction, when he might have seen something, noticed something?" She looked into Hamish's eyes. "Did I get him killed?"

"No." Hamish shook his head firmly. "Yes, you may have distracted him, but distracted him from what? From watching a young man he'd seen literally thousands of times walk into Flag Bridge on a perfectly legitimate errand?" He shook his head again. "Not even a Grayson armsman would have expected anything like this, love."

"But he was my friend," Honor half-whispered. "I . . . loved him."

"I know."

It was Hamish's turn to squeeze her, and she leaned into his embrace.

"Nonetheless," he went on, "the fact that you had to so little warning suggests a couple of things to me."

"Such as?"

"First, there's no way he was a Peep agent. He never could've concealed that from you—or Nimitz—for this long. Second, whatever happened to him, he hadn't been personality adjusted."

"Why not? I mean, why can you be so confident of that?"

"Partly because Mandel, however pigheaded you may've found him, was right. Adjustment takes time—lots of time, even without the safeguards built into our military security protocols. And partly because someone who's been adjusted knows he has. On some level, he's aware of the fact that he's not fully in control of his own actions. In fact, I made a quick flight out to your parent's house on Sphinx with Samantha and had her consult the Bright Water memory singers about the attempted assassination of Queen Adrienne."

"You know, I'd actually forgotten about that," Honor said in a chagrined voice.

"You've been under a lot of stress," Hamish told her. "But Samantha got the memory song of the entire episode. She says the assassin knew what was happening to him from the moment he came into Dianchect's mental reach. It wasn't like . . . turning on a switch. Dianchect picked him up before he ever got into visual range of the Princess, and he knew there was something badly wrong the instant he tasted the assassin's mind-glow. That wasn't the case here."

"No, it wasn't," Honor agreed. "He was perfectly cheerful when he stepped through the hatch. Everything was normal, exactly the way it always was. And then, suddenly, he went for Simon's pulser."

"So he wasn't *adjusted*," Hamish said thoughtfully, "but he was *programmed*."

"I suppose you could say that. But how could that be done?" Honor shook her head. "That's what I keep coming back to, again and again. How in the name of God could someone *program* another human being that way without the human in question even being aware it had happened?"

"I don't know the answer to that one," Hamish said grimly,

"but here's another one. Why did it happen *now*? Why not before this?"

"You're suggesting whatever was done to him was done during his last trip to Manticore?"

"It seems likely, although CID's been over his entire visit with a fine tooth comb without finding anything out of the ordinary. And leaving that point aside for the moment, why *that* moment, in *that* place? Why not in a staff meeting, or when you invited him to dinner?"

"Opportunity, maybe," Honor said thoughtfully. He looked at her, and she shrugged. "I think it was the first time he and I and a single armsman were in the same place at the same time. Or, at least, when there was a single armsman he had a legitimate reason to come within arm's length of so naturally that not even a Grayson armsman would think it was anything out of the ordinary."

"And why would that be significant?"

"Because," she said grimly, "my armsmen are the only people constantly in my presence who're armed. To kill me, he first had to have a weapon, and, secondly, he had to . . . disable my bodyguard. By taking Simon's weapon the way he did, he accomplished both."

"I see." Hamish frowned, then shrugged. "You may be onto something there. I don't know. But I do know where something like this happened before."

"Where—Oh! Colonel Hofschulte!"

"Exactly. Pat Givens has already sent a message to the Andermani requesting all their case files on Hofschulte, because it sounds like exactly the same thing. A totally trusted, totally loyal, longtime retainer who just suddenly snapped and tried to kill Prince Huang and his entire family. My understanding is that they very carefully considered the possibility of adjustment, but that Hofschulte was never out of sight long enough for that to happen. Which, again, sounds exactly like what happened here."

"But why should the Havenites have tried to kill the Andermani Crown Prince?" Honor asked in puzzlement.

"That I can't tell you," Hamish admitted. "I just know the *modus operandi* appears to be extremely similar. I can see some possible advantages for them, I suppose, in killing him now that they're at war with the Andies as well as us, but then?" He shook his head. "Of course, StateSec was still running their entire intelligence machine at that point. Maybe they did have some sort of motive we just can't see from here."

"That's hard to imagine," Honor said thoughtfully. "I wonder..."

"Wonder what?" Hamish asked after a few seconds.

"What? Oh!" Honor gave herself a shake. "I was just wondering if there's someone else out there, someone who's developed a technique that would let them do something like this, and made it available on a hire basis?"

"Possible." Hamish considered. "Quite possible, really. Because I can't think of anyone besides the Peeps who'd have both the motive and the resources to pull something like this off."

"I can't either," Honor agreed, but her expression was troubled.

Yes, assassination had always been a favorite tactic of the *People's* Republic, whether it was being run by InSec or StateSec. But it wasn't the sort of tactic she would have associated with Thomas Theisman. On the other hand, Eloise Pritchart had come up through the Havenite Resistance, and her Aprilists had been credited with several dozen assassinations of key Legislaturalists and InSec personnel. And however Honor wanted to look at it, she, as the commander of the Allied fleet which had done the most damage to the Republic's civilians, as well as its military, was clearly a legitimate military target.

And assassination didn't kill anyone deader than a bomb-pumped laser.

"Well," Hamish said finally, "one of the reasons I came out was to tell you that, although Pat would appreciate it if you'd go through channels next time, if you want Mandel out of the picture, he's gone. And she intimated to me that if he'd gotten out of line, instead of simply being dumb as a post, she'd see to it he was for the long drop, as well."

"No." Honor shook her head. "No, as much as the nasty side of me would like to see that happen, it really was just a matter of his being...unresponsive to novel hypotheses."

"My, what a diplomatic way to put it," her husband murmured. Then he grinned crookedly. "Her second question was whether or not this Commander Simon was acceptable to you?"

"She is. Just speaking to her is like prodding a wound with your finger, because of her name, but she's much more open-minded than Mandel. I don't say she agrees with me—yet, at least—but she hasn't ruled the possibility out. And she hasn't already wedded herself to some theory of her own. And she apparently does believe what the xenologists have been saying about the 'cats and their abilities for the past few years."

"Good, because in that case, I want Samantha to talk to her. I don't suppose we're lucky enough that she reads sign?"

"No, she doesn't."

"Pity. In that case, I'll just have to translate, I suppose." Hamish shrugged. "It may be an interesting conversation, especially when Samantha tells her about the memory song about Queen Adrienne. And at least I'll feel like I'm actually *doing* something about the bastards who tried to murder my wife."

His voice hardened on the last sentence, and she felt the fury—and fear—behind it.

"They may've tried, and they may have killed a lot of other people, but they didn't kill me, and they aren't going to," she promised him, reaching up to touch the side of his face with her right hand.

"Not with assassins, anyway," Hamish said with a slightly strained smile. "Not with both you and your furry shadow watching out for them."

Honor smiled back, then stiffened.

"That's it," she said softly.

" 'It' what?" he asked when she didn't say anything else immediately.

"It's just that if there *is* some new assassination technology out there, something they used to get to Tim without his disappearing long enough to be adjusted, then they could do it to anyone. Which means literally *anybody* could be a programmed assassin, without even realizing it."

"Talk about your security nightmares," Hamish muttered, and she nodded grimly.

"But at the moment whatever the programming is kicks in, they *do* know someone or something else is controlling them," she said, "and no treecat could miss something like that."

"Like food tasters," Hamish said slowly. "Or canaries in coal mines back on Old Earth."

"More or less," she agreed. "It wouldn't be much warning, but at least it would be some. And if the security types guarding the intended target knew to take their cue from the 'cat, it might be enough."

"Palace Security and the Queen's Own have been paying attention to treecats for centuries now," Hamish said. "They, at least, won't have any problems with the idea."

"No, and you need to get Dr. Arif and her commission involved in this. It's exactly the sort of thing she's been looking for, and she's already in position to coordinate with all the 'cat clans to come up with volunteers. We can't put treecats everywhere—there aren't enough of them, even if they were all prepared or mentally equipped to work that closely with so many humans in such proximity—but with her help, we can probably cover most of the major ministerial targets, for example."

"An excellent notion," Hamish approved, then smiled at her in quite a different way.

"What?" she demanded as she tasted the sudden shift in his emotions and a pleasant heat deep down inside her responded to it.

"Well," he said, turning sideways on the couch to take her face between the palms of his hands, "I can now truthfully tell my fellow Lords of Admiralty that I discharged official business when I was out here. So with that out of the way, why don't we discharge a little *un*official business, Ms. Alexander-Harrington?"

And he kissed her.

Chapter Thirty-Four

"So tell me, Boss. Are we sure this is a good idea this time around?" Captain Molly Delaney asked.

Admiral Lester Tourville looked at her with a slight frown, and she shrugged.

"I'm not saying it isn't," his chief of staff said. "It's just that the last time the Octagon sent us off on one of its little missions, it didn't work out so well."

Times had certainly changed, Tourville reflected. An officer who'd said what Delaney just had would have been arrested, charged with defeatism and treason against the People, and almost certainly shot—probably in less than twenty-four hours—under the old régime.

Not that she didn't have a point, he admitted to himself.

"Yes, Molly," he said aloud. "As a matter of fact, I *do* think it's a good idea. And," he added just a bit pointedly, "what you say to me in private like this is one thing."

"Understood, Sir," Delaney said a bit more formally—but, Tourville was pleased to note, without any trace of obsequiousness.

"I'll admit," the admiral continued after a moment, "that attacking a target like Zanzibar isn't exactly something for the weak-nerved, but at least this time we've got what looks like adequate—and accurate—operational intelligence. And assuming the numbers we've got are correct, we've also got a big enough hammer this time."

"I know," Delaney said, and there might have been just a bit of embarrassment in her smile. "It's just that we got caught with our trousers so thoroughly down around our ankles last time."

"That," Tourville conceded, "we certainly did. Of course, *this* time we can also be fairly certain Honor Harrington is going to be somewhere else. And while I'm not particularly superstitious, I have to admit that I consider that a good omen."

He and Delaney exchanged grins whose humor was more than a bit strained as they recalled the Battle of Sidemore. It was the second time Lester Tourville had crossed swords with Honor Harrington. The first time, units under his command had crippled her ship and captured her. The second time, she had—he acknowledged it freely—kicked his ass up between his ears.

His calm expression concealed an inner shudder as he remembered the nightmare in the Marsh System. Four hundred light-years from home, with a fleet which was supposed to have a decisive edge over its unprepared, unsuspecting opponents, only to discover that its opponents were anything but unsuspecting . . . and very well prepared, indeed.

When Harrington sprang her trap, he hadn't expected to get anything out. As it was, he'd somehow managed to extract almost a third of his total fleet. Which, of course, was another way of saying he'd *lost* over two-thirds of it. And he would have lost it all, if Shannon Foraker's defensive doctrine hadn't worked so well. Most of the ships he'd gotten out had been badly battered, and although he'd managed to evade any pursuit in the depths of hyper-space, the voyage home had been a nightmare all its own. Restricted by damage to the Delta bands, his maximum apparent velocity had been only 1,300 *c*, which meant the trip had taken over three months. Three months of dealing with damage out of limited onboard resources. Three months of watching his wounded recover—or not—when even his surviving units had lost thirty percent of their medical personnel. And three months without any idea at all how the *rest* of Operation Thunderbolt had gone.

It was fortunate that the answer to that last question was that it had gone quite well indeed. The success of the other fleet commanders might have rubbed a little more salt into the wound of his own failure, but at least the Manties had been hammered far harder overall than the Republic. It was a pity Javier Giscard hadn't gone ahead and attacked at Trevor's Star, but Tourville couldn't fault that decision—not on the basis of what Javier had known at the time. But the Grendelsbane attack, especially, had been a crushing success, and no one at the Octagon had blamed Tourville or his staff for what had happened to Fourth Fleet in Marsh.

One or two politicians had had a few things to say. In fact, a couple of them had been vocal enough to get themselves firmly onto Lester Tourville's personal shit list. That was one side of a living, breathing democracy which Tourville was honest enough to admit he could have done without. But the most telling evidence that he continued to enjoy the confidence of his superiors was his new assignment.

Second Fleet was a new organization. The old Second Fleet had been dissolved after Thunderbolt, and the new one's skeleton of veteran units was receiving primarily new construction, straight from completing working up exercises under Shannon Foraker's direction in Bolthole. When he'd been given the command, his understanding had been that it wouldn't be committed to action for at least a T-year, and probably somewhat longer. Second Fleet was supposed to be the knuckleduster no one on the other side knew existed until it landed in a devastating right cross.

But even the best plans were subject to change, and Operation Gobi was right down Lester Tourville's alley. Nor was it going to require him to commit his complete strength. He could put together the required strike force out of his more experienced, battle hardened units without exposing his newbies. In fact, he supposed he really could have handed the entire operation over to one of his task force commanders . . . if there'd been a single chance in hell he wouldn't be commanding it himself.

"It ought to be interesting, anyway," he said after a few moments. "I wasn't there when Icarus smashed Zanzibar last time, but somehow I don't think the Zanzibarans are going to be especially happy about getting run over by an air lorry a *second* time. And Zanzibar is at least as important to the Alliance's war effort as all of the systems Harrington has hit so far, combined, were to ours."

"I know, Boss." Delaney nodded. "As a matter of fact, I think that's one reason I may be feeling a little more anxious." Tourville quirked an eyebrow at her, and she shrugged. "They have to know Zanzibar's important to them, if we do. And they gave up an awful lot of intel on their defensive deployments the last time we hit them. If I were them, I'd have been making some changes since."

"Which is exactly what the operations plan assumes they've done," Tourville pointed out. "But unless they're prepared to make a major commitment of ships of the wall, they're going to be using some variant of what we already saw. And unlike them, we *are* prepared to make a major commitment of the wall." He smiled thinly. "I don't think they're going to enjoy the experience as much as we are."

Honor stood on *Imperator's* flag bridge, hands clasped loosely behind her, and watched her plot as Eighth Fleet headed out on Cutworm III. The bloodstains had been cleaned up long ago, of course, and the shattered consoles and command chairs had been replaced. But no one on the bridge was likely to forget that six people they'd all known well had died there. And Honor could feel Spencer Hawke, standing in Simon's spot beside the hatch.

She watched the silent, peaceful icons moving across the plot, accelerating steadily towards Trevor's Star's hyper limit, and tried to analyze her own emotions. Sorrow predominated, she thought. And then . . . not *guilt*, exactly, but something like it.

Too many of her armsmen had died in the line of duty, protecting her back, or simply caught in the crossfire of naval engagements they would never have been anywhere near if not for her. At first, she'd felt almost angry at them because of the way their deaths weighed upon her sense of responsibility. But gradually she'd come to understand it didn't really work that way. Yes, they'd died because they'd been *her* armsmen, but every one of them had been a volunteer. They'd served her because they'd chosen to, and they were content. They were no more eager to die than anyone else, but they were as confident that they had given their service to someone worthy of them as Honor Harrington had been confident of the same thing the first day she met Elizabeth III face to face. And because they were, it wasn't her job to keep them alive—it was her job to *be* worthy of the service they'd chosen to give.

And yet, despite that, she carried the weight of their deaths as she carried the weight of all her dead, and she desperately wanted them to live. And however she might feel about Simon

Mattingly's death, or the deaths of her other bridge personnel, there was Timothy Meares himself. The young man she'd killed.

She stood in almost exactly the same spot she'd stood then. She could turn around and see exactly where Simon had fallen, where Meares' body had slammed to the deck. She knew she'd had no choice, and that even as she killed him, Meares had understood that. But he'd been so young, had so much promise, and to die like that—killed by a friend to stop him from killing other friends . . .

Nimitz bleeked in her ear, the sound scolding, and she shook herself mentally as she tasted his emotions. He, too, grieved for Simon and for Meares, but he blamed neither her nor Meares. *His* hatred was reserved for whoever had sent Timothy Meares on his final horrifying mission, and Honor realized he was right.

She didn't know who had ordered her assassination, or planned its execution . . . but she would. And when she did, she would personally do something about it.

Nimitz bleeked again, and this time the sound was hungrier and soft with agreement.

"Sir, the task force is ready to proceed."

Lester Tourville turned his head to look down into the small com display. Captain Celestine Houellebecq, the commanding officer of RHNS *Guerriere*, flagship of Second Fleet, looked back out of it at him.

"What?" Tourville asked with a small smile. "No last-minute delays? No liberty parties still adrift?"

"None, Sir," Houellebecq replied deadpan. "I informed the shore patrol that anyone who reported in late was to be shot beside the shuttle pad as an object lesson to others."

"There's the spirit I like to see!" Tourville said, although, truth be told, he found the joke just a bit too pointed, given the previous régime's history. "Always find a positive way to motivate your personnel."

"That's what I thought, Sir."

"Well, in that case, Celestine, let's get them moving. We've got an appointment with the Manties."

"Aye, Sir."

Houellebecq disappeared from the display as she began issuing the orders necessary for Task Force 21 to break parking orbit, and Tourville turned his attention to his plot.

The slowly moving light codes wouldn't have meant much to a civilian, but they were an impressive sight to the trained eye. He picked out the ponderous might of his four battle squadrons, shaking down into cruising formation as they accelerated slowly. Ahead of them were the icons of a pair of battlecruiser squadrons, and six *Aviary*-class CLACs followed in their wake. A sprinkling of lighter units spread out in a necklace of jewels ahead of the main formation, watching alertly for any hint of an unidentified starship, and a trio of fast replenishment ships loaded with additional missile pods trailed along behind the carriers.

Not a capital ship on the display was more than three T-years old, and once again Tourville felt something suspiciously like awe. The Republican Navy might remain technologically inferior, in some ways, to the Royal Manticoran Navy, but unlike the Manties, it had risen from the ashes of defeat. Its officers, its senior personnel, had known what it meant to lose battle after battle, but now the same officers and personnel had learned what it was to win. More than that, they'd come to *expect* to win, and Lester Tourville wondered if the Manties truly realized just how true that was.

Well, he thought, *if they don't realize it now, we'll give them a hint in about two weeks.*

"Sir, we've just picked up a hyper footprint. It looks like at least two ships, probably destroyers or light cruisers."

"Where?" Captain Durand demanded, walking across the space station's command deck to Plotting.

"Forty-two light-minutes out from the primary, on our side and right on the ecliptic, Sir," Lieutenant Bibeau replied.

"So the foxes are scouting the hen house," Durand murmured.

The Plotting officer looked up at him a bit strangely; Charles Bibeau was from the slums of Nouveau Paris, whereas Durand came from the farming planet of Rochelle, and the Skipper kept coming up with oddball metaphors and similes. But the lieutenant caught his drift just fine, and nodded in agreement.

"All right, Lieutenant," Durand said after a moment, resting one hand lightly on Bibeau's shoulder as he watched the hyper footprints fade from the plot. "Keep an eye out. If we can pick up their platforms, so much the better, but the main thing I want to know is when anyone else hypers in."

"Aye, Sir."

Durand patted him on the shoulder once, then turned and walked slowly back to his own command chair.

Somewhere out there, he knew, Manty reconnaissance arrays were creeping stealthily inward, spying out the details of the Solon System's defenses. He knew what they were going to see, and it wasn't all that impressive: a single division of old-style superdreadnoughts, a slightly understrength battlecruiser squadron, and a couple of hundred LACs. Hardly enough to cause a Manty raiding force to break a sweat.

Which was fine with Captain Alexis Durand. Just fine.

Chapter Thirty-Five

"We have Commander Estwicke's report, Your Grace," Andrea Jaruwalski said.

"Good."

Honor turned away from the visual display's gorgeous imagery. Task Force 82 forged through hyper-space, closing in on its objective steadily in close enough formation for the display to show the glowing disks of the nearest ships' Warshawski sails. *Intolerant*, *Imperator*'s sister ship and the flagship of Rear Admiral Allen Morowitz, the division's CO, was the nearest vessel. Her sails—three hundred kilometers across—flickered with lambent fire, like a slice of heat lightning moving across the glowing depths of hyper-space in a visual spectacle Honor never tired of, but she turned her back upon it with what was almost a sense of relief at Jaruwalski's announcement.

"Let's see it," she said, crossing to the secondary plot at Jaruwalski's bridge station. The ops officer touched the keyboard, shunting the download from HMS *Ambuscade* onto the display, and then she and her admiral stood back and watched the data assemble itself.

"Not as much firepower as we'd anticipated, Your Grace," Jaruwalski observed after a moment.

"No."

Honor frowned and rubbed the tip of her nose. All their planning had assumed Lorn would be the target more likely to be covered by mobile units, which was why she'd swapped Alice Truman two of Alistair McKeon's superdreadnought divisions and

445

Matsuzawa Hirotaka's older battlecruisers in return for Michelle Henke's more modern but understrength squadron. She'd also given Alice Winston Bradshaw's Seventh Cruiser Squadron, with its four *Edward Saganami-C*-class cruisers, while she took Charise Fanaafi's CruRon 12, with its older *Saganami* and *Star Knight*-class cruisers. Still, they'd anticipated more defensive strength than this for a target as populous and economically important as Solon.

"I make it two superdreadnoughts," she continued after moment, "plus seven battlecruisers and roughly—" she consulted a display sidebar "—a hundred and ninety LACs."

"For mobile units, yes, Your Grace," Jaruwalski agreed. "But it looks like they've got a fairly dense shell of missile pods in close to the planetary industry around Arthur."

"And another little clutch here, around Merlin," Honor pointed out, and frowned some more. "That's a rather strange spot for them, wouldn't you say?"

"I certainly would."

Jaruwalski looked at the data and pursed her lips while she considered it.

"That's much too far out to cover the Nimue Belt's extraction centers," she said. "Is there something going on out among Merlin's moons that we don't know about?"

"I suppose there could be," Honor mused, gazing at the stupendous gas giant—only a bit smaller than Old Earth's Jupiter—in question. "According to the astro data, a couple of Merlin's moons are darned nearly the size of Manticore, and it's got a total of eleven. There could be something exploitable in among all of those. But whatever it is, it's on the far side of the primary from Arthur at the moment, anyway. So I think we'll just leave Merlin alone and concentrate on Arthur and the belter installations."

"That suits me just fine, Your Grace," Jaruwalski agreed.

"It looks like our best bet is probably Alpha Three," Honor continued. "I'd just as soon avoid any unnecessary bells and whistles."

"Alpha Three works for me, Your Grace," Jaruwalski agreed again. "Shall I pass the word to Admiral Miklós?"

"Go ahead." Honor nodded. "And tell him to doublecheck his alternate recovery points with his COLACs."

"Of course, Your Grace," Jaruwalski said, then paused, looking at her admiral thoughtfully. "Um, is there some particular reason you wanted to do that, Your Grace?"

"Nothing I can put a finger on," Honor said after a moment. "I guess I'm just a little antsy. As you say, we'd anticipated a significantly heavier defensive force for a system this important."

"Yes, Ma'am. You're thinking that whoever's in command here has tried to pull a Bellefeuille on us?"

"Not really," Honor said almost unwillingly, then shook her head at her own formless misgivings. "Estwicke knows her job, and everybody was thoroughly briefed on what happened at Chantilly."

And, she reminded herself, *that's one reason we gave her an extra eighteen hours to scout the system. If there'd been anything close enough to Arthur to pose a threat,* Ambuscade *and* Intruder *would have found it.*

"I suppose part of it could just be the fact that Solon lies right in the middle of a gravity wave," she continued aloud. "I always get a sort of uncomfortable feeling between my shoulder blades in a case like this."

Jaruwalski nodded. No flag officer really liked attacking a star system which lay in the middle of a hyper-space gravity wave—not unless she was totally confident she'd brought along enough firepower to take the system outright—for a very simple reason. A starship could not enter a gravity wave and survive without functioning Warshawski sails, and no ship could produce a Warshawski sail if it had lost an alpha node out of one of its impeller rings. Which meant a single unlucky hit could leave a warship with otherwise trifling damage unable to withdraw into hyper if the rest of its task force or fleet had to run for it.

Frankly, Jaruwalski suspected that was one reason Honor had assigned herself to command the Solon attack. Well, that and the fact that they'd anticipated—erroneously, as it turned out—that Solon, with its heavily populated planet and relatively thriving economy would have considerably heavier fixed defenses than Lorn.

"As I say," Honor continued, "I don't have any real reason to feel uneasy, but have Samuel doublecheck, anyhow." She smiled crookedly. "I'm not trying to develop a reputation for infallible intuition, so it won't hurt anything if I do a little excess worrying and people catch me at it."

✧   ✧   ✧

"Captain Durand! Captain Durand to the command deck immediately!"

Alexis Durand punched the flush button, yanked up his trousers, and hit the lavatory door running. One of the space station's civilian maintenance techs grinned as the naval officer charged past him, still sealing his trousers. Well, Durand could stand a little civilian amusement at his expense.

He came through the command deck hatch and slid to a stop at Plotting. Bibeau had the watch again, and he looked up as Durand appeared beside him.

"You wanted to know when anyone else turned up, Sir," the petty officer said grimly, waving at his display. "Well, here they are."

"So I see, Lieutenant. Have you informed Admiral Deutscher?"

"Yes, Sir. And passed to word to Moriarty, too."

"Good," Durand said softly, leaning closer to the display. "What does CIC make of it so far?"

"Twenty-eight point sources, Sir. It looks like seven super-dreadnoughts or carriers, eleven battlecruisers or heavy cruisers, and nine light cruisers or destroyers, all on our side of the primary and right on the limit. Plus, of course, whatever they left in-system to keep an eye on us."

"Of course." Durand nodded, and he and the lieutenant exchanged wolflike grins.

"Sir," a communications rating said respectfully, "Governor Mathieson wants to know if she should begin evacuating the platforms?"

"By all means," Durand said. "And remind her to be obvious about it."

"Aye, Sir."

Durand returned his attention to Bibeau's plot and folded his arms across his chest while he thought.

"No sign of LAC separation yet?" he asked after a few moments.

"No, Sir."

"Very good. Inform me as soon as you see it, as soon as their lead starship crosses the hyper limit, or as soon as any of them micro-jump."

"Aye, Sir."

Durand gazed at the plot for a few more moments, then walked slowly to his own command chair and seated himself in it.

Despite Rear Admiral Deutscher's seniority, this portion of the operation was officially Durand's responsibility, and part of him wanted to send the message now. But he made himself put the temptation firmly aside; they needed to let the situation settle down a bit first.

"Very well, Samuel, let's be about it," Honor said. "Launch your LACs."

"Aye, aye, Your Grace," Vice Admiral Miklós acknowledged, and turned away from his com pickup on the flag bridge of HMS *Succubus* to pass the order. A moment later, Honor saw the first LACs' icons appear on her tactical plot.

The six CLACs carried over six hundred and seventy LACs between them, but she was leaving HMS *Unicorn*'s wing behind to provide security for Miklós weakly armed carriers. She was also leaving three of Mary Lou Moreau's light cruisers—*Tisiphone*, *Samurai*, and *Clotho*—to help keep an eye on things, but the rest of the task force headed steadily in-system with her flagship.

She supposed she could have left a few main combatants, as well, given how sparse the defenses were, but she still felt that unaccountable itch between her shoulder blades. She was fairly certain she was jumping at shadows, but it wouldn't hurt anything to stay concentrated.

The five hundred and sixty LACs accompanying her starships spread out in a globe about them, and Andrea Jaruwalski sent an advanced guard of recon platforms out ahead as they shaped their course to intercept the planet Arthur's orbit.

"Sir, they're crossing the limit," Bibeau said. "Present velocity two-point-six-one thousand KPS. Range to Arthur ten-point-two light-minutes. Tracking makes their current accel four-point-eight-one KPS squared."

"They're staying concentrated? No detachments?"

"Pretty much, Sir. It looks like they're leaving their carriers behind with three cruisers and a LAC security patrol, but all the rest of them are headed in-system."

Durand nodded, not without a flicker of disappointment. Not that he was really surprised. He'd always thought the Merlin pods were unlikely to suck them in, but it had been worth a try. And they'd needed something to camouflage the *Tarantula* platforms, anway.

"Time to Arthur?" he asked.

"Assuming a zero/zero intercept and constant accelerations, approximately three hours and seventeen minutes, Sir. They'll make turnover niner-one-point-eight million klicks out in ninety-four minutes."

"Very good. Communications!"

"Yes, Sir?"

"Send Lieutenant Bibeau's data to *Tarantula* and instruct Lieutenant Sigourney to execute his orders."

"Aye, Sir."

"Their superdreadnoughts are starting to stir, Your Grace."

Honor broke off her conversation with Mercedes Brigham at Jaruwalski's announcement. Her own force had been headed in-system for thirty-seven minutes. Her velocity relative to the system primary was up to 13,191 KPS, and she'd come just over seventeen million kilometers since crossing the hyper limit . . . which meant she had a hundred and sixty-six million still to go.

She glanced at the plot, and noted the vector arrows which had appeared next to the tiny defensive force in orbit around Arthur. As Jaruwalski said, the starships—escorted by the swarm of LACs—were beginning to move. She studied their vector for a moment, then frowned.

"Odd," she murmured.

"Ma'am?" She looked up. Brigham stood at her elbow, where she'd been gazing at the same display, and the chief of staff arched one eyebrow as their eyes met.

"I said that's odd." Honor indicated the icons of the accelerating defenders. "They're coming to meet us, which is odd enough on its own. I would have expected them to wait for us as deep into the envelope of their system defense pods as they could. If they keep accelerating at that rate, they'll be right at the very fringe of their pods' effective range when we engage, which means accuracy will be even lower than usual. By the same token, the range to their ships will be lower for us, which means *our* accuracy will be greater. But not only are they coming to meet us, but from these acceleration numbers, they don't have many, if any, pods of their own on tow."

"You think they're up to something sneaky? Or is this just a panic reaction?"

"I don't see what kind of 'sneakiness' they could have in mind," Honor said after a second. "Estwicke's arrays got visual-range imagery off of both of the SDs, so we know they aren't pod-layers. That means they don't have any MDM capability, without towing pods, which they clearly aren't doing. Oh," she waved a hand, "they may have a few dozen tractored inside their wedges, but nowhere near enough to take us on in a missile duel, especially with the *Katanas* to thicken our point defense.

"On the other hand, this is a bit late in the game for a panic reaction. We've been in the system for over forty-five minutes. For them to be underway at all at this point, they must have been at at least standby readiness when we turned up—which makes sense, since they obviously realized Estwicke was scouting for a raid. But from standby readiness they *could* have been underway a good fifteen minutes sooner than this—a half-hour sooner, if they were sitting there with hot nodes. So why wait until now to 'panic'?"

"So what *do* you think they're doing?" Brigham asked.

"I don't know," Honor admitted, rubbing the tip of her nose once more. "It *looks* like they're reacting in confusion, and I suppose that could be what's happening. But that just doesn't feel right, somehow."

She contemplated the plot for a few more moments, then climbed out of her command chair, scooped a skinsuited Nimitz up in her arms, and crossed to Jaruwalski's station.

"How's their evacuation coming, Andrea?"

"It's still going full bore, Your Grace." Jaruwalski indicated a secondary display driven by transmissions from the stealthed arrays hovering near Arthur. "I wouldn't go so far as to call it panic stricken," she continued, "but they're obviously hauling everybody dirt-side as quick as they can."

"Still no word from the system authorities, Harper?" Honor asked, turning her head towards Communications.

"No, Your Grace," Harper Brantley replied, and Honor grimaced.

"But you're still picking up those grav-pulses?" she asked.

"Yes, Your Grace." The com officer nodded his head at Jaruwalski. "Captain Jaruwalski's arrays are actually picking up most of them, but we've been looking at them over here, as well. So far, it all looks like our own early-generation traffic, probably from fixed recon arrays scattered around the system. Their pulse repetition frequency rate's still on the low side, so the information they're passing is probably limited, but there are at least a couple of stations out there with a higher PRF."

"Can you localize the more capable transmitters?"

"We've nailed down two of them, Your Grace," Jaruwalski reported. "One of them seems to be aboard this space station."

A red sighting ring popped into existence around the system's main space station as she spoke. It was a big thing, though no more than twenty percent the size of *Hephaestus*, back home.

"And the other?" Honor asked, eyes narrowing intently.

"The other one is out here, Your Grace."

Jaruwalski dropped another icon into the display. This one appeared to be in orbit around Merlin, which put it over forty light-minutes outside the system hyper limit on the far side of the primary.

"Are they talking to each other, Harper?"

"I'd say, yes, Your Grace. I can't be positive, of course, but pattern analysis strongly suggests that they are."

"Thank you."

Honor nodded and walked slowly back across to her command chair, right hand gently caressing the plushy fur between Nimitz's ears.

"Your Grace, I know that expression," Brigham said quietly as Honor and Nimitz rejoined her.

"I beg your pardon?"

"I said I know that expression. May I ask what's provoking it this time?"

"I don't know, really." Honor shrugged. "There's just . . . something wrong. It's like they're going off in all directions at once—panicky evacuation of their orbital platforms, ships heading out to meet us without even bringing along heavy pod loads, no effort to communicate with us at all, and now this FTL message traffic."

"Maybe they really *are* going off in all directions at once, Your Grace," Brigham suggested. "It's one thing to know the other side is scouting your system; it's another to see a force this powerful coming down on you."

"I know, I know." Honor snorted. "Maybe I'm simply being

paranoid! But I just can't shake the feeling that there's something out of kilter."

"Well, Ma'am, even if Arthur is talking to someone out at Merlin, it's not like either of them were close enough to pose any sort of threat to us. For that matter, Merlin's on the entirely wrong side of Solon!"

"Exactly. So why—"

Honor broke off abruptly, her eyes suddenly widening.

"Your Grace?" Brigham asked sharply.

"Sidemore," Honor said. "They're taking a page from Sidemore!"

Brigham looked blank for a moment, then inhaled deeply.

"They'd have to have accurately predicted our objectives," she said.

"No reason they couldn't have," Honor replied almost absently, eyes intent as she stared into the depths of her tactical plot. "Not in a general sense, at least. Deciding what sorts of targets we'd be likely to hit wouldn't be that hard. Picking the exact, *specific* targets would probably come down to a guessing game, but it looks like someone guessed right."

She looked into the plot for a few more seconds, then turned away.

"Harper, get me a priority link to Admiral Miklós!"

"Too bad they didn't go for the cheese, Sir," Captain Marius Gozzi said as he and Javier Giscard studied the master plot aboard RHNS *Sovereign of Space*.

"I never figured there was more than one chance in three they would," Giscard replied. "Still, it was worth a try."

He stood back from the plot and folded his hands behind him while he thought. From the reports of his own sensor platforms, it was very likely that one of those Manty superdreadnoughts was Eighth Fleet's flagship. In which case, he was about to sit down across the table from the best the Manties had.

But this time I get to use my own cards, he reminded himself. *And they're marked.*

The one thing he wished he had was real-time intelligence on exactly what the Manties were up to, but that simply wasn't possible. The *Tarantula* net could get tactical information to him, but only by sending it aboard dispatch boats, and he didn't have an unlimited supply of them. Nor could he send any of the boats back after they'd reported to him, since the Manties would have been much too likely to detect their hyper footprints when they translated back into normal-space.

At least, so far, the raiders appeared to be doing what he wanted them to do. He would have preferred for them to take the "cheese," as Gozzi had called it. If they'd decided the missile pods planted around Merlin indicated there was something out there worth attacking, they might have divided their forces. Of course, the real reason for the pods had been to provide background clutter to hide the *Tarantula* platforms, because Shannon hadn't been able to get the new FTL coms into something small enough to count on evading the notice of Manty sensor arrays. But there'd always been the chance of killing multiple birds with a single stone. And once they'd come in close enough to Merlin, they would have been trapped inside the massive gas giant's own hyper limit, pinned while his units closed in behind them. Still, as he'd told his chief of staff, he'd never really had much confidence they would.

He checked the time display. Four minutes until the next dispatch boat was due.

"Selma, pass the preparatory signal for Ambush Three," he said.

"Aye, Sir," Commander Selma Thackeray, his operations officer responded.

"Yes, Your Grace?" Vice Admiral Samuel Miklós said as he appeared on Honor's com display.

"It's a trap, Samuel," Honor said flatly. The FTL com grav pulses meant there was no light-speed lag in their conversation at this short range, and Miklós' eyes widened in surprise. "I can't prove it—yet," she continued, "but I'm sure of it. Get your carriers out. Go to Omega One."

It was obvious from Miklós' expression that he wanted to ask her if she was certain that was what she really wanted to do, but he didn't. He only nodded.

"Yes, Your Grace. At once. And you?"

"And we, Samuel, are going to have our hands full, I'm afraid," she said grimly.

✧   ✧   ✧

"Captain Durand!"

"Yes, Charles?" Durand turned quickly towards Bibeau.

"Sir, their carriers just translated out!"

"Damn."

Durand thought furiously for perhaps ten seconds. There *could* be a perfectly innocent reason for the Manties to have suddenly decided to move their carriers, but he didn't believe it for a moment. No. Somehow, they'd guessed what was coming, and he suppressed a desire to swear yet again.

"Communications, pass Lieutenant Bibeau's current sensor data on to *Tarantula*. Tell them I recommend an immediate relay to Admiral Giscard."

The dispatch boat one light-minute outside Merlin's orbit received the Durand's FTL transmission, relayed to its light-speed communications arrays by the *Tarantula* net, seventy-two seconds after it was transmitted. The boat's computers updated, and it translated smoothly across the alpha wall. Javier Giscard's task force was waiting exactly where it had been for the past week and a half, and the dispatch boat quickly relayed the tactical update to his flagship.

"Sir, it looks like the Manties smelled a rat," Commander Thackeray reported. "Their CLACs just translated out."

"Damn it," Gozzi muttered, but Giscard only showed his teeth in a tight grin.

"Actually catching them that far outside the limit would have been problematical, at best, Marius," he said. "You know how hard it is a to plot a hyper jump this short. And they weren't exactly likely to be sitting there with their hyper generators off-line and their impeller nodes cold. Unless we'd translated down right on top of them, they'd have had time to get into hyper before we could range on them." He shrugged. "I'd figured we were going to lose them from the moment the Manties left them behind. However," his grin turned positively lupine, "if the carriers are gone, the LACs are stuck, aren't they?"

He looked at the updated plot for a few more seconds, then nodded decisively to himself.

"Selma, execute Ambush Three."

"Oh, *crap*," Commander Harriman muttered.

"Talk to me, Yolanda!" Raphael Cardones said quickly.

"CIC reports multiple hyper footprints, Skipper," *Imperator's* tactical officer reported harshly. "Three separate clusters—one dead astern of us at three-zero-point-four million clicks, one at polar north, and one at polar south. They've got us boxed, Sir."

Cardones felt his jaw muscles clench as his own tactical plot updated with the new icons.

Well, the Old Lady's been warning us the Peeps were eventually going to get wise, he told himself. *I could wish they hadn't gotten quite* this *wise, though!*

"It's confirmed, Your Grace," Andrea Jaruwalski said. "Three separate forces, a total of eighteen wallers and six CLACs, plus screening elements. We're designating the Arthur detachment Bogey One, the task group to system north is Bogey Two, the one to system south is Bogey Three, and the one astern of us is Bogey Four."

"And their units are evenly distributed between Two, Three, and Four?"

"That's what it looks like, Your Grace."

"So, three-to-one in wallers, at best," Mercedes Brigham said quietly, her expression taut. "Nine-to-one if they manage to concentrate. Plus the older ships in-system, of course!"

"If we let them concentrate on us, we'll deserve whatever happens to us." Honor's soprano was completely calm, almost detached.

The good news was that the three ambushing task groups had clearly been waiting in place in hyper, motionless relative to Solon. They'd come across the alpha wall with an effectively zero velocity, and though they were accelerating hard at five hundred and twenty-nine gravities, which meant their compensator safety margins must be down to zero, it was going to take them time to build a vector, whereas her own command was already up to over fourteen thousand kilometers per second. Moreover, her maximum acceleration rate was higher than theirs, so the force astern of them couldn't possibly overtake them unless they suffered drive damage. The bad news was that they were only thirty million kilometers back ... and on low-powered settings, current-generation Havenite MDMs had a powered range of almost *sixty-one* million kilometers from rest.

"Missile defense, go to Plan Romeo," she said crisply. "Shift to formation Charlie. Theo."

"Yes, Your Grace?" Lieutenant Commander Kgari said instantly.

"We'll break south," Honor told her staff astrogator. "Take us to military power and plot me a course that bends us the maximum distance away from Bogey One but maintains at least current separation from Bogey Four."

"Aye, aye, Ma'am."

Kgari bent over his console, and Honor returned her attention to the tactical plot, watching the icons of her formation shift rapidly.

It won't be long now, she thought.

"Sir, we've got about the best targeting solutions we're going to get," Commander Thackeray reported. Giscard looked at her, and she met his gaze frankly. "Our accuracy isn't going to be very good at such extended range," she said.

"Understood, Selma. On the other hand, we've got a lot of missiles. Let's start getting them into space. Fire Plan Baker."

"Aye, Sir!"

Chapter Thirty-Six

"Missile separation!" Andrea Jaruwalski announced. "I have multiple missile separations. Range at launch three-zero-point-four-five million kilometers. Time to attack range seven minutes!"

"Understood. Do *not* return fire."

"Do not return fire, aye, aye, Ma'am," Jaruwalski replied.

"Your Grace, I have that course," Kgari said.

"Give it to Andrea."

"Come to two-niner-three, zero-zero-five at six-point-zero-one KPS squared," Kgari said.

"Two-niner-three, zero-zero-five, six-point-zero-one KPS squared," Jaruwalski repeated, and the task force altered course while the first salvo howled up its wake.

Each of Javier Giscard's six SD(P)s could roll six pods simultaneously, one pattern every twelve seconds, and each pod contained ten missiles, each a bit larger than the Royal Manticoran Navy's own first-generation MDMs. The range was extremely long for accuracy, especially using Havenite fire control systems, so Giscard opted for maximum density salvos, both to saturate the enemy's defenses and to give him more possibilities of hits.

Each of his ships deployed six patterns—a total of one hundred and eight pods—programmed for staggered launch. And then, precisely on schedule, all of them launched and sent a total of almost eleven hundred multi-drive missiles screaming up Task Force 82's wake.

The range at launch was 30,450,000 kilometers. Given the relative

458

motion of the two forces, actual flight distance was 36,757,440 kilometers. At that distance, and an acceleration of 416.75 KPS^2, the MDMs attained a velocity relative to the primary of 175,034 KPS, which equated to an overtake velocity against Task Force 82 of 152,925 KPS, or fifty-three percent of light-speed.

Seventy-two seconds later, a second, identical salvo roared out of its pods.

And seventy-two seconds after *that*, a third.

In the space of just over thirteen minutes, eleven salvos—just under twelve thousand missiles—went hurtling after Task Force 82.

In a traditional engagement, the pursuing Republican super-dreadnoughts would have been able to fire only a handful of missiles from their bow-mounted chase tubes. In an era of pod-layers, that limitation had long since disappeared, but what remained true was that missiles closing from directly ahead or directly astern faced the weakest defensive fire. There simply wasn't room to mount as many point defense laser clusters and counter-missile tubes on a warship's ends as on her broadside. The clusters mounted were the most powerful ones in her entire armament, but there could be only a few of them. Telemetry links to counter-missiles were also limited, and the fact that her wedge offered no protection against fire from those angles only made the situation worse.

And, of course, just to make things even better from Task Force 82's perspective, Havenite MDMs carried bigger and more powerful warheads as compensation for their poorer accuracy and penetration aids.

"Why aren't they returning fire?" Gozzi asked quietly.

"I don't know," Giscard replied. "Maybe they don't want their own attack birds' wedges interfering with their fire control. Besides, unless they want to alter heading to open their broadsides, they can't have the control links to manage a salvo dense enough to get through our point defense."

Gozzi nodded, and Giscard turned his attention back to the plot. His hypothesis was at least superficially logical, but deep inside, he didn't believe it himself.

Bogey Four's first salvo's MDMs raced onward, crossing the vast gulf between the ships which had launched them and their targets. Seventy lost lock and arced off uselessly four minutes into their flight, due to a telemetry glitch. One thousand and ten continued on course.

"Enemy fire appears to be tracking in on *Imperator* and *Intolerant*," Jaruwalski reported tensely.

"Not surprising, I suppose," Mercedes Brigham muttered.

"But maybe not the smartest targeting," Honor replied calmly. Brigham looked at her, and Honor shrugged. "I admit, it would pay the highest dividend if they managed to knock out an alpha node on one of the superdreadnoughts, but their defenses are a lot tougher than anyone else's, and given the geometry, they'll have a long time to throw missiles at us. If I were in command over there, I'd start with the battlecruisers, or maybe even the heavy cruisers."

"Kill the weaker platforms first and attrit our missile defenses," Brigham said.

"Exactly. Each of them represents a smaller percentage of our total defensive capability, but they'd be a lot easier to kill or cripple." Honor shrugged again. "You could argue it either way, I suppose—go for the 'golden BB' on an SD(P), or chew up the weaker escorts first. Personally, I'd have done it the other way."

She stood gazing into the master tactical plot, left hand resting on the corner of a tactical rating's console, right hand slowly, gently stroking Nimitz's head, and her expression was calm, thoughtful.

"Counter-missile launch in . . . fifteen seconds," Jaruwalski announced.

The powered range from rest for the Mark 31 counter-missile was 3,585,556 kilometers, with a flight time of seventy-five seconds. Given the geometry of the engagement, effective range at launch was over 12.5 million kilometers, and the defensive missiles started to go out ninety seconds before the Havenite MDMs reached standoff attack range of their targets. The Mod-2-XR counter-missile launcher had a cycle time of eight seconds, which meant there was time for eleven launches per tube.

In the old days—all of four T-years ago—that wouldn't have mattered all that much, since the interference of the counter-missiles' own wedges would have blinded follow-up launches. Even now, that would have been true of a Havenite ship, although with the changes Shannon Foraker had made, any ship in a Havenite formation could now "manage" any other ship's counter-missiles, as long as both units had arranged the handoff prior to launch. That meant a Republican formation with the same degree of separation between units as Task Force 82 could have managed perhaps three times the number of counter-missiles it once could have.

But the Royal Manticoran Navy had added the Keyhole platforms to its bag of tricks.

Instead of a half-dozen or a dozen counter-missiles per ship, they could bring the fire of their *entire* broadside counter-missile batteries to bear. They weren't restricted to the telemetry links physically mounted on their after hammerheads; they had sufficient links to control *all* of their counter-missiles aboard *each* Keyhole, and each ship had two Keyholes deployed. And as missile defense Plan Romeo rolled Honor's ships up on their sides, those platforms gained sufficient "vertical" separation to see past the interference of subsequent counter-missile salvos fired at far tighter intervals than had ever before been possible.

They still couldn't control eleven salvos . . . but they *could* control eight, and each of those eight contained far more missiles than anyone else could have managed.

Javier Giscard's staff had anticipated no more than five CM launches, and they'd allowed for an average of only ten counter-missiles per ship, for a total of two hundred per launch. Their fire plans had been predicated on facing somewhere around a thousand ship-launched CMs, and perhaps another thousand or so from the *Katanas*.

What they got was over seventy-two hundred from Honor's starships alone.

"My God," Marius Gozzi said softly as the impeller signatures of their attack missiles vanished under the swarm of Manty counter-missiles. "How in the hell did they *do* that?"

"I don't know," Giscard gritted, "but that's why they didn't counter-launch MDMs. They figure their defenses can handle whatever we throw, and the bastards are simply conserving their ammo!"

He glared at the display, then looked up at Thackeray.

"Abort Baker. We're going to need a lot heavier salvos to get through *that*."

He jerked his head at the plot, where his second salvo had just disappeared as tracelessly as the first.

"I don't know if we can *throw* a dense enough salvo to get through it, Sir," Thackeray said. Her expression was almost shocked, but her eyes were intent, and it was obvious her brain was still working.

"Yes, we can," Giscard told her flatly. "Here's what I want you to do."

He explained for a few seconds, and Thackeray nodded sharply when she finished.

"It'll take me a little while to set it up, Sir."

"Understood. Go."

Giscard pointed at her console, and as she dived back into the tactical section, he returned his attention to Gozzi.

"I never counted on that level of defensive fire, either," he said. "But I think it means we're going to have to change our plans for Deutscher."

"What do you want him to do, Sir?"

"Their new vector is going to take them within fifty million kilometers of Arthur. Given that that's almost certainly Honor Harrington in command over there, I don't expect them to peg any missiles at the civilian orbital platforms as they go by. Of course, it may not *be* her, or I could be wrong about what she's going to do. At any rate, we're not going to be able to prevent her from passing that close. But given that, I don't want Deutscher getting any closer to her than he has to. Besides, if he stops accelerating now, he'll have extra time to build his own side of the trap."

"I understand, Sir."

"Your Grace, they've ceased fire!" Andrea Jaruwalski reported jubilantly.

"No, they haven't," Honor replied quietly. Jaruwalski looked at her, and Honor smiled thinly. "What they're doing over there right this minute, Andrea, is deploying a lot more pods. I'd guess they'll probably roll at least ten or twelve patterns each. Sequencing that many launches for a simultaneous time on target will be complicated, but not all that difficult."

"You're probably right, Your Grace," Jaruwalski conceded after only a moment's thought. "It's the obvious counter, now that you've pointed it out."

"So the next salvo is going to be just a bit more difficult to kill. In which case," Honor said grimly, "it may be time to distract them just a bit. I want the battlecruisers held in reserve—they don't have enough ammo capacity to use up pods at this range—but *Imperator* and *Intolerant* will engage the enemy. Pick one superdreadnought and pound it, Andrea."

"Aye, *aye*, Ma'am!"

"Admiral," one of Jaruwalski's ratings said, "Bogey One just killed its acceleration."

"I expected that," Honor said. "Bogey One was never strong enough to fight us. I suspect the only reason it headed towards us in the first place was to contribute to the impression of a system defense force that was thoroughly uncoordinated and panicked. Now that the trap's been sprung, they're not going to want to get any closer to us than they can help."

"We're ready, Admiral," Selma Thackeray said.

"Very well. Execute."

Javier Giscard's task group abruptly altered heading by ninety degrees, bringing its broadsides to bear on Task Force 82. The maneuver cut their acceleration towards the Manticoran ships to zero. But their relative velocity was losing ground steadily, anyway, and the turn also brought all of their broadside fire control to bear. Which meant they had many times as many control links as they'd had before. He was effectively conceding the pursuit in order to maximize his chances of crippling one or more of his foes.

"Missile launch!" Thackeray's assistant operations officer barked suddenly. "We have multiple missile separations, Admiral! Range at launch three-niner-point-four-oh-four million kilometers! Time to attack range seven-point-six minutes!"

"Well, that wasn't exactly unexpected," Giscard said, just a bit more calmly than he actually felt. "They've figured out what we're up to, and they want to force us to 'use them, or lose them.'"

"Launching now, Sir!" Thackeray said, and Giscard nodded.

"So, they have a few new wrinkles of their own," Honor observed.

Selma Thackeray had spent the last six minutes deploying

missile pods. In that time, she'd positioned 1,080 of them. Now she launched *all* of them simultaneously.

The next best thing to eleven thousand MDMs hurled themselves at Task Force 82. Given their lower acceleration rate, and the fact that TF 82 was continuing to accelerate away from them, their flight time would be twenty-five seconds longer than TF 82's, and their closing velocity would be almost nine thousand KPS lower when they arrived, but what they lacked in performance, they more than made up in sheer numbers.

They couldn't possibly have enough control links to manage that many missiles simultaneously, Honor thought. But the way the individual components of the enormous salvo were spreading out and separating, it looked as if they'd come up with a data sharing approach similar to that of the Alliance. If she was right, their control circuits were bouncing back and forth between individual sub flights of missiles, which was going to cost them even more in accuracy. But given the size of the attack wave it made possible, they probably figured the new technique was well worth it.

And they're probably right about that, too, she told herself.

"All units, Missile Defense Sierra!" Jaruwalski snapped. "Carter, stay on the attack birds!"

"Aye, aye, Ma'am!" one of her assistants replied, and Jaruwalski turned her full attention to the defensive engagement.

"We have a probable total of two hundred and eighty-eight incoming in each salvo, Sir," Thackeray reported.

Giscard nodded in understanding. Given the greater capacity per pod the Manties appeared to be getting out of their new, downsized MDMs, Thackeray's estimate worked out to a double pattern from each of the Manty superdreadnoughts. Of course, given the fiendishly capable EW capabilities of Manty missile penetration aids, an accurate count of the incoming was a virtual impossibility. Still, the interval between salvos—twenty-four seconds—accorded well with Thackeray's estimate.

"Get the *Cimeterres* into position," he said.

"Aye, Sir," Thackeray replied, and he heard her coaching the escorting LACs into positions from which their counter-missiles and laser clusters could engage the incoming warheads without fouling Thackeray's telemetry to her own attack birds.

✧   ✧   ✧

"They're moving their LACs in to intercept," Lieutenant Carter announced, his voice a bit hoarse.

Despite his superb instrumentation, he himself had absolutely no control over the attack. He was simply monitoring it for Honor while the tac officers of the individual ships executed the instructions Jaruwalski had already transmitted, and he was very young.

"It's to be expected," Honor told him quietly. She stood behind Jaruwalski, watching the ops officer's plot as the incredible Havenite missile storm roared towards her command. "Just take it as it comes, Jeff."

"Yes, Your Grace."

Carter drew a deep breath and settled himself in his chair, and Honor reached out to rest her right hand lightly on his shoulder for a moment. But even as she did, her eyes stayed on Jaruwalski's plot.

ONI estimated that the latest Havenite SD(P)s carried approximately the same number of missile pods as a *Medusa*-class. Assuming that was accurate, then each of the six superdreadnoughts pursuing her task force carried five hundred pods. They'd expended at least a hundred and sixty each in the first exchange, and there had to be at least a thousand pods in this monster salvo. That came to a total of somewhere around two thousand. So, if the six of them carried three thousand pods between them, that meant they'd have expended two-thirds of their total ammunition allotment by the time *these* missiles arrived.

They can't sustain this level of fire, she told herself. *On the other hand, if they get through with enough of it this time around, it may not matter.*

"They're targeting the battlecruisers this time, too, Your Grace," Brigham said softly, and Honor nodded curtly. They weren't ignoring the superdreadnoughts, but they'd clearly devoted at least some of their total fire to Henke's battlecruisers.

"Here it comes," someone said.

The voice was low, and Giscard didn't recognize it. Nor did he try to. He doubted whoever it was realized he'd spoken aloud, anyway.

Not that anyone had required the announcement.

The first Manticoran salvo streaked into his task group's teeth, and it was obvious the Manties had concentrated everything on a single target.

Task Force 82's missiles roared down on the superdreadnought RHNS *Conquete*. There were, in fact, two hundred and forty attack missiles and forty-eight EW platforms in the lead salvo. Half of the EW birds were Dragon's Teeth, and as they entered Bogie Four's counter-missile envelope, they suddenly appeared on the Havenite tracking displays as two hundred and forty additional attack missiles. Counter-missiles which had been locked onto them suffered massive confusion as their targets abruptly shoaled into literally dozens of false images. Other counter-missiles, which had been earmarked for genuine threats, diverted to the new targets, spending themselves uselessly.

Fourteen of the Dragon's Teeth survived to cross the first interception zone. Six of them survived to cross the second interception zone. Two of them made it halfway across the inner counter-missile zone. But before the last of them was destroyed, they'd carried a hundred and fifty-six attack missiles and fourteen Dazzler EW platforms with them.

Laser clusters tracked onto the surviving Manticoran missiles, but those missiles were closing at sixty-two percent of light-speed. Each cluster had an effective range of 150,000 kilometers, but Manticoran MDMs had a standoff attack range of 40,000 kilometers . . . and it took them barely half a second to cross the intervening 110,000 kilometers. There were literally thousands of laser clusters aboard the superdreadnoughts and their escorting *Cimeterres*, but they got at most one shot each.

And just before they fired, the fourteen surviving Dazzlers erupted in bursts of jamming that blinded sensors searching desperately for targets.

Despite everything the superior Manticoran EW could do, Shannon Foraker's defensive doctrine worked. Not as well as a Manticoran defense might have, perhaps, but sheer volume of firepower still made itself felt. Of the two hundred and forty attack missiles in the salvo, only eight survived to attack range.

Two of them detonated late, wasting their power on the roof of *Conquete*'s impenetrable impeller wedge. The other six detonated between fifteen and twenty thousand kilometers off the ship's port bow, and massive bomb-pumped lasers punched brutally through her sidewall.

Alarms howled as the *Temeraire*-class ship shuddered in anguish. Five point defense clusters, two counter-missile tubes, and three graser mounts, blew apart. Beta Nodes One, Three, and Five; Radar One; Gravitic One; and three of her fire control telemetry arrays were blotted away. Fifty-one members of her crew were killed, another eighteen were badly wounded, and splinters of armor—some the size of a pinnace—blasted away from her hull. But for all the horrific power of those hits, the damage was actually minor. Superdreadnoughts were designed and built to survive the most savage punishment imaginable, and *Conquete* went right on rolling missile pods.

"It looks like we got at least a couple of hits through, Your Grace," Lieutenant Carter reported. "It's hard to be certain at this range, even with the remote arrays, but CIC feels fairly confident."

"Good," Honor said. "Good."

"And here comes the response," Brigham said grimly. "What was that old wet-navy saying you told me about, Your Grace? 'For what we are about to receive—'?"

"'May we be truly thankful,'" Honor finished without looking away from the plot.

"That's it," Brigham agreed, and then the MDMs were upon them.

It was the Republic's turn, and the tsunami of missiles crashed into Task Force 82's outer counter-missile zone. Havenite EW might not be as good as the RMN's, but it did its best, and that best was much better than it once had been.

Almost eleven thousand MDMs had been launched. Six hundred and seventeen had simply become lost and wandered away as Bogie Four's fire control strained to meet the demands placed on it. The remaining 10,183 continued to charge forward as the Mark 31s came to meet them. Twenty-six hundred of them died in the outer interception zone. Another three thousand two hundred died in the intermediate zone, and the Mark 31s killed another two thousand nine hundred in the inner zone. But then it was *their* turn to slash across the laser clusters' engagement envelope in less than a second, and there were still 1,472 of them left. Two hundred were EW platforms, and the targeting solutions of the other twelve hundred were far poorer than Task Force 82's had been, but there were a great many of them.

The last-ditch lasers aboard the warships and their escorting LACs killed over nine hundred. Of the three hundred and seventy-two surviving attack missiles, a hundred and three wasted themselves uselessly against their targets' impeller wedges. Of the other two hundred and sixty-nine, a hundred and seventy-two attacked the two superdreadnoughts, and *Imperator* and *Intolerant* heaved as lasers ripped into them. Their sidewalls intercepted and blunted most of the lasers, but it was the turn of Manticoran armor to shatter under the pounding.

Imperator emerged with relatively minor damage, including the loss of three grasers and half a dozen laser clusters, but *Intolerant* staggered as dozens of hits hammered her thick, multi-ply armor. Huge splinters of it blew away, energy mounts and laser clusters were wiped out, and communication and fire control emitters, radar and gravitic arrays shattered. She bucked in agony under the pounding . . . and then a final, freak hit ripped straight into the gaping missile hatch in the center of her after hammerhead.

Rear Admiral Morowitz's flagship rocked as the powerful energy blast smashed forward along the unarmored, open central core of a pod-layer. Hundreds of missile pods were wrecked, turned into twisted and shattered alloy and wreckage. The missile handling rails were torn apart, and over thirty of her crew were killed.

Yet terrible as the damage was, BuShips had considered the possibility of just such a hit. Unlike the original *Medusa/Harrington*-class SD(P)s, the *Invictus*-class had been built from the beginning with a double-sided core hull wrapped around its hollow center, and the walls of her central missile well were armored almost as heavily as her flanks. The cofferdamming and compartmentalization weren't as deep, but they were far deeper than in the earlier classes, and the additional defenses proved their worth as a ring of vaporized and splintered alloy blasted back out of the shattered missile hatch, for the ship survived. Not only survived, but maintained her maximum acceleration while her antimissile defenses continued to engage the last of the incoming MDMs.

✧　　　✧　　　✧

"Your Grace, *Intolerant*'s lost her entire offensive missile armament and both Keyholes," Jaruwalski said in a tight voice. "Casualties are heavy, and her flag bridge took a heavy hit. Sounds like something blew back through CIC. Admiral Morowitz and most of his staff are down." She shook her head. "It doesn't sound good for the Admiral, Ma'am."

"Understood," Honor said quietly.

"*Star Ranger* also took a beating," Jaruwalski continued. "She's still combat capable, but she's already confirmed sixty-two dead, and her starboard sidewall is at less than half strength forward.

"Aside from that, the only other damage is to *Ajax*." Honor's expression didn't even flicker, but a cold fist seemed to touch her heart, and she looked quickly for the sidebar on Henke's flagship. "It's relatively minor," Jaruwalski went on. "She's got half a dozen wounded, only a couple of them seriously, and she's lost one graser and two point defense clusters out of her port broadside."

"Understood," Honor said again. She looked at Lieutenant Brantley.

"Harper, inform Captain Cardones that Admiral Morowitz is down and that I'm assuming tactical control of the division for now."

"Aye, aye, Your Grace."

"Andrea," Honor turned back to Jaruwalski, "drop the LACs back. With *Intolerant*'s damage, we'll need the *Ferrets* and the *Katanas*' Vipers.

Task Force 82's second wave of MDMs roared in on Bogey Four. Counter-missiles streamed to meet them, Dragon's Teeth spawned, targets proliferated, Dazzlers flared, counter-missile and MDM impeller wedges vanished in mutual self-destruction. And then the surviving attackers hurled themselves once again upon *Conquete*.

"Multiple hits aft!" *Conquete*'s captain listened to his senior engineering officer's report from Damage Control Central. "Heavy damage between frames one-zero-niner-seven and two-zero-one-eight. Graser Forty's gone—just *gone*; there's a hole you could park a fucking pinnace in where it used to be, and it looks like hundred percent casualties on the mount. Forty-Two's out of the fire control net, as well, and Sidewall Ten and Eleven are toast.

We've got a core hull breach at frame two-zero-zero-six, I've lost at least three more laser clusters, and they just took two beta nodes out of the after ring."

"Do what you can, Stew," the captain replied, looking at the scarlet-splashed damage control schematic on one of his secondary plots.

"We're on it," the engineer replied, and the captain nodded to himself. *Conquete* was hurt, no question about it, and he knew the pain of the people he'd just lost was waiting for him. But she was still combat capable, and that was what really mattered.

"*Conquete* reports moderate damage," Marius Gozzi told Giscard. "Captain Fredericks says she's still combat capable, but he's rolling ship to pull his starboard sidewall away from the Manties."

"Good," Giscard replied, never looking away from the main tactical plot. He didn't like the fact that the Manties had managed to hit *Conquete* that hard with only two salvos, but Fredericks was a solid, reliable CO. And by simply rolling ship rather than delaying to ask permission, he was showing the sort of intelligent initiative Giscard, Tourville, and Thomas Theisman had worked so hard to create.

The thoughts ran through the back of Giscard's mind, but virtually all of his attention was focused on the plot as he waited for the light-speed report on what his first huge salvo had accomplished.

"Sir, we're showing hits on multiple enemy units!" Selma Thackeray said suddenly, her voice jubilant, and Giscard's eyes narrowed as the same results appeared on the plot's sidebars.

"Hits on both SDs and at least two of the cruisers," Thackeray continued, listening to CIC's verbal report over her earbug. "And . . ."

She paused, listening intently, then turned her head to look directly at Giscard.

"Sir, the platforms confirm major damage to one of the SD(P)s!"

"Good work!" Giscard replied, but his pleasure at the report was not unalloyed. The third Manty MDM launch was coming in, and he watched the missiles slashing in on *Conquete*.

"At least five more hits, Your Grace," Jaruwalski reported. "Her wedge strength is dropping, and her point defense is weakening."

"Which would be nice, if we still had the missiles to pound her with," Mercedes Brigham said quietly to Honor. Honor glanced at her, and the chief of staff bobbed her head in Jaruwalski's direction. "Do you want to use the *Agamemnons* to make up for *Intolerant*'s pods?" she asked.

"No." Honor shook her head, watching Giscard's second stupendous missile wave overtake her ships from astern. "This has to be the last launch this size they can manage. They've shot themselves dry to manage this kind of density, and I won't do the same thing with Mike's battlecruisers just to try to kill a ship that can't shoot at us anymore, anyway. Not when we may need them worse shortly."

"Yes, Ma'am."

The attacking MDMs came sweeping in, like a comber rearing higher as it neared the beach, and Mark 31s, Vipers, and standard LAC counter-missiles from the *Ferrets*, slashed into it. The loss of *Intolerant*'s Keyhole platforms weakened the defensive umbrella significantly, but the time the Havenites' needed to "stack" patterns had increased the interval between salvos enough for Honor's LACs to drop back and take up optimum intercept positions astern of her starships.

Several dozen MDMs lost lock on their programmed targets as the LACs' impeller signatures cluttered the range. They quested for replacements, obedient to their onboard programming, and twenty-six of them found LACs. Nineteen of them got through, and seven *Shrikes*, nine *Ferrets* and three *Katanas*—along with the hundred and ninety men and women aboard them—died.

Thirty-seven other MDMs got through everything Task Force 82 could throw at them. Six of the leakers were EW platforms; the other thirty-one streaked in on *Imperator* and *Intolerant*.

"Four hits starboard aft," Commander Thompson reported to Rafe Cardones from Damage Control. "Two more midships, about frame niner-six-five. Graser Twenty-Three's out of the net, but the mount's undamaged; it's prepared to fire in local control. No major penetrations and no personnel casualties, but we've lost a couple of laser clusters from the after starboard quadrant, and we're down one beta node from the after ring. I think I can get the node back in about twenty minutes, but I could be wrong."

"Do what you can, Glenn," Cardones said, but his attention was on a secondary display. His own ship's wounds were minor, superficial, at worst. The same couldn't be said for *Intolerant*.

"*Intolerant* reports loss of her entire starboard sidewall aft of midships, Your Grace. She has at least three core hull breaches, and one fusion plant's off-line. Her shipboard fire control and point defense are seriously compromised."

Honor nodded, keeping her expression calm as she listened to Jaruwalski's report.

"Harper, get me Captain Sharif."

"Aye, aye, Ma'am."

"Captain," Honor said, moments later as Captain James Sharif appeared on her com display.

"Your Grace." Sharif's face was taut, but his expression and voice were under firm control.

"How bad is it over there, James?"

"Honestly?" Sharif shrugged. "Not good, Your Grace. I've got serious personnel casualties, and Engineering's lost about twenty-five percent of its damage control remotes—almost a hundred percent in the missile core. Our compensator's undamaged, and we've got enough node redundancy to maintain military power, but our offensive combat capability outside energy range is shot. And I'm afraid our missile defense pretty much sucks right now."

"That's what I was afraid of." Honor glanced at the astrogation display, then looked back at Sharif. "We've run out of Bogey Four's MDM range, and on our present heading, we'll just scrape by outside Bogey Three's envelope. But that's going to take us within range of the pods they've got deployed around Arthur in about another fourteen minutes. How much missile defense can you restore in that much time?"

"Not a lot," Sharif said grimly. "We've lost both Keyholes. I don't think we can get either of them back this side of an all-up shipyard visit, Your Grace, and we still have a major fire in secondary fire control. My shipboard control links to starboard have taken a real beating, too. We're mostly intact to port, so as long as I can keep that side of the ship towards the threat, we'll be able to control three or four CM salvos, but, at best, I figure we'll be at maybe forty percent of design missile defense capability."

"Do what you can," she said. "Go ahead and roll ship now. I'll try to adjust the formation to give you a little more cover."

"Thank you, Your Grace." Sharif smiled tightly. "I'm glad you're thinking about us."

"Take care, James," Honor replied. "Clear."

She looked over her shoulder at Lieutenant Brantley.

"Admiral Henke, Harper," she said.

"Aye, aye, Ma'am."

Less than ten seconds later, Michelle Henke's face had replaced Sharif's on the com display.

"Mike," Honor began without preamble, "*Intolerant*'s in trouble. Her missile defense is way below par, and we're headed into the planetary pods' envelope. I know *Ajax*'s taken a few licks of her own, but I want your squadron moved out on our flank. I need to interpose your point defense between *Intolerant* and Arthur. Are you in shape for that?"

"Of course we are." Henke nodded vigorously. "*Ajax*'s the only one who's been kissed, and our damage is all pretty much superficial. None of it'll have any effect on our missile defense."

"Good! Andrea and I will shift the LACs as well, but they've expended a lot of CMs against those two monster launches from Bogey Four." Honor shook her head. "I didn't think they could stack that many pods without completely saturating their own fire control. It looks like we're going to have to rethink a few things."

"That's the nature of the beast, isn't it?" Henke responded with a shrug. "We live and learn."

"Those of us fortunate enough to survive," Honor agreed, just a bit grimly. Then she gave herself a little shake. "All right, Mike. Get your people moving. Clear."

"They're shifting formation, Admiral," Selma Thackeray reported. "It looks like they're moving their battlecruisers between their damaged superdreadnought and Arthur."

"Sounds like we got a pretty good piece of her, Sir," Gozzi observed.

"I'd have preferred a better one," Giscard said, his eyes on the damage control report from *Conquete* scrolling up his display.

Despite the disparity in firepower, the Manties' stubborn concentration on a single target had paid them dividends. *Conquete* was the only one of Giscard's ships they'd damaged, but they'd hammered her severely. Her max acceleration was down by almost twenty-two percent, her point defense had been significantly degraded, she had over two hundred casualties, and like all Giscard's SD(P)s, she'd effectively exhausted her offensive missile capacity.

But superdreadnoughts were tough, and the Republic's damage control capabilities had improved dramatically over the past few years. *Conquete* might be hurt, but she would still have been combat capable . . . if there'd been anyone in range for her to fight.

"Their present course is going to carry them clear of Sewall, isn't it, Marius?" he asked after a moment.

"Yes, Sir, I'm afraid it is," Gozzi replied. Rear Admiral Hildegard Sewall commanded the Republican task group closing in from system south. "Not by very much, though," the chief of staff continued. "If Deutscher manages to inflict more impeller damage, I think she'll probably be able to bring them into her engagement envelope."

"And with one of their superdreadnoughts already beat up on." Giscard nodded. "Well, I suppose it's all up to Deutscher, then."

Chapter Thirty-Seven

Additional damage reports came in over the next several minutes, and Honor settled back in her command chair as she digested them. *Intolerant*'s damages were the worst, and from the medical reports, it sounded very much as if Alistair McKeon was going to require a new CO for his battle squadron's first division. Honor had never gotten to know Allen Morowitz as well as she would have liked ... and it didn't look as if she would ever have the chance to.

Star Ranger was the next most badly damaged. Her personnel casualties were even worse than *Intolerant*'s, but that was largely because she was one of the older, manpower-intensive *Star Knight*-class ships. From the reports, her people seemed to have things under control, but she, too, was going to require an extensive shipyard stay. Given her age, and how long repairs were likely to take, it was probable BuShips would simply write her off, but at least Honor should be able to get her home.

Ajax's damage was much less severe. Assuming nothing else happened to her, her repairs should be both routine and rapid.

Taken altogether, things could have been far worse, she told herself. She'd allowed her task force to be mousetrapped, and the fact that the Havenites had used a variant of her own Sidemore tactics to do it lent it an additional sting. But the thing which had made it effective at Sidemore was the same thing which had made it equally effective here: no one in normal-space could "see" into hyper-space to detect units there. And at least she'd gotten the carriers clear before the bad guys dropped in on her.

"Is *Rifleman* still clear, Mercedes?" she asked looking up from the damage reports.

"As far as we can tell, they don't haven't a clue where she is," Brigham replied.

"Good. But tell her to stay where she is until we clear the hyper limit." Brigham looked a question at her, and Honor smiled thinly. "Whoever's in charge on the other side has already demonstrated she's pretty good. At the moment, it looks like all her available units, aside from Bogey Four, are still accelerating in-system. They probably hope we'll take enough lumps from the Arthur pods to slow us down, let them overhaul. But if *I* were in command on the other side, and if I had enough hulls for it, I'd have at least one more task group waiting in hyper."

"To drop just outside the limit, right in our faces just when we think we're about to get away clean," Brigham said.

"Exactly. Mind you, I think the odds are good that they've committed everything they have already, but let's make sure before *Rifleman* hypers out to tell Samuel where to pick up his LACs."

"Yes, Your Grace. I'll see to it."

"Is Moriarty ready?" Rear Admiral Emile Deutscher asked his chief of staff.

"Yes, Sir," the chief of staff replied.

"Good." Deutscher returned his attention to his tactical display. His two obsolete wallers had almost certainly been completely dismissed by the Manties as a threat. And, by and large, the Manties would have been correct about that. After all, at this range, without pods on tow, they couldn't possibly have a weapon with the range to reach them.

But the superdreadnoughts' real purpose, from the beginning, had simply been to attract the Manties' attention away from the *real* threat.

"Sir?"

Deutscher looked back up at his chief of staff.

"Yes?"

"Sir, why did Admiral Foraker call it 'Moriarty'? I've been trying to figure it out for weeks now."

"I wondered that, myself," Deutscher admitted. "So I asked Admiral Giscard the same question. He said one of Admiral

Foraker's staffers had introduced her to some old, pre-space fiction. 'Detective stories,' he called them. Apparently this 'Moriarty' was some kind of mastermind character in one of them." He shrugged.

"Mastermind," the chief of staff repeated, then chuckled. "Well, I guess that does make sense, in a way, doesn't it?"

"We'll be entering the estimated range of Arthur's pods in another forty-five seconds, Your Grace," Jaruwalski said.

"Thank you." Honor turned her command chair to face the Ops officer. "Remind all of our tac officers of that."

"Yes, Ma'am."

"They're entering range now, Sir."

"Thank you," Deutscher said. "Send the execute."

"Aye, Sir!"

"Missile launch! Multiple missile launches, *multiple sources!*"

Honor snapped her command chair back around, staring at the master plot at Jaruwalski's sudden sharp announcement.

"Estimate *seventeen thousand*—I say again, one-seven *thousand*—inbound! Time to attack range, seven-point-one minutes!"

For just a moment, Honor's brain flatly refused to believe the numbers. Their scout ships' arrays had detected only four hundred pods in orbit around Arthur. The maximum number of missiles aboard them should only have been *four* thousand!

Her eyes darted across the plot, and then flared wide in sudden understanding. The others—*all* the others—were coming from the nine ships of Bogey One. Which was flatly impossible. Two superdreadnoughts and seven battlecruisers couldn't possibly have fired or controlled that many missiles, even if they'd all been pod designs! But—

"Where the hell did they all come from?" Brigham demanded, and Honor looked at her.

"The battlecruisers," she said, her mind going back to the Battle of Hancock.

"*Battlecruisers?*" Brigham looked incredulous, and Honor chuckled without any humor at all.

"They aren't battlecruisers, Mercedes; they're minelayers. The Havenites build their fast fleet minelayers on battlecruiser hulls, just like we do. And we were so busy worrying about superdreadnoughts and pod-layers it never occurred to us to look closely at the 'battlecruisers.' So they've been sitting there, ever since they stopped accelerating, doing nothing but lay pods."

"Jesus!" Brigham murmured softly, and it was a prayer, not an imprecation. Then she drew a deep breath. "Well, at least they can't have the fire control to *handle* it all!"

"Don't bet on it," Honor said grimly. "They wouldn't have gone to all the trouble of setting this up if they hadn't figured they could actually hit something with it after they did."

"Moriarty confirms control, Sir."

"Good," Deutscher said, and sat back with a hungry smile.

"Engage Bogey One!" Honor snapped.

"Aye, aye, Ma'am," Jaruwalski responded. "Should I use the *Agamemnons*, too?"

"Yes," Honor replied. "Gamma sequence."

"Aye, aye, Ma'am," Jaruwalski repeated, and began issuing orders over the task force's tactical net.

Given the geometry—the effective closing speed between TF 82 and the launch platforms was almost thirty-six thousand KPS—the battlecruisers' Mark 16 MDMs, with one less "stage" than *Imperator*'s larger missiles, had a maximum powered range of forty-two million kilometers. But the range was over fifty-three million, which meant the Mark 16s would have to coast ballistically for eleven million kilometers between stage activations. That would add an additional minute and a half to their flight time, bringing it to a total of thirteen and a half minutes, whereas *Imperator*'s more powerful missiles could make the entire run under power, in only seven. Moreover, the smaller missiles' closing speed relative to their targets would be over twenty thousand KPS lower.

But by using the gamma sequence she and Jaruwalski had worked out months ago, *Imperator* would roll her first half dozen patterns with missile settings which duplicated those of the Mark 16s. The *Agamemnons* would roll six patterns each at the same rate, which would take seventy-two seconds, and those six salvos—each of two hundred and seventy-six missiles—would make the crossing at the Mark 16s' speed.

Only after the smaller MDMs were away would *Imperator* begin firing full-power patterns of her own, one double pattern every twenty-four seconds. The first of *her* 120-strong salvos would arrive on target eight and a half minutes after she first began rolling pods, five minutes before the battlecruisers' fire.

In Arthur orbit, the installation codenamed Moriarty came fully on-line for the first time. It wasn't a very huge installation. In fact, it was no larger than a heavy cruiser, and it had been transported in two prefabricated modules aboard a fleet supply ship, then assembled in place in less than forty-eight hours.

As warship tonnages went, four hundred thousand wasn't a lot . . . unless *all* of it was dedicated to fire control.

Moriarty was Shannon Foraker's system defense answer to the individual inferiority of the Republic's missile pods. The control station was a flat, light-drinking black, constructed of radar absorbent materials. It was almost impossible to detect, as long as it practiced strict emission-control discipline, and the Manticoran recon arrays had missed it entirely.

Now it reached out through the *other* innocent-looking orbital platforms which had been seeded about the system at the same time. Each of those platforms was, in effect, a less capable, simpler minded version of the RMN's own Keyholes. They formed a network, an expanding spray of tentacles, which gave Moriarty literally thousands of fire control telemetry links. And what those links lacked in Manticoran-style sophistication they made up in numbers, because they could control the missiles assigned to them without break all the way to their targets.

Moriarty had only one real weakness, aside from the fact that if it *had* been detected, killing it would have been relatively simple. That weakness was the light-speed limitation on its telemetry. It simply couldn't provide real-time corrections as its missiles raced down range. On the other hand, neither could Honor's telemetry links. Aside from the superior seeking systems and more capable AIs aboard the Manticoran missiles, the accuracy playing field had just been leveled.

And the Republic's salvo contained sixty-two times as many missiles as the *largest* salvo TF 82 was firing.

✧　　　✧　　　✧

"Get on them! Get on them *now!*"

Captain Amanda Brankovski, Samuel Miklós' senior COLAC, knew her people didn't need any exhortations from her, but she couldn't help it. She watched the incredible cyclone of missile icons streaking across her plot towards the task force, and it seemed impossible that any of its ships could survive.

The five LAC wings, arranged "above" and "below" the heavier ships and fifty thousand kilometers closer to Arthur, belched an answering hurricane. Vipers and standard counter-missiles began to launch from the LACs as Mark 31s roared away from the starships, and incoming missiles began to vanish.

Brankovski had five hundred and sixty LACs, one for every thirty attack missiles, and they punched a steady stream of counter-missiles into their teeth. Tethered and free-flying Ghost Rider decoys sang to the Republican MDMs' sensors. Dazzlers were launched into their faces, exploding in bursts of blinding interference. And *Imperator* and her consorts punched out wave after wave of Mark 31s.

The front of the Republic's missile attack eroded under TF 82's defensive fire like a cliff, crumbling under the assault of a stormy sea. But, like the cliff, it was only the *front* of a far larger mass. Thousands of MDMs were killed, yet more thousands remained, and Honor Harrington watched them reaching out for her command.

Emile Deutscher watched Moriarty's fire race towards the enemy. Even from here, he could see that virtually none of the attack missiles were becoming lost in midflight, as normally happened in MDM combat. *All* of them held their courses, and he felt totally certain no defenses, not even the Manties', could stop them.

Which left the little problem of the fire coming at *him*.

It took the massive attack seven minutes to reach Task Force 82. Of the seventeen thousand missiles in the initial launch, only sixty lost their telemetry links and self-destructed after wandering off course. The Mark 31s killed over three thousand in the outermost intercept zone. In the middle zone, bolstered by the *Katanas'* Vipers and the standard counter-missiles from the *Shrikes* and *Ferrets*, they killed another four thousand. Jammers blinded another sixteen hundred missiles as they tried to settle into final acquisition, and the incredible cauldron of missile, starship, and LAC impeller wedges was too much for Moriarty's arthritic light-speed telemetry to sort out any longer.

The surviving eighty-three hundred MDMs dropped into autonomous mode as they hit the inner counter-missile zone. Shipboard EW did its best to spoof and blind the attackers, last-second decoy launches drew some of them astray, and a seemingly solid wall of Mark 31s met them head on.

Four thousand more MDMs were wiped out of space. Another eleven hundred fell prey to decoys or jamming. Three hundred of the survivors were penetration-aid EW platforms, without laser heads, and almost half the remaining twenty-nine hundred lost lock and reacquired not starships, but the nearer, more readily seen LACs. They streaked in to the attack, but Manticoran LACs were extraordinarily difficult targets. "Only" two hundred and eleven of them—and the twenty-one hundred of Honor's men and women aboard them—were killed.

And then the final sixteen hundred missiles attacked TF 82's starships, most of them targeted on the two superdread-noughts.

Only one thing saved HMS *Imperator*, and that was the damage already inflicted on *Intolerant. Imperator*'s consort's defenses and electronic warfare capability were simply far below par. She was both easier to see and easier to hit. The near-sighted autonomous-mode MDMs mobbed her in huge numbers, ignoring *Imperator*, and her last-ditch defenses weren't equal to the task of protecting her.

Warhead after warhead, literally hundreds of them, detonated in a hellish pattern of strobes—bubbles of nuclear fusion spitting deadly harpoons of coherent radiation that crashed through *Intolerant*'s wavering sidewalls and ripped deep, deep into her massively armored hull. Mike Henke's battlecruisers did their best to beat that tide of destruction aside, but they simply lacked the firepower, and they themselves were not immune from attack.

Honor clung to the arms of her command chair, feeling *Imperator* shudder under the pounding of her own hits, tasting Nimitz in the back of her brain, clinging to her with all his fierce love and devotion as death thundered and bellowed about their ship. Yet even as she did, her eyes were on the plot, watching the lethal wave of fire washing over *Intolerant*.

No one would ever know how many hits the superdread-nought took, but however many there were, it was too many. They ripped into her again, and again, and *again*, until, suddenly, she simply disappeared in the most brilliant, eye-tearing flash of them all.

Nor did she go alone. The light cruisers *Fury*, *Buckler*, and *Atum* vanished from Honor's plot, as did the battlecruisers *Priam* and *Patrocles*. The heavy cruisers *Star Ranger* and *Blackstone* were reduced to crippled hulks, coasting onward ballistically without power or drives. And HMS *Ajax* faltered suddenly as her entire after impeller ring went down.

Imperator took over a dozen direct hits of her own, yet the flagship's actual damage was incredibly light. Her thick armor shrugged off most of the hits with little more than superficial cratering, and despite the loss of half a dozen energy mounts, she remained fully combat capable.

Honor gazed into the bitter ashes of her display, tasting the cruel irony of her flagship's apparent inviolability as she saw the harrowed wreckage of the rest of her command. Of the twenty starships and five hundred and sixty LACs she'd taken across the hyper limit, only twelve starships, all but two of them damaged, and three hundred and forty-nine LACs survived. And even as she watched, *Ajax* and the heavy cruiser *Necromancer* were falling behind due to impeller damage.

"Your Grace," Andrea Jaruwalski said quietly. Honor looked at her. "The remote arrays confirm the destruction of two of their minelayers and heavy damage to one of their superdread-noughts."

"Thank you, Andrea." Honor was astounded by how calm, how *normal*, her own voice sounded. It was a pathetic return for what the Havenites had done to her, but she supposed it was better than nothing.

"Harper," she said, "get me a link to Admiral Henke."

"Yes, Your Grace."

Several seconds passed before Michelle Henke's strained face appeared on Honor's com.

"How bad is it, Mike?" Honor asked as soon as she saw her friend.

"That's an interesting question." Henke managed to produce at least the parody of a smile. "Captain Mikhailov is dead, and things are . . . a bit confused over here, just now. Our rails and pods are still intact, and our fire control looks pretty good, but our point defense and energy armament took a real beating. The worst of it seems to be the after impeller ring, though. It's completely down."

"Can you restore it?" Honor asked urgently.

"We're working on it," Henke replied. "The good news is that the damage appears to be in the control runs; the nodes themselves look like they're still intact, including the alphas. The bad news is that we've got one hell of a lot of structural damage aft, and just locating where the runs are broken is going to be a copperplated bitch."

"Can you get her out?"

"I don't know," Henke admitted. "Frankly, it doesn't look good, but I'm not prepared to just write her off yet. Besides," she managed another smile, this one almost normal-looking, "we can't abandon very well."

"What do you mean?" Honor demanded.

"Both boat bays are trashed, Honor. The Bosun says she thinks she can get the after bay cleared, but it's going to take at least a half-hour. Without that—" Henke shrugged, and Honor bit the inside of her lip so hard she tasted blood.

Without at least one functional boat bay, small craft couldn't dock with *Ajax* to take her crew off. There were emergency personnel locks, but trying to lift off a significant percentage of her crew that way would take hours, and the battlecruiser carried enough emergency life pods for little more than half her total complement. There was no point carrying more, since only half her crew's battle stations were close enough to the skin of the hull to make a life pod practical.

And her flag bridge was not among the stations which fell into that category.

"Mike, I—"

Honor's voice was frayed around the edge, and Henke shook her head quickly.

"Don't say it," she said, almost gently. "If we get the wedge back, we can probably play hide and seek with anything heavy enough to kill us. If we don't get it back, we're not getting out. It's that simple, Honor. And you know as well as I do that you can't hold the rest of the task force back to cover us. Not with

Bogey Three still closing. Even just hanging around for a half-hour while we try to make repairs would bring you into their envelope, and your missile defense has been shot to shit."

Honor wanted to argue, to protest. To find some way to make it not true. But she couldn't, and she looked her best friend straight in the eye.

"You're right," she said quietly. "I wish you weren't, but you are."

"I know." Henke's lips twitched again. "And at least we're in better shape than *Necromancer*," she said almost whimsically, "although I think her boat bays are at least intact."

"Well, yes," Honor said, trying to match Henke's tone even as she wanted to weep, "there is that minor difference. Rafe's coordinating the evacuation of her personnel now."

"Good for Rafe." Henke nodded.

"Break north," Honor told her. "I'm going to drop our acceleration for about fifteen minutes." Henke looked as if she were about to protest, but Honor shook her head quickly. "Only fifteen minutes, Mike. If we go back to the best acceleration we can sustain at that point and maintain heading, we'll still scrape past Bogey Three at least eighty thousand kilometers outside its powered missile range."

"That's cutting it too close, Honor!" Henke said sharply.

"No," Honor said flatly, "it isn't, Admiral Henke. And not just because *Ajax* is your ship. There are seven hundred and fifty other men and women aboard her."

Henke looked at her for a moment, then inhaled sharply and nodded.

"When they see our accel drop, they'll have to act on the assumption *Imperator* has enough impeller damage to slow the rest of the task force," Honor continued. "Bogey Three should continue to pursue *us* on that basis. If you can get the after ring back within the next forty-five minutes to an hour, you should still be able to stay clear of Bogey Two, and Bogey One is pretty much scrap metal at this point. But if you don't get it back—"

"If we don't get it back, we can't get into hyper anyway," Henke interrupted her. "I think it's the best we can do, Honor. Thank you."

Honor wanted to scream at her friend for *thanking* her, but she only nodded.

"Give Beth my best, just in case," Henke added.

"Do it yourself," Honor shot back.

"I will, of course," Henke said. Then, more softly, "Take care, Honor."

"God bless, Mike," Honor said equally quietly. "Clear."

Chapter Thirty-Eight

The communicator on her desk buzzed, and she looked up from the report and pressed the acceptance key.

"Yes?"

"Your Grace," Harper Brantley's voice said, "you have a message."

"What is it?"

"We've just been informed that the First Lord and First Space Lord are aboard the midday shuttle flight, Your Grace. Their pinnace will dock with *Imperator* in thirty-seven minutes."

"Thank you, Harper."

Honor's courteous voice was calm enough to fool anyone who didn't know her very well indeed. Harper Brantley was one of those who did.

"You're welcome, Your Grace," he said quietly, and cut the circuit.

Honor sat back in her float chair, and Nimitz crooned comfortingly from his perch. She looked up and smiled, acknowledging both his love and his effort to cheer her, but they both knew he hadn't succeeded.

She looked back at her terminal, and the latest in the merciless progression of reports floating in its display. There was never an end to any Queen's officer's paperwork, and she'd found that was even truer after a resounding defeat than it was after a victory. In many ways, she was grateful. It gave her something to do besides sitting in the stillness of her quarters, listening to her ghosts.

Nimitz hopped down onto the desk and rose on his haunches,

leaning forward to rest his true-hands on her shoulders while the tip of his nose just touched hers. He stared into her eyes, his own grass-green gaze as deep as the oceans of Sphinx they had sailed together in her childhood, and she felt him deep inside her. Felt his concern, and his scolding love as they both grappled with her sense of guilt and loss.

She reached out and folded her arms about him, holding him to her breasts while she buried her face in his soft, soft fur, and his croon sang gently, gently through her.

Honor stood in *Imperator*'s boat bay, Andrew LaFollet at her shoulder, as the pinnace settled into the docking arms. The green light glowed, the inner end of the personnel tube opened, and the bosun's pipes shrilled as Major Lorenzetti's Marine side party snapped to attention.

"First Lord, arriving!" the intercom announced, and Hamish Alexander, Samantha on his shoulder, swung himself through the tube first, as befitted his seniority as Sir Thomas Caparelli's civilian superior.

"Permission to come aboard, Captain?" he asked, as Rafe Cardones saluted.

"Permission granted, My Lord."

"Thank you." Hamish nodded and shook Cardones' proffered hand. Then he stepped past the captain and his eyes met Honor's for just a moment before he held out his hand to her. She shook it without speaking, her empathic sense clinging to the concern and love in his mind-glow, acutely aware of all the other, watching eyes, as the bay speakers spoke again.

"First Space Lord, arriving!"

"Permission to come aboard, Captain?" Sir Thomas Caparelli asked in the ancient ritual.

"Permission granted, Sir," Cardones gave the equally ritualistic response, and Caparelli stepped across the painted line on the deck.

"My Lord, Sir Thomas," Honor said in formal greeting as she released Hamish's hand to shake Caparelli's in turn.

"Your Grace," Caparelli replied for both of them, and Honor tasted his emotions, as well. The anger she'd half dreaded and yet half desired was absent. Instead, she tasted sympathy, concern, and something very like compassion. Part of her was glad, but another part—the wounded part—was almost angry, as if he were betraying her dead by not blaming her for their deaths. It was illogical and unreasonable, and she knew it. And it didn't change her emotions one bit.

"Would you and Earl White Haven care to join me in my quarters?"

"I think that's an excellent idea, Your Grace," Caparelli said after only the briefest glance at Hamish.

"In that case, My Lords," Honor said, and waved her right hand at the waiting lifts.

The short journey to Honor's quarters was silent, without the casual small talk which would normally have filled it. LaFollet peeled off outside the day cabin hatch, and Honor waved her visitors through it.

She followed them, and the hatch slid shut behind her.

"Welcome to *Imperator*, My Lords," she began, then chopped off in astonishment as Hamish turned and enfolded her in a fierce embrace. For just a moment, conscious of Caparelli's presence, she started to resist. But then she realized she tasted absolutely no surprise from the First Space Lord, and she abandoned herself—briefly, at least—to the incredible comfort of her husband's arms.

The embrace lasted several seconds, and then Hamish stood back, his left hand on her right shoulder, while his feather-gentle right hand brushed an errant strand of hair from her forehead.

"It's . . . *good* to see you, love," he said softly.

"And you." Honor felt her lower lip try to quiver and called it sternly to order. Then she looked past Hamish to Caparelli and managed a wry smile. "And it's good to see you, too, Sir Thomas."

"Although not, perhaps, quite *as* good, eh, Admiral Alexander-Harrington?"

"Oh, dear." Honor inhaled and looked back and forth between the two men. "Have we gone public while I was away, Hamish?"

"I wouldn't put it quite that way," he replied. "A few people have either figured it out or been informed because it's just so much simpler that way. Thomas here falls into both categories. I informed him . . . and he'd already figured it out. Essentially, at least."

"Your Grace—Honor," Caparelli said with a crooked smile, "your relationship with Hamish has to be one of the worst kept secrets in the history of the Royal Manticoran Navy." Alarm flickered in her eyes, but he only chuckled. "I might add, however, that I doubt very much that any Queen's officer would breathe a word about it. If nothing else, he'd be terrified of what the rest of us would do to him when we found out."

"Sir Thomas," she began, "I—"

"You don't have to explain anything to me, Honor," Caparelli cut her off. "First, because I think Hamish is probably right where the Articles of War are concerned. Second, because I've never seen any indication of your allowing personal feelings to influence your actions. Third, because you've made it crystal clear throughout your career that you have absolutely no interest in playing the patronage game and relying on 'interest' to further that career. And, fourth, and probably most importantly of all, the two of you—the *three* of you—have damned well earned it."

Honor closed her mouth, tasting the rock-ribbed sincerity behind his words. It was an enormous relief, but she made herself bite off any thanks. Instead, she simply waved for the two of them to be seated on the couch, then seated herself in one of the facing armchairs.

Hamish smiled faintly but said nothing as she deliberately separated the two of them from one another. Samantha hopped down from his shoulder, and she and Nimitz leapt up into the other armchair, curling down beside one another and purring happily.

"I imagine," Honor said after a moment, her mood darkening once more, "that you've come out to discuss my fiasco."

Hamish's expression never wavered, but she felt his internal wince at her choice of noun.

"I suppose that's one way to describe it," Caparelli said. "It's not the one I would've chosen, however."

"I don't see a better one." Honor knew she sounded bitter, but she couldn't quite help it. "I lost half my superdreadnoughts, sixty percent of my battlecruisers, half my heavy cruisers, thirty-eight percent of my *light* cruisers, and over forty percent of my LACs. In return for which I managed to destroy two minelayers and damage two superdreadnoughts, one of them a pre-pod relic. And to inflict absolutely no damage on the system's infrastructure which was my original objective." She smiled without a trace of humor. "That sounds like the dictionary definition of a 'fiasco' to me."

"I'm sure it does," Caparelli said calmly. "What struck *me* most strongly, however, was how light your losses were, given what you sailed into."

His raised hand stopped her protest, and his eyes met hers levelly.

"I know exactly what I'm talking about, Honor, so don't tell me I don't. You walked into a carefully prepared ambush. I've reviewed your reports, and those of your surviving captains, and the log recordings from your flag bridge and from *Imperator's* tactical section. I reviewed them very carefully, and whether you want to believe this or not, I also reviewed them very critically. And, on the basis of what you knew, *when* you knew it, I can't see a single thing you did wrong."

"What about sailing directly into that last missile launch?" Honor challenged. "If anyone should have seen that coming, *I* should have!"

"The fact that you and Mark Sarnow used similar tactics at Hancock Station sixteen T-years ago doesn't make you clairvoyant," Caparelli replied. "You *did* realize they were coming in out of hyper behind you, and I doubt very much most flag officers would have figured it out as quickly. And without knowing the size of the salvos Bogey One could throw, your decision to stay away from a force which outnumbered you three-to-one in ships of the wall was the only reasonable one you could have made."

"And what about abandoning *Ajax*?" Honor's voice was so low it was almost a whisper.

"That, too, was the proper decision, Your Grace," Caparelli said quietly. Honor looked up, meeting his eyes once more, tasting his sincerity. "It was hard. I know that. I know how close you and Admiral Henke were. But your overriding responsibility was to the ships you could still get out, and with the damage you'd already suffered, slowing to cover *Ajax* would have made that impossible. If you'd been able to evacuate her personnel, that might have been one thing. But you couldn't."

"But—" Honor began, eyes burning, and Caparelli shook his head.

"Don't. I've been there, too, and I know leaving people behind, however correct the tactical decision may have been, always hurts. You always ask yourself if there wasn't some way you could've gotten everyone out, and curse yourself at night for not having found one. The fact that you and Countess Gold Peak were so close, for so long, has to make that still worse, but I've come to know you. Whether Michelle Henke had been aboard that ship or not, you'd still feel what you're feeling right now."

Honor blinked, then looked away for just a moment. He was right, and she knew it. And yet, remembering Mike—

She closed her eyes, her memory replaying the last she'd seen—the last she would *ever* see—of Michelle Henke. She and her other survivors had gotten across the hyper limit, with Bogey Two and Bogey Three in hot pursuit. *Rifleman* had performed her part of Omega One by translating up into hyper to rejoin Samuel Miklós' CLACs at the designated rendezvous once the task force's other survivors were across the limit. And Miklós' squadron had executed a flawless micro-jump to rendezvous with Honor's survivors, in turn. They'd gotten the surviving LACs aboard the carriers and translated out less than fifteen minutes before Bogey Three crossed the hyper limit after them, but that hadn't been soon enough to prevent her from knowing what happened.

She wished there'd been time for at least one last personal message, but *Ajax*'s communications section had taken massive damage in the first salvo Bogey Two had fired into Henke's lamed flagship. There'd been no way to communicate—even the remote sensor arrays had been too far away to see it clearly—but from the sensor recordings, it looked as if *Ajax* had taken at least one battlecruiser with her. The explosion when her own fusion plants let go, however, had been far clearer.

"I left her," she said softly. "I left her behind to die."

"Because her drive was damaged," Caparelli said, deliberately misinterpreting the pronoun's antecedent. "Because you had no choice. Because you were a fleet commander, with a responsibility for the survival of the other ships under your command. It was the *right* decision."

"Maybe."

Honor looked back at him, and the First Space Lord cocked his head. She could taste him accepting that that "maybe" was as close as she could yet come to agreeing with him, and her mouth moved in an almost-smile.

"But whether it was the right decision or not, I still got my backside kicked right up between my ears and didn't take out my objective. Exactly what Eighth Fleet wasn't supposed to have happen to it."

"It's not given to us to simply command victory," Caparelli told her. "The other side has an interest in winning, as well, you know. And when you're consistently given the most difficult jobs to do, the chances of running into something like you ran into at Solon go up rather steeply.

"As for your failure to hit your objectives, yes, you did. Admiral Truman, on the other hand, operating according to your plan, blew the Lorn shipyard, every bit of its supporting industry, and every mobile unit in the system into scrap for the loss of six LACs."

"I know she did," Honor conceded. "And I also know our primary objective was to force the Republic to redeploy, which—on the evidence of Solon—they've certainly done. But I feel depressingly confident that the way this story is going to be spun for their civilian population will dwell on how hard they hit *my* task force, not how well Alice's did."

"I think we can all safely depend upon that," Caparelli agreed. "Especially since you've been the one blacking *their* eyes up until now. The defeat of 'the Salamander'—and I agree that, however well you did to salvage what you did, it *was* a defeat—is going to be page-one news in every Peep 'fax. They're going to play it up to the max, exactly the way our own 'faxes have been playing up Eighth Fleet's *successes*.

"Nor, I'm afraid," he said, much more bleakly, his emotions suddenly far darker, "is that the only thing they're going to have to play up."

"I beg your pardon?"

Honor looked at him, and he shrugged heavily.

"The initial report came in this morning. Their Admiral Tourville is apparently back from Marsh, and they've given him a new fleet to replace the one you trashed. Units under his command hit Zanzibar about the same time you were attacking Lorn and Solon."

Honor inhaled sharply, looking back and forth between Caparelli and Hamish.

"How bad was it?"

"About as bad as it could have been," Hamish replied. She looked at him, and he sighed. "He came in with four full battle squadrons of pod-layers, and their battle squadrons are still eight ships strong. He also had a couple of divisions of carriers and at least two battlecruiser squadrons to support them, and although we'd reinforced heavily after Admiral al-Bakr's fiasco—and I use the word deliberately," he added bitterly "—it wasn't heavily enough. He hit the defenses like a hammer, and he started right out by sweeping the asteroid belt with remote arrays of his own, followed by LAC strikes on our predeployed pods. Not only that, he'd brought along fast colliers stuffed with additional missile pods. He left them tucked away in hyper, came in just far enough to draw our mobile units away from their own support bases, and engaged them at long range until both sides had burned most of their ammo. Then he pulled back across the limit, reammunitioned, and came right back in before we could replace the expended defense pods or get our own pod-layers back in-system to rearm. It was a massacre."

"How bad?" she repeated.

"Eleven SD(P)s and seven older superdreadnoughts," Caparelli said grimly. "Plus seven hundred LACs, six battlecruisers, and two heavy cruisers. Those were *our* losses. Most of the Zanzibaran Navy went with them. Not to mention," the First Space Lord added harshly, "the near total destruction of Zanzibar's deep-space industry. For the *second* time."

Honor paled. Those losses made her own seem almost trivial.

"I think we can all safely agree," Caparelli continued, "that as things stand right this instant, it's going to be relatively easy for the Peeps to convince their public—and possibly even our own—that the momentum's just shifted. Which makes it even more imperative for *us* to convince them they're wrong."

"What do you have in mind, Sir Thomas?" Honor asked, watching his face closely.

"You know exactly what I have in mind, Honor," he told her. "That's one reason I came out here with Hamish. I know you're hurting, and I know your people have to be shocked by what happened at Solon. And I also know it's going to take at least several weeks for you to be in any position to plan and mount another op. But we need you—and your people—back in the saddle, and we need you there quickly. We'll do what we can to reinforce you and replace your losses, but it's essential, absolutely essential, that Eighth Fleet resume *offensive* operations at the earliest possible moment. We simply cannot afford to allow the enemy, or ourselves, to believe the initiative has passed into his hands."

Chapter Thirty-Nine

Thomas Theisman watched through the viewport as the shuttle made its final approach to the stupendous superdreadnought. The Republic's Secretary of War and Chief of Naval Operations smiled as he remembered the last time he'd made this trip. His waiting host had been in a somewhat different mood that time.

The shuttle slowed to a halt relative to the superdreadnought, and the boat bay's docking tractors locked onto it. They snubbed away the remainder of its motion, then drew it smoothly into the bay. It settled into the docking arms, the personnel tube ran out, and Theisman and Captain Alenka Borderwijk, his senior naval aide, climbed out of their seats.

"Don't lose that, Alenka," Theisman said, tapping the case under Borderwijk's left arm.

"Don't worry, Sir," the captain replied. "The thought of being shot at dawn holds absolutely no attraction for me."

Theisman grinned at her, then turned to lead the way down the tube into *Sovereign of Space*'s boat bay gallery.

"Chief of Naval Operations, arriving!" the announcement rang out, and Theisman smothered another grin.

Technically speaking, he should have been referred to as the Secretary of War, since the Secretary was the CNO's civilian superior. It was common knowledge throughout the Fleet, however, that he preferred to think of himself as still an honest admiral, not a politician, and he was always amused when the Navy's uniformed personnel chose to pander to that particular vanity of his.

"Welcome aboard, Sir," Captain Patrick Reumann said, stepping forward to greet him before he could request formal permission to board.

"Thank you, Pat." Theisman shook the tall captain's hand, then looked past him to Javier Giscard.

"Welcome aboard, Sir," Giscard said, echoing Reumann as they clasped hands.

"Thank you, Admiral." Theisman raised his voice slightly. "And while I'm at it, allow me to express my thanks—and the Republic's—to you and all the men and women under your command for a job very well done."

He still felt a bit silly playing the political leader, but he'd learned not to despise the role, and he saw the smiles on the faces of the officers and enlisted personnel in range of his voice. What he'd said would be relayed throughout the ship—and, later, throughout Giscard's entire command—with a speed which mocked the grav pulses of an FTL com. And although he knew Giscard understood what he was doing perfectly, he also saw the genuine pleasure in the other man's eyes as his ultimate service superior made certain his thanks had been publicly delivered.

"Thank you, Sir," Giscard said, after a moment. "That means a lot to me, just as I know it will to all our personnel."

"I'm glad." Theisman released Giscard's hand as Reumann finished greeting Alenka Borderwijk and she stepped forward to join him and Giscard. "And now, Admiral, you and I have a few things to discuss."

"Of course, Sir. If you'll accompany me to my flag briefing room?"

"I meant what I said, Javier," Theisman said, as the briefing room hatch closed behind them. "You and your people did a *damned* fine job. Combined with what Lester did to Zanzibar, the Manties have to be feeling as if they strayed in front of an out-of-control freight shuttle at the bottom of a gravity well."

"We aim to please, Tom," Giscard said, waving the CNO and his aide into chairs, then dropping into one himself. "Linda and Lewis are the ones who really made it possible by guessing right. Well, them and Shannon." He shook his head, his wry grimace less than amused. "If it had been just my mobile units, she'd have gotten away clean."

"I think that's a bit pessimistic," Theisman disagreed. "Based on the system sensor platforms' data, you got a hell of a good piece of one of the SDs before Moriarty ever got a shot at them."

"Yeah, and I shot *six* SD(P)s dry to do it," Giscard responded. "I'm not trying to denigrate what my people accomplished, and I'm not trying to poor mouth my own accomplishments. But that missile defense of theirs." He shook his head. "It's a bear, Tom. Really, really tough."

"Tell me about it!" Theisman snorted. "I know you haven't seen Lester's after-action report on Zanzibar yet, but he makes exactly the same point. In fact, he feels that the only reason he managed to carry through was the reloads he'd brought along for his superdreadnoughts. Basically, he ran them out of ammunition at extreme range, then closed in to almost *single*-drive missile range to get the best targeting solutions he could. And even then, he needed a superiority of three-to-one."

He shrugged.

"It's something we're going to have to deal with. The next-generation seekers are about ready to deploy—that should help some—and Shannon's already working on other solutions . . . in her copious free time." He and Giscard both chuckled at that one. "In the meantime, we're having to rethink our calculations over at the Bureau of Planning on the relative effectiveness of our units. At the moment, we're still confident we'll attain it, but it's beginning to look as if it will take longer than we'd anticipated."

"How much longer?" Giscard asked, his expression faintly alarmed.

"Obviously, I can't answer that definitively yet, but nothing we've seen so far indicates more than a few months slippage—six or seven at the outside—from our original schedule. We're not talking about requiring construction not already in the pipeline, only about needing more of that construction ready to go than we'd thought we would. And given that our margin of superiority was going to continue growing for a full year beyond our original target date, six or seven months is completely acceptable."

"I hope it doesn't run longer, but—" Giscard paused for a moment, then shrugged and continued. "The thing that concerns me, Tom, is that our projections are based on what they've already shown us and what we've been able to extrapolate on that basis. But we didn't correctly extrapolate the improvement in their defensive capability. We knew it was going to get better, but I think it's safe to say none of us anticipated the actual margin of improvement. Just like none of us anticipated this dogfighting missile of theirs. What if they do the same thing to us with their MDMs?"

"That's a completely valid point," Theisman said gravely, "and I'd be lying if I said I hadn't had the occasional qualm myself. I think, though, that what we've already seen with Moriarty and the steady improvement in our own FTL communication and coordination ability, indicates we're still making up ground faster than we're losing it. And at the moment, it appears both we and the Manties are up against a fairly hard limit on the accuracy of full-ranged MDM exchanges. Theirs is better than ours, but with improvements like the new seekers, ours is getting better faster than theirs is."

He tipped back in his chair and folded his arms across his chest.

"I've got Linda and Op Research running every combat report through every analysis we can think of. We're charting the qualitative and quantitative improvements on both sides as accurately as we can, and we're constantly readjusting our projections. It's possible something will come along to overturn all our calculations. I don't think it will, and I hope it doesn't. But if it does, we ought to spot it in time to rethink both our options and our plans. And the bottom line is that I have no intention of committing the Navy to a decisive offensive operation unless I'm confident our calculations *haven't* been invalidated."

"And, with all due respect, Admiral Giscard," Alenka Borderwijk put in, "what you accomplished at Solon completely validated the Moriarty concept. We're moving ahead rapidly with deployment in other star systems, beginning with the most vital ones. On the basis of Solon, we believe our *defensive* doctrine and capabilities are sufficient to make it impossible for the Manties to accept the attritional losses major offensives of their own would entail."

"It certainly looks that way right now," Giscard agreed. "On the other hand, remember that at Solon we were up against only one task force, with only a single division of *Invictuses*. The missile defense of an entire Manty *fleet* would be much deeper and more resilient. I think you're right that Moriarty represents what's currently our best option for fixed system defenses, but it's going to have to be deployed in even greater depth than it was at Solon if it's going to stand up to a major Manty offensive."

"Granted," Theisman said, amused—and deeply pleased—by the confidence and persistence of Giscard's arguments. It was a far and welcome cry from the way Giscard had persisted in second-guessing—and blaming—himself after Thunderbolt.

"Granted," the CNO repeated. "And we're working on that. In addition, Shannon has the new system defense missiles almost ready to go into actual production. We still haven't been able to figure out a way to fit them into something an SD(P) can handle, but they ought to give the Manties fits when they run into them. That's the plan, anyway."

"So what you're saying is we ought to have a firm enough defensive capability to be able to take a few chances operating *offensively*," Giscard said.

"Within limits," Theisman agreed. "But *only* within limits. The one thing we can't afford is to shoot ourselves in the foot through sheer overconfidence. Even if," he grinned suddenly, "you did just thoroughly trounce 'the Salamander.'"

"Well," Giscard admitted with a grin of his own, "I have to admit it *did* feel good. I don't have anything personally against her, you understand, but as I'm sure Lester would agree, playing the part of her round-bottomed doll gets old in a hurry."

"I've been going back over the combat reports—my own included—from the last round," Theisman said thoughtfully. "It's a bit early, but I'm inclined to think she's even better than White Haven was, tactically at least. I know he gave us conniptions, and God knows their damned 'Buttercup' was a fucking disaster, but Harrington is *sneaky*. There are times I don't think she's even bothered to *read* The Book, much less pay any attention to it. Look at that insane trick she pulled at Cerberus, for God's sake! And then what she did to Lester at Sidemore."

"Personally, and speaking as someone who gleefully used her own ideas against her," Giscard said, "I'm wondering how much of what happened at Hancock was Sarnow's idea, and how much was *hers*? I know NavInt gave Sarnow the credit, and everything I've seen indicates he was good enough to've come up with it on his own, but it has all the Harrington fingerprints."

"Now that you mention it, it does," Theisman said. He frowned, then shrugged. "Well, she's only one woman, and as you just demonstrated, she's not invincible. Tough, and not someone I want to go up against without a substantial advantage, but not invincible. Which, by the way, the newsies have been playing up with joyous abandon ever since your dispatches arrived. I warn you, if you turn up in public anywhere on Haven, be prepared to be embarrassed within a centimeter of your life."

"Oh, God," Giscard muttered in disgusted tones. "Just what Eloise and I needed—*smutsies*."

Theisman laughed. He shouldn't have, and he knew it, but smutsies—the modern heirs of the old pre-space paparazzi—had always been a particularly virulent fact of life in the People's Republic. In fact, they'd been almost a semi-official adjunct of the Office of Public Information's propagandists. They'd been used to titillate—and divert—the Mob with all sorts of intrusive, sensationalized stories about entertainment figures, supposed enemies of the People, and, especially, political leaders of opposition star nations. Some of the stories about Elizabeth III and her alleged . . . relations with her treecat, for example, had been decidedly over the top. Not to mention, he felt sure, anatomically impossible.

Unfortunately, the smutsies had survived the People's Republic's fall, and the new freedom of information and the press under the restored Constitution actually made them *more* intrusive, not less. So far, Giscard and President Pritchart had managed to keep their relationship more or less below the smutsies' radar horizon, and what the so-called "journalists" would do when they finally realized what they'd been missing formed the basis for the unofficial presidential couple's joint nightmares.

"Well," Theisman said, and held out his hand to Borderwijk, "I can understand why that would be a matter of some concern. And while I hate to do this, I'm afraid I may be going to make it just a bit worse."

"Worse?" Giscard regarded him suspiciously. "Just how are you going to make it worse? And don't bother telling me you regret it—I can see the gleam in your eye from here!"

"Well, it's just . . . *this*," Theisman said, opening the case Borderwijk handed him and extending it to Giscard.

The admiral took it with another suspicious glower, then glanced down into it. His expression changed instantly, and his eyes shot back up to Theisman's face.

"You're joking."

"No, Javier, I'm not." Theisman's smile had disappeared.

"I don't deserve it," Giscard said flatly. "This is what Jacques Griffith got for taking out *Grendelsbane*, for God's sake!"

"Yes, it is."

Theisman reached out to reclaim the case, and lifted the rather plain-looking silver medal out of it. It hung on a ribbon of simple blue cloth, and he held it up to catch the light. It was the Congressional Cross, a medal which had been abandoned a hundred and eighty T-years ago when the Legislaturalists "amended" the Constitution out of existence. It had been replaced, officially at least, by the Order of Valor, awarded to "Heroes of the People" under the People's Republic. But it had been resurrected, along with the Constitution, and so far, only two of them had been awarded.

Well, three of them, now.

"This is goddamned ridiculous!" Giscard was genuinely angry, Theisman saw. "I won one *small* engagement against a single task force, half of which got away, whereas Jacques took out their entire damned building program! And Lieutenant Haldane gave his life to save the lives of almost three hundred of his fellow crewmen!"

"Javier, I—"

"*No*, Tom! We can't demean it this way—not this soon! I'm telling you, and I'll tell Eloise, if I have to!"

"Eloise had nothing to do with it. Nor, for that matter, did I. *Congress* decides who gets this, not the President, and not the Navy."

"Well you tell *Congress* to shove it up—!"

"Javier!" Theisman cut the admiral off sharply, and Giscard settled back in his chair, mouth shut but eyes still angry.

"Better," Theisman said. "Now, by and large, I agree with everything you've just said. But, as I already pointed out, the decision is neither mine nor Eloise's. And, despite your personal feelings, there are some very valid arguments for your accepting this medal. Not least the public relations aspect of it. I know you don't want to hear that, but Harrington's raids have generated an enormous amount of anger. Not all of that anger's directed at the *Manties*, either, since the general view seems to be that we ought to be stopping her somehow. And her activities have also begun generating *fear*, as well. Now you've not only stopped one of her raids cold, but you've decisively defeated *her*, as well. All that pent-up frustration and anger—and fear—is now focused on what you've accomplished as *satisfaction*. To be frank, I'm certain that's a lot of the reason Congress decided in its infinite wisdom to award you the Cross."

"I don't *care* what its reasons were. I won't accept it. That's it. End of story."

"Javier—" Theisman began, then stopped and shook his head. "Damn, you're even more like 'the Salamander' than I thought!"

"Meaning what?" Giscard asked suspiciously.

"Meaning there are persistent rumors that *she* refused the Parliamentary Medal of Valor the first time they tried to give it to her."

"No, did she?" Giscard chuckled suddenly. "Good for her! And you can tell Congress that if they decide to offer me the Cross again, I may accept it. But not this time. Let them find something else, something that doesn't devalue the Cross. This is too important to the Navy we're trying to build to be turned into a *political* award."

Theisman sat there for several seconds, gazing at the admiral. Then he replaced the silver cross in the case, closed it, and sighed.

"You may be right. In fact, I'm inclined to agree. But the important point, I suppose, is that you genuinely intend to be stubborn about this."

"Count on it."

"Oh, I do." Theisman smiled without a great deal of humor. "You're going to put me and Eloise into a very difficult position with Congress."

"I'm genuinely and sincerely sorry about that. But I'm not going to change my mind. Not about this."

"All right. I'll go back to Congress—thank God the award hasn't been announced yet!—and suggest to them that your natural humility and overwhelming modesty make it impossible for you to accept it at this time. I'll further suggest that they might want to simply vote you the thanks of Congress. I trust that *that* won't be too highfalutin' for you?"

"As long as it's not the Cross. And—" Giscard's eyes gleamed as Theisman groaned at the qualifier "—as long as it includes thanks to all of my people, as well."

"That I think I can arrange." Theisman shook his head. "Jesus! Now I'm going to have to tell Lester about this."

"What do you mean?"

"Well, you know how long and hard he worked on that out-of-control cowboy image of his before we got rid of Saint-Just. How do you think he's going to react to the fact that Congress wants to give *him* the Cross for Zanzibar? Especially now that you've opened the way to turning the damn thing down!"

Chapter Forty

"Your Grace," Dr. Franz Illescue said stiffly, "on behalf of Briarwood Reproduction Center, I offer you my sincere and personal apologies for our inexcusable violation of your confidentiality. I've discussed the matter with our legal department, and I've instructed them not to contest any damages you may choose to seek because of our failure. Furthermore, in recognition of the media furor the unauthorized release of this information provoked, I have informed our billing department that all additional services will be billed at no charge to you."

Honor stood in the Briarwood foyer, facing Illescue, and tasted his genuine remorse. It was overlaid with more than a little resentment at finding himself in this position, especially in front of her. And there was no question that he also suspected—or feared, at least—that her parents would hold him personally responsible. Yet for all that, it was remorse and professional responsibility which truly drove his emotions. It was unlikely most people would have believed that, given his stiff-backed, tight-jawed body language and expression. Honor, however, had no choice but to accept it.

She rather regretted that. After running the gauntlet of newsies outside Briarwood—despite Solomon Hayes' fall from grace, the story was still grist for the mills of a certain particularly repulsive subspecies of newsy—she'd been positively looking forward to removing large, painful, bloody chunks of Franz Illescue's hide. Now she couldn't do that. Not when it was so obvious to her, at least, that he truly meant his apology.

"Dr. Illescue," she said after a moment, "I know you personally had nothing to do with the leakage of this information."

His eyes widened slightly, and she tasted his astonishment at her reasonable tone.

"In addition," she continued, "I've had quite a bit of experience with large, bureaucratic organizations. The Queen's Navy, for example. While I'm aware the captain is responsible for anything that happens aboard her ship, I'm also aware that things happen over which she has no actual control. I'm convinced this leak was an example of that sort of lapse.

"I won't pretend I'm not angry, or that I don't strongly resent what's happened. I feel confident, however, that you've done everything in your power to discover just how this information got into the hands of someone like Solomon Hayes. I see no point in punishing you or your facility for the criminal actions of some individual acting without your authority and against Briarwood's policies on patient confidentiality. I have no intention of seeking damages, punitive or otherwise, from you or Briarwood. I'll accept your offer to provide your future services without fee, and for my part, I'll consider the matter otherwise closed."

"Your Grace—" Illescue began, then stopped. He gazed at her for a moment, his clenched expression easing slightly, then drew a deep breath.

"That's extraordinarily generous and gracious of you, Your Grace," he said, with absolute sincerity. "I won't apologize further, because, frankly, no one could apologize adequately for this lapse. I would, however, be honored if you'd allow me to personally escort you to your son."

Honor stood in the small, pleasantly pastel room, Andrew LaFollet at her back, and gazed at the innocuous-looking cabinet at the room's center. She could have pressed a button which would have retracted the "cabinet's" housing and revealed the artificial womb in which her child was steadily maturing, but she chose not to. She'd viewed all the medical reports, and the medical imagery, and a part of her wanted to see the fetus with her own eyes. But she'd already decided she wouldn't do that until Hamish and Emily could accompany her. This was her child, but he was also *theirs*, and she would not take that moment from them.

She smiled at her own possible silliness, then walked across the room, seated herself beside the unit, and lowered Nimitz from her shoulder to her lap. The powered chair was luxuriously comfortable, and she leaned back, closing her eyes and listening. The volume wasn't turned very high on the speakers, but she could hear what her unborn son was hearing. The steady sound of her own recorded heart beat. Snatches of music—especially the works of Salvatore Hammerwell, her favorite composer—and the sound of her own voice reading. Reading, in fact, she realized with another, quite different smile, from *David and the Phoenix*.

She sat there for several minutes, listening, absorbing, sharing. This was the child of her body, the child she'd been unable to carry, and this quiet, comfortable room existed exactly for what she was doing. For bringing herself, at least temporarily, into the presence of the mystic process from which circumstance, fate, and duty had excluded her. And in Honor's case, there was even more to it than for other mothers.

She reached out from behind her eyes, listening with more than just her ears, and there, in the quiet of her mind, she found him. She felt him. He was a bright, drowsy, drifting presence. As yet unformed, yet moving steadily towards becoming. His mind-glow danced in the depths of her own mind and heart, glorious with the promise of what he would be and become, stirring to the sound of his parents' voices, yearning from his peaceful dreams towards the future which awaited him.

In that moment, she knew, at least partly, what a treecat mother felt, and a part of her quailed at the thought of ever leaving this room again. Of separating herself from that new, bright life glowing so softly and yet so powerfully in her perceptions. Her closed eyes prickled, and she remembered the verse Katherine Mayhew had found for her when she'd had Willard Neufsteiler arrange the funding for her first Grayson orphanage. It was an ancient poem, older than the Diaspora itself, carefully preserved on Grayson because of how perfectly it spoke to their society and beliefs.

> Not flesh of my flesh, or bone of my bone,
> But still miraculously my own.
> Never forget for a single minute;
> You didn't grow under my heart, but in it.

She supposed it didn't really apply to *her* in this case. And yet . . . it did. Because whatever else was true of this child, he was growing daily, stronger, more vibrant, more *real* within her heart. And she'd already asked Katherine to send her a presentation copy of it for Emily.

She blinked, then turned her head and looked at LaFollet. The colonel wasn't looking at her at that instant. His eyes, too, were on the unit at the center of the room, and his unguarded expression mirrored his emotions. This was *his* child, too, she realized. Unlike most Grayson males, LaFollet had never married. She knew why that was, too, and she felt a sudden fresh flicker of guilt. But perhaps in part because of that, the emotions flooding out of him as he gazed at the bland cabinet hiding his Steadholder's unborn son were more than simply fiercely protective. They were, in fact, very, very similar to the ones she tasted from Nimitz.

Honor savored her armsman's mind-glow, and as she did, something crystallized within her. She looked at LaFollet again, seeing the gray flecking his still thick auburn hair, the crows feet at the corners of his steady gray eyes, the lines etched in his face. He was eight T-years younger than she was, but physically he could have been her father.

And he was also the only surviving member of her original personal security team. Every one of the others, and all too many of their replacements, had been killed in the line of duty. Including Jamie Candless, who'd stayed behind aboard a ship he'd known was going to be blown up, to cover his Steadholder's escape.

There was no adequate recompense for that sort of loyalty, and she knew it would have insulted Andrew LaFollet if she'd suggested there ought to be one. But as she tasted his fierce devotion, his love for her unborn son—and for her—an equally fierce determination filled her.

"Andrew," she said quietly.

"Yes, My Lady?"

He looked at her, eyes slightly narrowed, and she tasted his surprise at her tone.

"Sit down, Andrew."

She pointed at the chair beside hers, and he glanced at it, then looked back at her.

"I'm on duty, My Lady," he reminded her.

"And Spencer is standing right outside that door. I want you to sit down, Andrew. Please."

He gazed at her for a moment longer, then slowly crossed the room and obeyed her. She tasted his growing concern, almost wariness, but he regarded her attentively.

"Thank you," she said, and reached out to lay one hand lightly on the artificial womb.

"A lot of things are going to change when this child is born, Andrew. I can't even begin to imagine what some of them are going to be, but others are pretty obvious to me. For one thing, Harrington Steading's going to have a new heir, with all the security details that involves. For another thing, there's going to be a brand new human being in this universe, one whose safety is far more important to me than my own could ever be. And because of that, I have a new duty for you."

"My Lady," LaFollet began quickly, his tone almost frightened, "I've been thinking about that, and I have several armsmen in mind who'd be—"

"Andrew."

The single word cut him off, and she smiled at him, then reached out and cupped the side of his face in her right hand. It was the first time she'd ever touched him quite like that, and he froze, like a frightened horse.

She smiled at him.

"I know who I want," she told him quietly.

"My Lady," he protested, "I'm *your* armsman. I'm flattered—honored—more than you could possibly imagine, but I belong with *you*. Please."

His voice wavered ever so slightly on the last word, and Honor caressed his cheek with her fingers. Then she shook her head.

"No, Andrew. You *are* my armsman—you always will be. My perfect armsman. The man who's saved my life not once, but over and over. The man who helped save my sanity more than once. The man whose shoulder I've wept on, and who's covered my back for fifteen years. I love you, Andrew LaFollet. And I know you love me. And you're the one man I trust to protect my son. The one man I *want* to protect my son."

"My Lady—" His voice was hoarse, shaky, and he shook his head slowly, almost pleadingly.

"Yes, Andrew," she told him, sitting back in her chair again, answering the unspoken question she tasted in his emotions. "Yes, I do have another motive, and you've guessed what it is. I want you as safe as I can make you. I've lost Simon, Jamie, Robert, and Eddy. I don't want to lose you, too. I want to know you're alive. And if, God forbid, something happens and I'm killed in action, I want to know you're still here, still protecting my son for me, because I know no one else in this universe will do it as well as you will."

He stared at her, his eyes brimming with tears, and then he laid his hand atop the artificial womb exactly as he'd once laid it atop a Bible the day he swore his personal fealty to her.

"Yes, My Lady," he said softly. "When your son is born. On that day, I'll become his armsman, too. And whatever happens, I swear I will protect him with my life."

"I know you will, Andrew," she told him. "I know you will."

"Well, that didn't work out too well, did it?" Albrecht Detweiler said conversationally.

Aldona Anisimovna and Isabel Bardasano glanced at one another, then turned back to the face displayed on the secure com. They sat in Anisimovna's office—one of her offices—on Mesa itself, and they had no doubt what Detweiler was referring to. Just over one T-month had passed since the attempt on Honor Harrington's life, and this was the first time since then that they'd been back in the Mesa System.

"I haven't had time to fully familiarize myself with the reports, Albert," Bardasano said after a moment. "As you know, we've only been back in-system for a few hours. On the basis of what I've seen so far, I'd have to agree it didn't work out *as planned*. Whether that's a good thing or a bad one remains to be seen."

"Indeed?" Detweiler cocked his head, one eyebrow rising, and Anisimovna tried to decide whether his expression was more one of amusement or irritation.

"Are you sure you aren't simply trying to put the best face possible on a failure, Isabel?" he asked after a moment.

"Of course I am, to some extent." Bardasano smiled slightly. "If I said I wasn't, I'd be lying. Worse, you'd *know* I was. That could be decidedly unhealthy for me. By the same token, however, you know what my usual success rate is. And I think you also recognize I'm valuable not simply for the operations I carry out successfully, but also for my brain."

"That's certainly been true up till now," he agreed.

"Well, then," she said, "let's look at what happened. The operation should have succeeded—*would* have succeeded, according to the reports I have had time to look over—if not for the fact that Harrington had a *pulser*, of all things, actually built into her artificial hand."

She shrugged.

"None of the intelligence available to us suggested any such possibility, so it was impossible to factor it into our plans. Apparently, our vehicle succeeded in taking out her bodyguard, exactly as we'd planned, and under circumstances which should have left him armed when she wasn't. And then, unfortunately, she shot him . . . with her *finger*."

Bardasano grimaced, and Detweiler actually chuckled, ever so slightly.

"So that's why the operation failed," she continued. "However, removing Harrington herself, while it would have been extremely satisfying personally to all of us on several levels, was never really the primary object of killing her. True, it would have been useful to deprive the Manties of one of their best naval commanders. And, equally true, the fact that she and Anton Zilwicki have become such good friends only adds to the reasons to want her dead. But what we were really after was killing her in a way which would convince the Manties generally, and Elizabeth Winton in particular, *Haven* had done it. And that, Albrecht, is exactly the conclusion which our Foreign Office agent informs us they all reached. After all, who else had a reason to want her killed?"

"I think Isabel has a point, Albrecht," Anisimovna put in. Technically, the Harrington assassination hadn't been Anisimovna's responsibility in any way. The fact that she and Bardasano were working together on several other projects—and that Bardasano's sudden demise would complicate those projects significantly—gave her a distinct vested interest in the younger woman's survival, however.

"You do?" Detweiler's eyes moved from Bardasano to Anisimovna.

"I do," she replied firmly. "It's well known that the Legislaturalists and Pierre and his lunatics all used assassination as a standard tool. Given that history, it was inevitable, I think, for the Manties to automatically assume that Pritchart—who's killed quite a few people herself, in her time—ordered Harrington's assassination. Especially given how successful Harrington's raids have been." She shrugged. "So as far as I can see, Isabel's right. The operation succeeded in its primary objective."

"And," Bardasano added almost diffidently, "the reports I've had a chance to view so far all agree that the Manties don't have any more clue as to how we managed it than the Andermani did."

"That's true enough." Detweiler pursed his lips thoughtfully for a moment, then shrugged. "All right, on balance I agree with you. I would, however, add that I was one of the individuals who expected to take considerable personal satisfaction in knowing she was dead. Should the opportunity to rectify that aspect of this operation present itself, I trust it will be taken."

"Oh, you can count on *that*," Bardasano promised with a thin smile.

"Good. Well, turning from that, how are things proceeding in Talbott?"

"Well, as of our last reports," Anisimovna said. "Obviously, we're several weeks behind here, thanks to the communications lag, but both Nordbrandt and Westman seem to be working out well, each in his or her own way. Personally, I think Nordbrandt is more useful to us where Solly public opinion is concerned, but Westman's probably the more effective, in the long term.

"Politically, the reports coming out of their constitutional convention indicate Tonkovic is still digging in to resist annexation terms which would be acceptable to Manticore. She doesn't have any intention of actually killing the annexation, but she's so genuinely stupid she doesn't realize she's playing her fiddle while the house burns down above her. And reports from our people in Manticore all confirm that the combination of Nordbrandt's attacks and Tonkovic's obstructionism are contributing to a small but growing domestic resistance to annexing the Cluster after all."

"And Monica?"

"Levakonic is effectively in charge of that part of the operation," Bardasano said. "Aldona and I did the original spadework, but Izrok is coordinating the delivery and refitting of the battlecruisers. According to his last dispatch, they're running behind schedule. Apparently the Monicans' shipyards are less capable than they assured Izrok they were. He's brought in some additional technicians to expedite matters, and even with the slippage to date, we're well within the originally projected timetable. I'm not totally comfortable with the fact that the schedule is slipping at all, but at the moment things appear to be under control."

"Verbs like 'appear' always make me uncomfortable," Detweiler observed in a whimsical tone.

"I realize that," Bardasano said calmly. "Unfortunately, in black ops like this, they crop up quite a lot."

"I know." Detweiler nodded. "And what about the propaganda offensive in the League?"

"There," Anisimovna admitted, "we're hitting some air pockets."

"Why?"

"Mostly because the Manties have replaced the complete incompetents High Ridge and Descroix had assigned to their embassy on Old Earth." Anisimovna grimaced. "I never would have picked Webster as an ambassador, but I have to admit that he's doing them proud. I suppose it has something to do with all the political experience he gained as First Space Lord. At any rate, he comes across as a very reassuring, solid, reliable, *truthful* fellow. Not only as a talking head on HD, either. Several of our sources tell us he comes across that way in one-on-one conversations with League officials, as well. At the same time, he—or someone on his staff, although all the indications are that he's the one behind it—has orchestrated a remarkably effective PR campaign.

"We're making progress, Albrecht. All the imagery of blood, explosions, and body parts coming out of Split are at least creating a widespread sense that someone in the Cluster objects to the annexation. And our own PR people tell us they're making some ground in convincing the Solly in the street to project Nordbrandt's activities onto *all* the Cluster's systems. But I'd be misleading you if I suggested Webster isn't doing some very successful damage control. In particular, he's succeeded in pointing out that actions like Nordbrandt's are those of a lunatic fringe, and that lunatics aren't exactly the best barometer for how the *sane* members of any society are reacting."

"And how serious is that?"

"For our purposes, not very, at this point," Anisimovna said confidently. "We're providing a justification for Frontier Security to do what we want. We don't have to convince the Solly public; we only have to provide a pretext OFS can use, and they've had lots of practice using far less graphic pretexts then Nordbrandt and Westman. Assuming President Tyler and his Navy hold up their end, Verrochio will have all the fig leaf he needs."

"I see." Detweiler pondered for several seconds, then shrugged.

"I see," he repeated. "Still, from what you're saying, this Webster is at least a minor irritant, yes?"

"I think that's fair enough," Anisimovna agreed.

"And he's popular on Manticore?"

"Quite popular. In fact, there was considerable pressure to reassign him to command their Home Fleet, rather than 'waste' him as a diplomat."

"Then having him assassinated by the Peeps would be more than mildly irritating?"

"It certainly would."

"Very well. Isabel."

"Yes, Albrecht?"

"I know you've got a lot on your plate, but I'd like you to see to this little matter, as well. And this time, when you choose your vehicle, pick someone from the Havenite diplomatic staff on Old Earth. Sometimes you have to be really obvious to convince neobarbs to draw the desired conclusion."

Chapter Forty-One

"Well, Honor. I believe you and Hamish have something you want to tell me about, don't you?"

Honor turned quickly, putting her back to the archaic, battlemented parapet of King Michael's Tower. She cursed herself silently for the suddenness of her movement, and hoped she didn't look too much like a Sphinx chipmunk suddenly confronted by treecat.

Sunlight poured down over the tower's flat roof, less warm than the sun had been for her last visit to Mount Royal Palace four months earlier, but still hot. The rooftop garden's flowers and shrubs were in full leaf, and the fringe of the sun awning over the garden chairs popped gently in the breeze. The sky was a deep, cloudless blue, and some of Mount Royal's flock of Old Earth ravens rode the wind in circles high overhead.

Queen Elizabeth and Crown Prince Justin sat in two of the garden chairs, their treecats stretched out comfortably on the old-fashioned wicker table between them. Hamish sat to one side, with Emily's life-support chair beside him, and Samantha and Nimitz lay sprawled together in a patch of shade on Emily's other side.

It was a charmingly tranquil domestic scene, Honor thought. Unfortunately, she tasted the gently malicious amusement behind the Queen's innocent brown eyes.

"What makes you think that, Elizabeth?" she asked, sparring for time and tasting Hamish's sudden consternation. She did *not*, she noticed, sense any such emotion from Emily.

"Honor," the Queen said patiently, "I'm the Queen, remember? I have thousands and thousands of spies whose sole job is to make sure I know things. More to the point, I've known Hamish and Emily since I was born, and you for—what? Fifteen T-years, now? You may not be aware of how your body language has changed around them, but I certainly am. So, which of you miscreants wants to confess that you and Hamish are in violation of the Articles of War?"

Honor felt Hamish's flicker of dismay, but there was too much devilish delight in Elizabeth's mind-glow for Honor to share it.

"As a matter of fact," she replied after a moment, "according to my attorney, Richard Maxwell, there's every reason to believe that since the First Lord is a civilian and I'm not, any relationship between us wouldn't be in violation of the Articles. Assuming, of course," she added with a smile, "that there was any such relationship."

"Oh, certainly *assuming* any such thing," Elizabeth agreed affably. "Ah, and would it happen there is such a relationship?"

"Actually, Beth," Emily said tranquilly, "there is. We're married."

"You shock me." Elizabeth chuckled and leaned back in her chair, fanning herself with one hand. "Oh, how my trust in all three of you has been betrayed! Woe and lamentations. And so forth."

"Very funny," Emily said politely.

"You don't seem surprised that *I'm* not surprised," Elizabeth pointed out.

"Unlike my lamentably overly trusting spouses, I felt more than a slight twinge of suspicion when you invited the three of us for a private audience. They, needless to say, walked in all innocent and unwary." Emily shook her head sadly. "Well, Honor may not have. She's really much more clever about these things than Hamish, but I'm fairly confident you managed to at least partially blindside her, as well."

"I certainly tried." Elizabeth looked at Honor, her eyes glinting in the awning's shade. "It's not always the easiest thing to do," she added.

"It's been happening to me with depressing regularity for the past several months, actually," Honor told her. "First the minor matter of that unexpected pregnancy. Then Solomon Hayes' helpful announcement of it. Then there was the little ambush Reverend Sullivan, Archbishop Telmachi, my mother, and my husband and wife—only they weren't my husband and wife at that point, you understand—set up. Did you know I was proposed to and married in less than two hours? The Reverend came all the way from Grayson to make an honest woman out of me. And then," despite herself, her mood darkened, "there've been a few other, less pleasant surprises since."

She felt a quick, sharp echo of her own darkness from Elizabeth as her words brought back the pain of losing Michelle Henke. Then Nimitz gave her a firm, scolding bleek, and she shook her head quickly.

"Sorry about that." She smiled almost naturally. "I don't mean to be the ghost at the banquet."

"Apology accepted," Elizabeth told her. She drew a breath, then shook herself and smiled back, banishing her own sense of loss and reaching back out for her previous mood.

"However," she continued, "the real devious reason I invited you three here and strong-armed your confession out of you, is that I'm wondering just how long you intend to wait before you publicly . . . regularize your situation?"

"We were waiting until Richard was able to confirm Hamish's interpretation of the legal complications," Honor said.

"And," Hamish admitted, "keeping quiet about it has sort of gotten to be a habit. I think we're all just a little bit nervous—no, a *lot* nervous—over how the public will react to this. Especially after High Ridge's smear campaign."

"Knowing you all, I assume there was no truth to Hayes' allegations at the time?"

"No, there wasn't," Hamish said firmly, then glanced at Emily and Honor. "Not," he added with scrupulous honesty, "that there wasn't considerable temptation, whether Honor and I had admitted it to ourselves or not."

"I thought as much." Elizabeth regarded them thoughtfully, then shrugged. "I'm sure a lot of people who don't know you will assume otherwise. Unfortunately, nothing you can do is going to change that, and waiting until after your son is born will only make it worse. You do realize that, don't you?"

"We do—even Hamish," Emily said, smiling demurely at her husband.

"Under some circumstances," Elizabeth continued just a bit more seriously, "this could have been a significant political liability. Not only is Hamish First Lord, but Willie is Prime Minister. Which, by the way, is the first time in the Star Kingdom's history two sibs have simultaneously held such important positions in a government. The idea that all of us were lying, whether we were or not, is going to present itself, and the Opposition would just love to pounce on it. At the moment, however, there *is* no effective Opposition. The only person who could put one together, really, is Cathy Montaigne, and given her own . . . irregular personal life—not to mention her basic personality—*she'll* be standing on top of the Parliament building toasting the brides and groom and leading choruses of obscene drinking songs in their honor.

"What I'm trying to say is that, politically speaking, there's no time like the present. I think you should go ahead and make your marriage public. Besides, I've consulted the Queen's Bench. They agree with Hamish's interpretation. And they also agree I have the authority as Queen to set aside Article One-Nineteen. For that matter, they tell me Admiral Caparelli could make the same decision 'for the good of the service' on the basis that the Crown can't afford to lose either of you at this particular time. So it's time to come out of the closet, you three."

"That's . . . a scary thought," Honor admitted softly, her smile just a bit tremulous. "One I'm really looking forward to, you understand, but still scary after so long. And I have to go back to Trevor's Star the day after tomorrow. I'll feel awfully guilty if we're all wrong and this blows up in everyone else's face while I'm off with the fleet and out of range!"

"If we wait until you can hang around to absorb your share of any slings and arrows, we'll never get it announced," Emily pointed out. "Eighth Fleet is eating up every minute of your time." She pouted. "It was bad enough when the Navy was only seducing one of my spouses away from me!"

"Hey, if you can't take a joke, you shouldn't follow the Fleet, girlie," Hamish said with a wicked grin, and Emily gurgled a laugh.

"I bet you say that to all your dirt-side dollies, spacer!" she growled.

"If we can return this conversation to a somewhat less salacious basis," Elizabeth said severely, eyes twinkling, "I have a suggestion."

"Which is?" Honor asked, ignoring Hamish and Emily as Emily reached out and smacked him on the head with her working arm.

"Which is that we can probably defuse at least some of any adverse public reaction if we make the announcement the right way."

"Which is?" Honor repeated.

"You three were already invited to tonight's state dinner," Elizabeth said. "It was going to be one of those boring but necessary evenings, full of ambassadors and toasts and looking confident for the newsies and HD cameras. And I'll be honest with you, looking confident is more necessary than usual at the moment."

Her expression darkened once more, and Ariel's ears flattened in reaction to her mood shift.

"What happened to you at Solon, Honor, and what the Peeps did to us at Zanzibar, have had a measurable impact on public morale. Events in Talbott aren't helping, either. At the moment, Admiral Sarnow seems to be getting on top of the situation in Silesia, but that butcher Nordbrandt is killing hundreds of people in Split. And what happened when the Peeps tried to assassinate you also has to be factored into the mix."

"My read is that the assassination attempt mainly pissed people off," Hamish said.

"It certainly did," Elizabeth agreed. "And if you think people were 'pissed off' here in the Star Kingdom, you don't even want to know how *Grayson* reacted! It was bad enough when they thought the Peeps had executed you, Honor—this is even worse, in a way. At the same time, though, all kinds of rumors are flying. In fairness to Lieutenant Meares and his family, I authorized the release of the information that he was acting under some form of compulsion. But the fact that we can't suggest how the compulsion was exerted is contributing to a climate of suspicion. Or fear, perhaps. After all, if the Peeps got to him, who else can they get to?

"At any rate, anything that pushes morale upward is very much worthwhile, and I think having your marriage announced here at Mount Royal, by me, with all the appropriate hoopla, ought to have a sort of festive effect. You three are probably among the dozen or so most popular public figures in the Star Kingdom right now, and that's going to more than compensate for anyone who might suspect Hamish and Honor were . . . dallying with one another before you actually were."

"Politics," Honor sighed, then laughed a trifle sadly.

"What?" Hamish asked.

"I was just recalling a discussion with Admiral Courvoisier before we deployed to Grayson for the first time," Honor said, shaking her head.

"Politics are always important at our level of responsibility, Honor," Elizabeth told her. "That doesn't necessarily make this a sordid decision."

"I wasn't trying to suggest it does. It's just that it gets so fatiguing sometimes."

"That it does. On the other hand, sometimes I get to combine things I genuinely want to do with political considerations. Of course, it works the other way around, too, sometimes. More often, I usually think. In this case, though, I have a belated wedding gift for the three of you."

Honor regarded the Queen warily. At the moment Elizabeth's idea of what she was "due"—especially after Solon—would leave an unpleasant taste in her mouth.

Elizabeth looked back at her as if the *Queen* were the empath, then reached under her chair and pulled out a small, flat case.

"Nothing excessive," she reassured her vassal with a slight smile. "I just asked Broughton and Stemwinder to make these up for me."

She handed the case to Emily, and Honor walked over so that Emily's life-support chair was between her and Hamish. Emily looked up at both of them, then looked back down and ran her finger across the raised, intertwined "B" and "S" crest of the firm which had been jewelers to the House of Winton for over three T-centuries.

She opened it, and Honor drew a deep breath as she saw the three rings nestled into the velvet interior. They were Grayson-style wedding bands, larger and heavier than the Manticoran norm, and exquisitely wrought, if not quite in the pure Grayson style. On Grayson, men's wedding rings were traditionally of yellow gold and women's of silver, but all three of these bands were made up of three interwoven strands, one each of yellow gold, white gold, and silver. They carried the Harrington Steading key on one side and the rampant White Haven stag on the other, and the flat-topped bezels bore the traditional circle of diamonds, each centered by a different semiprecious stone.

"I checked," Elizabeth said. "Honor, you were born in October, old-style. Hamish, you were born in March, and Emily was born in August. That makes your birthstones opal, jade, and sardonyx. So I had these made for you. They aren't quite Grayson, and they aren't quite Manticoran, just as the three of you no longer belong to just one of us."

"They're beautiful, Elizabeth." Emily looked up with bright eyes. "Thank you."

"As gifts go, they're small enough for people who mean as much to me as you do," Elizabeth said simply. "And these are from us—from Elizabeth and Justin, not the Crown."

Honor reached into the case and removed the opal-crested ring. She held it, glittering in the sun, gazing down at it for a few seconds. Then she tried it on the third finger of her left hand.

It was a bit large, and she felt a flicker of surprise. Elizabeth had obviously taken pains to get this gift right, and it should have been easy for her to get Honor's ring size, given that Honor's father had the exact dimensions of her prosthetic hand. But then she felt Elizabeth's eyes on her and sensed the Queen's waiting watchfulness. She thought about it for a moment, then removed the ring from her left hand and tried it on her right.

It fit perfectly, and she held it up, looking past it at Elizabeth.

"If you want it resized, it won't be a problem, Honor," Elizabeth told her. "But I think I know you pretty well by now, and it occurred to me that you might want to wear it on your flesh-and-blood hand."

"I think you're right," Honor said slowly, lowering her hand and looking down at it. She'd never been one to wear much jewelry, but that ring looked perfect, and she smiled. Then she took it back off and handed it to Emily.

"Please, Emily," she said, holding out her hand as well. "On Grayson, the senior wife gives the wedding band to her junior. I know that, as Elizabeth says, we're not really Manticoran or Grayson anymore, but it would mean a lot to me."

"Of course," Emily said gently, then looked up at her husband. "Hamish, would you help me?"

Hamish smiled at both of them, then reached down, gently holding Honor's wrist as Emily slid the ring back onto her finger. Emily gazed at it, then looked back up.

"It looks good there, doesn't it?" She moved her gaze to Elizabeth. "And I think I'll have mine resized for *my* right hand, too."

"No need," Elizabeth told her. "It already is."

"Such a clever person you are," Emily told her distant cousin, and Elizabeth chuckled.

"I have it on the best of authority that *all* queens named 'Elizabeth' are clever."

"Ha! Probably that sycophantic Crown Prince you're married to currying favor with you!" Emily retorted.

"Thereby proving," the maligned Crown Prince in question said equably, "how clever *he* is."

Chapter Forty-Two

"Congratulations, Your Grace," Mercedes Brigham said with a huge smile, waiting just inside the hatch as Honor and Nimitz swam the transfer tube between the shuttle from Manticore and her pinnace. Andrew LaFollet and Spencer Hawke followed the two of them, and Brigham chuckled as Honor raised an eyebrow at her greeting.

"The news is all over the Fleet by now." The chief of staff gestured at the ring glittering on Honor's right hand. "I was actually a bit surprised by how many people were surprised, if you know what I mean."

"And the reaction?" Honor asked.

"Ranges from mere approval to ecstatic, I'd say," Brigham told her.

"No concerns over One-Nineteen?"

"Of course not." Brigham chuckled again. "You know as well as I do that One-Nineteen is probably the most winked at of the Articles. Even if it weren't, nobody's going to suggest it applies to you and Earl White Haven. Or," Brigham cocked her head, "is he Steadholder Consort Harrington now?"

"Please!" Honor gave a deliberate shudder. "I can hardly wait for the Conclave of Steadholders to start in on this one! I seem to spend most of my time trying to find ways to give the real conservatives apoplexy."

"One can only hope it carries some of them off," Brigham said tartly, with all the fervor of the years she'd spent in the Grayson Space Navy.

"A most improper thought—with which I agree completely, however unofficially."

Honor looked demurely over her shoulder at LaFollet, who returned her gaze with a deadpan expression. Then she held out her arms, and Nimitz swarmed down into them from her shoulder as she moved towards her seat. Brigham followed her, and seated herself across the aisle as the flight engineer sealed the hatch and the transfer tube detached. She and Honor and Honor's armsmen were the pinnace's only two-legged passengers, and LaFollet and Hawke chose seats two rows in front of Honor, between her and the flight deck.

It wasn't their usual position, and Honor's cheerfulness dimmed slightly as she tasted their emotions. Simon Mattingly's death, and Honor's narrow escape, had left their mark. Her armsmen's professional paranoia had risen to new heights, and she didn't much like the hairtrigger on which they were poised. She made another mental note to discuss the situation with LaFollet, then returned her attention to Brigham.

"What's the word on our repairs?"

"*Imperator*'s going to be in yard hands for at least another month, Your Grace." Brigham's expression sobered. "Probably more, actually. None of the damage may've gotten through to the core hull, but her after graser mounts took a lot heavier beating than we thought before the yard survey. *Agamemnon*'s going to be out of service even longer than that. *Truscott Adams* and *Tisiphone* should be returning sometime in the next three to six weeks."

"I was afraid of that when I saw the preliminary yard surveys," Honor sighed. "Oh, well. What can't be cured must be endured, as we say on Grayson. And it's not as if repairs are the only thing that's going to be slowing us up."

"Your Grace?"

"I spent three days at Admiralty House, Mercedes. The situation after Zanzibar is even worse than we'd thought. The Caliph is apparently considering withdrawing from the Alliance."

"What?" Brigham sat upright abruptly, and Honor shrugged.

"It's hard to blame him, really. Look at it. His star system's been hammered flat twice, and he joined the Alliance in the first place for protection. It's kind of hard to argue we've protected his people successfully."

"And it's his own admiral's damned fault!" Brigham said hotly.

"If al-Bakr hadn't overruled Padgorny and given the Peeps a road-map of the system defenses, it never would have happened!"

"I know that's the general view in the Fleet, but I'm not sure it's fair."

Brigham looked at her semi-incredulously, and Honor shrugged.

"I'm not saying al-Bakr made the right decision, or that the decision he did make didn't help the Havenites considerably. But if they'd sent in the same attack force against our original defensive deployment, it would have steamrollered anything in its path anyway. Sure, the missile pods would've hurt them more than they did, but not enough to stop an attack that power-ful under Lester Tourville's command. The fact that they knew what we'd originally deployed may have inspired them to send a heavier force in the first place, but once they'd made that level of commitment, our original setup wouldn't have stopped them even if it had taken them completely by surprise."

"Maybe you're right." Brigham's concession was manifestly unwilling. "But even if you are, our losses would have been a lot lighter if we hadn't had to throw good money after bad by reinforcing."

"Mercedes," Honor said just a bit sternly, "we have an *alliance*. That implies mutual responsibilities and obligations—and I might remind you that High Ridge's idiotic failure to remember that has already cost us Erewhon. If we find our obligations under the treaty too onerous, then we should be happy to see Zanzibar withdraw from it. If we don't, then the Star Kingdom—and the Queen—have a direct, personal responsibility to discharge them. And that means reinforcing a threatened ally to the very best of our ability."

Brigham looked at her rebelliously for just a moment, then sighed.

"Point taken, Your Grace. It's just—" She broke off, shaking her head.

"I understand," Honor said. "But the Fleet's angry enough as it is. You and I have a special responsibility to avoid pumping any more hydrogen into that particular fire."

"Understood, Ma'am."

"Good. Having said that, however," Honor continued, "there are some members of the Government—and a few people at

Admiralty House, for that matter—who think we should actually be encouraging Zanzibar, and possibly Alizon, as well, to declare nonbelligerent status."

"They *what*?" Brigham blinked. "After all the trouble we went to to build the Alliance in the first place?"

"The situation was a bit different then," Honor pointed out. "We were on our own against the Peeps, and we were looking for strategic depth. Zanzibar and Alizon have both been net contributors to the Alliance—or would have been, if the need to rebuild both of them after McQueen's Operation Icarus hadn't cost so much—but what we really wanted them for was forward bases when everyone was still thinking in terms of system-by-system advances."

She shrugged.

"Strategic thinking's changed, as our own ops—and Tourville's attack on Zanzibar—demonstrate. Both sides are thinking in terms of deep strikes now, operating deep into 'enemy territory,' and simple strategic depth, unless you've got one heck of a lot of it, is looking less and less important. Not only that, but with Zanzibar effectively knocked out of the war for at least eight T-months to a T-year, the system's become a defensive obligation which offers no return. And Alizon, which also got hammered by Icarus, really only offers us the capacity to build a few dozen battlecruisers or lighter units at a time.

"So the new school of thought argues that freeing ourselves of the defensive commitments to protect relatively minor star systems would actually allow us to concentrate more strength in Home Fleet and here in Eighth Fleet. At the same time, assuming the Republic's willing to accept their neutrality and leave them alone, it gets them out of the line of fire. And the *important* allies at this moment are Grayson and the Andermani. We can protect Grayson more strongly if we can recall the forces currently tied down by commitments like Alizon, and the Andermani are effectively secure against direct attack simply because of how far away they are."

Brigham sat without speaking for almost two minutes, obviously considering what Honor had just said, then looked at her admiral.

"And do *you* agree with the 'new school of thought,' Your Grace?"

"I think it's a rational, fresh approach to the problem. And I think that if the Republic *is* willing to accept and respect the future neutrality of current members of the Alliance, it would be very much in our interest to pursue the possibility. My biggest reservation is whether or not the Republic will accept anything of the sort, though."

"They've been trying to split the Alliance for decades," Brigham pointed out.

"Yes, they have. But one thing Eloise Pritchart and Thomas Theisman obviously aren't is stupid, which means they're as well aware as we are of how the strategic and operational realities have changed. So, if I were they, I'd be very tempted to reject any easy out for our allies. I'd insist on their *surrender*, rather than simply allowing them to say they're tired of playing and want to go home."

"Or," Brigham said slowly, "you might agree to allow them to become neutral, when what you really intend to do is sweep them right up as soon as we withdraw our units and leave them on their own."

"That's certainly one possibility. And given the Pritchart Administration's apparent track record in interstellar diplomacy, quite a few people opposed to the idea are making the same point. Personally, I think that if Pritchart officially agreed to accept their neutrality, she'd almost have to stand by her word precisely because of the dispute over what happened to our diplomatic correspondence before the shooting started again. I've said as much, not without evoking quite a bit of incredulity. It's not a point on which the Government at large and I, or even my new brother-in-law and I, seem to be in close agreement." She grimaced. "Fortunately, perhaps, it's a decision I don't have to make."

"But it is going to affect our stance here, isn't it? That's why you brought it up."

"Yes, it is. As things stand now, we're being forced to make even heavier commitments to Alizon and the other secondary systems because of what happened at Zanzibar. Which means, of course, that finding replacements and reinforcements for Eighth Fleet just got even harder. And given what we blundered into in Solon, Admiralty House is insistent that we have to be reinforced before we resume offensive operations. We can't afford another hammering like the one Giscard gave us."

"So it's confirmed that it was Giscard?"

"The news came in just before my shuttle left. He's been officially voted the thanks of the Republic's Congress for his successful defense of Solon. And Tourville got the same thing for hammering Zanzibar."

"That's good to know," Brigham said thoughtfully. Honor looked at her, and the chief of staff shrugged. "It always makes me feel better, somehow, to be able to put a face on the enemy, Your Grace."

"Does it?" Honor shook her head. "It helps me when I consider their probable actions or reactions, but I really think I'd rather not know the people on the other side. It's easier to kill strangers."

"Don't fool yourself, Your Grace," Brigham said quietly. "I've known you a long time now. The fact that they're strangers doesn't make you feel any better about killing them."

Honor looked at her again, more sharply, and her chief of staff looked back levelly. And she was right, Honor thought.

"At any rate," she continued, her tone conceding the point, "we can't afford to let them do that to us again for several reasons. The losses themselves are painful enough, but we've got to regain the momentum, and we're not going to be able to do that if they keep bloodying our nose. So the decision's been taken that even though it's important to get back onto the offensive as quickly as we can, we're not going to do it until we've been able to reinforce Eighth Fleet significantly. Which means turning up additional modern wallers, among other things."

"Which is going to take how long?" Brigham asked anxiously.

"At least another six to eight weeks. That's why I said *Imperator*'s repair time wasn't going to set us back badly."

"New wallers sound good, but I hate the thought of giving them that much free time, Your Grace." Brigham's expression was worried. "They've got to be tempted to follow up their success against Zanzibar, and if we take the pressure off of them for a couple of months . . ."

She let her voice trail off, and Honor nodded.

"I made the same point to Admiral Caparelli and the Strategy Board. And I also made a suggestion about how we might alleviate some of the worse consequences of having to effectively stand down Eighth Fleet's offensive for that long."

"What sort of suggestion, Your Grace?" Brigham regarded her narrowly.

"We're going to try to keep them looking over their shoulders. Beginning next week—about the time we'd be doing it anyway, if we were following the cycle we established in Cutworm Two and Three—our destroyers are going to start scouting half a dozen of their systems. They'll do exactly what they've been doing as the preliminary for each of our earlier attacks. Except, of course, that there won't *be* any attacks."

"That's . . . deliciously nasty, Your Grace," Brigham said admiringly. "They'll have to assume we do plan to attack and react accordingly."

"Initially, at least. I suspect they're smart enough to wonder if that isn't exactly what we're doing, since they know they've hurt us badly. But I think you're right; they're going to have to honor the threat, at least the first time we do it to them. After that, they could change their minds."

"So if we do it to them two or three times while we aren't ready to attack," Brigham said, "get them accustomed to the idea that our scouts are just part of a strategy of bluffs, then when we *are* ready to attack—"

"Then hopefully, scouting the systems will actually give us a bit of an edge of surprise, since they'll *know* we aren't really going to hit them," Honor agreed. "And if we do it right, we may be able to convince them to do an al-Bakr and tip their hands on their current defensive thinking and deployments."

"I like it," Brigham said. "Obviously, I'd prefer not to have to suspend operations, but if we have to, let's make it work for us as much as we can."

"That's more or less what I was thinking. So why don't you and I spend some time thinking about which systems we'd like to make them most nervous about?

"Your Grace?"

Honor and Spencer Hawke broke immediately, stepping back towards opposite sides of the mat. They fell into rest positions, then Honor bowed and Hawke returned the courtesy before she turned towards James MacGuiness.

"Yes, Mac?"

MacGuiness stood just inside the gymnasium hatch. Like Honor's original flagship, HMS *Second Yeltsin* was an *Invictus*-class superdreadnought. Honor had transferred her flag to her while *Imperator* was undergoing repairs, but although she and her staff been aboard *Second Yeltsin* for almost two weeks now, ever since her return from Manticore, the ship still didn't feel like "home."

Still, it wasn't exactly like camping out in a hut in the woods, either. *Second Yeltsin*, like *Imperator*, had been built as a flagship from the keel out, and several of her amenities reflected her flagship status, including the small, well-equipped private "flag gym" one deck down from the admiral's personal quarters. Honor had preferred to use the main gymnasium aboard *Imperator*, where she could take the pulse of the flagship's crew's morale and attitudes, but since Simon Mattingly's and Timothy Meares' deaths, Andrew LaFollet had put his foot down firmly. He simply could not guarantee her security with so many people so close together, and his feelings—and concern—had been so strong that this time Honor had offered barely token resistance. Even now, she could taste her personal armsman's focused attention as he stood behind MacGuiness, of all people, tautly wary of any sudden move on the other man's part.

"There's a special courier boat, Your Grace." If MacGuiness was aware of LaFollet's scrutiny, and he almost certainly was, he gave no sign of it. Nor did Honor taste any resentment of her armsmen's heightened wariness in MacGuiness' mind-glow. "It's from Admiralty House," he continued. "It just came through the Junction, and Harper's already received a transmission from it. It has personal dispatches aboard for you."

Honor felt her eyebrows try to rise. The regular morning shuttle from Manticore had arrived barely three hours ago; the evening shuttle was due in another five. So what was so urgent that the Admiralty had sent it aboard a special dispatch boat?

She felt a sudden pang of anxiety, then forced herself to put it aside. If this had been some sort of personal bad news, it would have arrived aboard a private courier, not an official Admiralty dispatch boat.

"Thank you, Mac," she said calmly. "I'll grab a shower and take the dispatches in my quarters."

"Of course, Your Grace."

MacGuiness bobbed his head and departed, and Honor turned back to Hawke.

"I'm sorry to break this up, Spencer. I think you're starting to get the hang of it." Hawke grinned; he'd only been studying *coup de vitesse* for ten T-years. "Schedule permitting, maybe we can finish the session before supper," she said.

"As always, My Lady, I'm at your disposal," he told her with a bow, and she chuckled and looked at LaFollet.

"By golly, we're getting close to getting him civilized, aren't we?"

"'Close' only counts in horseshoes, hand grenades, and tactical nuclear weapons, My Lady," LaFollet replied gravely.

Honor slid the data chip into her desktop terminal. The display came up, and she frowned slightly as a header floated before her. The dispatch bore the electronic seal and personal cipher key of the First Lord, not the First *Space* Lord. Was it a personal message from Hamish, after all?

She input her own key and slid her right hand across the DNA sniffer. An instant later, the display blinked in acceptance, and the header disappeared, replaced by Hamish's face. He looked oddly excited, but not worried. In fact, if anything, the reverse.

"Honor," he said, "I suppose I could've let this come to you through normal channels, but I decided you'd hurt me if I did. So I pulled rank and got Tom Caparelli to agree to let me send you a special dispatch. Hold onto your socks, love."

He drew a deep breath, and Honor felt her shoulders tightening in anticipation of she knew not what.

"We just got an official message from the Peeps, delivered through Erewhon. It's an updated list of the names of POWs and of our personnel who they've confirmed as KIAs. According to it, Mike Henke is alive."

Honor sat back in her chair as abruptly as if someone had punched her in the chest. Which, she realized an instant later, as Nimitz reared up on his perch in reaction to her emotional spike, was exactly what it felt like. She stared at the display, and Hamish looked back out of it at her without speaking for several seconds, as if he'd anticipated her reaction and was giving her time to fight through it before he continued.

"We don't have many details," he went on after several seconds, "but it sounds as if *Ajax* must've gotten at least one of her boat bays cleared. From the list, it looks like about a third of her people got off, including Mike. She's hurt, we don't know how badly, but according to the Peeps' message, her injuries are definitely not life-threatening, and she's getting the best medical care they can provide. In fact, all of your wounded are.

"There's at least a suggestion, towards the end of their message, that they might be open to the idea of prisoner exchanges. You've been telling us all along that there's a big difference between the current régime and Pierre and his cutthroats. This certainly seems to bear that out. Of course, there are those—including the Queen—who argue that this is some sort of a trick, something designed to put us off guard, somehow, by a leopard who doesn't know how to change its spots. But whether they're right or not, I knew you'd want to know about Mike as soon as possible.

"According to their dispatch, the Peeps intend to allow personal messages from and to their POWs, strictly according to the Deneb Accords. Which is another refreshing change from StateSec or the Legislaturalists. I figured you'd probably want to start thinking about a message to her."

He paused again, giving her a few more seconds to think, then smiled.

"Whatever her suspicions, Elizabeth's overjoyed to know Mike is still alive. So is everyone who knows her. And Emily and I are almost happier for *you* than we are for ourselves. Be well, love. Clear."

The display blanked, and Honor sat staring at it. Nimitz swarmed down from his perch, climbed into her arms, and patted her on the cheek. She looked down, and his flying fingers began to sign.

<See? Told you things would get better. Now maybe your mind-glow will finish healing.>

"I'm sorry, Stinker." She stroked the back of his head. "I know I haven't been the best company since Solon."

<You lost a fight,> he signed back. <The first one you ever really lost. I don't think you knew how to do that. And you thought your friend was gone. Of course your mind-glow was darker. Strong Heart and Sees Clearly are good for you, they make you whole, but you have always been hardest on yourself.

Deep inside, you could not forgive yourself for Mike's death. Now you don't have to.>

"Maybe you're right." She hugged him gently. It was unusual for him to use Hamish and Emily's treecat names in normal conversation. The fact that he had reflected how concerned he'd been about her, she realized, and she hugged him again.

"Maybe you're right," she repeated, and her face blossomed in an enormous smile as she felt the realization that her best friend was still alive sinking home on an emotional as well as an intellectual basis. "In fact, Stinker, I think you *are* right. And I also think we'd better go find Mac and tell *him* about this before he finds out from someone else!"

"Admiral Henke."

Michelle Henke opened her eyes, then struggled hastily upright in the hospital bed as she saw the person who'd spoken her name. It wasn't easy, with her left leg still in traction while the quick heal rebuilt the shattered bone. But although they'd never met, she'd seen more than enough publicity imagery to recognize the platinum-haired, topaz-eyed woman standing at the foot of her bed.

"Don't bother, Admiral," Eloise Pritchart said. "You've been hurt, and this isn't really an official visit."

"You're a head of state, Madam President," Henke said dryly, getting herself upright and then settling back in relief as the elevating upper end of the bed caught up with her shoulders. "That means it *is* an official visit."

"Well, perhaps you're right," Pritchart acknowledged with a charming smile. Then she gestured at the chair beside the bed. "May I?"

"Of course. After all, it's your chair. In fact," Henke waved at the pleasant, if not precisely luxurious, room, "this is your entire hospital."

"In a manner of speaking, I suppose."

Pritchart seated herself gracefully, then sat there for several seconds, her head cocked slightly to the side, her expression thoughtful.

"To what do I owe the honor, Madam President?" Henke asked finally.

"Several things. First, you're our senior POW, in several

senses. You're the highest ranking, militarily speaking, and you're also—what? Fifth in the line of succession?"

"Since my older brother was murdered, yes," Henke said levelly, and had the satisfaction of seeing Pritchart flinch ever so slightly.

"I'm most sincerely sorry about the death of your father and your brother, Admiral Henke," she said, her voice equally level, meeting Henke's eyes squarely as she spoke. "We've determined from our own records that StateSec was, in fact, directly responsible for that assassination. The fanatics who actually carried it out may have been Masadans, but StateSec effectively recruited them and provided the weapons. As far as we're able to determine, all the individuals directly involved in the decision to carry out that operation are either dead or in prison. Not," she continued as Henke's eyebrows began to arch in disbelief, "because of that particular operation, but because of an entire catalog of crimes they'd committed against the people of their own star nation. In fact, while I'm sure it won't do anything to alleviate your own grief and anger, I'd simply point out that the same people were responsible for the deaths of untold thousands—no, millions—of their own citizens. The Republic of Haven has had more than enough of men and women like that."

"I'm sure you have," Henke said, watching the other woman carefully. "But you don't seem to have completely renounced their methods."

"In what way?" Pritchart asked a bit sharply, her eyes narrowing.

"I could bring up the little matter of your immediately prewar diplomacy, except that I'm reasonably certain we wouldn't agree on that point," Henke said. "So instead, I'll restrict myself to pointing out your attempt to assassinate Duchess Harrington. Who, I might remind you, happens to be a personal friend of mine."

"I'm aware of your close relationship with the Duchess," Pritchart said. "In fact, that's one of the several reasons I mentioned for this conversation. Some of my senior officers, including Secretary of War Theisman and Admiral Tourville and Admiral Foraker have met your 'Salamander.' They think very highly of her. And if they believed for a moment that my administration had ordered her assassination, they'd be very, very displeased with me."

"Forgive me, Madam President, but that's not exactly the same thing as saying you *didn't* authorize it."

"No, it isn't, is it?" Pritchart smiled. "I'd forgotten for a moment that you're used to moving at the highest level of politics in the Star Kingdom. You have a politician's ear, even if you are 'only a naval officer.' However, I'll be clearer. Neither I, nor anyone else in my administration, ordered or authorized an attempt to assassinate Duchess Harrington."

It was Henke's eyes' turn to narrow. As Pritchart said, she was accustomed to dealing with Manticoran *politicians*, if not politics *per se*. In her time, she'd met some extraordinarily adroit and polished liars. But if Eloise Pritchart was another of them, it didn't show.

"That's an interesting statement, Madam President. Unfortunately, with all due respect, I have no way to know it's accurate. And even if you think it is, that doesn't necessarily mean some rogue element in your administration didn't order it."

"I'm not surprised you feel that way, and we here in the Republic have certainly had more than enough experience with operations mounted by 'rogue elements.' I can only say I believe very strongly that the statement I just made is accurate. And I'll also say I've replaced both my external and internal security chiefs with men I've known for years, and in whom I have the greatest personal confidence. If any rogue operation was mounted against Duchess Harrington, it was mounted without their knowledge or approval. Of that much, I'm absolutely positive."

"And who else would you suggest might have a motive for wanting her dead? Or the resources to try to kill her in that particular fashion?"

"We don't have many specific details about how the attempt was made," Pritchart countered. "From what we have seen, however, speculation seems to be centering on the possibility that her young officer—a Lieutenant Meares, I believe—was somehow adjusted to make the attempt on her life. If that's the case, *we* don't have the resources to have done it. Certainly not in the time window which appears to have been available to whoever carried out the adjustment. Assuming that's what it was, of course."

"I hope you'll forgive me, Madam President, if I reserve judgment in this case," Henke said after a moment. "You're very convincing. On the other hand, like me, you operate at the highest level of politics, and politicians at that level *have* to be convincing. I will, however, take what you've said under advisement. Should I assume you're telling me this in hopes I'll pass your message along to Queen Elizabeth?"

"From what I've heard of your cousin, Admiral Henke," Pritchart said wryly, "I doubt very much that she'd believe any statement of mine, including a declaration that water is wet."

"I see you've got a fairly accurate profile of Her Majesty," Henke observed. "Although that's probably actually something of an understatement," she added.

"I know. Nonetheless, if you get the opportunity, I wish you'd tell her that for me. You may not believe this, Admiral, but I didn't really want this war, either. Oh," Pritchart went on quickly as Henke began to open her mouth, "I'll freely admit I fired the first shot. And I'll also admit that given what I knew then, I'd do the same thing again. That's not the same thing as *wanting* to do it, and I deeply regret all the men and women who have been killed or, like yourself, wounded. I can't undo that. But I would like to think it's possible for us to find an end to the fighting short of one of us killing *everyone* on the other side."

"So would I," Henke said levelly. "Unfortunately, whatever happened to our diplomatic correspondence, you did fire the first shot. Elizabeth isn't the only Manticoran or Grayson—or Andermani—who's going to find that difficult to forget or over-look."

"And are you one of them, Admiral?"

"Yes, Madam President, I am," Henke said quietly.

"I see. And I appreciate your honesty. Still, it does rather underscore the nature of our quandary, doesn't it?"

"I suppose it does."

Silence fell in the sunlit hospital room. Oddly enough, it was an almost companionable silence, Henke discovered. After perhaps three minutes, Pritchart straightened up, inhaled crisply, and stood.

"I'll let you get back to the business of healing, Admiral. The doctors assure me you're doing well. They anticipate a full recovery, and they tell me you can be discharged from the hospital in another week or so."

"At which point it's off to the stalag?" Henke said with a smile. She waved one hand at the unbarred windows of the hospital room. "I can't say I'm looking forward to the change of view."

"I think we can probably do better than a miserable hut behind a tangle of razor wire, Admiral." There was actually a twinkle in Pritchart's topaz eyes. "Tom Theisman has strong views on the proper treatment of prisoners of war—as Duchess Harrington may remember from the day they met in Yeltsin. I assure you that all our POWs are being properly provided for. Not only that, I'm hoping it may be possible to set up regular prisoner of war exchanges, perhaps on some sort of parole basis."

"Really?" Henke was surprised, and she knew it showed in her voice.

"Really." Pritchart smiled again, this time a bit sadly. "Whatever else, Admiral, and however hardly your Queen may be thinking about us just now, we really aren't Rob Pierre or Oscar Saint-Just. We have our faults, don't get me wrong. But I'd like to think one of them isn't an ability to forget that even enemies are human beings. Good day, Admiral Henke."

Chapter Forty-Three

The pinnace drifted slowly down the length of the spindle-shaped mountain of alloy. Honor, Nimitz, Andrew LaFollet, Spencer Hawke, Rafael Cardones, and Frances Hirshfield sat gazing out the armorplast viewport as the small craft reached the super-dreadnought's after hammerhead and braked to a complete halt, like a tadpole beside a slumbering whale.

Hard-suited construction workers, robotic repair units, and an ungainly webwork of girders and work platforms, all arranged with microgravity's grand contempt for the concept of "up and down," clustered about the ship as she floated against the stars. Powerful work lamps illuminated the frenetic activity of the repair crews and their robotic minions, and Honor frowned thoughtfully as she watched the bustling energy.

"Looks pretty terrible, doesn't it, Your Grace?" Cardones said, and she shrugged.

"I've seen lots worse. Remember the old *Fearless* after Basilisk?"

"Or the second one after Yeltsin," Cardones agreed. "But it's still like seeing your kid in the emergency room." He shook his head. "I hate seeing her in this shape."

"She looks a lot better than she did, Skipper," Hirshfield pointed out.

"Yes, she does," Cardones acknowledged, glancing at his executive officer. "On the other hand, there was a lot of *room* for improvement."

"The important thing is that the yard dogs say you can

have her back in another six days," Honor said, turning away from the viewport to look at him, "and that's good. Captain Samsonov's been perfectly satisfactory, but I want *my* flag captain back."

"I'm flattered, Your Grace. But even after I get her back, we're going to need some pretty serious exercises to blast the rust off."

"Oh, I've been keeping an eye on you, Rafe," Honor said with a smile. "You and Commander Hirshfield here have kept your people hopping in the simulators the entire time the ship's been down. I'm sure you will need a few days, at least, but I doubt you've let too much rust accumulate."

"We've tried not to," Cardones admitted. "And it's helped that we didn't have to completely shut down. Just being able to keep our people on board helped, and we've been able to drill regularly with the forward weapons mounts, at least."

"I know. I wish I'd been able to stay, myself. Unfortunately—"

Honor shrugged, and Cardones nodded in understanding. Honor could, theoretically, have remained on board *Imperator*, since the repair techs had been working primarily on exterior sections of the hull and, as Cardones had said, the rest of her crew had never had to leave her. Unfortunately, *Imperator* had been thoroughly immobilized, and if any emergency had turned up, Honor would have required a flagship capable of moving and fighting.

"Still," she went on, "I'm looking forward to moving back aboard. Mac is looking forward to it, too." She grinned. "Actually, he's got at least half my stuff already packed up!"

"We're ready whenever you are, Ma'am," Cardones told her.

"Unless the yard dogs manage to break something new, I think I'll make the move in about four days," Honor said. "I'll start then, anyway. It's going to take at least a couple of days for Mac to get everything moved and settled back into place, and I need to make another run to Admiralty House this week, anyway. I think I can schedule it to overlap with the move and let Mac get everything arranged while I'm on Manticore."

"That sounds fine to me, Your Grace," Cardones said, and Hirshfield—who, as *Imperator*'s XO, was actually in charge of all such housekeeping details—nodded in agreement.

"Good," Honor turned away from the viewport. "In that case,

let's get back over to *Yeltsin.* We'll just about have time for lunch before the staff meeting if we hurry."

"We're calling the new operation 'Sanskrit,'" Andrea Jaruwalski told the assembled admirals, commodores, and captains in HMS *Second Yeltsin*'s flag briefing room. "'Cutworm,' unfortunately, got leaked to the newsies, and it's been bandied about quite a bit over the last several weeks. Besides, we're going to be adopting an entirely new operational approach, so a new designation makes sense from a lot of perspectives."

She looked around the big compartment, and Honor reached up to gently rub Nimitz's ears while she listened. The next best thing to eight weeks had passed since Task Force 82 limped back into Trevor's Star, and as she'd feared, Eighth Fleet's reinforcement had taken a heavy hit in the wake of the Zanzibar disaster. Despite the fact that there was nothing left, really, to defend in the Zanzibar System, it had been politically impossible to refuse to station a powerful defensive force to keep an eye on the ruins. And Alizon, in particular, had been vociferous about the need to bolster *its* defenses. It was fortunate that over forty Andermani superdreadnoughts had finally completed their refits to handle Manticoran missile pods and reported for duty. But even with that reinforcement, finding the sheer number of hulls required had been extraordinarily difficult.

Now, though, things were beginning to look up. An entire division of *Invictuses*, with all the latest system updates, had arrived just yesterday, and two more superdreadnought divisions, all pod types, were anticipated before the end of the week. If things stayed on schedule, Eighth Fleet would have three entire squadrons of SD(P)s—eighteen ships—on its order of battle within the next two weeks. Additional battlecruisers, including the next five *Agamemnons*, had also come in, and Admiralty House was promising her three more *Saganami-Cs*, as well. And while all that had been going on, Alice Truman and Samuel Miklós had been reorganizing their carriers' LAC wings, incorporating twice as many *Katanas* into their orders of battle.

"This, of course," Jaruwalski continued, "is only a preliminary meeting. Her Grace wants us to be sure we're all thinking in the same direction. At the moment, we're planning on an execute date nineteen days from today. The preliminary operations plan, based on our anticipated units, will be drafted over the next ten days. At the end of that time, we'll conduct a dress rehearsal in the simulators. Any problems that come up will be discussed, and we'll draft a revised ops plan over the next three or four days. At that time we should know definitely what our unit availability will be, and we'll make any adjustments necessary. We'll run the revised plan through the simulator at X minus three days."

One or two of the people sitting at the table looked less than delighted at the timetable's tightness. In fact, Honor sensed several spikes of emotion which verged on consternation, and she couldn't blame the officers who were feeling them.

She looked up at Jaruwalski and made a tiny gesture with her right hand. The operations officer immediately turned to face her, and every other eye followed hers as if by magnetic attraction.

"I realize we're cutting things tight, people," Honor said, when she was sure she had everyone's attention. "That's particularly true for the new ships just joining us. And for those of you who've been with us from the beginning, it seems even more rushed, I'm sure, after our relative inactivity over the last couple of months.

"The problem is that we don't have a lot more time. Intelligence reports indicate the Havenites have been doing a lot of the same things we've been doing. They've been analyzing and considering what happened at Solon and Zanzibar, and they've also been adding new construction to their fleets. Those same reports strongly suggest they're getting ready to uncork a new offensive of their own. It's imperative that we get our punch in first and force them to worry about their rear areas again. Unfortunately, we haven't been able to do any definitive planning of our own because we simply haven't known what we'd have available at the time. And, frankly, because the operational change Captain Jaruwalski has already referred to required a substantial reinforcement of our wall of battle.

"The ships we need are finally becoming available, and the instant I have sufficient hulls to launch Sanskrit, it goes. I want that clearly understood. This operation *must* proceed as expeditiously as possible. ONI's latest estimate gives the Havenites over five hundred SD(P)s; the Alliance at this moment has less than three hundred. It's quite possible," her brown eyes were very level, "that the fate of the Star Kingdom may depend on our ability to make the Havenites anxious—anxious enough about their rear areas to divert heavy forces to protect them, and anxious enough about our new weapons capabilities to rethink the price they'll pay for any offensives of their own."

The compartment was very quiet, but Honor felt a sense of satisfaction as she tasted her subordinates' emotions. Concern still colored several individual mind-glows, but determination predominated, and she nodded.

"Andrea?" she said.

"Thank you, Your Grace."

Jaruwalski also surveyed the officers around the huge conference table, then keyed a holographic star map. It appeared above the conference table, and she tapped keys on her control pad, dropping a cursor into the map. It singled out a star, and Honor felt a fresh stir of surprise.

"Lovat, Ladies and Gentlemen," Jaruwalski said. "The system Admiral White Haven would have taken if High Ridge hadn't swallowed Saint-Just's bait hook, line, and sinker. We're going back there."

"You're confident you can do it with just three battle squadrons?" Admiral Caparelli asked.

"As confident as I can be," Honor replied, a bit more calmly than she actually felt.

She sat in a conference room deep inside Admiralty House, at a conference table surrounded by comfortable chairs, most of them empty at the moment. Honor herself was flanked by Mercedes Brigham on her right and Andrea Jaruwalski on her left. Nimitz lay stretched across the back of her chair, and Andrew LaFollet stood directly behind her.

Caparelli faced her across the table, flanked by Captain Dryslar, his chief of staff, and Patricia Givens. Admiral of the Green Sonja Hemphill was also present, along with Commander Coleman Hennessy, *her* chief of staff, but Hamish Alexander-Harrington was conspicuously absent. Technically, this was a matter for his uniformed subordinates, and he'd been extraordinarily careful ever since becoming First Lord to avoid stepping on those subordinates' toes, but under other circumstances he might have attended, anyway.

"This isn't going to be like Cutworm," Honor continued. "We're going to do to Lovat what Tourville did to Zanzibar. We're going to strike directly at one of the nodes they strengthened heavily post-Buttercup, and we're going to do it in a way which makes a declaration. Were going to tell them that they really, really don't want to screw around with us."

"That sounds like a very good idea, Your Grace," Admiral Givens said. "My only concern is how badly you may get hurt in the process of attempting to pull it off."

"We're not going to 'attempt' anything, Pat," Honor said flatly. "We're going to do it."

"Run through it for us again, please," Caparelli requested.

"A lot of our planning revolves around Admiral Hemphill's newest toys," Honor said, nodding respectfully to the BuWeaps CO. "The rest is predicated on three basic assumptions. First, that the Havenites are likely to believe our scouting destroyers are simply more of the misdirection we've been using to cover up our inability to mount actual operations. The second is that they know we've been forced to divert large numbers of wallers to thicken the defenses of Alizon, Zanzibar, and our other minor allies. And the third is that we established an operational pattern in Cutworm of operating in relatively light strength against relatively lightly defended star systems, and that they won't be surprised if we continue it . . . or appear to..

"Obviously, we can't absolutely rely on any of those premises, but we believe they should all hold true. In particular, although they've got to be concerned about the security of Lovat, we've consistently shied away from hitting targets that hard. That ought to generate at least some sense of false security, no matter how good they are.

"We know from our operations over the last sixty days that they've been reacting vigorously to our scouting operations. It's pretty obvious they've been trying to identify the systems we're likely to hit and stationing forces in hyper to cover them.

"As you know, we planned and executed a feint attack on the Suarez System three weeks ago. We sent in scouting destroyers, then, after a couple of days, sent in Admiral Truman's carrier squadron, escorted by a single squadron of battlecruisers and one of heavy cruisers. Admiral Truman launched half her LACs and sent them in-system, accompanied by a dozen Ghost Rider EW platforms simulating the emissions signatures of battlecruisers and superdreadnoughts, then translated back out with her hyper-capable units. Given the endurance on the Ghost Rider micro fusion plants, we estimated that they'd be able to continue their deception long enough to draw a response.

"We got one. It was a virtual repeat of what they did to me at Solon. This time, though, we'd expected what we got, and they'd planned their interception based on the maximum acceleration rates of the wallers they thought we'd sent in, not LACs. In addition, three-quarters of our LACs were *Katanas*, which made them extraordinarily difficult missile targets. Our LACs were able to avoid interception and break back out across the limit before any of the defenders could follow them. Admiral Truman recovered them at the prearranged rendezvous, and translated back out.

"The operation did several things. First, it confirmed that, at that time, at least, they were sticking with a doctrine which had worked. Second, it gave us an opportunity to evaluate how quickly this covering force, as compared to the one we encountered at Solon, responded. Third, we hope it made them even more confident that we've been essentially running a bluff, without the wherewithal—or the will—to mount a serious raid. And, fourth, while they were busy bringing up their defenses, and before they realized we were using drones on them, they activated the same sort of control network they must have used at Solon. We'd hoped they would, and Admiral Truman had sensor arrays deep enough in-system to see them do it, so now we know what to look for in our next op."

She paused and reached for the glass sitting at the corner of her blotter. Andrea Jaruwalski quickly topped it off with ice water from a carafe, and Honor smiled her thanks before she sipped. Then she set the glass down and looked back up at Caparelli, Givens, and Hemphill.

"We ran a few other ops, similar in nature but without the electronic warfare platforms. In two cases, we drew no response at all, which leads us to suspect that in those two cases there were picket forces hiding in hyper which never got called in because they never saw a threat. In most of the others, the arrival of our scout units was the signal for courier boats to translate out, and fairly hefty response forces turned up within anywhere from two to four days. So, it looks like they've adopted a nodal strategy, in addition to staking out the systems they believe we're most likely to attack.

"By picking Lovat, we believe we'll be striking directly at one of those nodal forces. If we can punch it out when we hit, there shouldn't be anything else close enough to be called in on us for at least seventy-two hours, if our analysis of their previous operations is accurate. In addition, since we'll be scouting a heavily defended system, and we've established a pattern of sending diversionary scouts into systems we have no intention of attacking, we believe they'll be skeptical about our intentions. Even if they aren't, there's no reason for them to call in additional reinforcements before we actually hit them.

"And this time around, especially since we know what to look for in their system defense control net, we ought to be able to neutralize it with Mistletoe before they ever get a chance to use it. In which case, it will be our wallers and our LACs against theirs, in a standup fight without the sort of missile launch which hammered us at Solon."

"So you're confident you can neutralize their system defense command and control systems?" Givens asked, but her attention was more than half on Hemphill, and Honor smiled.

"Admiral Hemphill and I haven't always been on the same page," she began, and Hemphill actually chuckled.

"You might say that, Your Grace," she said, "if you're given to understatement. I seem to recall a rather passionate debriefing you gave the Weapons Development Board after that little affair in Basilisk."

"I was younger then, Admiral," Honor said almost demurely. "And I was mildly irritated, at the time."

"And rightly so," Hemphill said with a nod. She shook her head. "I don't believe I've ever had the opportunity to actually tell you this, Your Grace, but I always envisioned *Fearless* as a testbed. I never expected her to be committed to combat, especially not totally unsupported. The fact that you managed to win was an impressive testimony to your tactical ability. And the fact that you were—'mildly irritated,' I believe you said—was certainly understandable. Besides," she chuckled again, "having watched your track record over the last few years, I'm inclined to doubt you've mellowed all that much since."

"Not mellowed," Honor said with another smile. "Just gained a greater sense of . . . diplomacy."

This time Caparelli and Givens joined Hemphill's laughter, and Caparelli tipped his chair back.

"I believe you are about to respond to Pat's question, Your Grace?" he said.

"Yes, I was," Honor agreed, turning her attention back to Admiral Givens. "What I was about to say, Pat, is that this time around, I'm convinced Admiral Hemphill's new wrinkles will do the job. I'd hoped to keep her new toys tucked away against a rainy day, without letting the Havenites know they exist until we really, really needed them. Unfortunately, 'really, really need them' is a pretty good description of where we are right now. At any rate, we've quietly tested the new hardware in exercises at Trevor's Star, and it's performed to specs. Obviously, that's not the same as using it operationally, but the exercise results look very good. In fact, they look much better than the original projections. We're really still just beginning to appreciate all the tactical possibilities, but even what we've already worked out is going to give whoever gets in our way at Lovat fits."

She smiled again, and this time there was no amusement at all in her expression.

"As a matter of fact," Admiral Lady Dame Honor Alexander-Harrington said softly, "I'm rather looking forward to the opportunity."

Chapter Forty-Four

"Well, that went pretty well, I thought, Your Grace."

Andrea Jaruwalski was trying very hard not to preen in satisfaction, and Honor smothered a smile. Jaruwalski, Brigham, Rafe Cardones, and Yolanda Harriman had joined her for dinner, and now they all sat back from the table, nursing after-dinner coffee—or cocoa, as the case might be.

"I *suppose* you could say that," Honor said slowly, pursing her lips with a dubious expression. "Of course, there were a few little glitches."

"There always are," Brigham pointed out. "Personally, Your Grace, I found myself wondering just who programmed the simulation to throw that extra squadron of superdreadnoughts at us."

She gave Honor an intensely speculative look, which Honor returned with one of total innocence. The chief of staff transferred her speculation to Commander Harriman, who suddenly seemed to find the bottom of her coffee cup extraordinarily interesting.

"It occurred to me, while I was wondering," Brigham continued, "that whoever might have decided to do it—and, I trust you'll note, I name no names—would have needed a minion somewhere in the flagship. Preferably, someone with access to the tactical computers. Of course, once that ignoble suspicion occurred to me, I womanfully put it behind me as one unworthy of our open and forthright command staff."

"Mac!" Honor called through the pantry hatch.

"Yes, Your Grace?"

"Bring me my hip-waders, would you? It's getting deep in here."

"Of course, Your Grace," MacGuiness replied with perfect aplomb. "Would you like your snorkel mask, as well?"

"I don't think it's going to get quite that deep," Honor said as her guests laughed.

"Very good, Your Grace," MacGuiness said as he stepped back out of the pantry and set a second serving of peach cobbler in front of Honor. She smiled her thanks and picked up her dessert fork again.

"Your Grace," Brigham said wistfully, watching Honor dig in, "there are times when I positively hate you and that metabolism of yours."

She patted her own reasonably flat stomach and shook her head sadly.

"You should try the downside of it sometime, Mercedes," Honor told her. "You may envy the way it lets me pander to my sweet tooth, but try waking up with the sort of middle-of-the-night munchies I got as, say, a twelve-year-old." She shuddered. "Trust me, as an adolescent, I seemed to spend *all* my time shoveling in food, not just half of it."

She felt a sudden jab of darker emotion from behind her and glanced over her shoulder.

Andrew LaFollet stood inside the dining cabin hatch. Before the attempt on Honor's life, he would have been content to stand his post outside the hatch, given the guest list. These days, that was out of the question as far as he was concerned, and she recognized the somberness radiating from him. He was remembering PNS *Tepes* and her own half-starved gauntness when he, Jamie Candless, and Robert Whitman broke her out of a StateSec holding cell.

She caught his eye long enough to smile gently at him, and he smiled back, shaking off his mood. Then she turned back to her guests, none of whom had picked up on that particular bit of byplay.

"Actually, Andrea, getting back to your original comment, I have to agree. Things did seem to go quite well, over all. I was especially pleased with the way Mistletoe worked."

"I was, too, Your Grace," Cardones said. "At the same time, I can't help worrying a little bit about the simulation's parameters.

If it turns out Mistletoe doesn't work as well in practice—or, even worse, gets picked up early—we could be in a world of hurt against another missile attack like the one they threw at us at Solon."

"You're right, of course." Honor nodded. She forked up another bite of cobbler, chewed, and swallowed, then continued. "We deliberately used the more pessimistic set of assumptions from Admiral Hemphill's testing programs, but we won't know for certain until we test it against active Havenite defenses. For the most part, though, BuWeaps has done a pretty good job of simulating enemy threat levels for quite some time now."

"I didn't say my worries were all that *reasonable*, Your Grace," Cardones said with a smile. "I just said I had them."

"Personally, Skipper," Harriman told him, "I'm looking forward to seeing Apollo in action." *Imperator*'s tactical officer smiled almost beatifically. "Their point defense better be *really* good if they expect to go home with a whole hide this time!"

"I only hope they don't figure out how few of the new pods we really have," Brigham said.

"Unless their spies have managed a lot better penetration than ONI thinks they have, they shouldn't realize that," Honor replied. "And if they do have that kind of penetration, we're in so much trouble already that it won't really matter if they figure out that particular point."

Brigham chuckled.

"You're right, Your Grace, I—"

"Excuse me, Your Grace."

Honor turned, eyebrows lowering, as MacGuiness stepped back out of his pantry.

"What is it, Mac?"

"Communications just buzzed. A special Admiralty courier boat just cleared the Junction. According to her captain, she has emergency dispatches onboard."

The levity and confidence of Honor's dinner guests was notable for its complete absence as she sat in her flag briefing room once again. Only Cardones, her staff, and Andrew LaFollet and Nimitz were physically present, but the huge com display above the conference table was divided into quadrants showing the faces of every squadron and divisional commander of her enlarged and more powerful Eighth Fleet.

The enlarged and more powerful fleet which wasn't going anywhere, after all, she thought grimly.

"I'm sorry to get you all up this late," she began. "Unfortunately, the Admiralty's news isn't good."

She saw no surprise on the tense faces in the display. That much, at least, they'd all obviously guessed.

"This afternoon, the Admiralty received an emergency dispatch from Admiral Khumalo in Talbott," she continued evenly. "A copy of that dispatch was included in the Admiralty download I received an hour ago. Commander Reynolds," she waved a hand at her intelligence officer, "will put together copies of most of the material and distribute it to all of you immediately after this conference. For the moment, to summarize, Admiral Khumalo's informed the Admiralty that Captain Aivars Terekhov has deduced that the apparently unrelated terrorist incidents in the Cluster have, in fact, been carefully orchestrated by outside elements. Specifically, the terrorist Nordbrandt and her 'Freedom Alliance of Kornati' are being armed with modern weapons by Mesa. The same apparently holds true for the terrorists operating in the Montana System, as well."

She clearly had everyone's attention, she noted with bitter amusement.

"Apparently, Captain Terekhov has physical proof of that part of his theory. He intercepted and captured a Jessyk Combine slaver being used to run in the weapons. Before he did so, however, it used a laser cluster to destroy one of his pinnaces and kill everyone aboard it."

She closed her eyes briefly in pain, recalling the bright promise and eagerness of Midshipwoman Ragnhild Pavletic. Then she opened them once more and continued.

"After interrogating the slaver's surviving crew and breaking into its computers, Terekhov concluded that the Republic of Monica is also involved. He believes the Monicans are being provided with modern warships in sufficient numbers to provoke a crisis in the Cluster. And he believes the Office of Frontier Security is also involved, and that OFS is prepared to commit Solly fleet units to 'restore order' in the Cluster after the Monicans have acted."

Every eye was riveted on her now, and she looked back steadily.

"At this moment, the last thing in the universe the Star

Kingdom needs is a shooting incident with the Solarian League Navy. Captain Terekhov is clearly well aware of that, because, on his own initiative, he's assembled a small squadron of cruisers and destroyers and moved directly on Monica."

"He's *what*?" Alistair McKeon asked sharply. Honor looked at him on the display, and he shook his head. "He's launched an unauthorized invasion of a sovereign star nation in time of peace. Is that what you're saying, Your Grace?"

"It's exactly what I'm saying," Honor replied flatly. "His report was obviously written with an eye towards publication. He's very careful to make it clear he's operating solely on his own, without authorization from any superior. He doesn't say so, but it's clear he's deliberately setting himself up to be disavowed if necessary. At the same time, he intends to personally investigate the situation in Monica and, if his suspicions are confirmed, to . . . neutralize the threat by any means necessary."

There was total silence, and her eyes moved across the display, examining the face of each of her senior subordinates in turn.

"Admiral Khumalo," she continued after a moment, "dispatched a courier boat to Admiralty House as soon as he received Terekhov's report to him. In his own dispatches, he informed the Admiralty that he fully endorsed Terekhov's actions and was moving to support him with all available units."

She wondered how many of her officers were as surprised by that as she was, but she allowed no sign of the thought to show itself.

"Under the circumstances, Admiral Khumalo felt he had no option but to request immediate reinforcement. Since it's possible Terekhov, or Khumalo, or both of them may find themselves in a shooting incident with Solarian units, the Admiralty felt it had no option but to dispatch a significant reinforcement from Home Fleet. Those units are already on their way to Monica.

"Obviously, all of these moves have implications for us. The most immediate one is that Home Fleet is now going to be understrength, and one of the functions of Eighth Fleet, like Third Fleet, is to serve as a ready reserve for Home Fleet. There's also the possibility that the Star Kingdom is about to find itself engaged against Solarian units, and no one is prepared to predict the possible ramifications of that.

"Because the entire strategic situation's suddenly been thrown into such a state of flux, Admiralty House has ordered the temporary stand down of Operation Sanskrit. For now, we're postponing the execution date by three weeks. That should give us time to receive dispatches from Terekhov or Khumalo from Monica. Hopefully, those dispatches will confirm that Terekhov was either wrong or that he and Khumalo have managed to defuse the situation. In either of those cases, Sanskrit will be reactivated, although we'll probably face some delay because of our need to factor in intelligence on any changes which may occur in the meantime."

She sat very still, looking at her flag officers, and her face was grimmer than any of them remembered ever having seen it.

"People, in my judgment, the Star Kingdom is now facing the greatest danger we have ever faced," she said quietly. "It's entirely conceivable that we could find ourselves simultaneously at war with the Republic of Haven and the Solarian League. Should that occur, our strategic situation would be about as close to desperate as any I can conceive of. The next month to six weeks may very possibly determine the fate of our kingdom."

"You wanted to see me, Kevin?" Eloise Pritchart asked warily.

"I wouldn't put it exactly that way," Kevin Usher said almost whimsically. "I'd say I *needed* to see you."

"Which means you're about to tell me something I don't want to hear."

"Which means I'm about to tell you something you don't want to hear," Usher agreed. "Actually, Senior Inspector Abrioux is about to tell you."

"Senior Inspector?" the President turned to the petite FIA officer, and Danielle Abrioux returned her look with an unhappy expression.

"Madam President," she said, "I'm sorry, but the Director and I both feel we've hit a stone wall. We've tried everything we can think of, and we can't give you the smoking gun you need."

"Why not?" Pritchart shook her head quickly. "I'm sorry. That came out sounding almost accusatory, and I didn't mean it that way. What I meant was, why is it a stone wall?"

"Because both our original suspects are dead, and we haven't been able to identify a single additional damned accomplice,"

Usher replied for Abrioux. "Grosclaude still looks like a suicide, although Danny and I are both positive it was actually homicide. Giancola, damn his black soul to hell, was a genuine accident, but no one's going to believe it. And Grosclaude's so-called 'evidence' is an obvious, if fairly clever, forgery. Those, unfortunately, are the only hard facts we have. We've tried every avenue, short of opening a very public exhaustive investigation, without being able to move beyond those points. And, frankly, I don't think going public would let us turn up anything we haven't already found.

"My own theory, and I think Danny agrees with me," he glanced at Abrioux, who nodded vigorously, "is still that Giancola pulled the entire thing off basically on his own, and that he's responsible for the 'forgeries' in Grosclaude's personal files. He needed Grosclaude to make the substitutions, and I can't escape the suspicion that he had someone else helping him out at *this* end, as well—at least with the computer access he needed. Unfortunately, there's no clue as to who that someone may have been, assuming he actually existed at all and that he's not simply someone I desperately *want* to exist so I can find him and choke a confession out of him with my bare hands. But even if he existed, it was Giancola's show."

"And you're convinced he never meant it to go as far as it did?"

"I'm . . . not as certain of that as I was," Usher said slowly, and Pritchart straightened in her chair, looking at him intently.

"Why not? What's changed?"

"Danny pointed something out to me the other day," Usher replied. "The Manty lieutenant who tried to kill Harrington three months ago was apparently acting under some form of compulsion. From all the information available to us, he was very close to Harrington. He'd been with her for quite some time, and NavInt's dossier on her suggests that her inner circle is almost always intensely loyal and personally devoted to her. So whatever the compulsion was, it had to be powerful enough to overcome that sort of personal devotion and push him into committing what was ultimately a suicidal act. But the Manties—whose medical and forensic establishments, let's face it, are both better than our own—haven't been able to come up with any explanation for how he was compelled. Doesn't that sound like what happened to Grosclaude to you?"

"You think the same people who killed Grosclaude—or, at

least, gave Arnold whatever *he* used to do the job—also tried to kill Harrington?"

"Let's just say I strongly suspect that whatever technique is being used came from the same source. Now, as the nasty and suspicious sort I am, it occurs to me that if it came from the same source, it's very possibly being used in support of some unified strategy. It's possible, I suppose, that it's simply a case of someone marketing the technology to whoever needs it and can afford it, but I'm beginning to doubt that's the case." Usher shook his head. "No, Eloise. There's a pattern here, I just haven't been able to figure out what it is yet. But what I have seen of it suggests that whoever is behind it doesn't much care for either us or the Manties."

"So now you're saying Arnold may have been actively working for someone else to provoke fresh hostilities between us and the Manties?" Pritchart wished she'd been able to sound more incredulous than she did.

"I think it's possible," Usher agreed. "But there are still way too many unanswered questions for me to suggest exactly *why* someone might want that. Did they have enough information on Bolthole to expect to us to roll right over the Manties for them? In that case, presumably Manticore is the primary target, and we're simply the blunt instrument. Or did they expect the Manties to roll over us, which would make *us* the primary target? Or do they, for some reason I can't currently envision, simply want the two of us shooting at one another again, which would make *both* of us the target of some third party with a completely unknown agenda of his own?"

"Jesus Christ, Kevin!" Pritchart stared at him in something very like horror. "That's so . . . so . . . so *twisty* just thinking about it makes my head hurt! What good could sending us back to war with Manticore do any hypothetical third party?"

"I just said I couldn't envision what their motives might be. If I could, I could make a pretty fair stab at figuring out who they were, as well. And it's entirely possible I'm totally out to lunch with the whole theory. It could be no more than my 'spook' experience making me see things because Danny and I have exhausted all of the potential domestic avenues we could see. I just don't *know*, Eloise. But I do know this—my instincts all tell me that so far all we've seen is the tip of an iceberg."

Chapter Forty-Five

"Good morning, everyone," Eloise Pritchart said as she walked briskly into the sunlit chamber.

The Cabinet Room was on the eastern side of the President's official residence, and the tide of morning light which flooded in through the extensive windows on the room's outer wall gleamed on the expensive, polished conference table, inlaid with half a dozen exotic species of wood. The thick, natural fiber carpet was like a deep pool of cobalt water, with the Presidential Seal floating on it like a golden reflection. All of the chairs, except for Pritchart's own, were upholstered in black; hers was the same blue as the carpet, with the seal of her office emblazoned on its back. Glasses and expensive crystal carafes of ice water sat at each place, and optical pickups on the roof of the building fed the chamber's interior smart walls, which were configured to give a panoramic view of the city of Nouveau Paris and its morning traffic.

"Good morning, Madam President," Thomas Theisman, as her Cabinet's acknowledged senior member, replied for all of them.

According to the presidential succession established by the Constitution, Leslie Montreau, Arnold Giancola's successor as Secretary of State, was technically senior to Theisman, but no one in this room was under any misapprehensions. Theisman's devotion to the Constitution, and his personal determination to avoid the office of President, had been accepted by even the most cynical cabinet secretaries. In a way, however, that only enhanced his powerbase. They knew he had absolutely no personal ambitions

553

and that he stood squarely behind Eloise Pritchart, the Republic's first elected president in three centuries.

And that the Republic's military stood squarely behind *him*.

Pritchart crossed to her chair, drew it out from the table, sat, and waited a moment while it adjusted to her body. Then she leaned forward very slightly and swept the members of her Cabinet with her eyes.

"I know you're all wondering what this unscheduled meeting is about," she began. "You're about to find out. You're also about to discover some things which only a few people in this room already knew. Those things are going to be shocking, and probably more than a little upsetting, to most of you. Despite that, I believe you'll understand why the details have been kept confidential, but I have a policy initiative in mind that's going to require the full—and fully *informed*—cooperation of every senior member of this Administration. I hope you'll give me that cooperation."

She had their full attention, she observed, and smiled almost whimsically.

"Denis," she looked at her Attorney General, "would you ask Kevin and Wilhelm to join us?"

"Of course, Madam President."

Denis LePic pressed a key on his terminal. A moment later, a door opened in the western wall, like a gap ripped from the heart of the living, breathing image of Nouveau Paris. Pritchart always found that particular image rather disturbing, and today it seemed more ominous than usual.

She nodded in greeting to them, then indicated the empty chairs provided to either side of LePic. They settled into them, and she returned her attention to her Cabinet, several of whose members were clearly perplexed . . . and not a little apprehensive.

"Kevin and Wilhelm are here to help explain things," she said. "In particular, Kevin is going to be briefing you on something which he brought to my attention almost six T-months ago. The short version of it, Ladies and Gentlemen, is that the High Ridge Government did *not* falsify our diplomatic correspondence."

The handful of people who'd already known that, like Rachel Hanriot, took it fairly calmly. The rest only stared at her, as if their minds simply weren't up to understanding what she'd said, for the first several seconds. After that, it was hard to say whether consternation, disbelief, or anger was the most predominant emotion. Whatever the emotional mix might have been, however, what it produced was something very like pandemonium.

She let them sputter and wave their hands for fifteen or twenty seconds, then rapped sharply on the table top. The crisp sound penetrated the upheaval, and people sank back in their chairs once again, still stunned-looking, but also more than a little embarrassed by their initial reactions.

"I don't blame you for being surprised," the President said into the renewed silence with generous understatement. "My own reaction when Kevin brought me his hypothesis was very similar. I'm going to ask him to brief you on a black investigation which I authorized. It was off the books, and, frankly, probably not particularly constitutional. Under the circumstances, however, I felt I had no choice but to green-light his efforts, just as I now have no choice but to bring all of you into it."

She looked at Usher.

"Kevin, if you would," she invited.

"So that's about the size of it," Pritchart said thirty minutes later.

Usher's actual briefing had taken less than ten minutes; the rest of the time had been occupied in answering questions—some incredulous, some hostile, most angry, and all worried—from the rest of the Cabinet.

"But it's all still just speculation," Tony Nesbitt, the Secretary of Commerce, objected. As one of Arnold Giancola's strongest allies in the Cabinet, he still seemed much inclined towards incredulity. "I mean, Director Usher just told us there's no proof."

"No, he didn't, Tony," Rachel Hanriot said.

Nesbitt looked at her, and she returned his gaze with one that was almost compassionate, although they'd generally found themselves on opposite sides of the power struggle between Pritchart and Giancola.

"What he said," she continued, "is that there's no way to prove *who* on our side did it, although given Arnold's position at State, it's impossible for me to believe he wasn't the prime mover. But even if the Grosclaude documents are forgeries, they're very convincing proof that *somebody* in the Republic's government falsified the correspondence. At any rate, they seem to me to clearly demonstrate that the Manties have been telling the exact, literal truth about their correspondence. Which strongly suggests they're also telling the truth about the correspondence they say they received from us. Which, again, points the finger squarely at Arnold."

"But . . . but my cousin Jean-Claude is—was—Arnold's security chief," Nesbitt protested. "I can't believe Arnold could've managed something like this without Jean-Claude at least suspecting." He looked at Montreau. "Leslie? Have you found *anything* at State to support all these allegations?"

Montreau looked acutely uncomfortable. Despite her position in the official hierarchy, she was the newest member of the Cabinet, and she cleared her throat a bit nervously.

"No, I haven't," she said. "On the other hand, Tony, it never would have occurred to me to look for any evidence of such . . . incredible criminal activities. I will say this, however," she added reluctantly. "The security measures in place at State may still be a bit too much like the ones the Legislaturalists and the Committee had in place."

"What do you mean?" Nesbitt asked.

"I mean too much control passes directly through the Secretary's hands," Montreau said bluntly. "I was frankly astonished when I found out how much access to and control of the Department's security processes goes directly through my office. It would never have occurred to me that Secretary Giancola might have done any such thing, but looking at the access *I* have, and assuming—as Director Usher does—that he had access to the Manties' Foreign Office validation codes, as well, he really could have done it. And I'm afraid that so far, at least, I can't think of anyone else who could have."

Nesbitt sat back in his chair, clearly dismayed. Pritchart regarded him thoughtfully, but as far as she could tell, he was at least as astonished as anyone else in the room. More to the point, he seemed horrified.

"Obviously," she said, after a moment, "I've had to proceed very cautiously where this entire incredible bucket of snakes is concerned. As Kevin and Denis have just explained in answer to your questions, we don't have—and probably never will have—the sort of smoking gun we'd need to convince Congress and the public that what we believe happened actually did. Without that sort of proof, going public would still be a highly risky decision, I believe."

"It may be the only option available to us, Madam President," Nesbitt said after a moment. Everyone looked at him, and he shrugged unhappily. "Don't think I like saying that. God knows if there's anyone in this room Arnold completely fooled, it's me, and I'm going to look like an utter idiot when the newsies finally get hold of this! But if you're right about what happened, then we're fighting a war we were maneuvered into by a member of our own administration." He shook his head. "We can't possibly justify not telling the truth."

"But the President's right," Henrietta Barloi, the Secretary of Technology, objected. "No one's going to believe us, and given what happened to Arnold, everyone is going to think we had him eliminated."

"But why would we have done that?" Nesbitt demanded.

"I'm afraid I can come up with several scenarios, Mr. Secretary," Kevin Usher said.

Everyone looked at him, and he shrugged.

"If I were a conspiracy theorist, or just someone with personal political ambitions or a desire to restore the old régime, my interpretation of what happened might well be that Secretary Giancola figured out what that arch traitor President Pritchart had done to justify seeking a declaration of war. When he learned the truth, she—and, by extension, all of you—ordered his execution. Now, however, we're afraid the truth is going to leak out, and so we're attempting to fasten the blame on the man who's safely dead because we murdered him. All of which demonstrates that our highflown principles and devotion to 'the rule of law' are so much crap. Which means this entire government—not just the administration—is a corrupt edifice built upon a Constitution which is nothing but yet another huge swindle perpetrated on the long-suffering people."

"That's insane," Nesbitt protested.

"Of course it is!" Usher snorted. "The best conspiracy theories usually are! How do you think Cordelia Ransom managed to stay in front of the Mob as long as she did? But if you don't like that one, here's another. Someone else, someone in the security area—probably me or Wilhelm, here—did all of this. Giancola found out, we killed him, and now through a sinister cabal, for reasons of our own, we're trying to bring the war to a less than fully successful conclusion and we've spun this whole theory of Giancola's responsibility as a way to do that. Or, if you don't like that one, it's all an attempt by someone—probably an alliance of some of the Cabinet secretaries and Wilhelm and me—to sabotage the President's fully justified and so far successful war against the evil Manties. Unfortunately, we've managed to pull the wool over her eyes, and she actually believes our preposterous tale about Giancola's doctoring the correspondence. Really, the Manties did it all along, and we murdered him because he was the one man who could have proved they had. Or—"

Nesbitt was looking more than a little cross-eyed by then, and Pritchart raised her hand at Usher.

"That's enough, Kevin," she said. Then she turned her attention fully to Nesbitt. "Kevin can't quite forget he used to be a spook, Tony. He's used to thinking in this kind of twisted, convoluted way. But the point he's making—that God only knows how this entire thing can be spun by power seekers or people simply hostile to the Constitution—is unfortunately valid. And don't any of you believe for a moment that there aren't people out there who fall into those categories. They're not just all ex-SS goons who've gone to earth, hoping for a change in the political climate more favorable to their objectives, either. Unless I'm very much mistaken, Arnold himself was one of the people who see themselves as players under the old Legislaturalist rules and would love to see the Constitution overturned, or at least gelded, so they can get on with it. There are more of them out there, and this situation could play directly into their hands."

"But if we can't go public, what *can* we do?" Nesbitt asked almost plaintively.

"And," Walter Sanderson, Secretary of the Interior, asked, his eyes narrow, "why tell us about it now? Some of us—like Tony and me—were very close to Arnold. You can't be certain none of us were involved in whatever he was up to. You also can't be certain we're not going to leave this room and immediately spill what you've just told us to the newsies."

"You're right." Pritchart nodded. "In fact, any or all of you could make an excellent case for having a constitutional responsibility to go public with it, whatever I ask you to do. There's no *official* investigation into it, yet, but I'm pretty sure a case could be made for my decisions to date amounting to an attempt to obstruct justice."

"So why tell us?" Sanderson pressed.

"Because we may have a window of opportunity to negotiate an end to the war," Pritchart told them all.

"What sort of window, Madam President?" Stan Gregory, the Secretary of Urban Affairs, asked, and several other people sat more upright, looking almost hopeful.

"According to Wilhelm and NavInt," Pritchart said, nodding towards Trajan, "the Manties are having serious problems in the Talbott Cluster. We don't have anything like complete information, you understand, but what we do have suggests they're looking at at least the possibility of a shooting confrontation with the League."

Someone inhaled audibly, and Pritchart gave a very thin smile.

The Solarian League was the galaxy's eight-kiloton gorilla. Although she strongly suspected that the League Navy had no idea what sort of vibro blade it would be reaching its fingers into if and when it tangled with the Royal Manticoran Navy, the possibility of the Star Kingdom's successfully standing up against such a towering monolith in the long term was remote, to say the least. *No one* wanted to take on the Sollies.

"This presents us with two separate possible opportunities," she continued. "On the one hand, if they do get into a war with the Solarian League, our problems, militarily speaking, are solved. They'd have to accept whatever peace terms we chose to offer if they were going to have any hope at all of resisting the League.

"On the other hand, if we offer to negotiate with them now, and let them know we're aware of the pressures they're under in Talbott, then they'll also be aware we aren't actively moving to take advantage of this diversion . . . but that we *could*, if we wanted to.

"So my idea is to propose a direct summit meeting, to be held at some mutually acceptable neutral site, between myself and Queen Elizabeth."

"Madam President, I don't think—"

"Wait, are you suggesting—?"

"But they'll feel like we're holding a pulser to their heads, and—"

"I think it could work, if—"

Pritchart rapped on the table top again, harder than before, until the babble subsided.

"I'm not suggesting this is going to be some sort of silver pulser dart," she said. "And, yes, Walter, I'm aware that they're going to know we're 'holding a pulser to their heads.' I don't say I expect them to be very happy about the idea, but if I can ever sit down across the table from Elizabeth Winton, I may have a chance of convincing her to agree to terms acceptable to both the Star Kingdom and to our own public."

"Excuse me, Madam President, but how much of that is realism, and how much is wishful thinking?" Nesbitt asked almost gently.

"Leslie?" Pritchart looked at the Secretary of State.

"That's very difficult to say, Madam President," Montreau said after a moment. "I take it you're thinking in terms of signing a peace treaty first, and then, after peace has had a chance to take hold, going public with our suspicions and holding an open investigation into them?"

"That's pretty much what I have in mind, yes."

"Well, it might actually work." Montreau frowned at the Nouveau Paris skyline, rubbing the tips of her right hand's fingers on her blotter.

"For one thing, you're right about the pressure the Manties are going to be under, assuming whatever's going on in Talbott is as serious as you're suggesting. They won't like that, but they'll have to be realistic, and in the final analysis, talking is less dangerous to them than shooting, especially if they're looking at the possibility of a two-front war.

"In addition," she continued with mounting enthusiasm, "a face-to-face meeting between the two of you would be such a dramatic departure that even if you came home with terms which might not be as good as our current military advantage could secure, the public would probably accept them. Which also means, of course, that you could go even further towards what the Manties consider acceptable than you've already offered."

"That's what I was thinking." Pritchart nodded. "And I'm also thinking, that if and when we do go public with this in the wake of a peace settlement, we candidly admit the way in which we allowed ourselves to be maneuvered and offer fairly hefty reparations to the Manties."

She started to go further, then stopped. This was no time to admit that she was seriously considering at least a partial admission of their current suspicions to the Manticoran Queen if the talks seemed to be going well. One or two of the people around the table looked outraged at the suggestion she'd already made, but she shook her head firmly.

"No," she said. "Think about it first. First, it's the right thing to do. Second, if we want any peace settlement with the Manties to stand up over the long haul, and if it turns out someone on our side was responsible for manipulating our correspondence with them, then we're going to have to make a substantial gesture towards them, especially since we're the ones who reinstituted hostilities. And finally, if we find what we all, I think, expect we'll find, it's going to do enormous diplomatic damage to us. By acknowledging our responsibility, and by offering to make amends as best we can, we'll have the best shot at damage control and rehabilitating ourselves in terms of interstellar diplomacy."

Most of the outrage faded, although several people still looked profoundly unhappy.

"May I make a suggestion, Madam President?" Thomas Theisman said formally.

"Of course you may."

"In that case, I'd suggest one additional point to include in your suggestion of a summit." Pritchart raised an eyebrow at him, and he shrugged. "I'd recommend that you specifically request Duchess Harrington's presence at the conference as a military adviser."

"Harrington? Why Harrington?" Sanderson asked.

"Several reasons," Theisman replied. "Including, in no particular order, the fact that our sources indicate she's consistently been a voice of political moderation, despite her position as one of their best fleet commanders. The fact that she's now married to the First Lord of their Admiralty, which also makes her a sister-in-law of their Prime Minister. The fact that although she and her Queen are clearly not in agreement where *we're* concerned, she remains one of Elizabeth's most trusted confidants, plus a Grayson Steadholder, and probably the one Benjamin Mayhew trusts most of all. The fact that she and I, and she and Lester Tourville, have met and, I think, established at least some sense of rapport. And the fact that all reports indicate she has a rather uncanny ability to tell when people are lying to her. Which suggests she can probably tell when they're telling the truth, as well. In short, I think she'd be a moderating influence on Elizabeth's temper, and the closest thing to a friend in court we're going to find."

"Madam President, I think that's an excellent idea," Montreau said. "It wouldn't have occurred to me, because I tend to think of her as a naval officer first, but Secretary Theisman's made some very telling points. I recommend you follow his advice."

"I agree, too, Madam President," Rachel Hanriot said.

"Very well, I think we can consider that a part of our suggestion." Pritchart looked around the table again. "And may I also assume we have a consensus that the summit ought to be pursued?"

"Yes," Nesbitt said, not without a certain obvious reluctance. Pritchart looked at him, and he shrugged. "I've invested so much in seeing the Manties *beaten* after what they did to us in the last war that a part of me just loathes the thought of letting them off the hook now. But if Arnold did what it looks like he did, we have no choice but to stop killing each other as quickly as we can. Just please don't expect me to ever *like* them."

"All right." Pritchart nodded. "And, as I'm sure I don't have to remind any of you, it's absolutely essential we keep our suspicions about all the rest of this to ourselves until after I've met with Elizabeth."

Vigorous nods responded, and she leaned back in her chair with a smile.

"Good. And since we're in agreement, I think I may have exactly the emissary to carry our offer to Manticore."

Chapter Forty-Six

"Skipper, we've got an unscheduled hyper footprint at six million kilometers!"

Captain Jane Timmons, CO, HMS *Andromeda*, spun her command chair towards her tactical officer. Six million kilometers was inside *single*-drive missile range!

She opened her mouth to demand more information, but the tac officer was already providing it.

"It's a single footprint, Ma'am. Very small. Probably a dispatch boat."

"Anything from it?" Timmons asked.

"Not FTL, Ma'am. And we wouldn't have anything light-speed for another—" he glanced at the time chop on the initial detection "—another couple of seconds. In fact—"

"Captain," the com officer said in a very careful voice, "I have a communications request I think you'd better take."

The communicator buzzed in the darkened cabin. Honor sat up quickly, with the instant wakefulness which had become the norm over the years. Except, perhaps, she thought with a fleeting smile, even as she reached for the com, when she was "home" in bed. Then her finger found the dimly illuminated voice-only acceptance button, and she pressed it.

"Yes?"

"Your Grace, I'm sorry to wake you." Honor's eyes narrowed. It wasn't MacGuiness, who almost always screened her after-hours calls; it was Mercedes Brigham.

"I don't suppose you did it without reasonably good cause," Honor said, when Brigham paused.

"Yes, Your Grace." Honor heard the chief of staff clear her throat. "One of the perimeter patrol battlecruisers just relayed a transmission to us. It's from an unscheduled courier boat." She paused again. "A *Peep* courier boat."

"A Havenite courier?" Honor repeated carefully. "Here?"

"That's correct, Your Grace." There was a very strange note in Brigham's voice, Honor noticed. But before she could probe, the chief of staff continued, "I think you should probably view the transmission we received from it, Your Grace. May I patch it through?"

"Of course," Honor said, feeling just a bit mystified, and pressed the button to accept a visual feed, as well. The display blinked alive with *Imperator*'s communications system's wallpaper, and then Honor twitched as a most familiar face appeared.

"I suppose this is all a bit irregular," Rear Admiral Michelle Henke said, "but I have a message for Her Majesty from the President of the Republic of Haven."

Honor was waiting behind the side party as *Andromeda*'s pinnace settled into the boat bay docking arms. She managed to look completely calm, although the slow, steady twitching of Nimitz's tail as he sat on her shoulder gave away her inner mood to those who knew the 'cat well.

The personnel tube ran out, the green light blinked, and then Michelle Henke swung gingerly through the interface from the tube's microgravity into *Imperator*'s internal grav field. She obviously favored her left leg as she landed, and Honor could taste her physical discomfort as she came to attention and saluted through the twitter of bosun's pipes.

"Battlecruiser Squadron Eighty-One, arriving!"

"Permission to come aboard, Sir?" she requested from the officer of the deck.

"Permission granted, Admiral Henke!"

Both hands fell from the salute, and Henke stepped past the BBOD with a noticeable limp.

"Mike," Honor said, very quietly, taking her friend's offered hand in a firm clasp. "It's good to see you again."

"And you, Your Grace," Henke said, her always husky contralto just a tad more husky than usual.

"Well," Honor released her hand at last, stepping back a bit from their mutual joy at the reunion, "I believe you said something about a message?"

"Yes, I did."

"Should I get Admiral Kuzak out here?"

"I don't believe that will be necessary, Ma'am," Henke said formally, aware of all of the watching eyes and listening ears.

"Then why don't you accompany me to my quarters?"

"Of course, Your Grace."

Honor led the way to the lift shaft, with an improbably wide awake-looking Andrew LaFollet coming along behind. She pressed the button, then smiled faintly and waved Henke through the opening door before her. She and LaFollet followed, the door slid shut behind her, and she reached out and gripped Henke's upper arms.

"My God," she said softly, "it *is* good to see you, Mike!"

Honor Alexander-Harrington had never been one for easy embraces, but she suddenly swept Mike Henke into a bear hug.

"Easy! *Easy!*" Henke gasped, returning the embrace. "The leg's bad enough, woman! Don't add crushed ribs to the list!"

"Sorry."

For a moment, Honor's soprano was almost as husky as Henke's contralto, but then she stood back and cleared her throat while Nimitz buzzed a happy, welcoming purr from her shoulder.

"Sorry," she repeated in a more normal voice. "It's just that I thought you were dead. And then, when we found out you weren't, I still expected months, or years, to pass before I saw you again."

"Then I guess we're even over that little Cerberus trip you took," Henke said with a crooked smile.

"I guess we are," Honor agreed with a sudden chuckle. "Although *you* at least weren't dead long enough for them to throw an entire state funeral for you!"

"Pity. I would've loved to watch the HD of it."

"Yes, you probably would have. You always have been just a bit peculiar, Mike Henke!"

"You only say that because of my taste in friends."

"No doubt," Honor said dryly, as the lift doors opened and deposited them in the passageway outside her quarters. Spencer

Hawke was standing guard outside them, and she paused and looked over her shoulder at LaFollet.

"Andrew, you and Spencer can't keep this up forever. We've got to get at least one other armsman up here to give the two of you some relief."

"My Lady, I've been thinking about that, but I haven't had the time to select someone. I'd have to go back to Grayson, really, and—"

"No, Andrew, you wouldn't." She paused to give him a moderately stern look. "Two points," she said quietly but firmly. "First, my son will be born in another month. Second," she continued, pretending she hadn't noticed the flicker of pain in his gray eyes, "Brigadier Hill is quite capable of selecting a suitable pool of candidates back on Grayson and sending them to us for you and me to consider together. I know you have a lot on your mind, and I know there are aspects of the situation you don't really like. But this needs to be attended to."

He looked back at her for perhaps two seconds, then sighed.

"Yes, My Lady. I'll send the dispatch to Brigadier Hill on the morning shuttle."

"Thank you," she said gently, touching him lightly on the arm, then turned back to Henke.

"I believe someone else is waiting to welcome you back," she said, and the hatch slid open to show a beaming James MacGuiness.

"So, Mike," Honor said fifteen minutes later, "just what induced the Havenites to send you home?"

She and Henke sat in facing chairs, Henke with a steaming cup of coffee, and Honor with a mug of cocoa. MacGuiness had seen to it that there was also a plate of sandwiches, and Honor nibbled idly on a ham and cheese, taking advantage of the opportunity to stoke her metabolism. Henke, on the other hand, was content with just her coffee.

"That's an interesting question," Henke said now, cradling her cup in both hands and gazing at Honor across it through a wisp of steam. "I think mostly they picked me because I'm Beth's cousin. They figured she'd have to listen to a message from me. And, I imagine, they hoped the fact that they'd given me back to her would at least tempt her to listen seriously to what they had to say."

"Which is? Or is it privileged information you can't share with me?"

"Oh, it's privileged all right—for now, at least. But I was specifically told I could share it with you, since it also concerns you."

"Mike," Honor said, with just a trace of exasperation as she tasted the teasing amusement behind Henke's admirably solemn expression, "if you don't come clean with me and quit tossing out tidbits, I'm going to choke it out of you. You do realize that, don't you?"

"Home less than an hour, and already threatened with physical violence," Henke observed in tones of profound sadness, shaking her head, then cowered dramatically as Honor started to stand.

"All right, all right! I'll talk!"

"Good. And," Honor added pointedly as she settled back, "I'm still waiting."

"Yes, well," Henke's amusement faded into seriousness, "it's not really a laughing matter, I suppose. But put most simply, Pritchart is using me as her messenger to suggest to Beth that the two of them meet in a face-to-face summit to discuss a negotiated settlement."

Honor sat abruptly further back in her chair. Despite the dramatic nature of Henke's return, the unanticipated radicalness of Pritchart's proposal was almost stunning. Sudden glittering vistas of an end to the killing spread out before her, and her heart leapt. But then she made herself step back and draw a deep breath of reality.

"That's a very interesting offer. Do you think she really means it?"

"Oh, I think she definitely wants to meet with Beth. Just what she intends to offer is another matter. On that front, I wish you'd been the one talking to her."

Henke glanced significantly at Nimitz, who raised his head from his comfortable sprawl on the back of Honor's chair.

"What sort of agenda did she propose?"

"That's one of the odd parts about the offer," Henke said. "Basically, she left it wide open. Obviously, she wants a peace treaty, but she didn't list any specific set of terms. Apparently, she's willing to throw everything into the melting pot if Beth will agree to negotiate with her one-on-one."

"That's a significant change from their previous stance, at least as I understood it," Honor observed.

"I hate to say it, but you're probably in a better position to know that than I am," Henke admitted. She shrugged, with a slightly sheepish grin. "I've been trying to pay more attention to politics since you tore a strip off me, but it's still not really a primary interest of mine."

Honor gave her an exasperated look and shook her head. Henke looked back, essentially unrepentant. Then she shrugged again.

"Actually, it's probably a good thing you *are* more interested in politics and diplomacy than I am," she said.

"Why?"

"Because one specific element of Pritchart's proposal is a request that you also attend the conference she wants to set up."

"Me?" Honor blinked in astonishment, and Henke nodded.

"You. I got the impression the original suggestion to include you may have come from Thomas Theisman, but I'm not sure about that. Pritchart did assure me, however, that neither she nor anyone in her administration had anything to do with your attempted assassination. And you can believe however much of that you want to."

"She'd almost have to say that, I suppose," Honor said thoughtfully, her mind racing as she considered Pritchart's proposal. Then she cocked her head. "Did she say anything about Ariel or Nimitz?"

"No, she didn't . . . and I thought that was probably significant," Henke said. "They know both you and Beth have been adopted, of course, and it was obvious that they have extensive dossiers on both of you. I'm sure they've been following the articles and other presentations on the 'cats capabilities since they decided to come out of the closet."

"Which means, in effect, that she's inviting us to bring a pair of furry lie detectors to this summit of hers."

"That's what I think." Henke nodded. "I guess it's always possible they haven't made that connection after all, but I think it's unlikely."

"So do I." Honor gazed off into the distance, thinking hard. Then she looked back at Henke.

"The timing on this is interesting. We've got several factors working here."

"I know. And so does Pritchart," Henke said. Honor looked a question at her, and the other woman snorted. "She made very certain I knew they know about this business in Talbott. She made the specific point that her offer of a summit is being made at a time when she and her advisers are fully aware of how tightly stretched we are. The unstated implication was that instead of an invitation to talk, they might have sent a battle fleet."

"Yes, they certainly could have."

"Have we heard any more from the Cluster?" Henke asked anxiously.

"No. And we won't hear anything back from Monica for at least another ten or eleven days. And that's one reason I said the timing on this was interesting. On the chance that the news we get may be good, I've been ordered to update our plans for Operation Sanskrit—that's the successor to the Cutworm raids," Honor explained when Henke raised an eyebrow "—with a tentative execution date twelve days from tomorrow. Well," she brought up the date/time display in her artificial eye, "from today, actually, now."

"You're thinking about the way Saint-Just derailed Buttercup by suggesting a cease-fire to High Ridge."

"Actually, I'm thinking about the fact that *Elizabeth* is going to remember it," Honor replied, shaking her head. "Unless they've got a lot more penetration of our security than I believe they do, they can't know what our operational schedule is. Oh, they've probably surmised that Eighth Fleet was just about ready to resume offensive operations, assuming we were going to do that at all, when Khumalo's dispatch arrived. And if they've done the math, they probably know we're about due to hear back from him. But they must have packed you off home almost the same day word of our diversions from Home Fleet could have reached them. To me, that sounds like they moved as quickly as possible to take advantage of an opportunity to negotiate seriously. I'm just afraid it's going to resonate with Buttercup in Elizabeth's thoughts."

"She's not entirely rational where Peeps are concerned," Henke admitted.

"With justification, I'm afraid," Honor said. Henke looked surprised to hear her say that, and Honor shook her head, wondering if Mike knew everything about her own family's experiences with various Havenite régimes.

"Well, I hope she doesn't get her dander up this time," Henke said after a moment. "God knows I love her, and she's one of the strongest monarchs we've ever had, but that temper of hers—!" It was Henke's turn to shake her head.

"I know everyone thinks she's a warhead with a hair trigger," Honor said a bit impatiently, "and I'll even acknowledge that she's one of the best grudge-holders I know. But she isn't really blind to her responsibilities as a head of state, you know!"

"You don't have to defend her to me, Honor! I'm just trying to be realistic. The fact is that she has got a temper from the dark side of Hell, when it's roused, and you know as well as I do how she hates yielding to pressure, even from people she knows are giving her their best advice. And speaking of pressure, Pritchart was careful to make sure I knew *she* knew the goings on in the Cluster have given the Republic the whip hand, diplomatically speaking. Not only that," Henke added with a combination of frustration and grudging admiration, "she told me to inform Beth that she's releasing an official statement tomorrow in Nouveau Paris informing the Republic and the galaxy at large that she's issued her invitation."

"Oh, lovely." Honor leaned back, resting the back of her head lightly against Nimitz's warm, furry weight. "That was a smart move. And you're right, Elizabeth is going to resent it. But she's played the interstellar diplomacy game herself—quite well, in fact. I don't think she'll be surprised by it. And I doubt very much that any resentment she feels over it would have a decisive impact on her decision."

"I hope you're right." Henke sipped coffee, then lowered her cup. "I hope you're right," she repeated, "because hard as I tried to stay cynical, I think Pritchart really means it. She really wants to sit down with Beth and negotiate peace."

"Then let's hope she manages to pull it off," Honor said softly.

"And *I* think I don't trust them as far as I could throw a superdreadnought!" Elizabeth III said angrily.

The power of her emotions was like a black thundercloud to Honor's perceptions, looming over the pleasant council chamber in Mount Royal Palace. None of the other humans could sense it, but all of the treecats were only too obviously aware of it.

She reached up to stroke Nimitz's spine, watching as Prince Justin did the same for Monroe. Ariel's half-flattened ears were an accurate barometer of the Queen's emotions, and Honor could sense Samantha buttressing herself against them from Hamish's chair back.

"Your Majesty—Elizabeth," William Alexander said, "nobody is asking you to trust them. Certainly not on no more basis than the fact that they've returned Michelle and that Pritchart is requesting a meeting with you. That's not really the point."

"Oh, yes, it is!" Elizabeth shot back.

"No, it isn't, Your Majesty," Sir Anthony Langtry disagreed firmly. The Queen glowered at him, and he shrugged. "Willie's right. The point is whether it's better for us to talk to them or shoot at them when we don't know what's happening in the Cluster."

"Which we'll know in another week or so!"

Honor very carefully did not sigh. Elizabeth had proven far more intransigent than she'd hoped over the four days since Michelle Henke's return to Manticore with Honor from Trevor's Star.

"Elizabeth," Honor said now, calmly, "four days from now is the soonest we could really hope to receive a dispatch boat, assuming Terekhov sent one off within twenty-four hours of his planned arrival at Monica. But the fact that we haven't already received one is a bad sign, and you know it."

Elizabeth looked at her, and Honor shrugged.

"We've known for two weeks, from the last dispatch boat he sent off, that *Copenhagen* confirmed his initial assumptions, at least in part, when she met him at his rendezvous point after scouting Monica."

"And?" Elizabeth said, when she paused.

"We also know, from the same dispatch, that he did continue to Monica, where he almost certainly violated Monican territorial space. Let's assume he managed to carry out his best-case plan without firing a shot, and the Monicans agreed to halt whatever preparations they were making until we could assure ourselves they had no designs against the Cluster. That's the *best* message we could be receiving in the next week."

"In which case the situation is under control," Elizabeth said.

"In which case we're effectively in control of Monican space," Honor corrected gently. "For now. It's also possible his dispatch is going to tell us he's fought a battle. In that case, he either won, or he lost. In either of *those* cases, we have a shooting incident with a sovereign star nation with a long-standing relationship with the Office of Frontier Security. In *that* case, it's going to be weeks, even months, before we know whether or not OFS is prepared to commit Solly naval units against us. In fact, even if no shots were exchanged, if Terekhov and Khumalo have occupied the Monica System under threat of force, we could still be looking at OFS intervention. And whatever Terekhov's dispatches might tell us a week from now, we're still going to be facing the same wait until we can be sure which way OFS is going to jump."

"Precisely what I'm trying to say." Baron Grantville looked gratefully at his sister-in-law and nodded vigorously. "I'm sure Pritchart didn't make it because of how much she loves us, but her point about the value of a cease-fire while we find out whether or not we're at war with the Solarian League is completely valid."

He turned back to the Queen.

"That's the same point Tony and I have been trying to make ever since Mike got home. Elizabeth," there was raw appeal in his eyes, "we're in serious trouble. The Peeps alone outnumber us two-to-one in ships of the wall. We all hope Terekhov and Khumalo have managed to nip whatever was happening in the Cluster in the bud, and that Admiral O'Malley's task force will be enough to keep a lid on things if they did. But we don't know that, and we *won't* know it until we know absolutely that OFS is going to back down. And don't forget the Mesan element in all this. We know they've got a cozy deal with a lot of Frontier Security commissioners, but we don't really know how much pressure they're going to be able to bring to bear to try to salvage whatever they were up to if Terekhov and Khumalo *have* spoked their wheel."

"And whether you trust them or not, and whether or not Pritchart really intends from the outset to negotiate in good faith, there's always the possibility a peace treaty would emerge, anyway," Hamish Alexander-Harrington pointed out in a neutral tone.

Elizabeth's eyes flashed at him, and he looked back steadily.

"She's the one who's told the newsies about the proposed

summit," he said. "That means the onus to make some sort of progress is at least largely on her if you do agree to meet with her. Unless the two of you are going to sit down somewhere, all alone, in a smoke-filled room and negotiate some sort of private deal, the whole thing's going to go forward in a positive glare of publicity. So if you make a reasonable offer, she may find herself hoist by her own petard and forced to entertain it seriously."

"You tell Emily not to try to manage me by remote control, Hamish!" Elizabeth snapped. "I've got enough *official* advisers trying to do that!"

Honor started to protest, then kept her mouth firmly closed. This being married business had its own complications, she'd discovered. The last thing she needed was to sound as if she were weighing in in concert with her spouses.

"Oh, be reasonable, Elizabeth!" the seventh human seated at the table said in a voice of considerable exasperation. The Queen turned her glare upon the speaker, only to be met by glittering eyes exactly the same color as her own.

"Stop pitching such a snit," Caitrin Winton-Henke told her niece sharply. "You don't like Peeps. You don't *trust* Peeps. Fine. Neither do I, and you know exactly why I don't. But you're the Queen of Manticore, not a schoolchild! Act like it."

Honor felt several people wincing in anticipation of a furious explosion from the Queen. But it didn't come. Instead, Elizabeth looked into her aunt's eyes and the tight shoulders and rigid spine of the woman the treecats had named Soul of Steel seemed to droop.

Honor felt her own eyes soften in sympathy, but she understood what Michelle Henke's mother had just done. The Dowager Countess of Gold Peak was Elizabeth's one-time regent. She was also the only person at the conference table who had lost even more deeply and personally to the Peeps than Elizabeth had . . . as she had just reminded her niece.

"And don't forget, Elizabeth," Honor said as she felt the Queen's adamantine resistance waver, "if you attend this summit, and if I attend it with you, there'll be at least two treecats present. Don't you think it would be worth getting Ariel and Nimitz close enough to taste Pritchart's mind-glow, whatever else happens?"

Elizabeth's eyes darted to Honor, and she frowned thoughtfully.

She was obviously thinking about the fact that it would also get *Honor* close enough to do the same thing, and Honor was cautiously pleased by the evidence that the Queen was finally stepping back far enough *to* think.

"Beth," Prince Justin said quietly. His wife looked at him, and he reached out to rest one hand lightly on hers where it lay on the tabletop. "Beth, think about it. Every single one of your advisers disagrees with you. Even," he smiled, "your husband. I think you need to factor that into your decision, don't you?"

She gazed into his eyes for several seconds, then sighed.

"Yes." She obviously hated making that admission, but Honor tasted her unwilling sincerity. The Queen looked around the council chamber, then shrugged her shoulders. "Very well. I'm sure you've all made valid points. I can even appreciate most of them, intellectually, at least. That doesn't mean I like it, because I don't. I *hate* it. But that doesn't make you wrong, however much I'd like it to. So I'll meet with Pritchart."

"Thank you, Your Majesty," Grantville said with quiet, thankful formality.

"Which raises the question of where you should meet," Langtry said. "Pritchart did invite you to name the site."

"Yes, and she suggested a 'neutral' one," Grantville agreed. "Although just exactly where she thinks we can find one is a bit of a puzzle."

"Nonsense," Elizabeth said with a hard little laugh. "That's the easiest part of all! If she wants a neutral meeting site, where better than Torch?"

"I don't know," Grantville began. "The security aspects would worry me, and—"

"Security would probably be the least of our worries," Honor interrupted. Grantville looked at her, and she grinned. "A planetful of freed slaves, Willie, invited to play host to the heads of state of the two star nations with the best track record for enforcing the Cherwell Convention? You'd need a couple of divisions of battle armor to get through them!"

"That," Langtry said, "is almost certainly true, Willie. They might not have the same technological capabilities we would, but they'd certainly have the motivation!"

"Yes, they would," Grantville agreed. "And I suppose there'd be ample time for us to make additional security arrangements."

"And," Elizabeth pointed out, "it would be an opportunity to draw Erewhon into the process. I know we've all been pissed off with the Erewhonese for the technology they transferred to the Peeps, but let's be honest. High Ridge did everything humanly possible to push them into doing it. If we ask them to dispatch units of their fleet to provide a neutral security umbrella in Congo for both sides, without either of us bringing in our own battle squadrons, it would be a demonstration that this Government—and the House of Winton—both trusts them and desires to patch up our differences."

Grantville looked at her with a slightly surprised expression, and she chuckled almost naturally.

"I may still have my reservations about this entire idea, Willie. But if we're going to do it anyway, we might as well accomplish as many objectives at once as we can."

Chapter Forty-Seven

Aldona Anisimovna tried to remind herself that she was one of the most successful organizers and executives Manpower Incorporated had ever produced. That she had a very nearly unrivaled record of successes. That she was a wealthy and powerful individual, who represented one of Mesa's star bloodlines.

None of it helped particularly.

She and Isabel Bardasano followed the "butler" (who sprang from a bloodline with far higher combat enhancements than the Anisimov genome) down the splendidly furnished hallway, past light sculptures, bronzes, paintings and handloomed textile wall hangings. The designer had deliberately eschewed smart walls or other modern visual technology, aside from the light sculptures, but soothing, unheard sonic vibrations seemed to caress her skin.

It was all very gracious and welcoming, but she drew a deep breath, trying to settle her nerves unobtrusively and hoping the invisible surveillance systems weren't noting her heightened pulse rate, as their guide opened the old-fashioned door at the end of the corridor.

"Ms. Anisimovna and Ms. Bardasano, Sir," he said.

"Thank you, Heinrich," a familiar voice said, and the "butler" who was actually a rather deadly bodyguard, when he wasn't being an assassin, bowed and stepped aside.

Anisimovna walked past him without even acknowledging his presence, but she was grateful when he closed the door behind her and Bardasano from the other side. Not that she'd really expected his . . . services to be required, she told herself firmly.

"Well, ladies," Albrecht Detweiler said from behind the desk workstation, without inviting either of them to be seated, "things don't appear to have gone very well in Talbott, after all."

"No, they haven't," Anisimovna agreed, her voice as level as possible. Detweiler regarded her thoughtfully, as if waiting for her to add something more to that bare agreement, but she knew better than to offer any hint of an excuse. Especially not when he'd kept the two of them waiting, and stewing in their own juice, for almost three standard days since their return from the Republic of Monica.

"Why not?" he asked after a moment.

"Because of a chain of circumstances we were unable to predict," Isabel Bardasano said, her voice as level as Anisimovna's had been.

"I was under the impression that proper planning allowed for all contingencies," Detweiler observed.

"Good planning allows for all the contingencies the planner can think of," Bardasano corrected in an amazingly calm tone. "This particular set of contingencies was impossible to anticipate, since no one can allow for freak circumstances which are inherently impossible to predict."

"That sounds remarkably like an excuse, Isabel."

"I prefer to think of it as an explanation, Albrecht," Bardasano said, while Anisimovna tried to focus her attention on one of Detweiler's pre-space oil paintings. "Under certain circumstances, explanations are also excuses, of course. You asked us why things didn't work out as planned, however. That's why."

Detweiler gazed at her, his lips very slightly pursed, his eyes narrowed, and she looked back squarely. One thing about her, Anisimovna thought; she didn't lack nerve. Whether her lack of fear was completely sane or not was another matter.

"Very well, Isabel," Detweiler said finally. " 'Explain' what happened."

"We don't know yet, not fully," she admitted. "We won't know for some time. The only hard fact we have at this time is that somehow a Manty cruiser captain named Terekhov and Bernardus Van Dort figured out what was happening. Terekhov put together what I strongly suspect was a completely unauthorized attack on Monica. And as Aldona and I told you at our last meeting, the program to refit the battlecruisers we—or, rather, Technodyne—were providing had fallen behind schedule."

"You also informed me that there was ample cushion in your timetable," Detweiler interrupted in a deceptively pleasant voice.

If he'd intended to put Bardasano off her pace, he failed. She simply looked at him for a moment, then nodded.

"Yes, we did. And it was an accurate statement. In fact, Izrok Levakonic and the Monicans had managed to get three of the battlecruisers completely refitted and manned before Terekhov showed up, and the biggest unit *he* had was a heavy cruiser. Had he delayed his arrival for another week, four more *Indefatigables* would have been ready for action, as well. Under normal circumstances, however, I believe most people would have felt three Solarian League battlecruisers, with up-to-date electronics and weapons fits, ought to have been able to deal with five cruisers and four destroyers."

"Apparently, they would have been wrong," Detweiler said. "And, I might point out to you, if I were inclined to pick nits, that one of the objectives of the operation was to obtain specimens of Manty hardware specifically because we knew it was better than Solly equipment."

"Granted," Bardasano replied. "I would submit, however, that its degree of superiority was greater than anyone had anticipated, including Technodyne."

"I'm much less well versed in technical matters than Isabel, Albrecht," Aldona said, speaking up in support of her colleague, "but we did discuss this with Levakonic. He felt confident of maintaining Monica's security with the combination of missile pods he'd deployed and the battlecruisers already in commission. That part of the operation was his responsibility, and we relied on his expert opinion."

Detweiler switched his gaze to her, and she made herself look back calmly. He appeared to consider her words for several seconds, then gave a tiny shrug.

"I suppose that was reasonable enough, under the circumstances," he said. "However," he continued before Anisimovna's nerves could begin to unknot themselves, "even granting that, the fact that the Manties and this Van Dort somehow tumbled to what was going on speaks poorly of your operational security."

"At this point," Bardasano said, "we don't know how our security was penetrated. I see two possibilities. One is that the penetration took place on the Monican side. President Tyler and his closest advisers had to be brought fully into the picture, at least as far as their part of the operation was concerned. Their security arrangements were beyond our control, and we don't know how or where they might have been breached.

"The second possibility," she continued unflinchingly, "is that the penetration was on our side of the operation. In that case, the most likely scenario is that this Terekhov literally stumbled over the *Marianne*."

"*Marianne?*" Detweiler repeated.

"The special ops ship we were using to deliver weapons to our proxies," Bardasano explained. "We've used her and her crew dozens of times before. They're reliable and experienced in this sort of covert operation, and using our own ship and our own people let us maintain a far lower profile and avoid an entire additional layer of potential leaks."

"So why do you think she could be involved?"

"Because she's the only direct link between our terrorist proxies and Monica." Bardasano shrugged. "Izrok needed emergency transportation for additional shipyard technicians. *Marianne* was already headed for the Cluster. He asked me if we could transport them for him, and I agreed. Apparently, I shouldn't have."

She made the admission without flinching, and a flicker of what might have been approval showed in Detweiler's eyes.

"If she is the clue the Manties picked up on," she continued, "they must have taken at least some of her personnel and sweated them. They don't actually *know* anything about the Monican side of the operation, but they do know they delivered technicians to Monica. That could have been enough. Unfortunately, we probably won't know whether or not that's what actually happened for some time. *Marianne's* movement schedule means we don't expect contact with her for another couple of weeks."

"This is all speculation," Detweiler remarked, and Bardasano and Anisimovna both nodded.

"We barely managed to get out of Monica, and take the only Frontier Security personnel directly involved in the operation with us," Anisimovna said. "We couldn't afford to wait around for any more details. If they'd captured Isabel or myself—"

She broke off, and it was Detweiler's turn to nod.

"Point taken," he acknowledged. He considered them silently for several more seconds, then seemed to reach a decision.

"Sit," he said, pointing at two of the chairs facing his desk, and Anisimovna hoped her enormous relief didn't show as she obeyed the command.

"None of us are happy about what's happened in the Cluster," Detweiler said. "I trust you're both prepared for the fact that you're going to face a lot of recrimination and accusations of incompetence?"

Anisimovna bobbed her head, and this time she didn't try to disguise her glum expression. Whatever else came of the Talbott fiasco, she'd be a long time rebuilding her prestige and repairing her damaged powerbase.

"Having said that, and assuming no new revelations suggest it really was your fault, I'm inclined to agree that the failure almost certainly stemmed from factors outside your control." He shrugged. "As I said at the beginning, it was always a crap shoot, and apparently we crapped out. So, starting from that, what's your feeling as to whether or not OFS is going to let this stand?"

"I think they are," Anisimovna said. Managing the Solly bureaucracies was her own area of expertise. "Verrochio is livid, and he's going to be even angrier if the Manties are able to prove his involvement. But he doesn't have the forces under his own command to take unilateral action, and the other Frontier Security commissioners won't support him. Not after something as spectacular as what the Manties did to Monica, and especially not if Tyler or any of his cronies roll over on us and cooperate with a Manty investigation."

"We don't need him to *win*," Detweiler pointed out. "You say he's 'livid' over this. Is there any probability of playing on that anger to maneuver him into a direct military confrontation? Whether the other commissioners approve or not, that would be something our friends in the League could probably spin into the pretext for intervention we need. Especially if he gets the crap shot out of him.."

"I don't see any way to do it," Anisimovna replied. "Angry as he is, he's not going to risk his own position. Neither is his vice-commissioner, Hongbo, who—unfortunately, perhaps in this instance—has a great deal of influence with him and is far less likely to let anger shape his decisions."

"I was afraid of that."

Detweiler tipped his chair back, folding his hands, fingers interlaced, across his midsection, and Anisimovna felt a sudden fresh pang of anxiety. That relaxed posture normally indicated that Albert Detweiler was quietly, icily, *dangerously* furious about something.

"Three weeks ago," he said, "Eloise Pritchart sent an invitation to Elizabeth Winton. She suggested the two of them meet in a face-to-face summit, in a neutral location of Winton's choosing."

Anisimovna felt her eyes widen and fought a sudden urge to turn and look at Bardasano in shock. Pritchart was proposing a *peace conference*?

"We found out about it from our mole in the Manties' Foreign Office," Detweiler continued. "The proposal itself arrived on Manticore nine days ago, and our mole's control did very well to get it to us this quickly, although he had to use the Beowulf conduit to do it. I'm not exactly delighted at that. That conduit is too valuable to lose. In this case, though, I think our man's decision was justified."

"Excuse me, Albrecht," Anisimovna said, "but do we have any idea what prompted Pritchart to do something like this?"

"Not specifically, no." Detweiler frowned. "At the moment, my best guess is that she found out about what was happening in Talbott. She's demonstrated she's a very shrewd politician, and she may well have calculated that the pressure of a potential conflict with the Solarian League would force Winton to accept terms."

Anisimovna nodded, but very carefully said nothing. From Detweiler's tone, it was unlikely he would have appreciated the observation that it might have been their own efforts which had offered the Republic the wedge which might bring their carefully nurtured war to a premature conclusion.

"According to our mole," Detweiler went on, "it took two days to convince Winton to accept the offer. In the end, however, she did. And guess what 'neutral site' she proposed for their little get together?"

Anisimovna frowned, but Bardasano snorted harshly.

"Verdant Vista," she said flatly, and Detweiler's chuckle was even harsher than her snort.

"On the money," he agreed.

"Do we have a date for this summit?" Bardasano asked.

"Not yet. I'm sure the Manties will be proposing one in their reply to Pritchart, but our mole doesn't have that level of access. Even after they propose one, messages are going to have to go back and forth between Manticore and Haven, and transit time is almost eleven days each way, even for a fast dispatch boat via

Trevor's Star. So it's not going to happen next week, but it looks like it is going to happen."

"Elizabeth Winton hates Haven's guts," Anisimovna said. "Even if the summit meets, how likely is it to result in an actual peace treaty? Especially after Haven initiated the attack, and given that everyone's convinced Haven was behind the Harrington assassination attempt?"

"Under normal circumstances, I might think along the same lines," Detweiler said. "But Winton's been adopted by one of those frigging treecats, and you can bet she won't attend a conference without the little monster."

"Oh." Anisimovna grimaced.

"Yes, we can't afford to overlook the little bastards any longer, can we?" Detweiler growled.

It was unusual, to say the least, for him to allow his ire to show that clearly, but Sphinx's treecats had been a sore point with Manpower and Mesa literally for centuries. The possibility of unlocking the secret of telepathy had been impossible for the bioengineers of Mesa to resist, but they'd been remarkably unsuccessful in obtaining specimens. In fact, they'd managed to obtain only one living treecat in over three hundred T-years, and they'd discovered quickly that a treecat in captivity simply died. They still had some of the creature's genetic material, and some work continued with it in a desultory fashion, but without much prospect of successfully building the ability into humans.

The fact that the wretched little animals were even more intelligent than Manpower's own worst-case assumptions had come as an unpleasant revelation. And the ability of a fully functional telempathic to communicate its observations about the mental state of someone on the other side of high-level diplomatic negotiations was something political analysts were going to take some getting used to.

"We know, even if Winton doesn't, that Pritchart never wanted to go back to war in the first place," Detweiler continued. "If some dammed treecat gets a chance to communicate that to Winton, it's entirely possible the two of them will agree to a *joint* examination of the disputed diplomatic correspondence. In which case peace is likely to start breaking out all over."

"Not exactly a desirable outcome," Bardasano murmured, and Detweiler rewarded her with a tight grin and another hard chuckle.

"Nicely put. Now, what do we do to prevent it?"

"Killing Winton or Pritchart would be the most effective solution," Bardasano said thoughtfully. "On the other hand, if we could get to either of them easily, we'd have already done it. Hmmm . . ."

She thought for several seconds, then nodded to herself.

"I see one possibility," she said.

"Which is?"

"I've already prepared the operation you wanted on Old Earth," she told him. "I haven't scheduled a date for it yet, however. And I've also set up the groundwork for Operation Rat Poison. I can activate both of them immediately, and set them up to happen simultaneously, or at least in close succession. Given Elizabeth Winton's existing attitude towards Haven, I'd say there's a pretty good chance it would destabilize any summit arrangements."

"Especially Rat Poison," Detweiler agreed, his eyes lighting with pleasure at the prospect. Then they narrowed. "Probability of success?" he demanded.

"On Old Earth, very high," Bardasano said promptly. "Probably approaching a hundred percent. Rat Poison's more problematical, I'm afraid. Our choice of vehicles is much more limited, and all the ones we're currently considering are outside the inner circle, so access is going to be more of a problem. To make it work with one of the present vehicles, we'll have to use a two-stage control, and that's going to up the chances of something going wrong. I'd say probably sixty percent, plus or minus five percent either way, if we mount the op immediately."

"I'd really rather wait, at least until we could get better odds," Detweiler murmured.

"We can do that," Bardasano told him. "In fact, given a few more months of prep work, I could improve the odds significantly. But if we wait, we lose the opportunity to derail the summit. And we also increase the risk that even Winton would blame *us* for it. If the attempt hits at the same time as someone with an obvious Havenite connection kills Webster, though, the Manties are almost certain to connect the two ops and blame *both* of them on Haven. And we also increase the risk that even Winton would blame *us* for it. If the attempt hits at the same time as someone with an obvious Havenite connection kills Webster, though, the

Manties are almost certain to connect the two ops and blame *both* of them on Haven. And I might point out, Albrecht, that even if the attempt itself fails, the mere fact that it was made ought to accomplish what we want."

"There is that," Detweiler agreed. He sat motionless for perhaps fifteen seconds, obviously thinking hard. Then he nodded his head sharply.

"All right. Do it."

Chapter Forty-Eight

"What do you think the Sollies are going to do, Your Grace?" Rafe Cardones asked quietly.

He and Honor stood side by side in the lift, along with Mercedes Brigham, Andrea Jaruwalski, Frances Hirshfield, Andrew LaFollet, Spencer Hawke, and Sergeant Jefferson McClure, one of the two Harrington Steading armsmen Andrew LaFollet had finally chosen to reinforce Honor's personal detail. Nimitz rode on Honor's shoulder, and even the spacious lift car felt more than a little crowded.

"That's hard to say, Rafe," Honor replied, after a moment. The long-awaited courier from Aivars Terekhov and Augustus Khumalo had finally arrived the day before, with news of Terekhov's crushing victory over the Monican Navy. And of the horrific price his hastily organized squadron had paid for it.

"It's pretty obvious," she continued after a moment, "that at least some Sollies had to be in on this up to their necks. The Solarian Navy doesn't just 'lose' more than a dozen modern battlecruisers."

"You think the League Navy was directly involved?" Cardones was more than a little worried by the thought, and Honor didn't blame him.

"Not the Navy as such." She shook her head. "I'm more inclined to think it was some rogue element within the Navy, or else some private interest, one of their big builders, like Technodyne or General Industries of Terra. Either of them could have provided

585

the ships, if they'd been willing to run some risks, although I'd bet on Technodyne, given their involvement with Mesa at Tiberian. We won't know who it was for certain for quite a while, though. Admiral O'Malley's detachment won't even get there for another four days, and until he arrives, Terekhov and Khumalo are going to have all they can do just to keep the system nailed down. They certainly aren't going to be able to start conducting any investigations."

Cardones nodded thoughtfully, and she gave a small shrug.

"On the other hand, Frontier Security must have signed off on this operation, at least unofficially," she pointed out. "Without assurance of OFS support, this President Tyler would never have run the level of risk he was prepared to court. Not only that, I can't see Mesa providing this kind of logistical and financial support unless they were pretty darn certain one of their pet Frontier Security commissioners was going to back their play.

"Probably the question comes down mainly to how quickly their OFS stooges can react. If they can get in before O'Malley gets there, they might have enough locally deployed firepower to force Khumalo and Terekhov out of Monica. If they can't get themselves organized quickly enough for that, though, I don't think they're going to want to tangle with his task force. And if they blink, the longer they delay a counterattack, the less likely they are to be able to mount one at all. So I'm actually reasonably confident that if they haven't hit us by the time O'Malley gets into position, they won't. Not unless somebody on their side screws up by the numbers."

Cardones nodded again.

"And what about this summit?" Honor didn't really need her empathic ability to feel the hope in his question. "You think it could really lead to something?"

"I think there's always that possibility, How likely it is I can't say. But like you, I spend a lot of time hoping."

The lift came to a halt, the doors slid open, and Honor stepped out, leading the way towards her flag briefing room and yet another conference with her senior officers.

"And the time I don't spend hoping," she said, just a bit grimly, "I spend planning for what we're going to do if it doesn't work out."

✧   ✧   ✧

"Thank you for seeing me, Madam President."

Secretary of State Leslie Montreau shook Eloise Pritchart's hand as the President walked around her desk to greet her. Pritchart smiled, and waved for the Secretary to be seated in one of her office's armchairs, then sat herself, facing her guest.

"Given the general tenor of your message when you requested a meeting, Leslie, I was delighted to make room for you in this morning's schedule. I take it we've heard back?"

"Yes, Madam President."

Montreau opened her thin briefcase and extracted a sheaf of old-fashioned hard copy. There were several documents, each with the matching electronic document's chip attached, and she laid them out on the coffee table.

"Basically," she went on, "we've gotten a very favorable response, overall. This," she tapped one document, "is a personal letter from Queen Elizabeth to you. It's mainly polite formulas, but she does specifically thank you for the care our people have taken of our POWs, and for releasing her cousin, Admiral Henke, as your messenger.

"This one," she indicated another, thicker document, "is an official response to our proposal, drafted by their Foreign Office over Foreign Secretary Langtry's signature. There's quite a bit of diplomatic boilerplate in it, but what it boils down to is that they officially welcome our suggestion of a conference, and they accept our offer of a military standdown until after the summit, to begin twenty-four standard hours after the expected arrival time of their response here in Nouveau Paris. I think you'll want to read it for yourself, especially since there are a couple of passages which are just a bit testy. Most of them, I'm afraid, refer to our decision to launch Thunderbolt without formal notice we intended to resort to military action, but I think it's significant that they don't mention our dispute over who did what to the official diplomatic correspondence.

"In addition," she went on, in a slightly different tone, "they've responded to our request that they nominate a neutral site."

"Which is?" Pritchart asked as Montreau paused.

"Torch, Madam President," the Secretary said, and Pritchart sat back in her chair with a suddenly thoughtful expression.

"You know," she said, after a few seconds, "that really should have occurred to us. It's the one neutral port where we both have contacts." She chuckled suddenly. "Of course, if it had occurred to me, I probably wouldn't have suggested it anyway. I'd have figured they wouldn't want to risk their monarch anywhere near our half-tame lunatic, Cachat!"

"Then you feel the site's acceptable?" Montreau asked, and Pritchart cocked her head to one side.

"You don't?"

"I think it's very inconveniently placed for us, Madam President," the Secretary of State replied after a brief hesitation. "Their delegation could make the trip in less than a week, thanks to their Junction and the Erewhon Junction. It's going to take over a month for *our* delegation to make the trip from Haven. And it's going to take over three weeks for our acceptance and their acknowledgment of our acceptance to travel back and forth between here and Manticore. So the absolute earliest we could actually sit down with them is the next best thing to two months from today."

"That sort of time constraint's going to be part and parcel of any peace conference, Leslie," Pritchart pointed out. "It always takes time, and finding a suitable site we can both agree to is worth going a little out of our way. I suppose," she smiled thinly, "that we could always ask them to guarantee our safe conduct and take *Haven One* through their Junction. That would cut about a week off of our total transit time."

"And Thomas Theisman would have me shot at dawn if I proposed any such thing, Madam President."

"Probably not," Pritchart disagreed.

"If it's all the same to you, Madam President, I'd prefer not to find out."

"Wise of you, I suppose." Pritchart sat for another moment, studying the Secretary of State's expression, then frowned very slightly. "Somehow, though, Leslie, I don't think the time element is the only issue you have."

"Well," Montreau began, then stopped. She seemed uncomfortable, but finally she inhaled and started again.

"Madam President, I have to confess I'm just a little anxious about the notion of the President of the Republic attending a peace conference on a planet inhabited almost exclusively by freed genetic slaves. As far as I can tell, at least half of them have some connection with the Audubon Ballroom, and their Secretary of

War is probably the galaxy's most notorious terrorist. Then there's the fact that they're a monarchy, with a queen who's the adopted daughter of one of Manticore's leading politicians and a man who used to be one of the Star Kingdom's best spies. And that same man is basically running Torch's intelligence community, with the Queen of Manticore's *niece* as his assistant."

She shook her head.

"Madam President, I question whether or not this planet can really be considered a 'neutral site,' and I have some fairly severe reservations about your personal security and safety on Torch."

"I see."

Pritchart leaned back in her chair, her own expression thoughtful, and considered what Montreau had said. Then she shrugged.

"I can see why you might be concerned," she said. "I think, though, that you're making a not unreasonable mistake by failing to recognize that Torch is something new and unique. Yes, Queen Berry is the daughter of Anton Zilwicki and Catherine Montaigne. She was born on Old Earth, though, not Manticore, and I'm quite confident her primary loyalty is to her new planet and her new subjects. I have . . . certain highly covert contacts within the Torch government which keep me quite well informed in that regard.

"As for my personal security and safety among a bunch of ex-terrorists, you might want to recall just exactly what the Aprilists were." Her smile this time was thin and cold. "I was a senior member of the Aprilists, Leslie. I personally killed over a dozen men and women, and InSec labeled all of us 'terrorists.' I'm not going to worry all that much about my safety among people someone like Manpower's labeled terrorists simply because they chose to strike back violently at the butchers who made their lives living hells. And while Anton Zilwicki may head their intelligence services, I have complete and total faith in the young woman who commands their military."

Montreau looked at her. Pritchart suspected the Secretary wanted to press her objections, but she had the good sense not to.

"Very well, Madam President," she said instead. "If the site's acceptable to you, I'm not going to raise any more objections. Although, with your permission, I intend to discuss my specific concerns with the Attorney General and Presidential Security, as well as my own security people."

"Of course you have my permission, Leslie."

"Thank you."

The Secretary smiled, then tapped the last stack of hard copy.

"This was perhaps the most surprising part of the entire package," she said. "It includes a copy of two official messages to Erewhon. One is from Foreign Secretary Langtry, and the other's from Queen Elizabeth. They're proposing that both sides agree to bring no military units into the Congo System, aside from a single escort vessel for the ships transporting our delegations, and that the Erewhonese Navy assume responsibility for the system's security during the conference. They've requested that neither we nor the Star Kingdom announce the actual site of the conference. Instead, they've asked us to leave the announcement up to Erewhon, to be made only after the summit is officially agreed to and Erewhon is confident that it has all of its security arrangements in order. The official messages they've copied to us are requests to Erewhon to agree to undertake that role."

"Now *that*, Leslie, was a clever move on someone's part," Pritchart said almost admiringly. "High Ridge blotted Manticore's copybook so thoroughly with Erewhon that he almost *drove* them into our arms, and he managed it mainly because he was too stupid to understand how Erewhonese think. Obviously, whoever came up with this notion doesn't suffer from that particular form of blindness. Given that the Star Kingdom knows Erewhon provided us with significant technology transfers before hostilities resumed, this is Manticore's way of telling Erewhon the current government recognizes its predecessors' mistakes and that *it* trusts the Republic of Erewhon to keep its word. That it trusts Erewhon enough to put the life of its Queen into Erewhonese hands, even after what happened when Elizabeth visited Grayson. Or, for that matter, when Princess Ruth visited Erewhon."

She shook her head, smiling.

"Whatever comes of the peace conference, asking Erewhon to guarantee our security is going to move it almost all the way back to a truly neutral position between us and Manticore."

"Should we object to the suggestion, then?" Montreau asked, and Pritchart shook her head again, more violently.

"Certainly not! Objecting to the suggestion, especially after Elizabeth and Langtry have already issued their request, would be the same as saying we *don't* trust the Erewhonese to play the role of honest neutral. Right off hand, I can't think of anything that would be more destructive to our own relationship with them."

"Then I take it you're prepared to approve the Manticoran proposal?"

"Yes, I think I am. As you suggested, I'll want to read over the correspondence myself, and we'll have to have Cabinet approval before I take the entire notion officially to the Senate. Under the circumstances, though, I don't see anyone raising any objections if I'm agreeable."

"Frankly, I don't either, Madam President. So, with your permission," Montreau stood, "I'll get back to my office. Colonel Nesbitt and I need to begin considering our own security recommendations."

"So the President is really serious about this, Madam Secretary?" Jean-Claude Nesbitt asked.

"She certainly is, Colonel," Secretary of State Montreau replied. "And while I admit I have a few reservations about the site myself, this initiative of hers also strikes me as our best chance for a negotiated settlement."

"I see."

Nesbitt frowned, and Montreau looked at him questioningly. He saw her expression and gave himself an impatient little shake.

"Sorry, Madam Secretary. I'm just thinking about all the things that could go wrong. And, if I'm going to be honest, I suppose I'm also thinking about the relative military positions. Given our current advantages, and the fact that the Manties appear to be tangled up with the Sollies in Talbott, I hope President Pritchart's planning on taking a fairly hard line."

"Our exact position at the summit is going to be up to the President's direction," Montreau's said just a bit coolly.

"Of course, Madam Secretary. I didn't mean to suggest it shouldn't be. It's just that, especially after Solon and Zanzibar, I'm afraid the man in the street's in a fairly bloodthirsty mood."

"I know. On the other hand, formulating long-term diplomatic policy on the basis of public opinion surveys isn't exactly a good idea."

"Of course, Madam Secretary," Nesbitt said again, bobbing his head with a pleasant smile. "In that case, suppose I go and pull everything we have on Torch? I'll request a full background

download from Director Trajan over at FIS, as well. Let me spend
a few days reviewing it with my senior people and possibly get
a few of your senior staffers involved for input from their side
of the aisle. After that, I'll be able to delineate specific areas of
concern and formulate proposals for dealing with them."

"That sounds like the best way to proceed," Montreau agreed,
and Nesbitt smiled again and climbed out of his chair.

"I'll go and get started, then. Good afternoon, Madam Secretary."

"Good afternoon, Colonel."

Nesbitt let himself out of the Secretary's office and started
towards the building's lift shafts, then paused. He stood there a
moment, then turned and crossed the hall to knock lightly on
the frame of an open door.

"Oh. Good afternoon, Colonel," Alicia Hampton said, looking
up from her workstation.

"Good afternoon, Ms. Hampton." Nesbitt stepped into the fairly
spacious, comfortably furnished office. "I was just finishing up
my meeting with Secretary Montreau, and I thought I'd poke my
head in and see how you're getting along."

"Thank you Colonel. That's very thoughtful of you." Hampton
smiled a bit tremulously. "It hasn't been easy. Secretary Montreau's
a perfectly nice person, and she takes her job seriously, but
she's just not Secretary Giancola." Her eyes were suspiciously
bright, and she shook her head. "I still can hardly believe he's
gone—him and his brother, both at once, just *gone* like that. It
was all such . . . such a *stupid* waste."

"I know exactly what you mean," Nesbitt said feelingly, although
not for quite the same reasons.

"And he was such a *good* man," Hampton continued.

"Well, Ms. Hampton—Alicia," Nesbitt said, "when we lose a
good man, a leader, we just have to hope someone else can step
into the gap. I think Secretary Montreau's going to try very hard,
and I hope all of us can help her as she does."

"Oh, I certainly agree, Colonel! And it was so good of her to
keep me on as her administrative assistant!"

"Please, I think we've known one another long enough now for
you to call me Jean-Claude," he said with a pleasant smile. "And
it *was* good of her to keep you on. Of course, it was also smart
of her. Secretary Giancola often told me how much he relied on

you to keep the Department running smoothly. Obviously, your background knowledge and experience must have been very valuable to Secretary Montreau during the transition."

"I like to think so, anyway . . . Jean-Claude," Hampton said, her eyes dropping shyly for just a moment. Then she looked back up at him and returned his smile. "I've tried. And she's beginning to delegate a little more than she was willing to when the Senate first confirmed her."

"Good!" Nesbitt nodded vigorously. "That's exactly what I was talking about, Alicia. And I hope you'll keep *me* in mind, as well. Secretary Giancola was more than just a boss to me, too, and I'd really like to see his work carried on. So if there's anything I can do for you or Secretary Montreau, any security or intelligence matter, or anything of that sort, please let me know. After all, part of my job is being able to intelligently anticipate what the Secretary's likely to need before she actually gets around to asking me."

"Of course, Jean-Claude. I'll bear that in mind."

"Fine. Well, I've got to be on my way now. I'll check back with you in a day or so, once this whole conference idea's had a chance to shake down a little more. Maybe we could discuss the Secretary's needs over lunch, down in the cafeteria."

"I think that would be a good idea . . . Jean-Claude," she said.

Chapter Forty-Nine

Honor Alexander-Harrington stood between her husband and her wife. Her left hand held Emily's right, and her right hand held Hamish's left, while the three of them watched through the outsized window as Dr. Knippschd's technicians carefully rolled the artificial womb into the room beyond. Dr. Franz Illescue and his team stood waiting, gowned and prepared outside the sterilizing field.

Honor felt her hands tightening on her spouses', and forced herself to relax—physically, at least—before she did any damage. Hamish leaned towards her, pressing the side of his head briefly and gently to hers, and she smiled. Then she bent beside Emily's life-support chair and pressed her own cheek against Emily's.

"I never thought I'd see this," Emily whispered in her ear.

"Just wait a couple of months," Honor whispered back, and Emily looked up at her with an enormous smile.

"It'll be hard. But at least it looks like you'll be able to be here then, too."

"We can hope," Honor agreed, and straightened back up.

She glanced over her shoulder, and her lips twitched as she glanced at Nimitz and Samantha. Dr. Illescue and she weren't exactly friends, and she doubted they ever would be, but their relationship had become much more cordial since his apology and her acceptance of it. Still, he and Briarwood had seemed a bit nonplussed by the notion of having a pair of six-limbed, furry arboreals in attendance during a birthing. And the passel of armed security personnel standing behind the parents—all three of them—and the living grandparents, seven-year-old aunt and uncle, plus the unofficial aunts and uncles and the godparents—had only added to the staff's consternation. They were accustomed to having the immediate family present at such times, but this "immediate family" had challenged them.

Which was why they were gathered in the observation gallery of a full-scale operating room, rather than one of the smaller, more intimate delivery rooms normally used. Briarwood simply hadn't had a regular delivery room large enough to accommodate the crowd.

Colonel Andrew LaFollet, Captain Spencer Hawke, Sergeant Jefferson McClure, Sergeant Tobias Stimson, and Corporal Joshua Atkins stood between the parents' family and the observation gallery's single entrance in a solid wall of Harrington green. Alfred and Allison Harrington stood side-by-side, each with an arm around the other, to Emily's left. Faith and James stood in front of their parents, watching with huge eyes and most imperfectly suppressed excitement. Lindsey Phillips, their nanny, stood beside them, keeping a watchful eye peeled, and Miranda LaFollet and James MacGuiness stood to Hamish's right, with Farragut cradled in Miranda's arms. Willard Neufsteiler and Austen Clinkscales had arrived from Grayson for the event, accompanied by Katherine Mayhew and Howard Clinkscales' widows, and Michelle Henke, Alice Truman, and Alistair McKeon completed the party.

Almost, that was. The Queen of Manticore and her Consort were also present, along with *their* treecats, and half a dozen of the Queen's Own to bolster the Harrington security cordon. Not to mention the additional security clamped around the *outside* of the building.

No wonder *Illescue's people seemed a bit boggled by the guest list*, Honor thought, suppressing a sudden, almost overwhelming temptation to giggle. *Nerves*, she told herself sternly. *That's nerves talking, Honor.*

As if Illescue had felt her thinking about him, the doctor looked up at the observation window, nodded once, and beckoned his team forward.

It's a routine procedure he performs every day, Honor reminded herself. *A routine procedure. Nothing to worry about. Shut up, pulse!*

She breathed deeply, drawing on decades of martial arts training, but it was hard, hard. She wanted to stand on tiptoe, press her nose to the glass, to strain for the first glance, the first sight. She wanted to wrap her arms around Emily and Hamish, to sing. She felt Nimitz and Samantha with her, sharing her excitement and her joy, and she suddenly realized no other human being had ever shared the moment of her child's birth with a mated pair of treecats.

On the other side of the glass, Illescue and his team opened the unit. The inner chamber rose smoothly, and Honor found herself holding her breath, knew that despite her best efforts she was crushing Hamish's hand—she'd engaged the governor on her left hand to protect Emily—as she saw their unborn son floating in the amniotic fluid. The child stirred, kicking, drifting, and she felt the thread of his own sleepy, unformed wonder, as if he sensed the impending moment, even through the corona of joy rising about her. The emotions of her family and friends were like some enormous sea, deep, intense, and powerful, yet focused. Not precisely *peaceful*, yet equally not tempestuous. They were vibrant, quivering with anticipation like a strummed guitar string, and so brightly, warmly supportive—so *happy* for her—that tears blurred Honor's vision.

Illescue tapped buttons on a console, and the top of the inner chamber slid open. A fibrous-looking mat floated on the fluid, and he used a vibro scalpel to slice it open. The umbilical cord had been attached to the mat, and it coiled lazily as his gloved, sterile hands reached down and lifted the tiny, fragile, infinitely precious body.

Honor's lungs insisted that she breathe. She ignored them, her entire being focused on Illescue's gentle, competent hands as he and his team severed the umbilical and cleaned the air passages, and the baby's emotions shifted abruptly.

She closed her eyes, reaching out with mental hands, trying to touch the infant mind-glow as drowsy contentment turned into fear and confusion, shock as he left the soft, warm safety of the womb for the cold and frightening unknown. She felt him protesting, squirming, fighting to return, and then, in a fashion she knew she would never be able to explain to another human being, Nimitz and Samantha were with her. And so was Farragut, and behind him came Ariel and Monroe.

The treecats reached out with her as the first, thin squall of protest sounded, and suddenly, as easily as slipping her hand into a glove, she touched him. Touched him as she had never touched another human being, even Hamish. It was as if her hand had reached out into the dark, and a smaller, warmer, utterly trusting hand had found it with unerring accuracy.

The squalling complaint stopped. The infant eyes moved, unable to focus and yet sensing the direction of the warm, comforting welcome, the love and the eagerness flowing from Honor into him. His was an unformed presence, and yet he knew her. He *recognized* her, and she felt the unhappiness and fear flowing out of him as he nestled close to her.

Her outer vision wavered, vanishing into the blur of tears, and she felt Hamish's arms around her. She tasted his love for her, for their son, for Emily, rising to engulf her. She clung to him, without ever releasing Emily's hand, and in that moment, she knew her entire life had been worthwhile.

The baby squirmed, protesting the intrusion of other hands, of instruments, as he was weighed, examined, evaluated. But even as he squirmed, face wrinkled in newborn concentration, tiny mouth moving, eyes squeezed indignantly shut, she cuddled him in immaterial, steel-strong hands of love. And then he was a tiny, red-faced, neatly wrapped bundle in Illescue's hands as the doctor carried him out of the delivery room to his waiting parents.

Illescue stepped into the gallery, his face one huge smile, and for once Honor tasted no trace of his prickly personality, his innate sense of superiority. There was only the pleasure, the sense of wonder and renewal, which had drawn an arrogant aristocrat into the world of medicine's most joyous specialization in the first place, and she smiled back at him, holding out her hands eagerly, as he crossed to her.

"Your Grace," he said softly, "meet your son."

Honor's lips trembled as she gathered the tiny, tiny weight carefully to her. She could have held him stretched along one forearm, his head cupped in the palm of her hand, and she stared down at the ancient, eternally new miracle in her arms. His eyes slipped open once again, moving, unfocused and yet seeking the loving presence wrapped about him like another blanket, and she lifted him to her breast. She held him close, inhaling the indescribable newborn smell of him, feeling the incredibly smooth, fragile skin against her own cheek. She crooned softly, and his lips moved, nuzzling her. Perhaps he was only searching for a nipple with newborn hunger, but fresh tears of joy spilled down her cheeks.

"Welcome to the world, baby," she whispered into his ear, then lowered him and brushed a kiss across his forehead. She turned to Hamish and Emily, stooping beside Emily's life-support chair, holding him out to them, and Emily brushed aside her own tears so that they could see their son together.

Honor looked up as her father and mother stepped close behind her, and her mother rested both hands on her shoulders.

"He's beautiful," Allison Harrington said, and smiled tenderly as she reached past her daughter to touch her first grandchild's cheek. "You may not believe that, right this minute," she continued, brushing the tip of her finger across the screwed-up, still somehow indignant face, "but give him a little while. He'll knock your socks off."

"He already has," Emily said, and looked up at Honor and Hamish. "My God, he already has."

Honor smiled at her, blinking on her own tears, and then she straightened and turned. She stepped past Emily and Hamish, past a beaming Elizabeth Winton and Justin Zyrr-Winton, past a crooning Nimitz and Samantha, and faced Andrew LaFollet.

"This is my son," she said to them all, her eyes locked with the man who had been her personal armsman for so many years, "Raoul Alfred Alistair Alexander-Harrington. Flesh of my flesh, bone of my bone, heir of heart and life, of power and title. I declare him before you all, as my witnesses and God's."

"He is your son," Austen Clinkscales replied, bowing deeply. "So witness we all."

"This is my son," she repeated more softly, speaking only to LaFollet, "and I name you guardian and protector. I give his life into your keeping. Fail not in this trust."

LaFollet looked back at her, then dropped to one knee, resting his hand lightly on the blanket-wrapped baby, and met her eyes unflinchingly.

"I recognize him," he said, his voice soft yet clear as he spoke the ancient formula, "and I know him. I take his life into my keeping, flesh of your flesh, bone of your bone. Before God, Maker and Tester of us all; before His Son, Who died to intercede for us all; and before the Holy Comforter, I will stand before him in the Test of life and at his back in battle. I will protect and guard his life with my own. His honor is my honor, his heritage is mine to guard, and I will fail not in this trust, though it cost me my life."

His voice fogged on the final sentence, and his eyes were suspiciously bright as he rose from his knee. Honor smiled at him, and worked one tiny, preposterously delicate hand free of the swaddling blanket. LaFollet extended his own hand, fingers opened, and she placed her son's palm against his.

"I accept your oath in his name. You are my son's sword and his shield. His steps are yours to watch and guard, to ward and instruct."

LaFollet said nothing more, only bent his head in a slight yet profound bow, and then stepped back. Honor bent her own head to him, tasting and sharing both his joy and his deep, bittersweet regret, and then she turned back to the others.

"Faith, James," she said to her brother and sister, going down on one knee, "come meet your nephew."

"This is still going to take some getting used to," Hamish murmured into Honor's ear as they walked slowly down the central aisle of King Michael's Cathedral on either side of Emily's life-support chair.

"What?" Honor murmured back, looking down at the sleeping infant clasped carefully in his arms. "Fatherhood?"

"That, too," he said from the corner of his mouth, and then somehow managed to flick his head without actually moving it to indicate the four green-uniformed men walking behind them.

Honor didn't have to look. Andrew LaFollet was there, of course, as Raoul's personal armsman. Spencer Hawke walked directly behind her, and she tasted the combination of his pride and apprehensive sense of responsibility at his promotion to *her* personal armsman. But she knew it was Tobias Stimson and Jefferson McClure to whom Hamish actually referred.

"I warned you and Emily both," she whispered to him as they approached the baptismal font. "And at least you each got off with only *one* armsman."

Emily snorted quietly between them, and Hamish glanced across at both of them eyes twinkling, then smoothed his expression into solemnity as they reached the font and Archbishop Telmachi turned to face them. Father O'Donnell stood beside the archbishop, prepared to assist, and Telmachi smiled and opened his arms in an inviting gesture.

There was a stir behind them as Raoul's godparents assembled.

"Beloved," Telmachi said, "we have gathered here to baptize this child. As he is the child of two planets, so also is he the child of God in two traditions. We have examined the doctrine of the Church of Humanity Unchained, as the Church of Humanity Unchained has examined that of Mother Church. We find no irreconcilable conflict between them, and as this child stands heir to high office and titles in both of his worlds, we baptize him here in God's most Holy Name for both Mother Church and the Church of Humanity Unchained."

He paused a moment, then smiled and turned his attention to the parents.

"Has this Child been already baptized, or not?"

"He has not," Honor, Hamish, and Emily replied in unison, and Telmachi nodded.

"Dearly beloved, inasmuch as our Savior has said none can enter into the kingdom of God, unless he be regenerate and born anew of Water and the Holy Ghost, I beseech you to call upon God, that through our Lord Jesus Christ, he will of his bounteous mercy grant to this Child that which by nature he cannot have; that he may be baptized with Water and the Holy Ghost, and received into Christ's holy Communion, and be made a living member of the same.

"Let us pray."

Honor bowed her head, and Telmachi's beautifully trained voice continued.

"Almighty and immortal God, the aid of all in need, the helper of all who flee to You for succor, the life of those who believe, and the resurrection of the dead; we call upon You for this child, that he, coming to Your holy Baptism, may receive remission of sin by spiritual regeneration. Receive him, O Lord, as You have promised by Your well-beloved Son, saying, ask, and you shall have; seek, and you shall find; knock, and it shall be opened unto you. So give now unto us who ask; let us who seek find; open the gate unto us who knock; that this Child may enjoy the everlasting benediction of Your heavenly washing, and may come to the eternal kingdom, which You have promised by Christ our Lord. Amen."

"Amen," the response came back, and he smiled, looking directly into the parents' eyes.

"Hear the word of the Gospel, written by Saint Mark, in the tenth Chapter, at the thirteenth Verse.

"They brought young children to Christ, that he should touch them: and his disciples rebuked those who brought them. But when Jesus saw it, he was much displeased, and said to them, Let the children come to me, and do not forbid them, for of such is the kingdom of God. Truly, I say to you, whosoever shall not receive the kingdom of God like a little child, he will not enter therein. And He took them up in His arms, put His hands upon them, and blessed them.

"And now, being persuaded of the good will of our heavenly Father towards this child, declared by His Son Jesus Christ; let us all faithfully and devoutly give thanks to Him, and say,

"Almighty and everlasting God," Telmachi prayed, joined by the gathered celebrants' voices, "heavenly Father, we give You humble thanks that You have vouchsafed to call us to the knowledge of Your Grace, and to faith in You. Increase this knowledge, and confirm this faith in us forever. Give Your Holy Spirit to this child, that he may be born again, and be made an heir of everlasting salvation. Through our Lord Jesus Christ, Who lives and reigns with You and the same Holy Spirit, now and forever. Amen."

Telmachi paused, then beckoned once more. In the Grayson tradition, there were four godparents: two godfathers and two godmothers, and Honor smiled as Elizabeth Winton, Justin Zyrr-Winton, Katherine Mayhew, and Alistair McKeon stepped up on either side of the parents.

"Dearly beloved," Telmachi said to them, "you have brought this child here to be baptized; you have prayed that our Lord Jesus Christ would receive him, would release him from sin, would sanctify him with the Holy Ghost, and would give to him the kingdom of heaven and everlasting life.

"Do you, therefore, in the name of this Child, renounce the devil and all his works, the vain pomp and glory of the world and all covetous desires of the same, and the sinful desires of the flesh, so that you will not follow, nor be led by them?"

"I renounce them all," the godparents replied in unison, "and by God's help, will endeavor not to follow nor be led by them."

"Do you believe all the articles of the Christian Faith, as contained in the Apostles' Creed?"

"I do."

"And will you be baptized in this Faith?"

"That is my desire."

"Will you obediently keep God's holy will and commandments, and walk in the same all the days of your life?"

"I will, by God's help."

"Having now, in the name of this Child, made these promises, will you also on your part take care that this Child learn the Creed, the Lord's Prayer, and the Ten Commandments, and all those things which a Christian ought to know and believe for his soul's health?"

"I will, by God's help."

"Will you take care that this Child, so soon as he may be sufficiently instructed and of an age to reaffirm these vows in his own right, and of his own will, be brought before the Bishop or Reverend to be confirmed by him?"

"I will, by God's help."

"Oh merciful God, grant that as Christ died and rose again, so this Child may die to sin and rise to newness of life. Amen."

"Amen."

"Grant that all sinful affections may die in him, and that all things belonging to the Spirit may live and grow. Amen."

"Amen."

"Grant that he may have power and strength to have victory, and to triumph against the devil, the world, and the flesh. Amen."

"Amen."

"Grant that whoever is here dedicated to You by our office and ministry, may also be imbued with heavenly virtues, and everlastingly rewarded to Your mercy, oh blessed Lord God, who lives, and governs all things, worlds without end. Amen."

"Amen."

"The Lord be with you."

"And with you."

"Lift up your hearts."

"We lift them up to God."

"Let us give thanks to our Lord God."

"It is meet and right to do so."

"It is very meet, right, and our bounden duty, that we should give thanks to You, Oh Lord, Holy Father, Almighty and Everlasting God, for Your dearly beloved Son, Jesus Christ, for the forgiveness of our sins, did shed out of His most precious side both water and blood, and gave commandment to His disciples, that they should go teach all nations, and baptize them in the Name of the Father, and of the Son, and of the Holy Ghost. Receive, we beseech You, the supplications of Your congregation. Sanctify this Water to the mystical washing away of sin, and grant that this Child, now to be baptized therein, may receive the fullness of Your Grace, and remain always in the number of Your faithful children; through the same Jesus Christ our Lord, to whom, with You, in the unity of the Holy Spirit, be all honor and glory, now and forever. Amen."

"Amen."

Telmachi reached out, and Raoul stirred, rolling his head as the Archbishop took him into his arms and looked once again at the godparents.

"Name this Child."

"Raoul Alfred Alistair," Elizabeth Winton replied clearly, and Telmachi bent to the font, cupping up some of the water in his palm. He poured it gently over Raoul's dark fuzz of hair, and the baby promptly began to wail.

"Raoul Alfred Alistair," Telmachi said through Raoul's lusty protests, "I baptize you in the name of the Father, and of the Son, and of the Holy Ghost. Amen."

"Amen."

"I've been wondering what to get Raoul for a christening gift," Elizabeth III said quietly to Honor as they walked out of the cathedral onto its well guarded front steps.

"You already gave it," Honor said, equally quietly, turning to look at her Queen.

"I did?" Elizabeth quirked one eyebrow.

"Yes, you did." Honor smiled. "It should be arriving in Nouveau Paris in about three more days."

"Oh. That." Elizabeth couldn't quite restrain a slight grimace, but Honor only nodded.

"I can think of much worse christening gifts than a peace treaty ending an interstellar war, Elizabeth."

Chapter Fifty

"It's on, Tom."

Thomas Theisman looked at the smiling face on his com and felt himself smiling in response.

"The official reply is here?" he asked, and Eloise Pritchart nodded.

"The dispatch boat got in about five hours ago. The Manticoran delegation will meet us on Torch in two months. We'll have to depart in about three weeks—twenty days, to be precise—to meet them."

"That's wonderful, Eloise!"

"Yes, it is," Pritchart agreed, but then her face sobered. "In a way, though, it's even worse."

"Worse?" Theisman repeated, surprised.

"I've got to sit down across the table from a woman who detests everything she thinks the Republic of Haven stands for and somehow convince her to make peace with the people who attacked her star nation on my personal orders." She shook her head. "I've had easier chores in my life."

"I know," he replied. "But we've got to try."

"We've got to do more than *try*, Tom." Pritchart's expression firmed up, and she shook her head again, this time with a completely different emphasis. "I'm coming home with a peace treaty. One way or the other. Even if it means telling Elizabeth what we suspect about Giancola."

"Are you certain about that? About telling her, I mean? It

could blow up in our faces, you know. We've all heard about her temper, and if anyone ever had a right to be pissed to the max, she does. If she finds out we let Giancola manipulate us, especially after we accused *her* government of being the guilty party, Lord only knows how she may react."

"She's going to find out eventually, anyway," Pritchart pointed out. "And as you suggested, Harrington's going to be present. Hopefully, she really will have a moderating influence. But I actually suspect the treecats are going to be even more important, assuming the Manty reports on their capabilities are accurate. I think I'm willing to take a chance on telling her the truth, as long as I can do it face-to-face, with the treecats there to prove to her that I *am* telling the truth."

"I hope you haven't mentioned this particular brainstorm to Leslie?" Theisman's smile was only half humorous, and Pritchart chuckled.

"She's unhappy enough about going to Torch for the summit in the first place. I don't think she needs to know exactly what sort of diplomatic *faux pas* I'm prepared to commit if it seems necessary after we get there."

Admiral Sir James Bowie Webster, Baron of New Dallas, and the Star Kingdom of Manticore's ambassador to the Solarian League, regarded his morning's schedule with scant favor.

"This is goddamned ridiculous," he grumbled to Sir Lyman Carmichael, his assistant ambassador.

"What's ridiculous?" Carmichael responded, as if they hadn't had this identical conversation every Monday morning since Webster's arrival on Old Earth.

"This." Webster thumped a rather large fist on the hardcopy printout of his agenda, then opened his hand and waved it around his palatial office. "*All* this crap! I'm a naval officer, not a frigging *diplomat*!"

"Traditional prejudices aside," Carmichael replied mildly, "a career in diplomacy isn't quite the same as seeking employment in a brothel. And *don't*—" he raised an admonishing index finger as Webster opened his mouth "—don't tell me that's because whores have more principles!"

"All right, I won't. Especially," Webster grinned, "since you already appear to realize that yourself."

"One of these days," Carmichael promised him. "One of these days."

Webster laughed and leaned back behind his desk.

"Actually, my cousin, the Duke, would be better at this than I am, Lyman. You know that as well as I do."

"I've had the pleasure of knowing your cousin for many years now," Carmichael said. "I have immense respect for him, and he really is a skilled diplomat. Having said all that, I truly don't think he could do the job you've been doing."

"Now *that*," Webster said, "really *is* ridiculous!"

"No, it isn't. Your status as a naval officer, especially one who's held the offices you've held, is part of the reason, of course." Carmichael smiled. "One reason the Star Kingdom's traditionally assigned military officers and ex-military officers as our ambassadors to the League is the fact that they have a certain fascinating effect on Solly politicos. They don't see very many real military people at this level, and that rather blunt directness you Navy types seem to acquire contrasts quite nicely with the mouthfuls of platitudes and careful political maneuvering they're accustomed to.

"But mostly, in your case, to be honest, it's the fact that you don't lie worth a damn, Jim."

"I beg your pardon?" Webster blinked, and Carmichael chuckled.

"I said you don't lie worth a damn. In fact, you're so bad at it that the two or three times I've seen you try, the people you were talking to simply assumed you were deliberately *pretending* to lie in order to make a point."

Webster regarded him narrowly, and Carmichael shrugged.

"You're simply an honest man. It comes across. And that's rare—very rare—for someone operating at the level you currently are. Especially here." Carmichael grimaced. "There's a taint of decadence in the air here on Old Earth, which may be why honesty's so rare. But why ever it is, they don't really understand you, in a lot of ways, because you do come out of the military, and very few of them do. But when you say something, personally or as the Queen's representative, they're confident you're telling them the truth. At the moment, especially with the dispute over our correspondence with the Peeps and the shenanigans in the Talbott Cluster, that's incredibly important, Jim. Don't undervalue yourself."

Webster waved one hand, as if he were uncomfortable with Carmichael's explanation.

"Maybe," he said, then shook himself. "Speaking of the Peeps, how do you feel about this summit meeting Pritchart's proposed?"

"I was surprised," Carmichael admitted, accepting the change of subject. "It's a very unusual departure, especially for the Havenites. In fact, it's so unusual, I'm inclined to think she really must be serious."

"God, that would be an enormous relief," Webster said frankly. "I don't like this Talbott business. There's more going on than we think. I'm sure of it. I just can't put my finger on what it is. But it's there, and I can't shake the feeling that in the long run, it may be even more dangerous to us than the Peeps are."

Carmichael sat back in his chair, even his trained diplomat's face showing surprise, and Webster barked a harsh laugh.

"I haven't lost my mind, Lyman. And I'm not blind to the current military situation—trust me on that one. But the Republic of Haven is small beer compared to the Solarian League, and if Mesa—and you know as well as I do that Terekhov is right about Mesa's involvement—can maneuver Frontier Security into doing its dirty work, the situation will be a thousand times worse. And the Sollies are arrogant enough that a lot of their so-called political leaders wouldn't even care."

"You're probably right," Carmichael said, forced to concede the point, however much he disliked doing so. "But you seriously think there's more to what's going on in Talbott than Mesa's traditional efforts to keep us as far away from them as possible?"

"Look at the scale of their effort," Webster said. "We're talking billions—*lots* of billions—of dollars worth of battlecruisers. Somebody ponied up the cash to pay for them, not to mention obviously orchestrating the efforts of OFS, local terrorists, and an entire star nation as a proxy. That's a huge effort, and it's also more direct then Mesa or Manpower have been in the last couple of centuries. Hell, since Edward Saganami!"

"But couldn't that simply be because of how threatening they find our proximity and because they know how distracted by Haven we are? I mean, they know we don't have a lot of resources to commit against them."

"I'm convinced that's an element in their thinking," Webster agreed, "but they're still coming further out of the shadows—not just with us; with the Sollies, as well. They're running the risk of coming to the surface, and they've always been bottom feeders before." He shook his head. "No. There's a whole new flavor to this one, and that makes me nervous."

"Now you're making *me* nervous," Carmichael complained. "Can't we just deal with one crisis at a time?" he added rather plaintively.

"I wish." Webster drummed on his desk for a moment, then shrugged. "Actually, I suppose we are, assuming this summit idea produces something. And in the meantime, I'm afraid it also means we have to make nice with the Peep ambassador and his people, at least in public."

"Well, we'll have the opportunity tonight," Carmichael said philosophically.

"I know," Webster said glumly. "And I *hate* the opera, too."

"Are we ready?"

"Yes." Roderick Tallman thought of himself as a "facilitator," and he was good at his job. Despite the fact that he was required to maintain an extremely low profile because of the nature of the things he "facilitated," there was always work waiting for him, and he knew without any sense of false modesty that he was indispensable.

"The money's in place?"

"Yes," Tallman said, managing not to sound wearily patient. He *did* know how to do his job, after all. "The credit transfers have been made, backdated, and then erased ... mostly. I handled the computer side myself." He smiled and shook his head. "The Havenites really ought to hire a good Solarian firm to update their systems security. It shouldn't have been this easy to hack."

"Count your blessings," his current employer said sourly. "Their accounting software may be vulnerable, but we've tried about four times to break into their other secured files without much luck. Actually, I suspect you got into their banking programs from the Solly end, didn't you?"

"Well, yes," Tallman admitted. "I invaded their interface with their banks."

"That's what I thought." His employer shook her head. "Don't take this personally, but a lot of Sollies make some rather unjustified assumptions about their technological superiority.

One of these days, that may turn around and bite all of you on the ass. Hard."

"I suppose anything's possible." Tallman shrugged. It wasn't as if anyone could *threaten* the League, after all. The very idea was preposterous.

"Well," his employer said, "if that's all taken care of, I suppose you'd appreciate your fee."

"You suppose correctly," Tallman told her.

"The most important thing of all," she said, not hurrying to hand over the untraceable hard copy bearer bond certificate, "is that this particular manipulation be completely untraceable. The *only* place it can lead is back to the Havenites."

"I understood that from the beginning." Tallman leaned back slightly in his chair. "You know my reputation. That's why you came to me in the first place, because my work is guaranteed and I've never had a client burned. The hard part wasn't making the actual changes. The *hard part* was simultaneously infiltrating four separate secure storage sites to get at the bank's backup files. Well that," he allowed himself the lazy, arrogant smile of a top professional, "and leaving exactly the right footprints. When the bank examiners pull their files, they're going to find that the Havenites managed to infiltrate *three* of their sites but failed to spot number four. That's where I nested the backup file that does show the transactions. It's actually rather neat, if I do say so myself. If they look *really* closely, they'll discover that those nasty Havenite hackers managed to erase the transactions from the sites they knew about, but the fourth file—that one is going to hang them. Trust me, when the examiners track this one back, they'll even be able to identify the terminal in the embassy where the transactions were supposed to have been entered."

"Good!" She smiled. "That's exactly what I needed to hear. And now, for your fee."

She reached into her smartly tailored jacket, and Tallman let his chair come back fully upright, reaching out his hand—then froze in shock.

"Wh—?" he began, but he never finished the question, for the pulser in her hand snarled. The burst of darts hit him at the base of the throat and tracked upwards across his neck and the left side of his face, with predictably gruesome results.

His employer grimaced with distaste, but she'd been careful to sit further back than usual. She was outside the splatter pattern, and she dropped the pulser on the desk, straightened her jacket fastidiously, and let herself out of the office. She walked down the hallway and took the lift to the parking garage, where she climbed into her air car and flew calmly off. Five minutes later, she landed several miles away from the late, lamented Tallman's office building.

This parking garage was in a much less desirable part of town. Most of the vehicles parked here were old, battered. The sort of things youth gangs looking for a quick credit would turn up their noses at.

She parked her own new-model, expensive sports vehicle in a stall beside one such battered, grimy air car, and climbed out into the shadows. She looked around carefully, then took a small handset from her pocket and pressed a button. Her face seemed to ripple and shudder indescribably, and her complexion—not just on her face, but everywhere—shifted abruptly, darkening and coarsening, as the nanotech which had coated every millimeter of her body turned itself off. The invisibly tiny machines released their holds, drifting away on the morning breeze, and in place of the rather tall, blonde woman who had murdered Roderick Tallman, there stood a dark-faced man, slightly below the average in height, with a wiry, muscular build and a bosom.

He grimaced and reached inside his shirt, removing the padding, and tossed it into the back seat of his air car. A quick squirt from a small aerosol can, and the padding dissipated into a wispy fog.

He adjusted his clothing slightly, then unlocked the grimy vehicle beside the air car in which he had arrived. He settled himself at the controls, brought up the counter-grav, and flew calmly away. He inserted the vehicle into one of the capital city's outbound traffic lanes, switched in the autopilot, and leaned back in his seat, wondering idly whether or not the vehicle he'd abandoned had been picked up and stripped yet.

If it hadn't, it would be very shortly, of that he was confident.

Sir James Bowie Webster smiled pleasantly, despite the fact that his teeth badly wanted to grit themselves, as he stepped out of his official diplomatic limousine in front of the Greater New Chicago Opera House. He'd never liked opera, even at the best of times, and the fact that the Sollies prided themselves that they did this—like everything else—better than anyone else in the known universe irritated him even more.

If pressed, Webster was prepared to admit that the citizens of planets like Old Earth and Beowulf at least meant well. The fact that they had little more clue than a medieval peasant about things that went on outside their own pleasant little star systems was unfortunate, but it didn't result from any inherent malevolence. Or even stupidity, really. They were simply too busy with the things that mattered to them to think much about problems outside their own mental event horizon. But the fact that they complacently believed that the Solarian League, with its huge, corrupt bureaucracies and self-serving, manipulative elites, was still God's gift to the galaxy made it difficult, sometimes, to remember that most of their sins were sins of omission, not commission.

At least he and Carmichael were making some progress dealing with the bloody events in Talbott. Accounts of the Battle of Monica were really only just beginning to trickle in to Old Earth, and from everything he'd seen so far, the revelations were going to get worse, before they got better. The good news, he supposed, was that it was remotely possible even the Solarian public might get exercised over such flagrant—

Webster never saw the pulser in the hand of the Havenite ambassador's chauffeur.

"*What?* What did you say?" William Alexander, Baron Grantville, demanded incredulously.

"I said Jim Webster's been shot," Sir Anthony Langtry said, his face ashen, his voice that of a man who couldn't—or didn't want to—believe what he heard himself saying.

"He's *dead?*"

"Yes. He and his bodyguard were killed almost instantly, right outside the Opera House, of all goddamned places!"

"Jesus." Grantville closed his eyes on a stab of pain. He'd known James Webster most of his life. They'd been personal friends, but not nearly so close as Webster and Hamish had been. This was going to hit his brother hard, and the entire Star Kingdom was going to be stunned—and enraged—by the highly popular admiral's death.

"What happened?" he asked after a moment.

"That's the really bad part," Langtry said grimly. The Foreign Secretary had come to Grantville's office in person with the news, and something about his tone sent a chill down Grantville's spine.

"Just the fact that he's dead is bad enough for me, Tony," the Prime Minister said a bit more tartly than he'd really intended to, and Langtry raised a hand, acknowledging the point.

"I know that, Willie. And I'm sorry if it sounded like I didn't. I didn't know him as well as you and Hamish, but what I did know about him, I liked a lot. Unfortunately, in this instance, the *way* he was killed really is worse."

The Foreign Secretary drew a deep breath.

"He and one of his bodyguards were shot and killed by the Peep ambassador's personal driver."

"*What?!*"

Despite all his years of political training and a basic personality which remained calm in the face of disaster, Grantville erupted to his feet behind his desk, leaning forward over it to brace both hands on its top. Eyes of Alexander blue blazed with consternation—and rage—and for just a moment it looked as if he intended to vault physically across the desk.

Langtry didn't reply. He simply sat, waiting for the Prime Minister to work through his shock the same way *he* had when the news first hit his office. It took several seconds, and then, slowly, Grantville settled back into his chair, still staring at Langtry.

"That's what happened," Langtry said finally, after the Prime Minister had seated himself once more. "In fact, it's pretty damned open and shut. The driver's dead, of course—Webster's second security man nailed him, and three Solly cops at the Opera as additional security saw the whole thing. In fact, one of them got his sidearm out in time to put at least one dart of his own into the driver, and one of the others got the entire thing on his shoulder cam. It's all on chip, and they sent the visual record out with the dispatch."

"My God," Grantville said, almost prayerfully.

"Wait, it gets better," Langtry said grimly. "The driver wasn't a Havenite national. He was a Solly, provided by the limo service with the transportation contract for the Peeps New Chicago embassy."

"A Solly," Grantville repeated carefully.

"A Solly," Langtry confirmed, "who's received the equivalent of just over a hundred and twenty-five thousand Manticoran dollars over the past half T-year—seventy-five thousand of them in the last three weeks—in unrecorded, unreported credit transfers from a Havenite diplomatic account."

Grantville stared at him, far beyond consternation and into the realm of pure shock.

"What could they have been *thinking*?" He shook his head. "Surely they didn't think they could get *away* with this?"

"I've asked myself both those questions. But, to be frank, there's another one that's far more pressing at the moment."

Grantville looked at the Foreign Secretary, who shrugged.

"Why?" he asked simply. "Why should they do this?"

"God *damn* them!" Elizabeth Winton snarled as she stormed back and forth like a caged tigress, pacing the carpet behind the chair in which she should have been sitting.

Her fury was a living, breathing thing in the conference room, and Ariel crouched on the back of her chair, ears glued flat to his skull, scimitar claws shredding its upholstery like kneading scalpels. Samantha was in little better condition, her eyes half-closed as she crouched on the back of Hamish Alexander-Harrington's chair and fought to resist the other 'cat's blazing rage.

"Don't these *fuckers* ever learn a goddamned *thing*?" Elizabeth hissed. "What the *hell* did they—"

"Just a minute, Elizabeth."

The Queen whirled back towards the table, her face still suffused with rage, as White Haven spoke.

"What?" she snapped.

"Just . . . calm down for a second," he said, his own expression that of a man who'd taken a physical wound. "Think. Jim Webster was my friend for over seventy T-years. You can't possibly be more furious about his murder than I am. But you just asked a very important question."

"What question?" she demanded.

"Don't they ever learn," he said. She glared at him, and he looked back steadily. "Don't misunderstand me. And don't think for an instant, if it turns out the Peeps did this, that I won't want them just as dead as you do. For God's sake, Elizabeth—they already tried to kill my *wife*!"

"And your point is?" she asked in a slightly more moderate tone.

"And my point is that this whole thing is *stupid*. Assume the

Peeps have access to whatever they used to make Timothy Meares try to kill Honor. In that case, why in *hell* would they choose their own ambassador's driver as their assassin? They could have picked someone with absolutely no connection to them, so they used *his* driver. Does that make any sense to you at all?"

"I—" Elizabeth began. Then she paused, obviously beginning to think at last.

"All right," she said, after a moment. "I'll grant that that's a legitimate question. But what about the credit transfers the Solly police turned up?"

"Ah, yes," White Haven said. "The credit transfers. Transfers made directly out of Havenite diplomatic funds. Not exactly the least incriminating payment method I've ever heard of. And if they used whatever they used against Honor, why bother to pay him at all? Let's not forget, that killer was on what anyone but an idiot must have recognized would be a suicide mission. Like the reports say, there were *police* eyewitnesses. At the very least, he was looking at certain arrest and conviction for murder. Would *you* do that for less than a hundred and fifty thousand dollars? How much good would the money do you lying dead on the sidewalk, or after it was confiscated by the courts when they convicted and sentenced you for murder? So if they could get him to do the job under those circumstances, the amount they could pay him certainly wasn't the controlling factor. And if it wasn't, why hand him money and establish a direct link between him and them in the first place?"

"Those are excellent questions, My Lord," Colonel Ellen Shemais acknowledged. Shemais' job as the head of Elizabeth's personal security detachment was at least half that of a spook. As a consequence, Elizabeth had made the colonel her liaison to the Special Intelligence Service, as well as her chief bodyguard.

"What do you mean, Ellen?" the Queen asked now.

"I mean Earl White Haven's objections are extremely well taken, Your Majesty," Shemais said. "It's got to be the stupidest way to arrange an ostensibly deniable assassination I've ever heard of, and the Queen's Own is something of an authority on the history of assassination."

"But according to this," Grantville said, tapping his own copy of the hard copy report from Old Earth, "they thought they'd erased all records of the payment. In fact, they did. It was only pure luck that they didn't pick up on the bank's extra security backup and change it, as well."

"I agree that it's possible we lucked out in that regard, Prime Minister," Shemais replied. "But the fact remains that they'd paid this man out of an official embassy account and then went back and *erased* the records. If they were going to pay him anything, why not pay him through a third-party cutout in the first place? For that matter, the Old Earth 'shadow' economy is riddled with conduits they could have used to pay him without leaving any record at all, much less one they'd have to go back and erase. Judging by the preliminary reports on the quality of the work they did on the backups they knew about, I'll grant that they probably felt completely confident that they'd buried their tracks. But why leave those tracks in the first place? And if they had a traceable connection to this man to begin with, why in God's name pick *him* as their assassin? They might as well have had their ambassador pull the trigger himself!"

"According to the last report ONI shared with the Foreign Office," Langtry said, "we still don't have a clue how they did whatever they did to Lieutenant Meares. There are all sorts of theories going around, but nothing solid. Still, at least one of them suggests that the lieutenant wasn't chosen just for his proximity to Duchess Harrington, but also because there was something unique about him. Possibly something in his medical or genetic background made him more vulnerable to whatever technique they're using. Is it possible that this fellow was the closest person they could lay hands on that fit whatever medical profile they need?"

"Possible, I suppose, Mr. Secretary," Shemais said. "And they did—or, at least, obviously thought they'd managed to—erase the direct financial connection between him and them. If it was a case of their needing someone with his specific profile, at least they went to a lot of effort to sanitize him. But to use their own ambassador's driver?" She shook her head. "Even granted that their hacker could eliminate the record of direct clandestine payments, the connection between him and their ambassador had to jump out and hit any investigator squarely between the eyes."

"Could they have counted on that?" Grantville wondered aloud. Everyone looked at him, and he shrugged. "If there's something to Tony's suggestion that this man may have had some quality they needed if they were going to use him the way they used

Lieutenant Meares, then maybe they decided to make the best of a bad bargain. If they had to use *him*, maybe they figured we'd be asking ourselves exactly these questions."

"A double-blind, you mean, Prime Minister?" Shemais said thoughtfully. "You're suggesting that they want us to think the connection is so obvious no halfway competent covert operations planner would go near it with a three-meter pole?"

"Something like that," Grantville agreed.

"I suppose it's remotely possible." Shemais frowned. "I don't say I think it's likely, though. But the bottom line is that either they didn't do it, and someone's gone to enormous lengths to convince us they did, or else they deliberately set it up this way to point a too obvious finger at themselves."

"Why would they do that, Ellen?" Elizabeth asked skeptically.

"As the Prime Minister already suggested, Your Majesty, making the best of a bad bargain. If there was some reason they *had* to use this particular man to pull the trigger, then they may have hoped the *surface* connection between them and him would be so blatant that they could scream they were being framed by a third-party. Which," she admitted, almost against her will, "I personally might have been inclined to place some credence in if it weren't for the history of payments and the fact that they went to such obvious pains to *erase* that history. Unfortunately for them, there was a previous financial relationship, plus the fact that, according to the bank investigators and the Solly police, they doctored the bank records at least a week *before* the assassination. Someone else might have found out that the man was on their payroll, which could have made him even more attractive from the prospect of framing them, but altering the records when they did indicates that they *knew* this was coming and wanted to be certain they'd cut the obvious linkage well ahead of time."

"So you think it *was* them, Colonel?" Langtry asked.

"I don't know what I think, Mr. Secretary. Not yet," the colonel said frankly. "I'd have to say there's a lot of circumstantial evidence indicating they did do it—as I say, the timing on the computer hack strongly suggests that they knew it was coming. But the tradecraft on this, assuming it was them, isn't just bad, it's atrocious. It's not just unprofessional, it's clumsy, especially for someone with as much institutional experience setting up assassinations as the old People's Republic. I suppose it's possible

Pritchart's purge of the old régime's security services cost them some expertise, but still . . . ."

"But if we're going to entertain the possibility that it wasn't them, who else could have wanted Jim dead?" Grantville asked.

"I can't answer that one, Prime Minister," Shemais admitted. "There could be any number of other people who might have had an interest in killing him. But an analyst can get herself into a lot of trouble by wandering off into too much speculation based on too little hard data, and there are two salient points which stand out to me. First, the timing. It could simply be a coincidence, but I'm naturally suspicious of coincidences, and while we're in the middle of a war with another star nation, the reasons *that* nation might want one of our ambassadors dead go to the head of my own queue. And second, this entire affair certainly does sound very similar to the attempt on Duchess Harrington's life. In that case, unlike this one, there's not much question about *why* the Peeps wanted her dead, but it's the similarity of technique that strikes me so strongly. When we think about who else could have wanted Admiral Webster dead, we also have to think about who would have the resources and technical capability to put his assassination together this way. From what happened in Duchess Harrington's case, it seems evident that the Peeps have it, but we don't have any evidence that anyone *else* does. And if it *wasn't* them, someone went to an awful lot of trouble to convince us it was."

"I don't think it was anyone else," Elizabeth growled. She was marginally less furious, and Ariel allowed her to lift him from the sadly shredded top of her chair as she seated herself at last. She settled the 'cat in her lap, and frowned harshly.

"I'm willing to admit at least the theoretical possibility that it wasn't the Peeps," she said, "but I don't believe it was someone else. I think it was them. I think they did it for some reason we can't know, possibly something Webster had found out on Old Earth that they didn't want us to learn about. Maybe even something he hadn't realized yet that he knew. Like you say, Ellen, we can't know what might have seemed like a logical reason to them. And as for the credit transfers, they could have had him doing something else before they picked him for this one."

"But—" Hamish began, only to have her cut him off with a quick, sharp shake of her head.

"No," she said. "I'm not going to play the think and double-think game. For now—for the moment—I'll operate on the assumption that it *may* not have been the Peeps. You've got that much. We'll go ahead with the summit, and we'll see what they have to say. I'd be lying if I said what's happened wasn't likely to make me a lot less willing to believe anything they say on Torch, but I'll go. But I'm getting incredibly tired of having these bastards murder people I care about, members of my government, and my ambassadors. This is it, as far as I'm willing to go."

Anthony Langtry looked as if he wanted to argue, but instead, he only closed his mouth and nodded, willing to settle for what he could get.

Elizabeth glared around the conference room one more time, then climbed back out of her damaged chair, nodded to her three cabinet secretaries, and left, accompanied by Colonel Shemais.

Chapter Fifty-One

"Where's Ruth?" Berry Zilwicki, Queen of Torch, asked plaintively.

"Saburo says she's running late, girl," Lara said, shrugging with the casual informality which was such a quintessential part of her.

The ex-Scrag was still about as civilized as a wolf, and she had a few problems grasping the finer points of court etiquette. Which, to tell the truth, suited Berry just fine. Usually, at least.

"If I've got to do this," the Queen said firmly, "Ruth has to do it with me."

"Berry," Lara said, "Kaja said she'll be here, and Saburo and Ruth are already on their way. We can go ahead and start."

"No." Berry flounced—that really was the only verb that fit—over to an armchair and plunked down in it. "I'm the Queen," she said snippily, "and I want my intelligence advisor there when I talk to these people."

"But your father isn't even on Torch," Lara pointed out with a grin. Thandi Palane's "Amazons" had actually developed senses of humor, and all of them were deeply fond of their commander's "little sister." Which was why they took such pleasure in teasing her.

"You *know* what I mean!" Berry shot back, rolling her eyes in exasperation. But there was a twinkle in those eyes, and Lara chuckled as she saw it.

"Yes," she admitted. "But tell me, why do you need Ruth? It's only a gaggle of merchants and businessmen." She wrinkled her nose in the tolerant contempt of a wolf for the sheep a bountiful nature had created solely to feed it. "Nothing to worry about in *that* bunch, girl!"

"Except for the fact that I might screw up and sell them Torch for a handful of glass beads!"

Lara looked at her, obviously puzzled, and Berry sighed. Lara and the other Amazons truly were trying hard, but it was going to take years to even begin closing the myriad gaps in their social skills and general background knowledge. Just as it had for *her*.

"Never mind, Lara," the teenaged Queen said after a moment. "It wasn't really all that funny a joke, anyway. But what I meant is that with Web tied up with Governor Barregos' representative, I need someone a little more devious to help hold my hand when I slip into the shark tank with these people. I need someone to advise me about what they really want, not just what they *say* they want."

"Make it plain anyone who cheats you gets a broken neck." Lara shrugged. "You may lose one or two, early, but the rest will know better. Want Saburo and me to handle it for you?"

She sounded almost eager, and Berry laughed. Saburo X was the ex-Ballroom gunman Lara had picked out for herself. Berry often suspected Saburo still didn't understand exactly how it had happened, but after a brief, wary, half-terrified, *extremely* . . . direct "courtship," he wasn't complaining. On the face of it, theirs was one of the most unlikely pairings in history—the ex-genetic-slave terrorist, madly in love with the ex-Scrag who'd worked directly for Manpower before she walked away from her own murderous past—and yet, undeniably, it worked.

"There *is* a certain charming simplicity to the idea of broken necks," Berry conceded, after a moment. "Unfortunately, that's not how it's done. I haven't been a queen for long, but I do know that much."

"Pity," Lara said, and glanced at her chrono. "They've been waiting over half an hour," she remarked.

"Oh, all right," Berry said. "I'll go—I'll go!" She shook her head and made a face. "You'd think a queen would at least be able to get away with *something* when her father is half a dozen star systems away!"

Harper S. Ferry stood in the throne room, arms crossed, watching the thirty-odd people standing about. He knew he didn't cut a particularly military figure, but that was fine with him. In fact, the ex-slaves of Torch had a certain fetish for *not* looking spit and polish. They were the galaxy's outcast mongrels, and they wanted no one—including themselves—to forget that.

Which didn't mean they took their responsibilities lightly.

Harper, for example. Looking at him, a casual observer would have seen a man, probably in his late thirties, of relatively average build—maybe just a bit more wiry than most—with dark hair and eyes, a swarthy complexion, and an expression arranged out of reasonably pleasant features. That same casual observer almost certainly wouldn't have realized that Harper S. Ferry had been one of the Audubon Ballroom's most efficient assassins since he was fourteen. In fact, Harper would have had to think very hard—and consult his diary—to recall all of the men and women he'd killed in his lifetime.

Nor did he regret what he'd done. Still, after long enough, a man got tired of killing, even when the scum he was removing from the universe were genetic slavers. Men and women who'd made fortunes off of the systematic sale, abuse, and torture of millions of genetic slaves just like Harper S. Ferry literally for centuries. If he could find another way to hurt them, he was prepared to embrace it, and the notion that jabbing a jagged, pointy stick directly into Manpower Incorporated's eye involved keeping an immensely lovable young girl alive had appealed to him from the beginning. And however casual he might look, he took absolutely no chances with Berry Zilwicki's safety.

And not just because she was so lovable. It wasn't often that a girl barely seventeen T-years old was critical to the survival of an entire planet of refuge, yet that was precisely what Berry Zilwicki was.

Judson Van Hale walked casually across the throne room, angling a bit closer to Harper. Judson had never been a slave himself, but his father had. Fortunately, the senior Van Hale had also found himself aboard a slave ship intercepted by a Royal Manticoran Navy light cruiser. The slaver in question had been equipped to jettison its crew of human beings into space to avoid embarrassing questions, and its crew had suffered a series of fatal exposures to vacuum themselves shortly after its interception. Most of the liberated slaves had become Manticoran subjects, and Judson had been born on Sphinx.

He was also one of exactly three of Torch's present citizens who'd been adopted by a treecat.

That made him an extremely valuable asset for the relatively small bodyguard force Queen Berry was prepared to tolerate. In addition, Harper suspected that the fact that Judson had come from Manticore also helped make him more acceptable to the Queen. He was like a breath of home, a reminder of the first place—the only place really—where Berry Zilwicki had ever felt completely safe.

"This is a lively bunch," Judson murmured disgustedly out of the corner of his mouth as he stopped beside Harper. "Genghis here is downright bored."

He reached up and caressed the cream-and-gray treecat riding on his shoulder, and the 'cat purred and pressed his head against Judson's hand.

"Boring is good," Harper replied quietly. "Exciting is bad."

"I know. Still, I'd sort of like to earn my magnificent salary. Nothing too exciting, you understand. Just enough to make me feel useful. Well, to make *us* feel useful," he corrected, scratching Genghis' chest.

"Thandi thinks you're useful," Harper pointed out. "That's good enough for me. *I'm* not going to argue with her, at any rate."

Judson laughed. Harper, unlike the Sphinx-born Judson, had rather fancied himself as a deadly hand-to-hand fighter. Having watched him in the training *salle*, Judson was inclined to agree with him. Unfortunately for Harper, Thandi Palane *wasn't* a deadly hand-to-hand fighter; she was a lethal force of nature who laughed at the merely deadly. As she'd demonstrated rather conclusively to Harper the first time he swaggered onto the mat with her.

She'd hardly hurt him at all, really. With quick heal, the broken bones had healed in just a few weeks.

"I think not arguing with Thandi is turning into Torch's planetary sport," Judson said now, and Harper chuckled.

"Aren't they running late?" Judson asked after a moment, and Harper shrugged.

"I don't have any place else I need to be today," he said. "And if Berry's running true to form, she's dragging her heels, waiting for Ruth. And Thandi, if she can get her here."

"Why *aren't* they here?"

"They're going over something to do with security for the summit, and according to the net," Harper tapped his personal com, "Thandi's sending Ruth on ahead while she finishes up." He shrugged again. "I'm not sure exactly what it is she's working on. Probably something about setting up liaison with Cachat."

"Oh, yeah. '*Liaison*,'" Judson said, rolling his eyes, and Harper slapped him lightly on the back of the head.

"No disrespectful thoughts about the Great Kaja, friend! Not unless you want her Amazons performing a double orchidectomy on you without anesthesia."

Judson grinned, and Genghis bleeked a laugh.

"Who's that guy over there?" Harper asked after a moment. "The fellow by the main entrance."

"The one in the dark blue jacket?"

"That's the one."

"Name's Tyler," Judson said. He punched a brief code into his memo pad and looked down at the display. "He's with New Age Pharmaceutical. It's one of the Beowulf consortiums. Why?"

"I don't know," Harper said thoughtfully. "Is Genghis picking up any sort of vibes from him?"

Both humans looked at the treecat, who raised a true hand in the thumb-folded, two-finger sign for the letter "N" and nodded it up and down. Judson looked back at Harper and shrugged.

"Guess not. Want us to stroll a bit closer and check him out again?"

"I don't know," Harper said again. "It's just—" He paused. "It's probably nothing," he went on after a moment. "It's just that he's the only one I see who's brought along a briefcase."

"Hm?"

Judson frowned, surveying the rest of the crowd.

"You're right," he acknowledged. "Odd, I suppose. I thought this was supposed to be primarily a 'social occasion.' Just a chance for them to meet Queen Berry as a group, before the individual negotiating sessions."

"That's what I thought, too," Harper agreed. He thought about it for a moment longer, then keyed a combination into his com.

"Yes, Harper?" a voice replied.

"The guy with the briefcase, Zack. You checked it out?"

"Ran the sniffer over it and had him open it," Zack assured

him. "Nothing in it but a microcomputer and a couple of perfume dispensers."

"Perfume?" Harper repeated.

"Yeah. I picked up some organic traces from them, but they were all consistent with cosmetics. Not even a flicker of red on the sniffer. I asked him about them, too, and he said they were gifts from New Age for the girls. I mean, Queen Berry and Princess Ruth."

"Had they been pre-cleared?" Harper asked.

"Don't think so. He said they were supposed to be surprises."

"Thanks, Zack. I'll get back to you."

Harper switched off the com and looked at Judson. Judson looked back, and the ex-Ballroom assassin frowned.

"I don't like surprises," he said flatly.

"Well, Berry and Ruth might," Judson countered.

"Fine. Surprise *them* all you want, but not their security. We're supposed to know about this kind of crap ahead of time."

"I know." Judson tugged at the lobe of his left ear, thinking. "It's almost certainly nothing, you know. Genghis would be picking up something from him by now if he had anything . . . unpleasant in mind."

"Maybe. But let's you and I sashay over that way and have a word with Mr. Tyler," Harper said.

William Henry Tyler stood in the throne room, waiting patiently with the rest of the crowd, and rubbed idly at his right temple. He felt a bit . . . odd. Not ill, really. He didn't even have a headache. In fact, if anything, he felt just a bit euphoric, although he couldn't think why.

He shrugged and checked his chrono. "Queen Berry"—he smiled slightly at the thought of the Torch monarch's preposterous youth; she was younger than the younger of Tyler's own two daughters—was obviously running late. Which, he supposed, was the prerogative of a head of state, even if she was only seventeen.

He glanced down at his briefcase and felt a brief, mild stir of surprise. It vanished instantly, in a stronger surge of that inexplicable euphoria. He'd actually been a bit startled when the security man asked him what was in the case. For just an instant, it had been as if he'd never seen it before, but then, of course, he'd remembered the gifts for Queen Berry and Prince Ruth. That had been a really smart idea on Marketing's part, he conceded. Every young woman he'd ever met had liked expensive perfume, whether she was willing to admit it or not.

He relaxed again, humming softly, at peace with the universe.

"All right, see? I'm here," Berry said, and Lara laughed.

"And so graceful you are, too," the Amazon said. "You who keep trying to 'civilize' us!"

"Actually," Berry said, reaching out to pat the older woman on the forearm, "I've decided I like you all just the way you are. My very own wolfpack. Well, Thandi's, but I'm sure she'll lend you to me if I ask. Just do me a favor and try not to get any blood on the furniture. Oh, and let's keep the orgies out of sight, too, at least when Daddy's around. Deal?"

"Deal, Little Kaja. I'll explain to Saburo about the orgies," Lara said, and it was perhaps an indication of the effect Berry Zilwicki had on the people about her that an ex-Scrag didn't even question the deep surge of affection she felt for her teenage monarch.

A slight stir went through the throne room as someone noticed the Queen and her lean, muscular bodyguard entering through the side door. The two of them moved across the enormous room, which had once been the ballroom of the planetary governor when Torch had been named Verdant Vista and owned by the planet Mesa. The men and women who'd come to meet the Queen of Torch were a little surprised by how very young she looked in person, and heads turned to watch her, although nobody was crass enough to start sidling in her direction until she'd seated herself in the undecorated powered chair which served her for a throne.

Harper S. Ferry and Judson Van Hale were still ten meters from the New Age Pharmaceutical representative when Tyler looked up and saw Berry. Unlike any of the other commercial representatives in the room, he took a step towards her the moment he saw her, and Genghis' head snapped up in the same instant.

The 'cat reared high, ears flattened and fangs bared in the sudden, tearing-canvas ripple of a treecat's war cry, and vaulted abruptly from his person's shoulder towards Tyler.

Tyler's head whipped around, and Harper felt a sudden stab of outright terror as he saw the terrible, fixed glare of the other man's eyes. There was something . . . insane about them, and Harper was suddenly reaching for the panic button on his gun belt.

The pharmaceutical representative saw the oncoming 'cat, and his free hand flashed across to the briefcase he was carrying. The briefcase with the "perfume" of which no one at New Age Pharmaceuticals had ever heard . . . and which Tyler didn't even remember taking from the man who'd squirted that odd mist in his face on Smoking Frog.

Genghis almost reached him in time. He launched himself from the floor in a snarling, hissing charge that hit Tyler's moving forearm perhaps a tenth of a second too late.

Tyler pressed the concealed button. The two canisters of "perfume" in the briefcase exploded expelling the binary neurotoxin which they had contained under several thousand atmospheres of pressure. Separated, its components had been innocuous, easily mistaken for perfume; combined, they were incredibly lethal, and they mingled and spread, whipping outward from Tyler under immense pressure even as the briefcase blew apart with a sharp, percussive crack.

Genghis stiffened, jerked once, and hit the floor a fraction of a second before Tyler, left hand mangled by the explosion of the briefcase, collapsed beside him. Harper's finger completed its movement to the panic button, and then the deadly cloud swept over him and Judson, as well. Their spines arched, their mouths opened in silent agony, and then they went down as a cyclone of death spread outward.

Lara and Berry did their best to maintain suitably grave expressions, despite their mutual amusement, as they walked towards Berry's chair. They were about halfway there when the sudden, high-pitched snarl of an enraged treecat ripped through the throne room.

They spun towards the sound, and saw a cream-and-gray blur streaking through the crowd. For an instant, Berry had no idea at all what was happening. But if Lara wasn't especially well socialized, she still had the acute senses, heightened musculature, and lightning reflexes of the Scrag she had been born.

She didn't know what had set Genghis off, but every instinct she had screamed "*Threat!*" And if she wouldn't have had a clue which fork to use at a formal dinner, she knew *exactly* what to do about that.

She continued her turn, right arm reaching out, snaking around Berry's waist like a python, and snatched the girl up. By the time Genghis was two leaps from Tyler, Lara was already sprinting towards the door through which they'd entered the throne room.

She heard the sharp crack of the exploding briefcase behind her just as the door opened again, and she saw Saburo and Ruth Winton through it. From the corner of her eye, she also saw the outrider of death scything towards her as the bodies collapsed in spasming agony, like ripples spreading from a stone hurled into a placid pool. The neurotoxin was racing outward faster than she could run; she didn't know what it was, but she knew it was invisible death . . . and that she could not outdistance it.

"*Saburo!*" she screamed, and snatched Berry bodily off the floor. She spun on her heel once, like a discus thrower, and suddenly Berry went arcing headfirst through the air. She flew straight at Saburo X, like a javelin, and his arms opened reflexively.

"The door!" Lara screamed, skittering to her knees as she overbalanced from throwing Berry. "Close the door! *Run!*"

Berry hit Saburo in the chest. His left arm closed about her, holding her tight, and his eyes met Lara's as her knees hit the floor. Brown eyes stared deep into blue, meeting with the sudden, stark knowledge neither of them could evade.

"I love you!" he cried . . . and his right hand hit the button to close the door.

Chapter Fifty-Two

"Not one word," Elizabeth Winton said flatly. "Not one word about why they might have done it, or who else might have wanted to do it."

Her Prime Minister and his Cabinet sat silently as she surveyed them with eyes of frozen brown ice. The different distances and travel times from the Sol System, via Beowulf, and Congo, via the Erewhon Junction, meant the messages had arrived just over twenty-four hours apart, and Queen Elizabeth was beyond fury now. She had entered a frozen realm, where hate burned colder then interstellar space.

"They killed Sir James and tried to kill Berry Zilwicki and my niece on the same damned *day*. All the available evidence from Old Terra says it was a Peep operation, and who else knew we were planning a summit meeting on Torch? The Peeps and the Erewhonese, and does anyone in this room believe the Erewhon honor code would have let them do something like this? Even assuming they'd had any conceivable *reason* to?"

Hamish Alexander-Harrington inhaled deeply and looked around the Cabinet Room. It was unusual for the monarch to come here instead of being attended upon at Mount Royal Palace by her chief minister and, perhaps, one of two of his colleagues. In fact, it had only happened seven times in the entire history of the Star Kingdom. Well, eight now. But Elizabeth hadn't wanted to speak only to her Prime Minister; she wanted all the members of his Cabinet to hear what she had to say.

He closed his eyes briefly, his face wrung with pain, and not just for his murdered friend. The heroic determination of Berry Zilwicki's bodyguard had saved her and Ruth Winton from certain death. The ex-slave who'd closed the door in the nick of time had literally dragged the two girls out of Berry's palace. He'd had to drag them; Berry had been hysterically trying to pry the door open with her bare hands.

Every individual in the throne room had died within fifteen seconds, and another two hundred and twenty-six other people had died as the neurotoxin spread beyond the throne room through other doors, windows, and the air conditioning system. And the death toll would have been at least three times that high if the security man who'd first noticed the assassin's briefcase hadn't sounded the alarm with his panic button. The almost immediate shutdown of the air conditioning had slowed the poison's spread long enough for the rest of the people in its path to evacuate. And the agent used was apparently as persistent as it had been fast-spreading. According to early reports, it was going to be simpler to simply burn the "palace" down and start over than to decontaminate it.

"I don't understand," Baroness Mourncreek, Grantville's Chancellor of the Exchequer, said in a troubled voice. "Why did they do it? I mean, what have they accomplished?"

"They've managed to kill our ambassador to the League," Elizabeth said coldly. "Admiral Webster was highly trusted by his contacts in the League. He'd become a relatively well known media figure from his appearances on various talk shows, as well, and he'd been very effective in moderating the more extremist newsies' versions of what's been going on in the Talbott Cluster ever since Nordbrandt started killing people. They probably figured he'd be equally effective in controlling the League's reaction to Terekhov's actions at Monica. By killing him, they intended to remove that possibility and increase the odds the League will take military action against us in Talbott."

"And what happened on Torch, Your Majesty?" Mourncreek said.

"They invited us—me—to a summit meeting. I don't think they actually expected me to accept. I think it was essentially planned as yet another of their damned diplomatic lies. They probably intended to publish the correspondence of their invitation and my refusal as proof that they're the 'reasonable party' in this war. It would have bolstered their claim that they've been telling the truth about our diplomatic correspondence from the beginning.

"But then I *accepted* their invitation, and we nominated Torch for the site and invited Erewhon to provide security, with the possibility of repairing the damage to our relations with the Erewhonese. They hadn't counted on that. And even though they'd probably never expected to sit down and negotiate seriously, they found themselves in a position where they might actually have to do that. Where it was even possible *we'd* sound like the voice of reason. So they decided to avoid the entire problem by killing Berry and Ruth—after all, what's the death of two more teenaged girls to bastards like Peeps? For that matter, if the girls' schedule hadn't slipped, they probably would have killed Thandi Palane and decapitated the Torch military, as well. Obviously, the confusion and chaos which would have resulted would have made Torch completely impossible as a conference site. And even if it hadn't, they could always point to their concern about security issues and the safety of their precious President Pritchart as reasons they couldn't *possibly* meet with me there. After, of course, sending me their lying condolences for my niece's death—just like Saint-Just did after he murdered Uncle Anson and Cal!"

Hamish felt a protest hovering on the tip of his tongue. Not because he wasn't almost as certain of Haven's complicity as Elizabeth herself, but because it still didn't make sense to him. The way Haven had attempted to kill Honor certainly seemed to indicate they saw assassination as a perfectly legitimate tool, and that accorded with the traditional policies of the Legislaturalists and the Committee of Public Safety, as well. Not to mention the fact that Pritchart herself had been credited with more than one assassination during her revolutionary days.

Not only that, he could follow Elizabeth's reasoning where James Webster's death was concerned. Webster *had* been effective, and his death certainly wasn't going to help manage the crisis in the Talbott Cluster. Given how the threat of that crisis hung over the Star Kingdom, inhibiting Manticore's freedom of action, preventing its resolution had to be attractive to Haven.

But her theory about Haven's motives for what had happened on Torch . . . That he found much harder to accept. Or, at least, to understand.

There was no need for the Republic to resort to Machiavellian diplomatic maneuvering. If anyone knew that, it was Hamish Alexander-Harrington. The sheer scale of the Peeps' numerical advantage was terrifying, and it was going to get only worse. It was possible new innovations like Mistletoe and Apollo would go a long way towards equalizing those odds, but Pat Givens swore there was no way Haven could have penetrated the security screen around those projects. So as far as Thomas Theisman and Eloise Pritchart knew, the weapons mix wasn't about to change radically, which meant they should have been supremely confident their advantage in numbers would prove decisive.

So why worry about diplomacy? Why not simply issue an ultimatum: surrender now, or face an overwhelming offensive from our side at the same time you're confronting Frontier Security in Talbott.

And yet . . .

And yet, Elizabeth had put her finger on the single most damning point. Who *else* had a motive?

If not for the similarity of the technique employed in this attack, Webster's assassination, and the attack on Honor, he would have been inclined to wonder if the Torch attack had been a Mesan operation. After all, an attack on Berry Zilwicki might well have made perfectly good sense from a Mesan perspective, given the fact that Torch was the only planet which had openly declared war upon Mesa. And Manpower and Mesa could, conceivably, have wanted Webster dead for exactly the same reasons Elizabeth had just ascribed to Haven.

But was that his reason talking, or simply his desire to find someone else—*anyone* else—to blame if it would preserve the possibility of a negotiated peace settlement?

If only the three assassination attempts hadn't been so damned similar! Yet, there it was. Three separate attacks, each of them a clearly suicidal assault by someone with absolutely no personal reason to want the intended victim dead . . . and no chance of surviving his own attack. And if Mesa clearly had reasons to want Berry Zilwicki dead, and *possibly* had reasons to want Jim Webster dead, what reason did they have for the attack on *Honor*? Try as he might, he couldn't come up with an answer for that question.

Occam's razor, he thought. The simplest answer that covered all the observed facts was most likely to be the truth. And the simplest answer was that the same people had to be behind all three attacks. And given the timing on Webster's murder and the attempt to kill Berry, whoever it was must have wanted to derail the peace conference. But for them to do that, they had to know where the conference was to be held, and no one *had* known outside the Cabinet and the highest echelons of the Foreign Ministry; the Kingdom of Torch; the Erewhonese . . . and Eloise Pritchart's administration. Everyone had known the conference was to be held, but not *where*, and he simply couldn't believe Erewhon would have allowed the information to leak. Not when they knew how sensitive Manticoran sensibilities must remain in the wake of their transfer of so much technological information to Haven. *Torch* certainly wouldn't have leaked it, and there hadn't been so much as a whisper of it in the Star Kingdom's press.

And the Peeps are the only people I can think of who'd want Honor dead, as well. For that matter, even if the Mesans might somehow have discovered the location, could they have found out in time to mount an operation like this? Besides, despite any delusions of grandeur on Manpower's part, Mesa is nothing more than a semi-legitimizing front for little more than common criminals. And would even Manpower be stupid enough to assassinate the Star Kingdom's accredited ambassador to the Solarian League on Old Earth itself at the very moment proof of Mesan involvement in Talbott is starting to come out?

No. There was a hell of a lot more involved here than just Manpower's failed operation in Talbott. And the only people who could have known when and where the summit was to be held and had a reason to want Honor dead were the Peeps. Elizabeth's theory as to why they might want to sabotage their own peace conference might not be completely logical, yet no other plausible theory offered itself at all.

"I suppose," William Alexander said heavily, "that the real question before us isn't whether or not we hold the Peeps responsible for their actions, but what we do about it.

"Hamish," he turned to his brother, "what are our military options?"

"Essentially what they were before Pritchart's invitation," Hamish replied. "One thing that's changed is that Eighth Fleet's had longer to receive munitions and train with them. We've got a few new wrinkles we think are going to make our ships considerably more effective, and the additional training time will stand Eighth Fleet in good stead. However, at this time, Eighth Fleet is the only formation we've got which is fully trained with the new weapons. It's also the only formation that's *equipped* with the new weapons, because only the *Invictuses* and the Graysons' late-flight *Harringtons*—" he smiled wryly at the class name, despite his somber mood "—can operate them without refitting."

"Why is that?" Grantville asked. "I thought the pods were the same dimensions?"

"They are, but only the ships built with Keyhole capability from the outset can handle the Mark Two platforms, and they're essential to making the new missiles work. We can refit with Keyhole II—in fact, the decision to build that in is part of what's delayed the Andermani refits—but it requires placing the ship in yard hands for at least eight to ten weeks. And, frankly, we can't stand down our existing ships that long when we're this tightly strapped. All our new construction is being altered on the ways to be Keyhole II-capable, and when it starts coming into commission, we can probably start pulling the older ships back for refit.

"But at the moment, only Eighth Fleet is really equipped to handle them, and even they have only partial loadouts on the new pods. We're attempting to get into full production on them as quickly as possible, but we've hit some bottlenecks, and security issues have restricted the number of production facilities we could commit to them."

"But Eighth Fleet could resume active operations immediately?"

"Yes," Hamish said firmly, trying to ignore the icy shiver which went through him at the thought of Honor going back into combat when he'd allowed himself to hope so hard for a diplomatic solution. And trying not to think about her bitter disappointment—and Emily's—if she found herself unable to be there for their daughter's birth after all.

"And what does our defensive posture look like?"

"That, too, is essentially what it was, but there are improvements on the horizon. We're pressing ahead with the system defense version of Apollo, and we ought to be able to begin deploying it very soon. We're still looking at some production bottlenecks, but once we get the system-defense pods deployed in numbers, we'll have much greater security at home.

"We're in a little better shape in Talbott, as well, because O'Malley's on station at Monica now. Given ONI's current estimates of Solarian capabilities, and bearing in mind Terekhov's after-action report on the performance of the Solly battlecruisers the Monicans used, O'Malley can almost certainly destroy anything Verrochio could assemble to throw at him for at least the next two to four months. In fact, Verrochio would have to be heavily reinforced before he'd have any chance at all of evicting us from Monica, much less the Cluster as a whole.

"As far as direct action against the home system by the League is concerned, sheer distance would work in our favor. They aren't going to invade us successfully through the Junction, not with the number of missile pods we've got covering the central nexus. That means they've got to do it the hard way, which leaves them with something on the order of a six-month voyage just to get here. Which doesn't even take into consideration the fact that they're going to have to mobilize, bring together, and logistically support a fleet with overwhelming numerical superiority if they expect to offset our tactical and technological advantages.

"To be honest, I'm reminded of something a wet-navy admiral from Old Earth once said. For eighteen months to two years, possibly even twice that long, we'd run wild. It's unlikely the Sollies recognize just how much things have changed in the last five to ten T-years, which probably means they'd commit grossly inadequate force levels, at least initially. Eventually, they'd realize what was happening, though. And if they had the stomach for it, they could use their sheer size to soak up whatever we did to them while they got their own R and D to work on matching weapons and cranked up their own building capacity.

"The bottom line is that my current estimate is that we could do enormous damage to them—far more, I'm certain, then any of their strategists or politicians would imagine was possible. But quantity has a quality all its own, and we simply aren't big enough to militarily defeat the Solarian League if it's prepared to buckle down and pay the cost to beat us. We don't have the ships or the manpower to occupy the number of star systems we'd have to occupy if we wanted to achieve military victory.

They, on the other hand, have effectively unlimited manpower and productive capacity. In the end, that would tell. And even if that weren't true, it overlooks the fact that the Peeps already have—or soon will have—enough wallers with broadly equivalent capabilities to pound us under. Especially if we're distracted by dealing with the League."

"But what I seem to hear you saying," Grantville said intently, "is that whatever the League *ultimately* does, nothing it can do in the next, say, six months is going to have a significant impact on us?"

"That time estimate's probably a bit optimistic, assuming we take any heavy losses against Haven," Hamish replied. "Overall, though, that's fairly accurate."

"Then it seems to me we've got to take the position that that six months—or whatever shorter period we actually have—represents our window for dealing with the Peeps," the Prime Minister said.

"Except for the fact that by the end of that window, their numerical advantage in SD(P)s will be on the order of three-to-one or even higher," Hamish said.

"Nothing we can do will change that," Elizabeth said flatly. "We're building as quickly as we can; they're doing the same thing. The threat zone until the ships we've laid down can equalize the numbers is beyond our control ... unless we can do something to whittle the Peeps down."

"You're thinking about Sanskrit," Hamish said, equally flatly.

Most of the people in the Cabinet Room had no idea what Sanskrit was. Grantville, Hamish, the Queen, and Sir Anthony Langtry did, and Elizabeth nodded.

"You just said Eighth Fleet has the new weapons. If we use them, if we can convince the Peeps we've got more of them—that we've reequipped with them across the board—that's got to affect their strategic thinking. It may force them to do what we wanted all along and fritter away their wall of battle defending rear area systems. Or it may even convince them they've gotten their sums wrong and they *don't* have sufficient numbers to offset our individual superiority. In which case, the bastards may actually have to sit down and talk to us after all."

"It's possible," Hamish agreed. "I can't predict how *probable* it might be. A lot would depend on how their analysts evaluate the situation after they run into Mistletoe and Apollo. They might not draw the conclusions we'd expect them to, since they won't have the same information we have about the systems' capabilities and availability. And I don't think anyone at Admiralty House would be prepared to predict exactly what their military reaction might be."

"That's a given," Elizabeth said, nodding. "But you say we'll be deploying the system-defense Apollos shortly. That would bolster our rear area security, wouldn't it?"

"Considerably," Hamish replied. "But we don't have them deployed *yet.*"

"Still, Eighth Fleet already has Apollo, and it's part of Home Fleet's strategic reserve, isn't it, Ham?" Grantville asked.

"Yes it is, but it can only be in one place at a time," Hamish pointed out. "If it's out raiding Peep star systems, then it can't be here, defending the home system."

"But if we launch Sanskrit, then immediately bring Eighth Fleet home to Trevor's Star, it would be back in its covering position before Theisman could react to the new weapons systems, wouldn't it? I mean, one of the advantages of basing Eighth Fleet at Trevor's Star is that it's ninety light-years closer to Haven than Manticore is. So even if we hit a target like Lovat, Eighth Fleet can be back in position to cover the home system a good three weeks before Theisman could get a fleet here to attack us, even if he sent it straight from Haven the instant he heard about Sanskrit, right?"

"That's the theory," Hamish agreed, with a silent curse for the Admiralty contingency studies his brother had clearly been reading a bit too closely. Then he gave himself a mental shake. Willie and Elizabeth were right. The possibility of a direct confrontation with the Solarian League was a far more deadly strategic threat to the Star Kingdom than the Republic of Haven's possible reaction to the new weapons systems.

"We don't have enough time to waste any more of it trying to talk to these . . . *people,*" Elizabeth said flatly. "We've just had fresh proof of the fact that we can't trust them, and given the situation in Talbott, we have to allow for a worst-case scenario. That means we have to make our plans with the understanding that we could be at war with the Solarian League at any time, and that, as Hamish says, they could have a fleet in the Talbott Cluster in weeks, and another all the way out here in six months. Not only that, but if the war drags on, then somebody like Verrochio is more likely to push when he shouldn't, on the theory that we'll be too distracted by the threat closer to home to respond forcefully to something far away, in a place like Talbott. We can't afford that possibility, and the only way to avoid it is to achieve a decision quickly. Do you see any approach—any *military* approach—which would give us a better chance of attaining that decision, Hamish?"

"No." Hamish shook his head. "Hitting them hard with Sanskrit and Apollo will have to make them stop and think. And even if they wanted to counterattack immediately, it would take them weeks, at least, to plan, deploy for, and mount an attack heavy enough to break the defenses covering our critical star systems. Their losses would be massive, even against our existing defenses, and we've seen no evidence that Theisman is prepared to launch some sort of do-or-die kamikaze attack or throw his people's lives away on forlorn hopes. I'm not saying that that couldn't change, but, as Willie's suggested, there's still the time factor involved. We'd have at least a month, probably two, to get the system-defense Apollo pods into initial deployment, while he organized any attack in response to Sanskrit. And Willie's right. We'd have Eighth Fleet back in its covering position at Trevor's Star long before any such attack could come through."

He looked around the conference room, his face grim.

"I'm not going to pretend that we aren't running a risk launching Sanskrit," he said. "But unless Theisman is prepared to lose literally hundreds of superdreadnoughts, there won't be a lot he can do even against the defenses we already have in position. Against the defenses we can have in place in another couple of months, his losses would be even higher. My own preference would be to wait at least another month to six weeks before we launch Sanskrit, just to give ourselves a little longer to get Apollo fully into production, bring at least a few more Apollo-capable wallers forward, and get the Apollo-capable system-defense pods into initial deployment. But if we're going to decide we can't wait that long because of the potential for an incident—or maybe I should say *another* incident—with the Sollies, then Sanskrit represents our best option."

"Very well." Elizabeth surveyed her ministers one more time, then nodded sharply, decisively.

"Willie, I'm going to draft a note to Pritchart. It's not going to be pretty. I'm going to officially and publicly denounce her actions and notify her that I have no intention of meeting anywhere with someone who uses assassination as a routine tool. And I'm also going to notify her that we intend to resume active military operations immediately."

Grantville nodded.

Technically, he might have rejected Elizabeth's policy decisions. In fact, it was clear from her attitude that the only way he could have opposed them would have been by resigning rather than accepting them. And he had absolutely no doubt that if the Queen explained to her subjects what had happened, and why she'd made the decisions she had, those decisions would enjoy overwhelming support and approval. She could readily have found another Prime Minister to put them into effect.

All that was true enough, but ultimately beside the point. Because the critical point was that *he* agreed with her.

"Tony," Elizabeth continued, turning to the Foreign Secretary, "I want our notice that we're going back to active operations very clearly stated. Unlike them, we're not going to be launching attacks without declaring hostilities first, and I want that point made to the galaxy at large by publishing our note in the 'faxes at the same time we send it. There's not going to be any room for anyone to accuse us of altering correspondence after the fact this time. Clear?"

"Clear, Your Majesty," Langtry said, and the Queen turned back to Hamish.

"Hamish, I want orders cut to Eighth Fleet immediately. Operation Sanskrit is reactivated, as of now. I want active planning to begin immediately, and I want Sanskrit to hit the Peeps as soon as physically possible."

The smile she produced was one a hexapuma might have worn.

"We'll give them their formal notice," she said grimly, "and I hope the bastards *choke* on it!"

Chapter Fifty-Three

The senior members of Eloise Pritchart's cabinet sat around the conference table in stunned silence. Leslie Montreau had just finished reading the formal text of Elizabeth Winton's savage note aloud, and everyone in the room felt as if he or she had just been punched in the belly.

Except Pritchart. *She'd* experienced that sensation ninety minutes earlier, when Montreau delivered the note to her office. Now she inhaled deeply, tipped her chair slightly forward, and rested her forearms on the conference table in a posture which she hoped bespoke confidence.

"There you have it," she said simply.

"Is she *insane*?" Tony Nesbitt's question could have sounded furious; instead, it sounded plaintive. "Why in God's name does she think *we* did it? What possible motive could we have had?"

"They already blamed us for the attempt to kill Harrington," Pritchart replied. "And to be fair, if the situation were reversed, I'd be convinced of our guilt in that case, too. After all, Harrington would be such a logical target for us to remove, if we could.

"The fact that we know we didn't do it gives us a rather different perspective, of course. It's obvious to *us* that it had to have been someone else. That's not readily apparent to them in Harrington's case, though, and I can think of several logical reasons for us to have attempted to assassinate Webster, as well, if we were willing to use assassination in the first place. The *evidence* that we were directly involved in the Webster assassination is pretty damning, too, even if we do know it was all fabricated.

"So now they have this assassination attempt on Queen Berry and, apparently, Princess Ruth. Who else are they going to blame for it?"

"But we'd offered to discuss peace with them," Walter Sanderson said. "Why would we have done that and then deliberately sabotaged our own proposed peace conference? It just doesn't make sense!"

"Actually, Secretary Sanderson," Kevin Usher said, "I'm afraid that however angry Elizabeth may be being at this moment, her suspicions of us aren't as illogical—or unreasonable, at least—as I'd like them to be."

"Meaning what?" Sanderson demanded.

"Madam President?" Usher looked at Pritchart with a questioning expression, and she nodded.

"Go ahead, Kevin. Tell them."

"Yes, Ma'am."

Usher turned back to the rest of the Cabinet.

"Some months ago, I was going through some of the older State Security files. As you know, we seized so many secure files it's going to take literally years to sort our way through them all. These, though, carried maximum-security flags—from both InSec *and* StateSec. That was unusual enough to pique my curiosity, so I took a look. And it turns out we have an even longer history with the House of Winton than I thought we did."

Sanderson scowled, as if impatient for the Federal Investigative Agency's director to get on with it, and Usher smiled thinly.

"I'm sure we're all aware that Saint-Just organized the attempt to kill Elizabeth and Benjamin Mayhew in Yeltsin. I'm sure we're all also aware that while the Masadans missed Elizabeth and Benjamin, they did get the Manticoran prime minister and foreign secretary. And, of course, the foreign secretary in question, Anson Henke, was Elizabeth's uncle. Her first cousin was also killed, and she'd been very close, emotionally as well as politically, to the Duke of Cromarty literally from the day she first took the throne.

"That would be bad enough, but we might convince her to associate that only with StateSec. Except, of course, for the minor difficulty that we also had her *father* assassinated."

"*What?*" Thomas Theisman jerked upright in his chair, his expression thunderstruck, and Usher nodded grimly.

"King Roger was the primary moving force behind the original Manticoran buildup against the Legislaturalists' Duquesne Plan. They'd assumed all along that Manticore would be the toughest of their intended victims, but Roger's activities were making their projections look much worse, so they decided to decapitate the opposition. InSec already had its hooks into several Manty politicians, and it used them to kill the king. Elizabeth was still a minor at the time, and according to the InSec files, they hoped to influence the regency and 'redirect' Manticoran foreign-policy. At the very least, they figured putting someone as young and inexperienced as she was on the throne would hamstring opposition to them.

"Unfortunately for them, the operation was blown somehow. InSec didn't have any idea how the Manties tumbled to it, but they were convinced they had. The plan to influence the regency went out the window when Elizabeth's Aunt Caitrin was named regent. Caitrin's as tough-minded as they come, and she pretty thoroughly fumigated their Foreign Office of anyone remotely sympathetic to the Legislaturalists. And Elizabeth—despite the fact that she must have known about InSec's involvement—settled for politically castrating the Manticoran politicos who actually did the dirty work. Which, if you think about it, *proves* she knew who was really behind it . . . and that, even then, she had the brains and self-discipline to not accuse the Legislaturalists before the Star Kingdom was ready for war."

"My God," Theisman said. "They killed King Roger because they expected Elizabeth to be *weaker*?" He barked a harsh laugh. "Well, that little brainstorm certainly fucked up!"

"I believe you could safely say that," Pritchart agreed. "But you see what Kevin's driving at, don't you? The Legislaturalists and Internal Security murdered her father. The Committee of Public Safety and *State* Security tried to murder her, and did murder her uncle, her cousin, and her prime minister. So if two totally different Havenite régimes were willing to murder members of her family, why shouldn't a *third* régime attempt to murder her niece? Is it any wonder she has to be thinking it's impossible for this particular leopard to ever change its spots?"

"I had no idea about King Roger's death." Sanderson shook his head, his expression reminiscent of that of a poleaxed steer. "I still can't think of any logical reason for us to have been behind what happened on Torch, but I suppose, under the circumstances, it really isn't—or shouldn't be—that surprising she's reacted this way."

"The thing *I* have to wonder, Mr. Secretary," Usher said, "is whether or not whoever did kill Webster and attempt to kill Berry Zilwicki and Ruth Winton also knew the truth about King Roger's death?"

He glanced at Wilhelm Trajan, and the Foreign Intelligence Service's chief shrugged unhappily.

"We're looking into that, Kevin," he said, then turned his attention to the Cabinet as a whole. "As Kevin knows, we have a very good man in Erewhon, with extraordinarily good contacts on Torch. Unfortunately, we haven't heard from him yet, and we won't for some time. Even if he was actually on Torch when it happened—which is unlikely, frankly, given how broad his area of responsibility is—it's still going to be at least a couple of weeks before a message from Torch or Erewhon reaches here.

"Having said that, it's glaringly obvious to us that someone else did know about the summit conference and didn't want it to happen. Kevin, have your people turned up anything more on Grosclaude's 'suicide'?"

"No," Usher admitted.

"I was afraid of that." Trajan sighed. "We've been collating reports and rumors over at FIS for some time now. We really started looking after the attempt to kill Harrington, since we knew we hadn't done it. It became apparent to us rather quickly that there were a lot of parallels between the attempt on her life and the Hofschulte affair in the Empire. In fact, it looks like whatever technique was used was identical in both cases. We haven't heard anything yet direct from Old Earth about the Webster assassination, but looking at the indictment Elizabeth attached to her note, it looks very much to me as if Ambassador DeClercq's driver may have been another application of the same technique. And the attack on Berry Zilwicki may have been yet another—notice that in all four cases, for example, the apparent assassin had no personal motive to kill his victims and no chance at all of surviving the mission.

"From the outside, and bearing in mind how little forensic evidence we have, it sounds as if the same technique was used on Grosclaude. Not to make him kill anyone else, but to make him kill *himself.*"

"Where are you headed with this, Wilhelm?" Pritchart asked, regarding him intently.

"Grosclaude was almost certainly Giancola's tool," Trajan said. "*Giancola* was killed in what was clearly a genuine traffic accident, but Grosclaude was intentionally eliminated. And on the face of it, by the same unknown party who seems to have been wandering around the galaxy murdering people virtually at will. As Kevin's demonstrated, it's extremely likely Grosclaude's death and the forged files implicating Giancola were actually intended to convince us of Giancola's *innocence.* So our unknown party was looking out for the late, lamented Arnold's interests when he—or they—killed Grosclaude."

"Jesus!" Rachel Hanriot pursed her lips in a low, soft whistle. "You're suggesting Arnold was working for this 'unknown party' of yours from the beginning. That this entire war with the Manties was *deliberately provoked* by someone else?"

"I think it's a distinct possibility." Trajan nodded. "And if it is what happened, then obviously the people who wanted us shooting at the Manties in the first place are going to do anything they can to prevent us from *stopping* the shooting."

"But who?" Nesbitt demanded, his face screwed up in frustration. "Who does it help for us to be killing one another?"

"I don't know that," Trajan admitted. "Given the operation on Torch, I'd be tempted to point the finger at Mesa. After all, Mesa and Manpower don't much like us *or* the Manties, for a lot of reasons. But I'm not sure why they would have used Hofschulte to try and kill the Andy Emperor's younger brother. For that matter, the real culprits may have figured we'd *automatically* assume it was Mesa if they attacked the ruler of Torch. It could have been a bit of misdirection on their part, and aside from getting us both out of Manpower's hair—keeping us from inhibiting their slaving operations, at least in our respective sectors—I just don't see what sort of reason Mesa could have for committing the obvious time and resources necessary to set all of this up."

"Are you saying there *isn't* a reason?"

"No, Secretary Nesbitt. I'm saying that neither I nor any of my senior analysts can think of what that reason might be. And that we need to be careful not to allow the Torch component of what's happened to stampede us into running off after what may very well be a false scent. We can't afford to concentrate our attention solely on the Mesa/Manpower possibility without something more to go on than the physical location of the attack on Berry Zilwicki."

"All of this is fascinating," Thomas Theisman said. "I mean that sincerely, and I dearly want the answers to the questions that're being asked. Unfortunately, we have a more pressing problem before us. Specifically, Manticore's decision to resume hostilities."

"That's certainly true, Admiral," Leslie Montreau said. "From the phrasing, it's clear they intend to resume operations at the earliest possible moment. It's even possible they're attacking us somewhere even as we sit here. Under the strict letter of international law, they'd be thoroughly justified in asserting that they'd given us notice of their intentions before they violated the cease-fire, since our original agreement *to* the cease-fire didn't define what 'timely notice' would be."

"Do you think they are already hitting us, Tom?" Pritchart asked.

"From a diplomatic perspective, I couldn't begin to answer that one," Theisman replied. "From a military perspective, I'd be surprised if they could get an operation off the ground this quickly. I'm assuming they probably had operational plans in the works before the cease-fire, and that they've continued to do precautionary updates on their planning, but it's still going to take them some time to dust those plans off, bring their operational units up to speed, and then actually reach their targets. We've got possibly another week or so, from that perspective. I could be wrong, but I think that's the most probable scenario."

"There's got to be some way to dodge this pulser dart," Nesbitt argued urgently. "If Wilhelm's suspicions are remotely accurate, then both of us are playing into someone else's hands if we go back to war!"

"But if Tom's time estimate is accurate," Henrietta Barloi said harshly, "there's nothing we can do. If the Manties hit us as hard and as fast as the tone of that note suggests, we're going to get pounded *somewhere* before we could possibly get a note from Haven to Manticore. Even assuming Elizabeth were prepared to believe any of this—and I'm not at all sure she would be—there's no way to tell her about it before she pulls the trigger."

"And if she does 'pull the trigger,'" Pritchart said grimly, "then it's going to be harder than hell to convince anyone in Congress to try for a second summit agreement."

"In addition," Montreau pointed out unhappily, "we couldn't expect the Manties to take any such second proposal seriously unless we badly defeat whatever operation they mount."

Everyone looked at the Secretary of State, and she shrugged.

"Right now, Elizabeth's assuming we set this entire thing up for some unknown, underhanded, devious reason of our own. If they attack us successfully, inflict more damage, and get off unscathed, or with only minor damage of their own, then as far as she'll be concerned, we'll have even more reason to stall, or whatever the hell it is we were trying to accomplish. If we beat *them* severely, though, then send her another message, along with at least a partial explanation of Director Trajan's suspicions, we'll be speaking from a position of strength, tactically and psychologically. If we say to them 'Look, we just knocked the crap out of your last attack, and we're telling you we think someone else is manipulating both of us. So if you'll at least sit down and talk to us, we won't press our immediate advantage while you do it' they're a lot more likely to actually take this seriously."

"I see what you mean." Pritchart nodded, and cocked her head at Theisman. "Tom, how likely an outcome is that?"

"That depends on far too many imponderables for me to even guesstimate," Theisman said frankly. "It depends on what they decide to do, where they decide to do it, and what's waiting for them when they do. We've managed to cover almost all of the star systems we've been able to identify as possible candidates for their targeting list with the new pods and control systems. During the period of the cease-fire, I also redeployed a fair percentage of our capital ship strength to cover the more valuable of those systems. The subunits I used were able to continue their training and working up on their new stations while giving us more defensive depth.

"All intelligence indications are that they've been working hard to reinforce their Eighth Fleet. On the basis of that, they ought to be able to attack in greater strength. They may choose to attack a greater number of targets, but personally, I think it's more likely they'll concentrate on one, especially after what happened at Solon. So I'm betting on a heavy attack on one, or at most two, of the more valuable target systems.

"Assuming I'm right, and assuming we've guessed correctly about their likely targets, and assuming they pick one of the ones I've assigned fleet units to *and* that they haven't come up with some new doctrine or hardware, we ought to hammer them. But please notice how many assumptions went into that statement."

He shook his head and met his colleagues' gazes levelly.

"I'd be lying if I told you flatly that they can't punch out whatever system they pick. I expect they'll get hurt, wherever they hit us, but I can't guarantee they'll be repulsed, with or without significant losses on their part."

"Understood." Pritchart nodded again, unhappily this time, and sat in obvious thought for several seconds. Then her nostrils flared, and she straightened slightly in her chair.

"All right. Personally, I think you're onto something, Wilhelm. I want all your resources committed to trying to figure out what the hell is going on and who's behind it."

"Yes, Madam President."

"Leslie, I think *you're* onto something about the circumstances we need before we can share our suspicions with the Manties. All the same, I want you to begin working now on a message we might send them if we can find or create the right conditions. We can't afford to sound weak, or as if their present intransigence is driving our policy—not if we expect to convince them we're telling the truth. At the same time, we need to be as persuasive as we can, so I want you and Kevin to sit down together. I want you as intimately familiar with his investigation as you can possibly be, since you're the one who's going to be drafting an explanation of it for the Manties. Do the same thing with Wilhelm. I want a preliminary draft of the note on my desk within the next five days."

"Yes, Madam President."

"Tom," Pritchart turned to Theisman, "I'm sorry to say that at this point it looks like it all comes down to you and your people. Leslie's right. We need a victory before we hand this bucket of snakes to the Manties. I need you to give me one."

"Madam President—"

"I know you just said you can't guarantee to defeat their next attack," Pritchart interrupted. "I understand why that is, and I accept your analysis. On the other hand, we may kick their ass, after all, in which case we can immediately send them Leslie's note. But if they kick *our* ass, then we need to stage an immediate and powerful comeback. So I need you to go back to the Octagon and sit down with Admiral Marquette and Admiral Trenis. Get back to me with an analysis of possible offensive actions on our part. I want a spectrum of options, ranging from the heaviest blow we can launch to a more graduated response we might use if they attack us and we drive them off without either side getting badly hurt."

"Yes, Madam President." Theisman was manifestly unhappily, but his voice and expression were both unflinching.

"I don't like our situation," Pritchart said grimly. "I don't like it one little bit, and I like it even less every time I realize that whoever's doing the manipulating Wilhelm's suggested got me personally to do *exactly* what they wanted. Unfortunately, at this moment, they've done exactly the same thing with Elizabeth Winton, as well, and given her obvious attitude, there's no prospect of explaining that to her. So the only option we have is to hit her hard enough to convince her she *has* to listen to us, however ridiculous our claims sound."

Chapter Fifty-Four

"We've got those plans for you, Eloise."

"Good . . . I think."

Eloise Pritchart smiled at Thomas Theisman and Arnaud Marquette without much humor as the Secretary of War and the Chief of the Naval Staff seated themselves at the table in the small conference room just off her office. Of late, she thought, she seemed to be spending a great many hours in rooms like this.

"As you requested, we've put together a range of possible options," Theisman continued. "In my opinion, two of them are most likely to meet your requirements. Arnaud and I have brought you summaries on all of them, but with your permission, I'd prefer to concentrate on the two I think are most likely: Beatrice and Camille."

"Well, the names sound nice, anyway," the President said wanly, and Theisman and Admiral Marquette showed their teeth in dutiful smiles. "All right, Tom. Go ahead."

"In that case, let's look at Camille first," Theisman said.

"Basically, Camille is intended for a situation in which the Manties attack one of our star systems, and we fight them off with relatively light losses on either side. The consequence of a sparring match, you might say, and not a death grapple.

"In that situation, as we understood your directive, what we want is an operation which will punish them, but without radically raising the stakes on either side. A declaration that we've absorbed and parried their blow, and that we're prepared to deliver similar blows of our own.

648

"The basic problem is that, despite the way they've been forced to divert battle squadrons to cover places like Zanzibar and Alizon, they have proportionately heavier system defense forces on most of their important targets than we do. They simply have fewer systems to defend, which lets them cover up in greater depth, despite their numerical inferiority. So even something we intend as a relatively minor attack is going to require a significant commitment of force on our side. We have the resources to do that; my only real concern is that using a task force or fleet of the size we need is likely to be perceived by the Manties as an escalation on our part, whether we want that or not.

"Bearing that in mind, what we propose under Camille is an attack on Alizon, similar to the one we launched against Zanzibar. We'd probably put Lester in command again, and we'd commit six battle squadrons—forty-eight podnaughts—with carrier support and screening elements. That's a significantly heavier force than the one we used against Zanzibar, but the Manties have shored up the Alizon defenses since then, and we'll need the additional firepower to break in.

"Assuming our force estimates are accurate, our six squadrons should be sufficient to get the job done, but their Office of Naval Intelligence has to have at least a fair notion of our current strength. They'll recognize that six battle squadrons represents only a small portion of our total deployable ships of the wall. Hopefully, they'll conclude from that that we're deliberately operating on a reduced scale, although they may not conclude that it's for the reasons we want them to think it is. In that case, we may require some diplomatic contact to underscore the point that we could have hit them harder. That's one reason we picked Alizon as our target. It's significant politically, diplomatically, and in terms of their public's morale; it's *not* especially significant any longer in terms of their actual war-fighting ability, though. What we hope is that taking out Alizon's military infrastructure will underscore our capabilities without being perceived as a mortal threat.

"Is that about what you wanted at this end of the spectrum?"

"It sounds like it," Pritchart replied. "I'll want to read your summary on it, and digest it further, of course, but it sounds like the sort of smack in the face that will get their attention without punching their lights out."

"That's about what we tried to design it to do. On the other hand," Theisman continued, "I hope you and Leslie are both remembering that using military operations as a way to shape a diplomatic climate is always problematical. It's much simpler—and more reliable, frankly—to think in terms of accomplishing specific *military* goals than it is to come up with ways to elicit specific desired political responses from your opponent. He's always going to find some way to screw up what it was you *thought* you were going to get, and any secretary of war or admiral who tells you differently is either a lunatic or a liar. In either of which cases, you should get rid of his sorry ass as quickly as possible."

"I'll . . . bear that in mind," Pritchart said, lips twitching as she womanfully resisted the temptation to smile.

"Good. In that case, let's look at Beatrice."

Theisman sat forward slightly in his chair, his palms on the tops of his thighs as he leaned towards the President, and his expression became very serious.

"Beatrice is no slap in the face, Madam President," he said quietly. "Beatrice is an all-out bid for outright military victory. You said you wanted one end of your spectrum of options to be the most powerful one we could put together. Beatrice is it."

Pritchart felt her own expression congealing into focused attention.

"Basically, Beatrice is a direct attack on the Manticoran home system," Theisman told her. "There's not much finesse to it. We'll take forty-two battle squadrons—three hundred and thirty-six SD(P)s; equal to eighty-plus percent of their entire modern wall of battle, including the Andies, according to NavInt's current estimates—and we'll throw it straight at their toughest defenses and their most critical defensive objective. They'll *have* to fight to defend Manticore, and the system astrography is going to leave Sphinx especially exposed. Essentially, we'll be able to get at Sphinx quickly enough their Home Fleet will have no choice but to meet us head-on, however bad the odds are from their perspective. And the odds *will* be bad. Because they've had to deploy so much of their strength to cover other, secondary objectives, they'll be significantly outnumbered at the point of contact.

"We'll take along several thousand LACs. The attack force, which will be under Javier's command, with Lester as his second, will also be accompanied by a full press fleet train—repair ships, ammunition ships, hospital ships, everything. We'll be prepared to repeat Lester's Zanzibar tactics, complete to reloading our SD(P)s several times, if necessary.

"Even in the best-case scenario," he said soberly, "our losses will be heavy—*very* heavy. Don't think they won't. We'll be hitting very hard, well-prepared defenses—probably the toughest in the explored galaxy, at the moment—manned by highly motivated people, and they'll still have the technological advantage, even though we've narrowed it. Not only that, but we don't estimate we'll be able to hold the system against counterattack, even after we win. Certainly not indefinitely.

"At the moment, their Home Fleet consists of about fifty SD(P)s and the same number of older superdreadnoughts, according to NavInt. They have another fifty of the wall in Third Fleet, and Eighth Fleet has another twenty-four to thirty. Against Home Fleet alone, we'll have a better than three-to-one advantage in total hulls, and seven-to-one in SD(P)s. Their fixed defenses and the LACs they've deployed for home system defense will offset some of that advantage, but not as much as you might think. According to NavInt's latest reports, some of the dispositions they've been forced to make to protect Manticore-B and the Junction have forced compromises in Manticore-A we think we can make work for us.

"If both Third Fleet and Eighth Fleet are called in from Trevor's Star, the numerical odds will shift from seven-to-one in pod-layers to approximately four-to-one, but we don't really know how likely it is that both of them will be committed. They've got to worry about the fact that the force we're throwing at Manticore, big as it is, represents only a portion of our total wall of battle. That means they'll have to be worried about the possibility that we've got an additional fleet sitting in hyper waiting to pounce on Trevor's Star if they uncover it. They may dither at least a little and commit one of the Trevor's Star forces first, hoping it will be enough. In some ways, that would be good—it would bring them in in smaller packets, easier to defeat in detail. But one variant of Beatrice we're considering—Beatrice Bravo—would try to entice them to come through together.

"If they stay concentrated and commit both of them, our margin of superiority will be far tighter. It should still be enough, because most of Javier's force will go in concentrated, whereas their Home Fleet and Trevor's Star forces would have to rendez-vous with one another before they can combine tactically. If Javier heads directly towards Sphinx, Home Fleet will have to honor the threat and move immediately to intercept him, which ought to let him engage that detachment on his own terms.

"After that, and if the Trevor's Star detachments come in together, he may have to break off the attack, if his own losses against Home Fleet and the fixed defenses have been significant. Otherwise, especially if we adopt the Bravo variant's deployment, he ought to be in a position to engage the remaining fleet elements in succession, utilizing his numerical advantage, *or* ignore the forces coming up behind him while he heads directly through the system, taking out industrial infrastructure—and especially their dispersed shipyards—as he goes. A lot will depend on how heavy his own losses were and whether or not he still has the firepower to deal with the inner defenses. Ammunition consumption is going to be an especially ticklish problem, I suspect.

"If he's able to inflict heavy damage on their infrastructure, Beatrice might not prove immediately fatal to the Manties, but the long term effects on the strategic balance would be clearly decisive. Without the Manticoran yards, their Alliance can't pos-sibly match our construction ability, and they'll know it. Which means they'll have no choice but to surrender.

"It he's able to engage Third Fleet and Eighth Fleet in detail, after already trashing Home Fleet, he'll probably be able to com-pletely destroy or cripple just under half the total modern Manty wall of battle and *then* take out the infrastructure. In that case, Beatrice would definitely be immediately decisive."

Theisman stopped speaking and sat back in his chair, and Pritchart gazed at him without speaking for what seemed an eternity. It was very quiet in the conference room.

Beatrice, she thought. *Such a pretty name for something so hideous. Is this what it's really come to, Eloise?*

She wanted to say no, to reject the notion. Yet she couldn't. She'd done her dead level best to avoid this, and she prayed she would still be able to avoid Beatrice. But deep in the secret places of her soul, she was afraid. So afraid. Not of defeat, but of the price of the alternative.

"You say we'd commit almost three hundred and fifty ships

of the wall," she said, finally. "What does that leave us if things go wrong?"

"We'll have a total of just over six hundred and twenty SD(P)s in commission at that point," Theisman told her. "There'll be another three hundred or so older superdreadnoughts to support them, although by that point we'll be decommissioning the older ships steadily to provide crews for the new construction."

"Why not take more of them to Manticore, then?"

"For four main reasons. First, out of that total number of pod-layers, something like a hundred will still be working up. They won't be up to full efficiency, their ships companies won't be fully integrated. In short, they won't really be fully combat-effective units.

"Second, the force we're committing ought to be enough to do the job, and it's going to be the biggest fleet of superdreadnoughts ever committed to action in a single battle by *anyone*, including the Solarian League. Even under a worst-case scenario, it should be more than powerful enough to beat an organized retreat with minimum losses. I realize Murphy's still likely to put in an appearance, but there would have to be some truly radical shift in the basic operational parameters for the Manties to seriously threaten its ability to look after itself.

"Third, we simply can't be certain where their Eighth Fleet is going to be at the moment we launch Beatrice. Suppose, for example, that they've sortied from Trevor's Star on another raiding expedition. In that case, our margin of superiority at Manticore would be even greater, but we've got to cover our own absolutely essential rear areas—like Bolthole, although there's no indication they've figured out where Bolthole is yet—against whatever Eighth Fleet might be doing while we're trashing Manticore.

"Fourth, there's the Andermani. The Manties and Graysons have lost about twenty superdreadnoughts—twelve of them pod-layers—since Thunderbolt wrapped up. That's about seven percent of their total podnoughts. But the Andies are still out there somewhere, and so far, we've seen very few of their capital ships. There are at least a couple of squadrons of them assigned to the Manties' Home Fleet, but that's about it. By our estimates, they should have somewhere around a hundred and twenty pod-layers by now—just about a third of the Manticoran Alliance's total—and we haven't seen them yet. We know they aren't at

Trevor's Star, and intelligence suggests there's still some technical problem with them. We know they were conducting a major refit program on the Andy wallers, and we're assuming that explains their continued absence. But it's possible more of them will come forward before we launch Beatrice. And whatever happens in Manticore, the Andy ships that aren't there can't be destroyed. So we've got to retain enough of our own forces uncommitted to provide a strategic reserve against the sudden appearance of the Andermani Navy."

Pritchart considered what he'd said for a moment, then nodded.

"How soon could you mount these operations?"

"Camille could go on very short notice," Theisman said. "Lester's already essentially positioned to mount and execute the operation. Beatrice is going to take longer. Frankly, we'll need at least seven to eight weeks to bring ourselves up to our stipulated force levels. It will take another three weeks or so for the designated units to combine and reach Manticore. So say we could hit Alizon within two weeks of the time you say go, and we could execute Beatrice anywhere from ten weeks to three months from today. If we begin making preliminary deployments for Beatrice now, we'd probably come out closer to the ten-week deadline."

" 'From today,' " Pritchart repeated, with a forlorn smile. "You realize this is the day I was supposed to depart for Torch, don't you?"

"Yes, I do," Theisman said sadly.

"This wasn't a conversation I wanted to be having. Not today. Not ever."

"I know that, Madam President. But," he met her eyes unflinchingly, "if the diplomatic option isn't available, this is the logical consequence of going to war in the first place."

"You're right, of course," she sighed, massaging her temples with the fingertips of both hands. "And you tried to warn me before we did it. Before *I* did it."

"Madam President," he said quietly, "I could have stopped you. We both know that."

"No, you couldn't have," she disagreed. "I'd like to think you could, because then I could spread around some of the guilt I'm feeling right now. But you couldn't have stopped me without killing the Constitution, Tom, and you could no more do that than you could fly without counter-grav . . . or strangle your own child with your bare hands. We both know that."

He started to open his mouth, as if to continue arguing the point. Then he closed it, instead, and she smiled again.

"But however we got here, we're here now," she said, and inhaled sharply.

"All right, Tom, Arnaud. I'll review your summaries. On the basis of what you've said so far, I'm inclined to think you're probably right about the two we're most likely to be choosing between, unfortunately. I hope it will be Camille, but go ahead and assume the worst. Start deploying your units on the basis that Beatrice will be necessary."

Chapter Fifty-Five

The warship which emerged from the Trevor's Star terminus of the Manticore Wormhole Junction did not show a Manticoran transponder code. Nor did it show a Grayson or an Andermani code. Nonetheless, it was allowed transit, for the code it did display was that of the Kingdom of Torch.

To call the vessel a "warship," was, perhaps, to be overly generous. It was, in fact, a frigate—a tiny class which no major naval power had built in over fifty T-years. But this was a very modern ship, less than three T-years old, and it was Manticoran built, by the Hauptman Cartel, for the Anti-Slavery League.

Which, as everyone understood perfectly well, actually meant it had been built for the Audubon Ballroom, before its lapse into respectability. And this particular frigate—TNS *Pottawatomie Creek*—was rather famous, one might almost have said notorious, as the personal transport of one Anton Zilwicki, late of Her Manticoran Majesty's Navy.

Everyone in the Star Kingdom knew about the attempt to murder Zilwicki's daughter, and given Manticore's current bloody-minded mood, no one was inclined to present any problems when *Pottawatomie Creek* requested permission to approach HMS *Imperator* and send across a couple of visitors.

"Your Grace, Captain Zilwicki and . . . guest," Commander George Reynolds announced.

Honor turned from her contemplation of the nearest drifting units of her command, one eyebrow rising, as she tasted the peculiar edge in Reynolds' emotions. She'd decided to meet with Zilwicki as informally as possible, which was why she'd had Reynolds greet him and escort him to the relatively small observation dome just aft of *Imperator*'s forward hammerhead. The panoramic view was spectacular, but it was symbolically outside her own quarters or the official precincts of Flag Bridge.

Now, however, that odd ripple in Reynolds' mind-glow made her wonder if perhaps Zilwicki wouldn't be just as glad as she was to keep this an "unofficial" visit. Reynolds, the son of a liberated genetic slave, was an enthusiastic supporter of the great experiment in Congo, not to mention a personal admirer of Anton Zilwicki and Catherine Montaigne. He'd worked remarkably well with Zilwicki immediately prior to Honor's deployment to the Marsh System, and he'd been delighted when she asked him to meet Zilwicki's cutter. Now, however, he seemed almost . . . apprehensive. That wasn't exactly the right word, but it came close, and she caught Nimitz's matching flicker of interest as the 'cat sat up to his full height on the back of the chair where she'd parked him.

"Captain," she said, holding out her hand.

"Your Grace." Zilwicki's voice was as deep as ever, but it was also a bit more abrupt. Clipped. And as she turned her attention fully to him, she tasted the seething anger his apparently calm exterior disguised.

"I was very sorry to hear about what happened on Torch," Honor said quietly. "But I'm delighted Berry and Ruth got out unscathed."

"'Unscathed' is an interesting word, Your Grace," Zilwicki rumbled in a voice like crumbling Gryphon granite. "Berry wasn't hurt, not physically, but I don't think 'unscathed' really describes what happened. She blames herself. She knows she shouldn't, and she's one of the sanest people I know, but she blames herself. Not so much for Lara's death, or for all the other people who died, but for having gotten out herself. And, I think, perhaps, for the *way* Lara died."

"I'm sorry to hear that," Honor repeated. She grimaced. "Survivor's guilt is something I've had to deal with a time or two myself."

"She'll work through it, Your Grace," the angry father said. "As I said, she's one of the sanest people in existence. But this one's going to leave scars, and I hope she'll draw the right lessons from it, not the wrong ones."

"So do I, Captain," Honor said sincerely.

"And speaking of drawing the right lessons—or, perhaps I ought to say *conclusions*," he said, "I need to talk to you about what happened."

"I'd be grateful for any insight you can give me. But shouldn't you be talking to Admiral Givens, or perhaps to the SIS?"

"I'm not certain any of the official intelligence organs are ready to hear what I've got to say. And I know they're not ready to listen to . . . my fellow investigator, here."

Honor turned her attention openly and fully to Zilwicki's companion as the captain gestured at him. He was a very young man, she realized. Not particularly distinguished in any way, physically. Of average height—possibly even a little shorter than that—with a build which was no more than wiry, almost callow-looking beside Zilwicki's massively impressive musculature. The hair was dark, the complexion also on the swarthy side, and the eyes were merely brown.

But as she gazed at him and reached out to sample his emotions, she realized *this* young man was anything but "undistinguished."

In her time, Honor Alexander-Harrington had known quite a few dangerous people. Zilwicki was a case in point, as, in his own lethal way, was young Spencer Hawke, standing alertly to watch her back even here. But this young man had the clear, clean uncluttered taste of a sword. In fact, his mind-glow was as close to that of a treecat as Honor had ever tasted in a human being. Certainly not evil, but . . . direct. *Very* direct. For treecats, enemies came in two categories: those who'd been suitably dealt with, and those who were still alive. This unremarkable-looking young man's mind-glow was exactly the same, in that regard. There was not a single trace of malice in it. In many ways, it was clear and cool, like a pool of deep, still water. But somewhere in the depths of that pool, Leviathan lurked.

Over the decades, Honor had come to know herself. Not perfectly, but better than most people ever did. She'd faced the wolf inside herself, the aptness to violence, the temper chained by discipline and channeled into protecting the weak, rather than preying upon them. She saw that aspect of herself reflected in the mirrored surface of this young man's still water, and realized with an inner shiver, that he was even more apt to violence than she was. Not because he craved it one bit more than she did, but because of his focus. His purpose.

He wasn't simply Leviathan; this man was also Juggernaut. Dedicated every bit as much as she to protecting the people and the things about which he cared, and far more ruthless. She could readily sacrifice herself for the things in which she believed; this man could sacrifice *anything* in their name. Not for personal power. Not for profit. But because his beliefs, and the integrity with which he held them, were too strong for anything else.

But although he was as clean of purpose as a meat-ax, he was no crippled psychopath or fanatic. He would bleed for what he sacrificed. He would simply do it anyway, because he'd looked himself and his soul in the eye and accepted what he found there.

"May I assume, Captain," she said calmly, "that this young man's political associations, shall we say, might make him ever so slightly *persona non gratis* with those official intelligence organs?"

"Oh, I think you might say that, Your Grace." Zilwicki smiled with very little humor. "Duchess Harrington, allow me to introduce you to Special Officer Victor Cachat of the Havenite Federal Intelligence Service."

Cachat watched her calmly, but she felt the tension ratcheting up behind his expressionless façade. Those "merely brown" eyes were much deeper and darker than she'd first thought, she observed, and they made an admirable mask for whatever was going on behind them.

"Officer Cachat," she repeated in an almost lilting voice. "I've heard some rather remarkable things about you. Including the part you played in Erewhon's recent . . . change of allegiance."

"I hope you don't expect me to say I'm sorry about that, Duchess Harrington." Cachat's voice was as outwardly calm as his eyes, despite a somewhat heightened prickle of apprehension.

"No, of course I don't."

She smiled and stepped back a half-pace, feeling the way Hawke had tightened internally behind her at the announcement of Cachat's identity, before she waved at the dome's comfortable chairs.

"Sit down, Gentlemen. And then, Captain Zilwicki, perhaps

you can explain to me exactly what you're doing here in company with one of the most notorious secret agents—if that's not an oxymoron—in the employ of the sinister Republic of Haven. I'm sure it will be fascinating."

Zilwicki and Cachat glanced at one another. It was a brief thing, more sensed than seen, and then they seated themselves in unison. Honor took a facing chair, and Nimitz flowed down into her lap as Hawke moved slightly to the side. She felt Cachat's awareness of the way in which Hawke's move cleared his sidearm and put Honor herself out of his line of fire. The Havenite gave no outward sign he'd noticed, but he was actually rather amused by it, she noted.

"Which of you gentlemen would care to begin?" she asked calmly.

"I suppose I should," Zilwicki said. He gazed at her for a moment, then shrugged.

"First, Your Grace, I apologize for not clearing Victor's visit with your security people ahead of time. I rather suspected that they'd raise a few objections. Not to mention the fact that he *is* a Havenite operative."

"Yes, he is," Honor agreed. "And, Captain, I'm afraid I have to point out that you've brought the aforesaid Havenite agent into a secure area. This entire star system is a fleet anchorage, under martial law and closed to all unauthorized shipping. There's a great deal of highly confidential information floating around, including what could be picked up by simple visual observation. I trust neither of you will take this wrongly, but I really can't permit a 'Havenite operative' to go home and tell the Octagon what he's seen here."

"We considered that point Your Grace," Zilwicki said, much more calmly than he actually felt, Honor observed. "I give you my personal word that Victor hasn't been allowed access to any of our sensor data, or even to *Pottawatomie Creek*'s bridge, since leaving Congo. Nor was he given any opportunity to make visual observations during the crossing from *Pottawatomie* to your vessel. This—" he raised one hand, waving it at the panoramic view from the observation dome "—is the first time he's actually had a look at anything which could be remotely construed as sensitive information."

"For what it's worth, Duchess," Cachat said, meeting her

eyes steadily, his right hand resting lightly in his lap, "Captain Zilwicki is telling you the truth. And while I'll confess that I was very tempted to attempt to hack into *Pottawatomie Creek*'s information systems and steal the information I'd promised him I wouldn't, I was able to suppress the temptation quite easily. He and Princess Ruth are both accomplished hackers; I'm not. I have to rely on other people to do that for me, and none of those other people happen to be along this time. If I'd tried, I would have bungled it and gotten myself caught. In which case I would have gotten no information and destroyed a valuable professional relationship. For that matter, my knowledge of naval matters in general is...limited. I know a lot more than the average layman, but not enough to make any worthwhile observations. Certainly not relying on what I can see from the outside."

Honor leaned back slightly, gazing at him thoughtfully. It was obvious from his emotions that he had no idea she could actually taste him. And it was equally obvious he was telling the truth. Just as it was obvious he actually *expected* to be detained, probably jailed. And—

"Officer Cachat," she said, "I really wish you would deactivate whatever suicide device you have in your right hip pocket."

Cachat stiffened, eyes widening in the first sign of genuine shock he'd given, and Honor raised her right hand quickly as she heard the snapping whisper of Spencer Hawke's pulser coming out of its holster.

"Calmly, Spencer," she told the young man who had replaced Andrew LaFollet, never looking away from Cachat herself. "Calmly! Officer Cachat doesn't want to hurt anyone else. But I'd feel much more comfortable if you weren't quite so ready to kill *yourself*, Officer Cachat. It's rather hard to concentrate on what someone's telling you when you're wondering whether or not he's going to poison himself or blow both of you up at the end of the next sentence."

Cachat sat very, very still. Then he snorted—a harsh, abrupt sound, nonetheless edged with genuine humor—and looked at Zilwicki.

"I owe you a case of beer, Anton."

"Told you so." Zilwicki shrugged. "And now, Mr. Super Secret Agent, would you *please* turn that damned thing off? Ruth and Berry would both murder me if I let you kill yourself. And I don't even want to think about what Thandi would do to me!"

"Coward."

Cachat looked back at Honor, head cocked slightly to one side, then smiled a bit crookedly.

"I've heard a great deal about you, Duchess Harrington. We have extensive dossiers on you, and I know Admiral Theisman and Admiral Foraker both think highly of you. If you're prepared to give me your word—*your* word, not the word of a Manticoran aristocrat or an officer in the Manticoran Navy, but *Honor Harrington's* word—that you won't detain me or attempt to force information out of me, I'll disarm my device."

"I suppose I really ought to point out to you that even if *I* give you my word, that doesn't guarantee someone else won't grab you if they figure out who you are."

"You're right." He thought for a moment longer, then shrugged. "Very well, give me *Steadholder* Harrington's word."

"Oh, very good, Officer Cachat!" Honor chuckled as Hawke stiffened in outrage. "You *have* studied my file, haven't you?"

"And the nature of Grayson's political structure," Cachat agreed. "It's got to be the most antiquated, unfair, elitist, theocratic, *aristocratic* leftover from the dustbin of history on this side of the explored galaxy. But a Grayson's word is inviolable, and a Grayson steadholder has the authority to grant protection to anyone, anywhere, under any circumstances."

"And if I do, I'm bound—both by tradition and honor and by law—to see to it you get it."

"Precisely . . . Steadholder Harrington."

"Very well, Officer Cachat. You have Steadholder Harrington's guarantee of your personal safety and return to *Pottawatomie Creek*. And, while I'm being so free with my guarantees, I'll also guarantee Eighth Fleet won't blow *Pottawatomie Creek* out of space as soon as you're 'safely' back aboard."

"Thank you," Cachat said, and reached into his pocket. He carefully extracted a small device and activated a virtual keyboard. His fingers twiddled for a moment, entering a complex code, and then he tossed the device to Zilwicki.

"I'm sure everyone will feel happier if you hang onto that, Anton."

"*Thandi* certainly will," Zilwicki replied, and slid the disarmed device into his own pocket.

"And now, Captain Zilwicki," Honor said, "I believe you were about to explain just what brings you and Officer Cachat to visit me?"

"Your Grace," Zilwicki's body seemed to incline towards Honor without actually moving, "we know Queen Elizabeth and her government hold the Republic of Haven responsible for the attempt on my daughter's life. And I trust you'll remember how my wife was killed, and that I have no more reason to love Haven than the next man. Rather less, in fact.

"Having said that, however, I have to tell you that I, personally, am completely satisfied Haven had nothing at all to do with the assassination attempt on Torch."

Honor gazed at Zilwicki for several seconds without speaking. Her expression was merely thoughtful, and then she leaned back and crossed her long legs.

"That's a very interesting assertion, Captain. And, I can tell, one you believe to be accurate. For that matter, interestingly enough, *Officer Cachat* believes it to be accurate. That, of course, doesn't necessarily make it true."

"No, Your Grace, it doesn't," Zilwicki said slowly, and Honor tasted both of her visitors' burning curiosity as to how she could be so confident—and accurately so—about what they believed.

"All right," she said. "Suppose you begin, Captain, by telling me why *you* believe it wasn't a Havenite operation?"

"First, because it would be a particularly stupid thing for the Republic to have done," Zilwicki said promptly. "Leaving aside the minor point that being caught would be disastrous for Haven's interstellar reputation, it was the one thing guaranteed to derail the summit conference *they'd* proposed. And coupled with the Webster assassination, it would have been the equivalent of taking out pop-up ads in every 'fax in the galaxy that said 'Look, *we* did it! Aren't we nasty people?'"

The massive Gryphon highlander snorted like a particularly irate boar and shook his head.

"I've had some experience with the Havenite intelligence establishment, especially in the last couple of years. Its current management is a lot smarter than that. For that matter, not even

Oscar Saint-Just would have been arrogant enough—and stupid enough—to try something like that!"

"Perhaps not. But, if you'll forgive me, all of that is based purely on your reconstruction of what people ought to have been smart enough to recognize. It's logical, I'll admit. But logic, especially when human beings are involved, is often no more than a way to go wrong with confidence. I'm sure you're familiar with the advice 'Never ascribe to malice what you can put down to incompetence.' Or, in this case perhaps, stupidity."

"Agreed," Zilwicki said. "However, there's also the fact that I'm rather deeply tapped into Havenite intelligence operations in and around Congo." He bobbed his head at Cachat. "The intelligence types operating there and in Erewhon are fully aware that they don't want to tangle with the Audubon Ballroom. Or, for that matter, with all due modesty, with *me*. And the Republic of Haven is fully aware of how Torch and the Ballroom would react if it turned out Haven was actually responsible for the murder of Berry, Ruth, and Thandi Palane. Believe me. If they'd wanted to avoid meeting with Elizabeth, they would simply have called the summit off. They wouldn't have tried to sabotage it this way. And if they *had* tried to sabotage it this way, Ruth, Jeremy, Thandi, and I would have known about it ahead of time."

"So you're telling me that in addition to your analysis of all the logical reasons for them not to have done it, your own security arrangements would have alerted you to any attempt on Haven's part?"

"I can't absolutely guarantee that, obviously. I believe it to have been true, however."

"I see."

Honor rubbed the tip of her nose thoughtfully, then shrugged.

"I'll accept the probability that you're correct. At the same time, don't forget that someone—presumably Haven—managed to get to my own flag lieutenant. ONI still hasn't been able to suggest how that might have been accomplished, and while I have the highest respect for you and your capabilities, Admiral Givens isn't exactly a slouch herself."

"Point taken, Your Grace. However, I have another reason to believe Haven wasn't involved. And given the . . . unusual acuity with which you appear to have assessed Victor and myself, you may be more prepared to accept that reason than I was afraid you would be."

"I see," Honor repeated, and turned her eyes to Cachat. "Very well, Officer Cachat. Since you're obviously Captain Zilwicki's additional reason, suppose you convince me, as well."

"Admiral," Cachat said, abandoning the aristocratic titles which, she knew, had been their own subtle statement of plebeian distrust, "I find you have a much more disturbing presence than I'd anticipated. Have you ever considered a career in intelligence?"

"No. And about that convincing?"

Cachat chuckled harshly, then shrugged.

"All right, Admiral. The most convincing piece of evidence Anton has is that if the Republic had ordered any such operation on Torch, it would have been *my* job to carry it out. I'm the FIS chief of station for Erewhon, Congo, and the Maya Sector."

He made the admission calmly, although Honor knew he was very unhappy to do so. With excellent reason, she thought. Knowing with certainty who the opposition's chief spy was would have to make your own spies' jobs a lot easier.

"There are reasons—reasons of a personal nature—why my superiors might have tried to cut me out of the loop for this particular operation," Cachat continued, and she tasted his painstaking determination to be honest. Not because he wouldn't have been quite prepared to lie if he'd believed it was his duty, but because he'd come to the conclusion that he simply couldn't lie successfully to *her*.

"Although it's true those reasons exist," he went on, "it's also true that I have personal contacts at a very high level who would have alerted me anyway. And with all due modesty, my own network would have warned me if anyone from Haven had invaded my turf.

"Because all of that's true, I can tell you that the chance of any Republican involvement in the attempt to assassinate Queen Berry is effectively nonexistent. The bottom line, Admiral, is that *we didn't do it.*"

"Then who did?" Honor challenged.

"Obviously, if it wasn't Haven, our suspicions are naturally going to light on Mesa," Zilwicki said. "Mesa, and Manpower, have plenty of reasons of their own to want Torch destabilized and Berry dead. The fact that the neurotoxin used in the attempt is of Solly origin also points towards the probability of Mesan involvement. At the same time, I'm painfully well aware that everyone in the official intelligence establishment is going to line up to point out to me that we're naturally prejudiced in favor of believing Mesa is behind any attack upon us. And, to be totally honest, they'd be right."

"Which doesn't change the fact that you really do believe it was Mesa," Honor observed.

"No, it doesn't."

"And do you have any evidence beyond the fact that the neurotoxin probably came from the League?"

"No," Zilwicki admitted. "Not at this time. We're pursuing a couple of avenues of investigation which we hope will provide us with that evidence, but we don't have it yet."

"Which, of course, is the reason for this rather dramatic visit to me."

"Admiral," Cachat said with the first smile she'd seen from him, "I *really* think you should consider a second career in intelligence."

"Thank you, Officer Cachat, but I believe I can exercise intelligence without having to become a spy."

She smiled back at him, then shrugged.

"All right, Gentlemen. I'm inclined to believe you. And to agree with you, for that matter. It's never made sense to me that Haven would do something like attack Berry and Ruth. But, while *I* may believe you, I don't know how much good it's going to do. I'm certainly willing to present what you've told me to Admiral Givens, ONI, and Admiralty House. I don't think they're going to buy it, though. Not without some sort of corroborating evidence besides the promise—however sincere—of the senior Havenite spy in the area that he really, *really* didn't have anything to do with it. Call me silly, but somehow I don't think they're going to accept that you're an impartial, disinterested witness, Officer Cachat."

"I know that," Cachat replied. "And I'm not impartial, or disinterested. In fact, I have two very strong motives for telling you this. First, because I'm convinced that what happened in Congo doesn't represent my star nation's policy or desires, and that it's clearly not in the Republic's best interests. Because it isn't, I have a responsibility to do anything I can do mitigate the consequences of what's happened. That includes injecting any voice of sanity and reason I can into the Star Kingdom's decision-making process at the highest level I can reach. Which, at this moment, happens to be *you*, Admiral Harrington.

"Second, Anton and I are, as he said, pursuing our own investigation into this. His motives, I think, ought to be totally understandable and clear. My own reflect the fact that the Republic is being blamed for a crime it didn't commit. It's my duty to find out who did commit it, and to determine why he—or they—wanted to make it appear *we* did it. In addition, I have some personal motives, tied up with who might have been killed in the process, which also give me a very strong reason to want the people behind this. However, if our investigation prospers, we're going to need someone—at the highest level of the Star Kingdom's decision-making process we can reach—who's prepared to listen to whatever we find. We need, for want of a better term, a friend at court."

"So it really comes down to self-interest," Honor observed.

"Yes, it does," Cachat said frankly. "In intelligence matters, doesn't it always?"

"I suppose so."

Honor considered them both again, then nodded.

"Very well, Officer Cachat. For whatever it's worth, you have your friend at court. And just between the three of us, I hope to heaven you can turn up the evidence we need before several million people get killed."

Chapter Fifty-Six

"You can't be *serious!*" Baron Grantville blurted, looking incredulously at his sister-in-law.

"Yes, I certainly can be, Willie," Honor replied, with just a hint of a chill in her tone. "I'm not exactly in the habit of making jokes about things like this, you know."

The Prime Minister colored, and shook his head apologetically.

"Sorry. It's just that to be bringing this up at this late date, and with no evidence to support the theory...."

He let his voice trail off, and Honor reached up and stroked Nimitz's ears while she looked at Grantville levelly. She could hardly pretend his attitude was a surprise, but she'd given her word. Besides, she'd cherished profound doubts of her own about this war from the outset. Not that she'd really expected to magically change *his* mind about it.

Perhaps that was the real reason she'd asked to meet with him privately, she thought. Even a profoundly unhappy Spencer Hawke had been excluded from the meeting. He and Sergeant Clifford McGraw stood flanking the other side of the conference room door, and she'd sensed Grantville's surprise—and apprehension—when she left them there.

On the other hand, he hadn't been as surprised as he might have been. Despite the example of the High Ridge Government, a total idiot didn't normally become Prime Minister of Manticore, and Honor was *officially* back on Manticore for a final meeting at Admiralty House before launching Operation Sanskrit. A request by a fleet commander for a direct, unscheduled personal meeting with the Prime Minister under those circumstances was, to say the very least, unusual.

"Willie," she said after a moment, "you and I have disagreed about the fundamental nature of the current Havenite régime from the beginning. That means we've both got mental baggage at this point, and I don't want to lock horns with you on this issue. First, because you're the Prime Minister, not me. Second, because I'm a serving officer, and Queen's officers take the orders of their civilian superiors. And third, frankly, because the fact that Hamish and I are married now puts me in an uncomfortable position when I'm arguing not simply with the Prime Minister, but with my brother-in-law.

"Despite that, I truly believe you need to reconsider the position of Her Majesty's Government on this particular issue. Anton Zilwicki's in a far better position than anyone here in the Star Kingdom to know whether or not there was direct Havenite involvement in the attempt to kill his daughter. He still has contacts in the area which we've lost, he's intimately familiar with the situation on Torch itself, and he has a direct relationship with a fairly senior Havenite spy. You know this man's reputation, what he's already accomplished. And you know he's going to be highly suspicious of anyone who explains to him that they didn't have anything to do with the attempt to murder his daughter, so would he kindly not shoot *them* on sight. Or do I have to remind you what happened on Old Earth when his older daughter was kidnapped?"

Grantville made a face. Not of disagreement, so much as of painful memory. The Manpower Scandal had splattered on the previous Prime Minister, for whom Grantville had never had anything but contempt, but the fallout had still been extreme . . . and Anton Zilwicki could not have cared less. The entire government could have fallen, and he *still* wouldn't have cared—just as he hadn't cared if he himself ended up in prison for his actions. The father who'd orchestrated that particular exercise in mayhem was unlikely to take the events on Torch lightly.

"No, you don't have to remind me," he said. "For that matter, you don't have to remind me what happened to the mercenaries who tried to kill Catherine Montaigne when *they* tangled with Zilwicki. I'll happily concede the man's competence and the fact that he's dangerous. I'll even concede that he has the ear of the Queen—or, at least, of her niece—where certain questions are concerned.

"But what you're asking me to believe now is that some hypothetical third party is responsible for what happened on Torch. And, probably, for murdering Jim Webster. For that matter, probably for trying to kill *you*, since the technique was so similar in all three cases. And whenever you ask me to believe that, I come back again and again to the question of who had the most motive? And, for that matter, who has an established national track record of employing assassination as a routine technique?"

"I realize that," Honor said patiently. "But *anyone* with the proper resources can stage an assassination, and everyone has to know the Star Kingdom's had painful experience with previous Havenite régimes' use of assassination. So just what would *you* have done differently if you were a 'hypothetical third party' and wanted us to *automatically* assume the Havenites were attempting to sabotage their own peace conference?"

"Nothing," Grantville conceded after a moment. He leaned back in his chair, regarding Honor intently. "On the other hand, Honor, I've known you a long time. There's more to this than just Zilwicki's unsupported word, isn't there?"

Honor returned his gaze, and he chuckled harshly.

"You've gotten much better at high-stakes politics, but you still have to work on maintaining your expression of total candor while you conceal your hole cards."

"There is more to it," she admitted. "I didn't bring it up because I was pretty sure it wouldn't do your blood pressure any good if I did. Are you sure you want to hear about what I've been up to?"

"As my sister-in-law, or as a Queen's officer?" he asked bit warily.

"Either—both," she said with a crooked smile.

"If it's that bad, you'd better go ahead and tell me," he said, bracing himself visibly.

"Anton Zilwicki didn't come to visit me by himself," she said. "He brought a Mr. Cachat with him."

"Cachat," Grantville repeated. It was apparent the name was ringing bells, but that he hadn't quite put his mental hand on the memory.

"*Victor* Cachat," Honor said helpfully. "As in the same Victor Cachat who engineered the entire Torch gambit in the first place."

"A Peep spy?" If Grantville's expression had been incredulous before, it was dumbfounded now. "You had a *Peep spy* aboard your *flagship*?"

"Not just any old spy." Honor couldn't help it. Despite the anger beginning to bubble under the shock in Grantville's mindglow, she felt a certain manic glee in the admission. "As a matter of fact, he's now the Havenite chief of station for their entire Erewhon-based intelligence net."

The Prime Minister stared at her. Then he shook himself.

"This isn't funny," he said coldly. "It's entirely possible someone could make a case for treason out of what you've just admitted to me."

"How?" she challenged.

"You had a known senior secret agent of a star nation with whom we're at war aboard your flagship in a restricted military area, and from what you're saying, I feel quite confident he's not still there in a cell. Is he?"

"No, he isn't," she said, meeting his cold anger with a hard eye.

"And just what information did you allow him to take away from this completely unauthorized meeting, Admiral?"

"None he didn't bring with him."

"And you're prepared to prove that before a court-martial, if necessary?"

"No, Prime Minister, I'm not," she said in a voice of matching ice. "If my word isn't sufficient for you, then file charges and be damned to you."

Grantville's nostrils flared, but then he closed his eyes. His right hand clenched into a fist where it lay on the table before him, and Honor tasted the enormous effort he made to pull his icy fury back under control.

Interesting, she thought. *So Willie has the Alexander temper, too.*

"Your word is good enough for me," he said finally, opening his eyes once more, "but it may not be good enough for everyone if word of this . . . meeting ever gets out. My God, Honor! What were you *thinking* of?"

"I was thinking of the fact that a man who'd never met me was willing to come aboard my ship, knowing exactly what could happen to him. That he came with a suicide device in his pocket, which he was fully prepared to use. That, in fact, he *expected* to use it, and he came anyway. And that he told me the *truth*, Willie. You know I *know* that everything I just told you is true."

His eyes narrowed, because he did know.

"You say he expected to use his suicide device," the Prime Minister said after a moment, and she nodded. "Then I presume you also know—or think you do—why he was willing to come anyway?"

"Because he's a patriot," Honor said simply. "He's probably one of the most dangerous men I've ever met, and not just because of how competent he is, either. But the bottom line is that he takes his beliefs and responsibilities seriously. He knows the attempt to kill Berry and Ruth didn't go through his operatives, nor did he pick up on any effort by someone in Nouveau Paris to do an end run around him. And now that I've met the man, I don't doubt for a moment that he has his entire area of responsibility so tightly wired he *would* have known if something like that had happened. So since he knows he didn't do it, and he's virtually certain no one else in the Havenite government did it, he has to assume whoever *did* do it did it for reasons inimical to the Republic of Haven's foreign-policy and security. So he put his life on the line, in the full expectation that he was going to lose it, to tell us. Not because he loves *us*, but because he's trying to protect his own star nation. Because he believes his President is trying to stop a war and someone else is trying to sabotage her effort."

"And you . . . know," Grantville waved one hand, "all of this is true?"

"I know he wasn't lying to me, and that everything he told me was the complete truth in so far as he *knows* the truth. Of course it's possible he's wrong. Even the best intelligence people screw up. But what he told me was the best information he had."

"I see."

Grantville rocked his chair slightly back and forth, his brain working hard while he gazed at her.

"Have you discussed this with Hamish?" he asked after a moment.

"No." Honor looked away. "I wanted to. But, as I said, the fact that I'm married to him puts me in a peculiar position. I . . . chose not to involve him."

"You chose not to involve him because you didn't want anything to splash on him if this little meeting blew up in your face as spectacularly as it could have. That's what you mean, isn't it?"

"Maybe. To some extent. But also because it's almost impossible for our personal relationship not to have an impact on any conversation or debate we have. To be perfectly honest," she looked back at Grantville, "I didn't want to take the chance he might agree with me simply because it was me saying it."

"But you were willing to take the chance with *me*?" Grantville asked, with a flicker of returning humor.

"I had no choice where you were concerned," she said with another crooked smile. "It was talk to you, or go direct to Elizabeth. And, frankly, I'm not at all sure how *she* would have reacted."

"Poorly." Grantville's voice was bleak. "I don't believe I've ever seen her this furious. Whether it was the Peeps or someone who simply wanted us to believe it was, she's out for blood. And the hell of it, Honor, is that even if every single thing Cachat told you was the truth—so far as he knows, as you yourself said—I agree with her."

"Even if Haven had nothing to do with any of the assassinations and assassination attempts?" she asked quietly.

"If I could be *certain* they hadn't, I might feel differently. But I can't be. All I can know for certain is that one man who *ought* to know is convinced they didn't. But he's got to have a huge vested interest, whether he realizes it or not, in believing the best about his own government. I'll accept that he has no evidence this was a Peep operation. But if I recall my briefings on what happened in Erewhon and Congo accurately, his superiors might have had a very good reason to keep him out of the loop on something like this, considering who would probably have been among the victims. Am I wrong?"

"No," she admitted.

"So what am I supposed to do, Honor? We're in the middle of a war, we've already announced we're resuming operations, the Peeps have probably *already* resumed operations on the basis of our note, and the fact that Cachat didn't have anything to do with the attempt to kill Berry and Ruth doesn't prove someone else from Haven didn't."

He shook his head slowly, his expression sad.

"I'd like to believe you're right. I *want* to believe you are. But I can't make my decisions, formulate the Star Kingdom's policy, based on what I'd like to believe. I believe you military people are familiar with the need to formulate plans based on the worst-case scenario. I'm in the same position. I can't dislocate our entire strategy on the basis of what Zilwicki and Cachat *believe* to be true. If they had one single scrap of hard evidence, that might not be so. But they don't, and it is."

Honor tasted his honesty . . . and also the impossibility of changing his mind.

"I'm sorry to hear that," she said. "I think they're right, at least about whether or not what's happened represents the official policy of the Pritchart Administration."

"I realize that," Grantville said, and looked into her eyes. "And because I know you genuinely feel that way, I have to ask you. Are you still prepared to carry out your orders, Admiral Alexander-Harrington?"

She looked back, hovering on the brink of the unthinkable. If she said no, if she refused to carry out the operation and resigned her commission in protest, it would almost certainly blow the entire question wide open. The consequences for her personally, and for her husband and wife, would be . . . severe, at least in the short term. Her relationship with Elizabeth might well be permanently and irreparably damaged. Her career, in Manticoran service, at least, would probably be over. Yet all of that would be acceptable—a small price, actually—if it ended the war.

But it wouldn't. Grantville had put his finger squarely on the one insurmountable weakness: the lack of proof. All she had was the testimony of two men, in private conversation. At best, anything she said about what they'd told her would be hearsay, and there was simply no way she could expect anyone outside her immediate circle to understand—or believe—why she *knew* they'd told her the truth.

So the war would continue, whatever she did, and her own actions would have removed her from any opportunity of influencing its conduct or its outcome. That would be a violation of her responsibility to the men and women of Eighth Fleet, to her

Star Kingdom. Wars weren't always fought for the right reasons, but they were fought anyway, and the consequences to the people fighting them and to their star nations were the same, whatever the reasons. And she was a Queen's officer. She'd taken an oath to stand between the Star Kingdom and its enemies, why ever they were enemies. If the Star Kingdom she loved was going back into a battle in which so many others who'd taken that oath would die, she couldn't simply abandon them and stand aside. No, she had no choice but to stand beside them and face the same tempest.

"Yes," she said quietly, her voice sad but without hesitation or reservation. "I'm prepared to execute my orders, Willie."

Chapter Fifty-Seven

"What's the latest on our visitors?" Admiral Alessandra Giovanni asked.

"Pretty much unchanged, Ma'am," Commander Ewan Mac-Naughton replied. "Their starships are still stooging around outside the hyper limit, but their platforms are dancing all over the damned place ... and making sure we know it."

He grimaced and waved one hand at the huge display showing the Lovat System's inner planets and the space about them.

The system's G-6 primary floated at the display's center, orbited by the innermost cinder—which had never attained the dignity of an actual name, aside from Lovat I—and then the planets Furnace, Forge, and Anvil. At seven light-minutes from the primary, Forge, the system's only habitable world, would have enjoyed a pleasant climate, if not for its pronounced axial tilt. Although, to be fair, if you liked severe seasonal weather changes (which MacNaughton didn't), Forge was still a lovely world.

It was also heavily industrialized.

The Lovat System had originally been settled by the Aamodt Corporation, one of the huge industrial concerns which had helped build the original Republic of Haven's enormous wealth and power only to go the way of the dinosaur under the *People's* Republic. The current system governor, however, Havard Ellefsen, was a direct descendent of the Aamodt Coporation's founder, and Lovat had somehow avoided the worst consequences of the PRH's efforts to kill every golden goose it could lay hands on. Despite the fact that it was less than fifty light-years from the Haven System,

676

Lovat had remained one of the unquestioned bright spots of the People's Republic's generally blighted economy, and the system's industrial concerns had played a major role in the Republic's industrial renaissance since the economic reforms Rob Pierre had forced through and the restoration of the Constitution.

Among other things, Forge's current population of almost three billion was deeply involved in the enormous naval construction programs Thomas Theisman had initiated after going public about the existence of the Republican Navy's new ship types. To be sure, the Lovat System wasn't one of the primary yard sites. Its local industry was much more heavily committed to the construction of light units—light attack craft and the new light cruiser classes—and fleet support vessels—ammunition ships, personnel transports, general cargo haulers, and repair ships. Despite that, it was among the Republic's twenty or so most important star systems, and its system defenses reflected that importance.

Just over eight thousand LACs were based on Forge and the system's orbital platforms. A permanent covering force of three battle squadrons—admittedly, of pre-pod types, but still a total of twenty-four superdreadnoughts—was assigned, and the system was liberally blanketed with system defense missile pods. In the last six months, Lovat had also received not just one Moriarty platform, but three, the second pair to serve solely as backups for the first.

And, MacNaughton thought, *there's also the defenses I* can't *see.*

All of which explained why Commander MacNaughton was as confident as his admiral that no Manty raiding force was going to stick its nose into Lovat.

"We've got their arrays in several quadrants of the inner system," he continued, indicating the wavering icons representing the ghostlike sensor traces which were the best his platforms could do against current-generation Manticoran stealth technology. "They've been buzzing around for over sixty hours now, and we've still got hyper footprints jumping in and out all around the periphery. It's starting to get on my nerves, Ma'am."

"Which is exactly what it's supposed to do," Giovanni pointed out.

"I know that, Ma'am. And so do our LAC crews. But that doesn't keep it from being irritating, and Commander Lucas reports that Moriarty's gold crew is beginning to suffer from fatigue."

"I told the Octagon we needed more personnel," Giovanni growled. "Unfortunately, we don't really have them yet—not for Moriarty. Or, rather, we could have complete backup crews . . . if we were willing to do without backup *platforms*."

MacNaughton nodded. Admiral Foraker and her Bolthole command continued to work miracles in their training programs, but the Navy's enormous expansion was taking its toll. Despite the steadily climbing educational levels of the Republic, the Navy still had to spend far more time than the Manties did providing its recruits with the basic education needed to perform their jobs. Fortunately, Foraker had gotten very, very good at doing just that. *Un*fortunately, it still put a bottleneck into the availability of fully trained manpower.

"Shall I instruct Lucas to stand the gold platform down and bring up silver or bronze?"

"Um." Giovanni ran a hand over her dark hair, eyes thoughtful, then shrugged. "Go ahead and shift to silver. I doubt we're really going to need them, but it won't hurt for silver to get a little more hands-on experience, anyway."

"Yes, Ma'am. I'll get on it right away, and—"

The rest of MacNaughton's sentence was slashed off by the sudden jangle of alarms as a massive hyper footprint exploded onto the plot.

"Well done, Theo," Honor Alexander-Harrington said.

Lieutenant Commander Kgari had dropped TF 81, Eighth Fleet's leading task force, into normal-space barely forty thousand kilometers outside the Lovat System's hyper limit. That was extraordinarily precise astrogation, and Kgari smiled in appreciation of the well-deserved praise.

Honor smiled back, but her true attention was focused on the huge flag bridge tactical display. She watched alertly, waiting for CIC to post any major changes, but the only differences from *Skirmisher's* last upload were insignificant.

Not that it's going to stay that way if we've got things figured right, she reminded herself.

"All right," she said. "Harper, pass the execute command."

"Aye, aye, Your Grace," Lieutenant Brantley acknowledged, and the eight CLACs of Alice Truman's reinforced carrier squadron launched almost nine hundred LACs as Alistair McKeon's BatRon 61 headed in-system, screened by fifteen Manticoran and Grayson BC(P)s and HMS *Nike* under the overall command of Rear Admiral Erasmus Miller. Michelle Henke would have had the command, except that the terms of her parole precluded her from serving against the Republic. So she'd been sent to Talbott, where Honor knew she would prove enormously useful, and Michael Oversteegen, promoted to Rear Admiral, had been given her squadron. But much as Honor approved of Oversteegen's demonstrated capability, he was junior to Miller. And the Grayson rear admiral was more than merely competent in his own right, she reminded herself.

Winston Bradshaw and Charise Fanaafi's twelve heavy cruisers, eight of them *Saganami-C*-class ships, backed Miller up, and six light cruisers under the command of Commodore George Ullman, who'd replaced Commodore Moreau when she died aboard HMS *Buckler* at Solon, thickened the screen.

It was a powerful force, by any measure, although Honor was fully aware that it was grossly outnumbered and outgunned by the system's defenders.

Just as it was supposed to be.

"Admiral Truman reports all LAC wings away, Your Grace," Andrea Jaruwalski announced.

"Very good. Instruct her to hyper out to the Alpha rendezvous."

"Aye, aye, Your Grace."

Honor watched the carriers' icons disappear, then settled herself into her command chair, a skinsuited Nimitz in her lap, and watched her thirty starships accelerate steadily in-system.

"Do you think this is another Suarez, Ma'am?" MacNaughton asked tensely as he watched the oncoming icons move steadily across the plot.

"I don't know."

Giovanni's own eyes were slitted in concentration, and he noticed she was wrapping a single lock of hair around her right index finger. It was a mannerism he'd grown accustomed to over the last three T-years, and he waited respectfully.

"No," she said after several moments of consideration. "I

don't know why, but I don't think so. These people are really here."

"It seems awfully gutsy of them," MacNaughton said, and she shrugged. "And not especially bright, after Solon."

"I'm inclined to agree. On the other hand, maybe they think they can get deep enough in to do significant damage and still avoid interception. This is the strongest raiding force they've sent in yet, assuming the outer platforms' analysis is correct. It's possible they figure they've got the firepower to fight their way out past the sort of interception Admiral Giscard managed at Solon."

"If they do, they're wrong, Ma'am," MacNaughton said.

"We *think* they are, Ewan," Giovanni corrected. "Although, if they've got the sense God gave a Legislaturalist, at least they'll stay out of our inner-system missile envelope!"

Honor glanced at the date/time display and smiled sadly. If Illescue was on schedule, her daughter would be born in almost exactly eight minutes.

Katherine Allison Miranda Alexander-Harrington. She sampled the name silently, wishing with all her heart that she were there, watching the miracle of life, tasting her daughter's newborn mind-glow, and not here, orchestrating the deaths of thousands. She inhaled deeply, and sent a thought winging across the light-years.

Happy birthday, baby. I hope God lets me watch you grow up . . . and that you never have to do something like this.

"Coming up on Point Samar in five minutes, Your Grace," Jaruwalski said.

"Thank you, Andrea."

Honor looked up and checked the time display. Her units had been accelerating towards rendezvous with Forge for thirty-five minutes at a steady 4.81 KPS^2 from their relatively low initial velocity. They were up to 11,750 KPS, and they'd traveled just over fourteen million kilometers. They were still seventy-four minutes from turnover for a zero/zero intercept, but the one thing she felt absolutely confident of was that none of the defenders expected her to be making any zero/zero rendezvous with Forge.

Of course, they might be wrong, she thought coldly.

She returned her attention to the tactical plot. The old-style superdreadnoughts, which Jaruwalski had designated Bogey One, were holding their positions in-system, close to Forge, but the forward sensor drones showed that their impeller wedges were up, and their sidewalls were active. The massive LAC force their scouts had reported was also clearly in evidence. Whoever the system commander here in Lovat was, she didn't appear to have opted for the sort of deceptiveness Admiral Bellefeuille had displayed at Chantilly.

But appearances can be . . . deceiving, Honor reminded herself, with a slight smile. *I hope they are, anyway. I'd hate to have wasted all this preparation if this is really all they've got.*

She pursed her lips slightly, looking down at the smaller repeater plot deployed from the side of her command chair. Unlike the main plot, it was configured to show the entire system, and her gaze rested on the green sphere which represented the Lovat hyper limit.

"Any time now, Your Grace. If we've got it figured right, at least." She looked up. Mercedes Brigham stood beside her command chair, looking down at the same repeater, and Honor nodded.

"If it were me, I'd figure I had the patsies right about where I wanted them," she agreed. "And by now, their recon platforms have to have gotten a good enough look at us to be sure we're not just drones."

Brigham nodded back, and the two of them watched the plot, waiting.

"Admiral, they're seventy minutes from turnover."

"Very good, Ewan. Send the execute to *Tarantula*."

"Hyper footprint! We have major hyper footprints directly astern and at system north and system south," Andrea Jaruwalski reported. "Designate these forces Bogey Two, Bogey Three, and Bogey Four! They're accelerating in-system at five-point-zero-eight KPS-squared."

"Very well," Honor said calmly.

She leaned back in her command chair and crossed her legs, stroking the plushy fur between Nimitz's ears.

"Admiral, Admiral Giovanni's platforms confirm that one of the superdreadnoughts matches the emissions signature of the ship that got away at Solon," Marius Gozzi said.

"So," Javier Giscard said softly, "'the Salamander' is back."

He shook his head with more than a trace of sadness. Eloise had tried to hide her despair in her last letter to him, but he knew her too well. When Elizabeth Winton had accepted her offer of the summit, it had been like watching the sun come out. And when whatever the hell had happened on Old Earth and Torch crushed any prospect of a negotiated settlement, it had been like watching a late blizzard bury the frozen blossoms of a murdered spring.

He supposed he couldn't really blame the Manties for leaping to the conclusion that the Republic was behind what had happened. It didn't make sense, in a lot of ways, yet people—and star nations—all too often did things that *didn't* make sense. But however well he might understand their reasoning, he still had to cope with the consequences of their actions.

And so do they, he thought grimly, watching that outnumbered force go to military power. Not that it was going to do it a great deal of good. Its six superdreadnoughts were thoroughly outgunned by the sixteen SD(P)s and four CLACs in each of his three intercepting forces; the inner-system's missile pods were far more numerous than they'd been at Solon; and he'd been able to plot his own translations much more closely. Unlike Solon, *these* Manties would be unable to avoid entering the effective missile envelope of at least one of his intercepting forces.

"Open fire, Sir?" Selma Thackeray asked, but Giscard shook his head.

"Harrington showed us at Solon what she could do to long-range missile fire," he told the ops officer, "and she's got a lot more defensive platforms than she had then. No. We'll just follow along. We're the beaters; Moriarty is the hunter. Once Giovanni chews them up, we'll worry about cleaning up the remnants."

"Yes, Sir," Thackeray acknowledged, and Giscard returned his attention to the plot.

They shouldn't have sent you out with so few ships, Your Grace, he told the light code of HMS *Imperator*.

"All right, Andrea," Honor said, glancing at the time display once more. Twelve minutes had passed since the Havenite ambush force had translated in behind her. "Execute Ozawa."

"Aye, aye, Your Grace!" Jaruwalski said, her voice sparkling with excitement, and tapped a single command into her console.

"There's the execute signal, Ma'am!" Lieutenant Harcourt announced.

"Understood," Commander Estwicke replied, and looked at her astrogator. "Take us out, Jerome."

"Aye, aye, Skipper," Lieutenant Weissmuller acknowledged, and HMS *Ambuscade* popped back up into hyper-space.

Weissmuller had plotted his translation with care, and he'd had plenty of time to position his ship perfectly in normal-space before executing it. *Ambuscade* arrived precisely where she was supposed to be, and her plot suddenly blossomed with the light codes of capital ships.

"Communications, pass the word to Admiral Yanakov," Estwicke said.

"Hyper footprint!"

Javier Giscard's head snapped up at the unanticipated announcement. Commander Thackeray was bent over her console, fingers flying as she massaged the contact, and then she looked up, her face taut.

"Admiral, we've got eighteen superdreadnoughts or CLACs, well outside the hyper limit, directly astern of us. Range five-three-point-nine million kilometers. Velocity relative to Lovat two-point-five-zero-one thousand KPS. They—"

She broke off for just a moment, looking back down at her plot, then cleared her throat.

"Update, Sir. It's twelve SD(P)s and six carriers. The carriers just launched full LAC complements."

Giscard nodded, and hoped he looked calmer than he felt.

So she did set up her own mousetrap, by God, he thought. *I wondered if she would, after what we did to her at Solon. And it looks like they've reinforced their Eighth Fleet more heavily than NavInt predicted.*

He frowned down at the plot, his mind busy. The twelve super-dreadnoughts behind him probably had the edge in total combat power, despite his numerical advantage, and the LACs they were deploying would be more effective in the missile-defense role. But they didn't have a big enough advantage, and their astrogation had been off. He was about to get hurt, but it was unlikely that they could have *destroyed* any of his wallers before he ran out of their effective range even if their astrogation had been perfect, and it hadn't been. They had him trapped deep enough inside the hyper limit that he couldn't avoid action, but they'd made their own alpha translation 2.8 light-minutes *outside* the limit. At that range, even Manty MDM accuracy was going to be significantly degraded, and he was too far ahead of them, with too great an advantage in base velocity, for them to overtake him.

And Harrington was still in *front* of him, driving steadily deeper into the waiting defensive missiles.

"Start rolling pods, Selma," he told his ops officer. "Fire Plan Gamma."

The outer-system FTL platforms reported the arrival of Admiral Yanakov's Task Force 82 to Alessandra Giovanni almost as quickly as Selma Thackeray reported it to Javier Giscard.

Despite a brief, instinctive panic reaction, Giovanni quickly reached the same conclusions Giscard had, and her smile was much more unpleasant than his expression had been.

So the great "Salamander" can fuck up just like the rest of us mere mortals, she thought. *Pity about that.*

"Range from Forge?" she asked.

"Still one-one-point-two light-minutes, Ma'am," MacNaughton replied. "Roughly another thirty-six minutes to missile range for Moriarty."

"Thank you," she said, and turned back to the outer-system plot as the multi-drive missiles began to launch.

The range was almost fifty-four million kilometers, and Bogey Two was running away from TF 82 at a relative velocity of more than four thousand KPS. Missile flight time was over eight minutes, and as Giscard had demonstrated at Solon, even Manticoran accuracy at that range was going to be poor.

Except . . .

"Sir, there's something . . . odd about the Manties' launch," Thackeray said.

"What do you mean, 'odd'?" Giscard asked sharply.

"Their attack birds are coming in . . . well, 'clumped' is the only word I can think of for it, Sir. They aren't spreading out in a proper dispersion pattern."

"What?"

Giscard punched a command into his own repeater plot and frowned. Thackeray was right. His own outgoing missiles were spreading out, distancing themselves from one another to reduce wedge interference with their telemetry links to the ships which had launched them. Everyone's missiles did that.

But the Manties' missiles weren't.

"Query CIC," he told Thackeray. "I want an analysis of this pattern. There's got to be some reason for it."

"CIC's already on it, Sir. So far, they don't have any explanation."

Giscard grunted in acknowledgment. Actually, he realized, the attack missiles *were* spreading out, just not the way they should have. They were coming in in discrete clusters, spread across an attack front which would bring them all in simultaneously in the end, but making the trip in relatively tight groups of about eight or ten missiles each.

No, he thought as a preliminary analysis from the Combat Information Center came up as a sidebar to his plot. *They're coming in in clusters of* exactly *eight missiles each. Which is stupid, since they have* twelve *missiles in each pod!*

It was called "Apollo," after the archer of the gods.

It hadn't been easy for the R&D types to perfect. Even for Manticoran technology, designing the components had required previously impossible levels of miniaturization, and BuWeaps had encountered more difficulties than anticipated in putting the system into production. This was its first test in actual combat, and the crews which had launched the MDMs watched with bated breath to see how well it performed.

Javier Giscard was wrong. There weren't twelve missiles in an Apollo pod; there were nine. Eight relatively standard attack missiles or EW platforms, and the Apollo missile—much larger than the others, and equipped with a down-sized, short-ranged two-way FTL communications link developed from the one deployed in the still larger Ghost Rider reconnaissance drones. It was a remote control node, following along behind the other eight missiles from the same pod, without any warhead or electronic warfare capability of its own.

The impeller wedges of the other missiles hid it and its pulsed transmissions from the sensors of Giscard's ships, and from his counter-missiles. But its position allowed it to monitor the standard telemetry links from the other missiles of its pod. And it also carried a far more capable AI than any standard attack missile—one capable of processing the data from all of the other missiles' tracking and homing systems and sending the result back to its mothership via grav-pulse.

The ships which had launched them had deployed the equally new Keyhole II platforms, equipped not with standard light-speed links for their offensive missiles, but with grav-pulse links. Virtually every Manticoran or Grayson ship which could currently deploy Keyhole II was in Eighth Fleet's order of battle, and Honor Alexander-Harrington had taken ruthless advantage of the capability when she formulated her attack plans.

The grav-pulse transmissions were faster than light, although they weren't *instantaneous*. Actual transmission speed was "only" about sixty-four times the speed of light, but that was enormously better than anyone had ever been able to do before. The updated sensor information from the on-rushing missiles crossed the distance to the tactical sections and massively capable computers of the superdreadnoughts which had launched them, and at this range, the transmission lag was less than three seconds. For all practical purposes, they might as well have made the trip instantaneously. As did the corrections those tactical sections sent back.

In effect, Apollo gave the Royal Manticoran Navy effectively real-time correction ability at any attainable powered missile range.

Javier Giscard's tactical officers didn't realize at first what they faced. In fact, most of them never did realize.

The Manty missiles ignored their decoys almost contemptuously, and those peculiar clumps of MDMs maneuvered with a precision no missile-defense officer had ever seen before. It was almost as if each clump were a single missile, one which bored in through the defensive shield of the task group's electronic warfare as if it didn't exist.

Counter-missiles began to fire, and something else very peculiar happened. The EW platforms seeded throughout the Manticoran salvo didn't come up simultaneously, or in groups, the way they ought to have. Instead, they came up individually, singly, almost as if they could actually *see* the counter-missiles and adjust their own sequences.

Dragon's Teeth activated at *precisely* the right moment to draw the maximum number of counter-missiles into attacking the false targets. Dazzlers blasted the onboard sensors of other counter-missiles . . . just as the attack missiles behind them arced upward, or dove downward, to drive straight through the gap the Dazzlers had burned in the defensive envelope.

Not all the defensive missiles could be blinded or evaded, of course. There were simply too many of them. But their effectiveness was slashed.

The twelve superdreadnoughts of Task Force 82 had rolled quadruple patterns before they launched. Two hundred and eighty-eight Apollo pods had launched nineteen hundred attack missiles and four hundred EW platforms, along with two hundred and eighty-eight control missiles.

Javier Giscard's counter-missiles stopped only three hundred of the attack birds. His desperate point defense clusters, in the single volley each of them got, killed another four hundred.

Twelve hundred got through.

Damage alarms screamed on *Sovereign of Space*'s command deck and flag bridge. The huge ship shuddered and bucked as not one, or two, but *scores* of Manticoran missiles ripped straight through the heart of the task group's missile defenses. Armor splintered, atmosphere spewed into space, weapons mounts and point defense clusters were blasted into shattered wreckage, and the drum roll of destruction went on and on and on.

All of Judah Yanakov's fire had been concentrated on only two ships. Partly, that was because no one had really known how effective Apollo would prove against live opposition, and partly it had been because superdreadnoughts were simply so inconceivably tough. Killing targets that rugged was *hard*, and Honor and Yanakov had been determined to do as much damage with the first salvo, before the enemy had any chance to adjust to the new threat, as they could.

They did.

Javier Giscard clung to the arms of his command chair, surrounded by the frantic combat chatter of his task group, listening to the shrilling alarms, the desperate reports of damage control parties fighting the tidal wave of damage. His link to Damage Control Central lacked the detail of Captain Reuman's displays, but huge swathes of crimson damage blasted their way across the ship's schematic as he watched.

And then there was one brief, terrible flash as something ripped into the far end of the flag bridge. His head whipped up, and he just had time to see Selma Thackery and her tactical party torn apart by the blast front screaming towards him. Just long enough for his brain to begin to realize what was happening.

"Eloi—" he began, his voice soft in the hurricane of alarms and devastation.

He never finished her name.

"Jesus Christ," Ewan MacNaughton whispered, his face white.

The first Manticoran missile salvo had killed two of Admiral Giscard's superdreadnoughts outright . . . including *Sovereign of Space*. The second salvo, rumbling in on the first launch's heels forty-eight seconds later, killed two more, and the one after that, two more.

It took a total of eleven salvos—less than eight minutes' fire—to kill every superdreadnought in Bogey Two.

"How the hell did they *do* that?"

MacNaughton didn't even realize he'd asked the question aloud, but Admiral Giovanni answered it anyway.

"I don't know," she said, her voice ugly. "But it's not going to help their lead ships in another twenty-five minutes."

"CIC estimates another twenty minutes until we hit the envelope for their inner-system pods, Your Grace," Mercedes Brigham said quietly, and Honor nodded.

Imperator's flag bridge was oddly silent. Far astern of them, Judah Yanakov's missile batteries had just finished off the helpless CLACs of Bogey Two. He wasn't wasting any of his fire on the orphaned LACs. Instead, he'd recovered his own LACs and translated back out, and Honor watched her display, waiting.

Then Task Force 82 translated back into normal-space yet again. This time, much closer to the limit, and directly behind Bogey Three.

"Admiral Yanakov is launching against Bogey Three, Your Grace," Jaruwalski reported, and Honor nodded.

"Too bad he won't have time to catch Bogey Four before it gets too far in-system for him to range on, as well, Your Grace," Brigham said. "I'd love to make a clean sweep."

Honor glanced at her, remembering what had happened to her own command at Solon. Part of her agreed entirely with Brigham, and not just because of the professional naval officer in her. But the taste of revenge had a bitter tang, and she looked back at the plot.

"We'll just have to settle for what we can get," she said calmly. "And it's about time to see how vulnerable Balder really is. Andrea," she looked back up at Jaruwalski.

"Yes, Your Grace?"

"Activate the Mistletoe platforms."

"What the—?"

Commander MacNaughton stiffened in consternation.

"Admiral Giovanni! We've got—"

Giovanni was still turning towards her display when the explosions began.

The Havenite tracking crews had become accustomed to the fact that they simply couldn't localize and destroy the highly stealthy Manticoran reconnaissance platforms used to scout their star systems. It was galling, but true. And so, aside from a certain deep-seated irritation, they'd actually paid relatively little attention to the long-endurance Ghost Rider reconnaissance drones the Manticorans had distributed throughout the inner system of Lovat.

Which was unfortunate.

Sonja Hemphill had personally chosen the name "Mistletoe" in honor of the dart which had killed the god Balder in Norse mythology, and the name proved apt.

"Where the hell are they *coming* from?" Giovanni demanded.

"I don't *know*, Ma'am!" MacNaughton replied, his voice as anguished as his expression as the Manticoran laser heads ripped into the Moriarty platforms. Not just *one* of the platforms; all three of them. The stealth and dispersion which were supposed to have protected them obviously hadn't, he thought, and closed his eyes for a moment as the relentless avalanche of fire blew them apart.

Alessandra Giovanni's face was white with shock. With the

Moriarty platforms gone, she had nothing that could control missile salvos of the size needed to batter down Manticoran missile defenses. And given what the Manties had already done to Admiral Giscard's forces, it was painfully obvious her own anti-missile defenses were going to be at best marginally effective.

"The recon platforms!" MacNaughton said suddenly. "The bastards put laser heads on their goddamned *recon* platforms!"

Giovanni blinked, then shook her head and looked sharply at MacNaughton. He was right, she realized. It was the only explanation.

"But how did they find Moriarty?" she demanded. "Unless—"

"Unless what, Ma'am?" MacNaughton asked when she broke off suddenly.

"Suarez," she said sharply. "That's what Suarez was all about! They figured out what happened to them at Solon, and they used their EW drones to trick us into activating the Moriarty net at Suarez after they'd already planted their recon platforms deep enough in-system to see them. They had complete, detailed fingerprints on what they were looking for!"

"And then they mixed in armed recon drones to kill them after they found them," MacNaughton said through clenched teeth.

"That's exactly what they did," Giovanni agreed harshly. "Damn! They can't have the acceleration to be very effective against moving targets at any sort of range, but against fixed targets, especially when the attack birds know *exactly* what to look for . . ."

"Commander MacNaughton!" a rating called, and MacNaughton whipped back to his own displays. His shoulders went absolutely rigid for a moment, then slumped, and he looked back at Giovanni.

"Not just Moriarty, Ma'am," he grated. "It looks like we're going to have to start deploying the system defense pods further apart. They just took out three-quarters of the Beta echelon and almost that many of the Delta birds."

"How?" Giovanni asked flatly.

"More of their damned recon platforms. It had to be. They got old-fashioned nukes—the yields are somewhere in the five-hundred-megaton range—close enough to the pods to take them out with proximity explosions."

Giovanni nodded silently. Of course. If you could put laser heads on the things, then why not regular nukes? Not that they'd really had to. Given the accuracy they'd just shown against Giscard, they could take the pods out with proximity-armed MDM launches from beyond any range at which she could possibly expect to score hits in return.

"Admiral Giovanni," a shaken communications officer said, "Admiral Trask is asking for you."

Alessandra Giovanni glanced once more at the plot where the heart and mind of her defenses had just been annihilated, then drew a deep breath. Of course Trask wanted to speak to her. His obsolescent superdreadnoughts were going to be little more than targets for Harrington's SD(P)s, and Giovanni wasn't optimistic about her LACs' chance to get through Harrington's defensive fire and damned *Katanas* without the support of massed attacks from the system defense missile pods.

Which meant that if she committed Admiral Wentworth Trask's ships, he and all of his people were going to die.

"According to the standard recon platforms, we just took out all three of their control stations, Your Grace!" Jaruwalski announced jubilantly.

"Very good, Andrea. In that case, we'll proceed with the Alpha plan. Let's whittle their deployed pods down as far as we can before we enter their envelope."

"Aye, aye, Your Grace."

Honor nodded and turned back to her plot, hoping that whoever was in command over there would realize how helpless her defensive starships were and surrender before she had to kill them all.

Chapter Fifty-Eight

"How bad is it?" Eloise Pritchart asked flatly.

Thomas Theisman looked at her for a moment before he replied.

She looked . . . broken, he thought. Not in spirit, not in her determination to meet her responsibilities. But if those remained intact, something else, deep inside was a bleeding wound, and his own heart ached in sympathy. She wasn't just his President. She was his friend, just as Javier had been, and Javier's death, after all he and she been through, all they'd faced and survived under the Committee of Public Safety, was a bitter, bitter blow.

She returned his gaze across her desk, her eyes as flat and lifeless as her voice, and he knew she knew what he was thinking. But she said nothing more. She simply waited, motionless.

"It's *very* bad," he said finally. "Lovat, and all the LACs, support ships, and munitions we were building there, are simply gone. Harrington took them *all* out. Not to mention destroying thirty-two podnaughts, four CLACs, all twenty-four of Admiral Trask's older superdreadnoughts, and something like ten thousand LACs. I can't even begin to compute the straight economic cost. Rachel's people are still in a state of shock just looking at the preliminary numbers, but I think you can safely assume that they just at least doubled the total economic and industrial cost of all their previous raids combined." He shook his head. "Compared to this, what we did to Zanzibar was a love tap."

Pritchart's face had tightened with fresh pain as the litany of destruction rolled out.

"Fortunately, the loss of life was much lower than it might have been," Theisman continued. "Admiral Giovanni had the sense to order Trask to stand down his superdreadnoughts when Harrington started punching out her system defense missile pods with proximity warheads. He scuttled them himself, to prevent their capture, but all of his people got off alive first. We lost more of the LAC crews. They had to at least try, and no one can fault Giovanni for thinking there ought to have been enough of them to let them swarm Harrington's lead task force. Except that every single one of the LACs covering that task force was a *Katana*. Combined with their new counter-missiles and whatever they used on our wallers, they massacred our *Cimeterres*. Even the new Alpha birds."

"How did they do it?" she asked in that same flat, terrible voice.

"We're still evaluating the preliminary reports. From what we've seen so far, it looks like they used two new weapons on us. What makes it hurt worse is that both their new systems appear to be absolutely logical progressions from their damned Ghost Rider technology, and we never even saw them coming.

"We should have realized that sooner or later they were going to strap weapons onto their recon drones. They've demonstrated they can operate them deep inside our defended areas with virtual impunity, and they probably took a certain pleasure from applying a variant of the same technique Saint-Just used to destroy Elizabeth's yacht in Yeltsin. The bad news is how close they can get them; the good news—such as it is—is that, even so, they can't get them all the way into attack range in stealth. They still have to get into range to execute their attacks, and not even Manty stealth systems can hide them during the last hundred thousand kilometers or so of their runs. They don't have the sort of acceleration rates missiles do, either, and to be used properly, they have to attack virtually from rest, or else they can't loiter until the proper moment. So they have relatively low closing velocities when they come in, and they can be engaged by counter-missiles and standard point defense, now that we know they're out there. Our intercept probabilities won't be good, especially given how little warning we'll have between the moment their drives peak and the moment they reach attack range, but we can probably cope with the threat."

He paused for a moment, then shrugged.

"Actually, this part of it's largely my own personal fault," he said unflinchingly. "Shannon warned me from the beginning that the Moriarty platforms' stealth wouldn't be good enough to hide them if the Manties figured out what they should be looking for. She wanted to build them into purpose-built superdreadnoughts, or at least add them as strap-on components to larger, more heavily defended platforms. I overruled her because of the need to get Moriarty into service as quickly as possible. I shouldn't have. She was right."

"So were you. We did—*do*—need them. You didn't see some sort of invisible attack coming, but neither did anyone else. Don't second-guess yourself on this one."

Theisman bobbed his head, but he knew that was one presidential directive he wasn't going to be able to obey.

"The other new weapon they deployed is actually much more frightening," he continued. "The accuracy it demonstrated is bad enough, but what it did to our EW capabilities and counter-missiles may even have been worse. I'm trying very hard to remember we're looking at *preliminary* reports, but I'll be frank, Eloise. It's hard not to panic over this one.

"I've talked it over with Linda Trenis and Victor Lewis. Obviously, we haven't been able to get Shannon's input yet, but I'll be surprised if she reaches any different conclusions on the basis of the data we have so far.

"They've obviously incorporated an FTL link into their missile telemetry. I'm guessing it has to be an entirely separate, dedicated platform—a roughly missile-sized bird they've managed to squeeze the grav-pulse com into—that serves as an advanced data processing node. Nobody ever considered doing anything like that before, because there really wasn't any point. Light-speed limitations were light-speed limitations, and using this sort of approach must tie all the missiles the command platform is controlling into a fairly tightly bunched cluster. That *should* make them more vulnerable to interception, and before the FTL com came along, any control platform would have been just as far from home and just as sluggish responding to telemetry commands as any other missile.

"But what they've done gives their missiles the next best thing to *real-time* command control input from their shipboard tac sections, Eloise. You aren't a professional naval officer, so you may not realize just what a huge advantage that is. Even with conventional single-drive missiles, there's *always* been a light-speed telemetry lag which makes it impossible to exert effective shipboard control at extended missile ranges. Or to get improved targeting data back from one set of your attack birds' sensors and use it to update the targeting of another set.

"But apparently that isn't true for the Manties anymore. They don't have to preprogram evasion maneuvers into their missiles. Don't have to launch with a locked-in attack profile, or even prepackaged EW profiles. They can use their shipboard computational ability to analyze counter-missile patterns, electronic warfare emissions, and then they can make changes on the fly, adjust *everything* as they get steadily closer, get steadily better data on the defenses they have to penetrate. They can command their electronic warfare missiles to activate at precisely the most effective moment—decided by the capabilities of a *superdreadnought's* tactical computers, not just what can be squeezed into a missile body. And on top of that, they can direct the flight of their attack missiles to take the greatest possible advantage of the holes their EW opens up.

"In short, their accuracy's going to be enormously greater than ours in any maximum-range engagement, and their missiles' ability to penetrate our defenses is going to be much higher, as well. So they're going to get through with more laser heads, and those laser heads are going to be much more accurate when they arrive."

"So our numerical superiority just evaporated," Pritchart said grimly.

"Not . . . necessarily," Theisman said, and for the first time since he'd entered her office, emotion flickered in her topaz eyes.

It was incredulity.

"You just said they can kill our ships—like they did Javier's—at ranges where we can't even hurt them," she said curtly.

"Yes, they can. With at least *some* of their ships."

"What do you mean?"

She cocked her head, eyes suddenly intent, and Theisman shrugged.

"Eloise, this is a new weapon, just deployed. Obviously, it's possible they've refitted with it across the board. I don't think they have, though."

"Why not?"

"Eighth Fleet's been their first team ever since they activated it. It's got their most modern ships, and what I believe is their best fleet commander. It's also been their primary offensive weapon. But Eighth Fleet obviously didn't have this capability at Solon, five and a half months ago. If they'd had it, they sure as hell would've used it when Javier blindsided them.

"For that matter, if they'd had it in general deployment *two* and a half months ago, when Elizabeth accepted your invitation to a summit, she probably wouldn't have accepted in the first place. You know how she feels about us, and why. Do you really think she would have agreed to sit down to negotiate if she'd had this broadly deployed and ready to go?" He snorted in harsh, bitter derision. "No, if this had been available to Elizabeth Winton on that sort of scale, she would have told us to pound sand. And then she would have gone onto the offensive, taken back every single thing we took away from them in Thunderbolt, and carried straight on through to punch out Haven and occupy Noveau Paris the way they should have at the end of the *last* war."

"Maybe she only accepted in the first place to buy time while they got it deployed," Pritchart countered.

"Possibly," Theisman conceded. "In fact, that's probably effectively what happened, at least on a small scale. But look at what they did with their new weapon. They swooped down on Lovat, which, admittedly, was a far more important target than anything they'd hit before. They came in, they mousetrapped and massacred the real defensive force when it came out of hyper," a part of his mind cursed himself for his choice of verb as fresh pain flashed through her eyes, but he continued steadily, "then headed in-system, wiped out the LACs and a batch of obsolete wallers, and wrecked the star system's industrial base. Right?"

"Yes," she said, her voice once again curt.

"Then why do it to Lovat?" he asked simply. "If they had enough ships capable of deploying and using this weapon, why not go directly for Haven? Hit us with their own version of Beatrice? Trust me, Eloise—Caparelli, White Haven, and Harrington are at least as good as strategists as anyone on our side. And if we had a weapon like this available in decisive quantities, or if we had any prospect of having it available in those quantities in the immediate future, we would never tell the other side we had it by taking out a secondary target, however attractive it might be. We'd save it, keep it completely under wraps, until we could use it in a single offensive which would end the war. Think about it. That's exactly what they did last time around, in Operation Buttercup—sat on their new ships and weapons until they were ready, then hammered us into scrap."

"So you're saying what they did at Lovat indicates they *don't* have it broadly deployed?"

"I think that's exactly what it indicates. I think they showed it to us early because they know as well as we do what the tonnage numbers look like right now, and they're really sweating the possible Solarian threat. They're not just still trying to force us to redeploy, to fritter away our strength. They probably won't *mind* if they can convince us to waste time doing that while they carry out their refits, or iron out the production bottlenecks, or whatever it is they need to do to get this thing deployed throughout their wall of battle. But they'd really prefer for us to think they already have. They want this war *over*, before the Sollies horn in, and they're hoping we'll decide we're screwed and throw in the towel. And when they *do* get it deployed, we *will* be screwed, make no mistake about that."

"So what are you suggesting, Tom?"

"I'm saying we have three options. First, get them to agree to talk to us again and settle this thing without anyone else getting hurt on either side. Second, surrender before they get their new weapon fully into service and slaughter thousands more of our personnel the way they did in Buttercup. The way they did to Javier at Lovat. Third, go ahead and hit them with the Bravo variant of Beatrice before they can get it into full deployment."

"My God, Tom. You can't be serious!"

"Eloise, we're out of other options, and we're out of time." He shook his head. "You know how I've felt about this war from the beginning. I want the *first* option. I want to talk to them, to tell them about Arnold, to settle this thing across a conference table, not with broadsides and gutted star systems. But they've rejected that option. I know why we think they did it. I know somebody's manipulating what's going on. But if they won't even talk to us, we can't *tell* them that.

"So, it's either surrender, or go for outright victory."

"And which of *those* two options would you prefer?" she asked softly.

"In a lot of ways," he admitted, "I'd almost prefer surrender. I've been fighting the Manticorans for a long time now, Eloise. Hell, I started fighting them in Yeltsin, before the *first* war ever began! My emotions where they're concerned are probably as tangled up and knotted as those of anyone else in the Republic, but I'm tired of seeing men and women under my command, men and women who follow my orders because they *trust* me, killed. Especially when they're being killed because of a stupid fucking misunderstanding."

"But I'm an admiral; you're the politician. Is a surrender to them possible?"

"I don't know." She inhaled deeply, her eyes glistening with unshed tears. "I just don't know. I could carry the Cabinet with me, but I don't see how I could possibly carry the Senate, even if I told them everything we suspect about Arnold at this point. And I don't have the power, as President, to declare war or conclude peace—or surrender—without the advice and consent of the Senate. God only knows what would happen if I tried. Our legal system and chains of authority are still so new, they might shatter outright if I ordered a surrender and Congress repudiated my orders. Everything we've worked for could collapse. Even your navy could come apart. A lot of it would probably obey the order if you endorsed it, but other parts might ignore it and try to keep prosecuting the war. We might even wind up with another round of civil war!"

"Can we send a private message to Elizabeth, then?" Theisman was almost pleading. "Can we tell her we want another cease-fire? A stand down in place of all units while we send a diplomatic mission direct to Manticore?"

"Do you *really* think they'd listen after all that's happened?" Pritchart said sadly. "That's exactly what I proposed *before*, Tom! And they're convinced it was only a ploy. That I set it up for some Machiavellian reason of my own, and then tried to murder two teenaged girls to sabotage my *own* summit. If I try it again now, they're going to see it as an exact replay of the way Saint-Just derailed their Buttercup offensive. It would only 'prove' to them that their new weapons have us panicked."

A single tear tracked down her cheek, and she shook her head.

"I want this war ended even more than you do, Tom. *I'm* the one Arnold got to with his goddamned forged correspondence. *I'm* the one who started this entire fucking mess. And now look at it. Hundreds of thousands of men and women dead, star systems wrecked from one end to another, and even Javier."

"Eloise, it wasn't just you." Theisman leaned forward, reaching across the desk, and captured her hand and gripped it fiercely. "Yes, he fooled you. Well, he fooled me, the rest of the Cabinet, and the entire goddamned *Congress*, as well! You just said it yourself—you didn't have the power to declare war without advice and consent, and you got both of them."

"But I *asked* for them. It was my policy," she said softly. "My administration."

"Maybe it was. But the way we got here doesn't change where we are, or the options we've got. So, if we can't negotiate, and we can't surrender, what *can* we do except launch Beatrice? It's an 'all-costs' situation, Eloise, and thanks to your preliminary authorization and the forward redeployments we've already carried out, we can launch it far sooner than the Manties probably expect any response to this. And Beatrice Bravo was specifically designed to take out Eighth Fleet, as well. If we manage that, we knock out the only force we *know* is equipped with the new missiles, but even that's pretty much beside the point if the main op succeeds. That's really what it comes down to, now. If we wait, we lose; if we attack and I'm wrong about their deployment status, we lose; but if we attack and I'm *right*, we'll almost certainly win. It's that simple."

He looked into her eyes once again, still holding her hand.

"So which way do we go, Madam President?"

Chapter Fifty-Nine

"Duchess Harrington!"

"Over here, Duchess Harrington!"

"Duchess Harrington, would you care to comment on—?"

"Duchess Harrington, did you know—?"

"Alvin Chorek, Duchess Harrington, *Landing Herald United Faxes*! Are you going—?"

"Duchess Harrington! *Duchess Harrington!*"

Honor ignored the newsies' shouts as she moved quickly across the shuttle pad's concourse. It wasn't easy. A last-minute conference aboard *Imperator* that ran well over its originally allotted time had her running over six hours behind her original schedule, but that had only given the mob more time to gather. Worse, someone had obviously leaked her adjusted arrival time, and the concourse was a madhouse. Capital Field security personnel, joined by hastily mobilized drafts of Landing City Police, formed a cordon, holding the reporters—and what looked, to her jaundiced eye, like at least ten million private citizens—at bay.

Mostly.

A trio of particularly enterprising newsies bolted suddenly out of a service doorway which had somehow been left unguarded. They charged towards her, shoulder-mounted cameras running, shouting questions, then skidded to a sudden halt as they found themselves face to face with a suddenly congealing, solid line of green-clad armsmen.

Armed armsmen.

Unsmiling armed armsmen.

Andrew LaFollet had guessed what might happen, and he'd sent an additional twelve-man team from the Bay House to the concourse. They'd reinforced Spencer Hawke, Clifford McGraw, and Joshua Atkins at the arrivals gate, and LaFollet himself could not have bettered the stony brown stare Captain Hawke turned upon the lead newsy.

"Ah, um, I mean—"

The reporter's brashness appeared to have deserted him. Hawke made absolutely no threatening gesture, but none was needed, and as Honor watched gravely, her own unsmiling expression hid an inner chuckle as she wondered if "Newsy Intimidation 101" was a course listing on an armsman's training syllabus somewhere.

"Excuse me, Sir," Hawke said with exquisite courtesy, "but you're blocking the Steadholder's way."

"We just wanted—" The newsy began, then stopped. He looked over his shoulder at his two fellows, as if for support. If that was what he'd been searching for, he didn't find it. They were busy looking in different directions.

Then, as if by the result of some telepathic communication, the three of them drifted aside as one.

"Thank you," Hawke said courteously, and looked at Honor. "My Lady?"

"Thank you, Spencer," she said with admirable gravity, and the entire cavalcade resumed its interrupted passage to the waiting air limos and escorting sting ships.

Spencer Hawke looked studiously out the limo window as Hamish Alexander-Harrington wrapped one arm about his wife in a crushing hug.

"God, I'm glad to see you!" he said quietly as Honor sat beside him in the limousine seat, her head on his shoulder. She pressed the top of her head against his cheek, and the treecats on their shoulders reached out to rub their cheeks together, as well.

"And you," she murmured into his ear. She let herself relax totally for a moment, then straightened and sat more upright, still in the circle of his arm, but far enough back to see his face.

"Emily?" she asked. "Katherine?"

"Fine, both of them fine," he reassured her quickly. "Emily wanted to come, but Sandra wouldn't hear of it. For that matter, Jefferson was ready to put his foot down if she'd tried." He shook his head and glanced at Hawke with a wry grin. "How the *hell* have you managed to retain any tattered illusion that you run your own life after having had Grayson armsmen looking after you for so long?"

"Jefferson's only doing his job, love," Honor told him primly, also watching Hawke from the corner of her eye. Her personal armsman seemed to have become remarkably hard of hearing, however.

"And Sandra was probably just exercising simple sanity, given the madhouse out there!" Honor continued.

She jabbed her head at the spaceport buildings, dwindling rapidly behind them, and he snorted.

"Better get used to it," he advised her. "The news broke yesterday. Coupled with what Terekhov did at Monica, Lovat has public morale and enthusiasm soaring to new heights. It's actually rebounded harder because of the contrast to what happened at Zanzibar before the cease-fire. Not to mention the fact that Her Majesty's subjects are in the most murderous mood I've seen since your 'execution' over what happened to Jim and almost happened to Berry and Ruth. And since Terekhov won't be back from Talbott for another month or so, all of it's going to be focusing on you, Madam Salamander."

"God, I hate this kind of stuff," she muttered.

"I know you do. Sometimes I wish you were the sort who ate it up with a spoon, instead. But then you wouldn't be you, I suppose."

"Then Nimitz would cut my throat in my sleep, you mean!" Honor laughed. "You have no idea how a ravening mob of newsies affects a treecat's empathic sense!"

"No, but I've been basking in the reflected glow of your glory enough lately for Samantha to give me a shrewd notion the effect isn't good."

"To put it mildly."

The limo banked, and she frowned, looking out the window.

"Where are we going?"

"I'm afraid we're going to Admiralty House," Hamish told her.

"No!" Honor said sharply. "I want to see Emily and Katherine!"

"I know you do. But Elizabeth wants—"

"I don't give a *damn* what Elizabeth wants!" Honor snapped. Hamish blinked, sitting back and looking at her in astonishment. "Not this time, Hamish!" she continued angrily. "I want to see my wife and daughter. The Queen of Manticore, the Protector of Grayson, and the Emperor of the Known Universe can all get in line and wait behind the two of them!"

"Honor," he began carefully, "she wants to *congratulate* you, and she arranged to do it at Admiralty House, not Mount Royal Palace, because she wants all the rest of the Navy to be part of it. And she scheduled it originally to give you at least five hours at Jason Bay before the ceremony."

"I don't care." Honor sat back and crossed her arms. "Not this time. I'm going to hug our daughter before I do one more thing. Elizabeth's hung all these honors and rewards and presents on me, but I've never asked her for a thing. Well, today I'm asking. And if she doesn't want to give it to me, then I'm *telling*, instead of asking."

"I see."

Hamish gazed at her for a moment, remembering the diffident, focused, professionally fearless yet personally unassertive young captain he'd first met in Yeltsin so many years before. *That* Honor Harrington would never have dreamed of telling the Queen of Manticore to get in line behind her infant daughter. This one, however . . .

He pulled out his personal communicator and activated it.

"Willie?" he said. "Hamish. I told you not rescheduling was a bad idea. She's really, *really* pissed, and I don't blame her."

He listened for a moment, then shrugged.

"You're the Prime Minister of Manticore. I think dealing with situations like this is part of the job. So you trot into your office, screen Elizabeth, and *suggest*, ever so respectfully, that we reschedule. Personally, I think she'll see the wisdom of the suggestion. I hope she does, anyway."

He paused, listening again, and Honor could taste his amusement. She could also actually hear Baron Grantville's raised voice rattling the receiver pressed to Hamish's ear.

"Well, that's your problem, brother dear," he said with a grin. "Personally, I'm not stupid enough to argue with my wife—either of my wives—over something like this. So, we're going home. Have a nice day."

He deactivated the com and dropped its back into his pocket, then rapped on the partition between them and the pilot's compartment. It opened, and Tobias Stimson looked back at him.

"Yes, My Lord?"

"Jason Bay, Tobias."

"Very good, My Lord," Stimson said with obvious approval, and Hamish smiled at Honor as the air limo banked again.

"Better?"

"Yes," she said, just a bit darkly. "And the fact that you came around so quickly means you'll live to see another day despite the fact that you were going to drag me off to Admiralty House in the first place."

"Um." He rubbed the side of his head for a moment, then nodded. "Fair enough. In my defense, I'll only plead that the schedule was set yesterday, before you ran late. I'd gotten the timing into my head then."

"Hmph." She looked at him, then gave her head a little toss. "Fair enough, I suppose," she agreed grudgingly. "Just . . . don't let it happen again."

Katherine Allison Miranda Alexander-Harrington was a red-faced, scowling, *beautiful* baby, Honor thought. And her opinion was, of course, completely unbiased. After all, Raoul Alfred Alistair was at least equally beautiful, even if he was an older man.

She sat with Katherine in her arms, parked in her favorite lounger on the terrace, overlooking Jason Bay. Umbrellas kept the direct sunlight off the babies, and Emily's life-support chair was parked beside her.

They weren't exactly alone. Sandra Thurston and Lindsey Phillips had been waiting with Emily when Honor arrived. Sandra had been cuddling Katherine until Honor and Hamish got there, and Lindsey still had Raoul in her arms, with his sleeping face pillowed on her shoulder. Nimitz and Samantha had draped themselves across the umbrella-shielded table, basking in the children's mind-glows, and Andrew LaFollet and Jefferson McClure had been keeping an eye on Emily and the babies. Tobias Stimson and Honor's three-man personal detail had joined them, and now the six of them stood along the outer edge of the terrace, not exactly unobtrusively but giving them a protected bubble of privacy.

"We do good work," Honor said, smiling as she sampled the still unformed mind-glow of the blanket-wrapped infant in her arms. She reached out, stroking the impossibly soft cheek with the tip of her right index finger, then looked up at Emily.

"Well, Dr. Illescue and his people had a little something to do with the mechanics," Emily replied with a huge smile of her own. "And your mother's willingness to kick me in the posterior played a part, too. Still," she continued judiciously, "I'd have to say, on balance—and only after due and careful consideration, you understand—that you have a point."

"I only wish I'd been there when she was born," Honor said softly.

"I know." Emily reached out and patted her on the thigh. "I guess not all aspects of technology are really progress. I mean, once upon a time the only people who had to worry about not being there when babies were born were the fathers. The *mothers* were always there."

"I hadn't really thought about it quite that way," Honor said.

"*I* had," Hamish said, coming out of the house behind them. James MacGuiness, Miranda LaFollet, and Farragut followed him, and Hamish raised his right hand, flourishing the beer steins in it proudly.

"Had what?" his senior wife asked as he reached them and bent to give each of them a quick kiss.

"Thought about whether or not it was really progress," he said, plunking the steins down and watching as MacGuiness carefully poured them full of Old Tilman.

"I got to be there for both of them," he continued, "and that was good. But I was really pissed at the Admiralty for sending Honor off at that particular time. In fact, I was so pissed I decided to take it up personally with the First Lord. The conversation was a little confusing."

"You're always a little confused, dear," Emily told him, watching as he and Honor sampled their beers.

"Nonsense!" he said briskly. "I'm always a *lot* confused."

"Well, don't confuse the babies," Honor advised.

"Lindsey won't let me," Hamish pouted, and Honor looked across at the nanny in surprise.

"*Lindsey* won't let you? That sounds suspiciously like she's become a permanent fixture!"

"I have, Your Grace," Lindsey said with a smile. "Unless you'd rather not, of course. Your mother told me you were going to need help, especially with your schedule, and since—as she rather charmingly put it—she had me 'nicely broken in,' she'd feel better if I was available to you and Lady Emily."

"Well, of course I'd rather! But can Mother really spare you from the twins?"

"I'll admit I'll miss them," Lindsey acknowledged, "but it's not like I won't see a lot of them, is it? And your mother has Jenny, not to mention their tutors and their armsmen, to help keep an eye on them. Even a pair of seven-year-olds is going to find it difficult to wear all of them down."

"If Mother is sure about this, I'm certainly not going to argue!"

"And if you'd been foolish enough to do so, Hamish and I would have hit you smartly over the head and confined you somewhere until you came to your senses," Emily said tranquilly.

"Spencer wouldn't have let you," Honor retorted.

"Spencer," Miranda said, settling into an unoccupied chair, "would have helped them. And if he hadn't, *I* would have."

Farragut leapt up into her lap with a bleek of satisfied agreement, and Honor laughed.

"All right. All right! I surrender."

"Good," Emily said. Then she looked at Hamish. "Was the carnage at Admiralty House very extreme when Honor failed to arrive on schedule?"

"Not really." Hamish swallowed more beer and laughed. "I just got off the com with Tom Caparelli. From what he had to say, Elizabeth was completely in agreement with Honor. She hadn't realized how late Honor was running, and she said something about star chambers, oubliettes, bread and water, and headsmen for anyone who dragged Honor away from Katherine before tomorrow morning."

"Not just from *Katherine*, I hope," Emily said with a lurking smile, and Hamish chuckled.

"Probably not," he agreed. "Probably not."

"Welcome back aboard, Admiral," Captain Houellebecq said quietly as RHNS *Guerriere*'s side party dismissed behind Lester Tourville.

"Thank you, Celestine."

Tourville met Houellebecq's blue eyes levelly as he shook her hand. He was well aware of the questions behind his flag captain's attentive expression, but he was less certain he had the answers to them all.

Uncertainty and shock were two emotions he was unaccustomed to feeling, but they summed up his own initial reaction to the Octagon briefing handily. He'd known Lovat had been an unmitigated disaster, and the personal loss of so many friends—including Javier Giscard and the entire company of *Sovereign of Space*—had hit home with excruciating force. But his worst nightmares had fallen short of the new weapons capabilities the Manties had revealed. The reports on those had brought back other nightmares, of the days when he and Javier had watched Operation Buttercup rumbling down upon them as they waited to defend the same star system where Javier had just died.

And then, hard on the heels of that shattering news, had come Tom Theisman's proposed operation. The Octagon had been playing its cards close to its vest for weeks now, and Tourville had wondered why so many of his own units had been redeployed so far forward. Now he knew; it placed them at least fifteen days closer to the Manticore System. Which was not, he conceded, an especially comfortable thought. On the other hand, he'd had to entertain quite a few uncomfortable thoughts over the past several years. And if nothing else, Theisman's "Operation Beatrice" showed an impressive audacity, even if the decision to actually execute it was based on the logic of desperation. Still, if Theisman's assumptions about the availability of the new weapons was valid—and Op Research's conclusions matched those of the Secretary of War on that head—then this all-or-nothing throw of the dice might just work.

Of course, it might not, too. And although he'd regained his mental balance, questions about the proposed operation's mechanics and basic assumptions were still rattling around inside his own brain.

"Molly," Houellebecq said, reaching out to shake Captain DeLaney's hand in turn. "I see you managed to get the Admiral back home again, after all."

"It wasn't easy to drag him away from Nouveau Paris' nightlife,"

DeLaney replied, with a smile which looked almost natural, and Houellebecq returned it before switching her attention back to Tourville.

"Everyone's waiting in the briefing room, as you requested, Admiral."

"In that case," Tourville said heartily, "let's get down to it."

"Of course, Sir. After you." Houellebecq stepped back half a pace and waved one hand at the lifts.

"Be seated," Tourville said briskly before the assembled staffers and flag officers could climb more than halfway to their feet. They settled back obediently, and he strode to his own place at the head of the table. He seated himself, followed by Houellebecq and DeLaney, and gazed out over their assembled faces.

"Our next meeting is going to be just a bit larger than this one," he said after a moment. "We're going to be rather substantially reinforced over the next couple of weeks."

"Reinforced, Sir?" Rear Admiral Janice Scarlotti asked.

Scarlotti was a short, sturdy, no-nonsense brunette, and Tourville felt the corners of his eyes crinkle in a smile. She'd obviously heard the same rumors as everyone else. Unlike his other officers, however, she'd never heard of tact, and she'd plainly been waiting to pounce.

"Yes, Janice," he said patiently. "Reinforced. As in additional ships assigned to our order of battle."

"I gathered that, Sir," Scarlotti replied, apparently completely oblivious to his irony. Personally, Tourville suspected she was fully aware of it. She was much too smart and competent to be as totally socially clueless as she chose to appear. Of course, there had been the old Shannon Foraker...

"What I was wondering," Scarlotti continued, "is exactly what sort of reinforcements we're going to receive?"

"According to the Octagon's latest numbers, we're going to be reinforced to a total strength of something over three hundred of the wall," Tourville said calmly.

More than one of the officers around the table sat back in his or her chair as the number hit them squarely between the eyes. Even Scarlotti blinked, and Tourville smiled thinly.

"I'm well aware of the sorts of rumors which have been

circulating around the fleet," he said. "Some of them have been so wild as to be outright ridiculous. For example, the one that says we're going to launch a direct attack on the Manticoran home system in response to Lovat. The very idea is preposterous."

Several people nodded, and he smiled toothily under his brushy mustache as saw relief in a few of the expressions.

"I was completely confident of that when Admiral Theisman invited Captain DeLaney and me down to the Octagon to brief us on something called Operation Beatrice, of course," he continued. "It was a very interesting conversation. He and Admiral Marquette and Admiral Trenis laid Beatrice out with remarkable clarity.

"Now Captain DeLaney and I are going to brief *you* on it."

Chapter Sixty

"Well, that wasn't *too* bad, I hope?" Elizabeth Winton asked with a smile as she and Honor stepped into the Admiralty House conference room.

"Not too bad," Honor agreed.

"I did think about hanging some more medals on you," Elizabeth continued lightly as William Alexander and his older brother, Sir Thomas Caparelli, and Patricia Givens followed the two of them into the room. "I decided to settle for another Monarch's Thanks, instead. How many *is* that for you? A couple of dozen now?"

"Not quite," Honor said dryly.

Spencer Hawke, Tobias Stimson, and Colonel Shemais followed Givens. Hawke and Stimson positioned themselves behind their principals; Shemais took the place waiting for her at the conference table as Elizabeth's intelligence liaison.

It wasn't, Honor thought as the various treecats settled down in their people's laps or chair backs and the door closed, leaving Joshua Atkins, Clifford McGraw, and three troopers from the Queen's Own on guard in the hallway outside, as if there wasn't enough security in place without requiring the colonel's personal involvement.

The other participants in the meeting waited until Elizabeth and Honor were seated, then found their own seats.

"First," Caparelli said as they all turned their attention to him, "I'd like to add my own thanks—and that of everyone at Admiralty House—for a job very well done, Your Grace."

"We tried," Honor said.

"Quite successfully," Caparelli observed. "We're still analyzing your after-action report, but it's already obvious you hurt them much worse than they've hurt us anywhere since their opening offensive. The amount of damage you did, coupled with the demonstrated efficacy of Apollo and Mistletoe, has to have knocked them back on their heels."

"I'd like to think so," Honor said when he paused, inviting comment. "In fact, I'm inclined to think it has. I'd feel more comfortable about that if I didn't know how tough-minded Thomas Theisman is, though." She shook her head. "He was bad enough as a destroyer skipper at Blackbird; nothing I've seen indicates that he's turned into any more of a pushover since."

"Agreed." Caparelli nodded vigorously. "On the other hand, Pat and I have discussed this at some length with her analysts. Pat?"

"No one in my shop, with the possible exception of one or two very junior officers who haven't yet learned the limits of their own mortality, is prepared to make any unqualified predictions at this point, Your Grace," Givens said. "The consensus, however, is that Apollo's effectiveness, in particular, has to have come as a significant shock to their systems. In fact, it was more effective in action than *we* expected, even after your exercises, and it came at *them* completely cold. Given the way Sanskrit has to resonate with what happened to them in Buttercup," she nodded at Hamish, "they've got to be wondering if we're prepared to do the same thing to them all over again."

"I don't doubt that," Honor replied. "And don't misunderstand me, I'm not trying to say the analysts are wrong. I'd just like everyone to remember that Thomas Theisman wasn't prepared to roll over and play dead when we introduced the missile pod, and they didn't have it. And when we introduced the SD(P) and MDM, he and Shannon Foraker simply sat down and came up with effective responses to both of them."

"We're remembering that," Caparelli assured her. "I assure you, no one in this building is ever likely to take Admiral Theisman lightly again."

"I'm glad to hear it," she said. "I wish, though, that we could at least find this 'Bolthole' of theirs. I know it's not likely to be as critical to their building capacity as it was, and it's got to be becoming steadily less so as the units under the construction in their other yards progress. But that seems to be where Admiral

Foraker and her little brain trust are working on their various new weapons and doctrines, and *that* makes it a target well worth hitting any time."

"We all agree, Your Grace," Givens told her feelingly. "Unfortunately, we still haven't found it. Which leads me to suspect that our fundamental assumptions were in error."

"How?" Honor asked curiously.

"We assumed it was located in a Peep star system," Givens said simply, and Honor blinked.

"We assumed that for two reasons," Givens continued. "First, because it has to have a certain level of industrial capacity, which suggests a certain level of population to support it, which, in turn, suggests that it has to be an established star system. Second, we assumed that because we were too intellectually lazy to consider anything else."

"You're still being too hard on yourself, Pat," Caparelli put in, and Givens shrugged.

"I'm not staying up nights kicking myself, but it's ONI's job to think outside the box, as well as in it."

"I think I probably agree with Sir Thomas," Honor said. "What they've accomplished there obviously requires the capacity you were talking about."

"Yes, it does. But I've been going over some of our older intelligence summaries looking for clues. Some of those summaries date clear back to before the Pierre Coup, and a couple of very interesting ones came out of debriefs of some of the people you brought back from Cerberus, as well. On the basis of that, I'm beginning to suspect they didn't move into any star system's existing infrastructure, at all. I think they built it from the ground up in one where no one already lived."

"What?"

"I also think I'd like to sit down and discuss it with Admiral Parnell," Givens told her with a crooked smile. "Unless I miss my guess, *he's* the one who actually started the project even before President Harris was assassinated. Some of the people you brought back from Cerberus have mentioned large labor drafts from the political prisoners there. There was always some of that going on, of course, but assuming their memory of the timing is accurate, we can't account for where quite a few of them might have gone. That's not conclusive; the People's Republic was a big place, and they always had 'black projects' of one sort or another going on somewhere. We couldn't possibly have identified or tracked all of them. But I'm beginning to think 'Bolthole' is actually a complete secret colony of theirs somewhere. One the Legislaturalists started. I wouldn't be a bit surprised to find out that Pierre and the Committee took it and ran with it—probably on a scale Harris had never initially contemplated. But if I'm right, the reason we haven't found it despite all of our scouting efforts is because we don't have any idea where to look for it in the first place. It may even be outside the Republic's official borders!"

"That's not a very reassuring thought," Honor remarked after a moment.

"Even if it's true, it doesn't actually make things that much worse, Your Grace," Caparelli said. "As you said, Bolthole as a physical production facility is becoming progressively less important to them. Mostly, it's just frustrating to think that the Peeps were thinking far enough ahead to do something like this that long ago."

"And," Givens added sourly, "from a professional viewpoint, it's a lot more than 'frustrating' to think about an intelligence failure on this scale. We ought to at least have known they were doing it, even if we didn't have a clue where!"

"Stop beating yourself up over it," Caparelli said, his tone just a bit sharper, and Givens nodded.

"Whether or not Pat's new theory about Bolthole is accurate, Your Grace," the First Space Lord continued, turning back to Honor, "your point about the Peeps' tough-mindedness in general, and Theisman's in particular, is well taken. In fact, we believe it's time to give Admiral Theisman another whack as quickly as possible. We need to drive home the fact of his tactical inferiority and, hopefully, confirm the Peeps' belief that we've deployed the new systems broadly across the fleet before he has the time he needs to plan and implement a revised offensive strategy of his own."

Honor regarded him thoughtfully. Emily's "no business talk when Honor's home" decree—and Hamish's efforts to avoid intruding into Caparelli's authority in the operational sphere—had foreclosed the sort of discussion she and Hamish might otherwise have had. But from the little he'd said, and the wisps of anxiety she'd tasted from him, she had a shrewd notion of where Caparelli was headed.

"Lovat," the First Space Lord continued, "was an important target, but secondary. It hurt them, no question of that, and it was a major escalation from the sorts of targets we'd been hitting. But as far as their economy and central war effort is concerned, it was still a peripheral target, in a lot of ways. The Strategy Board thinks it's time we went for a first-rank target, instead, and we think we've found one which may not be Bolthole but still ought to get their attention. Jouett."

He paused again, and despite her earlier suspicions, Honor's nostrils flared. The planet of Shadrach, in the Jouett System, was one of Haven's oldest daughter colonies. The system had been colonized from Haven less than fifty T-years after the colony ship *Jason* reached an uninhabited planet called Manticore, and the system's population was well up into the billions. It was also the site of the oldest of the Republican Navy's satellite shipyards, and its defenses were almost as heavy as those of the Haven System itself.

"Sir Thomas," she said, very carefully, into the waiting silence, "that's . . . a very audacious proposal. And I imagine it would certainly come under the category of 'whacking' them smartly. But Jouett's going to be a very, very tough target. We succeeded at Lovat in large part because they didn't have a clue what was coming. That won't be the case the next time we go in. Two things I think we're all agreed the new management in Nouveau Paris is demonstrating are resiliency and flexibility. My staff and I haven't looked at Jouett closely, since it never occurred to us to include it in our targeting list, given the parameters laid down for Cutworm and Sanskrit. Nonetheless, I'd be very surprised if its defenses haven't been upgraded much more comprehensively even than Solon's and Lovat's."

"We agree entirely," Caparelli said gravely. "And before you raise the point, yes, it's possible we're suffering from a degree of operational hubris here. We're trying to protect ourselves against that by being as skeptical as we can, and we're also determined to avoid pushing you and Eighth Fleet into a tactical situation you can't control."

"I'm certainly in favor of that," Honor said with a wry smile. Then her smile faded, and she shrugged. "Assuming it's possible, of course."

"Of course," Caparelli agreed. "First, we have no intention of sending you in without thoroughly scouting the system ahead of time.

"Second, we're getting a handle on the production bottlenecks we've been experiencing. We're going to have a lot more of the Mistletoe-modified drones available, starting in about three weeks, and production of the Apollo pods and control platforms is beginning to accelerate, as well. We've got enough now to completely re-ammunition your command and began establishing a modest stockpile to support your operations. The system-defense version is still lagging; we won't be able to begin deploying those pods for another couple of months. But things are definitely looking up on the offensive front.

"Third, we intend to support any attack on Jouett by shotgunning them with feints all over their inner perimeter. We're going to be scouting every system we can, and after what happened in Lovat, they aren't going to be able to disregard *any* scouting operation. Hopefully, that will induce them to spread their defenses thinner.

"Fourth, your battle plan will be designed from the beginning from the perspective of breaking off the attack and withdrawing if the opposition seems tougher than our threat analyses have projected. In other words, this won't be any sort of all-costs target, Your Grace. It's an operation we want to succeed; not one we *need* to succeed, and your instructions would reflect that."

He paused again, and Honor considered what he'd said carefully. All of it seemed to make sense, but she still couldn't shake the fear that they were overreaching themselves.

"All of that sounds good, Sir Thomas," she said after moment. "But whatever we do to prepare for and support the operation, there's still the question of force levels. I'm as impressed as anyone by what Apollo accomplished at Lovat, but at the moment, my entire order of battle is less than a hundred ships, and only fifteen of them can operate the new pods. And while it's true the effectiveness of each shot in their magazines has just gone up, it's also true that we've just taken a twenty-five percent hit on our total magazine capacity. In other words, my fifteen SD(P)s only have as many rounds onboard as *eleven* ships with standard pods."

"Understood." Caparelli nodded vigorously. "In fact, we've taken that into consideration in our preliminary brainstorming. And before we continue, I should have mentioned from the outset that *all* we've done so far is to consider this from a conceptual standpoint. Any actual operation against Jouett would be mounted only after the Strategy Board—and your own staff—have had an opportunity to look at the nuts and bolts very carefully. As I said, this is a desirable operation, not an essential one. We're not going to commit to it unless we're confident—unless we're *all* confident—that it's practical and that the risks are manageable, or, at least, acceptable."

Honor felt an undeniable sense of relief. If the operation was practical, it would obviously be worthwhile. She had no qualms on that point—except, perhaps, for concern over the continuing level of escalation it represented. Beyond that single qualification, though, it was only a question of whether or not it *was* practical, and what she tasted in Caparelli's and Givens' mind-glows was vastly reassuring. The First Space Lord meant it. As much as he wanted this operation, he had no intention of charging ahead in an excess of blind enthusiasm.

"And speaking of nuts and bolts, and although we haven't put together hard numbers yet," Caparelli continued, "we already know we'll be able to reinforce Eighth Fleet more strongly than we'd anticipated."

Honor felt her right eyebrow rise, and Caparelli chuckled.

"Your old friend Herzog von Rabenstrange contacted me a couple of weeks ago, just after you'd sortied for Sanskrit. Apparently the Emperor decided a month or two before that to express his displeasure at how long their refit programs seem to be dragging out. Apparently, he expressed it rather vigorously, and his navy decided they ought to take him seriously and reallocated their efforts. Basically, they pulled their yard dogs off of about a third of the total number of ships they'd been working on—the ones farthest from completion at this point—and concentrated the additional effort on the units which were already most advanced."

The First Space Lord shrugged.

"That decision has its downsides, of course. Among other things, it means the ships they were pulled off of are going to be even later in completing, and their concentration only covered about a quarter of their total SD(P) strength. Still, it means that somewhere between twenty-five and forty additional pod-layers, all refitted to handle the Keyhole II platforms and the flat-pack pods, are going to be coming forward over the next month and a half or so. Our intention at the moment is to assign all of them to Eighth Fleet. Which will just happen to finally make your command the biggest and most powerful we have. *That's* what we're planning to commit to Sanskrit II."

Honor sat back in her chair. The tardiness of the Andermani wallers' refits had led her to forget almost completely about them. But if they really were going to come forward in such numbers, double or triple the number of Apollo-capable ships under her command, then suddenly Jouett became a much more attractive target.

"How firm are the Andermani numbers?" she asked after a moment.

"At present, they look very good. Obviously, there's room for slippage—we've already seen that. Again, however, if the proposed reinforcements aren't forthcoming, then the operation doesn't go in. It's predicated on providing you with the strength you need."

"We'd have to pretty much stand down until they do arrive," she said thoughtfully. "I don't really like that. We'll be taking the pressure off of them. But if we're going to hit a target as hard as Jouett, I can't afford any avoidable losses in the interim. It won't do us much good to reinforce if I've lost offsetting numbers. And we'll need to train hard with the Andies if we're going to integrate them properly."

"The Strategy Board came to the same conclusion," Caparelli replied. "We don't believe you could plan on launching the operation for at least another seven to eight weeks. And you're absolutely right about the need to train with the Andies as they come forward. Fortunately, Trevor's Star is well suited for all our purposes. With the entire star system under military control, it's as secure a place to exercise and work up new units as we've got. You can conduct training operations on just about any scale you want, without worrying about anyone reporting what you're doing to the Peeps. At the same time, you'll be well placed for us to recall you and your Apollo-capable ships quickly to the home system if we start picking up any indications that Theisman is still feeling frisky. And, of course, you're still closer to your potential targets in the Republic than any of the Peeps' forward bases are to the home system or Yeltsin's Star.

"While you're getting your new Andy units worked up to operational standards, we'll try to keep the pressure on them by continuing your previous strategy of scouting their systems.

As I said, that's been part of our preliminary strategy concept from the beginning."

"In that case, I think it's doable," she said. "I'd be less than honest if I said I wasn't a little nervous at the prospect of attacking a target that heavily defended. But given a monopoly on Apollo and the force levels you're suggesting, I think we can do it."

"Good!" Caparelli beamed.

In fact, everyone around the conference table smiled... except for Hamish Alexander-Harrington. Honor tasted his concern—his fear for her—and wanted to reach out and take his hand. Which would scarcely have comported with proper naval professionalism.

"Again," Caparelli stressed, "we're not going to commit to Sanskrit II until we've got a detailed plan, based on hard numbers and the most recent intelligence and scouting reports on Jouett. With that proviso, however, Your Grace, you're officially directed to begin preliminary planning immediately for the operation. Your tentative execution date will be sixty days from today."

Chapter Sixty-One

Honor swam strongly down the exact center of the swimming lane, listening to the music playing over the underwater sound system. The pool, below the outer edge of the Bay House terrace, was what was still called "Olympic-sized," and she was on the thirtieth of her forty laps. Much as she enjoyed swimming, lap work could be excruciatingly boring, and she'd insisted on a first-class sound system when she had the pool put in. She'd gotten what she paid for, and now she chuckled inside as the music segued abruptly from classical Grayson to Manticoran shatter-rock. *That* transition was guaranteed to send anyone's boredom packing.

Her armsmen were accustomed to her mania for swimming, although most of them still thought it was a bit bizarre. All of them had grimly passed the various life-saving courses, just in case, but most of them were perfectly happy that their duties required them to stand alertly about the pool rather than splashing around in all that wet stuff themselves. Nimitz, of course, had always considered her taste for immersing herself in water peculiar, and he was stretched out comfortably, sunning on a poolside table while she indulged her water fetish.

She reached the end of the lap, tucked lithely through a flip-turn, pushed off strongly from the end of the pool, and headed back the way she'd come on lap thirty-one. She was beginning to feel the strain, especially in her legs. Not surprisingly, she supposed, given how much of her time she'd been spending aboard ship lately. But she'd be *back* aboard ship the day after tomorrow, and she was determined to enjoy her pool to the full before she had to leave it behind once more.

She'd gotten to within ten meters of the end of the lap when James MacGuiness' voice suddenly interrupted the music.

"I'm sorry to disturb you, Your Grace," he said over the sound system, "but you have a com call. It's from Ms. Montaigne."

Honor inhaled when she shouldn't have, surprised by the interruption. She coughed the water back out before she rotated back up to breathe again and swam the last few strokes to the end of the pool. She caught the lip, lifted, twisted, and landed sitting on the pool surround.

"Spencer!"

"Yes, My Lady?" Captain Hawke turned quickly towards her and didn't even flinch. He'd had time to get used to Manticoran swimsuits, and compared to the ones *Allison* Harrington delighted in wearing, Honor's were positively demure.

"Mac says I've got a com call."

"Of course, My Lady." Hawke reached into the bag sitting on the poolside table beside Nimitz and extracted Honor's personal communicator. He handed it to her, and she smiled in thanks and configured it for video, but without bringing up the holo display, then keyed the acceptance button. An instant later, MacGuiness' face appeared on the small flatscreen.

"I'm here, Mac," she said, reaching up with her free hand and stripping off the swimming cap she'd been wearing over her braided hair. "Go ahead and put Ms. Montaigne through."

"Of course, Your Grace."

Honor swirled her feet slowly in the pool to keep muscles from stiffening and gazed out across the sparkling blue vitality of Jason Bay at the towers of Landing. Her house's terrace ran to the very edge of the upper tier of the cliffs above the bay; if she looked up, she could see the outer balustrade clinging to its lip. The upper cliff fell away from the terrace in a sheer precipice for ten or fifteen meters to a flattened saddle, almost like a giant stair step halfway between the beach below and the house above. That was where she'd chosen to put the pool, with a vanishing "infinite edge" on the outer side. From where she sat, the illusion that the pool's water was spilling over in a cascade to the ocean below was almost perfect. Of all the many features of her Manticoran mansion, she often thought the pool was her favorite.

The com beeped softly, recalling her from her thoughts, as the golden-haired, blue-eyed Honorable Member of Parliament for High Threadmore appeared upon it.

"Good morning, Your Grace," Catherine Montaigne said.

"And good morning to you, Cathy," Honor replied. "To what do I owe the honor?"

"I hope I didn't screen at an inconvenient moment," Montaigne said as Honor's water-beaded face registered.

"Actually, you just rescued me from the last nine laps," Honor reassured her with a smile.

"That's right. You actually swim for exercise." Montaigne shuddered dramatically.

"You don't like swimming?"

"I don't like *exercise*," Montaigne said cheerfully. "I burn off sufficient energy just charging around in six or seven directions at once. I'm sure you've heard that about me."

"I believe your ability to . . . multitask enthusiastically has come up a time or two," Honor acknowledged, her smile becoming a grin.

"I thought it probably had." Montaigne looked pleased, and Honor chuckled. She knew how much pleasure Catherine Montaigne took from her public persona's reputation for shatter-brained confusion.

"Actually, though," the ex-Countess of the Tor said, her own smile fading, "I had a serious reason for screening you this morning. I have a message for you from Anton."

"Do you?" Honor arched her eyebrows, and Montaigne nodded.

"He asked me to tell you that he and his associate believe they may be on the trail of evidence which will confirm the hypothesis they discussed with you last month."

"Really?" Honor sat up a bit straighter. "You say he's 'on the trail' of the evidence. I take it that that means he doesn't actually have it in hand?"

"I'm afraid not. It's going to take them some time to confirm what they suspect, but they feel confident at this time that they will be able to."

"Do we have any idea how long we're talking about?"

"I'm afraid not. Not exactly, at any rate. There's quite a bit of travel involved."

"I see." Honor's eyes narrowed intently. "May I ask where they're traveling to?"

"Since I can't be certain our connection is completely secure, I'd prefer not to answer that one, Your Grace," Montaigne said. "However, I will say that they'll have to travel incognito this time."

"I see," Honor repeated, and she did. The planet of Mesa, which she was almost certain had to be Zilwicki's and Cachat's destination, would not be a very healthy place for either of them. Manpower had a long and nasty memory at the best of times, and the slavers weren't likely to forget what the team of Zilwicki & Cachat had produced for them on Old Earth.

She tried not to feel disappointed although, in some ways, it was even worse to know Zilwicki and Cachat believed they would be able to confirm their suspicions. Whatever they might be able to do in the future, she still didn't have any proof of it now, and without that proof, there was no way to derail the events proceeding inexorably towards Sanskrit II.

And after we trash Jouett, the Havenites are going to be a lot less inclined to be reasonable, whatever Zilwicki turns up, unless they do decide Apollo gives them no choice but to surender, she thought grimly.

"If you should happen to be sending any messages to Captain Zilwicki," she said aloud, "please tell him I very much hope his search prospers. I spoke to the individuals I assured him I'd contact. Unfortunately, they feel that without conclusive—or at least very persuasive—evidence actually in their hands, there isn't a great deal they can do about the problem."

"I was afraid of that," Montaigne said, blue eyes sad. "We'll just have to do our best to turn up the evidence they need. I hope we can find it in time."

"So do I," Honor said soberly. "I'm afraid, though, that events are taking on a momentum all their own. One we may not be able to deflect, regardless of what they discover, if their discovery's delayed too long."

"We'd already deduced that." Montaigne inhaled deeply. "Well, at least we still have one friend at court. We'll try hard not to disappoint you."

"Welcome back, Your Grace," Rafe Cardones said as the twitter of bosun's pipes died in *Imperator*'s boat bay gallery.

"I'd like to say I'm glad to *be* back," Honor replied with a small smile. "Unfortunately, that would be a lie. Not that I'm not glad to see *you*, of course. It's just that I had to leave a very charming young gentleman and lady behind."

"But you brought lots of pictures, I hope," he replied, and she chuckled.

"Only a couple of dozen gigs worth. And I've changed out my personal wallpaper, of course."

"Oh, of course!" Cardones laughed, and she clapped him on the upper arm and looked at Mercedes Brigham.

"We've got a lot to discuss, Mercedes," she said, and Brigham nodded.

"I'm sure we do, Your Grace. Just as soon as you're done showing those pictures to all of us. We do have a certain sense of proper priorities around here, you know."

"So I see," Honor said, and Nimitz bleeked an echoing laugh from her shoulder. "All right. The two of you have twisted my arm nearly to the point of dislocation. Solely because of your harshly insistent demands, I'll sacrifice my own desire to plunge imme-diately back into the official business of this command and *force* myself to sit through all those awful pictures all over again."

"That's an . . . impressive itinerary, Your Grace," Dame Alice Truman said.

Honor's staff and senior flag officers sat around the outsized table in her dining cabin. The familiar cups of coffee, tea, and cocoa had made their appearance on schedule, following the dessert dishes, and Judah Yanakov extracted a worn briar pipe from his tunic pocket. He held it up and raised an eyebrow at his hostess.

"That's a truly disgusting habit, Judah," she told him with a smile of affection, and he nodded.

"I know it is, My Lady. And we'd almost stamped it out on Grayson, until you Manties came along with all your modern medicine. Now I can indulge myself and know your decadent, worldly medical science will preserve me from the consequences of my own excesses."

"Does Reverend Sullivan know about this hedonistic streak of yours?" she asked severely.

"Alas," he replied sadly. "I'm afraid my family's always been known for its lapses. My first Grayson ancestor, for example.

There he was, the captain of the colony ship, supposed to be in charge of completely decommissioning and scrapping her as an example of the evil technology we'd fled Old Earth to escape. And what did he do? Kept her intact for almost sixty years. Transferred her computers and her auxiliary power plant down to Grayson, too. With that sort of a beginning, surely you know the Reverend is going to expect the worst out of me."

"Stop boasting," Brigham told him with a smile of her own. "I read that biography of your great-great-great-whatever your grand-aunt wrote. We all know the Yanakov family was instrumental in preserving human life on Grayson. Did I get that quotation right?"

"Almost," he corrected solemnly. "The actual passage you're thinking of says that our family was 'instrumental, by the Tester's grace, in preserving human life on Grayson *against overwhelming odds*.'" He smiled admiringly. "Aunt Letitia always had a fine, well-rounded way with a phrase, didn't she?"

"Oh, forgive me! How could I have forgotten that bit?"

"Stop it, you two!" Honor said with a laugh. "And, yes, Judah. You can light the reeking thing as soon as Mac readjusts the air circulation to protect the rest of us."

"I'm reconfiguring now, Your Grace," MacGuiness' voice said from the open pantry hatch.

"Thank God," Alistair McKeon murmured, careful to be sure the comment was loud enough for Yanakov to hear.

"Infidel." Yanakov raised his nose with a sniff, and McKeon threw a balled-up linen napkin at him across the table.

"Children. Children!" Honor scolded. "I should never have left the nanny back on Manticore!"

The laughter was general this time, and Honor was glad to hear it. She was especially glad since Yanakov's seniority in the Grayson Navy had made him her official second in command. Fortunately, he, Truman, and McKeon had known one another for years and worked smoothly together in the past. No one had gotten his or her nose out of joint following Yanakov's arrival.

Nor had Honor felt any qualms. Yanakov had matured considerably from the days when he'd been one of her brilliant but occasionally overenthusiastic divisional commanders in the Grayson Space Navy's second battle squadron. He'd lost none of the audacity, the ability to think quickly and see possibilities others might miss, but the enthusiasm had been tempered by experience and honed to an even keener, more dangerous edge. He still had a gambler's instincts, but now they were those of a coldly capable, calculating, and highly *professional* gambler.

"All right," she said as Yanakov got his pipe properly stoked, "I think we can all agree that what the Strategy Board has in mind is, as Alice says, an 'impressive itinerary.' It's also going to be the most powerful single attack the Alliance or any of its members has ever launched. I had a personal message from Herzog von Rabenstrange just before I returned to the fleet. His current estimate is that we should have at least thirty-five Andermani Apollo-capable SD(P)s and sixteen of their BC(P)s joining us here. The first ten or twelve wallers will actually be here within the next two weeks; the others will arrive as they complete their working up exercises with the new systems.

"Assuming he meets his minimum estimate of thirty-five, we'll have a total of fifty-three pod-superdreadnoughts, fifty of them Apollo-capable. That's fifteen percent of the Alliance's *total* SD(P)s. And until the rest of the Andermani superdreadnoughts complete their refits, it's over twenty-seven percent of the total actually available. It's also more pod-layers, not even counting the battlecruisers, than Earl White Haven had for Buttercup, and none of his ships had Apollo."

She paused to let that sink in, looking around the table at her staffers and flag officers, radiating her own confidence even as she tasted theirs. And they *were* confident, despite a certain completely understandable anxiety. Confident of their weapons, confident of their doctrine, and confident of their leadership.

She savored that confidence, even as she carefully concealed her own reservations. Not about the practicality of Sanskrit II. Not about the quality of the fleet which was her weapon, or the admirals who would wield it. But about *why* they were launching this operation in the first place, and what its consequences might be.

There's nothing they could do about it anyway, she reminded herself once again. *So there's no point worrying them with it. The last thing they need right now is to be looking over their shoulders, wondering whether or not we ought to be doing this.*

"Judah," she continued, breaking the small silence she had imposed, "you've actually had the most experience using Apollo ship-to-ship. I've spent quite a while reviewing your after-action report, and also your ops officer's report, and it seems to me that we overestimated the number of birds necessary to get through to a single target. Would you concur?"

"Yes, and no, My Lady. Yes, we overestimated the numbers we needed at Lovat, but that was a freebie. They didn't have any idea what was coming, and they never had time to adjust. That won't be the case next time."

"No, it won't," McKeon said. "On the other hand, how much good will it to do them to know what's coming? How the hell do you establish a viable defensive doctrine against something like this?"

"Admiral Hemphill and the ATC simulators are developing one right now, Alistair," Samuel Miklós pointed out.

"They're *trying* to develop one," McKeon corrected. "I'm willing to bet they aren't having a lot of luck so far, and unlike the Peeps, they know exactly what Apollo can do. I'm not saying no one will ever come up with a doctrine which won't at least knock back Apollo's effectiveness. I just don't see any way the Peeps can have done it yet. *I* certainly can't think of anything they could do about it, and I've spent the odd couple of dozen hours thinking about it."

"I think you've got a point, Alistair," Honor said. "But so does Judah. And let's not succumb to any hubris about Apollo, either. I agree that so far it's proved more effective than my most optimistic estimate, but it's not a god weapon. So far, they haven't had a really good look at it, but all it really does, if you want to come right down to it, is to extend our effective control loop by about a factor of sixty."

McKeon's eyebrows rose, and she shook her head.

"I'm not trying to downplay what an advantage that gives us, especially now. But once we get out beyond three or four light-minutes, even the grav-pulse com starts imposing a measurable lag in the real-time communications loop. We'll be able to adjust and adapt far more rapidly than anyone else can, which is still going to give us an enormous edge. But our powered missile envelope from rest is over three and a half light-minutes. At that range, the transmission lag, one-way, is going to be three-point-four seconds. That's a minimum command and control loop of six-point-eight seconds."

"Which equates to a range to target of eight and a half light-seconds, with a closing velocity of point-eight light-speed," McKeon pointed out. "That means that our *two-way* communications loop would be shorter than their *one-way* loop, even if their counter-missiles had that sort of engagement range."

"Of course it does." Honor shook her head again. "I admit it's going to give us a huge advantage, at least until someone else figures out how to do the same thing. I'm just saying that as the range extends, our ability to adapt in real-time to their electronic warfare, and to steer our birds around their counter-missiles, is going to degrade. That's why Mercedes, Andrea, and I have been stressing the need to get as close to the edge of the enemy's powered envelope as we can without quite crossing over into it in order to maximize our own effectiveness. And don't forget, we carry a lot fewer rounds than we used to. That means we've got to make each of them count. So even though the Lovat effectiveness numbers would support a pullback of at least fifty percent, I think we have to factor in Judah's concerns, and only cut our original density estimates by thirty or forty percent."

"All right." McKeon nodded cheerfully. "I'd rather err on the side of pessimism than be overly optimistic and get my . . . tail caught in a wringer."

"I've got a few concerns of my own," Truman said. "They don't have anything to do with Apollo, but the observed performance of the Peep LACs at Lovat has me a little concerned. I wish we'd had more time to examine the wreckage, maybe pick up a couple of intact examples for BuWeaps and ONI to play around with."

"What specifically worries you?" Honor asked.

"Well, we really didn't turn it up until we started our intensive post-battle analysis back here at Trevor's Star," Truman admitted. "But when we took a good hard look, it became fairly obvious that they've got at least one, and probably two, new LAC classes. And unless I miss my guess, they're using fission power plants."

"I don't like the sound of that," Vice Admiral Morris Baez, commander of Battle Squadron 23, said.

"From the acceleration numbers, they don't have the new beta nodes yet," Truman said. "But their energy budget is obviously higher than it used to be, and, defensively, I suspect they've added at least bow walls. One of the two possible new classes we've tentatively identified seems to be the closest they could come to a clone of the *Shrike*. It packs a laser, instead of a graser, but it's an awful lot more powerful than any energy weapons we've ever seen out of a Peep LAC before. We're not absolutely certain about the other possible new design. We *think* they've done their best to duplicate the *Ferret*, as well. If they have, they still can't get as much out of the design as we can, though, because of the inferiority of their missiles."

"The *Katanas* seem to have handled them fairly easily, though," Matsuzawa Hirotaka said.

"At Lovat, yes, Hiro." Truman nodded. "On the other hand, they were present in strictly limited numbers. The vast majority of what they threw at us in Lovat were old-style *Cimeterres*. That suggests to me that these new birds aren't yet available in huge numbers. But it doesn't take very long to build a LAC, and we're talking about not launching Sanskrit II for another two months. They could have a lot more of them available, by then. And since we hit Lovat, they're going to be reinforcing their central systems with everything they can, as quickly as they can."

"How seriously would you assess their threat to our wall of battle, Alice?" Honor asked.

"That's impossible to say without a better fix on their capabilities and the numbers we may be looking at. I'm not trying to waffle, Honor. We simply genuinely don't know. I've got some highly problematical performance parameters on them, but under the circumstances, I think we have to consider them minimal. They were operating with the older designs, and that would have restricted them to the *Cimeterres'* performance envelope. Scotty's been kicking our tentative numbers around with the rest of my COLACs, and what I'd really like to do is to have him set up some simulations built around our best estimates and game out what happens. I think the combination of the *Katanas* and our own wall's defensive fire ought to be able to manage the threat, but I'll feel better if we're able to confirm that, at least in the sims."

"I see." Honor regarded Truman thoughtfully, then nodded. "It makes sense to me. And let's be sure to draw BuWeaps' attention to the data you've managed to record on them."

"I'll see to it, Your Grace," Brigham said, punching a note to herself into her memo pad.

"Good. In that case, let's look at possible approach courses. Obviously, we're going to want to scout the system thoroughly, so it seems to me that—"

Her officers leaned forward, listening intently, as she began to sketch out her own preliminary thoughts on the operation.

Chapter Sixty-Two

Admiral of the Fleet Sebastian D'Orville walked slowly onto his flag bridge, hands clasped behind him, expression suitably grave, and contemplated the perversity of the universe.

He'd spent his entire career in the service of the Crown, honing his professional skills, amassing seniority, proving his abilities. And what had all those decades of perseverance and professional excellence bought him? The most prestigious command in the Royal Manticoran Navy, of course.

Which meant he'd spent the dreary months since the Peeps' sneak attack doing absolutely nothing.

That's not true, Sebastian, and you know it, he scolded himself as he nodded pleasantly to the flag bridge personnel and crossed to the visual display. *You've turned Home Fleet back into a proper weapon, after that asshole Janacek let training levels go straight into the crapper. And commanding the fleet charged with protecting the home star system hasn't exactly been the least stressful duty slot you've ever held down.*

Which hasn't kept it from being boring as hell, of course.

He chuckled inside at the thought, but that didn't make it untrue, and he suppressed an unworthy stab of envy as he thought of Honor Alexander-Harrington.

She always has had a way of putting your nose out of joint, hasn't she? he asked himself wryly. *Starting with the way she blew your flagship out of space in that Fleet maneuver back when she was—what? Just a commander, wasn't it?* He shook his head in memory. *On the other hand, I don't suppose it's really fair to*

729

blame her for being so good. And she is awfully junior to you. Junior enough she gets the fun *command—the one Admiralty House figures it can take chances with—while you get to be the Queen's one and only Admiral of the Fleet and stay stuck at home with the one command that* can't *be risked.*

He chuckled mentally again, and then his thoughts saddened as he remembered James Webster. The two of them had been friends since Saganami Island, and it had been Webster's unenviable lot to command Home Fleet last time around. D'Orville remembered how he'd teased Webster at the time, and he snorted. What went round, came around, he supposed, and he'd clearly laid up enough bad karma to deserve what had happened to him.

Of course, there were compensations.

He turned from the visual display to regard the huge master plot, and allowed himself a feeling of satisfaction as he studied the icons of the new fortresses. A year ago, the Manticoran Wormhole Junction's permanent fortifications had been virtually nonexistent. In fact, they'd been so sparse he'd been forced to hang Home Fleet all the way out at the Junction to cover the critical central nexus of the Star Kingdom's economy against attack.

He hadn't liked that, but the Janacek Admiralty's failure to update the fortresses had left him no choice. And at least the Manticore System's astrography had let him get away with it for a while.

Classic system-defense doctrine, developed over centuries of experience, taught that a covering fleet should be deployed in an interior position. Habitable planets inevitably lay inside any star's hyper limit, and habitable planets were generally what made star systems valuable. That being the case, the smart move was to position your own combat power where it could reach those habitable planets before any attacker coming in from outside the limit could do the same thing.

Unfortunately, one could argue that the *Wormhole Junction* was what truly made the Manticore System valuable. D'Orville didn't happen to like that argument, but he couldn't deny that it had a certain applicability. Without the Junction, the Star Kingdom would never have had the economic and industrial muscle to take on something the Republic of Haven's size. And it was certainly the Junction which made the Manticore System so attractive to potential aggressors like Haven in the first place.

And therein lay the problem. Or, at least, one of the problems.

The Junction was almost seven light-hours from Manticore-A. Which meant any fleet stationed to cover the Junction was light-hours away from the planets on which the vast majority of Queen Elizabeth III's subjects happened to live. As the man charged with protecting those subjects, that was ... inconvenient for one Sebastian D'Orville.

The Junction's position also put it over eleven light-hours from Manticore-B, which created Home Fleet's commander's second problem. But, fortunately, Manticore-B also lay far outside the resonance zone—the volume of space between the Junction and Manticore-A in which it was virtually impossible to translate between hyper-space and normal-space. *Any* wormhole terminus associated with a star formed a conical volume in hyper, with the wormhole at its apex and a base centered on the star and twice as wide as its hyper limit, in which hyper-space astrogation became less than totally reliable. The bigger the terminus or junction, the stronger the resonance effect ... and the Manticoran Wormhole Junction, with its *multiple* termini, was the largest ever discovered. The resonance zone *it* produced was more of a tsunami, and it didn't just make astrogation "less than reliable." It made it the next best thing to flatly impossible. Any translation out of the resonance zone risked serious astrogational uncertainty, and any translation *into* the zone would have been no more than a complicated way to commit suicide. But since the Manticore Binary System's secondary component lay outside the resonance (and would for the next few hundred years or so), Home Fleet had actually been closer from its position covering the Junction—in terms of travel time—to Manticore-B than to Manticore-A.

As for Manticore-A, the planets of Manticore and Sphinx—Home Fleet's major inner-system defensive obligations—had been well inside the same resonance zone when he took up command of Home Fleet, with Manticore, with its smaller orbital radius, steadily "overtaking" Sphinx as it moved towards opposition. Each planet spent half its year inside the zone, and Sphinx's year was more than five T-years long. That meant it took thirty-one T-months to cross through the RZ, and it had been almost in the middle of the zone when he took up his command.

Actually, Sphinx's position was the third, and in many ways

worst, problem confronting any Home Fleet CO, because the planet's orbital radius was only 15.3 million kilometers—less than nine-tenths of a light-minute—shorter than the G0 primary's twenty-two-light-minute hyper limit. In an era of MDMs, that meant an attacker could translate out of hyper with the planet, and its entire orbital infrastructure, already fifty million kilometers *inside* his missile range. Even a conventionally armed fleet, with old-style compensators, and a relative velocity on translation of zero, could have achieved a zero/zero intercept with the planet in under an hour. A fleet of superdreadnoughts with modern Alliance compensators could have done it in barely fifty minutes.

Which, all things considered, didn't leave the system defenses' commander a lot of time in which to react.

But with Sphinx so deep inside the zone, he'd actually had much more defensive depth. He'd still been able, at least in theory, to cover both habitable planets from his position at the Junction, since he could have micro-jumped away from the Junction (and the primary) and then jumped back in close enough to come in behind any fleet moving in on either planet. He would have found it difficult to actually overtake the attackers, perhaps, but the range of his MDMs would have compensated for that. And because it would have taken the attacker longer to reach engagement range of his target, Home Fleet had had time to make those jumps. In theory, at least.

But theory, as Sebastian D'Orville had learned over the years, had a nasty habit of biting one on the backside at the most inopportune moment. That was why he'd never really been happy with his enforced deployment. And now that Sphinx would clear the RZ in less than four T-months, he was even less comfortable with hanging his fleet on the Junction. The planet had lost too much of the additional "depth" the zone had created for him, and even in a best-case scenario, his need to make two separate hyper translations from the Junction would have placed him well astern of his hypothetical attacker, since he couldn't make even the first of them until after the aggressor force arrived and started accelerating towards its targets.

In effect, Home Fleet had been isolated from the rest of the inner-system's defenses, because any attacking fleet would be between D'Orville's ships and the fixed defenses which were supposed to support it. And that attacking fleet would have been able to begin building an acceleration advantage towards its objectives while Home Fleet was still getting itself organized.

Under those circumstances, an attacker without the strength to defeat both Home Fleet and the inner defenses together might well still have the strength to turn on Home Fleet—which would have no option but to pursue him—and crush it in a separate, isolated engagement.

Which was why D'Orville was so relieved the new forts were finally operational. Much smaller than the old prewar fortifications which had been decommissioned to provide the manpower to crew new construction, they were actually more powerfully armed, thanks to the same increased automation and weapons developments which had gone into the Navy's new warships. And each of those forts was surrounded by literally hundreds of missile pods, with the fire control to handle stupendous salvos. It would take an attack in overwhelming force to break those defenses, which had freed D'Orville to move Home Fleet closer to a more traditional covering position, locating his command in Sphinx orbit.

His new station provided Sphinx with badly needed, close-in protection. And with the planet of Manticore still trailing its orbital position, and so still deeper into the zone *and* (as always) further inside the hyper-limit, he was actually better placed to cover Manticore than he would have been anywhere else. Any least-time course to Manticore would require the attacker to get past his position at Sphinx, first, and he could easily intercept the opposing fleet short of its objective.

The solution wasn't perfect, of course. For one thing, the move left Manticore-B and its inhabited planet of Gryphon more exposed than it had been when Home Fleet was stationed at the Junction, since D'Orville would now have to get clear of the zone before he could hyper out to the system's secondary component. But the extra danger wasn't very great, now that Sphinx was within eight light-minutes of the zone's boundary. And more vulnerable or not, Gryphon had the smallest population and industrial base of any of the Star Kingdom's original inhabited worlds. If something had to be exposed, cold logic said Gryphon was a better choice than the other two planets, and the Admiralty had compensated as best it could by assigning the buildup of Manticore-B's fixed defenses a higher priority than Manticore-A's. In fact, Manticore-B's forts and space station were already refitting with Keyhole II and would begin deploying the first of the system-defense Apollo pods within the next three weeks, on the theory that it would need them worse since it couldn't call as readily on Home Fleet's protection.

And once Manticore-B's defenses were fully up to speed, Sphinx would receive the next highest priority, despite the fact that the planet of Manticore had the largest population and the greatest economic and industrial value of any of the binary system's worls. Like Manticore-B, Sphinx was simply more exposed than Manticore.

D'Orville agreed with both those decisions, although that didn't mean he was happy about the policy they implied. It was merely, in his opinion, the best of several options, none of which could have been completely acceptable. And at least the Strategy Board's decision that Gryphon would have to look after itself instead of relying upon immediate intervention by Home Fleet had enormously simplified D'Orville's responsibilities and problems.

But today, Sebastian D'Orville and half of Home Fleet were back out at the Junction, waiting. Waiting not for an enemy attack, but to welcome back two of the Manticoran Navy's own.

He had to admit that he felt a twinge or two of anxiety over taking his command so far from its new inner-system station, but his qualms were tiny things. And given the way the Solarian League seemed to be pulling in its horns over events in the Talbott Cluster, the entire Star Kingdom owed a stupendous debt of gratitude to the two ships who were coming home today. Queen Elizabeth and her government had chosen to acknowledge that debt, and Sebastian D'Orville was out here to do just that.

He glanced at the date/time display, and nodded in satisfaction. Another thirty-two minutes to go.

Honor Alexander-Harrington glanced at the date/time display, and nodded.

If she'd had the choice, she would have loved to have been back in the Manticore System in about half an hour. Unfortunately, she didn't really have that choice. *Vizeadmiral* Lyou-yung Hasselberg, Graf von Kreuzberg, and the leading elements of his Task Force 16, IAN, had arrived at Trevor's Star less than a week earlier. Two of his three battle squadrons were at full strength, and the Imperial Andermani Navy, like the Republic of Haven's, still used eight-ship squadron organizations. His third battle squadron remained short one of its four divisions, but what had already arrived had added twenty-two SD(P)s—every one of them Keyhole II-capable—to Eighth Fleet's order of battle.

Unfortunately, none of those ships had ever functioned as part of Eighth Fleet before, and eleven of them had finished their post-refit working up exercises less than two weeks before they deployed forward to Trevor's Star. And, just to add a little more interest to the situation, *Vizeadmiral* Bin-hwei Morser, Graffin von Grau, Hasselberg's second-in-command, was not one of the Royal Manticoran Navy's greater admirers. In fact, she was a holdover from the same anti-Manticoran faction within the IAN which had produced Graf von Sternhafen, who'd done so much to help make Honor's last duty assignment . . . interesting.

The rest of Hasselberg's senior flag officers seemed much more comfortable with the notion of their Emperor's decision to ally himself with the Star Kingdom, and she suspected that Chien-lu Anderman had had more than a little to do with their selection for their present assignments. Morser obviously had patrons of her own, however, since she'd received command of the very first squadron of refitted Andermani SD(P)s. And, Honor admitted just a bit grudgingly, she also appeared to be very good at her job. It was just unfortunate that she found it difficult to conceal the fact that she would have preferred to be shooting at the rest of Honor's fleet, rather than accepting her orders.

Still, the graffin's attitude only lent added point to the need to get TF 16 fully integrated into Eighth Fleet as quickly as possible. And the best way to do that was to drill the Andermani ships in conjunction with the rest of her units.

At least all of the arguments in favor of using Trevor's Star as a training site still held good. And *Vizeadmiral* Morser's professionalism was responding to the challenge. She couldn't have enjoyed admitting that the Andermani simply weren't quite up to Manticoran or Grayson standards of proficiency, but neither could she deny it. Of course, the IAN hadn't spent most of the last twenty T-years fighting for its survival against the People's Republic of Haven, either. A navy either got very, very good under those circumstances, or else the star nation it was charged to defend got very, very dead, and both Grayson and the Star Kingdom were still here. The complacency the Janacek Admiralty had allowed to blunt the RMN's finely honed edge during the cease-fire had been a major factor in what happened during the Republic's Operation Thunderbolt, but most of it had been scoured away by the grim sandblaster of combat. The less than brilliant but politically acceptable flag officers and captains Janacek had appointed to sensitive positions had been shuffled aside or eliminated in the opening battles, and the officers who remained had been given a rather brutally pointed refresher course.

The bottom line, though, was that the Manticoran and Grayson navies were the explored galaxy's most experienced, battle-hardened fleets. Their margin of superiority over the revitalized navy of Thomas Theisman was far narrower than it once had been, but it remained the Alliance's most significant advantage. And the Andermani, although they were very, very good by any less Darwinian standard, simply weren't up to their allies' weight.

Yet, at least.

Hasselberg appeared to have understood that even before his arrival, which was another bit of evidence that Herzog von Rabenstrange had handpicked him for his assignment. Hasselberg clearly intended to bring his command up to Manticoran standards as quickly as possible, and if any of his subordinates—including *Vizeadmiral* Morser—had entertained any reservations about that, they were smart enough to keep those reservations to themselves. And, in all fairness, they'd buckled down hard.

They still had a way to go, though, which was the real reason Honor had turned down Admiral D'Orville's invitation to join him aboard HMS *Invictus* for today's ceremony. She'd scheduled yet another in her series of increasingly rigorous training problems for Eighth Fleet, and she couldn't justify giving herself the day off while she made everyone else work.

She chuckled quietly at the thought, and Mercedes Brigham—standing beside her and watching the master plot with her—looked at her with a raised eyebrow.

"Nothing, Mercedes." Honor shook her head. "Just a passing thought."

"Of course, Your Grace."

Brigham's slightly mystified tone almost set Honor off on another chuckle, but she suppressed the temptation sternly.

"Anything yet from *Vizeadmiral* Hasselberg, Andrea?" she asked instead, turning her head to look at Jaruwalski.

"No, Your Grace. I think it's still a little early. His recon drones can't be fully into position yet."

"I realize that," Honor said quietly, pitching her voice low enough so that only Jaruwalski and Brigham could hear her, "but his first wave platforms have to be close enough by now to be picking up at least the outer edge of Alistair's screen."

"You think he's waiting until he has a more fully developed picture?" Brigham asked.

"I think so, yes." Honor nodded. "The question is why he's waiting. Is it strictly because he wants to watch the situation develop a little more, get a better feel for it himself, before he reports it to the flagship? And if that's why he's waiting, is it because he's exercising intelligent initiative or because he resents being tied so tightly to our apron strings?"

"And which do *you* think it is, Your Grace, if I can ask?"

"Honestly, if it were Morser, I'd call it a toss-up," Honor admitted. "In this case, though, I think it's probably the former. And that's good. But we need to find a way to tactfully suggest to him that it's more important to inform us immediately, even if he has only partial information."

"*Kapitan der Sterne* Teischer is a tactful sort," Brigham said. "I could probably have a little discussion with him—one chief of staff to another. He's pretty good at post-exercise analysis, too."

"That's an excellent idea, Mercedes," Honor approved. "I'd much rather have any suggestions come to him in-house, as it were, rather than sound as if I'm stepping on his toes. Especially when he's pulling out all the stops to make this work the way he is."

"I'll see to it, Your Grace."

"Astro Control reports that *Hexapuma* and *Warlock* are making transit, Admiral," Lieutenant Commander Ekaterina Lazarevna, Sebastian D'Orville's communications officer announced.

"Very good." D'Orville turned from the main plot to the screen which showed his flagship's captain. "Let's get it right, Sybil," he said.

"We'll get it done, Sir," Captain Gilraven assured him.

"Good."

"Junction transit completed, Admiral," Lazarevna said.

"Very good. Send the first message, Katenka."

"Aye, aye, Sir. Transmitting . . . now."

D'Orville watched his chrono carefully as his message congratulating Aivars Terekhov and his surviving personnel for their accomplishments in the Battle of Monica flashed across to HMS *Hexapuma*. The two damaged heavy cruisers' icons blinked on his plot, accelerating slowly out of the Junction, and D'Orville felt something he hadn't felt since the day he'd watched the broken and crippled light cruiser HMS *Fearless* limp painfully home from Basilisk station.

Odd, he thought. *The second time, and* Warlock *was involved in both of them. But a bit differently this time. I'm glad. She needed her name cleared.*

"Now, Sybil," he said quietly, and the hundred and thirty-eight starships and seventeen hundred LACs of the Home Fleet detachment brought up their impeller wedges in perfect sequence. The impeller signatures radiated outward from *Invictus*, but *Invictus* wasn't in the traditional flagship's slot at the center of that stupendous globe.

That space was occupied by HMS *Hexapuma* and HMS *Warlock*.

"Second message for *Hexapuma*," Fleet Admiral Sebastian D'Orville said quietly. "'Yours is the honor.'"

"Aye, aye, Sir," Lazarevna said, equally quietly, and Home Fleet moved steadily in-system around the two battered, half-crippled heavy cruisers which had saved their Star Kingdom from a two-front war it could not possibly have won.

"Admiral Fisher's task force just came in, Sir," Captain DeLaney said.

"I see. Thank you, Molly. I'll meet you on Flag Bridge in fifteen minutes."

"Yes, Sir. DeLaney, clear," she said, and broke the com connection.

Lester Tourville sat at his desk for several seconds, looking around his day cabin, feeling the massive megaton bulk of RHNS *Guerriere* around him. At that particular moment, his flagship felt oddly small, almost fragile.

He stood and walked across to the view screen configured to show him the diamond-studded depths of space. He gazed deep into it, seeing the dim sparks of reflected light from the nameless star system's red dwarf primary.

Each of those specks of light was a starship, most of them as massive and powerfully armed as *Guerriere* herself. Now that Fisher had arrived on schedule, the reinforced Second Fleet was complete, as was Admiral Chin's Fifth Fleet, and both were under Tourville's command. Three hundred and thirty-six SD(P)s, the flower of the reborn Republican Navy, and by any standards, the most powerful battle force ever assembled for a single operation by any known star nation. They lay all about him, floating in distant orbit around the star system's second gas giant, waiting for *his* orders, and he felt a shiver of apprehensive anticipation flow through him.

I never really thought it would all come together, even after Tom told me. But it has. And now it's all mine.

It should have been Javier Giscard's command, he thought. Javier should have had Second Fleet and overall command, while he had Fifth, but Javier was gone, and so the task had fallen to him.

He thought about his orders, the different sets of contingency instructions, the planning and coordination and incredible industrial effort his huge fleet represented. The Republic's defenses had been unflinchingly reduced everywhere, despite the Manties' widespread scouting activities. Hopefully, however, the enemy wasn't aware of that. Not yet. All of his units had been left where they were, each drilling relentlessly in the simulators, until the operation actually began expressly to *keep* the Manties blissfully unaware of what was coming.

He hadn't liked that. In fact, it was the one part of the operational plan which he'd actually protested. Simulations were all well and good, but no one had ever put a fleet this size together before. He'd needed to practice coordinating with Chin, needed to drill the actual units, put the subunit commanders physically through their paces where he could watch them, evaluate their strengths and weaknesses. He'd asked—almost pleaded—for the chance to do that, but his request had been turned down. And even though he was the one who'd asked for it, he'd understood why Thomas Theisman had refused it.

It wasn't because Theisman didn't understand exactly why Tourville had made the request in the first place. It wasn't because Theisman disagreed with him, either. But for Operation Beatrice to succeed, complete strategic surprise was an absolute prerequisite.

Indeed, surprise was so important it had trumped even the need to conduct extensive hands-on training exercises. Given the activity of the Manty scouting forces, they'd dared not withdraw their picket forces from the stations closest to the enemy early. Even more, they hadn't dared to combine Tourville's units somewhere where a Manty reconnaissance drone might have picked them up and started their Office of Naval Intelligence wondering just why the Republic might have concentrated such a huge percentage of its total battle fleet in one place.

But we still have over a week before we sortie, plus the transit time, he thought. *It won't be as good as I would have preferred, but we can do a lot in that much time. And we'd better, because at the end of it*...

He let the thought trail off, because he didn't really know what would be waiting "at the end of it."

Except for the biggest naval battle in human history, of course.

Chapter Sixty-Three

"How does it look now, Andrea?"

"Better, Your Grace."

Captain Jaruwalski flipped a sighting circle into the main plot, dropping it neatly around the icons of Battle Squadrons Thirty-Six and Thirty-Eight, Imperial Andermani Navy. The light codes of the sixteen superdreadnoughts burned steadily in the display, giving no indication of how hard they were to find, even for *Imperator*'s sensors. The numbers in the CIC sidebar giving detected signal strength were another story, however, indicating exactly how hard they would have been to detect had *Imperator* not known precisely where to look for them. Not quite as hard as Manticoran ships might have been, but harder than anyone else's, Honor noted, and nodded in approval. Not so much of the EW capabilities, as of *Vizeadmiral* Morser's tactics.

"She's slipped around behind Admiral Yanakov," Jaruwalski continued. "I don't think he knows she's there, but he's a sneaky one. He may just be playing dumb until she's got him right where he wants her."

"Why do you think that might be?"

"Partly because of where he's got his carriers, Your Grace. He's got them pulled around, further ahead of his trailing battle squadron than his usual cruising dispositions. That puts the SD(P)s' onboard point defense between them and Morser's batteries. But they're still far enough astern that he could get their *Katanas* launched to thicken his task force missile defenses in a hurry. It may not mean anything, but it looks to me as if he's at least thinking about the possibility of being jumped from astern."

"I see."

Honor folded her hands behind her, standing beside her command chair while Nimitz draped bonelessly over its back, and contemplated the plot. Andrea had a point, she decided. Both about Judah's sneakiness, and about his formation. Personally, Honor gave it a sixty-forty chance Yanakov *didn't* know Morser was back there. Or, at least, how close she was. For the purposes of this exercise, he'd been denied the use of Ghost Rider's extended platform endurance, his sensor capability had been stepped down to no more than twenty percent better than ONI's current best estimate of the Republic's capabilities, and his acceleration rate had been reduced to match that of Republican superdreadnoughts. That meant he was more myopic than he was accustomed to being, and he must feel heavy-footed, slow to maneuver. So it made sense for him to be particularly wary about the possibility of being overhauled from behind.

Still, he *was* sneaky. . . .

Then again, so was Bin-hwei Morser. Honor still didn't like her much, and she was aware—painfully, one might say, given her ability to taste mind-glows—that Morser's feelings for her went far beyond "didn't like much." But the *vizeadmiral* was a superior tactician, and her very dislike for Manticore had inspired her to drive her personnel even harder over the five days since Aivars Terekhov's return from Monica. She hadn't come off very well in that series of exercises, and she hadn't liked *that* much, either. The last thing she wanted was to look inferior to the RMN.

When you're number two, you try harder, Honor thought wryly. *Especially when you resent the heck out of your number two status. Well, whatever works. I don't really care why she does it, as long she does do it.*

She began to pace slowly back and forth, watching the gradually developing tactical situation. At the moment, *Imperator* was tagging along behind *Konteradmiral* Syou-tung Waldberg's Battle Squadron Thirty-Eight at the rear of Morser's formation. Yanakov had his own Fifteenth Battle Squadron and Vice Admiral Baez's Twenty-Third, plus Samuel Miklós' Fifth Carrier Squadron and all four of Eighth Fleet's Manticoran and Grayson battlecruiser squadrons. Alistair McKeon's Sixty-First Battle Squadron, most of Alice Truman's carriers, and the rest of Honor's cruisers and destroyers had stayed home, near the Trevor's Star terminus of the Junction with Admiral Kuzak's Third Fleet, for this one. The object was to give her Andermani units a significant force advantage, since they were tasked as the aggressors in this particular system defense exercise.

"Any word on *Vizeadmiral* Hasselberg's units?" she asked, after a moment.

"Welllll . . ." Jaruwalski said, and Honor looked at her sharply, one eyebrow rising as she tasted the ops officer's emotions.

"Spit it out, Andrea."

"Well, I know Admiral Yanakov can't use the all-up Ghost Rider capabilities, and I know we're supposed to be letting *Vizeadmiral* Morser call all the shots on this one. But I couldn't quite resist the temptation to deploy a few drones of my own, Your Grace. None of the take from them is going to Morser, but it sort of lets me keep an eye on things."

"I see. And no doubt you simply forgot to display the positions of *Vizeadmiral* Hasselberg and his ships. The fact that you were attempting to conceal your transgression from my eagle eye had *nothing* to do with the omission, right?"

"Well, maybe a little, Your Grace," Jaruwalski admitted with a grin. "You want to see him?"

"Go ahead and show me."

"Coming up now," Jaruwalski said, and the understrength Forty-First Battle Squadron of *Vizeadmiral* Hwa-zhyou Reinke, screened by the sixteen battlecruisers of *Konteradmiral* Hen-zhi Seifert and *Konteradmiral* Tswei-yun Wollenhaupt and accompanied by Rear Admiral Harding Stuart's *Mermaid* and *Harpy,* appeared suddenly on the master plot.

Mermaid and *Harpy* formed Carrier Division Thirty-Four, detached from Truman's CLAC squadron to give the Andermani a carrier element. At the moment, they and the superdreadnoughts they were accompanying were well ahead of Yanakov's force, closing in on an almost directly converging heading, and Honor frowned.

Reinke's squadron had only six SD(P)s, which meant Yanakov's wallers outnumbered him by better than two-to-one. Stuart's carriers were outnumbered by three-to-one, and even in battlecruisers, Hasselberg was outnumbered four-to-three. That was bad enough, but coming in as he was, he'd be in MDM engagement range at least a half-hour before Morser closed up from behind Yanakov, and a half-hour was a long time in an engagement between pod-layers.

She started to say something, then changed her mind. She didn't really care for tactics which split an attacking fleet up into penny packets. It was too good a way to fritter away a numerical advantage and invite defeat in detail, especially if your timing screwed up, and that seemed to be what was about to happen to Hasselberg and Morser. It looked as if Hasselberg had planned on a simultaneous attack, enveloping Yanakov from ahead and astern at the same time. If he had, however, his timing was decidedly off.

But that was a point for her to make to him privately, where he could be positive she wasn't criticizing him in front of his juniors. She wasn't afraid Jaruwalski would have let anything slip to anyone else even if she'd commented on Hasselberg's error, but it was a bad habit to get into, even with her own staff. And so she possessed her soul in silence, watching the situation unfold.

And then—

"Your Grace, look at this!" Jaruwalski said suddenly, and Honor frowned. It took her an instant to recognize what she was seeing, but when she did, she decided she was glad she hadn't criticized Hasselberg's timing after all.

"Is he doing what I *think* he's doing, Your Grace?" Jaruwalski asked, and Honor chuckled.

"He is, indeed, Andrea. And I'll be interested to see how Judah reacts. This is very like something *he* once pulled in a training exercise in Yeltsin."

She stepped over closer to Jaruwalski, resting her right hand lightly on the ops officer's shoulder as they both watched the plot. Hasselberg had obviously just deployed Ghost Rider drones of his own. These weren't sensor platforms, though; they were EW platforms configured to counterfeit the emissions signatures of Morser's superdreadnoughts. And he was being subtle about it. The signal strength off the drones was very weak—barely more than ten percent higher than what could have been expected to leak through a standard Andermani stealth field. Given the way Yanakov's sensor capabilities had been dialed back for the exercise, his tac officers were going to have a hard time recognizing what Hasselberg was doing.

In fact, as became apparent a few moments later, they *hadn't* recognized it. Yanakov was changing course, turning away from the threat he'd just detected, and launching his LACs. With only Republican levels of capability allowed to his reconnaissance drones, his LACs were his best long-range sensor platforms, despite their far lower acceleration rates, and he was sending them out to check out the suspect contacts. At the same time, as a precaution, he was deploying the bulk of his *Katanas* between his battle squadrons and Hasselberg. His battlecruisers were redeploying, as well, shifting to cover the threat axis with their anti-missile defenses.

It was clear Yanakov didn't intend to allow himself to be drawn into automatically assuming he was seeing what his tactical sections thought they were seeing. At the same time, he'd equally clearly decided he had to honor the threat and shift his formation to meet it.

Which was exactly what Hasselberg had wanted him to do.

The next thirty minutes passed slowly as Honor and Jaruwalski watched the shifting patterns in the plot. Yanakov's turn away from Hasselberg had the effect of closing the range to Morser even more rapidly, but at such ranges "rapid" was a purely relative term.

Hasselberg was playing the game well, Honor decided. Once he'd given Yanakov a sniff of his position and drawn an obvious response, he cycled down the power of his decoys' signatures. It looked exactly as if he wasn't positive he'd been detected and he was reducing acceleration to cut back the strength of his impeller signatures and make his stealth systems more effective. The maneuver both lent verisimilitude to his deception and made it even harder to penetrate by requiring the reconnaissance LACs to close to much shorter range for positive identification.

Honor pursed her lips thoughtfully as the range from Morser's squadrons to Yanakov's dropped steadily. Yanakov was already in MDM range, and in another few minutes his LACs were going to get close enough to see through Hasselberg's masquerade. So if she were Morser, she'd be firing just about—

"*Vizeadmiral* Morser's opened fire, Your Grace," Jaruwalski said, and Honor nodded.

"So I see," she said mildly, folded her hands behind her once again, and walked calmly back to her command chair.

Judah was going to be . . . irritated with himself, she thought with a mental grin. He'd obviously taken Hasselberg's bait, after all. He might not have allowed himself to go charging after it, but Hasselberg and his skillfully deployed drones had riveted Yanakov's attention on the smaller of the Andermani task groups. His tac crews hadn't been paying as much attention to other possible axes of threat, and when Morser launched, Yanakov's screen—and *Katanas*—were badly out of position, with very poor shots at the incoming tide of missiles. Moreover, Morser had stacked her pods deeply. Her sixteen superdreadnoughts had deployed almost six hundred pods; now they launched a total of 4,608 attack and EW missiles . . . and five hundred and seventy-six Apollo control missiles.

Flight time was still almost six minutes, which gave Yanakov some time to adjust, but it wasn't long enough to significantly reposition his units. And as the missiles came streaking in, for the first time, Eighth Fleet units found themselves on the *receiving* end of an Apollo attack.

It was not, Honor thought, watching the first few damage codes appear on her display, like the first drifting flakes of a Sphinx mountain blizzard, going to be a pleasant experience.

"Admiral, it's time," Captain DeLaney said quietly over the com, and Lester Tourville nodded.

"Yes, I suppose it is," he agreed. "Send the Fleet to battle stations, Molly. I'll be up directly."

"Yes, Sir."

Tourville terminated the connection and stood. He patted his skinsuit's cargo pocket automatically, checking to be certain his trademark cigars were where they were supposed to be. They'd become so much a part of his image that he probably could have demoralized his entire flag bridge crew by the simple expedient of giving up smoking.

The thought made him chuckle, and he was glad he was alone as he detected the edge of nervousness in the sound.

Let's just get that out of our system right here, Lester. No butterflies in front of the troops. They deserve a hell of a lot better than that out of you.

He glanced at himself in a bulkhead mirror. It was probably just as well none of his personnel knew he'd been sitting here, already skinsuited, for the last fifteen minutes. Not that it had been because of any opening-night jitters. Or, at least, not very much so. It was more calculating than that. By suiting up early, he could take the time to do it right and arrive on flag bridge calm and collected, looking as if he'd just stepped out of a training holo. Just another of those little tricks to inspire his subordinates to pretend, even to themselves, that he was an unflappable, calm, confident leader. So sure of himself he would turn up perfectly turned out, without a single hair out of place.

He ran one hand over the hair in question, and chuckled again, much more naturally . . . just as the music began to play.

One of Thomas Theisman's reforms had been to allow the captains of capital units the right to substitute more personalized selections for the stridency of the standard fleet alarms. Captain Houellebecq had a fondness for really old opera, much of it actually dating from pre-space Old Earth. Tourville had cherished private doubts when she decided to use some of it aboard *Guerriere*, but he had to admit she'd come up with a suitable selection for this particular signal. In fact, he'd thought it was an appropriate one even before she told him what it was called.

"Now here this! Now here this! All hands, man Battle Stations! Repeat, all hands man Battle Stations!" Captain Celestine Houellebecq's calm, crisp voice said through the ancient, surging strains of Wagner's *Ride of the Valkyries*.

"Ma'am, the Alpha Arrays are reporting—*sweet Jesus!*"

Lieutenant Commander Angelina Turner turned quickly, eyes flashing angrily.

"Just what the hell kind of report do you call that, Hellerstein?" she demanded harshly, even angrier because Chief Petty Officer Bryant Hellerstein was one of her best, steadiest people.

"Commander—Ma'am—this *can't* be right!" Hellerstein blurted, and Turner strode quickly towards his station. She'd opened her mouth in another, still sharper reprimand, but Hellerstein's shocked expression when he turned to look at her stopped it unspoken. She'd never seen the tough, competent noncom look . . . terrified before.

"What can't be right, Bryant?" she asked, much more gently than she'd intended to speak.

"Ma'am," Hellerstein said hoarsely, "according to the Alpha Arrays, *three hundred-plus* unidentified ships just made their alpha translations right on the limit."

Chapter Sixty-Four

"All right, Robert. Let's get those drones deployed."

"Aye, Sir!" Commander Zucker began punching in commands at his console, and Rear Admiral Oliver Diamato turned to his chief of staff.

"It's not going to take them long to figure out we're out here, Serena," he said, one hand gesturing at the master plot which showed the Manticoran Wormhole Junction. Just getting this close to the Junction made Diamato's skin crawl, because if there was one point—besides their home system's inhabited worlds—guaranteed to make the Manties respond like a wounded swamp tiger, it was the Junction.

"As a matter of fact, Sir," Commander Taverner replied with a mirthless smile, "I sort of suspect they already know, don't you?"

"I'm an admiral. That means I can put the best face on things if I want to." Diamato countered with a taut, answering smile.

In fact, as both he and Zucker knew perfectly well, the Mantie's system platforms had detected and pinpointed their hyper footprints the instant they arrived. There was no point trying to fool those stupendous arrays. With dimensions measured in thousands of kilometers on a side, they could pick up even the most gradual translation into normal-space at a range of literally light-weeks, much less the signatures of two battlecruiser squadrons only six light-hours from the primary.

"I suppose so, Sir," Taverner agreed. "Maybe that's why I'm just a commander."

"And don't you forget it." Diamato could almost feel his flag bridge crew relaxing at the banter between him and the chief of staff, and that was good. But there were more serious things to consider, as well.

"What I meant," he continued, "is that I'd like to put as much distance—very stealthily—as we can between us and our arrival points. I doubt we'll be able to drop off their systems, but it's worth a try."

"Yes, Sir," Taverner said more seriously. She gazed at the plot along with him. Their recon drones were out, racing for the Junction to keep a close eye on things, and already the faint sensor ghosts which were all they ever seemed to see of the Manties' all-too-aptly named "Ghost Rider" drones were appearing, headed (as nearly as they could tell) in their direction.

"What about going to Shell Game, Sir?" she asked after a moment.

"That's what I was thinking," Diamato agreed.

His ships' job was to keep as close an eye as possible on the Junction for Second Fleet. Even with the FTL com, his reports to Lester Tourville would still be over six minutes old when they arrived, but that was infinitely better than the six-*hour* delay light-speed transmissions would have imposed. And at least the Manty defenses had made it easy for the planners to decide against sending in recon LACs, since none of them could have hoped to survive long enough to see a damned thing. That meant he wouldn't have LAC crews' deaths on his conscience, but it didn't exactly solve his other problems. Specifically, his drones, while more capable than they'd ever been before as *recon* platforms, still were nowhere near as stealthy as the Manties' drones. That meant he had to stay close enough to keep sending in fresh waves as the defenders picked off the earlier ones.

At the same time, there was no point pretending his command could fight off what the Manties could send its direction if they so chose. So instead of any deluded notions of martial glory and stand-up battle, it was time—as Taverner had just suggested—to rely on speed and dispersal. This far out from the system primary (and well to the side of the resonance zone), Diamato's sixteen battlecruisers were free to bob and weave. And once their hyper generators finished cycling, they could always disappear into hyper if things looked like getting too hot anyway. The trick was to avoid letting anything with MDMs get within four or five light-minutes of them.

"Should I pass the orders, then, Sir?" Taverner asked, and he nodded.

"Do it," he said.

"Oh, shit," Admiral Stephania Grimm, Royal Astrogation Control Service, said to herself very, very quietly as a soft but urgent audio alarm sounded. The napkin she'd been using to brush cake crumbs from her tunic was suddenly a crushed ball in her hand, and the people who'd just been wishing her happy birthday turned as one to look at the plot.

Figures, a corner of her brain thought. *They* would *decide to come calling on* my *birthday!*

She looked around at the suddenly taut faces of her co-workers. ACS was a civil service organization, despite its military ranks, and most of her subordinates and staff had never imagined in their darkest nightmares that they might ever actually see combat. But Grimm's position as the commanding officer of the Manticoran Junction's traffic control service required her to cooperate closely with its military hierarchy. Not all ACS commanders had been comfortable fits for that side of their duties, but it helped that Grimm was herself ex-Navy. In fact, she'd reached the rank of captain of the list before transferring to ACS, and she'd quickly acquired a reputation among her military colleagues for efficiency and brains. That was especially welcome in the wake of her immediate predecessor, Admiral Allen Stokes, whose sole claim to his position had been his brother-in-law's close ties to Baron High Ridge and First Lord Janacek.

But right at this moment, knowing she was well thought of was remarkably little comfort to Admiral Grimm. The huge hyper footprint just outside the system hyper-limit was bad enough, but for her, personally, the scattered footprints and spreading impeller signatures eight light-minutes out from the Junction were just as bad. There were going to be incoming drones very shortly, and there might be more superdreadnoughts hovering out there on the other side of the hyper wall, waiting to pounce, depending on what those drones told their masters.

She wasn't the only one thinking dark thoughts, she noticed, watching the huge astro plot's sidebars as the Junction forts rushed to battle stations. It would take a *lot* of SDs to deal with *them*, she told herself, but that didn't make her feel a great deal better. There were several hundred freighters, passenger liners, mail boats, and exploration vessels either already in transit through the Junction's various termini or else lined up in the transit queues awaiting their turns, and the thought of MDMs tearing around amidst all that defenseless civilian shipping made her physically sick to her stomach.

She flipped up a plastic shield and punched a large, red button on her console. A harsh, strident buzzer sounded, and every other sound on the command deck of HMSS *DaGama*, the Junction's central ACS platform ceased abruptly. Every eye turned towards her as the saw-edged audio alarm jerked her personnel's attention to her.

"It hasn't been declared yet, but we have damned sure got ourselves a Case Zulu, people," she announced in a flat, tense voice. "I'm declaring Condition Delta on my own authority. Clear the Junction—*all* traffic, wherever it is in the queue, not just the outbounds already on final. I want anything that might draw an MDM's attention way the hell away from here ASAP.

"After that, Jordan," she continued, turning to her exec, who still held half a slice of cake, "get ready for the ride of your life. Unless I miss my guess, what Admiral Yestremensky had to deal with when Earl White Haven took Eighth Fleet to Basilisk was a walk in the park compared to what's coming *our* way. Get a dispatch boat away to Trevor's Star with a sitrep immediately. Then go ahead and start setting up for a minimum-interval transit of everything Admiral Kuzak and Duchess Harrington have. I'm not sure what their deployments are, but we could have close to a hundred wallers coming through that terminus nose-to-arse. And if a couple of SDs misjudge their intervals and collide—or bring their wedges up too close together—we are going to have one *hell* of a mess."

"No joke," Captain Jordan Lamar said feelingly.

"So I want our best controllers on that lane," Grimm said. "Forget about the standard watch schedule. Pull in the best from wherever the hell they are and get them at those consoles—" she jabbed a finger at the Trevor's Star traffic controllers' section "—ten minutes ago. Then see what we've got available for tugs."

"Yes, Ma'am. I'm on it," Lamar said. He looked down, saw the cake as if for the first time, and stared at it for just a moment.

Then he chuckled harshly, shoved it into his mouth, and turned to his own com to begin giving orders.

"Bradley," Grimm went on, turning to her official liaison to Admiral Thurston Havlicek, the Junction Defense Command's commanding officer, "bring Admiral Havlicek up to speed on what we've already done. I'm sure we're going to have drones incoming from these people in the next thirty or forty minutes, and I'm sure he's got his own plans for dealing with them, but ask him if there's anything *we* can do to help. I'm thinking we may need to be looking at ways to stack the incoming wallers to block the drones' LOS to the terminus, keep them from getting a close enough look to tell the Peeps what's coming or when. Whatever JDC needs and we can do, he's got, but I need to know what he wants now."

"Aye, aye, Ma'am!" Commander Bradley Hampton said with a grateful smile. "I'll get right on it."

"Good," Grimm said quietly, and looked back at the plot. The first Ghost Rider platforms were already twenty-five thousand kilometers out, accelerating at just over five thousand gravities. She couldn't see them, though she knew they were there. But she *could* see the blossoming impeller signatures of Junction Defense Command's LACs. Over thirty-five hundred were already in space, and more were appearing with metronome precision as the LAC platforms launched.

You bastards just go right ahead and come in on us, she thought venomously at the impeller signatures of the battlecruisers trying to spy on her command area. *Come right ahead. We've* got *something for you.*

Sebastian D'Orville's thoughts about the boredom of his assignment ran through the back of his brain like a bitter, distant echo as he strode onto HMS *Invictus'* flag bridge. Despite all his training, all his preparation, all the simulations and wargames and contingency planning, he suddenly discovered that he'd never really believed it would happen. That the Peeps would have the sheer, unadulterated nerve to actually *attack* the Star Kingdom of Manticore's home star system.

And why the hell didn't *you believe it?* his brain demanded contemptuously. *You were ready enough to think about invading* their *home system during Buttercup, weren't you? Pissed off because Saint-Just's "cease-fire" ploy stopped the operation, weren't you? Well, it seems they can think big too, can't they?*

"Talk to me, Maurice," he said harshly.

"They're coming straight down our throats, Sir," Captain Maurice Ayrault, his chief of staff, replied flatly. "The only finesse I can see is their approach vector. It looks like they think they're going to take out Home Fleet and Sphinx first, then roll on over Manticore, but they're trying to leave themselves an out just in case, and their astrogation was first rate. They came in right on the intersection of the resonance zone and the hyper limit and split the angle almost exactly. It's not a least-time approach, but it means they can break back across the zone boundary if it gets too deep instead of being committed to the inner-system. At the moment, they're eight light-minutes out, closing at fifteen hundred KPS, and they're pouring on the accel. They must be running their compensators at at least ninety percent of full military power, because current acceleration is right on four-point-eight KPS-squared."

"Well," D'Orville said, "that's why we deployed this way. What does it look like for a zero/zero intercept on the planet?"

"Just under three hours," Ayrault said. "Turnover in roughly eighty-six minutes. They'll be up to twenty-six thousand KPS at that point." The chief of staff grimaced. "I suppose we should be grateful for small favors, Sir. They could have cut their time by over thirty minutes if they'd come straight in across the zone boundary."

"Time to range on the planet if they decide to go for maximum-range shots?" D'Orville asked levelly, hoping his tone and expression hid the icy chill running down his spine at the thought of weapons as notoriously inaccurate as long-range MDMs screaming through the inner system.

"On a zero/zero profile, ninety-four minutes. If they go for a least-time approach, without turnover, they can shave roughly a minute off of that. Either way, it's about an hour and a half."

"I see."

D'Orville considered what Ayrault had said. Home Fleet was still rushing to Battle Stations, but at least it was standing policy to hold his ships' nodes permanently at standby readiness, despite the additional wear that put on the components. He'd be able to get underway in the next twelve to fifteen minutes. The question was what he did when he could.

No, he told himself. *There really isn't any question at all, is there? You can't let those missile pods get any closer to Sphinx than you can help. But, Jesus—over three hundred ships?*

"Does Tracking have a breakdown yet, Madelyn?" he asked, turning to his operations officer.

"It's just coming in now, Sir," Captain Madelyn Gwynett told him. She watched the information come up on her display, and he saw her shoulders tighten.

"Tracking makes it two hundred and forty superdreadnoughts, Sir. At this time, it looks like they're all pod-layers, but we're trying to get drones in closer to confirm that. They've also got what looks like sixteen CLACs and a screen of roughly ninety cruisers and lighter units, as well."

"Thank you, Madelyn."

D'Orville was pleased, in a distant sort of way, by how calm he sounded, but he understood why Gwynett's shoulders had stiffened. Home Fleet contained forty-two SD(P)s and forty-eight older superdreadnoughts. He was outnumbered by better than two and a half-to-one in capital ships, but the ratio was almost *six*-to-one in SD(P)s. He had twelve pod-laying battlecruisers, as well, but they'd be spit on a griddle against superdreadnoughts.

Still, he told himself as firmly as possible, the situation wasn't quite as bad as the sheer numbers suggested. The new tractor-equipped "flat-pack" missile pods would allow each of his older superdreadnoughts to "tow" almost six hundred pods inside their wedges, glued to their hulls like high-tech limpets. That was a hundred and twenty percent of a *Medusa*-class' internal pod loadout, and the ships were already loading up with them. Unfortunately, they didn't have the fire control to manage salvos as dense as a *Medusa* could throw. Worse, they'd have to flush the majority of their pods early in order to clear the sensor and firing arcs of their point defense and its fire control arrays. So he was going to have to use them at the longest range, where their accuracy was going to be lowest.

"Katenka," he said to Lieutenant Commander Lazarevna, "get me Admiral Caparelli."

"Aye, aye, Sir."

Caparelli appeared on D'Orville's com display almost instantly.

"Sebastian," he said, his voice level but his expression taut.

"Tom." D'Orville nodded back, thinking about how many times they'd greeted one another exactly the same way before . . . and wondering if they'd ever do it again.

"I think I've got to go out to meet them," D'Orville continued.

"If you do, you lose the inner-system pods," Caparelli countered, and D'Orville nodded grimly.

The inner system defenses relied heavily on MDM pods, and they'd been deployed in massive numbers. Unfortunately, he thought, the numbers weren't massive enough. They'd been designed to stop any *likely* attack cold, but the defensive planners hadn't counted on an adversary who was prepared to throw over two hundred modern podnaughts, and all the anti-missile defenses that implied, straight into their teeth. They might still be able to beat off the attack, but not without letting the attackers into their own missile range of the hideously vulnerable dispersed shipyards in which the Royal Manticoran Navy's entire next-generation of superdreadnoughts was approaching completion. He couldn't let the Peeps close enough to do to the home system shipyards what had already happened to Grendelsbane's.

And that doesn't even count what could happen if they open fire on the inner system from that far out and a couple of their missiles run into Manticore or Sphinx at seventy or eighty percent of light-speed, he thought with a shudder.

"If you go out to meet them," Caparelli continued, "you'll have to take them on without any support, and they've got a huge edge in numbers. You'll lose everything you've got if you meet them head-on."

"And if I don't take them head-to-head, I let them into range of the planet," D'Orville countered harshly.

"So far, they've stayed away from anything which might look like a violation of the Eridani Edict," Caparelli pointed out.

"And so far they haven't invaded our home system, either," D'Orville shot back. The Manticoran tradition was that the Admiralty did not second guess a fleet CO when battle threatened—not even Home Fleet's commander. What D'Orville did with his fleet was his decision. Admiralty House might advise, might provide additional intelligence or suggest tactics, but the decision was his, and it wasn't like Thomas Caparelli to try to change that.

But D'Orville wasn't really surprised by Caparelli's reluctance to admit what he knew as well as D'Orville did had to happen. The First Space Lord knew too many of the men and women aboard D'Orville's ships . . . and he couldn't join them. He would be safely back on Manticore when the hammer came down on Home Fleet, and

Sebastian D'Orville knew Caparelli too well, knew exactly what the other admiral was feeling, the miracle he wanted to find. But there were no miracles, not today, and so D'Orville shook his head.

"No, Tom," he said almost gently. "I'd like to hang back—believe me, I would. But we can't count on continued restraint where their targeting's concerned. This one is for all the marbles. They've got thirty *squadrons* of SD(P)s—the equivalent of forty of our squadrons, with over a million people aboard them—coming at us, right into the heart of our defenses. That means they're ready for massive losses. I don't think we can expect them to take that kind of punishment without handing out whatever they can in return, and even if they never intentionally fire a single shot at the planet, think about how damned inaccurate end-of-run MDMs are. I can't let hundreds of those things go flying around this close to Sphinx."

"I know." Caparelli closed his eyes for a moment, then inhaled deeply and opened them once more.

"I've ordered the Case Zulu message transmitted to all commands," he said, his voice more clipped, his dread of what was to come cloaked in reflex professionalism. "Theodosia can start responding from Trevor's Star in about fifteen minutes, but most of Eighth Fleet is off the terminus, on maneuvers. I don't know how quickly it can get back there, but I'm guessing it'll take at least a couple of hours just for Duchess Harrington to get to the terminus. I'm recalling Jessup Blaine's squadrons from the Lynx Terminus, as well, but our best estimate on his current response time is even longer than Eighth Fleet's."

"And even Theodosia can't do it in a mass transit," D'Orville said grimly. "She's going to have to do it one ship at a time, the same way Hamish did it when the bastards hit Basilisk, because we're going to need everything she's got."

Kuzak could have put almost thirty superdreadnoughts through the Junction in a single mass transit, but the destabilizing effect would have locked down the Trevor's Star-Manticore route for almost seventeen hours. Even in a sequenced transit, each ship of the wall would close the route for almost two minutes before the next in the queue could use it.

"You're right," Caparelli agreed. "Allowing for her screening units, she's going to need almost two hours just to make transit."

"By which time these people will be about an hour out from Sphinx, and she can't possibly catch them," D'Orville said.

"We're scrambling every LAC we've got," Caparelli said. "We should be able to get five or six thousand of them to you by the time you engage."

"That will help—a lot," D'Orville said. "But they've got sixteen carriers with them. That gives them over three thousand of their own."

"I know." Caparelli looked out of the display, his eyes and face grim. "All you can do is the best you can do, Sebastian. We'll do whatever we can to support you, but it isn't going to be much."

"Who would have thought they'd throw something this size at us?" D'Orville asked almost whimsically.

"Nobody on the Strategy Board, that's for sure." Caparelli's voice was briefly saw-edged with bitter self-reproach, as if there were some way he could have kept this nightmare from coming. Then he got control of it again. "Actually, I suspect Harrington's the only one who would have believed they might throw the dice this way. And I honestly don't think even she would have *expected* them to."

"Well, they're here now, and my nodes are coming up. It looks like we're going to be pretty busy in a little while, Tom. Clear."

"Your Grace!"

Honor stepped back from her sparring match with Clifford McGraw and looked up in astonishment as one of Major Lorenzetti's Marines came skidding through the gymnasium hatch. Spencer Hawke and Joshua Atkins wheeled towards the sudden, unexpected arrival, hands flashing to their pulsers, and she spat out her mouth protector and threw up her own hand.

"No threat!" she snapped.

Hawke continued his draw, but his pulser stayed pointed at the deck. He didn't even look at her; his attention was locked on the Marine, who, Honor knew, didn't begin to realize how close he'd just come to being shot. In fact, probably the only thing that had saved him was her armsmen's faith in her and Nimitz's ability to sense what was going on inside someone else.

But not even that faith was going to get Hawke's sidearm back into its holster until he *knew* positively what was happening.

At the moment, however, that was a completely secondary concern for Honor beside the consternation and turmoil boiling inside the Marine.

"Yes, Corporal . . . Thackston?" she said, reading the Marine's name off of his nameplate and deliberately pitching her voice into the most soothing register she could. "What is it?"

"Your Grace—" Thackston stopped and shook himself. "Beg pardon, Your Grace," he said after a moment, his voice under tight control. "Captain Cardones' compliments," he touched the communicator at his belt as if to physically indicate where Cardones' message had come from, "and we've just received a Case Zulu from the Admiralty."

Honor jerked fully upright. She couldn't have heard him correctly! But even as she told herself that, her memory flashed back to another day, aboard another ship. The last time someone had transmitted the code phrase "Case Zulu." In the Royal Manticoran Navy, those two words had only one meaning: "invasion imminent."

"Thank you, Corporal," she said, her voice crisp yet calm enough the Marine looked at her in something very like disbelief. She nodded to him, then wheeled to Hawke and Atkins while Nimitz came bounding across the gym towards her.

"Spencer, get on the com. Find Commodore Brigham. Tell her we're in the gymnasium, and that I'll see the staff on Flag Bridge in five minutes."

"Yes, My Lady!" Hawke reholstered his pulser with one hand and reached for his communicator with the other, and Honor opened her arms as Nimitz leapt into them, then turned to Atkins.

"Joshua, com Mac. Tell him I'll need my skinsuit and Nimitz's on Flag Bridge as soon as possible."

"Yes, My Lady!"

"Clifford," she said over her shoulder to her third armsman as she started for the hatch, "just grab your gunbelt. You can worry about the rest of your uniform later."

"Yes, My Lady!"

Sergeant McGraw snatched up his weapons belt and buckled it over his own *gi*.

Fifteen seconds after Corporal Barnaby Thackston, RMMC, had delivered Rafe Cardones' message, Admiral Lady Dame Honor Alexander-Harrington was headed purposefully for the lifts with her armsmen jog trotting to match her long-legged strides.

"It seems they've made up their minds, Sir," Commander Frazier Adamson observed, watching the icons of the Manticoran Home Fleet.

"It's not as if we've left them a lot of options," Lester Tourville said without looking at his operations officer.

Adamson was a highly competent tactician, an efficient organizer, and a loyal subordinate. He was also a pretty fair pinochle player, and Tourville liked him quite a lot, under normal circumstances. But outside his area of professional interest, the commander had about as much imagination as a wooden post. It wasn't that he was a shallow person, or insensitive in his personal relationships. It was simply that it would never have occurred to him to put himself inside the minds and emotions of the people aboard the ships accelerating away from Sphinx to meet Second Fleet.

At the moment, Lester Tourville, who was cursed with entirely too much imagination, bitterly envied that inner blind spot.

"They can't feel confident we won't bombard the planetary orbitals—or even the planet itself—from long range," he continued, "especially if they use the inner system pods. So they're going to come to meet us, try to thin us down to something which won't dare continue inward to hit the fixed defenses at all."

"Yes, Sir," Adamson said. "That's what I meant."

He seemed surprised by his admiral's restatement of the obvious, and Tourville made himself smile.

"I know it was, Frazier. I know it was."

He patted the ops officer on the shoulder and walked a couple of paces closer to the main tactical display. He stood gazing into it until he sensed a human presence at his side and looked down to see Captain DeLaney standing there.

"Frazier means well, Boss," his shorter chief of staff said quietly.

"I know he does." Tourville smiled again, more naturally, but it was a sad smile, all the same. One only those he knew and trusted were ever allowed to see, since it accorded so poorly with his "cowboy" persona.

"It's just that he only sees them as targets," Tourville continued, equally quietly. "Right now, I wish I did, too. But I don't. I know exactly what they're thinking over there, but they're going to come out to meet us, anyway."

"Like you said, Boss," DeLaney's smile was a mirror of his own, "we didn't leave them much choice, did we?"

✧   ✧   ✧

"Forget the screen!" Admiral Theodosia Kuzak snapped. "We can cut fifteen minutes off our total transit time if we leave them behind, and it's not like cruisers and destroyers are going to make any difference, is it?"

"No, Ma'am," Captain Gerald Smithson, her chief of staff replied. He was a tall, spare-looking man, his dark hair and complexion a stark contrast to Kuzak's red-hair and fair skin, and he seemed to be coming back on balance after the shock of the Admiralty's Case Zulu.

"Has Astro Control responded?" Kuzak demanded, wheeling around to Lieutenant Franklin Bradshaw, her communications officer.

"Yes, Ma'am," Bradshaw said. "As a matter of fact, Admiral Grimm's courier boat just came back though from the Manticore end. She'd already started clearing the Junction even before she sent it through the first time. Now she's working out the best dispositions for our units to help screen the arrival terminus from Peep drones. And she's also moving tugs to the inbound nexus in case any of our units require assistance."

"A nice thought," Kuzak said with a mirthless smile, "but if any of our wallers bump, tugs aren't going to be much help."

"Take what we can get, Ma'am," Smithson said with graveyard humor, and Kuzak snorted a harsh chuckle.

"Actually, Ma'am," Smithson continued in a low-pitched voice, "I've just had a rather nasty thought. What if this isn't their only fleet? What if they've got another one waiting to hit Trevor's Star as soon as we pull out for Manticore?"

"The same thought occurred to me," Kuzak replied, equally quietly. "Unfortunately, there's not a lot we can do about it, if they do. We've *got* to hold the home system. If they punch out *Hephaestus* and *Vulcan*, take out the dispersed yards, it'll be a thousand times worse than what happened at Grendelsbane. I hate to say it, but if it's a choice between San Martin and Sphinx or Manticore, San Martin loses."

"At least the system defenses are better than they were when the shooting started," Smithson said.

"They are. But that's another reason we can't afford to lock down the Junction with a mass transit. If they do have something like that in mind, we've got to be able to get *back* as quickly as we left."

"What about Duchess Harrington?" Smithson asked. "She's too

far out to rendezvous with us before we make transit. Should we ask her to stay behind and mind the store while we're gone?"

"I wish we could, but we'll have to see what happens with Home Fleet. And of course, I can't give her direct orders, since—"

"Excuse me, Ma'am. You have a com request from Duchess Harrington," Bradshaw interrupted suddenly.

"Throw it to Jerry's display," Kuzak said, bending over the chief of staff's console rather than waste time walking back to her own. An instant later, Smithson's flatscreen lit with the image of Eighth Fleet's commander.

Harrington had obviously been as surprised as everyone else, Kuzak thought, noting the *gi* she hadn't burned up time changing out of.

"Admiral Harrington," she said with a choppy nod. Eighth Fleet was almost seventy-eight million kilometers from the terminus. At that range, even the FTL com imposed a noticeable lag, and eight seconds passed before Honor nodded back.

"Admiral Kuzak," she replied, then continued, getting straight to business, in light of the delay. "I assume you're already planning an immediate transit to Manticore with Third Fleet. I'm sending my battlecruisers ahead, but it's going to take most of my units another two hours-plus to reach the terminus. With your permission, I'll temporarily assign Admiral McKeon's battle squadron and Admiral Truman's carriers to you."

"Thank you, Admiral," Kuzak said very, very sincerely.

"The sooner they get there, the better," Honor replied eight seconds later. "And please remember that three of Alistair's superdreadnoughts are Apollo-capable. I don't know how much difference it's going to make, but—"

She shrugged, and Kuzak nodded grimly.

"I'll remember, Your Grace. I only wish I had more of them."

"I'll bring the rest through as quickly as I can," Honor promised after the inevitable delay.

"And I'll try to make sure there's still a Star Kingdom when you do," Kuzak replied.

"Well, Sir," Commander Zucker said, "the good news is that they don't seem to be deploying anything but LACs to cover the Junction. The *bad* news is that they've got a hell of a lot of them."

"So I see," Oliver Diamato murmured. Like Zucker, he was

delighted he wasn't already having to play tag with hordes of Manty battlecruisers or—worse!—those damned MDM-armed heavy cruisers he'd heard so much about from NavInt since that business at Monica. But the shoals of LAC impeller signatures sweeping outward from the Junction were building a solid wall of interference which made it almost impossible for his shipboard sensors to see a damned thing, even at this piddling little range. The density of that LAC shell also augured poorly for the survival of his recon drones when they finally got close enough for a look of their own.

On the other hand...

"All right, Serena," he said quietly. "Think with me here. They're covering up big time with LACs, and they aren't sending a single hyper-capable unit after us. What does that suggest to you?"

"That we don't want to get much closer to them, Sir?" the chief of staff suggested with a tight grin, and he snorted a chuckle.

"Besides that," he said.

"Well," she frowned thoughtfully, running one hand over her hair, "I'd say they're probably trying to use the LACs as much to blind us, keep us guessing about what's going on on the Junction, as to actually defend it. Which suggests they're doing something they think we wouldn't like. Like bringing bunches of big, nasty ships through from Trevor's Star."

"Yes, it does. But what do you get when you add the fact that no one is heading our way? No battlecruisers or heavy cruisers swanning around trying to nail us, or at least push us further away from the Junction?"

"That they're bringing through wallers, not screen elements," Taverner said after a second or two.

"Exactly." It was Diamato's turn to frown. "Much as we may hate to admit it, a one-on-one engagement with one of us would be a Manty BC skipper's wet dream. So if they're not sending them after us, then they must've had wallers in place and ready to start coming through almost immediately, instead. And they're going right *on* doing it. Which suggests they have quite a few of them on call."

He frowned some more, then looked over his shoulder at his com officer.

"Record for transmission to *Guerriere*, attention Captain DeLaney."

❖   ❖   ❖

"So Kuzak or Harrington—or both—are officially on their way, Boss," Molly DeLaney said quietly, and Tourville nodded.

"So far, so good," he agreed, and looked at Adamson.

"Start deploying the donkeys, Frazier," he said.

Chapter Sixty-Five

"Sir, their acceleration's dropping," Captain Gwynett said.

D'Orville stepped across to her console, accompanied by Captain Ayrault, and she looked up at him.

"How much is it coming down?" he asked.

"Only about a half a KPS squared, so far, Sir."

"What the hell are they up to now?" Ayrault wondered aloud.

"Putting pods on tow, maybe," D'Orville replied.

"I suppose that could be it, Sir," Gwynett raid. "Their pods are almost as stealthy as ours are, and the recon platforms wouldn't be able to see them at this range. But those are superdreadnoughts. They'd have to have an awful lot of tractors to be able to tow so many pods they'd have to tow them outside their wedges."

D'Orville nodded. Pods towed inside a ship's wedge didn't degrade its acceleration. That, after all, was exactly what his own pre-pod designs were doing with the tractor-equipped pods glued to their hulls. But superdreadnought wedges were huge; for the Peeps to be towing so many pods they couldn't fit them all inside their wedges, they'd have to have hundreds of tractors per ship. So they had to be up to something else.

But what?

"Maybe they've got tech problems," Ayrault suggested. "Could be one of their SDs has lost a couple of beta nodes and had to reduce accel. The others might be reducing so she can stay in company."

"Possible," D'Orville conceded. "Or it could be even simpler than that. Maybe they've just decided to ease off on their compensator margins now that they know we're coming out to meet them."

Ayrault nodded, but D'Orville wasn't really satisfied with his own hypothesis. It made sense, but it just didn't *feel* right, somehow.

"How far do you want to close before opening fire, Sir?" Gwynett asked, after a moment, and he looked back down at her. Despite the fact that he and Ayrault were standing right beside her, she had to pitch her voice very low to keep it from being overheard, because it was very quiet on HMS *Invictus'* flag bridge. Everyone had had time to realize what was going to happen, and fear hung in the background. There was no panic, no hesitation, but they knew what they faced, and the people on that bridge wanted to live just as much as anyone else. The knowledge that they very probably wouldn't was a cold, invisible weight, pressing down upon them.

D'Orville knew it, and he wished there was something he could say or do. Not to make the fear go away, because no one could have done that. But to tell them how much they meant to him, how bitterly he regretted taking them on this death ride.

"We have to make them count," he told Gwynett, equally quietly. "We know our accuracy and penaids are better, but we've still got to get in close. They're going to bury us whenever we open fire, and according to the recon drones, every single one of their wallers is a pod design. They aren't going to face the same 'use them or lose them' constraints we are.

"So we're either going to wait until they open fire, or else until the range drops to sixty-five million klicks."

Gwynett looked at him for a moment, then nodded slowly.

"I know. I know," he said softly. "But we've got to get our hits through at all costs. We've *got* to, Madelyn. If we don't, all of this," a slight motion of his head, almost as much imagined as seen, indicated his flag bridge and the fleet beyond it, "is for nothing."

"Yes, Sir. I understand."

"Which fire plan do you want to use, Sir?" Ayrault asked.

"We'll go with Avalanche," D'Orville said grimly. "Madelyn, I want you to start shifting formation to Sierra Three. How many LACs have managed to overtake us?"

"Just over thirty-five hundred so far, Sir. Another five hundred will be here by the time we reach the range you've specified."

"How many are *Katanas*?"

"I'm not positive, Sir. Under half—I know that much."

"I wish we had more," D'Orville said, "but what we have is all we've got. Pull them forward and spread them vertically. I want their Vipers positioned for the best firing arcs we can build."

"Yes, Sir."

"And set up your firing sequences to have the older ships deploy their pods first. We'll try to hold the internal pods as long as we can. I want the Keyhole ships to manage as many of the other units' pods as possible in the opening salvos."

"Yes, Sir. I understand."

"Good, Madelyn. Good." D'Orville patted her gently on the shoulder. "I'll let you get on with it, then."

"Yes, Sir," Captain Gwynett said.

"We're in range, Admiral," Commander Adamson pointed out, and Lester Tourville nodded.

"I'm aware of that, Frazier, thank you."

"Yes, Sir."

Tourville tipped back in his command chair and glanced at Molly DeLaney.

"So Tom was right," he said quietly.

"It looks that way," DeLaney agreed, and Tourville wondered if the relief hidden behind her calm expression could possibly be as great as the one roaring through him.

He looked at the master plot, with its sprawl of light codes. Second Fleet had been accelerating towards Sphinx for the last hour. Given the system's geometry, Tourville's present vector cut a chord at an angle of almost exactly forty-five degrees to the outer wall of the hugely elongated, "skinny" resonance zone. His phalanx of superdreadnoughts was up to 18,560 KPS, relative to the system primary, and they'd traveled over 35,600,000 kilometers. The Manties' Home Fleet had been under acceleration for only forty-seven minutes, on an almost exactly reciprocal course, but with its higher base acceleration, its velocity relative to the primary was already up to better than 17,000 KPS, and it had traveled just over 24,000,000 kilometers from its initial station.

Although Tourville's command was still almost half an hour from its turnover point for a zero/zero intercept of Sphinx, the range between the opposing forces had fallen to just a shade over 84,000,000 kilometers, and their closing speed was up to 45,569 KPS. That geometry gave Tourville's MDMs an effective range of better than 85,369,000 kilometers, which, as Frazier

Adamson had just observed, meant they were in extreme missile range of Home Fleet.

But Manticoran MDMs' acceleration rate was just over thirty-four KPS^2 higher than his birds could pull. That gave *them* a current effective range of better than 90,370,000 kilometers, which meant he'd been in *their* effective range for over two minutes.

"It doesn't just *look* like he was right," he told DeLaney after a moment. "He was. If they had those God awful missiles, they'd already be launching. They'd have spent the last ten minutes doing nothing but rolling pods, and they'd be punching them down our throats right this instant. They'd still have a transmission lag, but it'd be less than five seconds one-way, while ours would be over five *minutes*. So they'd have started hitting us *now*, without letting us close into our own effective range."

"You don't think they might just be letting the range fall a little more for their own fire control, Boss?"

"That's exactly what they're doing, and that's another reason we can be confident that they don't have the new missiles. They've got less than a hundred wallers over there. Even assuming they've got heavy external pod loads—which they very well could, despite their accel, if NavInt's right about their new pod designs—they're outnumbered better than two-to-one. They wouldn't be closing straight into salvos the size they know we can throw if they had any choice at all. Or, at least, they wouldn't be doing it without trying to whittle us down a bit first. But without the new control system, their accuracy at this range will be almost as bad as ours. They wouldn't get the kills they needed to do any whittling. They've got to get closer to improve *their* accuracy, just like we do."

"It's going to be ugly when we *do* open fire," Delaney said quietly, and Tourville nodded again.

"That it certainly is," he agreed grimly. "On the other hand, we planned for it, didn't we?"

"Yes, Sir."

Tourville studied the icons of the oncoming Home Fleet super-dreadnoughts for another few moments, then looked at a secondary display and shook his head in admiration. He'd always known Shannon Foraker had a talent for thinking outside the box. Way back when she'd been his operations officer, he'd recognized her knack for coming up with solutions which simply didn't occur to other people—concepts so elegantly simple everyone wondered why *they* hadn't thought of them.

When NavInt reported that the new Manty pods incorporated onboard tractors as a way to allow their pre-pod ships to tow greater numbers of them, it had seemed impossible for the Republic to respond. Their pods were already too big, and they had too limited a power budget, to permit the designers to cram a tractor into them (and power the damned thing), as well. But Shannon had decided to turn the problem on its head. Instead of fitting additional tractors into the pods, she'd come up with the "donkey." That was what everyone was calling it, although it had a suitably esoteric alphabet-soup designation, and it was another of those elegantly simple Foraker specialties.

Instead of the typically Manty bells-and-whistles approach of putting the tractor inside the pod, Shannon had simply built a very stealthy pod-sized platform which consisted of nothing except a solid mass of tractor beams and a receiver for beamed power from the ships which deployed it. Each "donkey" had the capacity to tow ten pods, and a *Sovereign of Space*-class SD(P) had enough tractors to tow twenty of them. Better yet, they could actually be ganged together, as long as all the pods in the gang could be lined up for power transmission from the mother ship. In theory, they could have been stacked three tiers deep, with each donkey towing ten more donkeys, each towing ten more donkeys, each . . .

If Lester Tourville had so chosen, his two hundred and forty superdreadnoughts could—in theory—have towed 4.8 *million* pods. Except for the minor fact that the drag would have reduced them to negative acceleration numbers. Not to mention the fact that he didn't begin to have the power transmission capability to feed that many donkeys. Still, he could tow quite a lot of them, and the readiness numbers on the display gave him a sense of profound satisfaction. He studied them a moment longer, then looked at Lieutenant Anita Eisenberg, his absurdly youthful communications officer.

"What's the latest from Admiral Diamato, Ace?"

"No change, Sir. He still can't get a clear look. Their fortresses and the LACs deployed to cover the Junction are picking off his recon platforms before they get close enough for that. But he still hasn't seen any hyper-capable units headed his way, and he's positive they're still coming through from Trevor's Star. No one's started in-system yet, though."

"Thank you," Tourville said, and cocked an eyebrow at DeLaney.

The chief of staff clearly had been running through the same mental math he had, and she grimaced.

"They've been coming through for over forty-five minutes now, Boss. By my calculations, that means at least twenty-four wallers so far."

"And it means they're planning on bringing through a lot more than that," Tourville agreed. "They could have put twenty-*seven* through in a mass transit and been headed after us over half an hour ago. The only reason to delay this long is because they figure they can't afford to lock the Junction down . . . because they've got one hell of a lot more than twenty-seven wallers waiting to come up our backside."

"Still, Boss, if I were them, I might be thinking about sending some of the ships I've already got through the Junction after us."

"No way." Tourville shook his head. "I wish to hell they would, but the Manties picked their best people to command Home Fleet, Third Fleet, and Eighth Fleet. I've studied NavInt's files on all three of them, and they aren't going to cooperate with *our* plans worth a damn.

"D'Orville's probably the most conventional thinker of the three, but he's also got the simplest equation . . . and plenty of guts. He can't let us get any closer to Sphinx than he can possibly help, so he's going to hit us head on, as far out as he can. He's going to get clobbered. In fact, I'll be surprised if *any* of his superdreadnoughts survive. But like you just said, it's going to be ugly for both sides, and our own losses are going to be heavy. He knows that, and he probably figures he can score at least a one-for-one exchange rate, despite the tonnage ratios. I think he may be being a little optimistic, but not very much. So given the combat strength he thinks he's up against, he probably figures he'll hurt us so badly we won't be able to close through the fixed inner-system defenses and missile pods. And if his analysis of the balance of forces was correct, he'd be right."

Tourville and his chief of staff looked at one another, and this time their smiles were hard. It was entirely possible RHNS *Guerriere* would be among the "heavy losses" the admiral had just predicted his fleet was going to suffer. But at this moment, an even exchange rate was actually heavily in the Republic's favor in the merciless mathematics of war . . . and those losses were also part of the bait in the trap Thomas Theisman and his Octagon planning staff had crafted.

"Kuzak's more of a free-thinker than D'Orville," Tourville continued. "I'm sure what she's doing right now has their Admiralty's approval, but even if it didn't, she'd do it anyway, on her own initiative. She knows exactly what's going to happen to D'Orville, and to us, and she knows she can't possibly get here in time to affect that outcome. So she's not going to split up her forces and send them in where we could chop them up in detail. Yes, she could've sent a couple of battle squadrons ahead, micro-jumped out to the side and then come back in directly behind us, assuming their astrogation was good enough. But unless *she's* got those new missiles, any small force she sent after us would get torn apart by the weight of fire we could send back at it.

"So, she's going to wait until she gets everything she's got through the Junction. *Then* she's going to do her micro-jumping and come in behind us—or more likely on our flank, especially, if we're driven back from Sphinx by our losses—as quickly as she can. She'll be too far behind to overhaul us, even with her acceleration advantage, if she has to come in astern, but she'll figure to put enough time pressure on us to limit the amount of damage we can do even if we've got enough left to risk engaging the Sphinx system-defense pods. At least, she'll figure, she can keep us from moving on from Sphinx to Manticore, and that would save about seventy percent of the system's total industry.

"The fact that she's waiting is the conclusive proof that she doesn't have any—or not very many, at least—of the new missiles, either. If she had a couple of battle squadrons equipped with them, then it would have made enormous sense to send them in, even in isolation. Their accuracy advantage would have been crushing enough to let them do heavy damage to us before we ever met D'Orville. Probably not enough to stop us, but maybe enough to even the odds between us and Home Fleet."

"And what about Harrington, Boss?" DeLaney asked quietly, when he paused.

"Harrington's probably the most dangerous of the lot," Tourville said, "and not just because we *know* Eighth Fleet's reequipped with at least some of the new missiles. She's got more actual combat experience than D'Orville or Kuzak, and she's sneaky as hell.

"But what's happening out at the Junction is tempting me to hope we filled an inside straight on the draw. If Eighth Fleet had been in position to intervene, *Kuzak* wouldn't be coming through the Junction; Harrington would, and we'd have had two or three of her battle squadrons ripping our ass off already. Assuming of course that Admiral Chin didn't have a little to say about it. So it's beginning to look as if Eighth Fleet really may be off on an operation of its own. I'm not planning on counting on that just yet—there could be any number of other explanations—but that's not going to keep me from hoping."

"I think I agree with you, Boss," DeLaney said, then chuckled. "I know Beatrice Bravo was specifically planned to mousetrap Eighth Fleet, and I guess I ought to be disappointed if we're not going to get it, too. But having seen what the lady can do, I'll be just *delighted* if 'the Salamander' is somewhere else while we're taking on the Manty home system's defenses!"

"I'm tempted to concur," Tourville agreed. "Taking out Eighth Fleet on top of everything else would certainly be a deathblow, but even with Eighth Fleet intact and Harrington to run it, the Manties are done if we take out this system's shipyards and both of the fleets they have defending them."

"We're coming down on sixty-five and a half million kilometers, Sir," Commander Adamson said.

"Thank you, Frazier."

Lester Tourville drew a deep breath. Eight minutes had passed since Adamson first informed him that they were into MDM range of the Manties. Second Fleet was still nineteen minutes short of its projected turnover point, but the range couldn't keep dropping forever without the Manties firing. The range between the two fleets had already fallen to 65,767,000 kilometers. Second Fleet's velocity was up to 20,866 kilometers per second; Home Fleet's was 19,923 KPS, and they'd closed the range between them by almost seventy-seven million kilometers. Tourville was still better than 98,835,000 kilometers from Sphinx, but from his current base velocity, his MDMs' range against the planet was almost 72,030,000 kilometers. The Manties weren't going to let him get much closer unchallenged.

"Open fire, Frazier," he said.

✦   ✦   ✦

The first missile impeller signatures began to speckle the plot, and Sebastian D'Orville drew a deep breath as the first, massive salvo streaked towards his command. Obviously, they *had* had a lot of pods on tow, he thought as he contemplated its numbers. More than he'd thought they had tractors for, actually. But their first salvo would be the least accurate against his EW, he reminded himself. And in the meantime, he had a few missile pods of his own.

"Engage as specified, Captain Gwynett," he said formally and watched his own missile's icons streaking outward across the plot.

That was when the enemy launched his *second* impossibly dense salvo.

Sebastian D'Orville's forty-eight pre-pod superdreadnoughts carried 27,840 pods externally, and theoretically, they could have deployed all of them in a single massive wave. In fact, Home Fleet carried a total of almost forty-nine thousand pods, with well over half a million missiles. Lester Tourville's slightly larger superdreadnoughts carried fewer pods, and each of those pods carried fewer missiles, because of the size penalty their bulkier MDMs imposed. So although he had two and a half times as many ships, he had barely twice as many pods, and each of those pods carried seventeen percent fewer missiles. He actually had "only" sixty-four percent more total missiles than Home Fleet.

But Lester Tourville also had Shannon Foraker's "donkey," and that meant every one of Sebastian D'Orville assumptions about the number and size of the salvos he could throw was fatally flawed. And what *else* he had was far more control channels for the missiles he carried. Not all of the forty-two Manticoran, Grayson, and Andermani SD(P)s confronting him were Keyhole-capable. Still, the majority of them were, and the pod-layers as a group could simultaneously control an average of four hundred missiles each. But the older, pre-pod ships could control only a hundred apiece, whereas each of *Tourville's* ships had control links for three hundred and fifty missiles, and by using Shannon Foraker's rotating control technique, they could increase that number by approximately sixty percent. So whereas Home Fleet could effectively control a total of just under twenty-two thousand missiles per salvo, Second Fleet could control *eighty-four* thousand without rotating control links. Worse, it could have increased that total to almost a hundred and thirty-five thousand, if it was prepared to accept somewhat lower hit probabilities, and the "donkey" meant Tourville could actually have deployed the pods to fire that many.

Manticoran fire control was better, Manticoran electronic warfare capabilities and penetration aids were better, and Manticoran MDM's were both faster and more agile. Sebastian D'Orville could confidently expect to score a significantly higher *percentage* of hits, but that couldn't offset the fact that Second Fleet could control over six times as many missiles. Even if Tourville's hit probabilities had been only half as good as his, the Republic would have scored three times as many hits.

It wasn't quite as bad for the Alliance as the raw numbers suggested. For one thing, deploying that many missiles and launching them without allowing their impeller wedges to cut one another's telemetry links was a far from trivial challenge. In fact, Tourville had decided to limit himself to no more than eighty percent of his theoretical maximum weight of fire. And to clear the firing and control arcs for even that many missiles, he'd been forced to spread his squadrons and their lumpy trails of donkeys and pods more broadly than he'd really wanted to. The separation between his units, necessary for effective offensive fire control, made it more difficult for them to coordinate their *defensive* fire. On the other hand, Havenite counter-missile doctrine relied so much more heavily than Manticoran doctrine did on mass, as opposed to accuracy, that the sacrifice was less significant than it might have been.

Even now, no one on either side knew exactly what would happen when fleets of pod-layers this size engaged one another. There was simply no experiential meterstick, because no one had ever *done* it before. For that matter, no battle in history had yet seen almost three hundred and fifty superdreadnoughts of *any* kind engage in what could only be a fight to the death. Over the centuries, tactical formalism had become the rule, with indecisive battles and limited losses. That might have changed, at least in this corner of the galaxy, but even here, most of the combatants were still feeling their way into the changing realities of interstellar carnage.

The Battle of Manticore would be something new and unique in the annals of deep-space combat. Everyone in both fleets knew that.

But that was *all* they knew as the missiles began to launch.

✧   ✧   ✧

The range at launch was 65,770,000 kilometers. Flight time for Home Fleet's faster MDMs was 7.6 minutes, and their closing speed as they streaked into Second Fleet's teeth was 246,972 kilometers per second. Second Fleet's slower missiles took fifteen more seconds to reach their targets, and had a closing speed of "only" 237,655 KPS.

At those speeds, both sides' defenses were stretched to and beyond the theoretical limits of their capabilities. Manticore's longer-ranged counter-missiles, and the greater capability of the *Katanas* in the fleet defense role, gave D'Orville's ships a significant advantage, but not a big enough one. Not the one he'd anticipated against the weight of fire he'd expected.

Home Fleet's Fire Plan Avalanche called for the pre-pod superdreadnoughts to deploy their pods as quickly as possible. They had to jettison them anyway, in order to clear their own defensive systems, and D'Orville had known from the beginning that he was going to lose a huge percentage of their total pod loads without ever actually firing their missiles. There was nothing he could do about that, however, and the older ships passed control of as many of their additional missiles as they could to their more capable consorts.

The *Medusa*, *Harrington*, *Adler*, and *Invictus*-class ships didn't deploy a single pod of their own in the initial broadsides. They used solely the pods deployed by D'Orville's older ships, reserving their better protected, internally stowed pods for the follow-up salvos it was at least possible they might live to launch. And since they were firing pods which had been effectively deployed in a single massive pattern, Avalanche also fired its salvos in closer, more tightly spaced intervals than the Republican Navy had yet seen out of any Allied fleet. In fact, Avalanche was almost—not quite, but *almost*—conceptually identical to Shannon Foraker's rotating control doctrine.

Each fleet's salvo density took the other fleet by surprise. Neither had anticipated such heavy fire . . . but Tourville's projections had been closer than D'Orville's to what he actually got. D'Orville had expected the battle to be short and violent, lasting no more than fifteen or twenty minutes.

The first half of his expectations was more than fulfilled.

In the seven and a half minutes it took the lead salvo to cross between Home Fleet and Second Fleet, Sebastian D'Orville's ships fired seven salvos at sixty-five-second intervals, each of 1,800 pods, containing a total of 21,600 missiles. Over a hundred and fifty thousand missiles, the maximum Home Fleet's fire control could manage, went screaming through space . . . and 524,000 Havenite missiles rampaged out to meet them. Fire control sensors and reconnaissance platforms all over the star system found themselves half-blinded by the interference and massive impeller source of almost *seven hundred thousand* attack missiles and many times that many counter-missiles. And then the EW platforms began to add their own blinding efforts to the chaos.

No human could have hoped to sort it out, keep track of it. There was simply no way protoplasmic brains could do it. Tactical officers concentrated on their own tiny pieces of the howling maelstrom, guiding their attack missiles, allocating their defensive missiles. Counter-missiles and MDMs blotted one another from existence as their impeller wedges slammed together. Decoys, jammers, Dazzlers, and Dragon's Teeth matched electronic wiles against tactical officers' telemetry links and onboard control systems. Standard counter-missiles, Mark 31s, and Vipers hurled themselves into the teeth of the mighty salvos. Great gaps and gulfs appeared in the onrushing wavefronts of destruction, but the gaps closed. The gulfs filled in. Laser clusters blazed in desperate last-ditch efforts to intercept missiles with closing speeds eighty percent that of light. MDMs lost their targets, reacquired, lost them again in the howling confusion. Onboard AIs took whatever targets they could find, and the sudden, abrupt changes in their targeting solutions made their final approach runs even more erratic and unpredictable.

And then wave after wave of laser heads began to detonate. Not in scores, or hundreds, or even in thousands. In *tens* of thousands in each roaring comber of fury.

The battle no one had been able to adequately envision was over in 11.9 minutes from the moment the first missile launched.

"My God," someone whispered on HMS *King Roger III*'s flag bridge.

Theodosia Kuzak didn't know who it was. It didn't matter. The imagery coming in from the FTL surveillance platforms was brutally clear.

Home Fleet was . . . gone. Simply *gone*.

Ninety superdreadnoughts, thirty-one battlecruisers and heavy cruisers, and twenty-six light cruisers had been effectively destroyed in less than twelve minutes. At least twenty shattered, broken hulks continued to coast towards the hyper limit, but they were only wrecks, gutted hulls streaming atmosphere, debris, and life pods while deep within them frantic rescue parties raced against time, fighting with grim determination and courage about which all too often no one would ever know, to rescue trapped and wounded crewmates.

But Home Fleet had not died alone. Sebastian D'Orville mght have been taken by surprise by the weight of Second Fleet's fire, and his computation of the exchange rate might have been overly optimistic as a result, but his ships and people had struck back hard. Ninety-seven Republican ships of the wall had been destroyed outright or beaten into dead, shattered hulks. Nineteen more had lost at least one impeller ring completely. And of the remaining hundred and twenty-four SD(P)s Lester Tourville had taken into the battle, exactly eleven were undamaged.

Second Fleet's brutally winnowed ranks continued onward, but its acceleration had been reduced to less than 2.5 KPS² by its cripples. At that rate, it would be unable to decelerate for its zero/zero intercept with Sphinx, and the Manticoran System's defenders weren't done with it yet.

Home Fleet's LAC screen had suffered massive losses of its own, mostly from MDMs which had lost their original targets and taken whatever they could find in exchange. Despite that, over two thousand of them survived, and they were driving hard to get into their own range of Second Fleet. They could expect to take fewer losses, now that they were free to maneuver defensively and to protect themselves, not Home Fleet's superdreadnoughts, and their crews had only one thought in mind.

More LACs were still streaming towards Second Fleet from the inner system, as well, and it was obvious the Havenites had no desire to tangle with Sphinx's fixed defenses, at least until they could get their own damages sorted out and reammunition. Second Fleet was changing course, crabbing away from Sphinx as it shepherded its cripples protectively out of harm's way.

But that, Theodosia Kuzak thought grimly, was going to prove just a bit more difficult than the bastards thought.

"How much longer?" she asked harshly.

"Our last units should clear the Junction in the next eleven minutes, Ma'am," Captain Smithson said.

"Good." Kuzak nodded once, then turned to Commander Astrid Steen, her staff astrogator.

"Plot me a couple of micro jumps, Astrid," she said coldly. "Those *people* have just had the crap kicked out of them. Now we're going to finish the job Home Fleet began."

"Admiral Kuzak's preparing to head in-system, Your Grace," Harper Brantley said quietly.

"Thank you, Harper."

Honor looked up from the holographic com display hovering above the briefing room's table at which she, Nimitz, Mercedes Brigham, Rafael Cardones, and Andrea Jaruwalski sat under her armsmen's watchful eye. The display was separated into individual quadrants, showing the faces of *Vizeadmiral* Hasselberg, Judah Yanakov, Samuel Miklós, and the commanders of every squadron in company with *Imperator*. Alice Truman and Alistair McKeon weren't there, and she tried to hide the cold, bleak anxiety she felt at their absence.

"Please inform the Admiral that we're still on schedule for our own ETA," Honor continued.

"Of course, Your Grace," her communications officer said quietly, and withdrew. The briefing room hatch closed behind him, and Honor returned her attention to the discussion at hand.

Most of the faces on her display showed a greater or lesser degree of shock at the total destruction of Home Fleet, and no wonder. Not only had the sheer weight of the Havenites' fire come as a complete surprise, but *all* of the Alliance's partners had taken losses when it hit. Of the ninety superdreadnoughts which had just been destroyed, twelve had been units of the Grayson Space Navy, and another twenty-six had been Andermani.

Of all her subordinates, Yanakov seemed least shocked. Or, at least, the least affected by whatever shock he felt. But, then, Judah had been present when Giscard leveled the Basilisk System's infrastructure in the last war, and his command had been part of Hamish's fleet for Operation Buttercup. And before that, he'd been at the First and Fourth Battles of Yeltsin. Three quarters of the pre-Alliance Grayson Space Navy had been wiped out in First Yeltsin, and half its super-dreadnought strength had been destroyed at Fourth Yeltsin. And he was the man whose task force had crushed the defensive forces deployed to cover Lovat. Despite his youth—and he was almost as young as his prolong made him look—he'd seen more carnage than any other flag officer on Honor's display.

Hasselberg had looked almost stunned when the initial reports came in. It hadn't been just the scale of the destruction. It had also been its speed, for the Andermani Navy had never experienced anything like it. Well, to be fair, neither had the *Manticoran* Navy, until this afternoon, but at least Manticore and Grayson had been granted some prior experience. They'd had firsthand practice adjusting to abrupt, wrenching changes in the paradigm of combat. The Empire had not, and the reality had come to the *vizeadmiral* like some hideous nightmare, despite all the effort he'd spent conscientiously trying to prepare himself for the realities of modern warfare.

But of them all, Honor thought, Bin-hwei Morser's reaction was the most interesting. She wasn't simply an admiral; she was also Graffin von Grau. Like Hasselberg himself, she was a member of the Empire's warrior aristocracy, and she was clearly one of those who took the Andermani martial tradition seriously. She might cherish doubts about her Emperor's decision to ally himself with the Star Kingdom which had been the Empire's traditional rival in areas like Silesia for so long, but that didn't matter. Not anymore, not now. Her dark eyes—remarkably like Allison Harrington's, or Honor's own, now that Honor thought about it—were narrow and intense, focused and fiery with purpose.

"I wish Admiral Kuzak had waited for us," Miklós said after a moment. "I'd feel a lot better if we were going in with her, especially after seeing how many birds these people can launch. She's still outnumbered better than two-to-one in wallers, and Alice is going to be outnumbered almost that badly in LACs."

"She can't wait, Samuel," Yanakov disagreed. "I don't have any idea how long it took the Peeps to deploy that many pods, however the hell they did it, but they had to use up most of their ammo to do it. She needs to hit them before they can pull out and restock their magazines. And even if that weren't a consideration, right now, the Peeps are edging away from Sphinx. She can't be sure they'll continue to do that if she doesn't move in *now*. If they get themselves sorted out, decide their damages aren't that bad after all, they've still got the strength—or close to it—to stand up to Sphinx's close-in defenses. And even if the defenses destroyed everything they've got left, they'd last long enough to take out virtually all of the planet's orbital infrastructure."

He smiled thinly.

"We Graysons have had a lot of experience worrying about what might happen to our orbital habitats. Trust me, I know exactly what's going through Admiral Kuzak's mind. She's got to keep the pressure on if she's going to keep them running."

"Judah's right," Honor said. "Our lead superdreadnought won't even transit the Junction for another eight minutes. We'll need another *seventy-five* minutes just to get the superdreadnoughts and your carriers through, Samuel. That's almost an hour and a half. She can't give them that long to think about things, not when they're already so close to the planet."

She spoke calmly, almost dispassionately, but she tasted the emotions of her staffers and, especially, her flag captain. They knew what was hidden behind that façade, she thought. Knew she couldn't forget that the planet they were talking about was the world of her birth. That all too many of the people on it were people she'd known all her life—family, friends. That it was the homeworld of the entire treecat species.

But what not even they knew was that at this very moment, both of her parents, and her sister and brother, were on Sphinx visiting Honor's Aunt Clarissa.

"The question before us," she continued, "is what *we* do after we make transit."

"We'll probably have instructions from the Admiralty, Your Grace," Mercedes Brigham pointed out. She smiled without any humor at all. "Thanks to the grav com, the central command can actually give real-time orders at interplanetary distances now."

"You may be right," Honor acknowledged. "So far, though, Admiral Caparelli's been refraining from backseat driving. And even if he doesn't, I want all of us to be thinking on the same page."

"One thing I don't believe we can do, Your Grace," Cardones said, "is commit ourselves before all our units have passed through the Junction."

Despite his relatively junior rank, the flag officers listened carefully. As Honor's flag captain, he was her tactical deputy.

"I strongly agree, Your Grace," Brigham said. "And at least we should have time to see how the situation's developing before we commit."

"I agree, too," Honor said. "But two things. First, I want to start rolling pods now. Use their onboard tractors to limpet them to the hulls. I want a third of our total pod loadout out there, if we can manage it."

"Yes, Your Grace," Brigham acknowledged.

"And, second," Honor continued, "let's get some lighter units through as quickly as we can. Admiral Oversteegen, I want your squadron to take lead and transit as soon as you reach the terminus. Admiral Bradshaw and Commodore Fanaafi, you and your *Saganami-Cs* are attached to Admiral Oversteegen." She smiled grimly. "If the Havenites are still trying to keep an eye on the Junction, let's give whoever's minding their drones something else to worry about."

Chapter Sixty-Six

"Sir, we've got impeller signatures moving clear of the Junction!" Commander Zucker said sharply.

"How many?" Diamato asked tautly.

"Hard to say with all this wedge interference, Sir." Zucker grimaced. "I make it at least fifty, though."

"Right." Diamato nodded and looked at his com officer. "Immediate priority for the Flag. Tell them we have fifty-plus wallers deploying for a hyper translation! Tell them—"

He broke off, as the deploying impeller signatures abruptly vanished.

"Correction!" he said sharply. "Inform the Flag that fifty-plus wallers have just translated out!"

"Captain Houellebecq says damage control has that fire in CIC under control, Sir."

"Thank you, Ace." Lester Tourville nodded to Lieutenant Eisenberg, and then returned his attention to Captain DeLaney.

"The numbers are still coming in, Boss," the chief of staff told him, her expression grim. "So far, they don't sound good. At the moment, it sounds like we can write off over half our wall of battle. Probably more than that, if we don't control the star system when the dust settles."

"We always knew we were going to get hammered," Tourville said, his own voice and expression calmer than DeLaney's. And it was true. His losses were twelve percent higher than his prebattle estimate—almost twenty-five percent higher than the Octogan staff weenies had estimated—because he hadn't anticipated how tightly the Manties would bunch their salvos. But from the beginning, everyone had understood that Second Fleet was going to take severe losses.

"But we cost them almost as many ships of the wall as we lost," he continued, "and if NavInt's estimates are accurate, we've got damned near three times as many of them as they do. Did. Not to mention the fact that we're about to take at least temporary control of their home star system away from them."

"I know," DeLaney said. "But I'm a little concerned about their LACs. We've got twenty-three hundred of them still coming in on us, and we're a lot lower on ammo than I'd like. We've fired off sixty percent of our MDMs, and we've lost effectively half our wall. I don't have exact numbers, but the current availability has to be no more than about two hundred thousand rounds. If we burn them trying to keep their *Shrikes* out of knife range, we're going to be sucking vacuum against Third Fleet."

"Then we'll have to let the *Cimeterres* and the screen fend off their LACs," Tourville said unflinchingly. "They'll get hammered at least as badly as we did, but they'll do the job."

"Yes, Sir." DeLaney gave herself a little shake, then bobbed her head in agreement. "I know we're still on profile for the operation, Boss. I guess I just never really thought about the sheer scale of things. Not emotionally."

"I made myself sit down and do that the day Thomas Theisman and Arnaud Marquette explained Beatrice to us," Tourville said grimly. "I didn't like it then, and I don't like it now. For that matter, *they* didn't like it. But it's a price we can afford to pay if it *ends* this goddamned war."

"Yes, Sir."

"Frazier."

"Yes, Sir?"

"What's our—"

"Excuse me, Sir!" Lieutenant Eisenberg said suddenly, pressing her hand to her earbug as she listened intently. "Admiral Diamato says the Manties have translated into hyper!"

"And so it begins," Tourville murmured softly, then gave his head an irritated shake as he realized how pretentious that sounded.

But that didn't make it untrue, and he watched the master plot intently, waiting for Kuzak's ships to reappear upon it.

He didn't have to wait long. Less than fifteen minutes after they'd vanished from the Junction, eight and a half minutes after they recepted Diamoto's warning, they reappeared dangerously close to the RZ's boundary. It was an impressive display of pinpoint astrogation—one that showed a steel-nerved willingness to cut their margin razor thin. And one which also put the Manties well out on Second Fleet's flank and headed for Sphinx on a least-time course.

"Exactly where I would have placed them myself," he said quietly to DeLaney, who nodded vigorously.

Second Fleet had started edging away from its original Sphinx-bound vector from the moment the shooting stopped. Five minutes later, it had altered course much more sharply, and at the moment, it was very obviously retreating from its original objective. In fact, Tourville had made the decision to sacrifice his worst lamed cripples within ten minutes. Any ship which couldn't produce an acceleration of at least 370 g had been abandoned, scuttling charges set. He hadn't liked doing that, but he couldn't afford to be hampered by them even if the rest of Beatrice worked perfectly. Even without them, Second Fleet's current maximum acceleration was barely 3.6 KPS^2, and that was too low for it to completely avoid the Sphinx defenses' missile envelope, whatever he did. Which didn't even consider the vengeful presence of Third Fleet coming in from the side to pin him between Sphinx and its own batteries.

Under the circumstances, Tourville had had no choice—for several reasons—but to settle on a course which formed a sharp angle from his original vector. Since he couldn't avoid going at least as far as Sphinx, he had pitched up vertically, to climb above the plane of the ecliptic, while simultaneously changing heading by 135 degrees. That let him pile on side vector to generate as much separation from the planet as he could get as he slid past it . . . which also happened to be the fastest way out of the system. The Manticoran resonance zone was so much "taller" than it was "broad" that the faces of the cone were almost parallel to one another, even this close to its base. Sphinx lay 102,002,500 kilometers inside the zone, and his original heading had been directly towards the planet, which defined just how much side vector he actually needed.

Even on his current profile, his restricted acceleration meant he'd pass within less than forty million kilometers of Sphinx, but he'd be further out—and longer getting there—than almost any other heading would have produced. If he hadn't changed course at all, he would have overflown Sphinx (and its defenses) seventy minutes after the brief, titanic engagement with Home Fleet, at an effective range of zero. If he'd changed heading by ninety degrees, he would have made his closest approach to Sphinx eight minutes later than that, at a range of only thirty-five million kilometers. On his current heading, his units' closest approach would come eighty-three minutes after changing course, and the range would be 39,172,200 kilometers.

He didn't much care for any of those options, given the pounding Home Fleet had given him, but the one he'd chosen was the best of the lot. It was still going to give the planet's defenders a shot, which he'd hoped wouldn't happen—yet, at least—but it would be long-ranged enough to degrade the Manties' accuracy, and the fire wouldn't be coming straight into his teeth the way Home Fleet's had. His missile defenses would be far more effective against whatever Sphinx had, and he frankly doubted that it had anything as heavy as ninety SDs had been able to hand out, anyway. And he'd needed to break back out across the RZ boundary for several reasons. Partly to get his cripples safely out of harm's way, but mostly because—as Taverner had just pointed out—he was critically low on ammunition. He needed to rendezvous with his ammunition ships and restock his magazines before driving back into the system defenses.

But Sphinx wasn't all he had to worry about, and Kuzak had dropped her own units in further "up" the zone's outer surface than he had. That put her in a position to move quickly to Sphinx's relief, accelerating directly towards the planet on a least-time course along the shortest passage through the RZ . . . which would also catch him between her fire and Sphinx's. In fact, Third Fleet would be less than 33,000,000 kilometers from him at the moment of his closest approach to Sphinx. Yet if he turned away from *her*, he would have no choice but to flee deeper and deeper into the resonance zone (without reammunitioning), and her higher base acceleration would readily permit her to overhaul him there. So he had no choice but to hold his present course.

It was a masterful move on Kuzak's part . . . and exactly the one Lester Tourville had hoped for.

The orphaned LAC survivors of Sebastian D'Orville's fleet came slashing in towards Second Fleet's screening units.

The screen had taken losses of its own—heavy ones—during

the massive missile exchange, but, like the Manticoran LACs, the damage had been purely collateral. No one had been wasting missiles deliberately trying to hit battlecruisers when there were SD(P)s shooting back. But the inaccuracy for which long-range MDM fire had become justly famed had come into play, and "lost" missiles intended for superdreadnoughts had latched onto whatever targets they could find.

There were still thirty-three battlecruisers and forty-one heavy cruisers waiting for the incoming strike, ready to begin punching missiles at it as soon as they had the range. But the Manticoran LACs' closing velocity was over fifty thousand kilometers per second. Current-generation Havenite single-drive missiles had a powered range from rest of just over seven million kilometers. Given the geometry, they had a theoretical maximum range of almost 16.5 million, as did the LACs' attack missiles. That sounded like a lot . . . except that, at the Manticorans' closing velocity, they would streak straight across the entire engagement envelope in 317 seconds.

That wouldn't give much time for a lot of launches, and Republican accuracy against Alliance LAC electronic warfare capabilities was poor.

"Get on them! *Get on them!*" Captain Alice Smirnoff barked.

She was Second Fleet's senior surviving COLAC, and the crews of her twenty-seven hundred LACs, positioned between the cruisers screening Lester Tourville's battered ships of the wall and the incoming Manties, fought manfully to obey her orders.

Over two-thirds of Smirnoff's ships were *Cimeterre Alpha* and *Cimeterre Beta* birds, built around the new fission power plants and improved capacitors Shannon Foraker and her technical crews had been able to produce after the windfall of technical data from Erewhon.

The *Alphas* were equipped with lasers powerful enough to punch through the sidewalls and armor of destroyers and cruisers at normal engagement ranges. They couldn't match the performance of the massive grasers of the Alliance's *Shrikes*, but they were far more dangerous in energy range than any Republican LAC had ever been before. The *Betas* weren't a lot more combat capable than the original *Cimeterres* had been, since they were still armed solely with missiles and those missiles hadn't been significantly improved. But—like the *Alphas*—they had bow walls and vastly enhanced power budgets and endurance.

Now, for the first time, they went up against the Alliance in truly significant numbers.

The engagement was brief. It had to be, with the Manticorans barreling in at such a high closing velocity. Smirnoff had arranged her LACs "above" and "below" the sensor and firing arcs she'd left open for the screen, and her own shorter-legged missiles streaked towards the incoming strike. She had more units than the Manties did, but the Alliance's superior EW more than offset her sheer numerical advantage.

Her *Alphas* never really got the chance to use their lasers. Their targets were too hard to lock up, streaking across their engagement window too quickly, and her firing angle meant all too many of the laser shots which were fired wasted themselves on the roofs or bellies of their targets' wedges. But her *Betas'* missiles, although less accurate and capable than the *Katanas'* Vipers, were fired in enormous numbers.

Six hundred of the Alliance LACs were killed in the fleeting moments Smirnoff had to engage them, but at a price. It was the first time the Allied LAC crews had gone up against someone else's LAC bow walls, but Alice Truman's reports from Lovat had been taken to heart. *They* might never have encountered it before, but they'd allowed for the possibility, and although the new technology made the new Republican LACs far harder to kill, they still lost at a two-to-one rate as the Allied strike roared past them, into the teeth of the screen's fire.

The screen killed another three hundred, but the price it paid for its success was far higher than the one Smirnoff had paid. The Alliance lost six thousand men and women aboard the LACs Smirnoff's units had killed, and she'd lost roughly eighteen thousand, in return. Now the Alliance lost another three thousand people aboard the LACs the screen had killed. But as the surviving graser-armed *Shrikes* crashed over the screening cruisers which could not avoid them, they wreaked havoc.

There were "only" sixteen hundred Allied LACs left, but nine hundred of them were *Shrikes*, and they ignored the heavy cruisers. *Those* they left to the missile-armed *Ferrets*, whose light shipkillers were unlikely to do more than scratch the paint of a capital ship. Since they couldn't hurt wallers anyway, there was no point saving them, and three hundred *Ferrets* flung every missile they had into the teeth of Second Fleet's heavy cruisers. They fired at the last moment, at the shortest possible range, when their victims' defenses would have effectively no time at all to engage with anything except laser clusters. They paid heavily to get to that range, but when they reached it, they spewed out well over sixteen thousand shipkillers.

Those missiles carried only destroyer-weight laser heads, but a heavy cruiser's sidewalls were weaker than a battlecruiser's, and it mounted very little armor compared to any capital ship. Certainly not enough to survive against a fire plan which hit each ship with four hundred missiles from a range at which each laser cluster had time for—at most—a single shot.

The *Ferrets* fired at a range of 182,000 kilometers, and it took their missiles barely two seconds to cross the range. In those two seconds the heavy cruisers' desperate offensive fire killed another hundred and twelve LACs, but when the surviving *Ferrets* crossed the screen's position one and a half seconds behind their missiles, they did it in the glaring light of the failing fusion plants of the cruisers they had just slaughtered.

None of the screen's heavy cruisers, and very few of the fifty thousand men and women aboard them, survived.

The battlecruisers fared no better. There were fewer of them, and three times as many attackers. True, each of those attackers got only a single shot, but they were using grasers as powerful as most battlecruisers' chase weapons. They drove straight into the teeth of the battlecruisers' broadsides, closing with grim determination, and they fired at a white-knuckle range of less than seventy-five thousand kilometers.

Four hundred and eighty-one *Shrikes* and roughly another five thousand Allied personnel died, blown apart by the battlecruisers' energy weapons in the brief engagement window they had. In return, twenty-eight Republican battlecruisers were completely destroyed, five more were reduced to shattered, broken wrecks, and seventy-seven thousand more of Lester Tourville's personnel were killed.

But in its destruction, Second Fleet's screen had done its job. The LACs which survived the exchange were a broken force, streaming through and past Tourville's surviving superdreadnoughts so rapidly not even the *Shrikes* had time to inflict significant damage on such massively armored targets. Not without numbers they no longer had.

✧   ✧   ✧

"I've got the preliminary figures, Boss," Molly DeLaney said. Her expression and hoarse voice showed the strain they were all under, Tourville thought, and nodded for her to continue without ever taking his own attention from the plot.

"It looks like only about two hundred of their LACs got away," his chief of staff said. "The wall's energy weapons managed to nail most of the others as they crossed our vector."

"Thank you," Tourville said, and closed his eyes briefly.

My God, he thought. *I came into this thinking I knew what the casualties were going to be like, but I didn't. Neither did Tom Theisman, really. No one could have projected this kind of carnage, because no one's had any experience, even now, with this kind of fight. Both sides are so far outside our standard operational doctrines that we're in virtually unknown territory. Podnaughts aren't supposed to close head on until they get into mutual suicide range. And we're not supposed to let LACs get that close to our starships. Our wall is supposed to be able to kill them before they ever get to us. But I didn't have the missiles left to do it, and they whipped through our engagement window so quickly our energy weapons couldn't stop them in time, either.*

He opened his eyes again, looking back into the plot. In a galaxy where indecisive maneuvers had been the norm for so many centuries, two decades—even two decades like the ones which had begun at Hancock Station—simply hadn't been enough to prepare anyone for *this.*

But the galaxy had better get used to it, he thought grimly. Because one thing he knew: the lethal genies were out of the bottle, and no one was going to get them back inside it.

"Any new orders, Sir?" DeLaney asked, and he shook his head. "No."

"Hyper footprint at two-point-three-six million kilometers!" Commander Zucker barked. "Many footprints!"

Oliver Diamato's head whipped around as the erupting footprints speckled the plot. There were eighteen of them, and he swore with silent, vicious venom as they sparkled like curses in the display.

Whoever had taken the *Sherman* as his intended target had come in far closer than most of the others, but all of them showed remarkably good astrogation for such a short jump. Then the vector readouts came up, and he swore again. From their headings, and especially from their velocity numbers, they'd obviously managed to hyper out of the Junction without his ever noticing, then come back in after building their velocity in hyper, so the jump wasn't quite as short as he'd thought it was.

Not that he had much time to think about it.

"Missile launch!" Zucker said. "Many missiles, incom—!"

Diamato's mouth had opened before the ops officer spoke, and his order chopped off the end of Zucker's announcement.

"All units, Code Zebra!" he barked.

RHNS *William T. Sherman* blinked into hyper less than three seconds before HMS *Nike*'s missiles would have detonated. Two of Diamato's other battlecruisers were less fortunate, a bit slower off the mark. They took hits—RHNS *Count Maresuke Nogi* lost most of her after impeller ring—but they, too, managed to escape into hyper.

Diamato breathed a sigh of relief when he realized all his units had gotten out. But however relieved he was by their survival, the fact remained that he'd been driven off his station. Frustratingly incomplete as his observations had been, his had been the only eyes located to watch the Junction at all for Second Fleet.

"Admiral Diamato's been forced to fall back to the Alpha Rendezvous, Sir," Lieutenant Eisenberg reported.

"Damn," Molly DeLaney murmured, but Tourville only shrugged.

"It was bound to happen sooner or later, Molly. On the other hand, it may actually be good news."

"*Good* news, Sir?"

"Well, they didn't bother to send through screening units to chase him off before, because they were too busy bringing in their wallers. If they've sent in battlecruisers and cruisers now, it probably confirms that they've already got all their capital ships through the Junction. In which case, this—" he nodded at the oncoming rash of scarlet icons, already well inside their theoretical MDM range of his own battered survivors "—probably *is* all we've got to deal with."

"With all due respect, Sir, 'this' is quite enough for me."

"For all of us, Molly. For all of us."

Tourville considered the plot for several more seconds, then looked back at Eisenberg.

"Ace, message to *MacArthur*. 'Stand by to execute Paul Revere.'"

"Aye, Sir."

"Any change in his heading, Judson?" Admiral Kuzak asked.

"No, Ma'am. He's maintaining exactly the same heading and acceleration," Commander Latrell replied.

"What the hell does he think he's *doing*, Ma'am?" Captain Smithson asked quietly, and Kuzak shrugged in irritation.

"Damned if I know," she acknowledged frankly. "Maybe he just figures he's still got the firepower to take us. After all, he's still got a hundred and eighteen wallers, and we've only got fifty-five, even with Duchess Harrington's orphans."

"But he's had the crap hammered out of him, Ma'am," Smithson objected. "The recon platforms indicate he's got heavy battle damage to at least half his survivors, and his acceleration rate would be proof enough of that, even without the platforms' reports. So say he's got the equivalent of eighty wallers' combat power—which is generous, I'd say—and they're still *Peep* SD(P)s. We don't have as many units as Home Fleet had, but *all* of ours are *Medusas* or *Harringtons*, and that gives *us* the edge in real combat power. Not only that, but he's got to have used up a lot of ammo. Hell, he didn't fire a single MDM at the LACs, and you saw what they did to his screen. His magazines have to be close to empty."

"So if his situation is so desperate," Judson Latrell asked, "why didn't he abandon the rest of his ships with impeller damage and run for it at a higher acceleration rate in the first place?"

"I suppose the answer to that depends at least in part on exactly what their actual objective is," Kuzak said.

She glanced at the master plot. Twenty-six minutes had passed since Third Fleet had translated back into normal-space. It was hard to believe that barely two hours ago, Home Fleet and all of its units had been safely in orbit around Sphinx. Now they were gone, reduced to spreading patterns of wreckage, and her own command was accelerating steadily towards battle with their killers at 6.01 KPS². Her base velocity was up to almost ten thousand kilometers per second, she'd traveled the next best thing to eight million kilometers into the RZ, and the range to Second Fleet was coming down to right on sixty million kilometers. Which meant, of course, that they were already in her range, just as she was in theirs.

"Whatever they're up to," she said grimly, "I think you've got a point about their ammunition supply, Jerry. In which case, they aren't going to be hitting us with any more of those monster salvos. And it also means they haven't got enough birds left to waste them firing at long range, with their hit probabilities. *We*, on the other hand, have full magazines."

"You want to open fire now, Ma'am?" Commander Latrell asked, but she shook her head.

"Not just yet. In fact, not until *they* do." Her thin smile was cold. "Every kilometer the range drops increases our accuracy by a few thousandths of a percent. As long as they're willing not to shoot, so am I."

"They'll be coming into range of Sphinx in another ten minutes or so, Ma'am," Smithson said quietly.

"A good point." She nodded. "But that means the defense pods deployed around Sphinx are going to be coming into range of *them*, too, and the system reconnaissance platforms are going to give the defense pods very good accuracy."

"But if they open fire, the Peeps will return it," Latrell pointed out.

"I know," Kuzak agreed. "I've been thinking about that."

She considered numbers and ranges, then turned to Communications.

"Franklin, contact Admiral Caparelli. Tell him I recommend that the Sphinx defenses *not* fire on these people unless and until *they* launch against Sphinx."

"Yes, Ma'am," Lieutenant Bradshaw replied.

"Are you sure about that, Ma'am?" Smithson asked. Kuzak looked at him, and he looked back levelly. After all, one of a chief of staff's jobs was to play devil's advocate. "If they're going to bombard the planet, letting them get the first launch off unopposed is likely to cost us," he pointed out.

"But as Judson's just pointed out, if they *aren't* prepared to bombard the planet and the near-planet yards, and the orbital defenses open fire, they may go ahead and return it," Kuzak responded. "And they *have* been hammered hard. If Sphinx doesn't fire on them, they're probably going to reserve their fire for *us*, since we're obviously a much greater threat. Under the circumstances, I think it's worth risking letting them have one launch against the defenses, now that they're all on-line. Especially if they decide *not* to launch."

"Yes, Ma'am."

"No change in their dispositions, Your Grace," Andrea Jaruwalski reported, and Honor frowned.

"What is it, Your Grace?" a voice asked, and she looked up at her com display. Rafe Cardones looked back at her from it.

"What's what, Rafe?"

"That frown," her flag captain said. "I've seen it before. What's bothering you?"

"Besides the fact that somewhere around a million people have already been killed this fine afternoon, you mean?"

Cardones winced slightly, but he also shook his head.

"That's not what I meant, Ma'am, and you know it."

"Yes, I suppose I do," she agreed.

She reached up to stroke Nimitz's ears, and the 'cat pressed back against her hand, purr buzzing as his mind-glow caressed hers in reply. She treasured that small moment of unqualified support and love, clinging to its warmth against her cold, bleak awareness of so much death and devastation. Then she looked back at Cardones.

"I just can't escape the feeling that there's a shoe somewhere we haven't seen yet," she said slowly. "I know there's not a vector available to them which would let them avoid both Sphinx's envelope and Admiral Kuzak's. Under those circumstances, I guess it's not too surprising they're simply holding their course. What else can they do?"

"Not much, Your Grace," Mercedes Brigham said, when Honor paused. "From where I sit, it looks like they're screwed. The bastards hurt us badly enough, first, but they're in too deep to get out now, and Admiral Kuzak is going to hammer them into scrap."

"That's what's bothering me," Honor said slowly. "They didn't have to come in this way. They could have come in more slowly, left themselves a broader menu of maneuver options. Why did they simply come charging straight in towards Sphinx?"

"They didn't," Brigham pointed out. "They cut the angle on the limit and the zone so they could angle back out if they had to."

"No, Mercedes." Cardones shook his head on Honor's display. "I see what she means. It's the acceleration rate, isn't it, Your Grace?"

"That's exactly what it is," Honor agreed. "They can't have

known exactly what was going to happen when they ran into Home Fleet, but they had to have known they'd almost certainly be intercepted well short of the planet and hammered. But by charging in at such a high acceleration when they didn't have to, they built up a vector they couldn't possibly overcome before whatever we brought through from Trevor's Star hit them, as well. That's not like Theisman. He should have left his commander on the spot more freedom of maneuver, should have tried to protect his units from getting caught in this sort of trap."

"Then why didn't he?" Brigham frowned as she followed Honor's logic.

"I thought at first it probably did indicate they were going to try some sort of a two-pronged operation," Honor said. "Go ahead and hit us in Manticore, figuring we'd have to pull off of Trevor's Star to defend the home system, and then hit San Martin when we uncovered it. In that case, they might have hoped to catch us with Third Fleet and Eighth Fleet between two separate offensives, unable to respond adequately to either."

"Now that's an ugly thought, Your Grace," Brigham murmured.

"But that's not like Theisman, either," Honor pointed out. "He understands the KISS principle, and in their initial attacks, 'Operation Thunderbolt,' he planned each of his operations *independently* of one another. They all tied together into one overall design, but he was careful to avoid any attempt to coordinate widely dispersed fleets or require them to go after objectives in mutual support. The entire *offensive* was very carefully coordinated, except for the decision to send Tourville all the way to Marsh, but the success of any one operation didn't depend on the success of any *other* simultaneous operation."

"And hitting both Trevor's Star and Manticore would." Brigham nodded.

"It certainly would," Honor agreed. "And they wouldn't have any way to communicate with one another, so if either attack force screwed up its timing, it might blow the entire operation by alerting us early. It's still possible that that's what they're going to do, which is the main reason I still don't want to lock down the Trevor's Star terminus with a mass transit, but I don't think it's what's coming.

"But if they don't have something like that in mind, I'm at a loss to understand exactly what they're doing. According to ONI's estimate of their current fleet strength, this is a huge percentage of their total wall of battle, and they've rammed it straight into the teeth of our defenses on a vector which makes it impossible for them to avoid action with Third Fleet. That's what I don't like about it. It's stupid . . . and one thing Thomas Theisman *isn't*, is stupid."

"Boss, with all due respect," Molly Delaney said, "I think it's time."

"No, do you really?" Lester Tourville replied, his tone so dry that DeLaney looked up in surprise. Then, almost against her will, she chuckled.

It wasn't a very loud chuckle, but it sounded that way on *Guerriere*'s tense, silent flag deck. Heads came up all around the deck, eyes turned towards the chief of staff, and Tourville smiled. He could almost literally feel their astonishment that he could make even the smallest joke at a moment like this. And then he felt that same astonishment breaking at least a little of the taut fear and anxiety which had enveloped all of them as he continued to hold off on Paul Revere, continued to wait. They knew the Beatrice Bravo ops plan as well as he did, and they had to be wondering what the hell he was waiting for.

Which was fair enough. A part of *him* wondered what he was waiting for, as well.

He looked at the plot. The Manticoran response from Trevor's Star had been accelerating in-system for almost fifty minutes. Its velocity was up to just over eighteen thousand kilometers and it had traveled roughly 27,045,000 kilometers. The range to Second Fleet was falling rapidly towards thirty-three million kilometers, and he was frankly astonished that they hadn't already opened fire. Yet still that nagging little doubt, that voice of instinct, told him to wait.

He looked at a secondary plot, frozen with the last tactical data Oliver Diamato had been able to download before being forced off the Junction. He considered it for two or three seconds, careful to conceal his own mental frown lest it undo the beneficial consequences of DeLaney's chuckle.

You've got to get off the credit piece, Lester, he told himself. *You've already waited as long as you can; Molly's right about that. If Eighth Fleet were coming, it should already be here. And you can't justify holding off forever "just in case" it turns up. Because whether it's coming or not, you can't let the people you know about get any closer.*

"All right, Ace," he said in a calm, confident voice. "Send *MacArthur* the execute signal."

"Captain Higgins! We have the execute signal from *Guerriere!*"

"Maneuvering," Captain Edward Higgins said almost instantly, his voice sharp, "execute Paul Revere."

"Aye, Sir!" his astrogator replied, and the battlecruiser RHNS *Douglas MacArthur*, which had never accelerated in-system with the rest of Second Fleet's doomed screen, translated smoothly into hyper.

"I think we're just about ready to open the ball, whether they want to or not," Theodosia Kuzak told Commander Latrell. "How do our firing solutions look?"

"I think the old saying about fish in a barrel comes to mind, Ma'am," Latrell replied.

"Good. In that case—"

"*Hyper footprint!*" one of Latrell's ratings barked suddenly. "Hyper footprint at four-one-point-seven million kilometers, bearing one-eight-zero by one-seven-six!" He paused a second, then looked up, his face white. "Many point sources, Sir! It looks like at least *ninety* ships of the wall."

"Oh my God," Mercedes Brigham said softly as the plot abruptly altered. The FTL feed from the recon platforms made what had just happened all too hideously clear.

"You were right, Your Grace," Rafael Cardones said flatly. "They aren't stupid."

Honor didn't reply. She was already turning to the sidebars of her own tactical display. Sixteen of her thirty-two super-dreadnoughts were still in Trevor's Star, as were all of Samuel Miklós' carriers and thirty of her battlecruisers. She looked at the numbers for perhaps one heartbeat, then turned back to her staff.

"Mercedes, send a dispatch boat back to Trevor's Star. Inform Admiral Miller that he's in command and that he's to hold all of our battlecruisers there. Tell him he's responsible for covering Trevor's Star until we get back to him. Then instruct Judah to bring Admiral Miklós' carriers and all the rest of the wallers through in a single transit."

Her voice was crisp, calm, despite her own shock, and Brigham looked at her for a moment, then nodded sharply.

"Aye, aye, Your Grace!"

"Theo," she continued, pointing one index finger at Commander Kgari, "start plotting a new micro-jump. We'll go straight from here; no dogleg. I want us at least fifty million kilometers outside these newcomers. Seventy-five to a hundred would be better, but don't shave it any closer than fifty."

Kgari looked at her for a moment, and she tasted his shock. She was allowing him a much larger margin of error than Admiral Kuzak had allowed Third Fleet's units, but she was also requiring him to jump straight from a point _inside_ the RZ to one on its periphery. Safety margin or no, astrogation that precise was going to be extraordinarily difficult to deliver, given the fact that his start point's coordinates were going to be subject to significant uncertainty, whatever he did.

But despite his shock, his voice was clear.

"Aye, aye, Ma'am!"

"Harper," she continued, turning to the communications section. "Immediate priority message to Admiral Kuzak, copied to Admiralty House. Message begins: 'Admiral Kuzak, I will be moving to your support within—'" she looked at the chronometer, but nothing she could do could make time move more slowly "—fifteen minutes. If I can reduce that, I will.' Message ends."

"Aye, aye, Your Grace!"

Honor nodded, then sat back in her command chair and rotated it slowly to face the rest of her flag bridge personnel. She could see the echo of her own horror on their faces, taste it in their mind-glows, as they realized what was about to happen to Third Fleet, whatever _they_ might manage to do.

They stared back at her, but they saw no horror in her calm expression. They saw only determination and purpose.

"All right, people," she said. "We know what we have to do. Now let's be about it."

Chapter Sixty-Seven

Admiral Genevieve Chin, CO Fifth Fleet, stood on the flag bridge of RHNS *Canonnade* and let the background murmur of readiness reports wash over her.

"We've got them, Ma'am!" Commander Andrianna Spiropoulo announced exuberantly. "Astro put us less than fifty million klicks behind them—right on the money!"

"So I see." Chin might have quibbled with her operations officer's assessment of their astrogation, since they were several million kilometers further from the limit than they should have been. She suspected that Lieutenant Commander Julian had deliberately dropped them in a bit further out than she'd specified. But Spiropoulo's assessment of the tactical situation matched hers perfectly, and she fought hard to keep the exuberance out of her own voice.

She also knew she hadn't succeeded completely.

Well, maybe I didn't, she thought. *But if I didn't, I've earned it. We all have, after the way they pounded us in the last war. But it's more than that for me.*

"All right, Andrianna," she said, turning her back to the plot and the icons of the Manty wallers whose crews were beginning to realize they'd walked straight into a trap, "we don't have a lot of time before they run out of our envelope. Let's start rolling pods."

"Aye, Ma'am!"

Andrianna's dark eyes gleamed, and Chin glanced at Captain Nicodème Sabourin. Her chief of staff looked back, and then, unnoticed by the rest of Flag Bridge's personnel, he nodded, ever so slightly.

Chin nodded back. Sabourin was probably the only member of her staff who could fully savor her own sense of . . . completion. She'd come a long way to reach this point. She'd survived being scapegoated by the Legislaturalists for the disaster of Hancock Station at the very start of the last war. She'd survived long, dreary years in the service of the Committee of Public Safety—never quite trusted, too valuable to simply discard, always watched by her people's commissioner. She'd even survived Saint-Just's ascension to complete power . . . and the chaos following his overthrow.

She'd been "rehabilitated" twice now. Once by Rob Pierre's lunatics, solely *because* she'd been scapegoated by the previous régime. And once by the new Republic, because she'd damned well done a good job protecting her assigned sector despite the psychotic sadist they'd assigned as her people's commissioner.

This time, she actually believed it was going to stick. She'd still lost a lot of ground in the seniority game. Men and women who'd been junior officers, or even enlisted personnel, when she'd already been a flag officer, were senior to her now. Thomas Theisman, for one, who'd been a commander when she'd been a rear admiral. But she was one of only a handful of people who'd made admiral under the Legislaturalists who were still alive at all, so she supposed that was something of a wash.

And whether the universe was always a fair place or not, she couldn't complain about where she was today. The woman who'd been saddled with the blame for the Legislaturalists' disastrous opening campaign against the Star Kingdom of Manticore, was also the woman who'd been chosen to command the decisive jaw of the trap which would crush the Star Kingdom once and for all. She'd waited fifteen T-years for this moment, and it tasted sweet.

Nicodème Sabourin understood that. She hadn't known it for quite some time, but he'd been a second-class petty officer aboard one of her dreadnoughts at Hancock Station. Like her, he was looking forward to getting some of his own back this afternoon.

"How are your target solutions, Andrianna?" she asked calmly.

"They look good, Ma'am, considering their EW."

"In that case, Commander," Genevieve Chin said formally, "you may open fire."

"We walked right into it," Theodosia Kuzak said bitterly. "*I* walked right into it."

"It's not like we had much choice, Ma'am," Captain Smithson said.

The two of them stood staring into the plot, watching the overwhelmingly superior force which had suddenly cut in astern of them as it rolled pods. Waiting. The orders were already given. Their own missiles were already launching. There was, quite literally, nothing at all Kuzak could do at this point except watch other people execute her orders.

She turned her head, looking at her chief of staff, and Smithson shrugged.

"We couldn't let them punch out Sphinx, and we couldn't let them get away after the price D'Orville paid to stop them. That meant coming in after them," he said. "You did."

"I should have seen this coming," she shot back, but quietly, quietly, keeping her voice down. "After what Harrington did to them at Lovat, it was the logical response."

"Oh?" Smithson cocked his head, smiling ironically despite the hurricane of missiles rushing towards them. "And I suppose you were supposed to somehow use clairvoyance to realize they had *another* hundred wallers in reserve? That they were going to throw *three hundred and fifty* superdreadnoughts at us? Just you—not Admiral Caparelli, not ONI, not Admiral D'Orville, or Admiral Harrington. Just you. Because, obviously, this is all *your* fault."

"I didn't mean—" she began angrily, then stopped. She looked at him for a moment, then reached out and squeezed his shoulder.

"I guess I did deserve that. Thanks."

"Don't mention it." Smithson smiled sadly. "It's one of a chief of staff's jobs."

"All right, Alekan," Alistair McKeon told his ops officer harshly. "We're the only squadron with Apollo. Admiral Kuzak has authorized us for independent targeting to make best use of the system. That means it's going to be up to you."

"Understood, Sir." Commander Slowacki nodded hard.

"I want to concentrate on this new bunch," McKeon continued. "They haven't been hit yet, their fire control and their tactical departments are going to be in better shape. We'll take them one ship at a time."

"Understood, Admiral," Slowacki said again, and McKeon pointed at the icons of Genevieve Chin's task force.

"Good. Now go kill as many of those bastards as you can."

"Aye, aye, Sir!"

"I wish Her Grace were here, Sir," Commander Roslee Orndorff said quietly beside McKeon as Slowacki and his assistants began updating their targeting solutions.

"I don't," McKeon told Orndorff, his voice equally quiet, and shook his head. "This is one not even she could get us out of, Roslee."

"I guess not," Orndorff agreed. "And you're right. I shouldn't wish she was stuck in here with the rest of us. But—no offense, Sir—I . . . miss her."

"So do I." McKeon reached out and stroked the head of the treecat perched on Orndorff's shoulder. Banshee pressed back against his hand, but only for a moment. Then the 'cat pressed his cheek against the side of his person's head and crooned softly to her.

Orndorff reached up, caressing him tenderly, without ever taking her eyes from the plot.

Unlike Oliver Diamato's battlecruisers, Third Fleet couldn't dodge the pulser dart. Admiral Kuzak's command was too deep, pinned inside the RZ. Kuzak had intended to catch Second Fleet between her command and the Sphinx planetary defenses; now *she* was caught between the oncoming hammer of Genevieve Chin's MDMs and the battered anvil of Lester Tourville's surviving SD(P)s.

At least Third Fleet's base velocity was almost fourteen thousand kilometers per second higher than Fifth Fleet's, and almost directly away from it. Given that geometry, Chin's powered missile envelope was only fifty-one million kilometers. But the *range* was only 41,700,000 kilometers, and that meant Chin could keep Kuzak's ships under fire for eleven minutes before Third Fleet could run out of range.

Eleven minutes. It didn't sound like such a long time, but it was longer than Home Fleet had survived against Lester Tourville. And Home Fleet hadn't been running directly into the fire of one foe while the fire of a second came ripping into it from behind.

"Open fire!" Lester Tourville snapped.

"Aye, Sir!" Frazier Adamson acknowledged, and Tourville watched the icons of his missiles reaching out towards the Manties.

He'd almost left it too late, he thought. Chin's astrogation had been off by a good ten million kilometers, although it was hard to fault her for that. She'd had only a handful of minutes to adjust her position after *MacArthur*'s arrival, thanks in no small part to how long Tourville had waited, and making that kind of delicate, short-ranged micro-translation was always infernally difficult.

Given that any error placing her alpha translation on the wrong side of the zone boundary would have resulted in the destruction of every ship under her command, it was inevitable—and proper—that she should err on the side of caution. Besides, it had never been part of the ops plan for her ships to move inside the resonance zone or hyper limit until she and Tourville were certain they'd dealt with the defenses. *All* the defenses.

Still, eleven minutes of concentrated fire from ninety-six SD(P)s should smash the hell out of the Manties' combat capability, even if it failed to destroy them outright. And in the meantime, he could do a little something to help Chin along.

The range for *his* missiles was only 32,955,000 kilometers, and unlike the range from Chin's ships, it was dropping by over a million kilometers per minute. Not to mention the fact that unlike Chin, his tactical officers had been tracking the Manties steadily, updating their firing solutions for the last thirty or forty minutes.

He checked the time display. Flight time for his missiles was just under six minutes, two minutes less than for Chin. Although she'd fired first, his missiles would reach their targets before hers.

"We are truly and royally screwed, Skipper," Chief Warrant Officer Sir Horace Harkness said quietly from HMLAC *Dacoit*'s engineering station.

Scotty Tremaine glanced at him, then looked back at the plot, and wished there were some way he could disagree.

"You have a message from Admiral Truman, Captain," *Dacoit*'s com section AI said. "Personal to you."

"Accept, Central," Tremaine said. A moment later, Alice Truman appeared on his com display.

"Admiral," he said, watching the missile icons spreading like the tracks of pre-space wet-navy torpedoes.

"It looks like we're going to get hammered, Scotty," Truman told him bluntly. "I want you to detach your *Katanas*. Leave them behind to help thicken Admiral Kuzak's defenses. Then take all the rest of your birds and head for the in-system force now."

Tremaine looked at her for just a moment. He knew what

she had in mind. His *Ferrets* and *Shrikes*, especially the former, were preparing to help bolster Third Fleet's missile defenses, yet compared to his *Katanas*, their contribution would have been relatively minor. But by sending them against the survivors of the first Havenite attack force, she might compel it to divert its fire. It no longer had a screen, its attached LACs had taken severe losses, and it couldn't simply run away from him into hyper. It would have no choice but to stand and fight, and if it let him get into attack range without severe losses of his own . . .

"Understood, Dame Alice," he said. "We'll do our best to keep their heads down."

"Good, Scotty. Good hunting. Truman, clear."

"Crap," Molly DeLaney muttered, and Lester Tourville chuckled harshly.

"They're a little quicker off the mark with it than I expected," he said, watching the Manty LACs arc away from Third Fleet. Missile flight times were long enough—and the Manty reaction fast enough—that their course change was already evident, even though Second Fleet's first salvo had yet to reach attack range.

"Still," he continued, "it was the logical move, once we lost the screen. Frazier."

"Yes, Admiral?" Commander Adamson replied.

"Send Smirnoff out to meet these people."

"Captain Smirnoff is dead, Sir," Adamson said. "Commander West is COLAC now."

Tourville winced internally. He hadn't known Alice Smirnoff well. Only met the woman twice, actually, and then only in passing. But somehow her death, unnoticed in the general carnage, suddenly seemed to symbolize the hundreds of thousands of his personnel who had perished in the last three hours.

"Very well," he said, an edge of harshness burring his otherwise level response, "send West out to meet them."

"Aye, Sir."

"Is that going to be enough, Boss?" DeLaney asked quietly, and Tourville shook his head.

"No. They aren't sending in as many, but these people are fresh, and Smirnoff—*West*—and his people burned too many missiles stopping the last attack. We're going to have to take them with MDMs."

"Do you want to shift targeting?"

"Not yet." Tourville shook his head. "That's what they want us to do, and I'm not taking any pressure off Kuzak until we have to. But it's going to limit the number of salvos we can give her."

He punched in a command, calling up the fleet status display. He studied it for several seconds, then looked at Adamson.

"Frazier, tell Admiral Moore and Admiral Jourdain to abort their engagement of Third Fleet. I want their squadrons to reserve their total remaining pods for use against the Manty LACs."

"Yes, Sir."

Tourville nodded and sat back in his command chair. Moore and Jourdain had taken the lightest losses of any of his battle squadrons. Between them, they still had fourteen SD(P)s, and much as he hated taking them out of the firing queue at this particular moment, he had a feeling he was going to need their missiles badly in another half-hour or so.

"Here it comes," Wraith Goodrick murmured, and Alice Truman nodded.

Counter-missiles tore into the oncoming MDMs, and at least this time they hadn't been able to deploy whatever had let them throw such monster salvos at Home Fleet. These were merely "normal" double-pattern broadsides from over a hundred SD(P)s.

Nothing to worry about, she told herself; *only twelve thousand missiles or so. No more than a couple of hundred per ship. Just a walk in the park.*

Except, of course, that they weren't spreading them over all of Third Fleet's ships.

Scotty Tremaine's detached *Katanas* were tucked in close, hovering "above" Third Fleet, rather than going out to meet the incoming missiles as normal doctrine would have dictated. Normal doctrine, after all, hadn't anticipated a situation in which a fleet would screw up so badly it found itself squarely between two widely separated enemy fleets, each numerically superior to itself, and in range of both. The LACs couldn't place themselves between one threat and the rest of Third Fleet without leaving it uncovered against the other, and so they held their position, spitting Vipers against the wall of destruction crashing towards Theodosia Kuzak's command.

Thousands of Mark 31 counter-missiles went out with the Vipers, and Truman felt *Chimera* quiver as her own counter-missile tubes went to rapid fire, but nothing was going to stop all of that torrent of MDMs. Decoys and Dazzlers strove to bewilder or blind the incoming missiles, but still they came on.

"They're concentrating on the Nineteenth," Commander Janine Stanfield, Truman's operations officer, reported.

"They'll have a lot of strays at this range," Goodrick said, and Truman nodded agreement with her chief of staff. Not that having a few hundred MDMs wander off was going to do Vice Admiral Irene Montague and her command a lot of good. Not with two thousand missiles targeted on each of her six superdreadnoughts.

Even with its attention divided between the salvos rumbling down on it from opposite directions, Third Fleet's missile defense was far more effective than Home Fleet's had been. Partly that was simply the difference in the numbers of missiles in each incoming salvo. Another part was the difference in closing velocities, which improved engagement times. And, especially against Second Fleet, it was because so many of the ships launching those missiles had themselves been damaged, in many cases severely, before they launched. They'd lost control links, sensors, computational ability, and critical personnel out of their tactical departments, with inevitable consequences for the accuracy of their fire.

But twelve thousand missiles were still twelve thousand missiles.

Twenty percent were electronic warfare platforms. Another twelve percent simply lost lock, as Goodrick had predicted. The massed counter-missiles of Third Fleet and Alice Truman's *Katanas* killed almost four thousand, and the last-ditch fire of the 91st Battle Squadron and its escorts killed another fifteen hundred. It was a remarkable performance, but it still meant twenty-seven hundred got through.

The heavy laser heads detonated in rapid succession, bubbles of brimstone birthing X-ray lasers that ripped and tore at their targets. The superdreadnoughts' wedges intercepted many of those lasers. Their sidewalls bent and attenuated others. But nothing built by man could have stopped *all* of them.

The massively armored superdreadnoughts shuddered and bucked as transfer energy blasted into them. Armor and hull plating splintered, atmosphere gushed from gaping holes, and weapons, communications arrays, and sensors were torn apart. HMS *Triumph* staggered as her forward impeller ring went into emergency shutdown. Her wedge faltered, and then she staggered again, like a seasick galleon, as a half-dozen more laser heads detonated almost directly ahead of her. Her bow wall stopped most of the lasers, but at least twelve stabbed straight through it, hammering the massively armored face of her forward hammerhead. Her forward point defense clusters went down, her chase energy weapons were pounded into broken rubble, and one of her forward impeller rooms blew up as the massive capacitors shorted across.

For a moment, it looked like that was the extent of her damage. But deep inside her, invisible from the outside, the energy spike of that demolished impeller room drove deeper and deeper. Circuit breakers failed to stop it, control runs exploded, power conduits blew up in deadly sequence, and then, suddenly, the ship herself simply exploded.

There were no small craft, no life pods. No survivors. One moment she was there; the next she was an expanding sphere of fire.

Her squadron mates were more fortunate. None of them escaped unscathed, however, and HMS *Warrior* lost over half her port sidewall. HMS *Ellen D'Orville* lost half the beta nodes in her after impeller ring, and HMS *Bellona*'s port broadside point defense clusters and gravitic arrays were beaten into scrap. HMS *Regulus* escaped with only minor damage, but HMS *Marduk* lost a quarter of her broadside energy weapons. All of them survived, and their ability to deploy pods remained intact, but the follow-up salvo from Second Fleet was close on the heels of the first, and the first salvo from Fifth Fleet came crunching in almost simultaneously.

Third Fleet's defenses were simply spread too thin. Twelve thousand missiles came pounding down on it from Lester Tourville. Another 11,500 came crashing in from Genevieve Chin, and there simply weren't enough counter-missiles and *Katanas* to stop them all.

Second Fleet's second salvo concentrated on the same targets as the first, and those targets were already damaged, their defenses thinned. *Warrior* blew up, and *Marduk* took a catastrophic series of hits which virtually destroyed her starboard sidewall. *Bellona* staggered, impeller wedge dying, life pods beginning to fan out from her hulk. *Ellen D'Orville* took at least twenty more hits, but continued to run, and *Regulus* moved up on *Marduk*'s naked starboard flank, trying to shield her consort from the third salvo already streaking towards them.

The gallant effort to protect her sister cost *Regulus* her life twenty-three seconds later as over eight hundred laser heads took the only target they could see.

"We just lost *Bayard*, Sir," Molly DeLaney said, and Lester Tourville nodded, hoping his expression disguised his pain.

Second Fleet had sprung the trap exactly as planned, except for the fact that it had been supposed to close on Eighth Fleet, as well, and he tried to feel grateful. But it was hard. There came a time when phrases like "favorable rates of exchange," however accurate, were cold comfort in the face of so much death, so much destruction. And however hopeless Third Fleet's position, there was nothing at all wrong with the Manties' determination and sheer guts.

They recognized Second Fleet as the greater prize—and the greater threat—despite its previous damages. It was still the larger of Tourville's two task forces, and the one in the best position to strike Sphinx, and they were pouring fire into his bleeding ranks. He'd already lost three more superdreadnoughts, counting *Bayard*, and it was only a matter of time until he lost more.

Theodosia Kuzak stared into the master plot as the Havenites' task forces sledgehammered her fleet again and again. Battle Squadron Ninety-One was effectively destroyed in the first sixty seconds, and Second Fleet's follow-up salvos switched to BS 11. Her own missiles were striking back, and the system reconnaissance platforms showed fireballs glaring amid Second Fleet's formation, but she knew the exchange rate was completely in the Republic's favor, and there was nothing she could do about it.

"Incoming! Many incoming!" Commander Latrell barked suddenly, and HMS *King Roger III* heaved like a maddened animal as a storm of laser heads blasted into her.

"Jesus Christ! What the fuck *is* that?" Commander Spiropoulo demanded harshly as RHNS *Victorieux* blew up.

"It's got to be that new targeting system they used at Lovat," Captain Sabourin replied harshly. "Somebody over there has it, after all. But it can't be coming from more than a few of their ships, thank God!"

"Any is too goddamned *many*, Nicodème," Genevieve Chin grated. "And I don't like the targeting of whoever the hell it is!" she added, and Sabourin nodded.

Most of Fifth Fleet's wallers were more than holding their own against the Manties' fire. That was largely because at least three-quarters of that fire was still raining down on Lester Tourville's superdreadnoughts. Probably, Chin thought, because Tourville was still headed in-system. It looked as if Kuzak had decided stopping *him* was more important than shooting at ships which could vanish into hyper any time they chose, once their hyper generators had finished cycling from their last translation.

But if most of Third Fleet's missiles were headed in-system, three or four of Kuzak's ships were firing on Chin's wall with deadly accuracy. Their missiles threaded through the cauldron of counter-missiles, EW, and blazing laser clusters like awls. It was as if they could literally *see* where they were going, think for themselves, and they were coming in behind a deadly shield of closely coordinated electronic warfare platforms. Her missile defenses were hopelessly outclassed against them, and whoever was coordinating their targeting had chosen one of her battle squadrons and begun working her way through it.

Each individual salvo wasn't particularly large. Indeed, by the standards of pod-based combat, they were ludicrously tiny. But *all* of them seemed to be getting through. None of them wandered off. None wasted themselves by detonating high, or low, where their target's impeller wedge might stop them. And as they sent their avalanches of lasers through that target's wavering sidewall in deadly succession, they killed.

"God*damn* it!" she heard Sabourin say with soft, passionate venom as RHNS *Lancelot* slewed suddenly out of formation, impeller wedge dying.

"Is there *any* way to identify where this is coming from, Andrianna?" she demanded.

"No way, Ma'am," Spiropoulo said through gritted teeth. "They could be coming from anywhere in the middle of that mess." She jabbed an angry index finger at the crimson icons of Manticoran capital ships. "There's no way to localize who's actually firing the damned things!"

"Just thank God there aren't more of them, Ma'am," Sabourin said tightly. "It looks like Admiral Theisman was right. If we'd waited until they had that thing in general deployment, we'd have been toast."

Dame Alice Truman watched her plot sickly as missile after missile slammed its lasers into Third Fleet's superdreadnoughts. Her carriers were taking hits, too, but nothing compared to the agony of Kuzak's wall. It looked to Truman as if most of the hits on her carriers were overs or unders—MDMs which had lost the wallers on which they'd been targeted and found one of her carriers instead.

The bastards figure they can always get around to killing carriers later, she thought coldly, and felt an incredible stab of guilt as she realized how grateful she was. Yet she couldn't help it, for the people aboard her ships were *her* people, the people for whom *she* was responsible, and she wanted them to live.

"They're targeting Admiral McKeon, Ma'am!" Commander Stanfield said suddenly, and Truman's eyes snapped to the icon of HMS *Intransigent*.

"We nailed the son-of-a-bitch, Sir!" Commander Slowacki said, and despite his own fear, his voice was jubilant.

"Well done, Alekan!" Alistair McKeon replied, teeth bared in a wolfish grin of his own. His battle squadron had landed four salvos of Apollo-guided MDMs, and they'd killed a Havenite superdreadnought with each of them. In fact, they'd done better than that; the kill Slowacki had just announced was their fifth.

"Now go find another one," he said, and Slowacki nodded.

"Yes, Sir!"

The ops officer bent back over his displays, eyes bright, and McKeon felt a stab of envy. Slowacki was actually *doing* something, accomplishing something. In fact, the four Apollo-capable ships of McKeon's squadron were killing Havenite wallers in rapid succession, and Slowacki was too caught up in his task to realize that while he'd been killing five superdreadnoughts, the Havenites had already killed nine of Admiral Kuzak's. And it wouldn't be long before—

"Incoming!" someone shouted, and *Intransigent* lurched indescribably as the first deadly hits slammed home.

Alice Truman watched in horror as the Havenite flail came down on Alistair McKeon's squadron.

Was it deliberate? she wondered. *Were they able somehow to figure out where Apollo was coming from? Or was it just the luck of the draw?*

Not that it mattered.

Intransigent heaved madly as the lasers blasted into her. Astern of her, HMS *Elizabeth I* staggered as at least eighty direct hits slammed into her. She seemed to hesitate for a moment, and then, like her older sister *Triumph*, she vanished in a brief, terrible new star. *Second Yeltsin* and *Revenge* shuddered in agony of their own as the focused hurricane of destruction swept over McKeon's squadron. HMS *Incomparable*, *Imperator*'s division mate in place of the dead *Intolerant*, lurched out of formation, impellers dead, wreckage trailing, life pods launching. Then the last few hundred missiles of the concentrated salvo came punching in, and *Second Yeltsin* blew up while *Revenge*'s wedge went down. She started to fall behind, but before she could at least twelve lasers slammed directly into the unarmored top of her hull, which was supposed to be protected by her wedge. With no armor to stop them, the powerful lasers ripped deep into the superdreadnought's core, probing until they found her heart.

Thirty-one seconds after *Second Yeltsin*, HMS *Revenge* joined her in fiery death.

Intransigent survived. The only survivor of her entire squadron, Alistair McKeon's flagship staggered onward, little more than a wreck, but still alive.

Yet another hit slammed into HMS *King Roger III*. It stabbed deep, ripping through the wounds two of its predecessors had already torn. It breached the flagship's core hull, tearing its way into central engineering, and the superdreadnought's inertial compensator suddenly failed.

The emergency circuits shut down her impellers almost instantly, but "almost instantly" wasn't good enough for a ship under six hundred and twelve gravities of acceleration.

The ship sustained only moderate structural damage; none of her crew survived.

Chapter Sixty-Eight

"Ma'am, you're in command now," Captain Goodrick said.

"What?" Alice Truman looked at him in disbelief.

"The flagship's gone," Goodrick said harshly. "That puts you in command."

"What about Vice Admiral Emiliani?" Truman demanded.

"*Valkyrie* took a hit on flag bridge. Emiliani is dead. You're next most senior."

Truman stood for perhaps two heartbeats, then she shook herself.

"Very well," she said. "Franklin," she looked at Lieutenant Bradshaw. "General signal, all units. Inform them that command has passed to *Chimera*."

"Yes, Ma'am." Bradshaw seemed almost calm, anesthetized, perhaps, by the intensity of the carnage. "Any orders?" he asked.

"No." Truman shook her head. "Not at this time."

"Yes, Ma'am."

Bradshaw bent over his communications console, and Truman looked at the time/date display. Nine minutes. Only *nine* minutes since the Peeps had opened fire, and almost half of Third Fleet had already been destroyed.

She thought about Bradshaw's question. Orders. There *were* no orders for a situation like this one. Admiral Kuzak had already given the only ones anyone could. Now it was a matter of duty, not *orders*. A matter of Third Fleet's duty to fight to the death in defense of its home, and it would.

It's not my fleet, she thought, watching Third Fleet's bleeding ships, punching out missiles even as they died, and her eye unerringly found the icon of *Intransigent*, tagged with the jagged crimson code of critical damage. *Not my fleet . . . but by* God *if I've got to die, I couldn't have found a better one to die with.*

"That's two more of them, Ma'am," Commander Spiropoulo said, and Chin nodded.

Third Fleet was finished, she thought, her grim satisfaction tinged with more than a little horror as she contemplated the losses both navies had suffered this blood-soaked day. Thirty of the Manty SDs had been destroyed or hulked. Over half the survivors had critical damage, and whoever had been equipped with that new weapons system was among the dead or disabled.

Fifth Fleet would lose the range on Kuzak's battered remnants in another twenty-five seconds. The last salvo she could bring down on the fleeing Manties would land in another fifteen, but she found it hard to regret it. There'd already been enough blood, enough destruction, to satisfy anyone, she thought grimly.

She looked at the tally on one of her secondary displays. Second Fleet was down to only seventy-five ships—only fifty-six effectives, really—out of the two hundred and forty wallers and ninety escorts Lester Tourville had taken into the resonance zone. She herself had lost "only" eleven superdreadnoughts, and most of the crew had gotten out of three of them. But the back of the Star Kingdom's home system's defenses had been broken. She still had plenty of missile pods left aboard her remaining eighty-five wallers, and Second Fleet, despite its own brutal losses, had enough combat power to finish off Third Fleet's remnants. And then—

"Hyper footprint!" Spiropoulo said suddenly. "Multiple hyper footprints at seven-two-point-niner-three million kilometers!"

Honor Alexander-Harrington's eyes were brown ice as Theophile Kgari, in a virtuoso display of astrogation, dropped the massed superdreadnoughts of Eighth Fleet *exactly* where she'd told him to in a single jump right out of the center of the resonance zone.

She didn't look at the pathetic remnants of Third Fleet's icons. Didn't even glance at the other icons, representing Lester Tourville's task force. She had attention only for Genevieve Chin's superdreadnoughts, and her voice was a frozen soprano sword.

"Engage the enemy, Andrea," Lady Dame Honor Alexander-Harrington said.

Genevieve Chin's heart began beating once again, and her instant instinct to break off eased a bit as the range registered. At almost seventy-three million kilometers, the new arrivals were well outside even MDMs' powered range. Besides, there were only thirty-eight of them—less than half her own strength, even if all of them were wallers and not carriers.

"Turn us around, Andrianna," she said. "It looks like we've got some fresh customers."

Eighth Fleet released the five thousand Apollo pods which had been tractored to its SD(P)s' hulls, then spent another three minutes rolling additional pods. In all, it deployed a total of 7,776, almost exactly half its total ammunition allotment, given the Andermani ships' lighter magazine capacity.

Then it fired.

"What the—?" Andrianna Spiropoulo looked at the tracking report in disbelief. That didn't make any sense at all!

"Ma'am," she said, turning to Admiral Chin, "the Manties have just fired."

"They've what?" Genevieve Chin looked up from a discussion with Nicodème Sabourin.

"They've *fired*, Ma'am," Spiropoulo repeated. "It doesn't make any sense. They're still at least seven million kilometers out of range!"

"That *doesn't* make any sense," Chin agreed, walking across to stare at the preposterous missile icons in the master display.

"Maybe they're trying to panic us, Admiral," Sabourin suggested. She looked at him, eyebrows rising in disbelief, and he shrugged. "I know it sounds silly, Ma'am, but I don't have any *better* suggestion. I mean, we've just hammered two entire Manty fleets into so much scrap metal, and these people are outnumbered by at least three-to-one. Maybe they figure this is the only way to distract us from finishing off the system."

"I suppose it's possible," Chin said slowly, watching the icons come. "But it doesn't seem like a Manty sort of thing to do. On the other hand, I don't see what *else* they could expect to accomplish."

✧　　✧　　✧

Honor watched her own plot, sitting very still in her command chair. Nimitz sat upright in her lap, leaning back against her chest. She wrapped her right arm about him, holding him, and felt his cold, focused determination—an echo of her own—as his grass green eyes followed the same icons, watched the missiles speeding outward.

Apollo had done several things. It provided something verging on genuine real-time control of her missiles even at this range. By using the Apollo birds to control the other missiles from their pods, it effectively multiplied the number of MDMs each ship could control by a factor of eight. And it provided her tactical officers with unprecedented control over their missiles' fight profiles.

Eighth Fleet was the only formation in space fully equipped with the new system, and Honor and her captains had spent long, thoughtful hours exploring Apollo's ramifications. Now she was prepared to use them.

"They can't be serious," Spiropoulo said in exasperation as every single impeller signature disappeared simultaneously from her plot, six minues after launch. She glared at the plot with an affronted sense of professionalism, then punched a radical course change into the fleet tactical net.

Fifth Fleet obeyed the order immediately, rolling through a skew turn which would take it over thirty thousand kilometers from its predicted position by the time the Manticoran missiles reached it.

"What is it, Andrianna?" Chin asked, looking up from her com display and a hasty conference with her squadron commanders.

"Ma'am, you aren't going to believe this," Spiropoulo said, "but they're sending their birds in ballistic."

"What?" Chin looked back down at her com. "Excuse me for a moment, please," she told the flag officers on its compartmentalized display. "I think I need to see this for myself."

She climbed out of her command chair and walked over to stand beside Spiropoulo, her eyes seeking out the missile icons. She found them, but they were rapidly strobing flickers, not the steady light of the hard position fixes active impeller drives would have provided.

"They boosted for six minutes at forty-six thousand gravities,

Ma'am," Spiropoulo said. "Then they just shut the hell down. I altered course as soon as their impellers went down, which they have to know is going to play hell with whatever accuracy they might have achieved. And that's not the only screwy thing they're up to. Look at this."

The ops officer punched a macro, and Chin frowned as an additional cluster of impeller signatures blinked into existence. For some reason known only to itself and God, the Manty task force ahead of them had just fired another pattern of pods—*one* pattern of pods, with less than sixty missiles in it. And it hadn't fired them at *Chin's* ships; the missile vectors made it obvious the Manties had fired at Second Fleet, almost 150,000,000 kilometers away from them, inside the resonance zone.

"Well, at least now we know how they think they can get them to make attack runs once they get them into range," Sabourin said.

"I suppose," Chin said, but her expression was troubled.

Actually, it was their only real option, assuming they were going to fire from such a long range in the first place. At 46,000 g, their missiles had accelerated to almost 162,400 kilometers per second and traveled 29,230,000 kilometers before they'd shut down. That left the MDMs' third stage available for a powered attack run when they reached their targets. In sixty seconds of maximum acceleration, the remaining drive would add another 54,000 kilometers per second to the missiles' velocity. Or they could go for half that much power, and add another 81,000 over the space of three minutes. More importantly, it would permit the oncoming missiles to maneuver to engage their targets. She understood that. What she didn't understand was how they could believe it was anything but an utter waste of their missiles. They'd had to establish the targeting parameters when they launched. That meant they were gong to be looking for targets where Fifth Fleet would have been on its original heading and acceleration, and Spiropoulo's course change during the long ballistic portion in their flight profile's center would hopelessly compromise the weapons' already poor accuracy at long range.

She glanced at the time display while she did some mental math. Assume they waited until the birds were, say, eighty seconds out and then kicked in the last stage at 46,000 gravities. That would give them eighty seconds of maneuver time, for however much good that would do them at this extended range.

If they let the missiles come all the way in ballistic, flight time from shutdown would be about four and a half minutes. But they won't. So say they do bring the drives back up eighty seconds out—that would put them about three minutes before attack range on a straight ballistic profile—they'd still have about 13,000,000 kilometers to go. So if they kick the remaining drive at 46,000 gees at that point, they'll shave maybe seven seconds off their arrival time, and they'll be coming in somewhere around 200,000 KPS. But their accuracy will still suck. And what the hell *do they think they're doing with this* other *little cluster?*

Andrianna was right. It *didn't* make sense, unless Nicodème was right and they were trying to panic her. But if Third Fleet was what they'd just finished destroying, then these people had to be *Eighth* Fleet, which meant Honor Harrington. And Harrington didn't do things that didn't make sense. So what—?

Her eyes opened wide in horror.

"General signal all units!" she shouted, spinning towards her com section. "Hyper out immediately! Repeat, hyper out—"

But it had taken Genevieve Chin two minutes too long to realize what was happening.

"Drives going active . . . *now*, Your Grace," Andrea Jaruwalski said, and the missiles thirteen million kilometers short of Fifth Fleet suddenly brought their final drive stages on-line. Their icons burned abruptly bright and strong once again as they lit off their impellers . . . and hurled themselves at their targets under full shipboard control.

They blazed in across the remaining distance, tracking with clean, lethal precision, and their ballistic flight had dropped them off of the Republic's sensors. Chin's ships knew *approximately* where they were, but not exactly, and their supporting EW platforms and penetration aids came up with their impellers. They hurtled in across the Republican SD(P)s' defensive envelope at over half the speed of light, and the sudden eruption of jamming, of Dragon's Teeth spilling false targets, hammered those defenses mercilessly.

The fact that the missile defense crews aboard those ships had *known*, without question, that the attacking missiles would be clumsy, half-blind, only made a disastrous situation even worse.

Eighth Fleet had deployed almost eight thousand pods. Those

pods launched 69,984 missiles. Of that total, 7,776 were Apollo birds. Another 8,000 were electronic warfare platforms. Which meant that 54,208 carried laser heads—laser heads which homed on Genevieve Chin's ships with murderously accurate targeting.

Fifth Fleet's missile defenses did their best.

Their best was not good enough.

Honor sat hugging Nimitz and watched the tactical download from one of the Apollos. Despite the enormous range between *Imperator* and that missile, the transmission time was under four and a half seconds, and the clarity of the Apollo's enhanced sensors and data processing capability made the tactical feed crystal clear. It felt unnatural, as if she were right there, on top of the Havenite fleet, not over seventy million kilometers away. She watched the enemy counter-missiles fire late and wide. She watched the attack missiles' accompanying EW platforms beating down the defenses. She watched the missiles themselves sliding through those defenses like assassins' daggers.

Fifth Fleet stopped almost thirty percent of them, which was a truly miraculous total, under the circumstances. But over thirty-seven thousand got through.

It was, she decided coldly, a case of overkill.

Lester Tourville stared at his plot in horror as the impeller signatures of sixty-eight Republican ships of the wall abruptly vanished. Seventeen continued to burn on the display for another handful of seconds. Then they, too, vanished in what he devoutly hoped was a frantic hyper translation.

There was total silence on *Guerriere*'s flag bridge.

He never knew exactly how long he simply sat there, his mind a great, singing emptiness around a core of ice. It couldn't have been the eternity that it seemed to be, but eventually he forced his shoulders to straighten.

"Well," he said in a voice he couldn't quite recognize, "it would appear our time estimate on the deployment of their new system was slightly in error."

He turned his command chair to face Frazier Adamson.

"Cease fire, Commander."

Adamson blinked twice, then shook himself.

"Yes, Sir," he said hoarsely, and Second Fleet ceased firing at Third Fleet's tattered remnants as Adamson transmitted the order.

"Dear Lord," Dame Alice Truman murmured feelingly. "Talk about last-second reprieves."

"Did what I think happened really just happen, Ma'am?"

Wraith Goodrick's voice sounded shaky, and Truman didn't blame him a bit. Only seven of Theodosia Kuzak's superdreadnoughts were still in action, and all of them were brutally damaged. Another three had technically survived, but Truman doubted any of the ten would be worth repairing. All four of Kuzak's CLACs had been killed, and of Truman's own eight, three had been destroyed, one was a drifting cripple without impellers, and the other four—including *Chimera*—were severely damaged. For all intents and purposes, Third Fleet had been as totally destroyed as Home Fleet.

But the merciless hail of missiles had at least stopped pounding its remnants.

And, Truman thought with grim survivor's humor, *I don't blame whoever gave that order a bit, either.*

"Missile trace!" Frazier Adamson barked suddenly, and Lester Tourville's belly muscles clenched.

What was left of Third Fleet had stopped firing when he did. Were they insane enough to *resume* the action? If they did, he'd have no choice but to—

"Sir, they're coming in from *outside* the zone!" Adamson said.

"What?" Molly DeLaney demanded incredulously. "That's ridiculous! They're a hundred fifty *million* klicks away!"

"Well, they're coming in on us now anyway," Tourville said sharply as *Guerriere*'s missile defense batteries began to fire once more.

They didn't do much good. He watched sickly as the missiles which had suddenly brought up their impellers, appearing literally out of nowhere, hurtled down on his battered and broken command. They drove straight in, swerving, dancing, and his sick feeling of helplessness frayed around the edges as he realized there were less than sixty of them. Whatever they were, they weren't a serious attack on his surviving ships, so what—?

His jaw tightened as the missiles made their final approach. But they didn't detonate. Instead, they hurtled directly *through* his formation, straight through the teeth of his blazing laser clusters.

His point defense crews managed to nail two-thirds of them, despite the totality of the tactical surprise they'd acieved. The other twenty pirouetted, swerved to one side, then detonated in a perfectly synchronized, deadly accurate attack . . . on absolutely nothing.

Lester Tourville exhaled the breath he hadn't realized he was holding. He sensed the confusion of his flag bridge crew, and this time, he had no answer at all for them. Then—

"Sir," Lieutenant Eisenberg said in a very small voice, "I have a com request for you."

He turned his command chair to look at her, and she swallowed.

"It's . . . from Duchess Harrington, Sir."

The silence on *Guerriere*'s flag bridge was complete. Then Tourville cleared his throat.

"Throw it on my display, Ace," he said.

"Yes, Sir. Coming up now."

An instant later, a face appeared on Tourville's display. He'd seen that face before, when its owner surrendered to him. And again, when she had been clubbed down by the pulse rifle butts of State Security goons. Now she looked at him, her eyes like two more missile tubes.

"We meet again, Admiral Tourville," she said, and her soprano voice was cold.

"Admiral Harrington," he replied. "This is a surprise. I thought you were about eight light-minutes away."

He gazed at her hard eyes, eyes like leveled missile tubes, and waited. The transmission lag for light-speed communications should have been eight minutes—sixteen minutes, for a two-way exchange—at that range, but she spoke again barely fifteen seconds after he finished.

"I am. I'm speaking to you over what we call a 'Hermes buoy.' It's an FTL relay with standard sub-light communication capability." The expression she produced was technically a smile, but it was one that belonged on something out of deep, dark oceanic depths.

"We have several of them deployed around the system. I simply plugged into the nearest one so that I could speak directly to you," she continued in that same, icy-cold voice. "I'm sure you observed my birds' terminal performance. I'm also sure you understand I have the capability to blow every single one of your remaining ships out of space from my present position. I hope you aren't going to make it necessary for me to do so."

Tourville looked at her, and knew that last statement wasn't really accurate. Knew a part of her—the part behind those frozen eyes, that icy voice—hoped he *would* make it necessary. But too many people had already died for him to kill still more out of sheer stupidity.

"No, Your Grace," he said quietly. "I won't make it necessary."

Another endless fifteen seconds dragged past. Then—

"I'm glad to hear that," she told him, "however my acceptance of your surrender is contingent upon the surrender of your ships—and their databases—in their present condition. Is that clearly understood, Admiral Tourville?"

He hovered on the brink of refusing, of declaring that he would scrub his databases, as was customary, before surrendering a ship. But then he looked into those icy eyes again, and the temptation vanished.

"It's . . . understood, Your Grace," he made himself say, and sat there tasting the bitter poison of defeat. Defeat made all the more poisonous by how close Beatrice had come to success . . . and how completely it had failed, in the end.

"Good," she said at last, after yet another fifteen-second delay. "Decelerate to zero relative to the system primary. You'll be boarded by prize officers once you do. In the meantime," she smiled again, that same terrifying smile, "my ships will remain here, where we can . . . keep an eye on things."

"Your Grace," Andrea Jaruwalski said, as Honor turned away from her conversation with Lester Tourville.

"Yes, Andrea?"

Honor felt drained and empty. She supposed she should feel triumph. After all, she'd just destroyed almost seventy superdreadnoughts, and captured another seventy-five. That had to be an interstellar record, and for a bonus, her people had saved the Star Kingdom's capital system from invasion. But after so much carnage, so much destruction, how was a woman supposed to feel *triumphant*?

"Your Grace, we're getting IDs off Admiral Kuzak's surviving ships from the inner system recon platforms."

"Yes?" Honor felt herself tightening inside. The pitiful handful of icons where Third Fleet had been mocked her. If she'd been able to get her ships into position even a few minutes earlier, perhaps—

She forced that thought aside, and looked Andrea in the eye.

"Your Grace, most of our ships are gone," Jaruwalski said softly, "but I've got transponder codes on both *Chimera* and *Intransigent*."

Honor's heart spasmed, and the ice about her soul seemed to crack, ever so slightly. Nimitz stirred in her lap, sitting up once again, leaning back against her and reaching up to touch the side of her face with a long-fingered true-hand.

"I've been trying to contact them," Harper Brantley put in, drawing Honor's attention to him, and her eyes burned as she tasted his emotions. Like Jaruwalski, he wanted desperately to give her some sort of good news, to tell her someone she loved had survived. *Something* to balance at least some of the pain and the blood.

"I can't raise *Chimera*," Brantley continued. "It looks like she's actually in better general shape than *Intransigent*, but her grav com seems to be down. I've got Captain Thomas on the FTL, though."

"Put it on my screen," Honor said quickly, and turned to her com as it lit with the strained, exhausted face of Alistair McKeon's flag captain.

"Captain Thomas!" Honor said with a huge smile. "It's *good* to see you."

Intransigent was barely four hundred and thirteen light-seconds from *Imperator*—less than seven light-minutes—and the one-way transmission lag was barely six and a half seconds.

"And to see you, Your Grace," Thomas replied thirteen seconds later, and there was something just a bit odd about her voice.

"I've accepted the surrender of the remaining Havenite vessels," Honor continued. "Since you're so much closer to them than I am, it would make more sense to let Admiral McKeon or Admiral Truman handle the final details. Could I speak to Admiral McKeon, please?"

She sat there, waiting, her mind running ahead to all the things she needed to discuss with Alistair. If he could take over the actual surrender formalities, get some pinnaces loaded with Marines aboard Tourville's ships quickly, then—

"I—" Thomas began thirteen seconds later, then paused and closed her eyes for just a moment, her weary face wrung with pain.

"Your Grace," she said softly, "I'm sorry. We took a direct hit on Flag Bridge. There were . . . no survivors."

Chapter Sixty-Nine

It was very quiet in the nursery.

Her parents were downstairs, undoubtedly playing hearts with Hamish and Emily while they waited for her, and she didn't have much time. They were all due at Mount Royal Palace for a formal state dinner which was going to keep them out to all hours, and she'd come up to the nursery in uniform to save time changing later. In a lot of ways, she supposed, she really didn't have the time for this at all, but that was just too bad. The rest of the Star Kingdom—and the galaxy at large, for that matter—could just wait.

Lindsey Phillips had helped her get Raoul and Katherine changed and ready for bed while Emily supervised. Now she sat in her favorite chair—Raoul in her lap, Katherine asleep in the bassinet beside her—and adjusted the reading lamp, then looked at her sister and brother, curled like treecats on floor cushions in front of her.

"Are you ready?" she asked, and they nodded. "Where were we?"

"The pyre," Faith said, with a seven-year-old's assured, intimate familiarity with the story.

"Of course we were." She shook her head as she opened the book and began turning pages. "It's been so long, I'd forgotten where we'd gotten to."

Raoul began to fuss, with the quiet, stubborn, eyes-squeezed-shut intensity of a four-month-old. She reached out to his mind-glow, touching it gently, and smiled. He wasn't really unhappy,

821

just . . . bored with a world which wasn't focused exclusively on him. "Bored" wasn't really exactly the right word, she thought, but a baby's emotions, though clear and strong, were still in a formative stage, and it was difficult—even for her—to parse them exactly.

She felt Nimitz, stretched out across the chair back, reaching for the baby with her. There was something just a little odd about Raoul's mind-glow. Most of the time, Honor was convinced it was her imagination, just a difference in the way babies' emotions worked. Other times, she was far less certain of that, and this was one of those times.

Nimitz touched the baby's mind-glow, and Raoul stopped fussing instantly. His eyes opened, and that sense of boredom vanished. Honor turned her head, looking at Nimitz, and the treecat's grass-green eyes gleamed at her from the semi-darkness beyond the reading lamp's cone. She felt him radiating gentle reassurance, and Raoul gurgled happily.

Honor smiled at her younger siblings, then laid the book down long enough to maneuver Raoul into a seated position, supported against her shoulder, and looked at Nimitz.

"Did you do that with me, too, Stinker?" she asked him quietly. "I know we started later, but did you?"

Nimitz gazed back at her, and she felt the thoughtfulness behind those green eyes. Then, unmistakably, he nodded.

"Oh, my," Honor murmured, then looked down into Raoul's wide-open eyes. The baby was intent, focused . . . listening, and she shook her head. "Sweet pea," she told him tenderly, "fasten your seat belt. It's going to be an interesting ride."

Nimitz bleeked in cheerful agreement, and she felt long, agile fingers tug at something on the back of her neck. Then Nimitz lifted the Star of Grayson over her head on its crimson ribbon and dangled it above Raoul.

The baby's attention sharpened. He couldn't tell exactly what the star was at this point, but the bright sparkles of light dancing on its golden-starburst beauty drew his eyes like a magnet, and he reached up with one tiny, delicate hand while Nimitz crooned to him.

Honor watched for a moment, trying to imagine how the more stodgy of Grayson's steadholders would have reacted to the thought of an "animal" using their planet's highest, most solemn award for valor as a toy to distract a baby. No doubt the heart attacks would have come fast and thick, and she smiled slightly at the thought.

Then she looked back at Faith and James, and her smile turned a bit apologetic.

"Sorry. But now that Nimitz is keeping Raoul occupied, we can be about it."

She opened the book again, found her place, and began to read.

"'Behold, my boy.' The Phoenix opened the boxes and spread the cinnamon sticks on the nest. Then it took the cans and sprinkled the cinnamon powder over the top and sides of the heap, until the whole nest was a brick-dust red.

"'There we are, my boy,' said the Phoenix sadly. 'The traditional cinnamon pyre of the Phoenix, celebrated in song and story.'

"And with the third mention of the word 'pyre,' David's legs went weak and something seemed to catch in his throat. He remembered now where he had heard that word before. It was in his book of explorers, and it meant—it meant—

"'Phoenix,' he choked, "wh-wh-who is the pyre for?'

"'For myself,' said the Phoenix.

"'*Phoenix!*'"

Raoul gurgled happily, reaching for the shiny star, and Honor tasted Faith and James' rapt attention as they concentrated on the story. She'd always found it hard to read this final chapter without letting her voice fog up and waver just a bit around the edges.

That was harder than usual tonight.

She kept on reading the well-worn, beloved words, but under them were other thoughts, far removed from the peaceful quiet of this comforting, enfolding nursery.

Three weeks. Just three weeks since the carnage and destruction, the death. The Star Kingdom was still coming to grips with what had happened. No doubt, the Republic of Haven would soon be doing the same, when the word reached Nouveau Paris in another two weeks or so.

One hundred and thirty-nine Manticoran, Grayson, and Andermani superdreadnoughts and seven CLACs destroyed outright, and another seven superdreadnoughts and two CLACs so badly damaged they would never fight again. Twenty-seven battlecruisers, gone. Thirty-six heavy cruisers and two thousand eight hundred and six LACs, destroyed. The official death toll for the Alliance was 596,245, with another 3,512 wounded survivors. But for the Republic, it was even worse: two hundred and fifty-one superdreadnoughts destroyed, along with nine CLACs, sixty-four battlecruisers, fifty-four heavy cruisers, and 4,612 LACs, and sixty-eight superdreadnoughts, seven CLACs, and over three thousand LACs captured. The Star Kingdom was still trying to compute the true, shattering depth of Lester Tourville's casualties, but the numbers they'd already come up with stood at almost 1.7 *million* dead, 6,602 wounded, and 379,732 prisoners. The number of dead was almost certain to climb, according to Patricia Givens. It might even top two million before it was all done.

No one in history had ever seen a battle like it, and it ought to have been decisive. The walls of battle of both the Alliance and the Republic had been gutted. Yet despite Haven's horrific losses, the loss ratio was actually in the Republic's favor in hulls, and hugely so in terms of loss of life. Had it not been for the existence of Apollo—deployed so far only aboard Honor's ships—at this moment, no power in the universe could have prevented the Republic of Haven's remaining SD(P)s from rolling right over the Manticoran home system. Yet Apollo *did* exist, and what Honor had done to Genevieve Chin's fleet would serve as lethal notice to Thomas Theisman that he could not possibly take Manticore while Eighth Fleet survived.

Yet that also meant Eighth Fleet couldn't possibly uncover Manticore. And so, Eighth Fleet had been formally redesignated (for now, at least) as the Star Kingdom's Home Fleet, and Honor Alexander-Harrington, as its commander, found herself Fleet Admiral Alexander-Harrington, despite her relative lack of seniority. It was only an acting rank, of course; it went with Home Fleet, and as soon as they could find someone else to give the job to, she would revert to her permanent, four-star Manticoran rank. But they wouldn't be finding anyone else until they also managed to find another fleet with Apollo. And until they did that, she—like her ships—was as anchored to the capital system as if each of them had been welded to *Hephaestus* or *Vulcan*.

And Honor had emerged from the holocaust as the only surviving Allied fleet commander engaged. *She* was being given credit for the victory, lauded as "the greatest naval commander of her age" by the newsfaxes. A Manticoran public shocked to its very marrow by the audacity of the Havenite attack and its horrific casualties, terrified by how close Lester Tourville had come to success, had fastened on *her* as its heroine and savior.

Not Sebastian D'Orville, who'd given his life *knowing* he and all his people were going to die. If D'Orville hadn't decisively blunted the initial attack, it would have devastated everything in the Manticore System, no matter what Theodosia Kuzak or Honor had done, and he and his fleet had died where they stood to do it.

Not Theodosia Kuzak, whose Third Fleet had sailed straight into the jaws of death. Who'd done everything right, yet tripped the guillotine which would have destroyed Eighth Fleet, just as surely as it had destroyed the Third, if Honor had been in her place.

And not Alistair McKeon, who had died like so many thousands of others, doing what he always did—his duty. Protecting the star nation he loved, serving the Queen he honored. Obeying the orders of the admiral who'd sent him unknowingly to his death . . . and who'd never even had the chance to say goodbye.

The praise, the adulation, were as bitter on her tongue as the ashes of the Phoenix's pyre, and she felt the darkness outside this quiet nursery. The darkness of the future, with all its uncertainties, all its risks in the wake of such a savage display of combat power and such cruel losses to both combatants. The darkness of the new and terrible blood debt the Star Kingdom and the Republic had laid up between them. The hatred and the fear which had to come from such a cataclysmic encounter, with all its dark implications for where the war between them might go.

And the darkness of the past. The darkness of memory, of grief. Of remembering those who were gone, who she would never see again.

Her voice had continued, her eyes moving down the printed page out of reflex, guided by memory, but now she heard her own words once again.

"David noticed then that he was holding something in his hand, something soft and heavy. As he lifted it to look more closely, it flashed in the sunlight. It was the feather the Phoenix had given him, the tail feather. Tail feather? . . . But the Phoenix's tail had been a sapphire blue. The feather in his hand was of the purest, palest gold.

"There was a slight stir behind him. In spite of himself, he glanced at the remains of the pyre. His mouth dropped open. In the middle of the white ashes and glowing coals there was movement. Something within was struggling up toward the top. The noises grew stronger and more definite. Charred sticks were being snapped, ashes kicked aside, embers pushed out of the way. Now, like a plant thrusting its way out of the soil, there appeared something pale and glittering, which nodded in the breeze. Little tongues of flame, it seemed, licking out into the air . . . No, not flames! A crest of golden feathers! . . . A heave from below lifted the ashes in the center of the pile, a fine cloud of flakes swirled up into the breeze, there was a flash of sunlight glinting on brilliant plumage. And from the ruins of the pyre stepped forth a magnificent bird."

The ancient story's imagery touched her. It always had, but this time, it was different.

"It was the Phoenix," she heard herself read, "it must be the Phoenix! But it was a new and different Phoenix. It was young and wild, with a fierce amber eye; its crest was tall and proud, its body the slim, muscular body of a hunter, its wings narrow and long and pointed like a falcon's, the great beak and talons razor-sharp and curving. And all of it, from crest to talons, was a burnished gold that reflected the sun in a thousand dazzling lights.

"The bird stretched its wings, shook the ash from its tail, and began to preen itself. Every movement was like the flash of a silent explosion.

" 'Phoenix,' David whispered. 'Phoenix.' "

Honor saw Alistair in the Phoenix, heard herself in the ancient David. Heard the yearning, the hunger, the need for the rebirth of all she'd lost, all that had been taken from the universe.

"The bird started, turned toward him, looked at him for an instant with wild, fearless eyes, then continued its preening. Suddenly it stopped and cocked its head as if listening to something. Then David heard it too: a shout down the mountainside, louder and clearer now, excited and jubilant. He shivered and looked down. The Scientist was tearing up the goat trail as fast as his long legs would carry him—and he was waving a rifle.

" 'Phoenix!' David cried. 'Fly! Fly, Phoenix!'

"The bird looked at the Scientist, then at David, its glance curious but without understanding. Paralyzed with fear, David remained on his knees as the Scientist reached an open place and threw the gun up to his shoulder. The bullet went whining by with an ugly hornet-noise, and the report of the gun echoed along the scarp.

"'Fly, Phoenix!' David sobbed. A second bullet snarled at the bird, and spattered out little chips of rock from the inner wall of the ledge.

"'Oh, fly, fly!' David jumped up and flung himself between the bird and the Scientist. 'It's me!' he cried. 'It's David!' The bird gazed at him closely, and a light flickered in its eye as though the name had reached out and almost, but not quite, touched an ancient memory. Hesitantly it stretched forth one wing, and with the tip of it lightly brushed David's forehead, leaving there a mark which burned coolly.

"'*Get away from that bird, you little idiot!*' the Scientist shrieked. '*GET AWAY!*'

"David ignored him. 'Fly, Phoenix!' he cried, and he pushed the bird toward the edge."

No, she thought. She wasn't David, and Alistair wasn't simply the Phoenix. Alistair was David *and* the Phoenix, just as the Phoenix was all he had thrown himself in front of, like a shield, protecting it with his life, guarding it with his death.

And, like the Phoenix, he was forever gone beyond her touch again. She read the final paragraph through a blur of tears.

"Understanding dawned in the amber eyes at last. The bird, with one clear, defiant cry, leaped to an out-jutting boulder. The golden wings spread, the golden neck curved back, the golden talons pushed against the rock. The bird launched itself into the air and soared out over the valley, sparkling, flashing, shimmering; a flame, large as a sunburst, a meteor, a diamond, a star, diminishing at last to a speck of gold dust, which glimmered twice in the distance before it was gone altogether."

Fly, Alistair, Honor Alexander-Harrington thought. *Wherever you are, wherever God takes you, fly high. I'll guard the Phoenix for you, I promise. Goodbye. I love you.*

An Afterword . . .

In 1957, Follett Publishing Company of Chicago published a book by a fellow by the name of Edward Ormondroyd. That book was called *David and the Phoenix*, and in 1958, the Weekly Reader Children's Book Club brought out its own edition.

I was six years old that year, and *David and the Phoenix* is the very first book I can remember reading entirely to myself.

It made an impression.

Aside from the fact that the book's human protagonist had the best imaginable first name, it had several other things going for it. It was written for young people, but it wasn't written *down* to them. It was written in the sort of prose any writer could do well to learn from. And, most importantly of all, it told a marvelous story which taught that the world is full of wonder.

I can think back to most of the important, formative writers who first turned me into a reader, and, ultimately, into a writer myself. C. S. Lewis is on the list, and so are Walter Farley, Arthur Ransome, and Edward Ormondroyd. Indeed, for me, he came first; the others simply followed the trail he'd blazed and took me to other destinations.

Over the years, I hung on to the *Weekly Reader* copy of the book I purloined from my older brother Mike. I still have it, as a matter of fact, and I intend to go right on hanging onto it. (So there, Mike!) But in the last couple of years, I've revisited *David and the Phoenix*, and seen it from a rather different perspective.

I've been reading it aloud to my own children. Sharon and I

are both readers ourselves, of course, and we deliberately set out, with careful premeditation, to turn our kids into readers, as well. As part of our nefarious plan, Daddy reads to them every night. (After all, the first taste is always free.) Mommy gets the day shift's reading, and we double-team them fairly well, I think.

There *have* been a few evenings of slippage, especially since Michael Paul, our youngest, discovered *Finding Nemo*. Michael can be a bit . . . insistent, and he has a two-year-old's stubbornness. (Well, there's also that additional little streak of willfulness he gets from his mom, of course, but we won't talk about that.) Still, all three of the children have been through *David and the Phoenix* at least twice now. And when I went on a signing tour, I recorded the entire book on CD, so that Morgan Emily and Megan Elizabeth (and Mikey, although he was only five months old at the time) wouldn't miss their fix of Daddy-reading while I was gone.

In case you haven't already figured it out, I think this is one of the very best young-adult books ever written. And it's pretty amazing how many people I run into at science-fiction conventions who read the same book when they were younger.

Unhappily, it went out of print eventually. And it stayed out of print for a long time. But then, in 2000, Purple House Press in Cynthiana, Kentucky, reissued it in paperback. When I got my hands on a copy of the Purple House edition, I contacted them, and through them, got Mr. Ormondroyd's very kind permission to quote from the book in *At All Costs*. Not just because it was one of my most beloved childhood stories, but because the central imagery and theme of the book fitted so perfectly into the story I had to tell about Honor Harrington.

I take the reissue of this book after forty-three years as a good sign for the future. It's always possible, of course, that the Society for Creative Anachronism of two thousand years from now, *won't* have the good taste and good sense to keep it in print then. However, I understand that *Purple House* intends to keep it in print.

This is what is known as A Good Thing. It gives any of you haven't read it the opportunity to repair your oversight.

Take it.

Whether you have children to read it to or not, this is truly a work of wonder which will repay your time with Gryffins (and also Gryffons and Gryffens), Leprechauns, Banshees who feed their wails on heads of cabbage, Witches with racing broomsticks, Fauns, Sea Monsters, the pipes of Pan himself, and, most wondrous of all, the Phoenix. With that sense of both loss and perpetual renewal. Of friendship, love, the willingness to sacrifice for both, and the ability to let go at the end *because* of love.

It's a marvelous book, and like the Phoenix, its wonder will never really die.

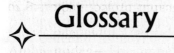 Glossary

Alpha nodes—The impeller nodes of a starship which both generate its normal-space impeller wedge and reconfigure to generate Warshawski sails in hyper-space.

Alpha translation—The translation into or out of the alpha (lowest) bands of hyper-space.

Andermani Empire—Empire founded by mercenary Gustav Anderman. The Empire lies to the "west" of the Star Kingdom, has an excellent navy, and is the Star Kingdom's primary competitor for trade and influence in the Silesian Confederacy.

Andies—Slang term for citizens and (especially) the military personnel and forces of the Andermani Empire.

Apollo—A Manticoran development utilizing forward-deployed FTL communications links to provide near real-time fire control for long-range missile fire.

BB—Battleship. At one time, the heaviest capital ship but now considered too small to "lie in the wall." Average tonnage is from 2,000,000 to 4,000,000 tons. Employed by some navies for rear area system security but no longer considered an effective warship type.

BC—Battlecruiser. The lightest unit considered a "capital ship." Designed to destroy anything it can catch and to outrun anything that can destroy it. Average tonnage is from 500,000–1,200,000 tons.

Beta node—Secondary generating nodes of a spacecraft's impeller wedge. They contribute only to the impeller wedge used for normal-space movement. Less powerful and less expensive than alpha nodes.

BLS—Basic Living Stipend. The welfare payment from the PRH government to its permanent underclass. Essentially, the BLS was a straight exchange of government services for a permanent block vote supporting the Legislaturalists who controlled the government.

DD—Destroyer. The smallest hyper-capable warship currently being built by most navies. Average tonnage is from 65,000–80,000 tons.

"Down the throat shot"—An attack launched from directly ahead of an impeller-drive spacecraft in order to fire lengthwise down its impeller wedge. Due to the geometry of the impeller wedge, this is a warship's most vulnerable single aspect.

DN—Dreadnought. A class of warship lying midway between battleships and superdreadnoughts. No major navy is currently building this type. Average tonnage is from 4,000,000 to 6,000,000 tons.

CA—Heavy cruiser (from Cruiser, Armored). Designed for commerce protection and long-endurance system pickets. Designed to stand in for capital ships against moderate level threats. Average tonnage is from 160,000–350,000 tons, although that has begun to creep upward towards traditional battlecruiser tonnage ranges in some navies.

Centrists—A Manticoran political party typified by pragmatism and moderation on most issues but very tightly focused on the Havenite threat and how to defeat it. The party supported by Honor Harrington.

CIC—Combat Information Center. The "nerve center" of a warship, responsible for gathering and organizing sensor data and the tactical situation.

CL—Light cruiser. The primary scouting unit of most navies. Also used for both commerce protection and raiding. Average tonnage is from 90,000–150,000 tons.

CLAC—LAC carrier. A starship of dreadnought or superdreadnought size configured to transport LACs through hyperspace and to service and arm them for combat.

COLAC—Commanding Officer, Light Attack Craft. The commander of the entire group of LACs carried by a CLAC.

Committee of Public Safety—The committee established by Rob S. Pierre after his overthrow of the Legislaturalists to control the PRH. It instituted a reign of terror and systematic purges of surviving Legislaturalists and prosecuted the war against the Star Kingdom.

Confederation Navy—Organized naval forces of the Silesian Confederacy.

Confeds—Slang term for citizens of the Silesian Confederacy and (especially) for members of the Confederation Navy.

Conservative Association—A generally reactionary Manticoran political party whose primary constituency is the extremely conservative aristocracy.

Coup de Vitesse—A primarily offensive, "hard style" martial art preferred by the RMN and RMMC. Main emphasis is on weaponless combat.

Crown Loyalists—A Manticoran political party united around the concept that the Star Kingdom requires a strong monarchy, largely as a counter balance to the power of the conservative element in the aristocracy. Despite this, the Star Kingdom's more progressive aristocracy is heavily represented in the Crown Loyalists.

Dolist—One of a class of Havenite citizens totally dependent on the government-provided Basic Living Stipend. As a group, undereducated and underskilled.

"Donkey," The—The popular name given by Havenite crews to the tractor-equipped platforms developed by Shannon Foraker to increase the number of missile pods the Republic's warships can tow.

Keyhole—A Manticoran-developed deployable platform mounting control links and telemetry channels for offensive and defensive missiles.

ECM—Electronic counter measures.

EW—Electronic warfare.

FIA—Federal Investigative Agency. The national police force of the restored Republic of Haven.

FIS—Federal Intelligence Service. The primary espionage agency of the restored Republic of Haven.

Ghostrider, Project—A Manticoran research project dedicated to the development of the multi-drive missile and associated technology. The original Ghostrider blossomed into a large number of sub-projects which emphasized electronic warfare and decoys as well as offensive missiles.

Gravity waves—A naturally occurring phenomenon in hyper-space consisting of permanent, very powerful regions of focused gravitic stress which remain motionless but for a (relatively) slow side-slipping or drifting. Vessels with Warshawski sails are capable of using such waves to attain very high levels of acceleration; vessels under impeller drive are destroyed upon entering them.

Grav pulse com—A communication device using gravitic pulses to achieve FTL communications over intrasystem ranges.

Grayson—Habitable planet of Yeltsin's Star. Star Kingdom of Manticore's most important single ally.

Hyper limit—The critical distance from a given star at which starships may enter or leave hyper-space. The limit varies with the mass of the star. Very large planets have hyper limits of their own.

Hyper-space—Multiple layers of associated but discrete dimensions which bring points in normal-space into closer congruence, thus permitting effectively faster than light travel between them. Layers are divided into "bands" of closely associated dimensions. The barriers between such bands are the sites of turbulence and instability which become increasingly powerful and dangerous as a vessel moves "higher" in hyper-space.

IAN—Imperial Andermani Navy.

Impeller drive—The standard reactionless normal-space drive of the Honor Harrington universe, employing artificially generated bands (or "wedges") of gravitic energy to provide very high rates of acceleration. It is also used in hyper-space outside gravity waves.

Impeller wedge—The inclined planes of gravitic stress formed above and below a spacecraft by its impeller drive. A military impeller wedge's "floor" and "roof" are impenetrable by any known weapon.

Inertial compensator—A device which creates an "inertial sump," diverting the inertial forces associated with acceleration into a starship's impeller wedge or a naturally occurring gravity wave, thus negating the g-force the ship's crew would otherwise experience. Smaller vessels enjoy a higher

compensator efficiency for a given strength of wedge or
gravity wave and thus can achieve higher accelerations than
larger vessels.

InSec—Internal Security. The secret police and espionage service
of the PRH under the Legislaturalists. Charged with security
functions and suppression of dissent.

Keyhole II—A successor to the original Keyhole platform which
is configured with FTL communications links instead of
light-speed telemetry.

LAC—Light Attack Craft. A sublight warship type, incapable of
entering hyper, which masses between 40,000 and 60,000
tons. Until recently, considered an obsolete and ineffective
warship good for little but customs duty and light patrol work.
Advances in technology have changed that view of it.

Laser clusters—Last-ditch, close-range anti-missile point defense
systems.

Liberal Party—A Manticoran political party typified by a belief
in isolationism and the need for social intervention and
the use of the power of the state to "level" economic and
political inequities within the Star Kingdom.

Legislaturalists—The hereditary ruling class of the PRH. The
descendants of the politicians who created the Dolist System
more than two hundred years before the beginning of the
current war.

Manties—Slang term for citizens of and (especially) military
personnel/forces of the Star Kingdom of Manticore.

Mark 31 Counter-missile—A new, longer-range counter-missile
developed by Manticore and deployed by the Alliance to
give greater stand off engagement range against MDMs. The
Mark 31 also provides the platform and missile drive for
the Viper (see below).

MDM—Multi-drive missile. A new Manticoran weapon development which enormously enhances the range of missile combat by providing additional drive endurance.

Mistletoe—Codename assigned by Sonja Hemphill to weapon-equipped "reconnaissance drones" used to creep into attack range of critical system defense infrastructure.

Moriarty—Codename assigned by Shannon Foraker to a specially developed centralized fire control node deployed to coordinate MDMs used in the system defense role.

NavInt—Shortened version of Naval Intelligence. The naval intelligence agency of the Republic of Haven.

New Men—A Manticoran political party headed by Sheridan Wallace. Small and opportunistic.

Office of Naval Intelligence (ONI)—The RMN's naval intelligence service, directed by the Second Space Lord.

Peeps—Slang term for citizens and (especially) military personnel of the Peoples' Republic of Haven.

Penaids—Electronic systems carried by missiles to assist them in penetrating their targets' active and passive defenses.

Pinnace—A general purpose military small craft capable of lifting approximately 100 personnel. Equipped with its own impeller wedge, capable of high acceleration, and normally armed. May be configured for ground support.

Powered Armor—Battle armor combining a vac suit with protection proof against most man-portable projectile weapons, very powerful exoskeletal "muscles," sophisticated on-board sensors, and maneuvering thrusters for use in vacuum.

Progressive Party—A Manticoran political party typified by what it considers a pragmatic acceptance of realpolitik. It is somewhat more socially liberal than the Centrists but has traditionally considered a war against Haven as unwinnable and believed that the Star Kingdom's interests would be best served by cutting some sort of "deal" with the PRH.

Protector—Title of ruler of Grayson. Equivalent to "emperor." The current protector is Benjamin Mayhew.

PubIn—Office of Public Information. Propaganda arm of the PRH under both the Legislaturalists and the Committee of Public Safety.

PRH—Peoples' Republic of Haven. The name applied to the Republic of Haven during the period when it was controlled by the Legislaturalists and/or the Committee of Public Safety. It was the PRH which began the current war by attacking the Star Kingdom of Manticore and the Manticoran Alliance.

Republic of Erewhon—Government of the Erewhon System. A single-system unit which controls the Erewhon Wormhole Junction connecting the Solarian League and the Phoenix Wormhole Junction. A member of the Manticoran Alliance since before the start of the current war.

Republic of Haven—The largest human interstellar political unit after the Solarian League itself. Until recently it was known as the Peoples' Republic of Haven, ruled by an hereditary governing class known as the Legislaturalists until they were overthrown by Rob S. Pierre. Thereafter controlled by Pierre through the Committee of Public Safety until it, too, was overthrown in turn and the original constitution of the Republic was reinstated.

RHN—Republic of Haven Navy. Navy of the Republic of Haven as reorganized by Thomas Theisman.

RMAIA—Royal Manticoran Astrography Investigation Agency. Agency created by High Ridge Government to explore the Manticoran Wormhole Junction searching for additional termini.

RMN—Royal Manticoran Navy.

RMMC—Royal Manticoran Marine Corps

SD—Superdreadnought. The largest and most powerful hyper-capable warship. Average tonnage is from 6,000,000–8,500,000 tons.

Shuttles—Small craft employed by starships for personnel and cargo movement from ship to ship or ship to surface. Cargo shuttles are configured primarily as freight haulers, with limited personnel capacity. Assault shuttles are heavily armed and armored and typically are capable of lifting at least a full company of ground troops.

Sidewalls—Protective barriers of gravitic stress projected to either side of a warship to protect its flanks from hostile fire. Not as difficult to penetrate as an impeller wedge, but still a very powerful defense.

Silesian Confederacy—A large, chaotic political entity lying between the Star Kingdom of Manticore and the Andermani Empire. Its central government is both weak and extremely corrupt and the region is plagued by pirates. Despite this, the Confederacy is a large and very important foreign market for the Star Kingdom.

Sillies—Slang term for Silesian citizens and/or military personnel.

Solarian League—Largest, wealthiest star nation of the explored galaxy, with decentralized government managed by extremely powerful bureaucracies.

Sollies—Slang term for citizens or military personnel of the Solarian League.

StateSec—Also "SS." Office of State Security. The successor to Internal Security under the Committee of Public Safety. Even more powerful than InSec. Headed by Oscar Saint-Just, originally second-in-command of InSec, who betrayed the Legislaturalists to aid Rob Pierre in overthrowing them.

Star Kingdom of Manticore—A small, wealthy star nation consisting of two star systems: the Manticore System and the Basilisk System. It is now in the process of radical expansion.

Treecats—The native sentient species of the planet Sphinx. Six-limbed, telempathic arboreal predators which average between 1.5 and 2 meters in length (including prehensile tail). A small percentage of them bond with "adopted" humans in a near symbiotic relationship. Although incapable of speech, treecats have recently learned to communicate with humans using sign language.

Triple Ripple—A Havenite defensive technique utilizing heavy concentrations of nuclear warheads to blind and disable enemy missile seekers and electronic warfare platforms.

"Up the kilt shot"—An attack launched from directly astern of a starship in order to fire down the length of its impeller wedge. Due to the geometry of the impeller drive, this is a warship's second most vulnerable aspect.

Viper—A Grayson-Manticoran-developed missile with shorter range but higher acceleration rates and better seeker systems and onboard AI to create a "launch and forget" weapon for use in the anti-LAC role. Vipers can also be used as standard counter-missiles.

Warshawski—Name applied to all gravitic detectors in honor of the inventor of the first such device.

Warshawski, Adrienne—The greatest hyper-physicist in human history.

Warshawski sail—The circular gravity "grab fields" devised by Adrienne Warshawski to permit starships to "sail" along gravity waves in hyper-space.

Wormhole junction—A gravitic anomaly. Effectively, a frozen flaw in normal space providing access via hyper-space as an instantaneous link between widely separated points. The largest known junction is the Manticoran Wormhole Junction with seven known termini.

Character List

Abercrombie, Captain Boniface, RHN—senior COLAC, Gaston System Defense Command.

Abrioux, Senior Inspector Danielle ("Danny")—a senior investigator for the Havenite FIA on personal assignment from Kevin Usher.

Anders, Captain William ("Five"), RHN—chief of staff, Bolthole.

Anisimovna, Aldona—Manpower Inc. board member; member of Mesan Strategy Council.

al-Bakr, Admiral Gammal, Zanzibar System Navy—CNO Zanzibar System Navy, CO Zanzibar System Defense Command.

Alexander, Emily—Countess White Haven, wife of Hamish Alexander, Earl White Haven.

Alexander, Admiral Hamish RMN (ret)—Earl White Haven, First Lord of Admiralty.

Alexander, William—Baron Grantville, Hamish Alexander's brother, Prime Minister of the Star Kingdom of Manticore.

Arbuckle, Senior Steward Clarissa—Michelle Henke's personal steward.

Atkins, Corporal Joshua—Harrington Steadholder's Guard, one of Honor Harrington's new personal armsmen.

Ariel—treecat companion of Queen Elizabeth III.

Ayrault—Captain Maurice, RMN, chief of staff, Home Fleet.

Banacek, Lieutenant Sally, RHN—Captain Boniface Abercrombie's tactical officer.

Banshee—treecat companion of Roslee Orndorff.

Bardasano, Isabel—Jessyk Combine Cadet board member; senior Mesan "wet work" specialist.

Barloi, Henrietta—Republic of Haven Secretary of Technology.

Bascou, Lieutenant Edouard, RHN—staff communications officer, Gaston System Defense Command.

Beach, Rear Admiral Everette, RHN—CO, Gaston System Defense Command.

Beauchamp, Captain Heinrich, RHN—CO, Hera System Defense Command's sensor net.

Begin, Camille—a Havenite security dispatcher.

Bellefeuille, Diana—Rear Admiral Bellefeuille's daughter.

Bellefeuille, Rear Admiral Jennifer, RHN—CO, Chantilly System Defense Command.

Bellefeuille, Matthew—Rear Admiral Bellefeuille's son.

Bellefeuille, Russell—Rear Admiral Bellefeuille's husband.

Bibeau, Lieutenant Charles, RHN—plotting officer of the watch, Alpha Station, Solon System.

Blackett, Corporal Luke, Harrington Steadholder's Guard—James Harrington's personal armsman.

Blaine, Admiral Jessup, RMN—CO, Task Force 14, Lynx Station.

Blumenthal, Commander Joel, RMN—executive officer, HMS *Nike*.

Bradshaw, Lieutenant Franklin, RMN—staff communications officer, Third Fleet.

Bradshaw, Rear Admiral Winston, RMN—CO, Cruiser Squadron 7.

Braga, Lieutenant Commander Antonio, RMN—astrogator, Battlecruiser Squadron 81.

Brankovski, Captain Amanda, RMN—senior COLAC, CLAC Squadron 6.

Brantley, Lieutenant Harper, RMN—staff communications officer, Eighth Fleet.

Bressand, Rear Admiral Baptiste, RHN—CO, Augusta System Defense Command.

Brigham, Commodore Mercedes, RMN—Chief of Staff Eighth Fleet.

Broughton, Captain Everard, RMN—CO, outer system LAC platforms, Zanzibar System Defense Command.

Bruckheimer, Admiral Arnold, RHN (ret)—Fordyce System governor, Republic of Haven.

Caparelli, Admiral Sir Thomas—First Space Lord, RMN.

Cardones, Captain Rafe, RMN—CO HMS *Imperator*; Honor Harrington's flag captain.

Carmouche, Commodore Desiree, RHN—CO, Fordyce System Defense Command.

Carter, Lieutenant Jeff, RMN—an officer on Andrea Jaruwalski's operations staff.

Chernitskaya, Lieutenant Veronika Dominikovna ("Vicki"), RMN—tactical officer, HMLAC Dacoit.

Clapp, Commander Mitchell, RHN—LAC development specialist assigned to Bolthole.

Chin, Admiral Genevieve, RHN—CO, Fifth Fleet.

Clinkscales, Austen MacGregor—Howard Clinkscales' nephew and successor as Regent of Harrington Steading.

Clinkscales, Bethany Judith—Howard Clinkscales' senior wife.

Clinkscales, Constance Marianne—Howard Clinkscales' third wife.

Clinkscales, Lieutenant Commander Carson Edward, GSN—Howard Clinkscales' nephew.

Clinkscales, Howard Samson Jonathan—Lord Clinkscales, Regent of Harrington Steading.

Clinkscales, Rebecca Tiffany—Howard Clinkscales' second wife.

Cortes, Admiral Sir Lucian—Fifth Space Lord, RMN.

Daniels, Lieutenant Commander Gunther, RMN—CO, HMS *Skirmisher*.

Dante, Lieutenant Commander Esmeralda, RMN—staff astrogator, CLAC Squadron 3.

Davidson, Monsignor Stuart—Archbishop Telmachi's personal representative on Grayson.

deCastro, Commander Ivan, RHN—chief of staff, Chantilly System Defense Command.

DeClercq, Travis—Republic of Haven's ambassador to the Solarian League.

DeLaney, Captain Molly, RHN—chief of staff, Second Fleet.

DePaul, Brother Matthew—Reverend Sullivan's personal secretary and aide.

Detweiler, Albrecht—Manpower, Inc., chairman of the Board; head of the Mesan governing council.

Detweiler, Evelina—Albrecht Detweiler's wife.

Deutscher, Rear Admiral Emile, RHN—CO, Task Group 36 ("Bogey One"), Third Fleet.

Diamato, Rear Admiral Oliver, RHN—CO, Battlecruiser Squadron 12.

D'Orville, Fleet Admiral Sebastian, RMN—CO, Home Fleet.

Dryslar, Captain Adam, RMN—Admiral Caparelli's chief of staff.

DuBois, Web—ex-genetic slave, Prime Minister of Torch.

DuPuy, Tabitha—White Haven's chief cook.

Durand, Captain Alexis, RHN—CO, Alpha Station, Solon System.

Duval, Rear Admiral Harold, RHN—CO, CLAC Division 19.

Eisenberg, Lieutenant Anita ("Ace"), RHN—staff communications officer, Second Fleet.

Ellefsen, Havard—Lovat System governor, Republic of Haven.

Ericsson, Commander Leonardo, RHN—operations officer, Chantilly System Defense Command.

Estwicke, Lieutenant Commander Bridget, RMN—CO, HMS *Ambuscade*.

Fanaafi, Commodore Charise, RMN—CO, Cruiser Squadron 12.

Farragut—treecat companion of Miranda LaFollet.

Ferry, Harper S.—ex-slave; ex-Audubon Ballroom terrorist; one of Queen Berry's bodyguards.

Foraker, Vice Admiral Shannon, RHN—CO, Bolthole.

Frazier, Doctor Janet—Honor Harrington's personal physician.

Fredericks, Captain Hal, RHN—CO, RHNS *Conquete*.

Genghis—treecat companion of Judson Van Hale.

Giancola, Arnold—Republic of Haven Secretary of State.

Giancola, Jason—Republic of Haven senator; Arnold Giancola's younger brother.

Gilraven, Captain Sybil, RMN—commanding officer, HMS *Invictus*, Admiral D'Orville's flag captain.

Giovanni, Commodore Alessandra, RHN—CO, Lovat System Defense Command inner defenses.

Giscard, Admiral Javier, RHN—CO, Third Fleet; President Eloise Pritchart's lover.

Givens, Admiral Patricia—Second Space Lord, RMN; CO, Office of Naval Intelligence.

Gohr, Lieutenant Commander Betty, RMN—tactical officer, HMS *Nike*.

Goldbach, Angelo—Axel Lacroix's best friend and fellow shipyard worker.

Goodrick, Captain Craig ("Wraith"), RMN—chief of staff, CLAC Squadron Three.

Gozzi, Captain Marius, RHN—chief of staff, Third Fleet.

Gregory, Stan—Republic of Haven Secretary of Urban affairs.

Grimm, Admiral Stephania, Royal Manticoran Astro Control Service—CO, Manticore Wormhole Junction ACS.

Grosclaude, Yves—ex-Havenite Special Ambassador to Manticore.

Guernicke, Liam—Second Lord of Admiralty (budgetary and fiscal management), RMN.

Guyard, Commander Claudette, RHN—chief of staff, Augusta System Defense Command.

Gwynett, Captain Madelyn, RMN—operations officer, Home Fleet.

Hampton, Alicia—Arnold Giancola's senior administrative assistant.

Hampton, Commander Bradley, RMN—navy liaison officer assigned to Manticore Wormhole Junction ACS.

Hanover, Captain Franklin, RMN—CO HMS *Hector*.

Hanriot, Rachel—Republic of Haven Secretary of the Treasury.

Harcourt, Lieutenant Emily, RMN—tactical officer, HMS *Ambuscade*.

Harkness, Chief Warrant Officer Sir Horace, RMN—engineer, HMLAC *Dacoit*.

Harrington, Doctor Alfred—Honor Harrington's father, ex-navy officer, one of the leading neurosurgeons of the Star Kingdom of Manticore.

Harrington, Doctor Allison—Honor Harrington's mother, born on the planet Beowulf, one of the leading geneticists of the Star Kingdom of Manticore.

Harrington, Clarissa—Alfred Harrington's younger sister; Honor Harrington's aunt.

Harrington, Faith Katherine Honor Stephanie Miranda—"Miss Harrington," Honor Harrington's younger sister and her designated heir.

Harrington, Lady Dame Honor Stephanie—Duchess Harrington; Steadholder Harrington; Admiral, RMN; Fleet Admiral, Grayson Space Navy; CO Protector's Own; CO Eighth Fleet; CO HMS *Unconquered*.

Harrington, James Andrew Benjamin—Honor Harrington's younger brother, younger twin of Faith Harrington.

Hartnett, Commander Thomasina, RMN—Rear Admiral Evelyn Padgorny's chief of staff.

Hasselberg, Vizeadmiral Lyou-yung, IAN—Graf Von Kreuzberg, CO, Task Force 16.

Hastings, Captain Josephus, RMN—Captain (Destroyers), Eighth Fleet.

Havenhurst, Nico—White Haven's majordomo.

Havlicek, Rear Admiral Thurston, RMN—CO, Manticore Wormhole Junction defenses.

Hawke, Captain Spencer—Harrington Steadholder' Guard. Honor Harrington's third personal armsman.

Hayes, Solomon—gossip columnist, *Landing Tattler*.

Hellerstein, Chief Petty Officer Bryant, RMN—chief of the watch, Manticore System Perimeter Sensor Watch.

Hemphill, Admiral Sonja, RMN—Baroness of Low Delhi, Fourth Space Lord, RMN.

Henke, Rear Admiral Michelle, RMN—Countess Gold Peak; CO, Battlecruiser Squadron 81.

Hennessy, Commander Coleman, RMN—Admiral Hemphill's chief of staff.

Hertz, Commander Eric, RMN—Captain Everard Broughton's COLAC, Zanzibar System Defense Command; CO, HMLAC *Ice Pick*.

Hipper—treecat companion of Rachel Mayhew.

Hirshfield, Commander Frances, RMN—executive officer, HMS *Imperator*.

Houellebecq, Captain Celestine, RHN—CO, RHNS *Guerriere*; Lester Tourville's flag captain.

Hovanian, Captain Arakel, RHN—CO, Destroyer Squadron 93.

Illescue, Doctor Franz—head of staff and senior partner, Briarwood Reproductive Center.

Inchman, Commander Sandra, RHN—operations officer, Gaston System Defense Command.

Isher, Julia—business manager, Briarwood Reproductive Center.

Jaruwalski, Captain (JG) Andrea, RMN—operations officer, Eighth Fleet.

Joubert, Captain Armand, RHN—CO, RHNS *Peregrine*.

Jourdain, Rear Admiral Franz, RHN—CO, Battle Squadron 27.

Julian, Lieutenant Commander James, RHN—staff astrogator, Fifth Fleet.

Kaminski, Lieutenant Albert, RMN—staff communications officer, Battlecruiser Squadron 81.

Kent, Lieutenant Janice, RMN—tactical officer, HMLAC *Ice Pick*.

Kgari, Lieutenant Commander Theophile, RMN—staff astrogator, Eighth Fleet.

Kleinman, Doctor Henry—Emily Alexander's personal physician.

Knippschd, Doctor Martijn ("Marty")—laboratory supervisor, Briarwood Reproductive Center.

Kochkarian, Captain Cyrus, RHN—CO, RHNS *Canonnade*; Genevieve Chin's flag captain.

Krenckel, Lieutenant Commander Ludwig, RHN—operations officer, Augusta System Defense Command.

Kuzak, Admiral Theodosia, RMN—CO, Third Fleet.

Kyprianou, Renzo—head of bio weapons research for Mesa and Manpower.

Lacroix, Axel—a young Havenite shipyard worker.

LaFollet, Colonel Andrew—Harrington Steadholder's Guard. Honor Harrington's chief personal armsman.

LaFollet, Jennifer—Allison Harrington's personal maid.

LaFollet, Miranda Gloria—Honor Harrington's personal maid; Andrew LaFollet's younger sister; adopted by treecat Farragut.

Lamar, Captain Jordan, Royal Manticoran Astro Control Service— executive officer, Manticore Wormhole Junction ACS.

Lapierre, Lieutenant Commander Hector, RHN—staff communications officer, Fifth Fleet.

Lara—one of Thandi Palane's ex-Scragg "Amazons"; assigned as a bodyguard to Queen Berry; Saburo X's lover.

Latrell, Commander Judson, RMN—operations officer, Third Fleet.

Lauder, Giuseppe—one of Arnold Giancola's senior bodyguards.

Lazarevna, Lieutenant Commander Ekaterina Gennadovna ("Katenka"), RMN—staff communications officer, Home Fleet,

LePic, Denis—Republic of Haven Attorney General.

le Vern, Mathilde—System Governor, Gaston System, Republic of Haven.

Lewis, Rear Admiral Victor, RHN—CO, Office of Operational Research.

Lorenzetti, Major Allen, RMMC—CO, Marine detachment, HMS *Imperator.*

Lowell, Petty Officer 1/c Peter, RHN—a noncommissioned officer assigned to the Hera System Defense Command sensor net.

Loyola, Lieutenant Justin, RHN—tactical officer, RHNS *Racer.*

MacGuiness, James—Honor Harrington's personal steward and friend.

MacNaughton, Commander Ewan, RHN—senior Sensor officer, Lovat System Defense Command.

Mandel, Captain Irving, RMN—Criminal Investigation Division.

Manfredi, Commander Oliver, RMN—chief of staff, Battlecruiser Squadron 81.

Mannock, Vice Admiral Sir Allen, RMN—Seventh space Lord, RMN; Surgeon General of the Star Kingdom of Manticore.

Marquette, Admiral Arnaud, RHN—chief of the naval staff, Republic of Haven.

Martinsen, Lieutenant Commander Astrid, RMN—staff communications officer, CLAC Squadron 3.

Mathieson, Georgina—Solon System governor, Republic of Haven.

Mattingly, Captain Simon—Harrington Steadholder's Guard. One of Honor Harrington's personal armsmen.

Matsuzawa, Rear Admiral Hirotaka, RMN—commanding officer, Battlecruiser Squadron 32.

Mayhew, Alexandra—Benjamin Mayhew's fifth child, by Elaine Mayhew. Goddaughter of Allison and Alfred Harrington.

Mayhew, Arabella Allison Wainwright—Benjamin Mayhew's eighth child, by Katherine Mayhew.

Mayhew, Benjamin Bernard Jason—Benjamin IX, Protector of Grayson.

Mayhew, Bernard Raoul—Lord Mayhew, Benjamin Mayhew's sixth child (and first son), by Katherine Mayhew. Heir Apparent to the Protectorship of Grayson.

Mayhew, Elaine Margaret—Benjamin Mayhew's junior wife.

Mayhew, Honor—Benjamin Mayhew's fourth child, by Elaine Mayhew. Honor Harrington's goddaughter

Mayhew, Jeanette—Benjamin Mayhew's second oldest child, by Elaine Mayhew.

Mayhew, Katherine Elizabeth—Benjamin Mayhew's senior wife; First Lady of Grayson.

Mayhew, Lawrence Hamish William—Benjamin Mayhew's seventh child, by Elaine Mayhew.

Mayhew, Rachel—Benjamin Mayhew's oldest child, by Katherine Mayhew, adopted by treecat Hipper, midshipwoman Saganami Island Naval Academy.

Mayhew, Teresa—Benjamin Mayhew's third oldest child, by Katherine Mayhew.

McClure, Sergeant Jefferson—Harrington Steadholder's Guard, Emily Alexander's personal armsman.

McGraw, Sergeant Clifford—Harrington Steadholder's Guard, one of Honor Harrington's new personal armsman.

McGwire, Commander Alan, RHN—chief of staff, Fordyce System Defense Command.

McGwire, Jackson—White Haven's butler.

McKeon, Rear Admiral Alistair, RMN—CO, Battle Squadron 61.

Meares, Lieutenant Timothy, RMN—Honor Harrington's flag lieutenant.

Meyers, Tajman—chief of security, Briarwood Reproductive Center.

Mikhailov, Captain Diego, RMN—CO, HMS *Ajax*, Michelle Henke's flag captain.

Miklós, Vice Admiral Samuel, RMN—CO, CLAC Squadron 6.

Milligan, Commodore Tom, RHN—CO, Hera System Defense Command.

Monroe—Prince Consort Justin Zyrr-Winton's treecat companion.

Montague, Vice Admiral Irene, RMN—CO, Battle Squadron 19.

Montaigne, Catherine—leader of the Manticoran Liberal Party; Manticoran leader of the Anti-slavery League; ex-Baroness of the Tor; Anton Zilwicki's lover.

Montreau, Leslie—Arnold Giancola's successor as the Havenite Secretary of State.

Moore, Rear Admiral Kenneth, RHN—CO, Battle Squadron 11.

Moreau, Commodore Mary Lou, RMN—CO, Light Cruiser Flotilla 18.

Morowitz, Rear Admiral Allen, RMN—CO, first division, Battle Squadron 61.

Morrison, Surgeon Commander Richenda, RMN—senior physician, HMS *Imperator*.

Morser, Vizeadmiral Bin-hewi, IAN—Graffin von Grau, CO, Battle Squadron 36, IAN.

Mueller, Travis—Steadholder Mueller.

Nesbitt, Tony—Republic of Haven Secretary of Commerce; Jean-Claude Nesbitt's cousin.

Nesbitt, Colonel Jean-Claude—chief of security, Republic of Haven Department of State; Tony Nesbitt's cousin.

Neukirch, Lieutenant Commander Harriet, RMN—astrogator, HMS *Imperator*.

Nielsen, Commander Petra, RHN—operations officer, Fordyce System Defense Command.

Nimitz—Honor Harrington's treecat companion; mate of Samantha.

O'Dell, Captain Harold, RMN—CO, HMS *King Roger III*; Theodosia Kuzak's flag captain.

O'Donnell, Father Jerome—parish priest, White Haven.

Orbach, Doctor Dame Jessica—Third Lord of Admiralty (health and Manpower), RMN

Orndorff, Commander Roslee, RMN—chief of staff, Battle Squadron 61; adopted by treecat Banshee.

Ormskirk, Admiral Sir Frederick—Earl Tanith Hill, Sixth Space Lord, RMN.

Oversteegen, Captain Michael, RMN—CO HMS Nike.

Padgorny, Rear Admiral Evelyn, RMN—CO Battle Squadron 31, Zanzibar System picket.

Palane, Thandi—"Great Kaja," uniformed commander-in-chief of the Torch military; Queen Berry's unofficial "big sister."

Pattison, Lieutenant Jayne, RMN—communications officer, HMS *Nike*.

Phillips, Lindsey—Manticoran nanny assigned to Faith and James Harrington.

Poykkonen, Joona—Augusta System governor, Republic of Haven.

Pritchart, Eloise—President of the Republic of Haven; Javier Giscard's lover.

Randall, Commander Myron, RHN—chief of staff, Gaston System Defense Command.

Reinke, Vizeadmiral Hwa-zhyou, IAN—Baron von Basaltberg, CO, Battlecruiser Squadron 31, IAN.

Reumann, Captain Patrick, RHN—CO, RHNS *Sovereign of Space*; Javier Giscard's flag captain.

Reynolds, Commander George, RMN—Honor Harrington's staff intelligence officer.

Rothschild, Lieutenant Jack, RHN—Captain Morton Schneider's tactical officer.

Sabourin, Captain Nicodème, RHN—chief of staff, Fifth Fleet.

Samantha—Hamish Alexander's treecat companion; mate of Nimitz.

Sanderson, Walter—Republic of Haven Secretary of the Interior.

Sandusky, Jerome—Mesan covert operations specialist with primary day-to-day responsibility for operations in Congo and the Republic of Haven.

Schneider, Captain Morton, RHN—COLAC for the first Havenite attack on Zanzibar.

Sebastian, Margaret—Chantilly System governor, Republic of Haven.

Sewall, Rear Admiral Hildegard, RHN—CO, Task Group 32 ("Bogey Two"), Third Fleet.

Sharif, Captain James, RMN—CO HMS *Intolerant*, Allen Morowitz' flag captain.

Shelburne, Captain Lavarenti, RMN—CO, HMS *Hecate*.

Shelton, Chester—system governor, Hera System, Republic of Haven.

Simon, Admiral Janos, Alizon Space Navy—CO, Alizon System Defense Command.

Simon, Commander Jean, RMN—ONI counter-espionage specialist.

Slowacki, Commander Alekan, RMN—operations officer, Battle Squadron 61.

Smirnoff, Captain Alice, RHN—Second Fleet's senior COLAC.

Smith, Gena—head of Protector's Palace childcare staff.

Smithson, Captain Gerald ("Jerry"), RMN—chief of staff, Third Fleet.

Snyder, Lieutenant Commander Henry, RMN—staff astrogator, Home Fleet.

Spiropoulo, Commander Andrianna, RHN—operations officer, Fifth Fleet.

Stackpole, Lieutenant Commander John, RMN—operations officer, Battlecruiser Squadron 81.

Stanfield, Commander Janine, RMN—operations officer, CLAC Squadron 3.

Stanton, Lieutenant Jethro, RMN—executive officer, HMS *Ambuscade*.

Staunton, Sandra—Republic of Haven Secretary of Biosciences.

Steen, Commander Astrid, RMN—staff astrogator, Third Fleet.

Stimson, Sergeant Tobias—Harrington Steadholder's Guard. Hamish Alexander's personal armsman.

Stokely, Commander Ellen, RHN—CO, RHNS *Racer*; Captain Arakel Hovanian's "flag captain."

Sullivan, The Reverend Jeremiah Winslow—First Elder, Church of Humanity Unchained.

Taverner, Commander Serena, RHN—chief of staff, Battlecruiser Squadron 12.

Taylor, Jasper—Steadholder Canseco.

Telmachi, Archbishop Robert—Archbishop of Manticore.

Tennard, Corporal Jeremiah—Harrington Steadholder's Guard; Faith Harrington's personal armsman.

Thackeray, Commander Alvin, RMN—Rear Admiral Padgorny's operations officer.

Thackery, Commander Selma, RHN—operations officer, Third Fleet.

Thackston, Corporal Barnaby, RMMC—Marine detachment, HMS *Imperator*.

Theisman, Admiral Thomas, RHN—Havenite CNO and Secretary of War.

Thiessen, Sheila—Presidential Security Force, President Pritchart's senior bodyguard.

Thomas, Captain Melinda, RMN—CO HMS *Intransigent*; Alistair McKeon's flag captain.

Thompson, Commander Glenn, RMN—chief engineer, HMS *Imperator*.

Thurston, Sandra—Emily Alexander's personal maid/nurse.

Timmons, Captain Jane, RMN—CO, HMS *Andromeda*.

Torricelli, Chief Petty Officer Andreas, RHN—chief of the watch, Hera System Defense Command sensor net.

Toscarelli, Vice Admiral Anton, RMN—Third Space Lord, RMN.

Tourville, Admiral Lester, RHN—CO, Second Fleet.

Trajan, Wilhelm—Director, Foreign Intelligence Service, Republic of Haven.

Tremaine, Captain Prescott ("Scotty"), RMN—CO HMLAC *Dacoit*; senior COLAC, CLAC Squadron 3.

Trenis, Vice Admiral Linda, RHN—CO, Bureau of Planning.

Truman, Vice Admiral Dame Alice, RMN—commanding officer, Third CLAC Squadron.

Tucker, Commander George, RHN—chief of staff, Hera System Defense Command.

Turner, Lieutenant Commander Angelina, RMN—watch officer, Manticore System Perimeter Sensor Watch.

Tyler, William Henry—New Age Pharmaceuticals commercial representative on Torch.

Usher, Kevin—Director, Federal Investigation Agency, Republic of Haven.

VanGuyles, Elfrieda—Countess Fairburn, Conservative Association insider.

Van Hale, Judson—Sphinx-born son of a genetic slave; one of Queen Berry's bodyguards; adopted by treecat Genghis.

Waldberg, Konteradmiral Syou-tung, IAN—CO, Battle Squadron 38, IAN.

Watson, Captain Diego, RHN—senior COLAC, Fordyce System Defense Command.

Webster, Admiral James Bowie, RMN (ret)—Manticoran ambassador to the Solarian League.

Weissmuller, Lieutenant Jerome, RMN—astrogator, HMS *Ambuscade*.

West, Commander Fred, RHN—Captain Alice Smirnoff's successor as Second Fleet's senior COLAC.

Willoughby, Lieutenant Sherwin, RMN—Rear Admiral Evelyn Padgorny's communications officer.

Winton, Elizabeth Adrienne Samantha Annette—Queen Elizabeth III, Queen of Manticore. Adopted by treecat Ariel.

Winton, Princess Ruth—adopted daughter of Michael Winton; Elizabeth III's niece; Queen Berry's friend and junior intelligence advisor.

Witcinski, Commander Sigismund, RMN—CO, LAC tender HMS *Marigold*, Zanzibar System Defense Command.

Wollenhaupt, Konteradmiral Tswei-yun, IAN—CO, Battle Squadron 56.

X., Jeremy—ex-genetic slave, ex-Audubon Ballroom terrorist; Queen Berry's Secretary of War.

X., Saburo—ex-genetic slave, ex-Audubon Ballroom terrorist, one of Queen Berry's bodyguards; Lara's lover.

Zilwicki, Captain Anton, RMN (ret)—ex-ONI agent; Queen Berry's adoptive father and senior intelligence advisor; Catherine Montaigne's lover.

Zilwicki, Berry—Queen Berry, first monarch of Torch.

Zucker, Commander Robert, RHN—operations officer, Battlecruiser Squadron 12.

Zyrr-Winton, Justin—Prince Consort of Manticore. Adopted by treecat Monroe.